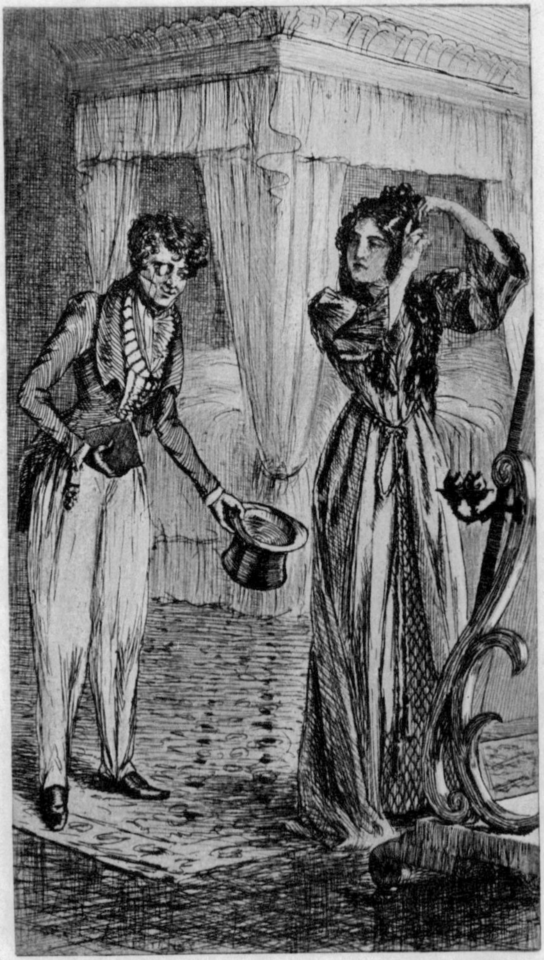

THE WORKS OF HONORÉ DE BALZAC

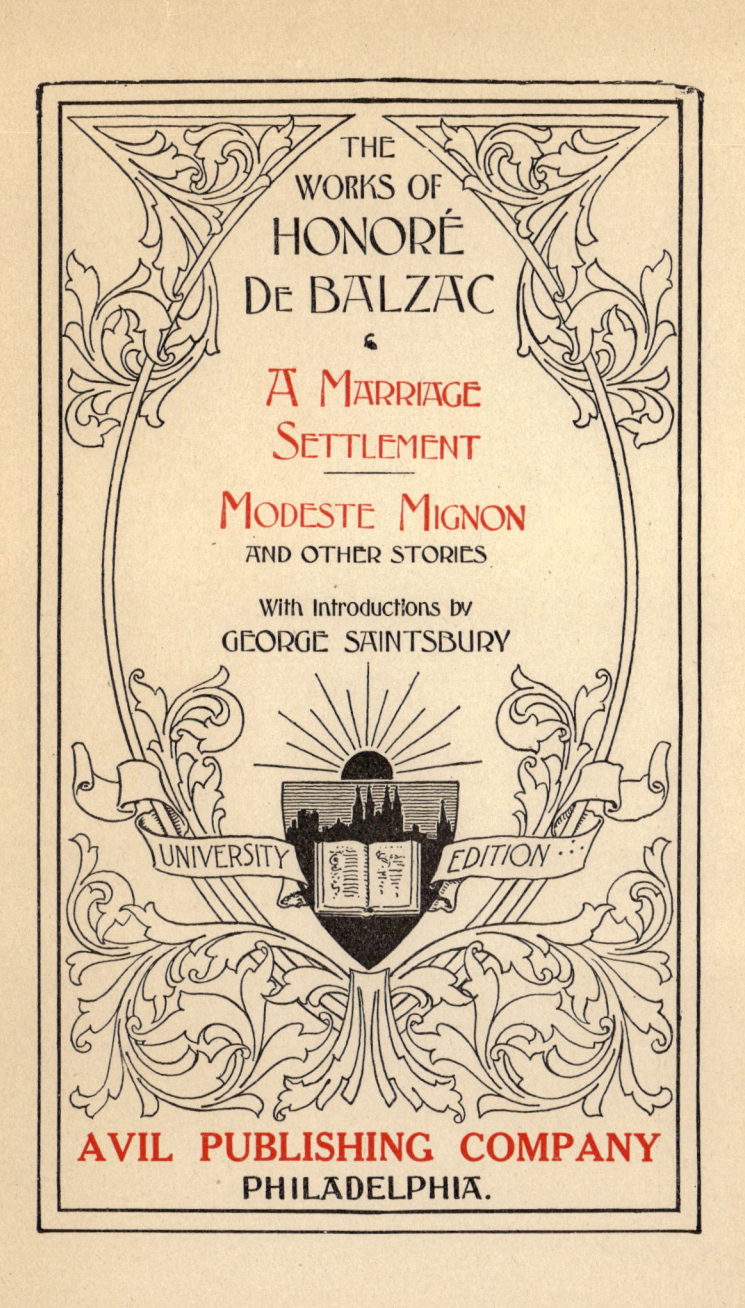

A MARRIAGE SETTLEMENT

MODESTE MIGNON
AND OTHER STORIES

With Introductions by
GEORGE SAINTSBURY

UNIVERSITY EDITION

AVIL PUBLISHING COMPANY
PHILADELPHIA.

COPYRIGHTED 1901
BY
John D. Avil
All Rights Reserved

CONTENTS

PART I

	PAGE
INTRODUCTION	ix
A MARRIAGE SETTLEMENT	1
(*Le Contrat de Mariage.*)	
A START IN LIFE	143
(*Un Début dans la Vie.*)	
A SECOND HOME	311
(*Une Double Famille.*)	

(Translator, CLARA BELL.)

PART II

INTRODUCTION	ix
MODESTE MIGNON	1
(*Modeste Mignon;* Translator, CLARA BELL.)	

THE HATED SON:
    (*L'Enfant Maudit;* Translator, JAMES WARING.)

I. HOW THE MOTHER LIVED	273
II. HOW THE SON DIED	329
THE ATHEIST'S MASS	379
(*La Messe de l'Athée;* Translator, CLARA BELL.)	

A MARRIAGE SETTLEMENT

AND OTHER STORIES

INTRODUCTION

If Balzac had been acquainted with the works of Chaucer (which would have been extremely surprising) he might have called *Le Contrat de Mariage* "A Legend of Bad Women." He has not been exactly sparing of studies in that particular kind; but he has surpassed himself here. Mme. de Maufrigneuse redeems herself by her character, however imperfectly supported, of *grande dame*, Béatrix de Rochefide by a certain naturalness and weakness, Flore Brazier by circumstances and education, others by other things. But Madame Evangelista and her daughter Natalie may be said to be bad all through—thoroughly poisonous persons who, much more than the actual Milady of *Les Trois Mousquetaires* (there was some charm in her), deserved to be taken and "justified" by lynch law. If the "Thirteen" (who were rather interested in the matter) had descended upon both in the fashion of d'Artagnan and his friends, I do not know that any one would have had much right to complain. How far the picture is exaggerated must be a question to be decided partly by individual experience, partly by other arguments. Although I am not always disposed to defend Balzac from the charge of exaggeration, I think he is fairly free from it here.

Madame Evangelista, besides the usual womanly desire to make a figure in the capital, has (not to excuse, but to explain her) the equally natural tendency to regard everybody outside her own family as an at least possible enemy to be "exploited" pitilessly, together with bad blood which, though luckily not common, is by no means impossible nor even extremely rare. Her daughter, as Balzac has acutely suggested, both here and elsewhere, is, like not a few women, destitute of that sense of abiding gratitude for pleasure mutually enjoyed which tempers the evil tendencies of the male sex to no considerable extent. She has never cared for her husband; she has no morals; and (as in another book and subject, her letter to Félix de Vandenesse, well deserved as it is in the particular instance, shows) she has the fortunately not universal but excessively dangerous combination of utter selfishness with very clear-sighted common-sense.

The men are equally true, and much more agreeable. It is noteworthy that here only does Balzac's pattern Byronic dandy Marsay cut a distinctly agreeable figure. He is still something of a coxcomb, but he is, as he is not very often, a gentleman; he is, as he is scarcely ever, a good fellow; and he deserves his character as *un homme très fort,* to say the least, better than he does in some places. The two family lawyers are excellent. As for Paul de Manerville, the unfortunate *fleur des pois* (the title for some time of the book) himself, he is one of the profoundest of Balzac's studies, and it was perhaps rather unkind of his creator to call him a *niais.* At any rate, he was not more so than that very creator when he committed slow suicide by waiting and working till a woman, who cannot have been worth the trouble, at last made up her mind to "derogate" a little, and, without any pecuniary sacrifice, to exchange the position of widow of a member of a second-rate aristocracy for that of wife of one of the foremost living men of letters in Europe, who was himself technically a gentleman. Marsay's letters to Paul only put pointedly what the whole story puts suggestively, the great truth that you may "see life" without knowing it, and that for a certain kind of respectable person the sowing of wild oats is a far more dangerous kind of husbandry than for the wildest profligate. It is true that Paul has exceedingly bad luck, and that in countries other than France he might have subsided into a most respectable and comfortable country gentleman. But as a great authority, whom he probably knew, Paul de Florac, his namesake and contemporary, remarked, "Do not adopt our institutions *à demi*," so it would seem to be a maxim that the two kinds of life cannot be combined—at least, that seems to be Balzac's moral.

The second story in the volume, a very slight touch of unnecessary cruelty excepted, is one of the truest and most amusing of all Balzac's *repertoire;* and it is conducted according to the orthodox methods of poetical justice. It is impossible not to recognize the justice of the portraiture of the luckless Oscar Husson, and the exact verisimilitude of the way in which he succumbs to the temptations and practical jokes (the first title of the story was *Le Danger des Mystifications*) of his companions. I am not a good authority on matters dramatic; but it seems to me that the story would lend itself to the stage in the right hands better than almost anything that Balzac has done. Half an *enfant terrible* and half a Sir Martin Mar-all, the luckless Oscar "puts his foot into it," and emerges in deplorable condition, with a sustained success which would do credit to all but the very best writers of farcical comedy, and would not disgrace the very best.

In such pieces the characters other than the hero have but to play contributory parts, and here they do not fail to do so. M. de Sérizy, whom it pleased Balzac to keep in a dozen books as his stock example of the unfortunate husband, plays his part with at least as much dignity as is easily possible to such a personage. Madame Clapart is not too absurd as the fond mother of the cub; and Moreau, her ancient lover, is equally commendable in the not very easy part of a "protector." The easy-going ladies who figure in Oscar's second collapse display well enough that rather facile generosity and good-nature which Balzac is fond of attributing to them. As for the "Mystificators," Balzac, as usual, is decidedly more lenient to the artist folk than he is elsewhere to men of letters. Mistigris, or Léon de Lora, is always a pleasant person, and Joseph Bridau always a respectable one. Georges Marest is no doubt a bad fellow, but he gets punished.

Nor ought we to omit notice of the careful study of the apprenticeship of a lawyer's clerk, wherein, as elsewhere no doubt, Balzac profited by his own novitiate. Altogether the story is a pleasant one, and we acquiesce in the tempering of the wind to Oscar when that ordinary person is consoled for his sufferings with the paradise of the French bourgeois —-a respectable place, a wife with no dangerous brilliancy, and a good *dot*.

Une Double Famille, which had an almost unusually complicated history and several titles, appears here (for reasons of practical convenience) out of its old place in conjunction with the *Chat qui Pelote*. It is a good specimen of Balzac's average work, neither much above nor much below the run of its fellows.

The first titles of the two main stories have been given above. *La Fleur des pois*, as such, appeared in no newspaper, but in the *Scènes de la Vie Privée* of 1834-35. It had three divisions, which disappeared in the first edition of the *Comédie*, when also the title was changed. Its companion was printed under its first title, and with fourteen chapter divisions, in a paper called *La Législature,* between July and September 1842. Balzac at first meant to call it *Les Jeunes Gens,* but changed this to *Le Danger des Mystifications,* and that again to the present form, when it appeared (with *La fausse Maîtresse*) as a book in 1844. Next year it was classed in the *Comédie,* undergoing the usual process of deletion of the chapter divisions and headings. G. S.

A MARRIAGE SETTLEMENT

To G. Rossini

MONSIEUR DE MANERVILLE the elder was a worthy gentleman of Normandy, well known to the Maréchal de Richelieu, who arranged his marriage with one of the richest heiresses of Bordeaux at the time when the old Duke held court in that city as Governor of Guienne. The Norman gentleman sold the lands he owned in Bessin, and established himself as a Gascon, tempted to this step by the beauty of the estate of Lanstrac, a delightful residence belonging to his wife. Towards the end of Louis XV.'s reign, he purchased the post of Major of the King's bodyguard, and lived till 1813, having happily survived the Revolution.

This was how. In the winter of 1790 he made a voyage to Martinique, where his wife had property, leaving the management of his estates in Gascony to a worthy notary's clerk named Mathias, who had some taint of the new ideas. On his return, the Comte de Manerville found his possessions safe and profitably managed. This shrewdness was the fruit of a graft of the Gascon on the Norman.

Madame de Manerville died in 1810. Her husband, having learned by the dissipations of his youth the importance of money, and, like many old men, ascribing to it a greater power in life than it possesses, Monsieur de Manerville became progressively thrifty, avaricious, and mean. Forgetting that stingy fathers make spendthrift sons, he allowed scarcely anything to his son, though he was an only child.

Paul de Manerville came home from college at Vendôme towards the end of 1810, and for three years lived under his father's rule. The tyranny exercised by the old man of sixty-nine over his sole heir could not fail to affect a heart and character as yet unformed. Though he did not lack the physical courage which would seem to be in the air of Gascony, Paul dared not contend with his father, and lost the elasticity of resistance that gives rise to moral courage. His suppressed feelings were pent at the bottom of his heart, where he kept them long in reserve without daring to express them; thus, at a later time, when he felt that they were not in accordance with the maxims of the world, though he could think rightly, he could act wrongly. He would have fought at a word, while he quaked at the thought of sending away a servant; for his shyness found a field in any struggle which demanded persistent determination. Though capable of much to escape persecution, he would never have taken steps to hinder it by systematic antagonism, nor have met it by a steady display of strength. A coward in mind, though bold in action, he preserved till late that unconfessed innocence which makes a man the victim, the voluntary dupe, of things against which such natures hesitate to rebel, preferring to suffer rather than complain.

He was a prisoner in his father's old house, for he had not money enough to disport himself with the young men of the town; he envied them their amusements, but could not share them. The old gentleman took him out every evening in an antique vehicle, drawn by a pair of shabbily-harnessed horses, attended to by two antique and shabbily-dressed men-servants, into the society of a royalist clique, consisting of the waifs of the nobility of the old Parlement and of the sword. These two bodies of magnates, uniting after the Revolution to resist Imperial influence, had by degrees become an aristocracy of landowners. Overpowered by the wealth and the shifting fortunes of a great seaport, this *Faubourg Saint-Germain* of Bordeaux responded with scorn to the magnificence of commerce and of the civil and military authorities.

Too young to understand social distinctions and the poverty hidden under the conspicuous vanity to which they give rise, Paul was bored to death among these antiques, not knowing that these associations of his youth would secure to him the aristocratic pre-eminence for which France will always have a weakness.

He found some little compensation for the dreariness of these evenings in certain exercises such as young men love, for his father insisted on them. In the old aristocrat's eyes, to be a master of all weapons, to ride well, to play tennis, and have fine manners—in short, the superficial training of the gentleman of the past—constituted the accomplished man. So, every morning Paul fenced, rode, and practised with pistols. The rest of his time he spent in novel-reading, for his father would not hear of the transcendental studies which put a finishing touch to education in these days.

So monotonous an existence might have killed the young man, but that his father's death delivered him from this tyranny at the time when it was becoming unendurable. Paul found that his father's avarice had accumulated a considerable fortune, and left him an estate in the most splendid order possible; but he had a horror of Bordeaux, and no love for Lanstrac, where his father had always spent the summer and kept him out shooting from morning till night.

As soon as the legal business was got through, the young heir, eager for pleasure, invested his capital in securities, left the management of the land to old Mathias, his father's agent, and spent six years away from Bordeaux. Attaché at first to the Embassy at Naples, he subsequently went as secretary to Madrid and London, thus making the tour of Europe. After gaining knowledge of the world, and dissipating a great many illusions, after spending all the money his father had saved, a moment came when Paul, to continue this dashing existence, had to draw on the revenues from his estate which the notary had saved for him. So, at this critical moment, struck by one of those impulses which are regarded as wisdom, he resolved to leave Paris, to return to Bordeaux, to manage his own affairs, to lead the life of a country gentleman, settling at Lanstrac and improving his estate—to marry, and one day to be elected Deputy.

Paul was a Count; titles were recovering their value in the matrimonial market; he could, and ought to marry well. Though many women wish to marry for a title, a great many more look for a husband who has an intimate acquaintance with life. And Paul—at a cost of seven hundred thousand francs, consumed in six years—had acquired this official knowledge, a qualification which cannot be sold, and which is worth more than a stockbroker's license; which, indeed, demands long studies, an apprenticeship, examinations, acquaintances, friends, and enemies, a certain elegance of appearance, good manners, and a handsome, tripping name; which brings with it success with women, duels, betting at races, many disappointments, dull hours, tiresome tasks, and indigestible pleasures.

In spite of lavish outlay, he had never been the fashion. In the burlesque army of the gay world, the man who is *the fashion* is the Field Marshal of the forces, the merely elegant man is the Lieutenant-General. Still, Paul enjoyed his little reputation for elegance, and lived up to it. His servants were well drilled, his carriages were approved, his suppers had some success, and his bachelor's den was one of the seven or eight which were a match in luxury for the finest houses in Paris. But he had not broken a woman's heart; he played without losing, nor had he extraordinarily brilliant luck; he was too honest to be false to any one, not even a girl of the streets; he did not leave his love-letters about, nor keep a boxful for his friends to dip into while he was shaving or putting a collar on; but, not wishing to damage his estates in Guienne, he had not the audacity that prompts a young man into startling speculations, and attracts all eyes to watch him; he borrowed of no one, and was so wrongheaded as to lend to friends, who cut him and never mentioned him again, either for good or evil. He seemed to have worked out the sum of his extravagance. The secret of his character lay in his father's tyranny, which had made him a sort of social hybrid.

One morning Paul de Manerville said to a friend of his named de Marsay, who has since become famous:

"My dear fellow, life has a meaning."

"You must be seven-and-twenty before you understand it," said de Marsay, laughing at him.

"Yes, I am seven-and-twenty, and for that very reason I mean to go to live at Lanstrac as a country gentleman. At Bordeaux I shall have my father's old house, whither I shall send my Paris furniture, and I shall spend three months of every winter here in my rooms, which I shall not give up."

"And you will marry?"

"I shall marry."

"I am your friend, my worthy Paul, as you know," said de Marsay, after a moment's silence; "well, be a good father and a good husband—and ridiculous for the rest of your days. If you could be happy being ridiculous, the matter would deserve consideration; but you would not be happy. You have not a strong enough hand to rule a household. I do you every justice: you are a perfect horseman; no one holds the ribbons better, makes a horse plunge, or keeps his seat more immovably. But, my dear boy, the paces of matrimony are quite another thing. Why, I can see you led at a round pace by Madame la Comtesse de Manerville, galloping, more often than not much against your will, and presently thrown —thrown into the ditch, and left there with both legs broken.

"Listen to me. You have still forty odd thousand francs a year in land in the Department of the Gironde. Take your horses and your servants, and furnish your house in Bordeaux; you will be King in Bordeaux, you will promulgate there the decrees we pronounce in Paris, you will be the corresponding agent of our follies. Well and good. Commit follies in your provincial capital—nay, even absurdities. So much the better; they may make you famous. But—do not marry.

"Who are the men who marry nowadays? Tradesmen, to

increase their capital or to have a second hand at the plough; peasants, who, by having large families, manufacture their own laborers; stockbrokers or notaries, to get money to pay for their licenses; the miserable kings, to perpetuate their miserable dynasties. We alone are free from the pack-saddle; why insist on loading yourself? In short, what do you marry for? You must account for such a step to your best friend.

"In the first place, if you should find an heiress as rich as yourself, eighty thousand francs a year for two are not the same thing as forty thousand for one, because you very soon are three—and four if you have a child. Do you really feel any affection for the foolish propagation of Manervilles, who will never give anything but trouble? Do you not know what the duties are of a father and mother? Marriage, my deal Paul, is the most foolish of social sacrifices; our children alone profit by it, and even they do not know its cost till their horses are cropping the weeds that grow over our graves.

"Do you, for instance, regret your father, the tyrant who wrecked your young life? How do you propose to make your children love you? Your plans for their education, your care for their advantage, your severity, however necessary, will alienate their affection. Children love a lavish or weak father, but later they will despise him. You are stranded between aversion and contempt. You cannot be a good father for the wishing.

"Look round on our friends, and name one you would like for a son. We have known some who were a disgrace to their name. Children, my dear boy, are a commodity very difficult to keep sweet.—Yours will be angels! No doubt!

"But have you ever measured the gulf that parts the life of a single man from that of a married one? Listen.—As you are, you can say: 'I will never be ridiculous beyond a certain point; the public shall never think of me excepting as I choose that it should think.' Married, you will fall into depths of the ridiculous!—Unmarried, you make your own happiness; you want it to-day, you do without to-morrow: married, you take it as it comes, and the day you seek it you have to do without it. Married, you are an ass; you calculate marriage portions, you talk about public and religious morality, you look upon young men as immoral and dangerous; in short, you are socially Academical. I have nothing but pity for you! An old bachelor, whose relations are waiting for his money, and who struggles with his latest breath to make an old nurse give him something to drink, is in paradise compared with a married man. I say nothing of all the annoying, irritating, provoking, aggravating, stultifying, worrying things that may come to hypnotize and paralyze your mind, and tyrannize over your life, in the course of the petty warfare of two human beings always together, united for ever, who have bound themselves, vainly believing that they will agree; no, that would be to repeat Boileau's satire, and we know it by heart.

"I would forgive you the absurd notion if you would promise to marry like a grandee, to settle your fortune on your eldest son, to take advantage of the honeymoon stage to have two legitimate children, to give your wife a completely separate establishment, to meet her only in society, and never come home from a journey without announcing your return. Two hundred thousand francs a year are enough to do it on, and your antecedents allow of your achieving this by finding some rich English woman hungering for a title. That aristocratic way of life is the only one that seems to me truly French; the only handsome one, commanding a wife's respect and regard; the only life that distinguishes us from the common herd; in short, the only one for which a young man should ever give up his single blessedness. In such an attitude the Comte de Manerville is an example to his age, he is superior to the general, and must be nothing less than a Minister or an Ambassador. He can never be ridiculous; he conquers the social advantages of a married man, and preserves the privileges of a bachelor."

"But, my good friend, I am not a de Marsay; I am, as you yourself do me the honor to express it, Paul de Manerville, neither more nor less, a good husband and father,

Deputy of the Centre, and perhaps some day a peer of the Upper House—altogether a very humble destiny. But I am diffident—and resigned."

"And your wife?" said the merciless de Marsay, "will she be resigned?"

"My wife, my dear fellow, will do what I wish."

"Oh! my poor friend, have you not got beyond that point—Good-bye, Paul. Henceforth you have forfeited my esteem. Still, one word more, for I cannot subscribe to your abdication in cold blood. Consider what is the strength of our position. If a single man had no more than six thousand francs a year, if his whole fortune lay in his reputation for elegance and the memory of his successes, well, even this fantastic ghost has considerable value. Life still affords some chances for the bachelor 'off color.' Yes, he may still aspire to anything. But marriage! Paul, it is the 'Thus far and no further' of social existence. Once married, you can never more be anything but what you are—unless your wife condescends to take you in hand."

"But you are always crushing me under your exceptional theories!" cried Paul. "I am tired of living for the benefit of others—of keeping horses for display, of doing everything with a view to 'what people will say,' of ruining myself for fear that idiots should remark: 'Why, Paul has the same old carriage!—What has he done with his money? Does he squander it? Gamble on the Bourse?—Not at all; he is a millionaire. Madame So-and-So is madly in love with him. —He has just had a team of horses from England, the handsomest in Paris.—At Longchamps, every one remarked the four-horse chaises of Monsieur de Marsay and Monsieur de Manerville; the cattle were magnificent.'—In short, the thousand idiotic remarks by which the mob of fools drives us.

"I am beginning to see that this life, in which we are simply rolled along by others instead of walking on our feet, wears us out and makes us old. Believe me, my dear Henri, I admire your powers, but I do not envy you. You are capable of judging everything; you can act and think as a statesman, you stand above general laws, received ideas, recognized prejudices, accepted conventionalities; in fact, you get all the benefits of a position in which I, for my part, should find nothing but disaster. Your cold and systematic deductions, which are perhaps quite true, are, in the eyes of the vulgar, appallingly immoral. I belong to the vulgar.

"I must play the game by the rules of the society in which I am compelled to live. You can stand on the summit of human things, on ice peaks, and still have feelings; I should freeze there. The life of the greatest number, of which I am very frankly one, is made up of emotions such as I feel at present in need of. The most popular lady's man often flirts with ten women at once, and wins the favor of none; and then, whatever his gifts, his practice, his knowledge of the world, a crisis may arise when he finds himself, as it were, jammed between two doors. For my part, I like the quiet and faithful intercourse of home; I want the life where a man always finds a woman at his side."

"Marriage is a little free and easy!" cried de Marsay.

Paul was not to be dashed, and went on:

"Laugh if you please; I shall be the happiest man in the world when my servant comes to say, 'Madame is waiting breakfast'—when, on coming home in the afternoon, I may find a heart——"

"You are still too frivolous, Paul! You are not moral enough yet for married life!"

"A heart to which I may confide my business and tell my secrets. I want to live with some being on terms of such intimacy that our affection may not depend on a *Yes* or *No,* or on situations where the most engaging man may disappoint passion. In short, I am bold enough to become, as you say, a good husband and a good father! I am suited to domestic happiness, and prepared to submit to the conditions insisted on by society to set up a wife, a family——"

"You suggest the idea of a beehive.—Go ahead, then. You will be a dupe all your days. You mean to marry, to have a wife to yourself? In other words, you want to solve, to your own advantage, the most difficult social problem presented in our day by town life as the French Revolution has left it, so you begin by isolation! And do you suppose that your wife will be content to forego the life you contemn? Will she, like you, be disgusted with it? If you do not want to endure the conjugal joys described by your sincere friend de Marsay, listen to my last advice. Remain unmarried for thirteen years longer, and enjoy yourself to the top of your bent; then, at forty, with your first fit of the gout, marry a widow of six-and-thirty; thus you may be happy. If you take a maid to wife, you will die a madman!"

"Indeed! And tell me why?" cried Paul, somewhat nettled.

"My dear fellow," replied de Marsay, "Boileau's Satire on Women is no more than a series of commonplace observations in verse. Why should women be faultless? Why deny them the heritage of the most obvious possession of human nature? In my opinion, the problem of marriage no longer lies in the form in which that critic discerned it. Do you really suppose that, to command affection in marriage, as in love, it is enough for a husband to be a man? You who haunt boudoirs, have you none but fortunate experiences?

"Everything in our bachelor existence prepares a disastrous mistake for the man who marries without having deeply studied the human heart. In the golden days of youth, by a singular fact in our manners, a man always bestows pleasure, he triumphs over fascinated woman, and she submits to his wishes. The obstacles set up by law and feeling, and the natural coyness of woman, give rise to a common impulse on both sides, which deludes superficial men as to their future position in the married state where there are no obstacles to be overcome, where women endure rather than allow a man's advances, and repel them rather than invite them. The whole aspect of life is altered for us. The unmarried man, free from care, and always the leader, has nothing to fear from a defeat. In married life a repulse is irreparable. Though a lover may make a mistress change her mind in his favor, such a rout, my dear boy, is Waterloo to a husband. A husband, like Napoleon, is bound to gain the victory; however often he may have won, the first defeat is his overthrow. The woman who is flattered by a lover's persistency, and proud of his wrath, calls them brutal in a husband. The lover may choose his ground and do what he will, the master has no such license, and his battlefield is always the same.

"Again, the struggle is the other way about. A wife is naturally inclined to refuse what she ought; a mistress is ready to give what she ought not.

"You who wish to marry (and who will do it), have you ever duly meditated on the Civil Code? I have never soiled my feet in that cave of commentary, that cockloft of gabble called the Law Schools; I never looked into the Code, but I see how it works in the living organism of the world. I am a lawyer, as a clinical professor is a doctor. The malady is not in books, it is in the patient.—The Code, my friend, provides women with guardians, treats them as minors, as children. And how do we manage children? By fear. In that word, my dear Paul, you have the bit for the steed.— Feel your pulse, and say: Can you disguise yourself as a tyrant; you who are so gentle, so friendly, so trusting; you whom at first I used to laugh at, and whom I now love well enough to initiate you into my science. Yes, this is part of a science to which the Germans have already given the name of Anthropology.

"Oh! if I had not solved life by means of pleasure, if I had not an excessive antipathy for men who think instead of acting, if I did not despise the idiots who are so stupid as to believe that a book may live, when the sands of African deserts are composed of the ashes of I know not how many unknown Londons, Venices, Parises, and Romes now in dust, I would write a book on modern marriages and the influence of the Christian system; I would erect a beacon on the heap of sharp stones on which the votaries lie who devote themselves to the social *multiplicamini*. And yet—is the human race worth a quarter of an hour of my time? Is not the sole rational use of pen and ink to ensnare hearts by writing love letters?

"So you will introduce us to the Comtesse de **Manerville**?"

"Perhaps," said Paul.

"We shall still be friends?" said de Marsay.

"Sure!" replied Paul.

"Be quite easy; we will be very polite to you, as the Maison Rouge were to the English at Fontenoy."

Though this conversation shook him, the Comte de Manerville set to work to carry out his plans, and returned to Bordeaux for the winter of 1821. The cost at which he restored and furnished his house did credit to the reputation for elegance that had preceded him. His old connections secured him an introduction to the Royalist circle of Bordeaux, to which, indeed, he belonged, alike by opinion, name, and fortune, and he soon became the leader of its fashion. His knowledge of life, good manners, and Parisian training enchanted the Faubourg Saint-Germain of Bordeaux. An old marquise applied to him an expression formerly current at Court to designate the flower of handsome youth, of the dandies of a past day, whose speech and style were law; she called him *la fleur des pois*—as who should say Pease-blossom. The Liberal faction took up the nickname, which they used in irony, and the Royalists as a compliment.

Paul de Manerville fulfilled with glory the requirements of the name. He was in the position of many a second actor; as soon as the public vouchsafes some approval, they become almost good. Paul, quite at his ease, displayed the qualities of his defects. His banter was neither harsh nor bitter, his manners were not haughty; in his conversation with women, he expressed the respect they value without too much deference or too much familiarity. His dandyism was no more than an engaging care for his person; he was considerate of rank; he allowed a freedom to younger men which his Paris experience kept within due limits; though a master with the sword and pistol, he was liked for his feminine gentleness.

Then his medium height, and a figure not lean but not yet rotund—two obstacles to personal elegance—did not hinder his playing the part of a Bordelais Brummel. A fair skin, with a healthy color, fine hands, neat feet, blue eyes with good eyelashes, black hair, an easy grace, and a chest-voice always pleasantly modulated and full of feeling,—all combined to justify his nickname. Paul was in all things the delicate flower which needs careful culture, its best qualities unfolding only in a moist and propitious soil, which cannot thrive under rough treatment, while a fierce sun burns it and a frost kills it. He was one of those men who are made to accept rather than give happiness, to whom woman is a great factor in life, who need understanding and encouraging, and to whom a wife's love should play the part of Providence.

Though such a character as this gives rise to trouble in domestic life, it is charming and attractive in society. Paul was a success in the narrow provincial circle, where his character, in no respect strongly marked, was better appreciated than in Paris.

The decoration of his town-house, and the necessary restoration of the château of Lanstrac, which he fitted up with English comfort and luxury, absorbed the capital his agent had saved during the past six years. Reduced, therefore, to his exact income of forty odd thousand francs in stocks, he thought it wise to arrange his housekeeping so as to spend no more than this. By the time he had duly displayed his carriages and horses, and entertained the young men of position in the town, he perceived that provincial life necessitated marriage. Still too young to devote himself to the avaricious cares or speculative improvements in which provincial folk ultimately find employment, as required by the need for providing for their children, he ere long felt the want of the various amusements which become the vital habit of a Parisian.

At the same time, it was not a name to be perpetuated, an heir to whom to transmit his possessions, the position to be gained by having a house where the principal families of the neighborhood might meet, nor weariness of illicit connections, that proved to be the determining cause. He had on arriving fallen in love with the queen of Bordeaux society, the much-talked-of Mademoiselle Evangelista.

Early in the century a rich Spaniard named Evangelista had settled at Bordeaux, where good introductions, added to a fine fortune, had won him a footing in the drawing-rooms of the nobility. His wife had done much to preserve him in good odor amid this aristocracy, which would not, perhaps, have been so ready to receive him but that it could thus annoy the society next below it. Madame Evangelista, descended from the illustrious house of Casa-Real, connected with the Spanish monarchs, was a Creole, and, like all women accustomed to be served by slaves, she was a very fine lady, knew nothing of the value of money, and indulged even her most extravagant fancies, finding them always supplied by a husband who was in love with her, and who was so generous as to conceal from her all the machinery of money-making. The Spaniard, delighted to find that she could be happy at Bordeaux, where his business required him to reside, bought a fine house, kept it in good style, entertained splendidly, and showed excellent taste in every respect. So, from 1800 till 1812, no one was talked of in Bordeaux but Monsieur and Madame Evangelista.

The Spaniard died in 1813, leaving a widow of two-and-thirty with an enormous fortune and the prettiest little daughter in the world, at that time eleven years old, promising to become, as indeed she became, a very accomplished person. Clever as Madame Evangelista might be, the Restoration altered her position; the Royalist party sifted itself, and several families left Bordeaux. Still, though her husband's head and hand were lacking to the management of the business, for which she showed the inaptitude of a woman of fashion and the indifference of the Creole, she made no change in her mode of living.

By the time when Paul de Manerville had made up his mind to return to his native place, Mademoiselle Natalie Evangelista was a remarkably beautiful girl, and apparently the richest match in Bordeaux, where no one knew of the gradual diminution of her mother's wealth; for, to prolong her reign, Madame Evangelista had spent vast sums of money. Splendid entertainments and almost royal display had kept up the public belief in the wealth of the house.

Natalie was nearly nineteen, no offer of marriage had as yet come to her mother's ear. Accustomed to indulge all her girlish fancies, Mademoiselle Evangelista had Indian shawls and jewels, and lived amid such luxury as frightened the speculative, in a land and at a time when the young are as calculating as their parents. The fatal verdict, "Only a prince could afford to marry Mademoiselle Evangelista," was a watchword in every drawing-room and boudoir. Mothers of families, dowagers with granddaughters to marry, and damsels jealous of the fair Natalie, whose unfailing elegance and tyrannous beauty were an annoyance to them, took care to add venom to this opinion by perfidious insinuations. When an eligible youth was heard to exclaim with rapturous admiration on Natalie's arrival at a ball—"Good Heavens, what a beautiful creature!"—"Yes," the mammas would reply, "but very expensive!" If some newcomer spoke of Mademoiselle Evangelista as charming, and opined that a man wanting a wife could not make a better choice—"Who would be bold enough," some one would ask, "to marry a girl to whom her mother allows a thousand francs a month for dress, who keeps horses and a lady's maid, and wears lace? She has Mechlin lace on her dressing-gowns. What she pays for washing would keep a clerk in comfort. She has morning capes that cost six francs apiece to clean!"

Such speeches as these, constantly repeated by way of

eulogium, extinguished the keenest desire a youth might feel to wed Mademoiselle Evangelista. The queen of every ball, surfeited with flattery, sure of smiles and admiration wherever she went, Natalie knew nothing of life. She lived as birds fly, as flowers bloom, finding every one about her ready to fulfil her least wish. She knew nothing of the price of things, nor of how money is acquired or kept. She very likely supposed that every house was furnished with cooks and coachmen, maids and men-servants, just as a field produces fodder and trees yield fruit. To her the beggar, the pauper, the fallen tree, and the barren field were all the same thing. Cherished like a hope by her mother, fatigue never marred her pleasure; she pranced through the world like a courser on the Steppe, a courser without either bridle or shoes.

Six months after Paul's arrival the upper circles of the town had brought about a meeting between "Pease-blossom" and the queen of the ballroom. The two flowers looked at each other with apparent coldness, and thought each other charming. Madame Evangelista, as being interested in this not unforeseen meeting, read Paul's sentiments in his eyes, and said to herself, "He will be my son-in-law"; while Paul said to himself, as he looked at Natalie, "She will be my wife!" The wealth of the Evangelistas, proverbial in Bordeaux, remained in Paul's memory as a tradition of his boyhood, the most indelible of all such impressions. And so pecuniary suitability was a foregone conclusion, without all the discussion and inquiry, which are as horrible to shy as to proud natures.

When some persons tried to express to Paul the praise which it was impossible to refuse to Natalie's manner and beauty and wit, always ending with some of the bitterly mercenary reflections as to the future to which the expensive style of the household naturally gave rise, Pease-blossom replied with the disdain that such provincialism deserves. And this way of treating the matter, which soon became known, silenced these remarks; for it was Paul who set the *ton* in ideas and speech as much as in manners and appearance. He had imported the French development of the British stamp and its ice-bound barriers, its Byronic irony, discontent with life, contempt for sacred bonds, English plate and English wit, the scorn of old provincial customs and old property; cigars, patent leather, the pony, lemon-colored gloves, and the canter. So that befell Paul which had happened to no one before—no old dowager or young maid tried to discourage him.

Madame Evangelista began by inviting him to several grand dinners. Could Pease-blossom remain absent from the entertainments to which the most fashionable young men of the town were bidden? In spite of Paul's affected coldness, which did not deceive either the mother or the daughter, he found himself taking the first steps on the road to marriage. When Manerville passed in his tilbury, or riding a good horse, other young men would stop to watch him, and he could hear their comments: "There is a lucky fellow; he is rich, he is handsome, and they say he is to marry Mademoiselle Evangelista. There are some people for whom the world seems to have been made!" If he happened to meet Madame Evangelista's carriage, he was proud of the peculiar graciousness with which the mother and daughter bowed to him.

Even if Paul had not been in love with Mademoiselle Natalie, the world would have married them whether or no. The world, which is the cause of no good thing, is implicated in many disasters; then, when it sees the evil hatching out that it has so maternally brooded, it denies it and avenges it. The upper society of Bordeaux, supposing Mademoiselle Evangelista to have a fortune of a million francs, handed her over to Paul without awaiting the consent of the parties concerned—as it often does. Their fortunes, like themselves, were admirably matched. Paul was accustomed to the luxury and elegance in which Natalie lived. He had arranged and decorated his house as no one else could have arranged a home for Natalie. None but a man accustomed to the expenses of Paris life and the caprices of Paris women could escape the pecuniary difficulties which might result from marrying a girl who was already quite as much a Creole and a fine lady as her mother. Where a Bordelais in love with Mademoiselle Evangelista would be ruined, the Comte de Manerville, said the world, would steer clear of disaster.

So the affair was settled; the magnates of the tiptop royalist circle, when the marriage was mentioned in their presence, made such civil speeches to Paul as flattered his vanity.

"Every one says you are to marry Mademoiselle Evangelista. You will do well to marry her; you will not find so handsome a wife anywhere, not even in Paris; she is elegant, pleasing, and allied through her mother with the Casa-Reals. You will be the most charming couple; you have the same tastes, the same views of life, and will keep the most agreeable house in Bordeaux. Your wife will only have to pack up her clothes and move in. In a case like yours a house ready to live in is as good as a settlement. And you are lucky to meet with a mother-in-law like Madame Evangelista. She is a clever woman, very attractive, and will be an important aid to you in the political career you ought now to aspire to. And she has sacrificed everything for her daughter, whom she worships, and Natalie will no doubt be a good wife, for she is loving to her mother.—And then, everything must have an end."

"That is all very fine," was Paul's reply; for, in love though he was, he wished to be free to choose, "but it must have a happy end."

Paul soon became a frequent visitor to Madame Evangelista, led there by the need to find employment for his idle hours, which he, more than other men, found it difficult to fill. There only in the town did he find the magnificence and luxury to which he had accustomed himself.

Madame Evangelista, at the age of forty, was handsome still, with the beauty of a grand sunset, which in summer crowns the close of a cloudless day. Her blameless reputation was an endless subject of discussion in the "sets" of Bordeaux society, and the curiosity of women was all the more alert, because the widow's appearance suggested the sort of temperament which makes Spanish and Creole women notorious. She had black eyes and hair, the foot and figure of a Spaniard—the slender serpentine figure for which the Spaniards have a name. Her face, still beautiful, had the fascinating Creole complexion, which can only be described by comparing it with white muslin over warm blood-color, so equably tinted is its fairness. Her form was round, and attractive for the grace which combines the ease of indolence with vivacity, strength with extreme freedom. She was attractive, but imposing; she fascinated, but made no promises. Being tall, she could at will assume the port and dignity of a queen.

Men were ensnared by her conversation, as birds are by bird-lime, for she had by nature the spirit which necessity bestows on intriguers; she would go on from concession to concession, arming herself with what she gained to ask for something more, but always able to withdraw a thousand yards at a bound if she were asked for anything in return. She was ignorant of facts, but she had known the Courts of Spain and of Naples, the most famous persons of the two Americas, and various illustrious families of England and of the Continent, which gave her an amount of information superficially so wide that it seemed immense. She entertained with the taste and dignity that cannot be learned, though to certain refined minds they become a second nature, assimilating the best of everything wherever they find it. Though her reputation for virtue remained unexplained, it served the purpose of giving weight to her actions, speech, and character.

The mother and daughter were truly friends, apart from filial and maternal feeling. They suited each other, and their perpetual contact had never resulted in a jar. Thus many persons accounted for Madame Evangelista's self-sacrifice by her love for her daughter. However, though Natalie may have consoled her mother for her unalleviated widowhood, she was not perhaps its only motive. Madame Evangelista was said to have fallen in love with a man whom the second Restoration had reinstated in his title and peerage. This man, who would willingly have married her in 1814, had very decently thrown her over in 1816.

Now Madame Evangelista, apparently the best-hearted creature living, had in her nature one terrible quality which can be best expressed in Catherine de' Medici's motto, *Odiate e aspettate*—Hate and wait. Used always to be first, always to be obeyed, she resembled royal personages in being amiable, gentle, perfectly sweet and easy-going in daily life; but terrible, implacable, when offended in her pride as a woman, a Spaniard, and a Casa-Real. She never forgave. This woman believed in the power of her own hatred; she regarded it as an evil spell which hung over her enemies. This fateful influence she had cast over the man who had been false to her. Events which seemed to prove the efficacy of her *jettatura* confirmed her in her superstitious belief in it. Though he was a minister and a member of the Upper Chamber, ruin stole upon him, and he was utterly undone. His estate, his political and personal position—all was lost. One day Madame Evangelista was able to drive past him in her handsome carriage while he stood in the Champs-Elysées, and to blight him with a look sparkling with the fires of triumph.

This misadventure, occupying her mind for two years, had hindered her marrying again; and afterwards her pride constantly suggested comparisons between those who offered themselves and the husband who had loved her so truly and generously. And thus, from disappointment to hesitancy, from hope to disenchantment, she had come to an age when women have no part to fill in life but that of a mother, devoting themselves to their daughters, and transferring all their interests from themselves to the members of another household, the last investment of human affection.

Madame Evangelista quickly read Paul's character and concealed her own. He was the very man she hoped for as a son-in-law, as the responsible editor of her influence and authority. He was related through his mother to the Maulincours; and the old Baronne de Maulincour, the friend of the Vidame de Pamiers, lived in the heart of the Faubourg Saint-Germain. The grandson of the Baronne, Auguste de Maulincour, had a brilliant position in society. Thus Paul would advantageously introduce the Evangelistas to the World of Paris. The widow had at rare intervals visited Paris under the Empire; she longed to shine in Paris under the Restoration. There only were the elements to be found of political success, the only form of fortune-making in which a woman of fashion can allow herself to co-operate.

Madame Evangelista, obliged by her husband's business to live in Bordeaux, had never liked it; she had a house there, and every one knows how many obligations fetter a woman's life under such circumstances; but she was tired of Bordeaux, she had exhausted its resources. She wished for a wider stage, as gamblers go where the play is highest. So, for her own benefit, she dreamed of high destinies for Paul. She intended to use her own cleverness and knowledge of life for her son-in-law's advancement, so as to enjoy the pleasures of power in his name. Many men are thus the screen of covert feminine ambitions. And, indeed, Madame Evangelista had more than one motive for wishing to govern her daughter's husband.

Paul was, of course, captivated by the lady, all the more certainly because she seemed not to wish to influence him in any way. She used her ascendency to magnify herself, to magnify her daughter, and to give enhanced value to everything about her, so as to have the upper hand from the first with the man in whom she saw the means of continuing her aristocratic connection.

And Paul valued himself the more highly for this appreciation of the mother and daughter. He fancied himself wittier than he was, when he found that his remarks and his slightest jests were responded to by Mademoiselle Evangelista, who smiled or looked up intelligently, and by her mother, whose flattery always seemed to be involuntary. The two women were so frankly kind, he felt so sure of pleasing them, they drove him so cleverly by the guiding thread of his conceit, that, before long, he spent most of his time at their house.

Within a year of his arrival Count Paul, without having declared his intentions, was so attentive to Natalie, that he was universally understood to be courting her. Neither mother nor daughter seemed to think of marriage. Mademoiselle Evangelista did not depart from the reserve of a fine lady who knows how to be charming and converse agreeably without allowing the slightest advance towards intimacy. This self-respect, rare among provincial folks, attracted Paul greatly. Shy men are often touchy, unexpected suggestions alarm them. They flee even from happiness if it comes with much display, and are ready to accept unhappiness if it comes in a modest form, surrounded by gentle shades. Hence Paul, seeing that Madame Evangelista made no effort to entrap him, ensnared himself. The Spanish lady captivated him finally one evening by saying that at a certain age a superior woman, like a man, found that ambition took the place of the feelings of earlier years.

"That woman," thought Paul, as he went away, "would be capable of getting me some good embassy before I could even be elected deputy."

The man who, under any circumstances, fails to look at everything or at every idea from all sides, to examine them under all aspects, is inefficient and weak, and consequently in danger. Paul at this moment was an optimist; he saw advantages in every contingency, and never remembered that an ambitious mother-in-law may become a tyrant. So every evening as he went home he pictured himself as married, he bewitched himself, and unconsciously shod himself with the slippers of matrimony. He had enjoyed his liberty too long to regret it; he was tired of single life, which could show him nothing new, and of which he now saw only the discomforts; whereas, though the difficulties of marriage sometimes occurred to him, he far more often contemplated its pleasures; the prospect was new to him.

"Married life," said he to himself, "is hard only on the poorer classes. Half its troubles vanish before wealth."

So every day some hopeful suggestion added to the list of advantages which he saw in this union.

"However high I may rise in life, Natalie will always be equal to her position," he would say to himself, "and that is no small merit in a wife. How many men of the Empire have I seen suffering torment from their wives! Is it not an important element of happiness never to feel one's pride or vanity rubbed the wrong way by the companion one has chosen? A man can never be utterly wretched with a well-bred woman; she never makes him contemptible, and she may be of use. Natalie will be a perfect mistress of a drawing-room."

Then he fell back on his recollections of the most distinguished women of the Faubourg Saint-Germain, to convince himself that Natalie could at least meet them on a footing of perfect equality, if not eclipse them. Every comparison was to Natalie's advantage. The terms of the comparisons indeed, derived from his imagination, yielded to his wishes. In Paris some new figure would each day have crossed his path, girls of different styles of beauty, and the variety of such impressions would have given balance to his mind; but at Bordeaux Natalie had no rival, she was the single flower, and had blossomed very cleverly at the juncture when Paul was under the tyranny of an idea to which most men fall victims. These conditions of propinquity, added to the reasoning of his vanity and a genuine affection, which could find no issue but in marriage, led Paul on to an increasing passion, of which he was wise enough to keep the secret to himself, construing it as a wish simply to get married.

He even endeavored to study Mademoiselle Evangelista in a way that would not compromise his ultimate decision in his own eyes, for his friend de Marsay's terrible speech rang in his ears now and again. But, in the first place, those who are accustomed to luxury have a tone of simplicity that is very deceptive. They scorn it, they use it habitually, it is the means and not the object of their lives. Paul, as he saw that these ladies' lives were so similar to his own, never for an instant imagined that they concealed any conceivable source of ruin. And then, though there are a few general rules for mitigating the worries of married life, there are none to enable us to guess or foresee them.

When troubles arise between two beings who have undertaken to make life happy and easy each for the other, they are based on the friction produced by an incessant intimacy which does not arise between two persons before marriage, and never can arise till the laws and habits of French life are changed. Two beings on the eve of joining their lives always deceive each other; but the deception is innocent and involuntary. Each, of course, stands in the best light; they are rivals as to which makes the most promising show, and at that time form a favorable idea of themselves which they cannot afterwards come up to. Real life, like a changeable day, consists more often of the gray, dull hours when Nature is overcast than of the brilliant intervals when the sun gives glory and joy to the fields. Young people look only at the fine days. Subsequently they ascribe the inevitable troubles of life to matrimony, for there is in man a tendency to seek the cause of his griefs in things or persons immediately at hand.

To discover in Mademoiselle Evangelista's demeanor or countenance, in her words or her gestures, any indication that might reveal the quota of imperfection inherent in her character, Paul would have needed not merely the science of Lavater and of Gall, but another kind of knowledge for which no code of formulas exists, the personal intuition of the observer, which requires almost universal knowledge.

Like all girls, Natalie's countenance was impenetrable. The deep, serene peace given by sculptors to the virgin heads intended to personify Justice, Innocence, all the divinities who dwell above earthly agitations—this perfect calm is the greatest charm of a girlish face, it is the sign-manual of her purity; nothing has stirred her, no repressed passion, no betrayed affection has cast a shade on the placidity of her features; and if it is assumed, the girl has ceased to exist. Living always inseparable from her mother, Natalie, like every Spanish woman, had had none but religious teaching, and some few lessons of a mother to her daughter which might be useful for her part in life. Hence her calm expression was natural; but it was a veil, in which the woman was shrouded as a butterfly is in the chrysalis.

At the same time, a man skilled in the use of the scalpel of analysis might have discerned in Natalie some revelation of the difficulties her character might present in the conflict of married or social life. Her really wonderful beauty was marked by excessive regularity of features, in perfect harmony with the proportions of her head and figure. Such perfection does not promise well for the intellect, and there are few exceptions to this rule. Superior qualities show in some slight imperfections of form which become exquisitely attractive, points of light where antagonistic feelings sparkle and rivet the eye. Perfect harmony indicates the coldness of a compound nature.

Natalie had a round figure, a sign of strength, but also an infallible evidence of self-will often reaching the pitch of obstinacy in women whose mind is neither keen nor broad. Her hands, like those of a Greek statue, confirmed the forecast of her face and form by showing a love of unreasoning dominion—Will for will's sake. Her brows met in the middle, which, according to observers, indicates a disposition to jealousy. The jealousy of noble souls becomes emulation and leads to great things; that of mean minds turns to hatred. Her mother's motto, *Odiate e aspettate,* was hers in all its strength. Her eyes looked black, but were in fact dark hazel-brown, and contrasted with her hair of that russet hue, so highly prized by the Romans, and known in English as auburn, the usual color of the hair in the children of two black-haired parents like Monsieur and Madame Evangelista. Her delicately white skin added infinitely to the charm of this contrast of colors in her hair and eyes, but this refinement was purely superficial; for whenever the lines of a face have not a peculiar soft roundness, whatever the refinement and delicacy of the details, do not look for any especial charms of mind. These flowers of delusive youth presently fade, and you are surprised after the lapse of a few years to detect hardness, sternness, where you once admired the elegance of lofty qualities.

There was something august in Natalie's features; still, her chin was rather heavy—a painter would have said thick in *impasto,* an expression descriptive of a type that shows pre-existing sentiments of which the violence does not declare itself till middle life. Her mouth, a little sunk in her face, showed the arrogance no less expressed in her hand, her chin, her eyebrows, and her stately shape. Finally, a last sign which alone might have warned the judgment of a connoisseur, Natalie's pure and fascinating voice had a metallic ring. However gently the brazen instrument was handled, however tenderly the vibrations were sent through the curves of the horn, that voice proclaimed a nature like that of the Duke of Alva, from whom the Casa-Reals were collaterally descended. All these indications pointed to passions, violent but not tender, to sudden infatuations, irreconcilable hatred, a certain wit without intellect, and the craving to rule, inherent in persons who feel themselves below their pretensions.

These faults, the outcome of race and constitution, sometimes compensated for by the impulsions of generous blood, were hidden in Natalie as ore is hidden in the mine, and would only be brought to the surface by the rough treatment and shocks to which character is subjected in the world. At present the sweetness and freshness of youth, the elegance of her manners, her saintly ignorance, and the grace of girlhood, tinged her features with the delicate veneer that always must deceive superficial observers. Then her mother had given her the habit of agreeable talk which lends a tone of superiority, replies to argument by banter, and has a fascinating flow under which a woman hides the tufa of a shallow mind, as nature hides a barren soil under a luxuriant growth of ephemeral plants. And Natalie had the charm of spoilt children who have known no griefs; her frankness was seductive, she had not the prim manners which mothers impress on their daughters by laying down a code of absurd reserve and speech when they wish to get them married. She was sincere and gay, as a girl is, who, knowing nothing of marriage, expects happiness only, foresees no disaster, and believes that as a wife she will acquire the right of always having her own way.

How should Paul, who loved as a man does when love is seconded by desire, foresee in a girl of this temper, whose beauty dazzled him, the woman as she would be at thirty, when shrewder observers might have been deceived by appearances? If happiness were difficult to find in married life, with this girl it would not be impossible. Some fine qualities shone through her defects. In the hand of a skilful master any good quality may be made to stifle faults, especially in a girl who can love.

But to make so stern a metal ductile, the iron fist of which de Marsay had spoken was needed. The Paris dandy was right. Fear, inspired by love, is an infallible tool for dealing with a woman's spirit. Those who fear, love; and fear is more nearly akin to love than to hatred.—Would Paul have the coolness, the judgment, the firmness needed in the contest of which no wife should be allowed to have a suspicion? And again, did Natalie love Paul?

Natalie, like most girls, mistook for love the first impulses of instinct and liking that Paul's appearance stirred in her, knowing nothing of the meaning of marriage or of housewifery. To her the Comte de Manerville, who had seen diplomatic service at every court in Europe, one of the most fashionable men of Paris, could not be an ordinary man devoid of moral strength, with a mixture of bravery and shyness, energetic perhaps in adversity, but defenceless against the foes that poison happiness. Would she develop tact enough to discern Paul's good qualities among his superficial defects? Would she not magnify these and forget those, after the manner of young wives who know nothing of life?

At a certain age a woman will overlook vice in the man who spares her petty annoyances, while she regards such annoyances as misfortunes. What conciliatory influence and what experience would cement and enlighten this young couple? Would not Paul and his wife imagine that love was all in all, when they were only at the stage of affectionate grimacing in which young wives indulge at the beginning of their life, and of the compliments a husband pays on their return from a ball while he still has the courtesy of admiration?

In such a situation would not Paul succumb to his wife's tyranny instead of asserting his authority? Would he be able to say "No"? All was danger for a weak man in circumstances where a strong one might perhaps have run some risk.

The subject of this study is not the transition of an unmarried to a married man—a picture which, broadly treated, would not lack the interest which the inmost storm of our feelings must lend to the commonest facts of life. The events and ideas which culminated in Paul's marriage to Mademoiselle Evangelista are an introduction to the work, and only intended as a study to the great comedy which is the prologue to every married life. Hitherto this passage has been neglected by dramatic writers, though it offers fresh resources to their wit.

This prologue, which decided Paul's future life, and to which Madame Evangelista looked forward with terror, was the discussion to which the marriage settlements give rise in every family, whether of the nobility or of the middle class; for human passions are quite as strongly agitated by small interests as by great ones. These dramas, played out in the presence of the notary, are all more or less like this one, and its real interest will be less in these pages than in the memory of most married people.

Early in the winter of 1822 Paul de Manerville, through the intervention of his grand-aunt, Madame la Baronne de Maulincour, asked the hand of Mademoiselle Evangelista. Though the Baroness usually spent no more than two months in Médoc, she remained on this occasion till the end of October to be of use to her grand-nephew in this matter, and play the part of a mother. After laying the overtures before Madame Evangelista, the experienced old lady came to report to Paul on the results of this step.

"My boy," said she, "I have settled the matter. In discussing money matters I discovered that Madame Evangelista gives her daughter nothing. Mademoiselle Natalie marries with but her barest right.—Marry, my dear; men who have a name and estates to transmit must sooner or later end by marriage. I should like to see my dear Auguste do the same.

"You can get married without me, I have nothing to bestow on you but my blessing, and old women of my age have no business at weddings. I shall return to Paris to-morrow. When you introduce your wife to society, I shall see her much more comfortably than I can here.—If you had not your house in Paris, you would have found a home with me. I should have been delighted to arrange my second-floor rooms to suit you."

"Dear aunt," said Paul, "thank you very warmly. . . . But what do you mean by saying her mother gives her nothing, and that she marries only with her bare rights?"

"Her mother, my dear boy, is a very knowing hand, who is taking advantage of the girl's beauty to make terms and give you no more than what she cannot keep back—the father's fortune. We old folks, you know, think a great deal of 'How much has he? How much has she?' I advise you to give strict instructions to your notary. The marriage contract, my child, is a sacred duty. If your father and mother had not made their bed well, you might now be without sheets.—You will have children—they are the usual result of marriage—so you are bound to think of this. Call in Maître Mathias, our old notary."

Madame de Maulincour left Paul plunged in perplexity. —His mother-in-law was a knowing hand! He must discuss and defend his interests in the marriage contract!—Who, then, proposed to attack them? So he took his aunt's advice and entrusted the matter of settlements to Maître Mathias.

Still, he could not help thinking of the anticipated discussion. And it was not without much trepidation that he went to see Madame Evangelista with a view to announcing his intentions. Like all timid people, he was afraid lest he should betray the distrust suggested by his aunt, which he thought nothing less than insulting. To avoid the slightest friction with so imposing a personage as his future stepmother seemed to him, he fell back on the circumlocutions natural to those who dare not face a difficulty.

"Madame, you know what an old family notary is like," said he, when Natalie was absent for a minute. "Mine is a worthy old man, who would be deeply aggrieved if I did not place my marriage contract in his hands——"

"But, my dear fellow," said Madame Evangelista, interrupting him, "are not marriage contracts always settled through the notaries on each side?"

During the interval while Paul sat pondering, not daring to open the matter, Madame Evangelista had been wondering, "What is he thinking about?" for women have a great power of reading thought from the play of feature. And she could guess at the great-aunt's hints from the embarrassed gaze and agitated tone which betrayed Paul's mental disturbance.

"At last," thought she, "the decisive moment has come; the crisis is at hand; what will be the end of it?—My notary," she went on, after a pause, "is Maître Solonet, and yours is Maître Mathias; I will ask them both to dinner to-morrow, and they can settle the matter between them. Is it not their business to conciliate our interests without our meddling, as it is that of the cook to feed us well?"

"Why, of course," said he, with a little sigh of relief.

By a strange inversion of parts, Paul, who was blameless, quaked, while Madame Evangelista, though dreadfully anxious, appeared calm. The widow owed her daughter the third of the fortune left by Monsieur Evangelista, twelve hundred thousand francs, and was quite unable to pay it, even if she stripped herself of all her possessions. She would be at her son-in-law's mercy. Though she might override Paul alone, would Paul, enlightened by his lawyer, agree to any compromise as to the account of her stewardship? If he withdrew, all Bordeaux would know the reason, and it would be impossible for Natalie to marry. The mother who wished to secure her daughter's happiness, the woman who from the hour of her birth had lived in honor, foresaw the day when she must be dishonest.

Like those great generals who would fain wipe out of their lives the moment when they were cowards at heart, she wished she could score out that day from the days of her life. And certainly some of her hairs turned white in the course of the night when, face to face with this difficulty, she bitterly blamed herself for her want of care.

In the first place, she was obliged to confide in her lawyer, whom she sent for to attend her as soon as she was up. She had to confess a secret vexation which she had never admitted even to herself, for she had walked on to the verge of the precipice, trusting to one of those chances that never happen. And a feeling was born in her soul, a little animus against Paul that was not yet hatred, nor aversion, nor in any way evil—but, was not he the antagonistic party in this family suit? Was he not, unwittingly; an innocent enemy who must be defeated? And who could ever love any one he had duped?

Compelled to deceive, the Spanish woman resolved, like any woman, to show her superiority in a contest of which the entire success could alone wipe out the discredit. In the silence of the night she excused herself by a line of argument, in which her pride had the upper hand. Had not Natalie benefited by her lavishness? Had her conduct ever been actuated by one of the base and ignoble motives that degrade the soul? She could not keep accounts—well, was that a sin, a crime? Was not a man only too lucky to win such a wife as Natalie? Was not the treasure she had preserved for him worth a discharge in full? Did not many a man pay for the woman he loved by making great sacrifices? And why should he do more for a courtesan than for a wife?—Besides, Paul was a commonplace, incapable being; she would support him by the resources of her own cleverness; she would help him to make his way in the world; he would owe his position to her; would not this amply pay the debt? He would be a fool to hesitate! And for a few thousand francs more or less? It would be disgraceful!

"If I am not at once successful," said she to herself, "I leave Bordeaux. I can still secure a good match for Natalie by realizing all that is left—the house, my diamonds, and the furniture, giving her all but an annuity for myself."

When a strongly tempered spirit plans a retreat, as Richelieu did at Brouage, and schemes for a splendid finale, this alternative becomes a fulcrum which helps the schemer to triumph. This escape, in case of failure, reassured Madame Evangelista, who went to sleep indeed, full of confidence in her second in this duel. She trusted greatly to the aid of the cleverest notary in Bordeaux, Maître Solonet, a young man of seven-and-twenty, a member of the Legion of Honor as the reward of having contributed actively to the restoration of the Bourbons. Proud and delighted to be admitted to an acquaintance with Madame Evangelista, less as a lawyer than as belonging to the Royalist party in Bordeaux,

A MARRIAGE SETTLEMENT

Solonet cherished for her sunset beauty one of those passions which such women as Madame Evangelista ignore while they are flattered by them, and which even the prudish allow to float in their wake. Solonet lived in an attitude of vanity full of respect and seemly attentions. This young man arrived next morning with the zeal of a slave, and was admitted to the widow's bedroom, where he found her coquettishly dressed in a becoming wrapper.

"Now," said she, "can I trust to your reticence and entire devotion in the discussion which is to take place this evening? Of course, you can guess that my daughter's marriage contract is in question."

The young lawyer was profuse in protestations.

"For the facts, then," said she.

"I am all attention," he replied, with a look of concentration.

Madame Evangelista stated the case without any finessing.

"My dear madame, all this matters not," said Maître Solonet, assuming an important air when his client had laid the exact figures before him. "How have you dealt with Monsieur de Manerville? The moral attitude is of greater consequence than any questions of law or finance."

Madame Evangelista robed herself in dignity; the young notary was delighted to learn that to this day his client, in her treatment of Paul, had preserved the strictest distance; half out of real pride, and half out of unconscious self-interest, she had always behaved to the Comte de Manerville as though he were her inferior, and it would be an honor for him to marry Mademoiselle Evangelista. Neither she nor her daughter could be suspected of interested motives; their feelings were evidently free from meanness; if Paul should raise the least difficulty on the money question, they had every right to withdraw to an immeasurable distance—in fact, she had a complete ascendency over her would-be son-in-law.

"This being the case," said Solonet, "what is the utmost concession you are inclined to make?"

"The least possible," said she, laughing.

"A woman's answer!" replied Solonet. "Madame, do you really wish to see Mademoiselle Natalie married?"

"Yes."

"And you want a discharge for the eleven hundred and fifty-six thousand francs you will owe her in accordance with the account rendered of your guardianship?"

"Exactly!"

"How much do you wish to reserve?"

"At least thirty thousand francs a year."

"So we must conquer or perish?"

"Yes."

"Well, I will consider the ways and means of achieving that end, for we must be very dexterous, and husband our resources. I will give you a few hints on arriving; act on them exactly, and I can confidently predict complete success.—Is Count Paul in love with Mademoiselle Natalie?" he asked as he rose.

"He worships her."

"That is not enough. Is he so anxious to have her as his wife that he will pass over any little pecuniary difficulties?"

"Yes."

"That is what I call having personal property in a daughter!" exclaimed the notary. "Make her look her best this evening," he added, with a cunning twinkle.

"We have a perfect dress for her."

"The dress for the Contract, in my opinion, is half the settlements," said Solonet.

This last argument struck Madame Evangelista as so cogent that she insisted on helping her daughter to dress, partly to superintend the toilet, but also to secure her as an innocent accomplice in her financial plot. And her daughter, with her coiffure à la Sévigné, and a white cashmere dress with rose-colored bows, seemed to her handsome enough to assure the victory.

When the maid had left them, and Madame Evangelista

A MARRIAGE SETTLEMENT

was sure that nobody was within hearing, she arranged her daughter's curls as a preliminary.

"My dear child, are you sincerely attached to Monsieur de Manerville?" said she in a steady voice.

The mother and daughter exchanged a strangely meaning glance.

"Why, my little mother, should you ask to-day rather than yesterday? Why have you allowed me to imagine a doubt?"

"If it were to part you from me for ever, would you marry him all the same?"

"I could give him up without dying of grief."

"Then you do not love him, my dear," said the mother, kissing her daughter's forehead.

"But why, my dear mamma, are you playing the grand inquisitor?"

"I wanted to see if you cared to be married without being madly in love with your husband."

"I like him."

"You are right; he is a Count, and, between us, he shall be made peer of France. But there will be difficulties."

"Difficulties between people who care for each other?—No! Pease-blossom, my dear mother, is too well planted there," and she pointed to her heart with a pretty gesture, "to make the smallest objection; I am sure of that."

"But if it were not so?"

"I should utterly forget him."

"Well said! You are a Casa-Real.—But though he is madly in love with you, if certain matters were discussed which do not immediately concern him, but which he would have to make the best of for your sake and mine, Natalie, heh? If, without proceeding in the least too far, a little graciousness of manner might turn the scale?—A mere nothing, you know, a word? Men are like that—they can resist sound argument and yield to a glance."

"I understand! A little touch just to make Favorite leap

the gate," said Natalie, with a flourish as if she were whipping a horse.

"My darling, I do not wish you to do anything approaching to invitation. We have traditions of old Castilian pride which will never allow us to go too far. The Count will be informed of my situation."

"What situation?"

"You would not understand if I told you.—Well, if after seeing you in all your beauty his eyes should betray the slightest hesitancy—and I shall watch him—at that instant I should break the whole thing off; I should turn everything into money, leave Bordeaux, and go to Douai, to the Claës, who, after all, are related to us through the Temnincks. Then I would find a French peer for your husband, even if I had to take refuge in a convent and give you my whole fortune."

"My dear mother, what can I do to hinder such misfortunes?" said Natalie.

"I never saw you lovelier, my child! Be a little purposely attractive, and all will be well."

Madame Evangelista left Natalie pensive, and went to achieve a toilet which allowed her to stand a comparison with her daughter. If Natalie was to fascinate Paul, must not she herself fire the enthusiasm of her champion Solonet?

The mother and daughter were armed for conquest when Paul arrived with the bouquet which for some months past had been his daily offering to Natalie. Then they sat chatting while awaiting the lawyers.

This day was to Paul the first skirmish in the long and weary warfare of married life. It is necessary, therefore, to review the forces on either side, to place the belligerents, and to define the field on which they are to do battle.

To second him in a struggle of which he did not in the least appreciate the consequences, Paul had nobody but his old lawyer Mathias. They were each to be surprised unarmed by an unexpected manœuvre, driven by an enemy whose plans were laid, and compelled to act without having time for reflection. What man but would have failed even with Cujas and Barthole to back him? How should he fear perfidy when everything seemed so simple and natural?

What could Mathias do single-handed against Madame Evangelista, Solonet, and Natalie, especially when his client was a lover who would go over to the enemy as soon as his happiness should seem to be imperiled? Paul was already entangling himself by making the pretty speeches customary with lovers, to which his passion gave an emphasis of immense value in the eyes of Madame Evangelista, who was leading him on to commit himself.

The matrimonial *condottieri,* who were about to do battle for their clients, and whose personal prowess would prove decisive in this solemn contest—the two notaries—represented the old and the new schools, the old and the new style of notary.

Maître Mathias was a worthy old man of sixty-nine, proud of twenty years' practice in his office. His broad, gouty feet were shod in shoes with silver buckles, and were an absurd finish to legs so thin, with such prominent knee-bones, that when he crossed his feet they looked like the cross-bones on a tombstone. His lean thighs, lost in baggy black knee-breeches with silver buckles, seemed to bend under the weight of a burly stomach and the round shoulders characteristic of men who live in an office! a huge ball, always clothed in a green coat with square-cut skirts, which no one remembered ever to have seen new. His hair, tightly combed back and powdered, was tied in a rat's tail that always tucked itself away between the collar of his coat and that of his flowered white waistcoat. With his bullet head, his face as red as a vine-leaf, his blue eyes, trumpet-nose, thick lips, and double chin, the dear little man, wherever he went, aroused the laughter so liberally bestowed by the French on the grotesque creations which Nature sometimes allows herself and Art thinks it funny to exaggerate, calling them caricatures.

But in Maître Mathias the mind had triumphed over the body, the qualities of the soul had vanquished the eccentricity of his appearance. Most of the townsfolk treated him with friendly respect and deference full of esteem. The notary's voice won all hearts by the eloquent ring of honesty. His only cunning consisted in going straight to the point, oversetting every evil thought by the directness of his questions. His sharply observant eye, and his long experience of business, gave him that spirit of divination which allowed him to read consciences and discern the most secret thoughts. Though grave and quiet in business, this patriarch had the cheerfulness of our ancestors. He might, one felt, risk a song at table, accept and keep up family customs, celebrate anniversaries and birthdays, whether of grandparents or children, and bury the Christmas log with due ceremony; he loved to give New Year's gifts, to invent surprises, and bring out Easter eggs; he believed, no doubt, in the duties of a godfather, and would never neglect any old-time custom that gave color to life of yore.

Maître Mathias was a noble and respectable survival of the notaries, obscure men of honor, of whom no receipt was asked for millions, and who returned them in the same bags, tied with the same string; who fulfilled every trust to the letter, drew up inventories for probate with decent feeling, took a paternal interest in their client's affairs, put a bar sometimes in the way of a spendthrift, and were the depositaries of family secrets; in short, one of those notaries who considered themselves responsible for blunders in their deeds, and who gave time and thought to them. Never, in the whole of his career as a notary, had one of his clients to complain of a bad investment, of a mortgage ill chosen or carelessly managed. His wealth, slowly but honestly acquired, had been accumulated through thirty years of industry and economy. He had found places for fourteen clerks. Religious and generous in secret, Mathias was always to be found where good was to be done without reward. He was an acting member of the Board of Asylums and the Charitable Committee, and the largest subscriber to the voluntary rates for the relief of unexpected disaster, or the establishment of some useful institution. Thus, neither he nor his wife had a carriage; his word was sacred; he had as much money deposited in his cellar as lay at the bank; he was known as "Good Monsieur Mathias"; and when he died, three thousand persons followed him to the grave.

Solonet was the youthful notary who comes in humming a tune, who affects an airy manner, and declares that business may be done quite as efficiently with a laugh as with a serious countenance; the notary who is a captain in the National Guard, who does not like to be known for a lawyer, and aims at the Cross of the Legion of Honor, who keeps his carriage and leaves the correcting of his deeds to his clerks; the notary who goes to balls and to the play, who buys pictures and plays *écarté,* who has a cash drawer into which he pours deposit-money, repaying in notes what he receives in gold; the notary who keeps pace with the times and risks his capital in doubtful investments, who speculates, hoping to retire with an income of thirty thousand francs after ten years in his office; the notary whose acumen is the outcome of duplicity, and who is feared by many as an accomplice in possession of their secrets; the notary who regards his official position as a means of marrying some blue-stocking heiress.

When the fair and elegant Solonet—all curled and scented, booted like a lover of the Vaudeville, and dressed like a dandy whose most important business is a duel—entered the room before his older colleague, who walked slowly from a touch of the gout, the two were the living representatives of one of the caricatures entitled "Then and Now," which had great success under the Empire.

Though Madame and Mademoiselle Evangelista, to whom "Good Monsieur Mathias" was a stranger, at first felt a slight inclination to laugh, they were at once touched by the perfect grace of his greeting. The worthy man's speech was full of the amenity that an amiable old man can infuse both into what he says and the manner of saying it.

The younger man, with his frothy sparkle, was at once thrown into the shade. Mathias showed his superior breeding by the measured respect of his address to Paul. Without humiliating his white hairs, he recognized the young man's rank, while appreciating the fact that certain honors are due to old age, and that all such social rights are interdependent. Solonet's bow and "How d' do?" were, on the contrary, the utterance of perfect equality, which could not fail to offend the susceptibilities of a man of the world, and to make himself ridiculous in the eyes of a man of rank.

The young notary, by a somewhat familiar gesture, invited Madame Evangelista to speak with him in a window-recess. For some few moments they spoke in whispers, laughing now and then, no doubt to mislead the others as to the importance of the conversation, in which Maître Solonet communicated the plan of battle to the lady in command.

"And could you really," said he, in conclusion, "make up your mind to sell your house?"

"Undoubtedly!" said she.

Madame Evangelista did not choose to tell her lawyer her reasons for such heroism, as he thought it, for Solonet's zeal might have cooled if he had known that his client meant to leave Bordeaux. She had not even said so to Paul, not wishing to alarm him prematurely by the extent of the circumvallations needed for the first outworks of a political position.

After dinner the plenipotentiaries left the lovers with Madame Evangelista, and went into an adjoining room to discuss business. Thus two dramas were being enacted: by the chimney corner in the drawing-room a love scene in which life smiled bright and happy; in the study a serious duologue, in which interest was laid bare, and already played the part it always fills under the most flowery aspects of life.

"My dear sir, the deed will be in your hands; I know what I owe to my senior." Mathias bowed gravely. "But," Solonet went on, unfolding a rough draft, of no use whatever, that a clerk had written out, "as we are the weaker party, as we are the spinster, I have drafted the articles to save you the trouble. We propose to marry with all our rights on a footing of possession in common, an unqualified settlement of all estate, real and personal, each on the other in case of decease without issue; or, if issue survive them, a settlement of one-quarter on the surviving parent, and a life-interest in one quarter more. The sum thrown into common stock to be one-quarter of the estate of each contracting party, the survivor to have all furniture and movables without exception and duty free. It is all as plain as day."

"Ta, ta, ta, ta," said Mathias, "I do not do business as you would sing a ballad. What have you to show?"

"What on your side?" asked Solonet.

"We have to settle," said Mathias, "the estate of Lanstrac, producing twenty-three thousand francs a year in rents, to say nothing of produce in kind: *Item* the farms of le Grassol and le Guadet, each let for three thousand six hundred francs. *Item* the vineyards of Bellerose, yielding on an average sixteen thousand—together forty-six thousand two hundred francs a year. *Item* a family mansion at Bordeaux, rated at nine hundred. *Item* a fine house in Paris, with a forecourt and garden, Rue de la Pépinière, rated at fifteen hundred. These properties, of which I hold the title-deeds, we inherit from our parents, excepting the house in Paris acquired by purchase. We have also to include the furniture of the two houses and of the château of Lanstrac, valued at four hundred and fifty thousand francs. There you have the table, the cloth, and the first course. Now what have you for the second course and the dessert?"

"Our rights and expectations," said Solonet.

"Specify, my dear sir," replied Mathias. "What have you to show? Where is the valuation made at Monsieur Evangelista's death? Show me your valuations, and the investments you hold. Where is your capital—if you have any? Where is your land—if you have land! Show me your guardian's accounts, and tell us what your mother gives or promises to give you."

"Is Monsieur le Comte de Manerville in love with Mademoiselle Evangelista?"

"He means to marry her if everything proves suitable," said the old notary. "I am not a child; this is a matter of business and not of sentiment."

"The business will fall through if you have no sentiment —and generous sentiment; and this is why," said Solonet. "We had no valuation made after our husband's death. Spanish, and a Creole, we knew nothing of French law. And we were too deeply grieved, to think of the petty formalities which absorb colder hearts. It is a matter of public notoriety that the deceased gentleman adored his wife, and that we were plunged in woe. Though we had a probate and a kind of valuation on a general estimate, you may thank the surrogate guardian for that, who called upon us to make a statement and settle a sum on our daughter as best we might just at a time when we were obliged to sell out of the English funds to an enormous amount which we wished to reinvest in Paris at double the interest."

"Come, do not talk nonsense to me. There are means of checking these amounts. How much did you pay in succession duties? The figure will be enough to verify the amounts. Go to the facts. Tell us plainly how much you had, and what is left. And then, if we are too desperately in love, we shall see."

"Well, if you are marrying for money, you may make your bow at once. We may lay claim to more than a million francs; but our mother has nothing of it left but this house and furniture and four hundred odd thousand francs, invested in 1817 in five per cents, and bringing in forty thousand francs a year."

"How then do you keep up a style costing a hundred thousand?" cried Mathias in dismay.

"Our daughter has cost us vast sums. Besides, we like display. And, finally, all your jeremiads will not bring back two sous of it."

"Mademoiselle Natalie might have been very handsomely

brought up on the fifty thousand francs a year that belonged to her without rushing into ruin. And if you ate with such an appetite as a girl, what will you not devour as a wife?"

"Let us go then," said Solonet. "The handsomest girl alive is bound to spend more than she has."

"I will go and speak two words to my client," said the older lawyer.

"Go, go," thought Maître Solonet, "go, old Father Cassandra, and tell your client we have not a farthing." For in the silence of his private office he had strategically disposed of his masses, formed his arguments in columns, fixed the turning-points of the discussion, and prepared the critical moment when the antagonistic parties, thinking all was lost, would jump at a compromise which would be the triumph of his client.

The flowing dress with pink ribbons, the ringlets *à la Sévigné,* Natalie's small foot, her insinuating looks, her slender hand, constantly engaged in rearranging the curls which did not need it—all the tricks of a girl showing off, as a peacock spreads its tail in the sun—had brought Paul to the point at which her mother wished to see him. He was crazy with admiration, as crazy as a schoolboy for a courtesan; his looks, an unfailing thermometer of the mind, marked the frenzy of passion which leads a man to commit a thousand follies.

"Natalie is so beautiful," he whispered to Madame Evangelista, "that I can understand the madness which drives us to pay for pleasure by death."

The lady tossed her head.

"A lover's words!" she replied. "My husband never made me such fine speeches; but he married me penniless, and never in thirteen years gave me an instant's pain."

"Is that a hint for me?" said Paul, smiling.

"You know how truly I care for you, dear boy," said she, pressing his hand. "Besides, do you not think I must love you well to be willing to give you my Natalie?"

"To give me! To give me!" cried the girl, laughing and

waving a fan of Indian feathers. "What are you whispering about?"

"I," said Paul, "was saying how well I love you—since the proprieties forbid my expressing my hopes to you."

"Why?"

"I am afraid of myself."

"Oh! you are too clever not to know how to set the gems of flattery. Would you like me to tell you what I think of you?—Well, you seem to me to have more wit than a man in love should show. To be Pease-blossom and at the same time very clever," said she, looking down, "seems to me an unfair advantage. A man ought to choose between the two. I, too, am afraid."

"Of what?"

"We will not talk like this.—Do not you think, mother, that there is danger in such a conversation when the contract is not yet signed?"

"But it will be," said Paul.

"I should very much like to know what Achilles and Nestor are saying to each other," said Natalie, with a glance of childlike curiosity at the door of the adjoining room.

"They are discussing our children, our death, and I know not what trifles besides," said Paul. "They are counting out our crown-pieces, to tell us whether we may have five horses in the stable. And they are considering certain deeds of gift, but I have forestalled them there."

"How?" said Natalie.

"Have I not given you myself wholly and all I have?" said he, looking at the girl, who was handsomer than ever as the blush brought up by her pleasure at this reply mounted to her cheeks.

"Mother, how am I to repay such generosity?"

"My dear child, is not your life before you? If you make him happy every day, is not that a gift of inexhaustible treasures? I had no other furniture."

"Do you like Lanstrac?" asked Paul.

"How can I fail to like anything that is yours?" said she. "And I should like to see your house."

"Our house," said Paul. "You want to see whether I have anticipated your tastes, if you can be happy there? Your mother has made your husband's task a hard one; you have always been so happy; but when love is infinite, nothing is impossible."

"Dear children," said Madame Evangelista, "do you think you can remain in Bordeaux during the early days of your marriage? If you feel bold enough to face the world that knows you, watches you, criticises you—well and good! But if you both have that coyness which dwells in the soul and finds no utterance, we will go to Paris, where the life of a young couple is lost in the torrent. There only can you live like lovers without fear of ridicule."

"You are right, mother; I had not thought of it. But I shall hardly have time to get the house ready. I will write this evening to de Marsay, a friend on whom I can rely, to hurry on the workmen."

At the very moment when, like all young men who are accustomed to gratify their wishes without any preliminary reflection, Paul was recklessly pledging himself to the expenses of a residence in Paris, Maître Mathias came into the room and signed to his client to come to speak with him.

"What is it, my good friend?" said Paul, allowing himself to be led aside.

"Monsieur le Comte," said the worthy man, "the lady has not a sou. My advice is to put off this discussion till another day to give you the opportunity of acting with propriety."

"Monsieur Paul," said Natalie, "I also should like a private word with you."

Though Madame Evangelista's face was calm, no Jew in the Dark Ages ever suffered greater martyrdom in his cauldron of boiling oil than she is her violet velvet dress. Solonet had pledged himself to the marriage, but she knew not by what means and conditions he meant to succeed, and she endured the most dreadful anguish of alternative courses. She really owed her triumph perhaps to her daughter's disobedience.

Natalie had put her own interpretation on her mother's words, for she could not fail to see her uneasiness. When she perceived the effect of her advances, her mind was torn by a thousand contradictory thoughts. Without criticising her mother, she felt half ashamed of this manœuvring, of which the result was obviously to be some definite advantage. Then she was seized by a very intelligible sort of jealous curiosity. She wanted to ascertain whether Paul loved her well enough to overlook the difficulties her mother had alluded to, and of which the existence was proved by Maître Mathias' cloudy brow. These feelings prompted her to an impulse of honesty which, in fact, became her well. The blackest perfidy would have been less dangerous than her innocence was.

"Paul," said she in an undertone, and it was the first time she had addressed him by his name, "if some difficulties of money matters could divide us, understand that I release you from every pledge, and give you leave to ascribe to me all the blame that could arise from such a separation."

She spoke with such perfect dignity in the expression of her generosity, that Paul believed in her disinterestedness and her ignorance of the fact which the notary had just communicated to him; he pressed the girl's hand, kissing it like a man to whom love is far dearer than money.

Natalie left the room.

"Bless me! Monsieur le Comte, you are committing great follies," growled the old notary, rejoining his client.

But Paul stood pensive; he had expected to have an income of about a hundred thousand francs by uniting his fortune and Natalie's; and however blindly in love a man may be, he does not drop without a pang from a hundred thousand to forty-six thousand francs a year when he marries a woman accustomed to every luxury.

"My daughter is gone," said Madame Evangelista, advancing with royal dignity to where Paul and the notary were standing. "Can you not tell me what is going on!"

"Madame," said Mathias, dismayed by Paul's silence, and forced to break the ice, "an impediment—a delay——"

On this, Maître Solonet came out of the inner room and interrupted his senior with a speech that restored Paul to life. Overwhelmed by the recollection of his own devoted speeches and lover-like attitude, Paul knew not how to withdraw or to modify them; he only longed to fling himself into some yawning gulf.

"There is a way of releasing Madame Evangelista from her debt to her daughter," said the young lawyer with airy ease. "Madame Evangelista holds securities for forty thousand francs yearly in five per cents; the capital will soon be at par, if not higher; we may call it eight hundred thousand francs. This house and garden are worth certainly two hundred thousand. Granting this, madame may, under the marriage contract, transfer the securities and title-deeds to her daughter, reserving only the life-interest, for I cannot suppose that the Count wishes to leave his mother-in-law penniless. Though madame has spent her own fortune, she will thus restore her daughter's, all but a trifling sum."

"Women are most unfortunate when they do not understand business," said Madame Evangelista. "I have securities and title-deeds? What in the world are they?"

Paul was enraptured as he heard this proposal. The old lawyer, seeing the snare spread and his client with one foot already caught in it, stood petrified, saying to himself:

"I believe we are being tricked!"

"If madame takes my advice, she will at least secure peace," the younger man went on. "If she sacrifices herself, at least she will not be worried by the young people. Who can foresee who will live or die?—Monsieur le Comte will then sign a release for the whole sum due to Mademoiselle Evangelista out of her father's fortune."

Mathias could not conceal the wrath that sparkled in his eyes and crimsoned his face.

"A sum of —— ?" he asked, trembling with indignation.

"Of one million one hundred and fifty-six thousand francs, according to the deed——"

"Why do you not ask Monsieur le Comte *hic et nunc* to renounce all claims on his wife's fortune?" said Mathias. "It would be more straightforward.—Well, Monsieur le Comte de Manerville's ruin shall not be accomplished under my eyes. I beg to withdraw."

He went a step towards the door, to show his client that the matter was really serious. But he turned back, and addressing Madame Evangelista, he said:

"Do not suppose, madame, that I imagine you to be in collusion with my colleague in his ideas. I believe you to be an honest woman—a fine lady, who knows nothing of business."

"Thank you, my dear sir!" retorted Solonet.

"You know that there is no question of offence among lawyers," said Mathias.—"But at least, madame, let me explain to you the upshot of this bargain. You are still young enough and handsome enough to marry again. Oh, dear me!" he went on, in reply to a gesture of the lady's, "who can answer for the future?"

"I never thought, monsieur," said she, "that after seven years of widowhood in the prime of life, and after refusing some splendid offers for my daughter's sake, I should, at nine-and-thirty, be thought capable of such madness.—If we were not discussing business, I should regard such a speech as an impertinence."

"Would it not be a greater impertinence to assume that you could not remarry?"

"Can and will are very different words," said Solonet, with a gallant flourish.

"Well," said Mathias, "we need not talk about your marrying. You may—and we all hope you will—live for five-and-forty years yet. Now, since you are to retain your life-interest in the income left by Monsieur Evangelista as long as you live, must your children dine with Duke Humphrey?"

"What is the meaning of it all?" said the widow. "Who is Duke Humphrey, and what is life-interest?"

Solonet, a speaker of elegance and taste, began to laugh.

"I will translate," said the old man: "If your children wish to be prudent, they will think of the future. To think of the future means to save half one's income, supposing there are no more than two children, who must first have a good education, and then a handsome marriage portion. Thus, your daughter and her husband will be reduced to living on twenty thousand francs a year when they have each been accustomed to spend fifty thousand while unmarried. And even that is nothing. My client will be expected to hand over to his children in due course eleven hundred thousand francs as their share of their mother's fortune, and he will never have received any of it if his wife should die and madame survive her—which is quite possible. In all conscience, is not this to throw himself into the Gironde, tied hand and foot? You wish to see Mademoiselle Natalie made happy? If she loves her husband—which no lawyer allows himself to doubt—she will share his troubles. Madame, I foresee enough to make her die of grief, for she will be miserably poor. Yes, madame, miserably poor; for it is poverty to those who require a hundred thousand francs a year to be reduced to twenty thousand. If love should lead Monsieur le Comte into extravagance, his wife would reduce him to beggary by claiming her share in the event of any disaster.

"I am arguing for your sake, for theirs, for that of their children—for all parties."

"The good man has certainly delivered a broadside," thought Solonet, with a glance at his client, as much as to say, "Come on!"

"There is a way of reconciling all these interests," replied Madame Evangelista. "I may reserve only such a small allowance as may enable me to go into a convent, and you will become at once possessed of all my property. I will renounce the world if my death to it will secure my daughter's happiness."

"Madame," said the old man, "let us take time for mature consideration of the steps that may smooth away all difficulties."

"Bless me, my dear sir," cried Madame Evangelista, who foresaw that by delay she would be lost, "all has been considered. I did not know what marriage meant in France; I am a Spanish Creole. I did not know that before I could see my daughter married, I had to make sure how many days longer God would grant me to live, that my child would be wronged by my living, that I have no business to be alive, or ever to have lived.

"When my husband married me I had nothing but my name and myself. My name alone was to him a treasure by which his wealth paled. What fortune can compare with a great name? My fortune was my beauty, virtue, happy temper, birth, and breeding. Can money buy these gifts? If Natalie's father could hear this discussion, his magnanimous spirit would be grieved for ever, and his happiness would be marred in Paradise. I spent millions of francs, foolishly I daresay, without his ever frowning even. Since his death I have been economical and thrifty by comparison with the life he liked me to lead. Let this end it! Monsieur de Manerville is so dejected that I——"

No words can represent the confusion and excitement produced by this exclamation "end it!" It is enough to say that these four well-bred persons all talked at once.

"In Spain you marry Spanish fashion, as you will; but in France, you marry French fashion—rationally, and as you can," said Mathias.

"Ah, madame," Paul began, rousing himself from his stupor, "you are mistaken in my feelings——"

"This is not a question of feelings," said the old man, anxious to stop his client; "this is business affecting three generations. Was it we who made away with the missing millions—we, who merely ask to clear up the difficulties of which we are innocent?"

"Let us marry without further haggling," said Solonet.

"Haggling! Haggling! Do you call it haggling to defend the interests of the children and of their father and mother?" cried Mathias.

"Yes," Paul went on, addressing his mother-in-law, "I deplore the recklessness of my youth, which now hinders my closing this discussion with a word, as much as you deplore your ignorance of business-matters and involuntary extravagance. God be my witness that at this moment I am not thinking of myself; a quiet life at Lanstrac has no terrors for me; but Mademoiselle Natalie would have to give up her tastes and habits. That would alter our whole existence."

"But where did Evangelista find his millions?" said the widow.

"Monsieur Evangelista was a man of business, he played the great game of commerce, he loaded ships and made considerable sums; we are a landed proprietor, our capital is sunk, and our income more or less fixed," the old lawyer replied.

"Still, there is a way out of the difficulty," said Solonet, speaking in a high-pitched key, and silencing the other three by attracting their attention and their eyes.

The young man was like a dexterous coachman who, holding the reins of a four-in-hand, amuses himself by lashing and, at the same time, holding in the team. He spurred their passions and soothed them by turns, making Paul foam in his harness, for to him life and happiness were in the balance; and his client as well, for she did not see her way through the intricacies of the dispute.

"Madame Evangelista may, this very day, hand over the securities in the five per cents, and sell this house. Sold in lots, it will fetch three hundred thousand francs. Madame will pay you one hundred and fifty thousand francs. Thus, madame will pay down nine hundred and fifty thousand francs at once. Though this is not all she owes her daughter, can you find many fortunes to match it in France?"

"Well and good," said Mathias; "but what is madame to **live on?**"

At this question, which implied assent, Solonet said within himself:

"Oh, ho! old fox, so you are caught."

"Madame?" he said aloud. "Madame will keep the fifty thousand crowns left of the price of the house. That sum, added to the sale of her furniture, can be invested in an annuity, and will give her twenty thousand francs a year. Monsieur le Comte will arrange for her to live with him. Lanstrac is a large place. You have a good house in Paris," he went on, addressing Paul, "so madame your mother-in-law can live with you wherever you are. A widow who, having no house to keep up, has twenty thousand francs a year, is better off than madame was when she was mistress of all her fortune. Madame Evangelista has no one to care for but her daughter; Monsieur le Comte also stands alone; your heirs are in the distant future, there is no fear of conflicting interests.

"A son-in-law and a mother-in-law under such circumstances always join to form one household. Madame Evangelista will make up for the deficit of capital by paying a quota out of her annuity which will help towards the housekeeping. We know her to be too generous, too large-minded, to live as a charge on her children.

"Thus, you may live happy and united with a hundred thousand francs a year to spend—a sufficient income, surely, Monsieur le Comte, to afford you, in any country, all the comforts of life and the indulgence of your fancies?—And, believe me, young married people often feel the need of a third in the household. Now, I ask you, what third can be more suitable than an affectionate, good mother?"

Paul, as he listened to Solonet, thought he heard the voice of an angel. He looked at Mathias to see if he did not share his admiration for Solonet's fervid eloquence; for he did not know that, under the assumed enthusiasm of impassioned words, notaries, like attorneys, hide the cold and unremitting alertness of the diplomatist.

"A petty Paradise!" said the old man.

Bewildered by his client's delight, Mathias sat down on an ottoman, resting his head on one hand, lost in evidently grieved meditations. He knew too well the ponderous phrases in which men of business purposely shroud their tricks, and he was not the man to be duped by them. He stole a glance at his fellow-notary and at Madame Evangelista, who went on talking to Paul, and he tried to detect some indications of the plot of which the elaborate design was beginning to be perceptible.

"Monsieur," said Paul to Solonet, "I have to thank you for the care you have devoted to the conciliation of our interests. This arrangement solves all difficulties more happily than I had dared to hope—that is to say, if it suits you, madame," he added, turning to Madame Evangelista, "for I will have nothing to say to any plan that is not equally satisfactory to you."

"I?" said she. "Whatever will make my children happy will delight me. Do not consider me at all."

"But that must not be," said Paul eagerly. "If your comfort and dignity were not secured, Natalie and I should be more distressed about it than you yourself would be."

"Do not be uneasy on that score, Monsieur le Comte," said Solonet.

"Ah!" thought Maître Mathias, "they mean to make him kiss the rod before they scourge him."

"Be quite easy," Solonet went on; "there is such a spirit of speculation in Bordeaux just now, that investments for annuities are to be made on very advantageous terms. After handing over to you the fifty thousand crowns due to you on the sale of the house and furniture, I believe I may guarantee to madame a residue of two hundred thousand francs. This I undertake to invest in an annuity on a first mortgage or an estate worth a million, and to get ten per cent, twenty-five thousand francs a year. Thus we should unite two very nearly equal fortunes. Mademoiselle Natalie will bring forty thousand francs a year in five per cents, and a hundred and fifty thousand francs in money, which will yield seven thousand francs a year; total, forty-seven as against your forty-six thousand."

"That is quite plain," said Paul.

As he ended his speech, Solonet had cast a sidelong glance at his client, not unseen by Mathias, and which was as much as to say, "Bring up your reserve."

"Why!" cried Madame Evangelista, in a tone of joy that seemed quite genuine, "I can give Natalie my diamonds; they must be worth at least a hundred thousand francs."

"We can have them valued," said Solonet, "and this entirely alters the case. Nothing, then, can hinder Monsieur le Comte from giving a discharge in full for the sums due to Mademoiselle Natalie as her share of her father's fortune, or the betrothed couple from taking the guardian's accounts as passed, at the reading of the contract. If madame, with truly Spanish magnificence, despoils herself to fulfill her obligations within a hundred thousand francs of the sum-total, it is but fair to release her."

"Nothing could be fairer," said Paul. "I am only overpowered by so much generosity."

"Is not my daughter my second self?" said Madame Evangelista.

Maître Mathias detected an expression of joy on Madame Evangelista's face when she saw the difficulties so nearly set aside; and this, and the sudden recollection of the diamonds, brought out like fresh troops, confirmed all his suspicions.

"The scene was planned between them," thought he, "as gamblers pack the cards when some pigeon is to be rooked. So the poor boy I have known from his cradle is to be plucked alive by a mother-in-law, done brown by love, and ruined by his wife? After taking such care of his fine estate, am I to see it gobbled up in a single evening? Three millions and a-half mortgaged, in fact, to guarantee eleven hundred thousand francs of her portion, which these two women will make him throw away——"

As he thus discerned in Madame Evangelista's soul a scheme which was not dishonest or criminal—which was not thieving, or cheating, or swindling—which was not based on any evil or blamable feeling, but yet contained the germ of every crime, Maître Mathias was neither shocked nor generously indignant. He was not a misanthrope; he was an old lawyer, inured by his business to the keen self-interest of men of the world, to their ingenious treachery, more deadly than a bold highway murder committed by some poor devil who is guillotined with due solemnity. In the higher ranks these passages of arms, these diplomatic discussions, are like the little dark corners in which every kind of filth is shot.

Maître Mathias, very sorry for his client, cast a long look into the future, and saw no hope of good.

"Well, we must take the field with the same weapons," said he to himself, "and beat them on their own ground."

At this juncture Paul, Solonet, and Madame Evangelista, dismayed by the old man's silence, were feeling the necessity of this stern censor's approbation to sanction these arrangements, and all three looked at him.

"Well, my dear sir, and what do you think of this?" asked Paul.

"This is what I think," replied the uncompromising and conscientious old man, "you are not rich enough to commit such princely follies. The estate of Lanstrac, valued at three per cent, is worth one million of francs, including the furniture; the farms of le Grassol and le Guadet, with the vineyards of Bellerose, are worth another million; your two residences and furniture a third million. To meet these three millions, yielding an income of forty-seven thousand two hundred francs, Mademoiselle Natalie shows eight hundred thousand francs in the funds, and let us say one hundred thousand francs' worth of diamonds—at a hypothetical valuation! Also, one hundred and fifty thousand francs in cash—one million and fifty thousand francs in all. Then, in the face of these facts, my friend here triumphantly asserts that we are uniting equal fortunes! He requires us to stand indebted in a hundred thousand francs to our children, since we are to give the lady a discharge in full, by taking the guardian's accounts as passed, for a sum of eleven hundred and fifty-six thousand francs, while receiving only one million and fifty thousand!

"You can listen to this nonsense with a lover's rapture; and do you suppose that old Mathias, who is not in love, will forget his arithmetic and fail to appreciate the difference between landed estate of enormous value as capital, and of increasing value, and the income derivable from money in securities which are liable to variations in value and diminution of interest. I am old enough to have seen land improve and funds fall.—You called me in, Monsieur le Comte, to stipulate for your interests; allow me to protect them or dismiss me."

"If monsieur looks for a fortune of which the capital is a match for his own," said Solonet, "we have nothing like three millions and a half; that is self-evident. If you can show these overpowering millions, we have but our one poor little million to offer—a mere trifle! three times as much as the dower of an Archduchess of Austria. Bonaparte received two hundred and fifty thousand francs when he married Marie Louise."

"Marie Louise ruined Napoleon," said Maître Mathias in a growl.

Natalie's mother understood the bearing of this speech.

"If my sacrifices are in vain," she exclaimed, "I decline to carry such a discussion any further; I trust to the Count's discretion, and renounce the honor of his proposals for my daughter."

After the manœuvres planned by the young notary this battle of conflicting interests had reached the point where the victory ought to have rested with Madame Evangelista. The mother-in-law had opened her heart, abandoned her possessions, and was almost released. The intending husband was bound to accept the conditions laid down beforehand by the collusion of Maître Solonet and his client, or sin against every law of generosity, and be false to his love.

Like the hand of the clock moved by the works, Paul came duly to the point.

"What, madame," cried he, "you could undo in one moment——"

"Why, monsieur, to whom do I owe my duty? To my daughter.—When she is one-and-twenty she will pass my accounts and release me. She will have a million francs, and can, if she pleases, choose among the sons of the peers of France. Is she not the daughter of a Casa-Real?"

"Madame is quite justified. Why should she be worse off to-day than she will be fourteen months hence? Do not rob her of the benefits of her position," said Solonet.

"Mathias," said Paul, with deep grief, "there are two ways of being ruined—and at this moment you have undone me!"

He went towards the old lawyer, no doubt intending to order that the contract should be at once drawn up. Mathias forefended this disaster by a glance which seemed to say, "Wait!" He saw tears in Paul's eyes—tears of shame at the tenor of this debate, and at the peremptory tone in which Madame Evangelista had thrown him over—and he checked them by a start, the start of Archimedes crying *Eureka!*

The words *Peer of France* had flashed light on his mind like a torch in a cavern.

At this instant Natalie reappeared, as lovely as the dawn, and said with an innocent air:

"Am I in the way?"

"Strangely in the way, my child!" replied her mother, with cruel bitterness.

"Come, dear Natalie," said Paul, taking her hand and leading her to a chair by the fire, "everything is settled!" for he could not endure to think that his hopes were overthrown.

And Mathias eagerly put in:

"Yes, everything can yet be settled."

Like a general who in one move baffles the tactics of the enemy, the old lawyer had had a vision of the Genius that watches over notaries, unfolding before him in legal script

a conception that might save the future prospects of Paul
and of his children. Maître Solonet knew of no other issue
from these irreconcilable difficulties than the determination
to which the young Count had been led by love, and by this
storm of contending feelings and interests; so he was excessively surprised by his senior's remark.

Curious to know what remedy Maître Mathias had to
suggest for a state of things which must have seemed to him
past all hope, he asked him:

"What have you to propose!"

"Natalie, my dear child, leave us," said Madame Evangelista.

"Mademoiselle is not *de trop*," replied Maître Mathias,
with a smile. "I speak as much for her as for Monsieur le
Comte."

There was a solemn silence, each one in great excitement
awaiting the old man's speech with the utmost curiosity.

"In our day," Mathias went on after a pause, "the notary's
profession has changed in many ways. In our day political
revolutions affect the future prospects of families, and this
used not to be the case. Formerly life ran in fixed grooves,
ranks were clearly defined——"

"We are not here to listen to a lecture on political economy,
but to arrange a marriage contract," said Solonet, with flippant impatience, and interrupting the old man.

"I beg you to allow me to speak in my turn," said
Mathias.

Solonet took his seat on the ottoman, saying to Madame
Evangelista in an undertone:

"Now you will learn what we lawyers mean by rigmarole."

"Notaries are consequently obliged to watch the course of
politics, since they now are intimately concerned with private
affairs. To give you an instance: Formerly noble families
had inalienable fortunes, but the Revolution overthrew them;
the present system tends to reconstructing such fortunes,"
said the old man, indulging somewhat in the twaddle of the

tabellionaris boa constrictor. "Now, Monsieur le Comte, in virtue of his name, his talents, and his wealth, is evidently destined to sit some day in the lower Chamber; destiny may perhaps lead him to the upper and hereditary Chamber; and as we know, he has every qualification that may justify our prognostics.—Are you not of my opinion, madame?" said he to the widow.

"You have anticipated my dearest hope," said she. "Manerville must be a Peer of France, or I shall die of grief."

"All that may tend to that end——?" said Maître Mathias, appealing to the mother-in-law with a look of frank good humor.

"Answers to my dearest wish," she put in.

"Well, then," said Mathias, "is not this marriage a fitting opportunity for creating an entail? Such a foundation will most certainly be an argument in the eyes of the present government for the nomination of my client when a batch of peers is created. Monsieur le Comte will, of course, dedicate to this purpose the estate of Lanstrac, worth about a million. I do not ask that Mademoiselle should contribute an equal sum; that would not be fair; but we may take eight hundred thousand francs of her money for the purpose. I know of two estates for sale at this moment, bordering on the lands of Lanstrac, in which those eight hundred thousand francs, to be sunk in real estate, may be invested at four and a half per cent. The Paris house ought also to be included in the entail. The surplus of the two fortunes, wisely managed, will amply suffice to provide for the younger children.—If the contracting parties can agree as to these details, Monsieur de Manerville may then pass your guardian's accounts and be chargeable for the balance. I will consent."

"*Questa coda non è di quetso gatto!*" (this tail does not fit that cat) exclaimed Madame Evangelista, looking at her sponser Solonet, and pointing to Maître Mathias.

"There is something behind all this," said Solonet in an undertone.

"And what is all this muddle for?" Paul asked of **Mathias**, going with him into the adjoining room.

"To save you from ruin," said the old notary in a whisper. "You are quite bent on marrying a girl—and her mother—who have made away with two millions of francs in seven years; you are accepting a debt of more than a hundred thousand francs to your children, to whom you will some day have to hand over eleven hundred and fifty-six thousand francs on their mother's behalf, when you are receiving hardly a million. You run the risk of seeing your whole fortune melt away in five years, leaving you as bare as St. John the Baptist, while you will remain the debtor in enormous sums to your wife and her representatives.—If you choose to embark in that boat, go on, Monsieur le Comte; but at least allow your old friend to save the house of Manerville."

"But how will this save it?" asked Paul.

"Listen, Monsieur le Comte; you are very much in love?"

"Yes," replied Paul.

"A man in love is about as secret as a cannon shot; I will tell you nothing!—If you were to repeat things, your marriage might come to nothing, so I place your love under the protection of my silence. You trust to my fidelity?"

"What a question!"

"Well, then, let me tell you that Madame Evangelista, her notary, and her daughter were playing a trick on us all through, and are more than clever. By Heaven, what sharp practice!"

"Natalie?" cried Paul.

"Well, I will not swear to that," said the old man. "You want her—take her! But I wish this marriage might fall through without the smallest blame to you!"

"Why?"

"That girl would beggar Peru. . . . Besides, she rides like a circus-rider; she is what you may call emancipated. Women of that sort make bad wives."

Paul pressed his old friend's hand and replied with a little fatuous smile.

"Don't be alarmed.—And for the moment, what must I do?"

"Stand firm to these conditions; they will consent, for the bargain does not damage their interests. And besides, all Madame Evangelista wants is to get her daughter married; I have seen her hand; do not trust her."

Paul returned to the drawing-room, where he found the widow talking in low tones to Solonet, just as he had been talking to Mathias. Natalie, left out of this mysterious conference, was playing with a screen. Somewhat out of countenance, she was wondering, "What absurdity keeps me from all knowledge of my own concerns?"

The younger lawyer was talking in the general outlines and remote effects of a stipulation based on the personal pride of the parties concerned, into which his client had blindly rushed. But though Mathias was now nothing else but a notary, Solonet was still to some degree a man, and carried some juvenile conceit into his dealings. It often happens that personal vanity makes a young lawyer forgetful of his client's interests. Under these circumstances, Maître Solonet, who would not allow the widow to think that Nestor was beating Achilles, was advising her to conclude the matter at once on these lines. Little did he care for the ultimate fulfilment of the contract; to him victory meant the release of Madame Evangelista with an assured income, and the marriage of Natalie.

"All Bordeaux will know that you have settled about eleven hundred thousand francs on your daughter, and that you still have twenty-five thousand francs a year," said Solonet in the lady's ear. "I had not hoped for such a brilliant result."

"But," said she, "explain to me why the creation of an entail should so immediately have stilled the storm."

"Distrust of you and your daughter. An entailed estate is inalienable: neither husband nor wife can touch it."

"That is a positive insult."

"Oh, no. We call that foresight. The good man caught you in a snare. If you refuse the entail, he will say, 'Then you want to squander my client's fortune'; whereas, if he creates an entail, it is out of all risk, just as if the couple were married under the provisions of the trust."

Solonet silenced his own scruples by reflecting:

"These stipulations will only take effect in the remote future, and by that time Madame Evangelista will be dead and buried."

She, for her part, was satisfied with Solonet's explanation; she had entire confidence in him. She was perfectly ignorant of the law; she saw her daughter married, and that was all she asked for the nonce; she was delighted at their success. And so, as Mathias suspected, neither Solonet nor Madame Evangelista as yet understood the full extent of his plan, which had incontrovertible reasons to support it.

"Well, then, Monsieur Mathias," said the widow, "everything is satisfactory."

"Madame, if you and Monsieur le Comte agree to these conditions, you should exchange pledges.—It is fully understood by you both, it is not," he went on, "that the marriage takes place only on condition of the creation of an entail, including the estate of Lanstrac and the house in the Rue de la Pépinière, both belonging to the intending husband, *item* eight hundred thousand francs deducted in money from the portion of the intending wife to be invested in land? Forgive me, madame, for repeating this; a solemn and positive pledge is necessary in such a case. The formation of an entail requires many formalities—it must be registered in Chancery and receive the royal signature; and we ought to proceed at once to the purchase of the lands, so as to include them in the schedule of property which the royal patent renders inalienable.—In many families a document would be required; but, as between you, verbal consent will no doubt be sufficient. Do you both consent?"

"Yes," said Madame Evangelista.

"Yes," said Paul.

"And how about me?" asked Natalie, laughing.

"You, mademoiselle, are a minor," replied Solonet, "and that need not distress you!"

It was then agreed that Maître Mathias should draw up the contract, and Maître Solonet audit the guardian's accounts, and that all the papers should be signed, in agreement with the law, a day or two before the wedding.

After a few civilities the lawyers rose.

"It is raining, Mathias; shall I take you home? I have my cab here," said Solonet.

"My carriage is at your service," said Paul, preparing to accompany the good man.

"I will not rob you of a minute," said the old man; "I will accept my friend's offer."

"Well," said Achilles to Nestor, as the carriage rolled on its way, "you have been truly patriarchal. Those young people would, no doubt, have ruined themselves."

"I was uneasy about the future," said Mathias, not betraying the real motive of his proposal.

At this moment the two lawyers were like two actors who shake hands behind the scenes after playing on the stage a scene of hatred and provocation.

"But is it not my business," said Solonet, who was thinking of technicalities, "to purchase the lands of which you speak? Is it not our money that is to be invested?"

"How can you include Mademoiselle Evangelista's land in an entail created by the Comte de Manerville?" asked Mathias.

"That difficulty can be settled in Chancery," said Solonet.

"But I am the seller's notary as well as the buyer's," replied Mathias. "Besides, Monsieur de Manerville can purchase in his own name. When it comes to paying, we can state the use of the wife's portion."

"You have an answer for everything, my worthy senior," said Solonet, laughing. "You have been grand this evening, and you have beaten us."

"Well, for an old fellow unprepared for your batteries loaded with grape-shot, it was not so bad, heh?"

"Ah, ha!" laughed Solonet.

The tedious contest in which the happiness of a family had

been so narrowly risked was to them no more than a matter of legal polemics. "We have not gone through forty years of chicanery for nothing," said Mathias. "Solonet," he added, "I am a good-natured fellow; you may be present at the sale and purchase of the lands to be added to the estate."

"Thank you, my good friend! You will find me at your service in case of need."

While the two notaries were thus peaceably going on their way, with no emotion beyond a little dryness of the throat, Paul and Madame Evangelista were suffering from the nervous trepidation, the fluttering about the heart, the spasm of brain and spine, to which persons of strong passions are prone after a scene when their interests or their feelings have been severely attacked. In Madame Evangelista these mutterings of the dispersing storm were aggravated by a terrible thought, a lurid gleam that needed explanation.

"Has not Maître Mathias overthrown my six months' labors?" she wondered. "Has he not destroyed my influence over Paul by filling him with base suspicions during their conference in the inner room?"

She stood in front of the fireplace, her elbow resting on the corner of the mantelpiece, lost in thought.

When the outer gate closed behind the notary's carriage, she turned to her son-in-law, eager to settle her doubts.

"This has been the most terrible day of my life," cried Paul, really glad to see the end of all these difficulties. "I know no tougher customer than old Mathias. God grant his wishes and make me peer of France! Dear Natalie, I desire it more for your sake than for my own. You are my sole ambition. I live in and for you."

On hearing these words spoken from the heart, and especially as she looked into Paul's clear eyes, whose look was as free from any concealment as his open brow, Madame Evangelista's joy was complete. She blamed herself for the somewhat sharp terms in which she had tried to spur her son-in-law, and in the triumph of success determined to make all smooth for the future. Her face was calm again, and her eyes expressed the sweet friendliness that made her so attractive as she replied:

"I may truly say the same. And perhaps, my dear boy, my Spanish temper carried me further than my heart intended. Be always what you are—as good as gold! And owe me no grudge for a few ill-considered words. Give me your hand——"

Paul was overwhelmed; he blamed himself in a thousand things, and embraced Madame Evangelista.

"Dear Paul," said she with emotion, "why could not those two scriveners arrange matters without us, since it has all come right in the end?"

"But then," said Paul, "I should not have known how noble and generous you could be."

"Well said, Paul!" cried Natalie, taking his hand.

"We have several little matters to settle yet, my dear boy," said Madame Evangelista. "My daughter and I are superior to the follies which some people think so much of. For instance, Natalie will need no diamonds—I give her mine."

"Oh! my dear mother, do you suppose I should accept them?" cried Natalie.

"Yes, my child, they are a condition of the contract."

"I will not have them! I will never marry!" said Natalie vehemently. "Keep what my father gave you with so much pleasure. How can Monsieur Paul demand——"

"Be silent, dear child," said her mother, her eyes filling with tears; "my ignorance of business requires far more than that."

"What?"

"I must sell this house to pay you what I owe you."

"What can you owe to me," said the girl—"to me, who owe my life to you? Can I ever repay you, on the contrary? If my marriage is to cost you the smallest sacrifice, I will never marry!"

"You are but a child!"

"My dear Natalie," said Paul, "you must understand that it is neither I, nor you, nor your mother who insists on these sacrifices, but the children——"

"But if I do not marry," she interrupted.

"Then you do not love me?" said Paul.

"Come, silly child," said her mother; "do you suppose that a marriage contract is a house of cards to be blown down at your pleasure? Poor ignorant darling, you do not know what trouble we have been at to create an entailed estate for your eldest son. Do not throw us back into the troubles we have escaped from."

"But why ruin my mother?" said Natalie to Paul.

"Why are you so rich?" he said, with a smile.

"Do not discuss the matter too far, my children; you are not married yet," said Madame Evangelista. "Paul," she went on, "Natalie needs no wedding gifts, no jewels, no trousseau; she has everything in profusion. Save the money you would have spent in presents to secure to yourselves some permanent home luxuries. There is nothing to my mind so foolishly vulgar as the expenditure of a hundred thousand francs in a *corbeille*,* of which nothing is left at last but an old white satin-covered trunk. Five thousand francs a year, on the other hand, as pin-money, save a young wife many small cares, and are hers for life. And indeed you will want the money of the *corbeille* to refurnish your house in Paris this winter. We will come back to Lanstrac in the spring; Solonet will have settled all our affairs in the course of the winter."

"Then all is well," said Paul, at the height of happiness.

"And I shall see Paris!" cried Natalie, in a tone that might indeed have alarmed a de Marsay.

"If that is quite settled, I will write to de Marsay to secure a box for the winter season at the Italian opera."

"You are most nice! I dared not ask it of you," said Natalie. "Marriage is a delightful institution if it gives husbands the power of guessing their wives' wishes."

---

*The bridegroom's presents of lace, jewels, and apparel constitute the *corbeille.*

"That is precisely what it is," said Paul. "But it is midnight—I must go."

"Why so early this evening?" said Madame Evangelista, who was lavish of the attentions to which men are so keenly alive.

Though the whole business had been conducted on terms of the most refined politeness, the effect of this clashing of interests had sown a germ of distrust and hostility between the lady and her son-in-law, ready to develop at the first spark of anger, or under the heat of a too strong display of feeling.

In most families the question of settlements and allowances under the marriage contract is prone to give rise to these primitive conflicts, stirred up by wounded pride or injured feelings, by some reluctance to make any sacrifice, or the desire to minimize it. When a difficulty arises, must there not be a conqueror and a conquered? The parents of the plighted couple try to bring the affair to a happy issue; in their eyes it is a purely commercial transaction, allowing all the tricks, the profits, and the deceptions of trade. As a rule, the husband only is initiated into the secret of the transaction, and the young wife remains, as did Natalie, ignorant of the stipulations which make her rich or poor.

Paul, as he went home, reflected that, thanks to his lawyer's ingenuity, his fortune was almost certainly secured against ruin. If Madame Evangelista lived with her daughter, the household would have more than a hundred thousand francs a year for ordinary expenses. Thus his hopes of a happy life would be realized.

"My mother-in-law seems to me a very good sort of woman," he reflected, still under the influence of the wheedling ways by which Madame Evangelista had succeeded in dissipating the clouds raised by the discussion. "Mathias is mistaken. These lawyers are strange beings; they poison everything. The mischief was made by that contentious little Solonet, who wanted to be clever."

While Paul, as he went to bed, was recapitulating the advantages he had won in the course of the evening, Madame Evangelista was no less confident of having gained the victory.

"Well, darling mother, are you satisfied?" said Natalie, following her mother into her bedroom.

"Yes, my love, everything has succeeded as I wished, and I feel a weight taken off my shoulders, which crushed me this morning. Paul is really an excellent fellow. Dear boy! Yes, we can certainly give him a delightful life. You will make him happy, and I will take care of his political prospects. The Spanish ambassador is an old friend of mine. I will renew my acquaintance with him and with several other persons. We shall soon be in the heart of politics, and all will be well with us. The pleasure for you, dear children; for me the later occupations of life—the game of ambition.

"Do not be alarmed at my selling this house; do you suppose we should ever return to Bordeaux? To Lanstrac—yes. But we shall spend every winter in Paris, where our true interests now lie.—Well, Natalie, was what I asked you so difficult to do?"

"My dear mother, I was ashamed at moments."

"Solonet advises me to buy an annuity with the price of the house," said Madame Evangelista, "but I must make some other arrangement. I will not deprive you of one sou of my capital."

"You were all very angry, I saw," said Natalie. "How was the storm appeased?"

"By the offer of my diamonds," replied her mother. "Solonet was in the right. How cleverly he managed the business! But fetch my jewel-box, Natalie. I never seriously inquired what those diamonds were worth. When I said a hundred thousand francs, it was absurd. Did not Madame de Gyas declare that the necklace and earrings your father gave me on the day of our wedding were alone worth as much? My poor husband was so lavish!—And then the family diamond given by Philip II. to the Duke of Alva, and left to me by my aunt—the *Discreto*—was, I believe, valued then at four thousand quadruples."

A MARRIAGE SETTLEMENT

Natalie brought out and laid on her mother's dressing-table pearl necklaces, sets of jewels, gold bracelets, gems of every kind, piling them up with the inexpressible satisfaction that rejoices the heart of some women at the sight of these valuables, with which, according to the Talmud, the fallen angels tempted the daughters of men, bringing up from the bowels of the earth these blossoms of celestial fires.

"Certainly," said Madame Evangelista, "although I know nothing of precious stones but how to accept them and wear them, it seems to me that these must be worth a great deal of money. And then, if we all live together, I can sell my plate, which is worth thirty thousand francs at the mere value of the silver. I remember when we brought it from Lima that was the valuation at the Custom House here.—Solonet is right. I will send for Élie Magus. The Jew will tell me the value of these stones. I may perhaps escape sinking the rest of my capital in an annuity."

"What a beautiful string of pearls!" said Natalie.

"I hope he will give you that if he loves you. Indeed, he ought to have all the stones reset and make them a present to you. The diamonds are yours by settlement.—Well, good-night, my darling. After such a fatiguing day, we both need sleep."

The woman of fashion, the Creole, the fine lady, incapable of understanding the conditions of a contract that was not yet drawn up, fell asleep in full content at seeing her daughter the wife of a man she could so easily manage, who would leave them to be on equal terms the mistresses of his house, and whose fortune, combined with their own, would allow of their living in the way to which they were accustomed. Even after paying up her daughter, for whose whole fortune she was to receive a discharge, Madame Evangelista would still have enough to live upon.

"How absurd I was to be so worried!" said she to herself. "I wish the marriage was over and done with."

So Madame Evangelista, Paul, Natalie, and the two lawyers were all delighted with the results of this first meeting. The

Te Deum was sung in both camps—a perilous state of things! The moment must come when the vanquished would no longer be deluded. To Madame Evangelista her son-in-law was conquered.

Next morning Élie Magus came to the widow's house, supposing, from the rumors current as to Mademoiselle Natalie's approaching marriage to Count Paul, that they wanted to purchase diamonds. What, then, was his surprise on learning that he was wanted to make a more or less official valuation of the mother-in-law's jewels. The Jewish instinct, added to a few insidious questions, led him to conclude that the value was to be included in the property under the marriage contract.

As the stones were not for sale, he priced them as a merchant selling to a private purchaser. Experts alone know Indian diamonds from those of Brazil. The stones from Golconda and Vizapur are distinguishable by a whiteness and clear brilliancy which the others have not, their hue being yellower, and this depreciates their selling value. Madame Evangelista's necklace and earrings, being entirely composed of Asiatic stones, was valued by Élie Magus at two hundred and fifty thousand francs. As to the *Discreto,* it was, he said, one of the finest diamonds extant in private hands, and was worth a hundred thousand francs.

On hearing these figures, which showed her how liberal her husband had been, Madame Evangelista asked whether she could have that sum at once.

"If you wish to sell them, madame," said the Jew, "I can only give you seventy thousand francs for the single stone, and a hundred and sixty thousand for the necklace and earrings."

"And why such a reduction?" asked Madame Evangelista in surprise.

"Madame," said he, "the finer the jewels, the longer we have to keep them. The opportunities for sale are rare in proportion to the greater value of the diamonds. As the dealer cannot lose the interest on his money, the recoupment for that interest, added to the risks of rise and fall in the market, accounts for the difference between the selling and purchasing value.—For twenty years you have been losing the interest of three hundred thousand francs. If you have worn your diamonds ten times a year, it has cost you a thousand crowns each time. How many handsome dresses you might have had for a thousand crowns! Persons who keep their diamonds are fools; however, happily for us, ladies do not understand these calculations."

"I am much obliged to you for having explained them to me; I will profit by the lesson."

"Then you want to sell?" cried the Jew eagerly.

"What are the rest worth?" said Madame Evangelista.

The Jew examined the gold of the settings, held the pearls to the light, turned over the rubies, the tiaras, brooches, bracelets, clasps, and chains, and mumbled out:

"There are several Portuguese diamonds brought from Brazil. I cannot give more than a hundred thousand francs for the lot. But sold to a customer," he added, "they would fetch more than fifty thousand crowns."

"We will keep them," said the lady.

"You are wrong," replied Élie Magus. "With the income of the sum now sunk in them, in five years you could buy others just as fine, and still have the capital."

This rather singular interview was soon known, and confirmed the rumors to which the discussion of the contract had given rise. In a provincial town everything is known. The servants of the house, having heard loud voices, supposed the dispute to have been warmer than it was; their gossip with other folks' servants spread far and wide, and from the lower depths came up to the masters. The attention of the upper and citizen circles was concentrated on the marriage of two persons of equal wealth. Everybody, great and small, talked the matter over, and within a week the strangest reports were afloat in Bordeaux.—Madame Evangelista was selling her house, so she must be ruined.—She had offered her diamonds to Élie Magus.—Nothing was yet final between her and the

Comte de Manerville.—Would the marriage ever come off? Some said, Yes; others said, No. The two lawyers, on being questioned, denied these calumnies, and said that the difficulties were purely technical, arising from the formalities of creating an entail.

But when public opinion has rushed down an incline, it is very difficult to get it up again. Though Paul went every day to Madame Evangelista's, and in spite of the assertions of the two notaries, the insinuated slander held its own. Several young ladies, and their mothers or their aunts, aggrieved by a match of which they or their families had dreamed for themselves, could no more forgive Madame Evangelista for her good luck than an author forgives his friend for a success. Some were only too glad to be avenged for the twenty years of luxury and splendor by which the Spaniards had crushed their vanities. A bigwig at the Préfecture declared that the two notaries and the two parties concerned could say no more, nor behave otherwise, if the rupture were complete. The time it took to settle the entail confirmed the suspicions of the citizens of Bordeaux.

"They will sit by the chimney-corner all the winter; then, in the spring, they will go to some watering-place; and in the course of the year we shall hear that the match is broken off."

"You will see," said one set, "in order to save the credit of both parties, the obstacles will not have arisen on either side; there will be some demur in Chancery, some hitch discovered by the lawyers to hinder the entail."

"Madame Evangelista," said the others, "has been living at a rate that would have exhausted the mines of Valenciana. Then, when pay-day came round there was nothing to be found."

What a capital opportunity for calculating the handsome widow's expenditure, so as to prove her ruin to a demonstration! Rumor ran so high that bets were laid for and against the marriage. And, in accordance with the accepted rules of society, this tittle-tattle remained unknown to the interested parties. No one was sufficiently inimical to Paul or Madame Evangelista to attack them on the subject.

Paul had some business at Lanstrac and took advantage of it to make up a shooting-party, inviting some of the young men of the town as a sort of farewell to his bachelor life. This shooting-party was regarded by society as a flagrant confirmation of its suspicions.

At this juncture Madame de Gyas, who had a daughter to marry, thought it well to sound her way, and to rejoice sadly over the checkmate offered to Madame Evangelista. Natalie and her mother were not a little astonished to see the Marquise's badly-assumed distress, and asked her if anything had annoyed her.

"Why," said she, "can you be ignorant of the reports current in Bordeaux? Though I feel sure that they are false, I have come to ascertain the truth and put a stop to them, at any rate in my own circle of friends. To be the dupe or the accomplice of such a misapprehension is to be in a false position, which no true friend can endure to remain in."

"But what in the world is happening?" asked the mother and daughter.

Madame de Gyas then had the pleasure of repeating everybody's comments, not sparing her intimate friends a single dagger-thrust. Natalie and her mother looked at each other and laughed; but they quite understood the purpose and motives of their friend's revelation. The Spanish lady revenged herself much as Célimène did on Arsinoé.

"My dear—you who know what provincial life is—you must know of what a mother is capable when she has a daughter on her hands who does not marry, for lack of a fortune and a lover, of beauty and talent—for lack of everything sometimes!—She would rob a diligence, she would commit murder, waylay a man at a street corner, and give herself away a hundred times, if she were worth giving. There are plenty such in Bordeaux, who are ready, no doubt, to attribute to us their thoughts and actions.—Naturalists have described the manners and customs of many fierce animals, but they have overlooked the mother and daughter in quest of a husband. They are hyænas who, as the Psalmist has it, seek whom they may devour, and who add to the nature of the wild beast the intelligence of man and the genius of woman.

"That such little Bordeaux spiders as Mademoiselle de Belor, Mademoiselle de Trans, and their like, who have spread their nets for so long without seeing a fly, or hearing the least hum of wings near them—that they should be furious I understand, and I forgive them their venomous tattle. But that you, who have a title and money, who are not in the least provincial, who have a clever and accomplished daughter, pretty and free to pick and choose—that you, so far above everybody here by your Parisian elegance, should have taken such a tone, is really a matter of astonishment. Am I expected to account to the public for the matrimonial stipulations which our men of business have considered necessary under the political conditions which will govern my son-in-law's existence? Is the mania for public discussion to invade the privacy of family life? Ought I to have invited the fathers and mothers of your province, under sealed covers, to come and vote on the articles of our marriage contract?"

A torrent of epigrams was poured out on Bordeaux.

Madame Evangelista was about to leave the town; she could afford to criticise her friends and enemies, to caricature them, and lash them at will, having nothing to fear from them. So she gave vent to all the remarks she had stored up, the revenges she had postponed, and her surprise that any one should deny the existence of the sun at noonday.

"Really, my dear," said the Marquise de Gyas, "Monsieur de Manerville's visit to Lanstrac, these parties to young men —under the circumstances——"

"Really, my dear," retorted the fine lady, interrupting her, "can you suppose that we care for the trumpery proprieties of a middle-class marriage? Am I to keep Count Paul in leading-strings, as if he would run away? Do you think he needs watching by the police? Need we fear his being spirited away by some Bordeaux conspiracy?"

"Believe me, my dear friend, you give me infinite pleasure——"

The Marquise was cut short in her speech by the man-servant announcing Paul. Like all lovers, Paul had thought it delightful to ride eight leagues in order to spend an hour with Natalie. He had left his friends to their sport, and came in, booted and spurred, his whip in his hand.

"Dear Paul," said Natalie, "you have no idea how effectually you are answering madame at this moment."

When Paul heard the calumnies that were rife in Bordeaux, he laughed instead of being angry.

"The good people have heard, no doubt, that there will be none of the gay and uproarious doings usual in the country, no midday ceremony in church, and they are furious.—Well, dear mother," said he, kissing Madame Evangelista's hand, "we will fling a ball at their heads on the day when the contract is signed, as a fête is thrown to the mob in the square of the Champs-Elysées, and give our good friends the painful pleasure of such a signing as is rarely seen in a provincial city!"

This incident was of great importance. Madame Evangelista invited all Bordeaux on the occasion, and expressed her intention of displaying in this final entertainment a magnificence that should give the lie unmistakably to silly and false reports. She was thus solemnly pledged to the world to carry through this marriage.

The preparations for this ball went on for forty days, and it was known as the "evening of the camellias," there were such immense numbers of these flowers on the stairs, in the ante-room, and in the great supper-room. The time agreed with the necessary delay for the preliminary formalities of the marriage, and the steps taken in Paris for the settlement of the entail. The lands adjoining Lanstrac were purchased, the banns were published, and doubts were dispelled.

Friends and foes had nothing left to think about but the preparation of their dresses for the great occasion.

The time taken up by these details overlaid the difficulties raised at the first meeting, and carried away into oblivion the words and retorts of the stormy altercation that had arisen over the question of the settlements. Neither Paul nor his mother-in-law thought any more of the matter. Was is not, as Madame Evangelista had said, the lawyers' business? But who is there that has not known, in the rush of a busy phase of life, what it is to be suddenly startled by the voice of memory, speaking too late, and recalling some important fact, some imminent danger?

On the morning of the day when the contract was to be signed, one of these will-o'-the-wisps of the brain flashed upon Madame Evangelista between sleeping and waking. The phrase spoken by herself at the moment when Mathias agreed to Solonet's proposal was, as it were, shouted in her ear: *Questa coda non è di questo gatto.* In spite of her ignorance of business, Madame Evangelista said to herself, "If that sharp old lawyer is satisfied, it is at the expense of one or other of the parties." And the damaged interest was certainly not on Paul's side, as she had hoped. Was it her daughter's fortune, then, that was to pay the costs of the war? She resolved to make full inquiries as to the tenor of the bargain, though she did not consider what she could do in the event of finding her own interests too seriously compromised.

The events of this day had so serious an influence on Paul's married life, that it is necessary to give some account of the external details which have their effect on every mind.

As the house was forthwith to be sold, the Comte de Manerville's mother-in-law had hesitated at no expense. The forecourt was graveled, covered with a tent, and filled with shrubs, though it was winter. The camellias, which were talked of from Dax to Angoulême, decked the stairs and vestibules. A wall had been removed to enlarge the supper-

Paul and Natalie sat by the fire on a little sofa

room and ballroom. Bordeaux, splendid with the luxury of many a colonial fortune, eagerly anticipated a fairy scene. By eight o'clock, when the business was drawing to a close, the populace, curious to see the ladies' dresses, formed a hedge on each side of the gateway. Thus the heady atmosphere of a great festivity excited all concerned at the moment of signing the contract. At the very crisis the little lamps fixed on yew-trees were already lighted, and the rumbling of the first carriages came up from the forecourt.

The two lawyers had dined with the bride and bridegroom and the mother-in-law. Mathias' head-clerk, who was to see the contract signed by certain of the guests in the course of the evening, and to take care that it was not read, was also one of the party.

The reader will rack his memory in vain—no dress, no woman was ever to compare with Natalie's beauty in her satin and lace, her hair beautifully dressed in a mass of curls falling about her neck; she was like a flower in its natural setting of foliage.

Madame Evangelista, in a cherry-colored velvet, cleverly designed to set off the brilliancy of her eyes, her complexion, and her hair, with all the beauty of a woman of forty, wore her pearl necklace clasped with the famous *Discreto,* to give the lie to slander.

Fully to understand the scene, it is necessary to remark that Paul and Natalie sat by the fire on a little sofa, and never listened to one word of the guardian's accounts. One as much a child as the other, both equally happy, he in his hopes, she in her expectant curiosity, seeing life one calm blue heaven, rich, young, and in love, they never ceased whispering in each other's ear. Paul, already regarding his passion as legalized, amused himself with kissing the tips of Natalie's fingers, or just touching her snowy shoulders or her hair, hiding the raptures of these illicit joys from every eye. Natalie was playing with a screen of peacock feathers, a gift from Paul—a luckless omen in love, if we may accept the superstitious belief of some countries, as fatal as that of scissors, or any other cutting instrument, which is based, no doubt, on some association with the mythological Fates.

Madame Evangelista, sitting by the notaries, paid the closest attention to the reading of the two documents. After hearing the schedule of her accounts, very learnedly drawn out by Solonet, which showed a reduction of the three millions and some hundred thousand francs left by Monsieur Evangelista, to the famous eleven hundred and fifty-six thousand francs constituting Natalie's portion, she called out to the young couple:

"Come, listen, children; this is your marriage contract."

The clerk drank a glass of sugared water; Solonet and Mathias blew their noses; Paul and Natalie looked at the four personages, listened to the preamble, and then began to talk together again. The statements of revenues; the settlement of the whole estate on either party in the event of the other's death without issue; the bequest, according to law, of one-quarter of the whole property absolutely to the wife, and of the interest of one-quarter more, however many children should survive; the schedule of the property held in common; the gift of the diamonds on the wife's part, and of the books and horses on the husband's—all passed without remark. Then came the settlement for the entail. And when everything had been read, and there was nothing to be done but to sign, Madame Evangelista asked what would be the effect of the entail.

"The entailed estate, madame, is inalienable; it is property separated from the general estate of the married pair, and reserved for the eldest son of the house from generation to generation, without his being thereby deprived of his share of the rest of the property."

"And what are the consequences to my daughter?" she asked. Maître Mathias, incapable of disguising the truth, made reply:

"Madame, the entail being an inheritance derived from both fortunes, if the wife should be the first to die, and leaves one or several children, one of them a boy, Monsieur le

Comte de Manerville will account to them for no more than three hundred and fifty-six thousand francs, from which he will deduct his one absolute fourth, and the fourth part of the interest of the residue. Thus their claim on him is reduced to about a hundred and sixty thousand francs independently of his share of profits on the common stock, the sums he could claim, etc. In the contrary case, if he should die first, leaving a son or sons, Madame de Manerville would be entitled to no more than three hundred and fifty-six thousand francs, to her share of all of Monsieur de Manerville's estate that is not included in the entail, to the restitution of her diamonds, and her portion of the common stock."

The results of Maître Mathias' profound policy were now amply evident.

"My daughter is ruined," said Madame Evangelista in a low voice.

The lawyers both heard her exclamation.

"Is it ruin," said Maître Mathias in an undertone, "to establish an indestructible fortune for her family in the future?"

As he saw the expression of his client's face, the younger notary thought it necessary to state the sum of the disaster in figures.

"We wanted to get three hundred thousand francs out of them, and they have evidently succeeded in getting eight hundred thousand out of us; the balance to their advantage on the contract is a loss of four hundred thousand francs to us for the benefit of the children.—We must break it off or go on," he added to Madame Evangelista.

No words could describe the silence, though brief, that ensued. Mathias triumphantly awaited the signature of the two persons who had hoped to plunder his client. Natalie, incapable of understanding that she was bereft of half of her fortune, and Paul, not knowing that the house of Manerville was acquiring it, sat laughing and talking as before. Solonet and Madame Evangelista looked at each other, he concealing his indifference, she disguising a myriad angry feelings.

After suffering from terrible remorse, and regarding Paul as the cause of her dishonesty, the widow had made up her mind to certain discreditable manœuvres to cast the blunders of her guardianship on his shoulders, making him her victim. And now, in an instant, she had discovered that, instead of triumphing, she was overthrown, and that the real victim was her daughter. Thus guilty to no purpose, she was the dupe of an honest old man, whose esteem she had doubtless sacrificed. Was it not her own secret conduct that had inspired the stipulations insisted on by Mathias?

Hideous thought! Mathias had, doubtless, told Paul.

If he had not yet spoken, as soon as the contract should be signed that old wolf would warn his client of the dangers he had run and escaped, if it were only to gather the praises to which everybody is open. Would he not put him on his guard against a woman so astute as to have joined such an ignoble conspiracy? Would he not undermine the influence she had acquired over her son-in-law? And weak natures, once warned, turn obstinate, and never reconsider the circumstances.

So all was lost!

On the day when the discussion was opened, she had trusted to Paul's feebleness and the impossibility of his retreating after advancing so far. And now it was she who had tied her own hands. Paul, three months since, would not have had many obstacles to surmount to break off the marriage; now, all Bordeaux knew that the lawyers had, two months ago, smoothed away every difficulty. The banns were published; the wedding was fixed for the next day but one. The friends of both families, all the town were arriving, dressed for the ball—how could she announce a postponement? The cause of the rupture would become known, the unblemished honesty of Maître Mathias would gain credence, his story would be believed in preference to hers. The laugh would be against the Evangelistas, of whom so many were envious. She must yield!

These painfully accurate reflections fell on Madame Evangelista like a waterspout and crushed her brain. Though she maintained a diplomatic impassibility, her chin showed the nervous jerking by which Catherine II. betrayed her fury one day when, sitting on her throne and surrounded by her Court, she was defied by the young King of Sweden under almost similar circumstances. Solonet noted the spasmodic movement of the muscles that proclaimed a mortal hatred, a storm without a sound or a lightning-flash; and, in fact, at that moment, the widow had sworn such hatred of her son-in-law, such an implacable feud as the Arabs have left the germs of in the atmosphere of Spain.

"Monsieur," said she to her notary, "you called this a rigmarole—it seems to me that nothing can be clearer."

"Madame, allow me——"

"Monsieur," she went on, without listening to Solonet, "if you did not understand the upshot of this bargain at the time of our former discussion, it is at least extraordinary that you should not have perceived it in the retirement of your study. It cannot be from incapacity."

The young man led her into the adjoining room, saying to himself:

"More than a thousand crowns are due to me for the schedule of accounts, and a thousand more for the contract; six thousand francs I can make over the sale of the house— fifteen thousand francs in all.—We must keep our temper."

He shut the door, gave Madame Evangelista the cold look of a man of business, guessing the feelings that agitated her, and said:

"Madame, how, when I have perhaps overstepped in your behalf the due limits of finesse, can you repay my devotion by such a speech?"

"But, monsieur——"

"Madame, I did not, it is true, fully estimate the amount of our surrender; but if you do not care to have Count Paul for your son-in-law, are you obliged to agree? The contract is not signed.—Give your ball and postpone the signing. It is better to take in all Bordeaux than to be taken in yourself."

"And what excuse can I make to all the world—already prejudiced against us—to account for this delay?"

"A blunder in Paris, a document missing," said Solonet.

"But the land that has been purchased?"

"Monsieur de Manerville will find plenty of matches with money."

"He! Oh, he will lose nothing; we are losing everything on our side."

"You," said Solonet, "may have a Count, a better bargain, if the title is the great point of this match in your eyes."

"No, no; we cannot throw our honor overboard in that fashion! I am caught in the trap, monsieur. All Bordeaux would ring with it to-morrow. We have solemnly pledged ourselves."

"You wish Mademoiselle Natalie to be happy?" asked Solonet.

"That is the chief thing."

"In France," said the lawyer "does not being happy mean being mistress of the hearth? She will lead that nincompoop Manerville by the nose. He is so stupid that he has seen nothing. Even if he should distrust you, he will still believe in his wife. And are not you and his wife one? Count Paul's fate still lies in your hands."

"If you should be speaking truly, I do not know what I could refuse you!" she exclaimed, with delight that glowed in her eyes.

"Come in again, then, madame," said Solonet, understanding his client. "But, above all, listen to what I say; you may regard me as incapable afterwards if you please."

"My dear friend," said the young lawyer to Mathias, as he re-entered the room, "for all your skill you have failed to foresee the contingency of Monsieur de Manerville's death without issue, or, again, that of his leaving none but daughters. In either of those cases the entail would give rise

A MARRIAGE SETTLEMENT 83

to lawsuits with other Manervilles, for plenty would crop up, do not doubt it for a moment. It strikes me, therefore, as desirable to stipulate that in the former case the entailed property should be included in the general estate settled by each on either, and in the second that the entail should be cancelled as null and void. It is an agreement solely affecting the intending wife."

"The clause seems to me perfectly fair," said Mathias. "As to its ratification, Monsieur le Comte will make the necessary arrangements with the Court of Chancery, no doubt, if requisite."

The younger notary took a pen and wrote in on the margin this ominous clause, to which Paul and Natalie paid no attention. Madame Evangelista sat with downcast eyes while it was read by Maître Mathias.

"Now to sign," said the mother.

The strong voice which she controlled betrayed vehement excitement. She had just said to herself:

"No, my daughter shall not be ruined—but he shall! My daughter shall have his name, title, and fortune. If Natalie should ever discover that she does not love her husband, if some day she should love another man more passionately—Paul will be exiled from France, and my daughter will be free, happy, and rich."

Though Maître Mathias was expert in the analysis of interests, he had no skill in analyzing human passions. He accepted the lady's speech as an honorable surrender, instead of seeing that it was a declaration of war. While Solonet and his clerk took care that Natalie signed in full at the foot of every document—a business that required some time—Mathias took Paul aside and explained to him the bearing of the clauses which he had introduced to save him from inevitable ruin.

"You have a mortgage on this house for a hundred and fifty thousand francs," he said in conclusion, "and we foreclose to-morrow. I have at my office the securities in the funds, which I have taken care to place in your wife's name.

Everything is quite regular.—But the contract includes a receipt for the sum represented by the diamonds; ask for them. Business is business. Diamonds are just now going up in the market; they may go down again. Your purchase of the lands of Auzac and Saint-Froult justifies you in turning everything into money so as not to touch your wife's income. So, no false pride, Monsieur le Comte. The first payment is to be made after the formalities are concluded; use the diamonds for that purpose; it amounts to two hundred thousand francs. You will have the mortgage value of this house for the second call, and the income on the entailed property will help you to pay off the remainder. If only you are firm enough to spend no more than fifty thousand francs for the first three years, you will recoup the two hundred thousand francs you now owe. If you plant vines on the hill slopes of Saint-Froult, you may raise the returns to twenty-six thousand francs. Thus the entailed property, without including your house in Paris, will some day be worth fifty thousand francs a year—one of the finest estates I know of.—And so you will have married very handsomely."

Paul pressed his old friend's hands with warm affection. The gesture did not escape Madame Evangelista, who came to hand the pen to Paul. Her suspicion was now certainty; she was convinced that Paul and Mathias had an understanding. Surges of blood, hot with rage and hatred, choked her heart. Paul was warned!

After ascertaining that every clause was duly signed, that the three contracting parties had initialed the bottom of every page with their usual sign-manual, Maître Mathias looked first at his client and then at Madame Evangelista, and observing that Paul did not ask for the diamonds, he said:

"I suppose there will be no question as to the delivery of the diamonds now that you are but one family?"

"It would, no doubt, be in order that Madame Evangelista should surrender them. Monsieur de Manerville has given his discharge for the balance of the trust values, and no one can tell who may die or live," said Maître Solonet, who thought this an opportunity for inciting his client against her son-in-law.

"Oh, my dear mother, it would be an affront to us if you did so!" cried Paul. *"Summum jus, summa injuria,* monsieur," said he to Solonet.

"And I, on my part," said she, her hostile temper regarding Mathias' indirect demand as an insult, "if you do not accept the jewels, will tear up the contract."

She went out of the room in one of those bloodthirsty furies which so long for the chance of wrecking everything, and which, when that is impossible, rise to the pitch of frenzy.

"In Heaven's name, take them," whispered Natalie. "My mother is angry; I will find out why this evening, and will tell you; we will pacify her."

Madame Evangelista, quite pleased at this first stroke of policy, kept on her necklace and earrings. She brought the rest of the jewels, valued by Élie Magus at a hundred and fifty thousand francs. Maître Mathias and Solonet, though accustomed to handling family diamonds, exclaimed at the beauty of these jewels as they examined the contents of the cases.

"You will lose nothing of mademoiselle's fortune, Monsieur le Comte," said Solonet, and Paul reddened.

"Ay," said Mathias, "these jewels will certainly pay the first instalment of the newly purchased land."

"And the expenses of the contract," said Solonet.

Hatred, like love, is fed on the merest trifles. Everything adds to it. Just as the one we love can do no wrong, the one we hate can do nothing right. Madame Evangelista scorned the hesitancy to which a natural reluctance gave rise in Paul as affected airs; while he, not knowing what to do with the jewel-cases, would have been glad to throw them out of the window. Madame Evangelista, seeing his embarrassment, fixed her eyes on him in a way which seemed to say, "Take them out of my sight!"

"My dear Natalie," said Paul to his fiancée, "put the

jewels away yourself; they are yours; I make them a present to you."

Natalie put them into the drawers of a cabinet. At this instant the clatter of carriages and the voices of the guests waiting in the adjoining rooms required Natalie and her mother to appear among them. The rooms were immediately filled, and the ball began.

"Take advantage of the honeymoon to sell your diamonds," said the old notary to Paul, as he withdrew.

While waiting for the dancing to begin, everybody was discussing the marriage in lowered tones, some of the company expressing doubts as to the future prospects of the engaged couple.

"Is it quite settled?" said one of the magnates of the town to Madame Evangelista.

"We have had so many papers to read and hear read, that we are late; but we may be excused," replied she.

"For my part, I heard nothing," said Natalie, taking Paul's hand to open the ball.

"Both those young people like extravagance, and it will not be the mother that will check them," said a dowager.

"But they have created an entail, I hear, of fifty thousand francs a year."

"Pooh!"

"I see that our good Maître Mathias has had a finger in the pie. And certainly, if that is the case, the worthy man will have done his best to save the future fortunes of the family."

"Natalie is too handsome not to be a desperate flirt. By the time that she has been married two years, I will not answer for it that Manerville will not be miserable in his home," remarked a young wife.

"What, the peas will be stuck you think?" replied Maître Solonet.

"He needed no more than that tall stick," said a young lady.

"Does it not strike you that Madame Evangelista is not best pleased?"

"Well, my dear, I have just been told that she has hardly twenty-five thousand francs a year, and what is that for her?"

"Beggary, my dear."

"Yes, she has stripped herself for her daughter. Monsieur has been exacting——"

"Beyond conception!" said Solonet. "But he is to be a peer of France. The Maulincours and the Vidame de Pamiers will help him on; he belongs to the Faubourg Saint-Germain."

"Oh, he visits there, that is all," said a lady, who had wanted him for her son-in-law. "Mademoiselle Evangelista, a merchant's daughter, will certainly not open the doors of the Chapter of Cologne to him."

"She is grand-niece to the Duc de Casa-Real."

"On the female side!"

All this tittle-tattle was soon exhausted. The gamblers sat down to cards, the young people danced, supper was served, and the turmoil of festivity was not silenced till morning, when the first streaks of dawn shone pale through the windows.

After taking leave of Paul, who was the last to leave, Madame Evangelista went up to her daughter's room, for her own had been demolished by the builder to enlarge the ball-room. Though Natalie and her mother were dying for sleep, they spoke a few words.

"Tell me, darling mother, what is the matter?"

"My dear, I discovered this evening how far a mother's love may carry her. You know nothing of affairs, and you have no idea to what suspicions my honesty lies exposed. However, I have trodden my pride underfoot; your happiness and our honor was at stake."

"As concerned the diamonds, you mean?—He wept over it, poor boy! He would not take them; I have them."

"Well, go to sleep, dearest child. We will talk business

when we wake; for we have business—and now there is a third to come between us," and she sighed.

"Indeed, dear mother, Paul will never stand in the way of our happiness," said Natalie, and she went to sleep.

"Poor child, she does not know that the man has ruined her!"

Madame Evangelista was now seized in the grip of the first promptings of that avarice to which old folks at last fall a prey. She was determined to replace, for her daughter's benefit, the whole of the fortune left by her husband. She regarded her honor as pledged to this restitution. Her affection for Natalie made her in an instant as close a calculator in money matters as she had hitherto been a reckless spendthrift. She proposed to invest her capital in land after placing part of it in the State funds, purchasable at that time for about eighty francs.

A passion not unfrequently produces a complete change of character; the tattler turns diplomatic, the coward is suddenly brave. Hatred made the prodigal Madame Evangelista turn parsimonious. Money might help her in the schemes of revenge, as yet vague and ill-defined, which she proposed to elaborate. She went to sleep, saying to herself:

"To-morrow!" And by an unexplained phenomenon, of which the effects are well known to philosophers, her brain during sleep worked out her idea, threw light on her plans, organized them, and hit on a way of ruling over Paul's life, devising a scheme which she began to work out on the very next day.

Though the excitement of the evening had driven away certain anxious thoughts which had now and again invaded Paul, when he was alone once more and in bed they returned to torment him.

"It would seem," said he to himself, "that, but for that worthy Mathias, my mother-in-law would have taken me in. Is it credible? What interest could she have had in cheating me? Are we not to unite our incomes and live together!—After all, what is there to be anxious about? In a few days Natalie will be my wife, our interests are clearly defined, nothing can sever us. On we go!—At the same time, I will be on my guard. If Mathias should prove to be right—well, I am not obliged to marry my mother-in-law."

In this second contest, Paul's future prospects had been entirely altered without his being aware of it. Of the two women he was marrying, far the cleverer had become his mortal enemy, and was bent on separating her own interests from his. Being incapable of appreciating the difference that the fact of her Creole birth made between his mother-in-law's character and that of other women, he was still less able to measure her immense cleverness.

The Creole woman is a being apart, deriving her intellect from Europe, and from the Tropics her vehemently illogical passions, while she is Indian in the apathetic indifference with which she accepts good or evil as it comes; a gracious nature too, but dangerous, as a child is when it is not kept in order. Like a child, this woman must have everything she wishes for, and at once; like a child, she would set a house on fire to boil an egg. In her flaccid everyday mood she thinks of nothing; when she is in a passion she thinks of everything. There is in her nature some touch of the perfidy caught from the negroes among whom she has lived from the cradle, but she is artless too, as they are. Like them, and like children, she can wish persistently for one thing with ever-growing intensity of desire, and brood over an idea till it hatches out. It is a nature strangely compounded of good and evil qualities; and in Madame Evangelista it was strengthened by the Spanish temper, over which French manners had laid the polish of their veneer.

This nature, which had lain dormant in happiness for sixteen years, and had since found occupation in the frivolities of fashion, had discovered its own force under the first impulse of hatred, and flared up like a conflagration; it had broken out at a stage in her life when a woman, bereft of what is dearest to her, craves some new material to feed the energies that are consuming her.

For three days longer Natalie would remain under her mother's influence. So Madame Evangelista, though vanquished, had still a day before her, the last her child would spend with her mother. By a single word the Creole might color the lives of these two beings whose fate it was to walk hand in hand through the thickets and highways of Paris society—for Natalie had a blind belief in her mother. What far-reaching importance would a hint of advice have on a mind thus prepared! The whole future might be modified by a sentence. No code, no human constitution can forefend the moral crime of killing by a word. That is the weak point of social forms of justice. That is where the difference lies between the world of fashion and the people; these are outspoken, those are hypocrites; these snatch the knife, those use the poison of words and suggestions; these are punished with death, those sin with impunity.

At about noon next day, Madame Evangelista was half sitting, half reclining on Natalie's bed. At this waking hour they were playing and petting each other with fond caresses, recalling the happy memories of their life together, during which no discord had troubled the harmony of their feelings, the agreement of their ideas, or the perfect union of their pleasures.

"Poor dear child," said the mother, shedding genuine tears, "I cannot bear to think that, after having had your own way all your life, to-morrow evening you will be bound to a man whom you must obey!"

"Oh, my dear mother, as to obeying him!" said Natalie, with a little wilful nod expressive of pretty rebellion. "You laugh!" she went on, "but my father always indulged your fancies. And why? Because he loved you. Shall not I be loved?"

"Yes, Paul is in love with you. But if a married woman is not careful, nothing evaporates so quickly as conjugal affection. The influence a wife may preserve over her husband depends on the first steps in married life, and you will want good advice."

"But you will be with us."

"Perhaps, my dear child.—Last evening, during the ball, I very seriously considered the risks of our being together. If my presence were to be disadvantageous to you, if the little details by which you must gradually confirm your authority as a wife should be ascribed to my influence, your home would become a hell. At the first frown on your husband's brow, should not I, so proud as I am, instantly quit the house? If I am to leave it sooner or later, in my opinion, I had better never enter it. I could not forgive your husband if he disunited us.

"On the other hand, when you are the mistress, when your husband is to you what your father was to me, there will be less fear of any such misfortune. Although such a policy must be painful to a heart so young and tender as yours, it is indispensable for your happiness that you should be the absolute sovereign of your home."

"Why, then, dear mother, did you say I was to obey him?"

"Dear little girl, to enable a woman to command, she must seem always to do what her husband wishes. If you did not know that, you might wreck your future life by an untimely rebellion. Paul is a weak man; he might come under the influence of a friend, nay, he might fall under the control of a woman, and you would feel the effects of their influence. Forefend such misfortunes by being mistress yourself. Will it not be better that you should govern him than that any one else should?"

"No doubt," said Natalie. "I could only aim at his happiness."

"And it certainly is my part, dear child, to think only of yours, and to endeavor that, in so serious a matter, you should not find yourself without a compass in the midst of the shoals you must navigate."

"But, my darling mother, are we not both of us firm enough to remain together under his roof without provoking the frowns you seem so much to dread? Paul is fond of you, mamma."

"Oh, he fears me more than he loves me. Watch him narrowly to-day when I tell him I shall leave you to go to Paris without me, and, however carefully he may try to conceal his feelings, you will see his secret satisfaction in his face."

"But why?" said Natalie.

"Why, my child? I am like Saint John Chrysostom—I will tell him why, and before you."

"But since I am marrying him on the express condition that you and I are not to part?" said Natalie.

"Our separation has become necessary," Madame Evangelista replied. "Several considerations affect my future prospects. I am very poor. You will have a splendid life in Paris; I could not live with you suitably without exhausting the little possessions that remain to me; whereas, by living at Lanstrac, I can take care of your interests and reconstitute my own fortune by economy."

"You, mother! you economize?" cried Natalie, laughing. "Come, do not be a grandmother yet.—What, would you part from me for such a reason as that?—Dear mother, Paul may seem to you just a little stupid, but at least he is perfectly disinterested——"

"Well," replied Madame Evangelista, in a tone big with comment, which made Natalie's heart beat, "the discussion of the contract had made me suspicious and suggested some doubts to my mind.—But do not be uneasy, dearest child," she went on, putting her arm round the girl's neck and clasping her closely, "I will not leave you alone for long. When my return to you can give him no umbrage, when Paul has learned to judge me truly, we will go back to our snug little life again, our evening chats——"

"Why, mother, can you live without your Ninie?"

"Yes, my darling, because I shall be living for you. Will not my motherly heart be constantly rejoiced by the idea that I am contributing, as I ought, to your fortune and your husband's?"

"But, my dear, adorable mother, am I to be alone there

A MARRIAGE SETTLEMENT

with Paul? At once?—Quite alone?—What will become of me? What will happen? What ought I to do—or not to do?"

"Poor child, do you think I mean to desert you forthwith at the first battle? We will write to each other three times a week, like two lovers, and thus we shall always live in each other's heart. Nothing can happen to you that I shall not know, and I will protect you against all evil.—And besides, it would be too ridiculous that I should not go to visit you; that would cast a reflection on your husband; I shall always spend a month or two with you in Paris——"

"Alone—alone with him, and at once!" cried Natalie in terror, interrupting her mother.

"Are you not to be his wife?"

"Yes, and I am quite content; but tell me at least how to behave.—You, who did what you would with my father, know all about it, and I will obey you blindly."

Madame Evangelista kissed her daughter's forehead; she had been hoping and waiting for this request.

"My child, my advice must be adapted to the circumstances. Men are not all alike. The lion and the frog are less dissimilar than one man as compared with another, morally speaking. Do I know what will happen to you to-morrow? I can only give you general instructions as to your general plan of conduct."

"Dearest mother, tell me at once all you know."

"In the first place, my dear child, the cause of ruin to married women who would gladly retain their husband's heart —and," she added, as a parenthesis, "to retain their affection and to rule the man are one and the same thing,—well, the chief cause of matrimonial differences lies in the unbroken companionship, which did not subsist in former days, and which was introduced into this country with the mania for family life. Ever since the Revolution vulgar notions have invaded aristocratic households. This misfortune is attributable to one of their writers, Rousseau, a base heretic, who had none but reactionary ideas, and who—how I know not—

argued out the most irrational conclusions. He asserted that all women have the same rights and the same faculties; that under the conditions of social life the laws of Nature must be obeyed—as if the wife of a Spanish Grandee—as if you or I—had anything in common with a woman of the people. And since then women of rank have nursed their own children, have brought up their daughters, and lived at home.

"Life has thus been made so complicated that happiness is almost impossible; for such an agreement of two characters as has enabled you and me to live together as friends is a rare exception. And perpetual friction is not less to be avoided between parents and children than between husband and wife. There are few natures in which love can survive in spite of omnipresence; that miracle is the prerogative of God.

"So, place the barriers of society between you and Paul; go to balls, to the opera, drive out in the morning, dine out in the evening, pay visits; do not give Paul more than a few minutes of your time. By this system you will never lose your value in his eyes. When two beings have nothing but sentiment to go through life on, they soon exhaust its resources, and ere long satiety and disgust ensue. Then, when once the sentiment is blighted, what is to be done? Make no mistake; when love is extinct, only indifference or contempt ever fills its place. So be always fresh and new to him. If he bores you—that may occur—at any rate, never bore him. To submit to boredom on occasion is one of the conditions of every form of power. You will have no occasion to vary your happiness either by thrift in money matters or the management of a household; hence, if you do not lead your husband to share your outside pleasures, if you do not amuse him, in short, you will sink into the most crushing lethargy. Then begins the spleen of love. But we always love those who amuse us or make us happy. To give and to receive happiness are two systems of wifely conduct between which a gulf lies."

"Dear mother, I am listening, but I do not understand."

"If you love Paul so blindly as to do everything he desires, and if he makes you really happy, there is an end of it; you will never be the mistress, and the wisest precepts in the world will be of no use."

"That is rather clearer; but I learn the rule without knowing how to apply it," said Natalie, laughing. "Well, I have the theory, and practice will follow."

"My poor Ninie," said her mother, dropping a sincere tear as she thought of her daughter's marriage and pressed her to her heart, "events will strengthen your memory.—In short, my Natalie," said she after a pause, during which they sat clasped in a sympathetic embrace, "you will learn that each of us, as a woman, has her destiny, just as every man has his vocation. A woman is born to be a woman of fashion, the charming mistress of her house, just as a man is born to be a General or a poet. Your calling in life is to attract. And your education has fitted you for the world. In these days a woman ought to be brought up to grace a drawing-room, as of old she was brought up for the Gynecæum. You, child, were never made to be the mother of a family or a notable housekeeper.

"If you have children, I hope they will not come to spoil your figure as soon as you are married. Nothing can be more vulgar—and besides, it casts reflections on your husband's love for you. Well, if you have children two or three years hence, you will have nurses and tutors to bring them up. You must always be the great lady, representing the wealth and pleasures of the house; but only show your superiority in such things as flatter men's vanity, and hide any superiority you may acquire in serious matters."

"You frighten me, mamma!" cried Natalie. "How am I ever to remember all your instructions? How am I, heedless and childish as I know I am, to reckon on results and always reflect before acting?"

"My darling child, I am only telling you now what you would learn for yourself later, paying for experience by wretched mistakes, by misguided conduct, which would cause you many regrets and hamper your life."

"But how am I to begin?" asked Natalie artlessly.

"Instinct will guide you," said her mother. "What Paul feels for you at this moment is far more desire than love; for the love to which desire gives rise is hope, and that which follows its gratification is realization. There, my dear, lies your power, there is the heart of the question. What woman is not loved the day before marriage? Be still loved the day after, and you will be loved for life. Paul is weak; he will be easily formed by habit; if he yields once, he will yield always. A woman not yet won may insist on anything. Do not commit the folly I have seen in so many wives, who, not knowing the importance of the first hours of their sovereignty, waste them in folly, in aimless absurdities. Make use of the dominion given you by your husband's first passion to accustom him to obey you. And to break him in, choose the most unreasonable thing possible, so as to gauge the extent of your power by the extent of his concession. What merit would there be in making him agree to what is reasonable? Would that be obeying you? 'Always take a bull by the horns,' says a Castilian proverb. When once he sees the uselessness of his weapons and his strength, he is conquered. If your husband commits a folly for your sake, you will master him."

"Good Heavens! But why?"

"Because, my child, marriage is for life, and a husband is not like any other man. So never be so foolish as to give way in anything whatever. Always be strictly reserved in your speech and actions; you may even go to the point of coldness, for that may be modified at pleasure, while there is nothing beyond the most vehement expressions of love. A husband, my dear, is the only man to whom a woman must grant no license.

"And, after all, nothing is easier than to preserve your dignity. The simple words, 'Your wife must not, or cannot do this thing or that,' are the great talisman. A woman's whole life is wrapped up in 'I will not!—I cannot!'—'I cannot' is the irresistible appeal of weakness which succumbs, weeps, and wins. 'I will not' is the last resort. It is the crowning effort of feminine strength; it should never be used but on great occasions. Success depends entirely on the way in which a woman uses these two words, works on them, and varies them.

"But there is a better method of rule than these, which sometimes involve a contest. I, my child, governed by faith. If your husband believes in you, you may do anything. To inspire him with this religion, you must convince him that you understand him. And do not think that this is such an easy matter. A woman can always prove that she loves a man, but it is more difficult to get him to confess that she has understood him. I must tell you everything, my child; for, to you, life with all its complications, a life in which two wills are to be reconciled and harmonized, will begin to-morrow. Do you realize the difficulty? The best way to bring two wills into agreement is to take care that there is but one in the house. People often say that a woman makes trouble for herself by this inversion of the parts; but, my dear, the wife is thus in a position to command events instead of submitting to them, and that single advantage counterbalances every possible disadvantage."

Natalie kissed her mother's hands, on which she left her tears of gratitude. Like all women in whom physical passion does not fire the passion of the soul, she suddenly took in all the bearings of this lofty feminine policy. Still, like spoilt children who will never admit that they are beaten even by the soundest reasoning, but who reiterate their obstinate demands, she returned to the charge with one of those personal arguments that are suggested by the logical rectitude of children.

"My dear mother, a few days ago you said so much about the necessary arrangements for Paul's fortune, which you alone could manage; why have you changed your views in thus leaving us to ourselves?"

"I did not then know the extent of my indebtedness to you, nor how much I owed," replied her mother, who would not confess her secret. "Besides, in a year or two I can give you my answer.

"Now, Paul will be here directly. We must dress. Be as coaxing and sweet, you know, as you were that evening when we discussed that ill-starred contract, for to-day I am bent on saving a relic of the family, and on giving you a thing to which I am superstitiously attached."

"What is that?"

"The *Discreto*."

Paul appeared at about four o'clock. Though, when addressing his mother, he did his utmost to seem gracious, Madame Evangelista saw on his brow the clouds which his cogitations of the night and reflections on waking had gathered there.

"Mathias has told him," thought she, vowing that she would undo the old lawyer's work.

"My dear boy," she said, "you have left your diamonds in the cabinet drawer, and I honestly confess that I never want to see the things again which so nearly raised a storm between us. Besides, as Mathias remarked, they must be sold to provide for the first instalment of payment on the lands you have purchased."

"The diamonds are not mine," rejoined Paul. "I gave them to Natalie, so that when you see her wear them you may never more remember the trouble they have caused you."

Madame Evangelista took Paul's hand and pressed it cordially, while restraining a sentimental tear.

"Listen, my dear, good children," said she, looking at Natalie and Paul. "If this is so, I will propose to make a bargain with you. I am obliged to sell my pearl necklace and earrings. Yes, Paul; I will not invest a farthing in an annuity; I do not forget my duties to you. Well, I confess my weakness, but to sell the *Discreto* seems to me to portend disaster. To part with a diamond known to have belonged to Philip II., to have graced his royal hand—a historical gem which the Duke of Alva played with for ten years on the hilt of his sword—no, it shall never be. Élie Magus valued my necklace and earrings at a hundred odd thousand francs; let us exchange them for the jewels I have handed over to you to cancel my debts to my daughter; you will gain a little, but what do I care; I am not grasping. And then, Paul, out of your savings you can have the pleasure of procuring a diadem or hairpins for Natalie, a diamond at a time. Instead of having one of those fancy sets, trinkets which are in fashion only among second-rate people, your wife will thus have magnificent stones that will give her real pleasure. If something must be sold, is it not better to get rid of these old-fashioned jewels, and keep the really fine things in the family?"

"But you, my dear mother?" said Paul.

"I," replied Madame Evangelista, "I want nothing now. No, I am going to be your farm-bailiff at Lanstrac. Would it not be sheer folly to go to Paris just when I have to wind up my affairs here? I am going to be avaricious for my grandchildren."

"Dear mother," said Paul, much touched, "ought I to accept this exchange without compensation?"

"Dear Heaven! are you not my nearest and dearest? Do you think that I shall find no happiness when I sit by my fire and say to myself, 'Natalie is gone in splendor to-night to the Duchesse de Berri's ball. When she sees herself with my diamond at her throat, my earrings in her ears, she will have those little pleasures of self-satisfaction which add so much to a woman's enjoyment, and make her gay and attractive.'— Nothing crushes a woman so much as the chafing of her vanity. I never saw a badly-dressed woman look amiable and pleasant. Be honest, Paul! we enjoy much more through the one we love than in any pleasure of our own."

"What on earth was Mathias driving at?" thought Paul. "Well, mother," said he, in a low voice, "I accept."

"I am quite overpowered," said Natalie.

Just now Solonet came in with good news for his client.

He had found two speculators of his acquaintance, builders, who were much tempted by the house, as the extent of the grounds afforded good building land.

"They are prepared to pay two hundred and fifty thousand francs," said he; "but if you are ready to sell, I could bring them up to three hundred thousand. You have two acres of garden."

"My husband paid two hundred thousand for the whole thing," said she, "so I agree; but you will not include the furniture or the mirrors."

"Ah, ha!" said Solonet, with a laugh, "you understand business."

"Alas! needs must," said she, with a sigh.

"I hear that a great many persons are coming to your midnight ceremony," said Solonet, who, finding himself in the way, bowed himself out.

Madame Evangelista went with him as far as the door of the outer drawing-room, and said to him privately:

"I have now property representing two hundred and fifty thousand francs; if I get two hundred thousand francs for myself out of the price of the house, I can command a capital of four hundred and fifty thousand francs. I want to invest it to the best advantage, and I trust to you to do it. I shall most likely remain at Lanstrac."

The young lawyer kissed his client's hand with a bow of gratitude, for the widow's tone led him to believe that this alliance, strengthened by interest, might even go a little further.

"You may depend on me," said he. "I will find you trade investments, in which you will risk nothing, and make large profits."

"Well—till to-morrow," said she; "for you and Monsieur le Marquis de Gyas are going to sign for us."

"Why, dear mother, do you refuse to come with us to Paris?" asked Paul. "Natalie is as much vexed with me as if I were the cause of your determination."

"I have thought it well over, my children, and I should

be in your way. You would think yourselves obliged to include me as a third in everything you might do, and young people have notions of their own which I might involuntarily oppose. Go to Paris by yourselves.—I do not propose to exercise over the Comtesse de Manerville the mild dominion I held over Natalie. I must leave her entirely to you. There are habits which she and I share, you see, Paul, and which must be broken. My influence must give way to yours. I wish you to be attached to me; believe me, I have your interests at heart more than you think perhaps. Young husbands, sooner or later, are jealous of a wife's affection for her mother. Perhaps they are right. When you are entirely united, when love has amalgamated your souls into one —then, my dear boy, you will have no fears of an adverse influence when you see me under your roof.

"I know the world, men and things; I have seen many a household rendered unhappy by the blind affection of a mother who made herself intolerable, as much to her daughter as to her son-in-law. The affection of old people is often petty and vexatious; perhaps I should not succeed in effacing myself. I am weak enough to think myself handsome still; some flatterers try to persuade me that I am lovable, and I might assume an inconvenient prominence. Let me make one more sacrifice to your happiness.—I have given you my fortune; well, now I surrender my last womanly vanities.—Your good father Mathias is growing old; he cannot look after your estates. I will constitute myself your bailiff. I shall make such occupation for myself as old folks must sooner or later fall back on; then, when you need me, I will go to Paris and help in your plans of ambition.

"Come, Paul, be honest; this arrangement is to your mind? Answer."

Paul would not admit it, but he was very glad to be free. The suspicions as to his mother-in-law's character, implanted in his mind by the old notary, were dispelled by this conversation, which Madame Evangelista continued to the same effect.

"My mother was right," thought Natalie, who was watching Paul's expression. "He is really glad to see me parted from her.—But why?"

Was not this *Why?* the first query of suspicion, and did it not add considerable weight to her mother's instructions?

There are some natures who, on the strength of a single proof, can believe in friendship. In such folks as these the north wind blows away clouds as fast as the west wind brings them up; they are content with effects, and do not look for the causes. Paul's was one of these essentially confiding characters, devoid of ill-feeling, and no less devoid of foresight. His weakness was the outcome of kindness and a belief in goodness in others, far more than of want of strength of mind.

Natalie was pensive and sad; she did not know how to do without her mother. Paul, with the sort of fatuity that love can produce, laughed at his bride's melancholy mood, promising himself that the pleasures of married life and the excitement of Paris would dissipate it. It was with marked satisfaction that Madame Evangelista encouraged Paul in his confidence, for the first condition of revenge is dissimulation. Overt hatred is powerless.

The Creole lady had made two long strides already. Her daughter had possession of splendid jewels which had cost Paul two hundred thousand francs, and to which he would, no doubt, add more. Then, she was leaving the two young people to themselves, with no guidance but unregulated love. Thus she had laid the foundations of revenge of which her daughter knew nothing, though sooner or later she would be accessory to it.

Now, would Natalie love Paul?—This was as yet an unanswered question, of which the issue would modify Madame Evangelista's schemes; for she was too sincerely fond of her daughter not to be tender of her happiness. Thus Paul's future life depended on himself. If he could make his wife love him, he would be saved.

Finally, on the following night, after an evening spent with the four witnesses whom Madame Evangelista had invited to the lengthy dinner which followed the legal ceremony, at midnight the young couple and their friends attended mass by the light of blazing tapers in the presence of above a hundred curious spectators.

A wedding celebrated at night always seems of ill-omen; daylight is a symbol of life and enjoyment, and its happy augury is lacking. Ask the staunchest spirit the cause of this chill, why the dark vault depresses the nerves, why the sound of footsteps is so startling, why the cry of owls and bats is so strangely audible. Though there is no reason for alarm, every one quakes; darkness, the forecast of death, is crushing to the spirit.

Natalie, torn from her mother, was weeping. The girl was tormented by all the doubts which clutch the heart on the threshold of a new life, where, in spite of every promise of happiness, there are a thousand pitfalls for a woman's feet. She shivered with cold, and had to put on a cloak.

Madame Evangelista's manner and that of the young couple gave rise to comments among the elegant crowd that stood round the altar.

"Solonet tells me that the young people go off to Paris to-morrow morning alone."

"Madame Evangelista was to have gone to live with them."

"Count Paul has got rid of her!"

"What a mistake!" said the Marquise de Gyas. "The man who shuts his door on his mother-in-law opens it to a lover. Does he not know all that a mother is?"

"He has been very hard on Madame Evangelista. The poor woman has had to sell her house, and is going to live at Lanstrac."

"Natalie is very unhappy."

"Well, would you like to spend the day after your wedding on the highroad?"

"It is very uncomfortable."

"I am glad I came," said another lady, "to convince myself of the necessity of surrounding a wedding with all the usual ceremonies and festivities, for this seems to me very cold and dismal. Indeed, if I were to tell the whole truth," she whispered, leaning over to her neighbor, "it strikes me as altogether unseemly."

Madame Evangelista took Natalie in her own carriage to Count Paul's house.

"Well, mother, it is all over——"

"Remember my advice, and you will be happy. Always be his wife, and not his mistress."

When Natalie had gone to her room, Madame Evangelista went through the little farce of throwing herself into her son-in-law's arms and weeping on his shoulder. It was the only provincial detail Madame Evangelista had allowed herself; but she had her reasons. In the midst of her apparently wild and desperate tears and speeches, she extracted from Paul such concessions as a husband will always make.

The next day she saw the young people into their chaise, and accompanied them across the ferry over the Gironde. Natalie, in a word, had made her mother understand that if Paul had won in the game concerning the contract, her revenge was beginning. Natalie had already reduced her husband to perfect obedience.

CONCLUSION

Five years after this, one afternoon in November, the Comte Paul de Manerville, wrapped in a cloak, with a bowed head, mysteriously arrived at the house of Monsieur Mathias at Bordeaux. The worthy man, too old now to attend to business, had sold his connection, and was peacefully ending his days in one of his houses.

Important business had taken him out at the time when his visitor called; but his old housekeeper, warned of Paul's advent, showed him into the room that had belonged to Madame Mathias, who had died a year since.

Paul, tired out by a hurried journey, slept till late. The

old man, on his return, came to look at his erewhile client, and was satisfied to look at him lying asleep, as a mother looks at her child. Josette, the housekeeper, came in with her master, and stood by the bedside, her hands on her hips.

"This day twelvemonth, Josette, when my dear wife breathed her last in this bed, I little thought of seeing Monsieur le Comte here looking like death."

"Poor gentleman! he groans in his sleep," said Josette.

The old lawyer made no reply but *"Sac à papier!"*—an innocent oath, which, from him, always represented the despair of a man of business in the face of some insuperable dilemma.

"At any rate," thought he, "I have saved the freehold of Lanstrac, Auzac, Saint-Froult, and his town house here."

Mathias counted on his fingers and exclaimed, "Five years! —Yes, it is five years this very month since his old aunt, now deceased, the venerable Madame de Maulincour, asked on his behalf for the hand of that little crocodile in woman's skirt's who has managed to ruin him—as I knew she would!"

After looking at the young man for some time, the good old man, now very gouty, went away, leaning on his stick, to walk slowly up and down his little garden. At nine o'clock supper was served, for the old man supped; and he was not a little surprised to see Paul come in with a calm brow and an unruffled expression, though perceptibly altered. Though at three-and-thirty the Comte de Manerville looked forty, the change was due solely to mental shocks; physically he was in good health. He went up to his old friend, took his hands, and pressed them affectionately, saying:

"Dear, good Maître Mathias! And you have had your troubles!"

"Mine were in the course of nature, Monsieur le Comte, but yours——"

"We will talk over mine presently at supper."

"If I had not a son high up in the law, and a married daughter," said the worthy man, "believe me, Monsieur le Comte, you would have found something more than bare hospitality from old Mathias.—How is it that you have come to Bordeaux just at the time when you may read on every wall bills announcing the seizure and sale of the farms of le Grassol and le Guadet, of the vine land of Bellerose and your house here? I cannot possibly express my grief on seeing those huge posters—I, who for forty years took as much care of your estates as if they were my own; I, who, when I was third clerk under Monsieur Chesneau, my predecessor, transacted the purchase for your mother, and in my young clerk's hand engrossed the deed of sale on parchment; I, who have the title-deeds safe in my successor's office; I, who made out all the accounts. Why, I remember you so high——" and the old man held his hand two feet from the floor.

"After being a notary for more than forty years, to see my name printed as large as life in the face of Israel, in the announcement of the seizure and the disposal of the property —you cannot imagine the pain it gives me. As I go along the street and see the folks all reading those horrible yellow bills, I am as much ashamed as if my own ruin and honor were involved. And there are a pack of idiots who spell it all out at the top of their voices on purpose to attract idlers, and they add the most ridiculous comments.

"Are you not master of your own? Your father ran through two fortunes before making the one he left you, and you would not be a Manerville if you did not tread in his steps.

"And besides, the seizure of real property is foreseen in the Code, and provided for under a special *capitulum;* you are in a position recognized by law. If I were not a white-headed old man, only waiting for a nudge to push me into the grave, I would thrash the men who stand staring at such abominations—'At the suit of Madame Natalie Evangelista, wife of Paul François Joseph Comte de Manerville, of separate estate by the ruling of the lower Court of the Department of the Seine,' and so forth."

"Yes," said Paul, "and now separate in bed and board——"

"Indeed!" said the old man.

"Oh! against Natalie's will," said the Count quickly. "I had to deceive her. She does not know that I am going away."

"Going away?"

"My passage is taken; I sail on the *Belle-Amélie* for Calcutta."

"In two days!" said Mathias. "Then we meet no more, Monsieur le Comte."

"You are but seventy-three, my dear Mathias, and you have the gout, an assurance of old age. When I come back I shall find you just where you are. Your sound brain and heart will be as good as ever; you will help me to rebuild the ruined home. I mean to make a fine fortune in seven years. On my return I shall only be forty. At that age everything is still possible."

"You, Monsieur le Comte!" exclaimed Mathias, with a gesture of amazement. "You are going into trade!—What are you thinking of?"

"I am no longer Monsieur le Comte, dear Mathias. I have taken my passage in the name of Camille, a Christian name of my mother's. And I have some connections which may enable me to make a fortune in other ways. Trade will be my last resource. Also, I am starting with a large enough sum of money to allow of my tempting fortune on a grand scale."

"Where is that money?"

"A friend will send it to me."

The old man dropped his fork at the sound of the word *friend*, not out of irony or surprise; his face expressed his grief at finding Paul under the influence of a delusion, for his eye saw a void where the Count perceived a solid plank.

"I have been in a notary's office more than fifty years," said he, "and I never knew a ruined man who had friends willing to lend him money."

"You do not know de Marsay. At this minute, while I speak to you, I am perfectly certain that he has sold out of the funds if it was necessary, and to-morrow you will receive a bill of exchange for fifty thousand crowns."

"I only hope so.—But then could not this friend have set your affairs straight? You could have lived quietly at Lanstrac for five or six years on Madame la Comtesse's income."

"And would an assignment have paid fifteen hundred thousand francs of debts, of which my wife's share was five hundred and fifty thousand?"

"And how, in four years, have you managed to owe fourteen hundred and fifty thousand francs?"

"Nothing can be plainer, my good friend. Did I not make the diamonds a present to my wife? Did I not spend the hundred and fifty thousand francs that came to us from the sale of Madame Evangelista's house in redecorating my house in Paris? Had I not to pay the price of the land we purchased, and of the legal business of my marriage contract? Finally, had I not to sell Natalie's forty thousand francs a year in the funds to pay for d'Auzac and Saint-Froult? We sold at 87, so I was in debt about two hundred thousand francs within a month of my marriage.

"An income was left of sixty-seven thousand francs, and we have regularly spent two hundred thousand francs a year beyond it. To these nine hundred thousand francs add certain money-lenders' interest, and you will easily find it a million."

"Brrrr," said the old lawyer. "And then?"

"Well, I wished at once to make up the set of jewels for my wife, of which she already had the pearl necklace and the *Discreto* clasp—a family jewel—and her mother's earrings. I paid a hundred thousand francs for a diadem of wheat-ears. There you see eleven hundred thousand francs. Then I owe my wife the whole of her fortune, amounting to three hundred and fifty-six thousand francs settled on her."

"But then," said Mathias, "if Madame la Comtesse had pledged her diamonds, and you your securities, you would have, by my calculations, three hundred thousand with which to pacify your creditors——"

"When a man is down, Mathias; when his estates are loaded with mortgages; when his wife is the first creditor for her settlement; when, to crown all, he is exposed to having writs against him for notes of hand to the tune of a hundred thousand francs—to be paid off, I hope, by good prices at the sales—nothing can be done. And the cost of conveyancing!"

"Frightful!" said the lawyer.

"The distraint has happily taken the form of a voluntary sale, which will mitigate the flare."

"And you are selling Bellerose with the wines of 1825 in the cellars?"

"I cannot help myself."

"Bellerose is worth six hundred thousand francs."

"Natalie will buy it in by my advice."

"Sixteen thousand francs in ordinary years—and such a season as 1825! I will run Bellerose up to seven hundred thousand francs myself, and each of the farms up to a hundred and twenty thousand."

"So much the better; then I can clear myself if my house in the town fetches two hundred thousand."

"Solonet will pay a little more for it; he has a fancy for it. He is retiring on a hundred odd thousand a year, which he has made in gambling in *trois-six*. He has sold his business for three hundred thousand francs, and is marrying a rich mulatto. God knows where she got her money, but they say she has millions. A notary gambling in *trois-six!* A notary marrying a mulatto! What times these are! It was he, they say, who looked after your mother-in-law's investments."

"She has greatly improved Lanstrac, and taken good care of the land; she has regularly paid her rent."

"I should never have believed her capable of behaving so."

"She is so kind and devoted.—She always paid Natalie's debts when she came to spend three months in Paris."

"So she very well might, she lives on Lanstrac," said Mathias. "She! Turned thrifty! What a miracle! She has just bought the estate of Grainrouge, lying between Lanstrac and Grassol, so that if she prolongs the avenue from Lanstrac down to the highroad you can drive a league and a half through your own grounds. She paid a hundred thousand francs down for Grainrouge, which is worth a thousand crowns a year in cash rents."

"She is still handsome," said Paul. "Country life keeps her young. I will not go to take leave of her; she would bleed herself for me."

"You would waste your time; she is gone to Paris. She probably arrived just as you left."

"She has, of course, heard of the sale of the land, and has rushed to my assistance.—I have no right to complain of life. I am loved as well as any man can be in this world, loved by two women who vie with each other in their devotion to me. They were jealous of each other; the daughter reproached her mother for being too fond of me, and the mother found fault with her daughter for her extravagance. This affection has been my ruin. How can a man help gratifying the lightest wish of the woman he loves? How can he protect himself? And, on the other hand, how can he accept self-sacrifice?—We could, to be sure, pay up with my fortune and come to live at Lanstrac—but I would rather go to India and make my fortune than tear Natalie from the life she loves. It was I myself who proposed to her a separation of goods. Women are angels who ought never to be mixed up with the business of life."

Old Mathias listened to Paul with an expression of surprise and doubt.

"You have no children?" said he.

"Happily!" replied Paul.

"Well, I view marriage in a different light," replied the old notary quite simply. "In my opinion, a wife ought to share her husband's lot for good or ill. I have heard that young married people who are too much like lovers have no families. Is pleasure then the only end of marriage? Is it not rather the happiness of family life? Still, you were but eight-and-twenty, and the Countess no more than twenty; it was excusable that you should think only of love-making. At the same time, the terms of your marriage-contract, and your name—

you will think me grossly lawyer-like—required you to begin by having a fine handsome boy. Yes, Monsieur le Comte, and if you had daughters, you ought not to have stopped till you had a male heir to succeed you in the entail.

"Was Mademoiselle Evangelista delicate? Was there anything to fear for her in motherhood?—You will say that is very old-fashioned and antiquated; but in noble families, Monsieur le Comte, a legitimate wife ought to have children and bring them up well. As the Duchesse de Sully said—the wife of the great Sully—a wife is not a means of pleasure, but the honor and virtue of the household."

"You do not know what women are, my dear Mathias," said Paul. "To be happy, a man must love his wife as she chooses to be loved. And is it not rather brutal to deprive a woman so early of her charms and spoil her beauty before she has really enjoyed it?"

"If you had had a family, the mother would have checked the wife's dissipation; she would have stayed at home——"

"If you were in the right, my good friend," said Paul, with a frown, "I should be still more unhappy. Do not aggravate my misery by moralizing over my ruin; let me depart without any after bitterness."

Next day Mathias received a bill payable at sight for a hundred and fifty thousand francs, signed by de Marsay.

"You see," said Paul, "he does not write me a word. Henri's is the most perfectly imperfect, the most unconventionally noble nature I have ever met with. If you could but know how superior this man—who is still young—rises above feeling and interest, and what a great politician he is, you, like me, would be amazed to find what a warm heart he has."

Mathias tried to reason Paul out of his purpose, but it was irrevocable, and justified by so many practical reasons, that the old notary made no further attempt to detain his client.

Rarely enough does a vessel in cargo sail punctually to the day; but by an accident disastrous to Paul, the wind being favorable, the *Belle-Amélie* was to sail on the morrow. At the moment of departure the landing-stage is always crowded with relations, friends, and idlers. Among these, as it happened, were several personally acquainted with Manerville. His ruin had made him as famous now as he had once been for his fortune, so there was a stir of curiosity. Every one had some remark to make.

The old man had escorted Paul to the wharf, and he must have suffered keenly as he heard some of the comments.

"Who would recognize in the man you see there with old Mathias the dandy who used to be called Pease-blossom, and who was the oracle of fashion here at Bordeaux five years since?"

"What, can that fat little man in an alpaca overcoat, looking like a coachman, be the Comte Paul de Manerville?"

"Yes, my dear, the man who married Mademoiselle Evangelista. There he is ruined, without a sou to his name, going to the Indies to look for the roc's egg."

"But how was he ruined? He was so rich!"

"Paris—women—the Bourse—gambling—display——"

"And besides," said another, "Manerville is a poor creature; he has no sense, as limp as papier-maché, allowing himself to be fleeced, and incapable of any decisive action. He was born to be ruined."

Paul shook his old friend's hand and took refuge on board. Mathias stood on the quay, looking at his old client, who leaned over the netting, defying the crowd with a look of scorn.

Just as the anchor was weighed, Paul saw that Mathias was signaling to him by waving his handkerchief. The old housekeeper had come in hot haste, and was standing by her master, who seemed greatly excited by some matter of importance. Paul persuaded the captain to wait a few minutes and send a boat to land, that he might know what the old lawyer wanted; he was signaling vigorously, evidently desiring him to disembark. Mathias, too infirm to go to the ship, gave two letters to one of the sailors who were in the boat.

"My good fellow," said the old notary, showing one of the

letters to the sailor, "this letter, mark it well, make no mistake—this packet has just been delivered by a messenger who has ridden from Paris in thirty-five hours. Explain this clearly to Monsieur le Comte, do not forget. It might make him change his plans."

"And we should have to land him?"

"Yes," said the lawyer rashly.

The sailor in most parts of the world is a creature apart, professing the deepest contempt for all land-lubbers. As to townsfolk, he cannot understand them; he knows nothing about them; he laughs them to scorn; he cheats them if he can without direct dishonesty. This one, as it happened, was a man of Lower Brittany, who saw worthy old Mathias' instructions in only one light.

"Just so," he muttered, as he took his oar, "land him again! The captain is to lose a passenger! If we listened to these land-lubbers, we should spend our lives in pulling them between the ship and shore. Is he afraid his son will take cold?"

So the sailor gave Paul the letters without any message. On recognizing his wife's writing and de Marsay's, Paul imagined all that either of them could have to say to him; and being determined not to risk being influenced by the offers that might be inspired by their regard, he put the letters in his pocket with apparent indifference.

"And that is the rubbish we are kept waiting for! What nonsense!" said the sailor to the captain in his broad Breton. "If the matter were as important as that old guy declared, would Monsieur le Comte drop the papers into his scuppers?"

Paul, lost in the dismal reflections that come over the strongest man in such circumstances, gave himself up to melancholy, while he waved his hand to his old friend, and bid farewell to France, watching the fast disappearing buildings of Bordeaux.

He presently sat down on a coil of rope, and there night found him, lost in meditation. Doubt came upon him as twilight fell; he gazed anxiously into the future; he could see nothing before him but perils and uncertainty, and wondered whether his courage might not fail him. He felt some vague alarm as he thought of Natalie left to herself; he repented of his decision, regretting Paris and his past life.

Then he fell a victim to sea-sickness. Every one knows the miseries of this condition, and one of the worst features of its sufferings is the total effacement of will that accompanies it. An inexplicable incapacity loosens all the bonds of vitality at the core; the mind refuses to act, and everything is a matter of total indifference—a mother can forget her child, a lover his mistress; the strongest man becomes a mere inert mass. Paul was carried to his berth, where he remained for three days, alternately violently ill, and plied with grog by the sailors, thinking of nothing or sleeping; then he went through a sort of convalescence and recovered his ordinary health.

On the morning when, finding himself better, he went for a walk on deck to breathe the sea-air of a more southern climate, on putting his hands in his pockets he felt his letters. He at once took them out to read them, and began by Natalie's. In order that the Comtesse de Manerville's letter may be fully understood, it is necessary first to give that written by Paul to his wife on leaving Paris.

PAUL DE MANERVILLE TO HIS WIFE.

"My best Beloved,—When you read this letter I shall be far from you, probably on the vessel that is to carry me to India, where I am going to repair my shattered fortune. I did not feel that I had the courage to tell you of my departure. I have deceived you; but was it not necessary? You would have pinched yourself to no purpose, you would have wished to sacrifice your own fortune. Dear Natalie, feel no remorse; I shall know no repentance. When I return with millions, I will imitate your father; I will lay them at your feet as he laid his at your mother's, and will say, 'It is all yours.'

"I love you to distraction, Natalie; and I can say so without fearing that you will make my avowal a pretext for exerting a power which only weak men dread. Yours was unlimited from the first day I ever saw you. My love alone has led me to disaster; my gradual ruin has brought me the delirious joys of the gambler. As my money diminished my happiness grew greater; each fraction of my wealth converted into some little gratification to you caused me heavenly rapture. I could have wished you to have more caprices than you ever had.

"I knew that I was marching on an abyss, but I went, my brow wreathed with joys and feelings unknown to vulgar souls. I acted like the lovers who shut themselves up for a year or two in a cottage by a lake, vowing to kill themselves after plunging into the ocean of happiness, dying in all the glory of their illusions and their passion. I have always thought such persons eminently rational. You have never known anything of my pleasures or of my sacrifices. And is there not exquisite enjoyment in concealing from the one we love the cost of the things she wishes for?

"I may tell you these secrets now. I shall be far indeed away when you hold this sheet loaded with my love. Though I forego the pleasure of your gratitude, I do not feel that clutch at my heart which would seize me if I tried to talk of these things. Alas, my dearest, there is deep self-interest in thus revealing the past. Is it not to add to the volume of our love in the future? Could it indeed ever need such a stimulus? Do we not feel that pure affection to which proof is needless, which scorns time and distance, and lives in its own strength?

"Ah! Natalie, I just now left the table where I am writing by the fire, and looked at you asleep, calm and trustful, in the attitude of a guileless child, your hand lying where I could take it. I left a tear on the pillow that has been the witness of our happiness. I leave you without a fear on the promise of that attitude; I leave you to win peace by winning a fortune so large that no anxiety may ever disturb our joys, and that you may satisfy your every wish. Neither you nor I could ever dispense with the luxuries of the life we lead. I am a man, and I have courage; mine alone be the task of amassing the fortune we require.

"You might perhaps think of following me! I will not tell you the name of the ship, nor the port I sail from, nor the day I leave. A friend will tell you when it is too late.

"Natalie, my devotion to you is boundless; I love you as a mother loves her child, as a lover worships his mistress, with perfect disinterestedness. The work be mine, the enjoyment yours; mine the sufferings, yours a life of happiness. Amuse yourself; keep up all your habits of luxury; go to the Italiens, to the French opera, into society and to balls; I absolve you beforehand. But, dear angel, each time you come home to the nest where we have enjoyed the fruits that have ripened during our five years of love, remember your lover, think of me for a moment, and sleep in my heart. That is all I ask.

"I—my one, dear, constant thought—when, under scorching skies, working for our future, I find some obstacle to overcome, or when, tired out, I rest in the hope of my return—I shall think of you who are the beauty of my life. Yes, I shall try to live in you, telling myself that you have neither cares nor uneasiness. Just as life is divided into day and night, waking and sleeping, so I shall have my life of enchantment in Paris, my life of labors in India—a dream of anguish, a reality of delight; I shall live so completely in what is real to you that my days will be the dream. I have my memories; canto by canto I shall recall the lovely poem of five years; I shall remember the days when you chose to be dazzling, when by some perfection of evening-dress or morning-wrapper you made yourself new in my eyes. I shall taste on my lips the flavor of our little feasts.

"Yes, dear angel, I am going like a man pledged to some high emprise when by success he is to win his mistress! To me the past will be like the dreams of desire which anticipate realization, and which realization often disappoints. But you have always more than fulfilled them. And I shall return to find a new wife, for will not absence lend you fresh charms?— Oh, my dear love, my Natalie, let me be a religion to you. Be always the child I have seen sleeping! If you were to betray my blind confidence—Natalie, you would not have to fear my anger, of that you may be sure; I should die without a word. But a woman does not deceive the husband who leaves her free, for women are never mean. She may cheat a tyrant; but she does not care for the easy treason which would deal a deathblow. No, I cannot imagine such a thing—forgive me for this cry, natural to a man.

"My dearest, you will see de Marsay; he is now the tenant holding our house, and he will leave you in it. This lease to him was necessary to avoid useless loss. My creditors, not understanding that payment is merely a question of time, might have seized the furniture and the rent of letting the house. Be good to de Marsay; I have the most perfect confidence in his abilities and in his honor. Make him your advocate and your adviser, your familiar. Whatever his engagements may be, he will always be at your service. I have instructed him to keep an eye on the liquidation of my debts; if he should advance a sum of which he presently needed the use, I trust to you to pay him. Remember I am not leaving you to de Marsay's guidance, but to your own; when I mention him, I do not force him upon you.

"Alas, I cannot begin to write on business matters; only an hour remains to me under the same roof with you. I count your breathing; I try to picture your thoughts from the occasional changes in your sleep, your breathing revives the flowery hours of our early love. At every throb of your heart mine goes forth to you with all its wealth, and I scatter over you the petals of the roses of my soul, as children strew them in front of the altars on Corpus Christi Day. I commend you to the memories I am pouring out on you; I would, if I could, pour my life-blood into your veins that you might indeed be mine, that your heart might be my heart, your thoughts my thoughts, that I might be wholly in you!—And you utter a little murmur as if in reply!

"Be ever as calm and lovely as you are at this moment. I would I had the fabled power of which we hear in fairy tales, and could leave you thus to sleep during my absence, to wake you on my return with a kiss. What energy, what love, must

I feel to leave you when I behold you thus.—You are Spanish
and religious; you will observe an oath taken even in your
sleep when your unspoken word was believed in beyond doubt.

"Farewell, my dearest. Your hapless Pease-blossom is
swept away by the storm-wind; but it will come back to you
for ever on the wings of Fortune. Nay, dear Ninie, I will
not say farewell, for you will always be with me. Will you not
be the soul of my actions? Will not the hope of bringing
you such happiness as cannot be wrecked give spirit to my
enterprise and guide all my steps? Will you not always be
present to me? No, it will not be the tropical sun, but the
fire of your eyes, that will light me on my way.

"Be as happy as a woman can be, bereft of her lover.—I
should have been glad to have a parting kiss, in which you
were not merely passive; but, my Ninie, my adored darling,
I would not wake you. When you wake, you will find a tear
on your brow; let it be a talisman.—Think, oh! think of him
who is perhaps to die for you, far away from you; think of
him less as your husband than as a lover who worships you
and leaves you in God's keeping."

REPLY FROM THE COMTESSE DE MANERVILLE TO HER HUSBAND

"MY DEAREST,—What grief your letter has brought me!
Had you any right to form a decision which concerns us
equally without consulting me? Are you free? Do you not
belong to me? And am I not half a Creole? Why should I not
follow you?—You have shown me that I am no longer indispensable to you. What have I done, Paul, that you should rob
me of my rights? What is to become of me alone in Paris?
Poor dear, you assume the blame for any ill I may have done.
But am I not partly to blame for this ruin? Has not my
finery weighed heavily in the wrong scale? You are making
me curse the happy, heedless life we have led these four years.
To think of you as exiled for six years! Is it not enough to
kill me? How can you make a fortune in six years? Will
you ever come back? I was wiser than I knew when I so

strenuously opposed the separate maintenance which you and my mother so absolutely insisted on. What did I tell you? That it would expose you to discredit, that it would ruin your credit! You had to be quite angry before I would give in.

"My dear Paul, you have never been so noble in my eyes as you are at this moment. Without a hint of despair, to set out to make a fortune! Only such a character, such energy as yours could take such a step. I kneel at your feet. A man who confesses to weakness in such perfect good faith, who restores his fortune from the same motive that has led him to waste it—for love, for an irresistible passion—oh, Paul, such a man is sublime! Go without fear, trample down every obstacle, and never doubt your Natalie, for it would be doubting yourself. My poor dear, you say you want to live in me? And shall not I always live in you? I shall not be here, but with you wherever you may be.

"Though your letter brought me cruel anguish, it filled me too with joy; in one minute I went through both extremes; for, seeing how much you love me, I was proud too to find that my love was appreciated. Sometimes I have fancied that I loved you more than you loved me; now I confess myself outdone; you may add that delightful superiority to the others you possess; but have I not many more reasons for loving?— Your letter, the precious letter in which your whole soul is revealed, and which so plainly tells me that between you and me nothing is lost, will dwell on my heart during your absence, for your whole soul is in it; that letter is my glory!

"I am going to live with my mother at Lanstrac; I shall there be dead to the world, and shall save out of my income to pay off your debts. From this day forth, Paul, I am another woman; I take leave for ever of the world; I will not have a pleasure that you do not share.

"Besides, Paul, I am obliged to leave Paris and live in solitude. Dear boy, you have a twofold reason for making a fortune. If your courage needed a spur, you may now find another heart dwelling in your own. My dear, cannot you guess? We shall have a child. Your dearest hopes will be crowned, monsieur. I would not give you the deceptive joys which are heart-breaking; we have already had so much disappointment on that score, and I was afraid of having to withdraw the glad announcement. But now I am sure of what I am saying, and happy to cast a gleam of joy over your sorrow. This morning, suspecting no evil, I had gone to the Church of the Assumption to return thanks to God. How could I foresee disaster? Everything seemed to smile on me. As I came out of church, I met my mother; she had heard of your distress, and had come by post with all her savings, thirty thousand francs, hoping to be able to arrange matters. What a heart, Paul! I was quite happy; I came home to tell you the two pieces of good news while we breakfasted under the awning in the conservatory, and I had ordered all the dainties you like best.

"Augustine gave me your letter.—A letter from you, when we had slept together! It was a tragedy in itself. I was seized with a shivering fit—then I read it—I read it in tears, and my mother too melted into tears. And a woman must love a man very much to cry over him, crying makes us so ugly.—I was half dead. So much love and so much courage! So much happiness and such great grief! To be unable to clasp you to my heart, my beloved, at the very moment when my admiration for your magnanimity most constrained me! What woman could withstand such a whirlwind of emotions? To think that you were far away when your hand cn my heart would have comforted me; that you were not there to give me the look I love so well, to rejoice with me over the realization of our hopes;—and I was not with you to soften your sorrow by the affection which made your Natalie so dear to you, and which can make you forget every grief!

"I wanted to be off to fly at your feet; but my mother pointed out that the *Belle-Amélie* is to sail to-morrow, that only the post could go fast enough to overtake you, and that it would be the height of folly to risk all our future happiness on a jolt. Though a mother already, I ordered horses, and my mother cheated me into the belief that they would be brought round. She acted wisely, for I was already unfit to move. I could not bear such a combination of violent agitations, and I fainted away. I am writing in bed, for I am ordered perfect rest for some months. Hitherto I have been a frivolous woman, now I mean to be the mother of a family. Providence is good to me, for a child to nurse and bring up can alone alleviate the sorrows of your absence. In it I shall find a second Paul to make much of. I shall thus publicly flaunt the love we have so carefully kept to ourselves. I shall tell the truth.

"My mother has already had occasion to contradict certain calumnies which are current as to your conduct. The two Vandenesses, Charles and Félix, had defended you stoutly, but your friend de Marsay makes game of everything; he laughs at your detractors instead of answering them. I do not like such levity in response to serious attacks. Are you not mistaken in him? However, I will obey and make a friend of him.

"Be quite easy, my dearest, with regard to anything that may affect your honor. Is it not mine?

"I am about to pledge my diamonds. My mother and I shall strain every resource to pay off your debts and try to buy in the vine land of Bellerose. My mother, who is as good a man of business as a regular accountant, blames you for not having been open with her. She would not then have purchased—thinking to give you pleasure—the estate of Grainrouge, which cut in on your lands; and then she could have lent you a hundred and thirty thousand francs. She is in despair at the step you have taken, and is afraid you will suffer from the life in India. She entreats you to be temperate, and not to be led astray by the women!—I laughed in her face. I am as sure of you as of myself. You will come back to me wealthy and faithful. I alone in the world know your womanly refinement and those secret feelings which make you an exquisite human flower, worthy of heaven. The Bordeaux folks had every reason to give you your pretty nickname. And who will take care of my delicate flower? My heart is racked by dreadful ideas. I, his wife, his Natalie, am here, when already perhaps he is suffering! I, so entirely one with you, may not share your troubles, your annoyances, your dangers? In whom can you confide? How can you live without the ear into which you whisper everything? Dear, sensitive plant, swept away by the gale, why should you be transplanted from the only soil in which your fragrance could ever be developed! I feel as if I had been alone for two centuries, and I am cold in Paris! And I have cried so long——

"The cause of your ruin! What a text for the meditations of a woman full of love! You have treated me like a child, to whom nothing is refused that it asks for; like a courtesan, for whom a spendthrift throws away his fortune. Your delicacy, as you style it, is an insult. Do you suppose that I cannot live without fine clothes, balls, operas, successes? Am I such a frivolous woman? Do you think me incapable of a serious thought, of contributing to your fortune as much as I ever contributed to your pleasures? If you were not so far away and ill at ease, you would here find a good scolding for your impertinence. Can you disparage your wife to such an extent? Bless me! What did I go out into society for? To flatter your vanity; it was for you I dressed, and you know it. If I had been wrong, I should be too cruelly punished; your absence is a bitter expiation for our domestic happiness. That happiness was too complete; it could not fail to be paid for by some great sorrow; and here it is! After such delights, so carefully screened from the eyes of the curious; after these constant festivities, varied only by the secret madness of our affection, there is no alternative but solitude. Solitude, my dear one, feeds great passions, and I long for it. What can I do in the world of fashion; to whom should I report my triumphs?

"Ah, to live at Lanstrac, on the estate laid out by your father, in the house you restored so luxuriously—to live there with your child, waiting for you, and sending forth to you night and morning the prayers of the mother and child, of the woman and the angel—will not that be half happiness? Cannot you see the little hands folded in mine? Will you still remember, as I shall remember every evening, the happiness of which your dear letter reminds me? Oh, yes, for we love each other equally. I no more doubt you than you doubt me.

"What consolations can I offer you here, I, who am left desolate, crushed; I, who look forward to the next six years as a desert to be crossed? Well, I am not the most to be pitied for will not that desert be cheered by our little one? Yes—a boy—I must give you a boy, must I not? So farewell, dearly beloved one, our thoughts and our love will ever follow you. The tears on my paper will tell you much that I cannot express, and take the kisses you will find left here, below my name, by your own   NATALIE."

This letter threw Paul into a day-dream, caused no less by the rapture into which he was thrown by these expressions of love than by the reminiscences of happiness thus intentionally called up; and he went over them all, one by one, to account for this promise of a child.

The happier a man is, the greater are his fears. In souls that are exclusively tender—and a tender nature is generally a little weak—jealousy and disquietude are usually in direct proportion to happiness and to its greatness. Strong souls are neither jealous nor easily frightened: jealousy is doubt, and fear is small-minded. Belief without limits is the leading attribute of a high-minded man; if he is deceived—and strength as well as weakness may make him a dupe—his scorn serves him as a hatchet, and he cuts through everything. Such greatness is exceptional. Which of us has not known what it is to be deserted by the spirit that upholds this frail machine, and to hear only the unknown voice that denies everything?

Paul, caught as it were in the toils of certain undeniable facts, doubted and believed both at once. Lost in thought, a prey to terrible but involuntary questionings, and yet struggling with the proofs of true affection and his belief in Natalie, he read this discursive epistle through twice, unable to come to any conclusion for or against his wife. Love may be as great in wordiness as in brevity of expression.

Thoroughly to understand Paul's frame of mind, he must be seen floating on the ocean as on the wide expanse of the past; looking back on his life as on a cloudless sky, and coming back at last after whirlwinds of doubt to the pure, entire, and untarnished faith of a believer, of a Christian, of a lover convinced by the voice of his heart.

It is now not less necessary to give the letter to which Henri de Marsay's was a reply.

LE COMTE PAUL DE MANERVILLE TO MONSIEUR LE MARQUIS HENRI DE MARSAY.

"HENRI,—I am going to tell you one of the greatest things a man can tell a friend: I am ruined. When you read this I shall be starting from Bordeaux for Calcutta on board the good ship *Belle-Amélie*. You will find in your notary's hands a deed which only needs your signature to ratify it, in which I let my house to you for six years on a hypothetical lease; you will write a letter counteracting it to my wife. I am obliged to take this precaution in order that Natalie may remain in her own house without any fear of being turned out of it. I also empower you to draw the income of the entailed property for four years, as against a sum of a hundred and fifty thousand francs that I will beg you to send by a bill, drawn on some house in Bordeaux, to the order of Mathias. My wife will give you her guarantee to enable you to draw the income. If the revenue from the entail should repay you sooner than I imagine, we can settle accounts on my return. The sum I ask of you is indispensable to enable me to set out to seek my fortune; and, if I am not mistaken in you, I shall receive it without delay at Bordeaux the day before I sail. I have acted exactly as you would have acted in my place. I have held out till the last moment without allowing any one to suspect my position. Then, when the news of the seizure of my salable estates reached Paris, I had raised money by notes of hand to the sum of a hundred thousand francs, to try gambling. Some stroke of luck might reinstate me.—I lost.

"How did I ruin myself? Voluntarily, my dear Henri. From the very first day I saw that I could not go on in the way I started in; I knew what the consequence would be; I persisted in shutting my eyes, for I could not bear to say to my wife, 'Let us leave Paris and go to live at Lanstrac.' I have ruined myself for her, as a man ruins himself for a mistress, but knowing it.

"Between you and me, I am neither a simpleton nor weak. A simpleton does not allow himself to be governed, with his eyes open, by an absorbing passion; and a man who sets out to reconstitute his fortune in the Indies, instead of blowing his brains out, is a man of spirit. And so, my dear friend, as I care for wealth only for her sake, as I do not wish to be any man's dupe, and as I shall be absent six years, I place my wife in your keeping. You are enough the favorite of women to respect Natalie, and to give me the benefit of the honest friendship that binds us. I know of no better protector than you will be. I am leaving my wife childless; a lover would be a danger. You must know, my dear de Marsay, I love Natalie desperately, cringingly, and am not ashamed of it. I could, I believe, forgive her if she were unfaithful, not because I am certain that I could be revenged, if I were to die for it! but because I would kill myself to leave her happy if I myself could not make her happy.

"But what have I to fear? Natalie has for me that true regard, independent of love, which preserves love. I have treated her like a spoiled child. I found such perfect happiness in my sacrifices, one led so naturally to the other, that she would be a monster to betray me. Love deserves love.

"Alas! must I tell you the whole truth, my dear Henri? I have just written her a letter in which I have led her to believe that I am setting out full of hope, with a calm face; that I have not a doubt, no jealousy, no fears; such a letter as sons write to deceive a mother when they go forth to die.

Good God! de Marsay, I had hell within me, I am the most miserable man on earth. You must hear my cries, my gnashing of the teeth. To you I confess the tears of a despairing lover. Sooner would I sweep the gutter under her window for six years, if it were possible, than return with millions after six years' absence. I suffer the utmost anguish; I shall go on from sorrow to sorrow till you shall have written me a line to say that you accept a charge which you alone in the world can fulfil and carry out.

"My dear de Marsay, I cannot live without that woman; she is air and sunshine to me. Take her under your ægis, keep her faithful to me—even against her will. Yes, I can still be happy with such half-happiness. Be her protector; I have no fear of you. Show her how vulgar it would be to deceive me; that it would make her like every other woman; that the really brilliant thing will be to remain faithful.

"She must still have money enough to carry on her easy and undisturbed life; but if she should want anything, if she should have a whim, be her banker—do not be afraid, I shall come home rich.

"After all, my alarms are vain, no doubt; Natalie is an angel of virtue. When Félix de Vandenesse fell desperately in love with her and allowed himself to pay her some attentions, I only had to point out the danger to Natalie, and she thanked me so affectionately that I was moved to tears. She said that it would be awkward for her reputation if a man suddenly disappeared from her house, but that she would find means to dismiss him; and she did, in fact, receive him very coldly, so that everything ended well. In four years we have never had any other subject of discussion, if a conversation as between friends can be called a discussion.

"Well, my dear Henri, I must say good-bye like a man. The disaster has come. From whatever cause, there it is; I can but bow to it. Poverty and Natalie are two irreconcilable terms. And the balance of my debts and assets will be very nearly exact; no one will have anything to complain of. Still, in case some unforeseen circumstance should threaten my honor, I trust in you.

"Finally, if any serious event should occur, you can write to me under cover to the Governor-General at Calcutta. I have friends in his household, and some one will take charge of any letters for me that may arrive from Europe. My dear friend, I hope to find you still the same on my return—a man who can make fun of everything, and who is nevertheless alive to the feelings of others when they are in harmony with the noble nature you feel in yourself.

"You can stay in Paris! At the moment when you read this I shall be crying, 'To Carthage!'"

THE MARQUIS HENRI DE MARSAY IN REPLY TO THE COMTE PAUL DE MANERVILLE.

"And so, Monsieur le Comte, you have collapsed! Monsieur the Ambassador has turned turtle! Are these the fine things you were doing? Why, Paul, did you keep any secret from me? If you had said but one word, my dear old fellow, I could have thrown light on the matter.

"Your wife refuses her guarantee. That should be enough to unseal your eyes. And if not, I would have you to know that your notes of hand have been protested at the suit of one Lécuyer, formerly head-clerk to one Solonet, a notary at Bordeaux. This sucking money-lender, having come from Gascony to try his hand at stock-jobbing, lends his name to screen your very honorable mother-in-law, the real creditor to whom you owe the hundred thousand francs, for which, it is said, she gave you seventy thousand. Compared to Madame Evangelista, Daddy Gobseck is soft flannel, velvet, a soothing draught, a *meringue à la vanille,* a fifth-act uncle. Your vineyard of Bellerose will be your wife's booty; her mother is to pay her the difference between the price it sells for and the sum-total of her claims. Madame Evangelista is to acquire le Guadet and le Grassol, and the mortgages on your house at Bordeaux are all in her hands under the names of men of straw, found for her by that fellow Solonet. And in this way these two worthy women will secure an income of a hundred and twenty thousand francs, the amount derivable from your estates, added to thirty odd thousand francs a year in the funds which the dear hussies have secured.

"Your wife's guarantee was unnecessary. The aforenamed Lécuyer came this morning to offer me repayment of the money I have sent you in exchange for a formal transfer of my claims. The vintage of 1825, which your mother-in-law has safe in the cellars at Lanstrac, is enough to pay me off. So the two women have calculated that you would be at sea by this time; but I am writing by special messenger that this may reach you in time for you to follow the advice I proceed to give you.

"I made this Lécuyer talk; and from his lies, his statements, and his concealments, I have culled the clues that I needed to reconstruct the whole web of domestic conspiracy that has been working against you. This evening at the Spanish Embassy I shall pay my admiring compliments to your wife and her mother. I shall be most attentive to Madame Evangelista, I shall throw you over in the meanest way, I shall abuse you, but with extreme subtlety; anything strong would at once put this Mascarille in petticoats on the scent. What did you do that set her against you? That is what I mean to find out. If only you had had wit enough to make love to the mother before marrying the daughter, you would at this moment be a peer of France, Duc de Manerville, and Ambassador to Madrid. If only you had sent for me at the time of your marriage! I could have taught you to know, to analyze, the two women you would have to fight, and by comparing our observations we should have hit on some good counsel. Was not I the only friend you had who would certainly honor your wife? Was I a man to be afraid of?—But after these women had learned to judge me, they took fright and divided us. If you had not been so silly as to sulk with me, they could not have eaten you out of house and home.

"Your wife contributed largely to our coolness. She was talked over by her mother, to whom she wrote twice a week, and you never heeded it. I recognized my friend Paul as I heard this detail.

"Within a month I will be on such terms with your mother-in-law that she herself will tell me the reason for the Hispano-Italian *vendetta* she has evidently vowed on you—you, the best fellow in the world. Did she hate you before her daughter was in love with Félix de Vandenesse? or has she driven you to the Indies that her daughter may be free, as a woman is in France when completely separated from her husband? That is the problem.

"I can see you leaping and howling when you read that your wife is madly in love with Félix de Vandenesse. If I had not taken it into my head to make a tour in the East with Montriveau, Ronquerolles, and certain other jolly fellows of your acquaintance, I could have told you more about this intrigue, which was incipient when I left. I could then see the first sprouting seed of your catastrophe. What gentleman could be scurvy enough to open such a subject without some invitation, or dare to blow on a woman? Who could bear to break the witch's mirror in which a friend loves to contemplate the fairy scenes of a happy marriage? Are not such illusions the wealth of the heart?—And was not your wife, my dear boy, in the widest sense of the word, a woman of the world? She thought of nothing but her success, her dress; she frequented the Bouffons, the Opera, and balls; rose late, drove in the Bois, dined out or gave dinner-parties. Such a life seems to me to women what war is to men; the public sees only the victorious, and forgets the dead. Some delicate women die of this exhausting round; those who survive must have iron constitutions, and consequently very little heart and very strong stomachs. Herein lies the reason of the want of feeling, the cold atmosphere of drawing-room society. Nobler souls dwell in solitude; the tender and weak succumb. What are left are the boulders which keep the social ocean within bounds by enduring to be beaten and rolled by the breakers without wearing out. Your wife was made to withstand this life; she seemed inured to it; she was always fresh and beautiful. To me the inference was obvious—she did not love you, while you loved her to distraction. To strike the spark of love in this flinty nature a man of iron was required.

"After being caught by Lady Dudley, who could not keep him (she is the wife of my real father), Félix was obviously the man for Natalie. Nor was there any great difficulty in guessing that your wife did not care for you. From indifference to aversion is but a step; and, sooner or later, a discussion, a word, an act of authority on your part, a mere trifle, would make your wife overleap it.

"I myself could have rehearsed the scene that took place between you every night in her room. You have no child, no boy. Does not that fact account for many things to an observer? You, who were in love, could hardly discern the coldness natural to a young woman whom you have trained to the very point for Félix de Vandenesse. If you had discovered that your wife was cold-hearted, the stupid policy of married life would have prompted you to regard it as the reserve of innocence. Like all husbands, you fancied you could preserve her virtue in a world where women whisper to each other things that men dare not say, where all that a husband would never tell his wife is spoken and commented on behind a fan, with laughter and banter, à propos to a trial or an adventure. Though your wife liked the advantages of a married life, she found the price a little heavy; the price, the tax, was yourself!

"You, seeing none of these things, went on digging pits and covering them with flowers, to use the time-honored rhetorical figure. You calmly submitted to the rule which governs the common run of men, and from which I had wished to protect you.

"My dear boy, nothing was wanting to make you as great an ass as any tradesman who is surprised when his wife deceives him; nothing but this outcry to me about your sacrifices and your love for Natalie: 'How ungrateful she would be to betray me; I have done this and that and the other, and I will do more yet, I will go to India for her sake——' etc., etc.—My dear Paul, you have lived in Paris, and you have had the honor of the most intimate friendship of one Henri de Marsay, and you do not know the commonest things, the first principles of the working of the female mechanism, the alphabet of a woman's heart!—You may slave yourself to death, you may go to Sainte-Pélagie, you may kill two-and-twenty men, give up seven mistresses, serve Laban, cross the Desert, narrowly escape the hulks, cover yourself with disgrace; like Nelson, refuse to give battle because you must kiss Lady Hamilton's shoulder, or, like Bonaparte, fight old Wurmser, get yourself cut up on the Bridge of Arcole, rave like Rolando break a leg in splints to dance with a woman for five minutes! —But, my dear boy, what has any of these things to do with her loving you? If love were taken as proven by such evidence, men would be too happy; a few such demonstrations at the moment when he wanted her would win the woman of his heart.

"Love, you stupid old Paul, is a belief like that in the immaculate conception of the Virgin. You have it, or you have it not. Of what avail are rivers of blood, or the mines of Potosi, or the greatest glory, to produce an involuntary and inexplicable feeling? Young men like you, who look for love to balance their outlay, seem to me base usurers. Our legal wives owe us children and virtue; but they do not owe love. Love is the consciousness of happiness given and received, and the certainty of giving and getting it; it is an ever-living attraction, constantly satisfied, and yet insatiable. On the day when Vandenesse stirred in your wife's heart the chord you had left untouched and virginal, your amorous flourishes, your outpouring of soul, and of money, ceased even to be remembered. Your nights of happiness strewn with roses— fudge! Your devotion—an offering of remorse. Yourself— a victim to be slain on the altar! Your previous life—a blank! One impulse of love annihilated your treasures of passion, which were now but old iron. He, Félix, has had her beauty, her devotion—for no return perhaps; but, in love, belief is as good as reality.

"Your mother-in-law was naturally on the side of the lover against the husband; secretly or confessedly she shut her eyes

—or she opened them; I do not know what she did, but she took her daughter's part against you. For fifteen years I have observed society, and I never knew a mother who, under such circumstances, deserted her daughter. Such indulgence is hereditary, from woman to woman. And what man can blame them? Some lawyer, perhaps, responsible for the Civil Code, which saw only formulas where feelings were at stake. —The extravagance into which you were dragged by the career of a fashionable wife, the tendencies of an easy nature, and your vanity too, perhaps, supplied her with the opportunity of getting rid of you by an ingenious scheme of ruin.

"From all this you will conclude, my good friend, that the charge you put upon me, and which I should have fulfilled all the more gloriously because it would have amused me, is, so to speak, null and void. The evil I was to have hindered is done —*consummatum est.*—Forgive me for writing *à la de Marsay,* as you say, on matters which to you are so serious. Far be it from me to cut capers on a friend's grave, as heirs do on that of an uncle. But you write to me that you mean henceforth to be a man, and I take you at your word; I treat you as a politician, and not as a lover.

"Has not this mishap been to you like the brand on his shoulder that determines a convict on a systematic antagonism to society, and a revolt against it? You are hereby released from one care—marriage was your master, now it is your servant. Paul, I am your friend in the fullest meaning of the word. If your brain had been bound in a circlet of brass, if you had earlier had the energy that has come to you too late, I could have proved my friendship by telling you things that would have enabled you to walk over human beings as on a carpet. But whenever we talked over the combinations to which I owed the faculty of amusing myself with a few friends in the heart of Parisian civilization, like a bull in a china shop; whenever I told you, under romantic disguises, some true adventure of my youth, you always regarded them as romances, and did not see their bearing. Hence, I could only think of you as a case of unrequited passion. Well,

on my word of honor, in the existing circumstances, you have
played the nobler part, and you have lost nothing, as you
might imagine, in my opinion. Though I admire a great
scoundrel, I esteem and like those who are taken in.

"A propos to the doctor who came to such a bad end,
brought to the scaffold by his love for his mistress, I remember
telling you the far more beautiful story of the unhappy lawyer
who is still living on the hulks, I know not where, branded as
a forger because he wanted to give his wife—again, an adored
wife—thirty thousand francs a year, and the wife gave him
up to justice in order to get rid of him and live with another
gentleman. You cried shame, you and some others too who
were supping with us. Well, my dear fellow, you are that
lawyer—minus the hulks.

"Your friends do not spare you the discredit which, in our
sphere of life, is equivalent to a sentence pronounced by the
Bench. The Marquise de Listomère, the sister of the two
Vandenesses, and all her following, in which little Rastignac
is now enlisted—a young rascal who is coming to the front;
Madame d'Aiglemont and all her set, among whom Charles
de Vandenesse is regnant; the Lenoncourts, the Comtesse
Féraud, Madame d'Espard, the Nucingens, the Spanish Embassy;
in short, a whole section of the fashionable world, very
cleverly prompted, heap mud upon your name. 'You are a
dissipated wretch, a gambler, a debauchee, and have made
away with your money in the stupidest way. Your wife—
an angel of virtue!—after paying your debts several times,
has just paid off a hundred thousand francs to redeem bills
you had drawn, though her fortune is apart from yours. Happily,
you have pronounced sentence on yourself by getting out
of the way. If you had gone on so, you would have reduced
her to beggary, and she would have been a martyr to conjugal
devotion!' When a man rises to power, he has as many
virtues as will furnish an epitaph; if he falls into poverty,
he has more vices than the prodigal son; you could never
imagine how many vices *à la* Don Juan are attributed to you
now. You gambled on the Bourse, you had licentious tastes,

which it cost you vast sums to indulge, and which are mentioned with comments and jests that mystify the women. You paid enormous interest to the money-lenders. The two Vandenesses laugh as they tell a story of Gigonnet's selling you an ivory man-of-war for six thousand francs, and buying it of your man-servant for five crowns only to sell it to you again, till you solemnly smashed it on discovering that you might have a real ship for the money it was costing you. The adventure occurred nine years ago, and Maxime de Trailles was the hero of it; but it is thought to fit you so well, that Maxime has lost the command of his frigate for good. In short, I cannot tell you everything, for you have furnished forth a perfect encyclopædia of tittle-tattle, which every woman tries to add to. In this state of affairs, the most prudish are ready to legitimatize any consolation bestowed by *Comte* Félix de Vandenesse—for their father is dead at last, yesterday.

"Your wife is the great success of the hour. Yesterday Madame de Camps was repeating all these stories to me at the Italian Opera. 'Don't talk to me,' said I, 'you none of you know half the facts. Paul had robbed the Bank and swindled the Treasury. He murdered Ezzelino, and caused the death of three Medoras of the Rue Saint-Denis, and, between you and me, I believe him to be implicated in the doings of the Ten Thousand. His agent is the notorious Jacques Collin, whom the police have never been able to find since his last escape from the hulks; Paul harbored him in his house. As you see, he is capable of any crime; he is deceiving the government. Now they have gone off together to see what they can do in India, and rob the Great Mogul.'—Madame de Camps understood that a woman of such distinction as herself ought not to use her pretty lips as a Venetian lion's maw.

"Many persons, on hearing these tragi-comedies, refuse to believe them; they defend human nature and noble sentiments, and insist that these are fictions. My dear fellow, Talleyrand made this clever remark, 'Everything happens.' Certainly even stranger things than this domestic conspiracy

A MARRIAGE SETTLEMENT

happens under our eyes; but the world is so deeply interested in denying them, and in declaring that it is slandered, and besides, these great dramas are played so naturally, with a veneer of such perfect good taste, that I often have to wipe my eyeglass before I can see to the bottom of things. But I say once more, when a man is my friend with whom I have received the baptism of Champagne, and communion at the altar of Venus Commoda, when we have together been confirmed by the clawing fingers of the croupier, and when then my friend is in a false position, I would uproot twenty families to set him straight again.

"You must see that I have a real affection for you; have I ever to your knowledge written so long a letter as this is? So read with care all that follows.

"Alack! Paul; I must take to writing, I must get into the habit of jotting down the minutes for dispatches; I am starting on a political career. Within five years I mean to have a Minister's portfolio, or find myself an ambassador where I can stir public affairs round in my own way. There is an age when a man's fairest mistress is his country. I am joining the ranks of those who mean to overthrow not merely the existing Ministry, but their whole system. In fact, I am swimming in the wake of a prince who halts only on one foot, and whom I regard as a man of political genius, whose name is growing great in history; as complete a prince as a great artist may be. We are Ronquerolles, Montriveau, the Grandlieus, the Roche-Hugons, Sérizy, Féraud, and Granville, all united against the priestly party, as the silly party that is represented by the *Constitutionnel* ingeniously calls it. We mean to upset the two Vandenesses, the Ducs de Lenoncourt, de Navarreins, de Langeais, and de la Grande-Aumônerie. To gain our end, we may go so far as to form a coalition with la Fayette, the Orleanists, the Left—all men who must be got rid of as soon as we have won the day, for to govern on their principles is impossible; and we are capable of anything for the good of the country—and our own.

"Personal questions as to the King's person are mere sentimental folly in these days; they must be cleared away. From that point of view, the English, with their sort of Doge, are more advanced than we are. Politics have nothing to do with that, my dear fellow. Politics consist in giving the nation an impetus by creating an oligarchy embodying a fixed theory of government, and able to direct public affairs along a straight path, instead of allowing the country to be pulled in a thousand different directions, which is what has been happening for the last forty years in our beautiful France—at once so intelligent and so sottish, so wise and so foolish; it needs a system, indeed, much more than men. What are individuals in this great question? If the end is a great one, if the country may live happy and free from trouble, what do the masses care for the profits of our stewardship, our fortune, privileges, and pleasures?

"I am now standing firm on my feet. I have at the present moment a hundred and fifty thousand francs a year in the Three per Cents, and a reserve of two hundred thousand francs to repair damages. Even this does not seem to me very much ballast in the pocket of a man starting left foot foremost to scale the heights of power.

"A fortunate accident settled the question of my setting out on this career, which did not particularly smile on me, for you know my predilection for the life of the East. After thirty-five years of slumber, my highly-respected mother woke up to the recollection that she had a son who might do her honor. Often when a vine-stock is eradicated, some years after shoots come up to the surface of the ground; well, my dear boy, my mother had almost torn me up by the roots from her heart, and I sprouted again in her head. At the age of fifty-eight, she thinks herself old enough to think no more of any men but her son. At this juncture she has met in some hot-water cauldron, at I know not what baths, a delightful old maid—English, with two hundred and forty thousand francs a year; and, like a good mother, she has inspired her with an audacious ambition to become my wife. A maid of six-and-thirty, my word! Brought up in the strictest puritanical

A MARRIAGE SETTLEMENT

principles, a steady sitting hen, who maintains that unfaithful wives should be publicly burnt. 'Where will you find wood enough?' I asked her. I could have sent her to the devil, for two hundred and forty thousand francs a year are no equivalent for liberty, nor a fair price for my physical and moral worth and my prospects. But she is the sole heiress of a gouty old fellow, some London brewer, who within a calculable time will leave her a fortune equal at least to what the sweet creature has already. Added to these advantages, she has a red nose, the eyes of a dead goat, a waist that makes one fear lest she should break into three pieces if she falls down, and the coloring of a badly painted doll. But—she is delightfully economical; but—she will adore her husband, do what he will; but—she has the English gift; she will manage my house, my stables, my servants, my estates better than any steward. She has all the dignity of virtue; she holds herself as erect as a confidante on the stage of the Français; nothing will persuade me that she has not been impaled and the shaft broken off in her body. Miss Stevens is, however, fair enough to be not too unpleasing if I must positively marry her. But—and this to me is truly pathetic—she has the hands of a woman as immaculate as the sacred ark; they are so red that I have not yet hit on any way to whiten them that will not be too costly, and I have no idea how to fine down her fingers, which are like sausages. Yes; she evidently belongs to the brew-house by her hands, and to the aristocracy by her money; but she is apt to affect the great lady a little too much, as rich English women do who want to be mistaken for them, and she displays her lobster's claws too freely.

"She has, however, as little intelligence as I could wish in a woman. If there were a stupider one to be found, I would set out to seek her. This girl, whose name is Dinah, will never criticise me; she will never contradict me; I shall be her Upper Chamber, her Lords and Commons. In short, Paul, she is indefeasible evidence of the English genius; she is a product of English mechanics brought to their highest pitch of perfection; she was undoubtedly made at Manchester, between the manufactory of Perry's pens and the workshops for steam-engines. It eats, it drinks, it walks, it may have children, take good care of them, and bring them up admirably, and it apes a woman so well that you would believe it real.

"When my mother introduced us, she had set up the machine so cleverly, had so carefully fitted the pegs, and oiled the wheels so thoroughly, that nothing jarred; then, when she saw I did not make a very wry face, she set the springs in motion, and the woman spoke. Finally, my mother uttered the decisive words, 'Miss Dinah Stevens spends no more than thirty thousand francs a year, and has been traveling for seven years in order to economize.'—So there is another image, and that one is silver.

"Matters are so far advanced that the banns are to be published. We have got as far as 'My dear love.' Miss makes eyes at me that might floor a porter. The settlements are prepared. My fortune is not inquired into; Miss Stevens devotes a portion of hers to creating an entail in landed estate, bearing an income of two hundred and forty thousand francs, and to the purchase of a house, likewise entailed. The settlement credited to me is of a million francs. She has nothing to complain of. I leave her uncle's money untouched.

"The worthy brewer, who has helped to found the entail, was near bursting with joy when he heard that his niece was to be a marquise. He would be capable of doing something handsome for my eldest boy.

"I shall sell out of the funds as soon as they are up to eighty, and invest in land. Thus, in two years I may look to get six hundred thousand francs a year out of real estate. So, you see, Paul, I do not give my friends advice that I am not ready to act upon.

"If you had but listened to me, you would have an English wife, some Nabob's daughter, who would leave you the freedom of a bachelor and the independence necessary for playing the whist of ambition. I would concede my future wife to you if you were not married already. But that cannot be helped, and I am not the man to bid you chew the cud of the **past.**

"All this preamble was needful to explain to you that for the future my position in life will be such as a man needs if he wants to play the great game of pitch-and-toss. I cannot do without you, my friend. Instead of going to pickle in the Indies, you will find it much simpler to swim in my convoy in the waters of the Seine. Believe me, Paris is still the spot where fortune crops up most freely. Potosi is situated in the Rue Vivienne or the Rue de la Paix, the Place Vendôme, or the Rue de Rivoli. In every other country, manual labor, the sweat of the perspiring agent, marches and countermarches, are indispensable to the accumulation of a fortune; here intelligence is sufficient. Here a man, even of moderate talent, may discover a gold-mine as he puts on his slippers, or picks his teeth after dinner, as he goes to bed or gets up in the morning. Find me a spot on earth where a good commonplace idea brings in more money, or is more immediately understood than it is here? If I climb to the top of the tree, am I the man to refuse you a hand, a word, a signature? Do not we young scamps need a friend we can rely on, if it were only to compromise him in our place and stead, to send him forth to die as a private, so as to save the General? Politics are impossible without a man of honor at hand, to whom everything may be said and done.

"This, then, is my advice to you. Let the *Belle-Amélie* sail without you; return here like a lightning flash, and I will arrange a duel for you with Félix de Vandenesse, in which you must fire first, and down with your man as dead as a pigeon. In France an outraged husband who kills his man is at once respectable and respected. No one ever makes game of him! Fear, my dear boy, is an element of social life, and a means of success for those whose eyes never fall before the gaze of any other man. I, who care no more for life than for a cup of ass's milk, and who never felt a qualm of fear, have observed the strange effects of that form of emotion on modern manners. Some dread the idea of losing the enjoyments to which they are fettered, others that of parting from some woman. The adventurous temper of past times, when a man threw away his life like a slipper, has ceased to exist. In many men courage is merely a clever speculation on the fear that may seize their adversary. None but the Poles now, in Europe, ever fight for the pleasure of it; they still cultivate the art for art's sake, and not as a matter of calculation. Kill Vandenesse, and your wife will tremble; your mother-in-law will tremble, the public will tremble; you will be rehabilitated, you will proclaim your frantic passion for your wife, every one will believe you, and you will be a hero. Such is France.

"I shall not stickle over a hundred thousand francs with you. You can pay your principal debts, and can prevent utter ruin by pledging your property on a time bargain with option of repurchase, for you will soon be in a position that will allow you to pay off the mortgage before the time is up. Also, knowing your wife's character, you can henceforth rule her with a word. While you loved her you could not hold your own; now, having ceased to love her, your power will be irresistible. I shall have made your mother-in-law as supple as a glove; for what you have to do is to reinstate yourself with the hundred and fifty thousand francs those women have saved for themselves.

"So give up your self-exile, which always seems to me the charcoal-brazier of men of brains. If you run away, you leave slander mistress of the field. The gambler who goes home to fetch his money and comes back to the tables loses all. You must have your funds in your pocket. You appear to me to be seeking fresh reinforcements in the Indies. No good at all!—We are two gamblers at the green table of politics; between you and me loans are a matter of course. So take post-horses, come to Paris, and begin a new game; with Henri de Marsay for a partner you will win, for Henri de Marsay knows what he wants and when to strike.

"This, you see, is where we stand. My real father is in the English Ministry. We shall have connections with Spain through the Evangelistas; for as soon as your mother-in-law and I have measured claws, we shall perceive that when devil meets devil there is nothing to be gained on either side

Montriveau is a Lieutenant-General; he will certainly be War Minister sooner or later, for his eloquence gives him much power in the Chamber. Ronquerolles is in the Ministry and on the Privy Council. Martial de la Roche-Hugon is appointed Minister to Germany, and made a peer of France, and he has brought us as an addition Marshal the Duc de Carigliano and all round 'rump' of the Empire, which so stupidly held on to the rear of the Restoration. Sérizy is leader of the State Council; he is indispensable there. Granville is master of the legal party, he has two sons on the Bench. The Grandlieus are in high favor at Court. Féraud is the soul of the Gondreville set, low intriguers who, I know not why, are always at the top.—Thus supported, what have we to fear? We have a foot in every capital, an eye in every cabinet; we hem in the whole administration without their suspecting it.

"Is not the money question a mere trifle, nothing at all, when all this machinery is ready? And, above all, what is a woman? Will you never be anything but a schoolboy? What is life, my dear fellow, when it is wrapped up in a woman? A ship over which we have no command, which obeys a wild compass though it has indeed a lodestone; which runs before every wind that blows, and in which the man really is a galley-slave, obedient not only to the law, but to every rule improvised by his driver, without the possibility of retaliation. Phaugh!

"I can understand that from passion, or the pleasure to be found in placing our power in a pair of white hands, a man should obey his wife—but when it comes to obeying Médor—then away with Angelica!—The great secret of social alchemy, my dear sir, is to get the best of everything out of each stage of our life, to gather all its leaves in spring, all its flowers in summer, all its fruits in autumn. Now we—I and some boon companions—have enjoyed ourselves for twelve years, like musketeers, black, white, and red, refusing ourselves nothing, not even a filibustering expedition now and again; henceforth we mean to shake down ripe plums, at an age when experience has ripened the harvest. Come, join us; you shall have a share of the pudding we mean to stir.

"Come, and you will find a friend wholly yours in the skin of

"HENRI DE M."

At the moment when Paul de Manerville finished reading this letter, of which every sentence fell like a sledge-hammer on the tower of his hopes, his illusions, and his love, he was already beyond the Azores. In the midst of this ruin, rage surged up in him, cold and impotent rage.

"What had I done to them?" he asked himself.

This question is the impulse of the simpleton, of the weak natures, which, as they can see nothing, can foresee nothing.

"Henri, Henri!" he cried aloud. "The one true friend!"

Many men would have gone mad. Paul went to bed and slept the deep sleep which supervenes on immeasurable disaster; as Napoleon slept after the battle of Waterloo.

PARIS, *September–October* 1835.

A START IN LIFE

TO LAURE

To whose bright and modest wit I owe the idea of this Scene, Hers be the honor!

> Her brother,
> DE BALZAC.

RAILROADS, in a future now not far distant, must lead to the disappearance of certain industries, and modify others, especially such as are concerned in the various modes of transport commonly used in the neighborhood of Paris. In fact, the persons and the things which form the accessories of this little drama will ere long give it the dignity of an archæological study. Will not our grandchildren be glad to know something of a time which they will speak of as the old days?

For instance, the picturesque vehicles known as *Coucous,* which used to stand on the Place de la Concorde and crowd the Cours-la-Reine, which flourished so greatly during a century, and still survived in 1830, exist no more. Even on the occasion of the most attractive rural festivity, hardly one is to be seen on the road in this year 1842.

In 1820 not all the places famous for their situation, and designated as the environs of Paris, had any regular service of coaches. The Touchards, father and son, had however a monopoly of conveyances to and from the largest towns within a radius of fifteen leagues, and their establishment occupied splendid premises in the Rue du Faubourg Saint-Denis. In spite of their old standing and their strenuous efforts, in spite of their large capital and all the advantages of strong centralization, Touchards' service had formidable rivals in the *Coucous* of the Faubourg Saint-Denis for distances of seven or eight leagues out of Paris. The Parisian has indeed such a passion for the country, that local establishments also held their own in many cases against the *Petites Messageries,* a name given to Touchards' short-distance coaches, to distinguish them from the *Grandes Messageries,* the general conveyance company, in the Rue Montmartre.

At that time the success of the Touchards stimulated speculation; conveyances were put on the road to and from the smallest towns—handsome, quick, and commodious vehicles, starting and returning at fixed hours; and these, in a circuit of ten leagues or so, gave rise to vehement competition. Beaten on the longer distances, the *Coucou* fell back on short runs, and survived a few years longer. It finally succumbed when the omnibus had proved the possibility of packing eighteen persons into a vehicle drawn by two horses. Nowadays the *Coucou,* if a bird of such heavy flight is by chance still to be found in the recesses of some store for dilapidated vehicles, would, from its structure and arrangement, be the subject of learned investigations, like Cuvier's researches on the animals discovered in the lime-quarries of Montmartre.

These smaller companies, being threatened by larger speculations competing, after 1822, with the Touchards, had nevertheless a fulcrum of support in the sympathies of the residents in the places they plied to. The master of the concern, who was both owner and driver of the vehicle, was usually an innkeeper of the district, to whom its inhabitants were as familiar as were their common objects and interests. He was intelligent in fulfilling commissions; he asked less for his little services, and therefore obtained more, than the employés of the Touchards. He was clever at evading the necessity for an excise pass. At a pinch he would infringe the rules as to the number of passengers he might carry. In fact, he was master of the affections of the people. Hence, when a rival appeared in the field, if the old-established conveyance ran on alternate days of the week, there were persons who would postpone their journey to take it in the company of the original driver, even though his vehicle and horses were none of the safest and best.

One of the lines which the Touchards, father and son, tried hard to monopolize, but which was hotly disputed—nay, which is still a subject of dispute with their successors the Toulouses—was that between Paris and Beaumont-sur-Oise, a highly profitable district, since in 1822 three lines of conveyances worked it at once. The Touchards lowered their prices, but in vain, and in vain increased the number of services; in vain they put superior vehicles on the road, the competitors held their own, so profitable is a line running through little towns like Saint-Denis and Saint-Brice, and such a string of villages as Pierrefitte, Groslay, Écouen, Poncelles, Moiselles, Baillet, Monsoult, Maffliers, Franconville, Presles, Nointel, Nerville, and others. The Touchards at last extended their line of service as far as to Chambly; the rivals ran to Chambly. And at the present day the Toulouses go as far as Beauvais.

On this road, the highroad to England, there is a place which is not ill named *la Cave* [the Cellar], a hollow way leading down into one of the most delightful nooks of the Oise valley, and to the little town of l'Isle-Adam, doubly famous as the native place of the now extinct family de l'Isle-Adam, and as the splendid residence of the Princes of Bourbon-Conti. L'Isle-Adam is a charming little town, flanked by two large hamlets, that of Nogent and that of Parmain, both remarkable for the immense quarries which have furnished the materials for the finest edifices of Paris, and indeed abroad too, for the base and capitals of the theatre at Brussels are of Nogent stone.

Though remarkable for its beautiful points of view, and for famous châteaux built by princes, abbots, or famous architects, as at Cassan, Stors, le Val, Nointel, Persan, etc., this district, in 1822, had as yet escaped competition, and was served by two coach-owners, who agreed to work it between them. This exceptional state of things was based on causes easily explained. From la Cave, where, on the highroad, begins the fine paved way due to the magnificence of the Princes of Conti, to l'Isle-Adam, is a distance of two leagues:

no main line coach could diverge so far from the highroad, especially as l'Isle-Adam was at that time the end of things in that direction. The road led thither, and ended there. Of late, a highroad joins the valley of Montromency to that of l'Isle-Adam. Leaving Saint-Denis it passes through Saint-Leu-Taverny, Méru, l'Isle-Adam, and along by the Oise as far as Beaumont. But in 1822 the only road to l'Isle-Adam was that made by the Princes de Conti.

Consequently Pierrotin and his colleague reigned supreme' from Paris to l'Isle-Adam, beloved of all the district. Pierrotin's coach and his friend's ran by Stors, le Val, Parmain, Champagne, Mours, Prérolles, Nogent, Nerville, and Maffliers. Pierrotin was so well known that the residents at Monsoult, Moiselles, Baillet, and Saint-Brice, though living on the highroad, made use of his coach, in which there was more often a chance of a seat than in the Beaumont *diligence,* which was always full. Pierrotin and his friendly rival agreed to admiration. When Pierrotin started from l'Isle-Adam, the other set out from Paris and *vice-versâ.* Of the opposing driver, nothing need be said. Pierrotin was the favorite in the line. And of the two, he alone appears on the scene in this veracious history. So it will suffice to say that the two coach-drivers lived on excellent terms, competing in honest warfare, and contending for customers without sharp practice. In Paris, out of economy, they put up at the same inn, using the same yard, the same stable, the same coach-shed, the same office, the same booking clerk. And this fact is enough to show that Pierrotin and his opponents were, as the common folks say, of a very good sort.

That inn, at the corner of the Rue d'Enghien, exists to this day, and is called the *Silver Lion.* The proprietor of this hostlery—a hostlery from time immemorial for coach-drivers—himself managed a line of vehicles to Dammartin on so sound a basis that his neighbors the Touchards, of the *Petites Messageries* opposite, never thought of starting a conveyance on that road.

Though the coaches for l'Isle-Adam were supposed to set

out punctually, Pierrotin and his friend displayed a degree of indulgence on this point which, while it won them the affections of the natives, brought down severe remonstrances from strangers who were accustomed to the exactitude of the larger public companies; but the two drivers of these vehicles, half *diligence,* half *coucou,* always found partisans among their regular customers. In the afternoon the start fixed for four o'clock always dragged on till half-past; and in the morning, though eight was the hour named, the coach never got off before nine.

This system was, however, very elastic. In summer, the golden season for coaches, the time of departure, rigorously punctual as concerned strangers, gave way for natives of the district. This method afforded Pierrotin the chance of pocketing the price of two places for one when a resident in the town came early to secure a place already booked by a bird of passage, who, by ill-luck, was behind time. Such elastic rules would certainly not be approved by a Puritan moralist; but Pierrotin and his colleague justified it by the hard times, by their losses during the winter season, by the necessity they would presently be under of purchasing better carriages, and finally, by an exact application of the rules printed on their tickets, copies of which were of the greatest rarity, and never given but to those travelers who were so perverse as to insist.

Pierrotin, a man of forty, was already the father of a family. He had left the cavalry in 1815 when the army was disbanded, and then this very good fellow had succeeded his father, who drove a *coucou* between l'Isle-Adam and Paris on somewhat erratic principles. After marrying the daughter of a small innkeeper, he extended and regulated the business, and was noted for his intelligence and military punctuality. Brisk and decisive, Pierrotin—a nickname, no doubt—had a mobile countenance which gave an amusing expression and a semblance of intelligence to a face reddened by exposure to the weather. Nor did he lack the "gift of the gab" which is caught by intercourse with the world, and by seeing different parts of it. His voice, by dint of talking to his horses, and shouting to others to get out of the way, was somewhat harsh, but he could soften it to a customer.

His costume, that of coach-drivers of the superior class, consisted of stout, strong boots, heavy with nails, and made at l'Isle-Adam, trousers of bottle-green velveteen, and a jacket of the same, over which, in the exercise of his functions, he wore a blue blouse, embroidered in colors on the collar, shoulder-pieces, and wristbands. On his head was a cap with a peak. His experience of military service had stamped on Pierrotin the greatest respect for social superiority, and a habit of obedience to people of the upper ranks; but while he was ready to be on familiar terms with the modest citizen, he was always respectful to women, of whatever class. At the same time, the habit of "carting folks about," to use his own expression, had led him to regard his travelers as parcels; though, being on feet, they demanded less care than the other merchandise, which was the aim and end of the service.

Warned by the general advance, which since the peace begun to tell on his business, Pierrotin was determined not to be beaten by the progress of the world. Ever since the last summer season he had talked a great deal of a certain large conveyance he had ordered of Farry, Breilmann and Co., the best diligence builders, as being needed by the constant increase of travelers. Pierrotin's plant at that time consisted of two vehicles. One, which did duty for the winter, and the only one he ever showed to the tax-collector, was of the *coucou* species. The bulging sides of this vehicle allowed it to carry six passengers on two seats as hard as iron, though covered with yellow worsted velvet. These seats were divided by a wooden bar, which could be removed at pleasure or refixed in two grooves in the sides, at the height of a man's back. This bar, perfidiously covered by Pierrotin with yellow velvet, and called by him a back to the seat, was the cause of much despair to the travelers from the difficulty of moving and readjusting it. If the board was painful to fix, it was far more so to the shoulder-blades when it was fitted; on the other hand, if it was not unshipped, it made entrance and egress equally perilous, especially to women.

Though each seat of this vehicle, which bulged at the sides like a woman before childbirth, was licensed to hold no more than three passengers, it was not unusual to see eight packed in it like herrings in a barrel. Pierrotin declared that they were all the more comfortable, since they formed a compact and immovable mass, whereas three were constantly thrown against each other, and often ran the risk of spoiling their hats against the roof of the vehicle by reason of the violent jolting on the road. In front of the body of this carriage there was a wooden box-seat, Pierrotin's driving-seat, which could also carry three passengers, who were designated, as all the world knows, as *lapins* (rabbits). Occasionally, Pierrotin would accommodate four *lapins,* and then sat askew on a sort of box below the front seat for the *lapins* to rest their feet on; this was filled with straw or such parcels as could not be injured.

The body of the vehicle, painted yellow, was ornamented by a band of bright blue, on which might be read in white letters, on each side, *L'Isle-Adam—Paris;* and on the back, *Service de l'Isle-Adam.* Our descendants will be under a mistake if they imagine that this conveyance could carry no more than thirteen persons, including Pierrotin. On great occasions three more could be seated in a square compartment covered with tarpaulin in which trunks, boxes, and parcels were generally piled; but Pierrotin was too prudent to let any but regular customers sit there, and only took them up three or four hundred yards outside the barrier. These passengers in the *poulailler,* or hen-coop, the name given by the conductors to this part of a coach, were required to get out before reaching any village on the road where there was a station of gendarmerie; for the overloading, forbidden by the regulations *for the greater safety of travelers,* was in these cases so excessive, that the gendarme—always Pierrotin's very good friend—could not have excused himself from reporting such a flagrant breach of rules. But thus Pierrotin's vehicle, on certain Saturday evenings and Monday mornings, carted out fifteen passengers; and then to help pull it, he gave his large but aged horse, named Rougeot, the assistance of a second nag about as big as a pony, which he could never sufficiently praise. This little steed was a mare called Bichette; and she ate little, she was full of spirit, nothing could tire her, she was worth her weight in gold!

"My wife would not exchange her for that great lazy beast Rougeot!" Pierrotin would exclaim, when a traveler laughed at him about this concentrated *extract of horse.*

The difference between this carriage and the other was, that the second had four wheels. This vehicle, a remarkable structure, always spoken of as "the four-wheeled coach," could hold seventeen passengers, being intended to carry fourteen. It rattled so preposterously that the folks in l'Isle-Adam would say, "Here comes Pierrotin!" when he had but just come out of the wood that hangs on the slope to the valley. It was divided into two lobes, one of which, called the *intérieur,* the body of the coach, carried six passengers on two seats, and the other, a sort of cab stuck on in front, was styled the *coupé.* This coupé could be closed by an inconvenient and eccentric arrangement of glass windows, which would take too long to describe in this place. The *four-wheeled coach* also had at top a sort of gig with a hood, into which Pierrotin packed six travelers; it closed with leather curtains. Pierrotin himself had an almost invisible perch below the glass windows of the coupé.

The coach to l'Isle-Adam only paid the taxes levied on public vehicles for the *coucou,* represented to carry six travelers, and whenever Pierrotin turned out the "four-wheeled coach" he took out a special license. This may seen strange indeed in these days; but at first the tax on vehicles, imposed somewhat timidly, allowed the owners of coaches to play these little tricks, which gave them the pleasure of "putting their thumbs to their noses" behind the collector's back, as they phrased it. By degrees, however, the hungry Exchequer grew strict: it allowed no vehicle to take the road without displaying the two plates which now certify that their capacity is registered and the tax paid. Everything, even a tax, has its age of innocence, and towards the end of 1822 that age was not yet over. Very often, in summer, the four-wheeled coach and the covered chaise made the journey in company, carrying in all thirty passengers, while Pierrotin paid only for six.

On these golden days the convoy started from the Faubourg Saint-Denis at half-past four, and arrived in style at l'Isle-Adam by ten o'clock at night. And then Pierrotin, proud of his run, which necessitated the hire of extra horses, would say, "We have made a good pace to-day!" To enable him to do nine leagues in five hours with his machinery, he did not stop, as the coaches usually do on this road, at Saint-Brice, Moisselles, and la Cave.

The *Silver Lion* inn occupied a plot of ground running very far back. Though the front to the Rue Saint-Denis has no more than three or four windows, there was at that time, on one side of the long yard, with the stables at the bottom, a large house backing on the wall of the adjoining property. The entrance was through an arched way under the first floor, and there was standing-room here for two or three coaches. In 1822, the booking-office for all the lines that put up at the *Silver Lion* was kept by the innkeeper's wife, who had a book for each line; she took the money, wrote down the names, and good-naturedly accommodated passengers' luggage in her vast kitchen. The travelers were quite satisfied with this patriarchally free-and-easy mode of business. If they came too early, they sat down by the fire within the immense chimney-place, or lounged in the passage, or went to the cafe *de l'Echiquier,* at the corner of the street of that name, parallel to the Rue d'Enghien, from which it is divided by a few houses only.

Quite early in the autumn of that year, one Saturday morning, Pierrotin, his hands stuffed through holes in his blouse and into his pockets, was standing at the front gate of the *Silver Lion,* whence he had a perspective view of the inn kitchen, and beyond it of the long yard and the stables at the end, like black caverns. The Dammartin diligence had just started, and was lumbering after Touchard's coaches. It was past eight o'clock. Under the wide archway, over which was inscribed on a long board, HOTEL DU LION D'ARGENT, the stableman and coach-porters were watching the vehicles start at the brisk pace which deludes the traveler into the belief that the horses will continue to keep it up.

"Shall I bring out the horses, master?" said Pierrotin's stable-boy, when there was nothing more to be seen.

"A quarter-past eight, and I see no passengers," said Pierrotin. "What the deuce has become of them? Put the horses to, all the same.—No parcels neither. Bless us and save us! This afternoon, now, *he* won't know how to stow his passengers, as it is so fine, and I have only four booked. There's a pretty outlook for a Saturday! That's always the way when you're wanting the ready! It's dog's work, and work for a dog!"

"And if you had any, where would you stow 'em? You have nothing but your two-wheel cab," said the luggage-porter, trying to smooth down Pierrotin.

"And what about my new coach?"

"Then there is such a thing as your new coach?" asked the sturdy Auvergnat, grinning and showing his front teeth, as white and as broad as almonds.

"You old good-for-nothing! Why, she will take the road to-morrow, Sunday, and we want eighteen passengers to fill her!"

"Oh, ho! a fine turnout! that'll make the folk stare!" said the Auvergnat.

"A coach like the one that runs to Beaumont, I can tell you! Brand new, painted in red and gold, enough to make the Touchards burst with envy! It will take three horses. I have found a fellow to Rougeot, and Bichette will trot unicorn like a good 'un.—Come, harness up," said Pierrotin, who was looking towards the Porte Saint-Denis while cramming his short pipe with tobacco, "I see a lady out there, and a little man with bundles under his arm. They are looking for the

Pierrotin sat down on one of the enormous curbstones

Silver Lion, for they would have nothing to say to the *coucous* on the stand. Hey day, I seem to know the lady for a customer."

"You often get home filled up after starting empty," said his man.

"But no parcels!" replied Pierrotin. "By the Mass! What devil's luck!"

And Pierrotin sat down on one of the enormous curbstones which protected the lower part of the wheels from the friction of the axles, but he wore an anxious and thoughtful look that was not usual with him. This dialogue, apparently so trivial, had stirred up serious anxieties at the bottom of Pierrotin's heart. And what could trouble Pierrotin's heart but the thought of a handsome coach? To cut a dash on the road, to rival the Touchards, extend his service, carry passengers who might congratulate him on the increased convenience due to the improvements in coach-building, instead of hearing constant complaints of his drags, this was Pierrotin's laudable ambition.

Now the worthy man, carried away by his desire to triumph over his colleague, and to induce him some day perhaps to leave him without a competitor on the road to l'Isle-Adam, had overstrained his resources. He had ordered his coach from Farry, Breilmann, and Co., the makers who had lately introduced English coach-springs in the place of the swan's-neck and other old-fashioned French springs; but these hard-hearted and mistrustful makers would only deliver the vehicle for ready cash. Not caring, indeed, to build a conveyance so unsalable if it were left on their hands, these shrewd tradesmen had not undertaken the job till Pierrotin had paid them two thousand francs on account. To satisfy their justifiable requirements, Pierrotin had exhausted his savings and his credit. He had bled his wife, his father-in-law, and his friends. He had been to look at the superb vehicle the day before in the painter's shop; it was ready, and waiting to take the road, but in order to see it there on the following day he must pay up.

Hence Pierrotin was in need of a thousand francs! Being in debt to the innkeeper for stable-room, he dared not borrow the sum of him. For lack of this thousand francs, he risked losing the two thousand already paid in advance, to say nothing of five hundred, the cost of Rougeot the second, and three hundred for new harness, for which, however, he had three months' credit. And yet, urged by the wrath of despair and the folly of vanity, he had just declared that his coach would start on the morrow, Sunday. In paying the fifteen hundred francs on account of the two thousand five hundred, he had hoped that the coachmakers' feelings might be touched so far that they would let him have the vehicle; but, after three minutes' reflection, he exclaimed:

"No, no! they are sharks, perfect skinflints.—Supposing I were to apply to Monsieur Moreau, the steward at Presles—he is such a good fellow, that he would, perhaps, take my note of hand at six months' date," thought he, struck by a new idea.

At this instant, a servant out of livery, carrying a leather trunk, on coming across from the Touchards' office, where he had failed to find a place vacant on the Chambly coach starting at one o'clock, said to the driver:

"Pierrotin?—Is that you?"

"What then?" said Pierrotin.

"If you can wait less than a quarter of an hour, you can carry my master; if not, I will take his portmanteau back again, and he must make the best of a chaise off the stand."

"I will wait two—three-quarters of an hour, and five minutes more to that, my lad," said Pierrotin, with a glance at the smart little leather trunk, neatly strapped, and fastened with a brass lock engraved with a coat-of-arms.

"Very good, then, there you are," said the man, relieving his shoulder of the trunk, which Pierrotin lifted, weighed in his hand, and scrutinized.

"Here," said he to his stable-boy, "pack it round with soft hay, and put it in the boot at the back.—There is no name on it," said he.

"There are monseigneur's arms," replied the servant.

"Monseigneur? worth his weight in gold!—Come and have a short drink," said Pierrotin, with a wink, as he led the way to the café of the *Echiquiers*.—"Two of absinthe," cried he to the waiter as they went in.—"But who is your master, and where is he bound? I never saw you before," said Pierrotin to the servant as they clinked glasses.

"And for very good reasons," replied the footman. "My master does not go your way once a year, and always in his own carriage. He prefers the road by the Orge valley, where he has the finest park near Paris, a perfect Versailles, a family estate, from which he takes his name.—Don't you know Monsieur Moreau?"

"The steward at Presles?" said Pierrotin.

"Well, Monsieur le Comte is going to spend two days at Presles."

"Oh, ho, then my passenger is the Comte de Sérizy!" cried Pierrotin.

"Yes, my man, no less. But, mind, he sends strict orders. If you have any of the people belonging to your parts in your chaise, do not mention the Count's name; he wants to travel *incognito*, and desired me to tell you so, and promise you a handsome tip."

"Hah! and has this hide-and-seek journey anything to do, by any chance, with the bargain that old Léger, the farmer at les Moulineaux, wants to make?"

"I don't know," replied the man; "but the fat is in the fire. Last evening I was sent to the stables to order the chaise *à la Daumont*, by seven this morning, to drive to Presles; but at seven my master countermanded it. Augustin, his valet, ascribes this change of plan to the visit of a lady, who seemed to have come from the country."

"Can any one have had anything to say against Monsieur Moreau? The best of men, the most honest, the king of men, I say! He might have made a deal more money than he has done if he had chosen, take my word for it!——"

"Then he was very foolish," said the servant sententiously.

"Then Monsieur de Sérizy is going to live at Presles at last? The château has been refurnished and done up," said Pierrotin after a pause. "Is it true that two hundred thousand francs have been spent on it already?"

"If you or I had the money that has been spent there, we could set up in the world.—If Madame la Comtesse goes down there, and Moreaus' fun will be over," added the man, with mysterious significance.

"A good man is Monsieur Moreau," repeated Pierrotin, who was still thinking of borrowing the thousand francs from the steward; "a man that makes his men work, and does not spare them; who gets all the profit out of the land, and for his master's benefit too. A good man! He often comes to Paris, and always by my coach; he gives me something handsome for myself, and always has a lot of parcels to and fro. Three or four a day, sometimes for monsieur and sometimes for madame; a bill of fifty francs a month say, only on the carrier's score. Though madame holds her head a little above her place, she is fond of her children; I take them to school for her and bring them home again. And she always gives me five francs, and your biggest pot would not do more. And whenever I have any one from them or to them, I always drive right up to the gates of the house—I could not do less, now, could I?"

"They say that Monsieur Moreau had no more than a thousand crowns in the world when Monsieur le Comte put him in as land steward at Presles?" said the servant.

"But in seventeen years' time—since 1806—the man must have made something," replied Pierrotin.

"To be sure," said the servant, shaking his head. "And masters are queer too. I hope, for Moreau's sake, that he has feathered his nest."

"I often deliver hampers at your house in the Chaussée-d'Antin," said Pierrotin, "but I have never had the privilege of seeing either the master or his lady."

"Monsieur le Comte is a very good sort," said the man confidentially; "but if he wants you to hold your tongue about his *cognito,* there is a screw loose you may depend.—At least, that is what we think at home. For why else should he counter-order the traveling carriage? Why ride in a public chaise? A peer of France might take a hired chaise, you would think."

"A hired chaise might cost him as much as forty francs for the double journey; for, I can tell, if you don't know our road, it is fit for squirrels to climb. Everlastingly up and down!" said Pierrotin. "Peer of France or tradesman, everybody looks at both sides of a five-franc piece.—If this trip means mischief to Monsieur Moreau—dear, dear, I should be vexed indeed if any harm came to him. By the Mass! Can no way be found of warning him? For he is a real good 'un, an honest sort, the king of men, I say——"

"Pooh! Monsieur le Comte is much attached to Monsieur Moreau," said the other. "But if you will take a bit of good advice from me, mind your own business, and let him mind his. We all have quite enough to do to take care of ourselves. You just do what you are asked to do; all the more because it does not pay to play fast and loose with monseigneur. Add to that, the Count is generous. If you oblige him that much," said the man, measuring off the nail of one finger, "he will reward you that much," and he stretched out his arm.

This judicious hint, and yet more the illustrative figure, coming from a man so high in office as the Comte de Sérizy's second footman, had the effect of cooling Pierrotin's zeal for the steward of Presles.

"Well, good-day, Monsieur Pierrotin," said the man.

A short sketch of the previous history of the Comte de Sérizy and his steward is here necessary to explain the little drama about to be played in Pierrotin's coach.

Monsieur Hugret de Sérizy is descended in a direct line from the famous Président Hugret, ennobled by Francis the First. They bear as arms *party per pale or and sable, an orle and two lozenges counterchanged.* Motto, *I Semper Melius eris,* which, like the two winders assumed as supporters, shows the modest pretence of the citizen class at a time when each rank of society had its own place in the State, and also the artlessness of the age in the punning motto, where *eris* with the *I* at the beginning, and the final *S* of *Melius,* represent the name Serisi of the estate, whence the title.

The present Count's father was a President of *Parlement* before the Revolution. He himself, a member of the High Council of State in 1787, at the early age of two-and-twenty, was favorably known for certain reports on some delicate matters. He did not emigrate during the Revolution, but remained on his lands of Sérizy, near Arpajon, where the respect felt for his father protected him from molestation.

After spending a few years in nursing the old President, whom he lost in 1794, he was elected to the Council of Five Hundred, and took up his legislative functions as a distraction from his grief.

After the eighteenth Brumaire, Monsieur de Sérizy became the object—as did all the families connected with the old *Parlements*—of the First Consul's attentions, and by him he was appointed a Councillor of State to reorganize one of the most disorganized branches of the Administration. Thus this scion of a great historical family became one of the most important wheels in the vast and admirable machinery due to Napoleon. The State Councillor ere long left his department to be made a Minister. The Emperor created him Count and Senator, and he was pro-consul to two different kingdoms in succession.

In 1806, at the age of forty, he married the sister of the *ci-devant* Marquis de Ronquerolles, and widow, at the age of twenty, of Gaubert, one of the most distinguished of the Republican Generals, who left her all his wealth. This match, suitable in point of rank, doubled the Comte de Sérizy's already considerable fortune; he was now the brother-in-law of the *ci-devant* Marquis du Rouvre, whom Napoleon created Count and appointed to be his chamberlain.

In 1814, worn out with incessant work, Monsieur de Sérizy, whose broken health needed rest, gave up all his appointments, left the district of which Napoleon had made him Governor, and came to Paris, where the Emperor was compelled by ocular evidence to concede his claims. This indefatigable master, who could not believe in fatigue in other people, had at first supposed the necessity that prompted the Comte de Sérizy to be simple defection. Though the Senator was not in disgrace, it was said that he had cause for complaint of Napoleon. Consequently, when the Bourbons came back, Louis XVIII., whom Monsieur de Sérizy acknowledged as his legitimate sovereign, granted to the Senator, now a peer of France, the highly confidential post of Steward of his Privy Purse and made him a Minister of State.

On the 20th March, Monsieur de Sérizy did not follow the King to Ghent; he made it known to Napoleon that he remained faithful to the House of Bourbon, and accepted no peerage during the hundred days, but spent that brief reign on his estate of Sérizy. After the Emperor's second fall, the Count naturally resumed his seat in the Privy Council, was one of the Council of State, and Liquidator on behalf of France in the settlement of the indemnities demanded by foreign powers.

He had no love of personal magnificence, no ambition even, but exerted great influence in public affairs. No important political step was ever taken without his being consulted, but he never went to Court, and was seldom seen in his own drawing-room. His noble life, devoted to work from the first, ended by being perpetual work and nothing else. The Count rose at four in the morning in all seasons, worked till midday, then took up his duties as a Peer, or as Vice-President of the Council, and went to bed at nine.

Monsieur de Sérizy had long worn the Grand Cross of the Legion of Honor; he also had the orders of the Golden Fleece, of Saint Andrew of Russia, of the Prussian Eagle; in short, almost every order of the European Courts. No one was less conspicuous or more valuable than he in the world of politics. As may be supposed, to a man of his temper the flourish of Court favor and worldly success were a matter of indifference.

But no man, unless he is a priest, can live such a life without some strong motive; and his mysterious conduct had its key—a cruel one. The Count had loved his wife before he married her, and in him this passion had withstood all the domestic discomforts of matrimony with a widow who remained mistress of herself, after as well as before her second marriage, and who took all the more advantage of her liberty because Monsieur de Sérizy indulged her as a mother indulges a spoilt child. Incessant work served him as a shield against his heartfelt woes, buried with the care that a man engaged in politics takes to hide such secrets. And he fully understood how ridiculous jealousy would be in the eyes of the world, which would certainly never have admitted the possibility of conjugal passion in a time-worn official.

How was it that his wife had thus bewitched him from the first days of marriage? Why had he suffered in those early days without taking his revenge? Why did he no longer dare to be revenged? And why, deluded by hope, had he allowed time to slip away? By what means had his young, pretty, clever wife reduced him to subjection? The answer to these questions would require a long story, out of place in this "Scene," and women, if not men, may be able to guess it. At the same time, it may be observed that the Count's incessant work and many sorrows had unfortunately done much to deprive him of the advantages indispensable to a man who has to compete with unfavorable comparisons. The saddest perhaps of all the Count's secrets was the fact that his wife's repulsion was partly justified by ailments which he owed entirely to overwork. Kind, nay, more than kind, to his wife, he made her mistress in her own house; she received all Paris, she went into the country, or she came back again, precisely as though she were still a widow; he took care of her money, and supplied her luxuries as if he had been her agent.

The Countess held her husband in the highest esteem, indeed, she liked his turn of wit. Her approbation could give him pleasure, and thus she could do what she liked with the poor man by sitting and chatting with him for an hour. Like the great nobles of former days, the Count so effectually protected his wife that he would have regarded any slur cast on her reputation as an unpardonable insult to himself. The world greatly admired his character, and Madame de Sérizy owed much to her husband. Any other woman, even though she belonged to so distinguished a family as that of Ronquerolles, might have found herself disgraced for ever. The Countess was very ungrateful—but charming in her ingratitude. And from time to time she would pour balm on the Count's wounds.

We must now explain the cause of the Minister's hurried journey and wish to remain unknown.

A rich farmer of Beaumont-sur-Oise, named Léger, held a farm of which the various portions were all fractions of the estate owned by the Count, thus impairing the splendid property of Presles. The farm-lands belonged to a townsman of Beaumont-sur-Oise, one Margueron. The lease he had granted to Léger in 1799, at a time when the advance since made in agriculture could not be foreseen, was nearly run out, and the owner had refused Léger's terms for renewing it. Long since, Monsieur de Sérizy, wanting to be quit of the worry and squabbling that come of such enclosed plots, had hoped to be able to buy the farm, having heard that Monsieur Margueron's sole ambition was to see his only son, a modest official, promoted to be collector of the revenue at Senlis.

Moreau had hinted to his master that he had a dangerous rival in the person of old Léger. The farmer, knowing that he could run up the land to a high price by selling it piecemeal to the Count, was capable of paying a sum so high as to outbid the profit derivable from the collectorship to be bestowed on the younger Margueron. Two days since, the Count, who wanted to have done with the matter, had sent for his notary Alexandre Crottat, and Derville his solicitor, to inquire into the state of the affair. Though Crottat and Derville cast doubts on the Steward's zeal—and, indeed, it was a puzzling letter from him that gave rise to this consultation—the Count defended Moreau, who had, he said, served him faithfully for seventeen years.

"Well," Derville replied, "I can only advise your lordship to go in person to Presles and ask this Margueron to dinner. Crottat will send down his head-clerk with a form of sale ready drawn out, leaving blank pages or lines for the insertion of descriptions of the plots and the necessary titles. Your Excellency will do well to go provided with a cheque for part of the purchase-money in case of need, and not to forget the letter appointing the son to the collectorship at Senlis. If you do not strike on the nail, the farm will slip through your fingers. You have no idea, Monsieur le Comte, of peasant cunning. Given a peasant on one side and a diplomate on the other, the peasant will win the day."

Crottat confirmed this advice, which, from the footman's report to Pierrotin, the Count had evidently adopted. On the day before, the Count had sent a note to Moreau by the Beaumont diligence, desiring him to invite Margueron to dinner, as he meant to come to some conclusion concerning the Moulineaux farm-lands.

Before all this, the Count had given orders for the restoration of the living-rooms at Presles, and Monsieur Grindot, a fashionable architect, went down there once a week. So, while treating for his acquisition, Monsieur de Sérizy proposed inspecting the works at the same time and the effect of the new decorations. He intended to give his wife a surprise by taking her to Presles, and the restoration of the château was a matter of pride to him. What event, then, could have happened, that the Count, who, only the day before, was intending to go overtly to Presles, should now wish to travel thither *incognito,* in Pierrotin's chaise?

Here a few words are necessary as to the antecedent history of the steward at Presles.

This man, Moreau, was the son of a proctor in a provincial town, who at the time of the Revolution had been made a magistrate (*procureur-syndic*) at Versailles. In this position the elder Moreau had been largely instrumental in saving the property and life of the Sérizys, father and son. Citizen Moreau had belonged to the party of Danton; Robespierre, implacable in revenge, hunted him down, caught him, and had him executed at Versailles. The younger Moreau, inheriting his father's doctrines and attachments, got mixed up in one of the conspiracies plotted against the First Consul on his accession to power. Then Monsieur de Sérizy, anxious to pay a debt of gratitude, succeeded in effecting Moreau's escape after he was condemned to death; in 1804 he asked and obtained his pardon; he at first found him a place in his office, and afterwards made him his secretary and manager of his private affairs.

Some time after his patron's marriage, Moreau fell in love with the Countess' maid and married her. To avoid the unpleasantly false position in which he was placed by this union —and there were many such at the Imperial Court—he asked to be appointed land steward at Presles, where his wife could play the lady, and where, in a neighborhood of small folks, they would neither of them be hurt in their own conceits. The Count needed a faithful agent at Presles, because his wife preferred to reside at Sérizy, which is no more than five leagues from Paris. Moreau was familiar with all his affairs, and he was intelligent; before the Revolution he had studied law under his father. So Monsieur de Sérizy said to him:

"You will not make a fortune, for you have tied a millstone round your neck; but you will be well off, for I will provide for that."

And, in fact, the Count gave Moreau a fixed salary of a thousand crowns, and a pretty little lodge to live in beyond the outbuildings; he also allowed him so many cords of wood a year out of the plantations for fuel, so much straw, oats, and hay for two horses, and a certain proportion of the payments in kind. A sous-préfet is less well off.

During the first eight years of his stewardship, Moreau managed the estate conscientiously, and took an interest in his work. The Count, when he came down to inspect the domain, to decide on purchases or sanction improvements, was struck by Moreau's faithful service, and showed his approbation by handsome presents. But when Moreau found himself the father of a girl—his third child—he was so completely established at his ease at Presles, that he forgot how greatly he was indebted to Monsieur de Sérizy for such unusually liberal advantages. Thus in 1816, the steward, who had hitherto done no more than help himself freely, accepted from a wood-merchant a bonus of twenty-five thousand francs, with the promise of a rise, for signing an agreement for twelve years allowing the contractor to cut fire-logs in the woods of Presles. Moreau argued thus: He had no promise of a pension; he was the father of a family; the Count certainly owed him so much by way of premium on nearly ten years' service. He was already lawfully possessed of sixty thousand francs in savings; with this sum added to it he could purchase for a hundred and twenty thousand a farm in the vicinity of Champagne, a hamlet on the right bank of the Oise a little way above l'Isle-Adam.

The stir of politics hindered the Count and the country-folks from taking cognizance of this investment; the business was indeed transacted in the name of Madame Moreau, who was supposed to have come into some money from an old great-aunt in her own part of the country, at Saint-Lô.

When once the steward had tasted the delicious fruits of ownership, though his conduct was still apparently honesty itself, he never missed an opportunity of adding to his clandestine wealth; the interests of his three children served as an emollient to quench the ardors of his honesty, and we must do him the justice to say that while he was open to a bribe, took care of himself in concluding a bargain, and strained his rights to the last point, he was still honest in the eye of the law; no proof could have been brought in support of any accusation. According to the jurisprudence of the least dishonest of Paris cooks, he shared with his master the profits due to his sharp practice. This way of making a fortune was a matter of conscience—nothing more. Energetic, and fully alive to the Count's interests, Moreau looked out all the more keenly for good opportunities of driving a bargain, since he was sure of a handsome douceur. Presles was worth sixty-two thousand francs in cash rents; and throughout the district, for ten leagues round, the saying was, "Monsieur de Sérizy has a second self in Moreau!"

Moreau, like a prudent man, had, since 1817, invested his salary and his profits year by year in the funds, feathering his nest in absolute secrecy. He had refused various business speculations on the plea of want of money, and affected poverty so well to the Count that he had obtained two scholarships for his boys at the Collège Henri IV. And, at this moment, Moreau owned a hundred and twenty thousand francs in reduced consuls, then paying five per cent, and quoted at eighty. These unacknowledged hundred and twenty thousand francs, and his farm at Champagne, to which he had made additions, amounted to a fortune of about two hundred and eighty thousand francs, yielding an income of sixteen thousand francs a year.

This, then, was the steward's position at the time when the Count wished to purchase the farm of les Moulineaux, of which the possession had become indispensable to his comfort. This farm comprehended ninety-six plots of land, adjoining, bordering, and marching with the estate of Presles, in many cases indeed completely surrounded by the Count's property, like a square in the middle of a chess-board, to say nothing of the dividing hedges and ditches, which gave rise to constant disputes when a tree was to be cut down if it stood on debatable ground. Any other Minister of State would have fought twenty lawsuits a year over the lands of les Moulineaux.

Old Léger wanted to buy them only to sell to the Count; and to make the thirty or forty thousand francs of profit he hoped for, he had long been endeavoring to come to terms with Moreau. Only three days before this critical Saturday, farmer Léger, driven by press of circumstances, had, standing out in the fields, clearly demonstrated to the steward how he could invest the Comte de Sérizy's money at two and a half per cent in purchasing other plots, that is to say, could, as usual, seem to be serving the Count's interests while pocketing the bonus of forty thousand francs offered him on the transaction.

"And on my honor," said the steward to his wife as they went to bed that evening, "if I can make fifty thousand francs on the purchase of les Moulineaux—for the Count will give me ten thousand at least—we will retire to l'Isle-Adam to the Pavillon de Nogent."

This *pavillon* is a charming little house built for a lady by the Prince de Conti in a style of prodigal elegance.

"I should like that," said his wife. "The Dutchman who has been living there has done it up very handsomely, and he will let us have it for thirty thousand francs, since he is obliged to go back to the Indies."

"It is but a stone's throw from Champagne," Moreau went on. "I have hopes of being able to buy the farm and mill at Mours for a hundred thousand francs. We should thus have ten thousand francs a year out of land, one of the prettiest places in all the valley, close to our farm lands, and six thousand francs a year still in the funds."

"And why should you not apply to be appointed Justice of the Peace at l'Isle-Adam? It would give us importance and fifteen hundred francs a year more."

"Yes, I have thought of that."

In this frame of mind, on learning that his patron was coming to Presles, and wished him to invite Margueron to dinner on Saturday, Moreau at once sent off a messenger, who delivered a note to the Count's valet too late in the evening for it to be delivered to Monsieur de Sérizy; but Augustin laid it, as was usual, on his master's desk. In this letter Moreau begged the Count not to take so much trouble; to leave the matter to his management. By his account Margueron no longer wished to sell the lands in one lot, but talked of dividing the farm into ninety-six plots. This, at any rate, he must be persuaded to give up; and perhaps, said the steward, it might be necessary to find some one to lend his name as a screen.

Now, everybody has enemies. The steward of Presles and his wife had given offence to a retired officer named de Reybert and his wife. From stinging words and pin-pricks they had come to daggers drawn. Monsieur de Reybert breathed nothing but vengeance; he aimed at getting Moreau deposed from his place and filling it himself. These two ideas are twins. Hence the agent's conduct, narrowly watched for two years past, had no secrets from the Reyberts. At the very time when Moreau was despatching his letter to Monsieur de Sérizy, Reybert had sent his wife to Paris. Madame de Reybert so strongly insisted on seeing the Count, that, being refused at nine in the evening, when he was going to bed, she was shown into his study by seven o'clock next morning.

"Monseigneur," said she to the Minister, "my husband and I are incapable of writing an anonymous letter. I am Madame de Reybert, *née* de Corroy. My husband has a pension of no more than six hundred francs a year, and we live at Presles, where your land-steward exposes us to insult upon insult though we are gentlefolks.—Monsieur de Reybert, who has no love of intrigue—far from it!—retired as a Captain of Artillery in 1816 after twenty years' service, but he never came under the Emperor's eye, Monsieur le Comte; and you must know how slowly promotion came to those who did not serve under the Master himself; and besides, my husband's honesty and plain speaking did not please his superiors.

"For three years my husband has been watching your steward for the purpose of depriving him of his place.—We are outspoken, you see. Moreau has made us his enemies, and we have kept our eyes open. I have come therefore to tell you that you are being tricked in this business of the Moulineaux farm lands. You are to be cheated of a hundred thousand francs, which will be shared between the notary, Léger, and Moreau. You have given orders that Margueron is to be asked to dinner, and you intend to go to Presles to-morrow; but Margueron will be ill, and Léger is so confident of getting the farm that he is in Paris realizing enough capital. As we have enlightened you, if you want an honest agent, engage my husband. Though of noble birth, he will serve you as he served his country. Your steward has made and saved two hundred and fifty thousand francs, so he is not to be pitied."

The Count thanked Madame de Reybert very coldly and answered her with empty speeches, for he detested an informer; still, as he remembered Derville's suspicions, he was shaken in his mind, and then his eye fell on Moreau's letter; he read it, and in those assurances of devotion, and the respectful remonstrances as to the want of confidence implied by his intention of conducting this business himself, he saw the truth about Moreau.

"Corruption has come with wealth, as usual," said he to himself.

He had questioned Madame de Reybert less to ascertain the details than to give himself time to study her, and he had then written a line to his notary to desire him not to send his clerk to Presles, but to go there himself and meet him at dinner.

"If you should have formed a bad opinion of me, Monsieur le Comte, for the step I have taken unknown to my husband," said Madame Reybert in conclusion, "you must at least be convinced that we have obtained our knowledge as concerning your steward by perfectly natural means; the most sensitive conscience can find nothing to blame us for."

Madame de Reybert *née* de Corroy held herself as straight as a pikestaff.

The Count's rapid survey took in a face pitted by the smallpox till it looked like a colander, a lean, flat figure, a pair of eager, light-colored eyes, fair curls flattened on an anxious brow, a faded green silk bonnet lined with pink, a white stuff dress with lilac spots, and kid shoes. Monsieur de Sérizy discerned in her the wife of the poor gentleman; some Puritanical soul subscribing to the *Courrier Français,* glowing with virtue, but very well aware of the advantages of a fixed place, and coveting it.

"A pension of six hundred francs, you said?" replied the Count, answering himself rather than Madame de Reybert's communication.

"Yes, Monsieur le Comte."

"You were a de Corroy?"

"Yes, monsieur, of a noble family of the Messin country, my husband's country."

"And in what regiment was Monsieur de Reybert?"

"In the 7th Artillery."

"Good!" said the Count, writing down the number.

He thought he might very well place the management of the estate in the hands of a retired officer, concerning whom he could get the fullest information at the War Office.

"Madame," he went on, ringing for his valet, "return to Presles with my notary, who is to arrange to dine there to-night, and to whom I have written a line of introduction; this is his address. I am going to Presles myself, but secretly, and will let Monsieur de Reybert know where to call on me."

So it was not a false alarm that had startled Pierrotin with the news of Monsieur de Sérizy's journey in a public chaise, and the warning to keep his name a secret; he foresaw imminent danger about to fall on one of his best customers.

On coming out of the café, Pierrotin perceived, at the gate of the *Silver Lion,* the woman and youth whom his acumen had recognized as travelers; for the lady, with outstretched neck and an anxious face, was evidently looking for him. This lady, in a re-dyed black silk, a gray bonnet, and an old French cashmere shawl, shod in open-work silk stockings and kid shoes, held a flat straw basket and a bright blue umbrella. She had once been handsome, and now looked about forty; and her blue eyes, bereft of the sparkle that happiness might have given them, showed that she had long since renounced the world. Her dress no less than her person betrayed a mother entirely given up to her housekeeping and her son. If the bonnet-strings were shabby, the shape of it dated from three years back. Her shawl was fastened with a large broken needle, converted into a pin by means of a head of sealing-wax.

This person was impatiently awaiting Pierrotin to commend her son to his care; the lad was probably traveling alone for the first time, and she had accompanied him as far as the coach office, as much out of mistrust as out of motherly devotion. The son was in a way supplementary to his mother; and without the mother the son would have seemed less comprehensible. While the mother was content to display darned gloves, the son wore an olive-green overcoat, with sleeves rather short at the wrists, showing that he was still growing, as lads do between eighteen and nineteen. And his blue trousers, mended by the mother, showed that they had been new-seated whenever the tails of his coat parted maliciously behind.

"Do not twist your gloves up in that way," she was saying when Pierrotin appeared, "you wear them shabby.—Are you the driver?—Ah! it is you, Pierrotin!" she went on, leaving her son for a moment and taking the coachman aside.

"All well, Madame Clapart?" said Pierrotin, with an expression on his face of mingled respect and familiarity.

"Yes, Pierrotin. Take good care of my Oscar; he is traveling alone for the first time."

"Oh! if he is going alone to Monsieur Moreau's——?" said Pierrotin, to discover whether it were really there that the fellow was being sent.

"Yes," said the mother.

"Has Madame Moreau a liking for him, then?" said the man, with a knowing look.

"Oh! it will not be all roses for the poor boy; but his future prospects make it absolutely necessary that he should go."

Pierrotin was struck by this remark, and he did not like to confide his doubts concerning the steward to Madame Clapart; while she, on her part, dared not offend her son by giving Pierrotin such instructions as would put the coachman in the position of a mentor.

During this brief hesitation on both sides, under cover of a few remarks on the weather, the roads, the stopping places on the way, it will not be superfluous to explain the circumstances which had thrown Pierrotin and Madame Clapart together and given rise to their few words of confidential talk.

Frequently—that is to say, three or four times a month—Pierrotin, on his way to Paris, found the steward waiting at la Cave, and as the coach came up he beckoned to a gardener, who then helped Pierrotin to place on the coach one or two baskets full of such fruit and vegetables as were in season, with fowls, eggs, butter, or game. Moreau always paid the carriage himself, and gave him money enough to pay the excise duties at the barrier, if the baskets contained anything subject to the *octroi*. These hampers and baskets never bore any label. The first time, and once for all, the steward had given the shrewd driver Madame Clapart's address by word of mouth, desiring him never to trust anybody else with these precious parcels. Pierrotin, dreaming of an intrigue between some pretty girl and the agent, had gone as directed to No. 7 Rue de la Cerisaie, near the Arsenal, where he had seen the Madame Clapart above described, instead of the fair young creature he had expected to find.

Carriers, in the course of their day's work, are initiated into many homes and trusted with many secrets; but the chances of the social system—a sort of deputy providence—having ordained that they should have no education or be unendowed with the gift of observation, it follows that they are not dangerous. Nevertheless, after many months Pierrotin could not account to himself for the friendship between Madame Clapart and Monsieur Moreau, from what little he saw of the household in the Rue de la Cerisaie. Though rents were not at that time high in the neighborhood of the Arsenal, Madame Clapart lived on the third floor on the inner side of a courtyard, in a house which had been in its day the residence of some magnate, at a period when the highest nobility in the kingdom lived on what had been the site of the Palais des Tournelles and the Hôtel Saint-Paul. Towards the close of the sixteenth century the great families spread themselves over vast plots previously occupied by the King's Palace Gardens, of which the record survives in the names of the streets, Rue de la Cerisaie, Rue Beautreillis, Rue des Lions, and so on. This apartment, of which every room was paneled with old wainscot, consisted of three rooms in a row —a dining-room, a drawing-room, and a bedroom. Above were the kitchen and Oscar's room. Fronting the door that opened on to the landing was the door of another room at an angle to these, in a sort of square tower of massive stone built out all the way up, and containing besides a wooden staircase. This tower room was where Moreau slept whenever he spent a night in Paris.

Pierrotin deposited the baskets in the first room, where he could see six straw-bottomed, walnut-wood chairs, a table, and a sideboard; narrow russet-brown curtains screened the windows. Afterwards, when he was admitted to the drawing-room, he found it fitted with old furniture of the time of the Empire, much worn; and there was no more of it at all than the landlord would insist upon as a guarantee for the rent. The carved panels, painted coarsely in distemper of a dull pinkish white, and in such a way as to fill up the mouldings and thicken the scrolls and figures, far from being ornamental, were positively depressing. The floor, which was never waxed, was as dingy as the boards of a schoolroom. If the carrier by chance disturbed Monsieur and Madame Clapart at a meal, the plates, the glasses, the most trifling things revealed miserable poverty; they had silver plate, it is true, but the dishes and tureen, chipped and riveted like those of the very poor, were truly pitiable. Monsieur Clapart, in a dirty short coat, with squalid slippers on his feet, and always green spectacles to protect his eyes, as he took off a horrible peaked cap, five years old at least, showed a high-pointed skull, with a few dirty locks hanging about it, which a poet would have declined to call hair. This colorless creature looked a coward, and was probably a tyrant.

In this dismal apartment, facing north, with no outlook but on a vine nailed out on the opposite wall, and a well in the corner of the yard, Madame Clapart gave herself the airs of a queen, and trod like a woman who could not go out on foot. Often, as she thanked Pierrotin, she would give him a look that might have touched the heart of a looker-on; now and again she would slip a twelve-sou piece into his hand. Her voice in speech was very sweet. Oscar was unknown to Pierrotin, for the boy had but just left school, and he had never seen him at home.

This was the sad story which Pierrotin never could have guessed, not even after questioning the gate-keeper's wife, as he sometimes did—for the woman knew nothing beyond the fact that the Claparts' rent was but two hundred and fifty francs; that they only had a woman in to help for a few hours in the morning; that Madame would sometimes do her own little bit of washing, and paid for every letter as it came as if she were afraid to let the account stand.

There is no such thing—or rather, there is very rarely such a thing—as a criminal who is bad all through. How much more rare it must be to find a man who is dishonest all through! He may make up his accounts to his own advantage rather than his master's, or pull as much hay as possible to his end of the manger; but even while making a little fortune by illicit means, few men deny themselves the luxury of some good action. If only out of curiosity, as a contrast, or perhaps by chance, every man has known his hour of generosity; he may speak of it as a mistake, and never repeat it; still, once or twice in his life, he will have sacrificed to well-doing, as the veriest lout will sacrifice to the Graces. If Moreau's sins can be forgiven him, will it not be for the sake of his constancy in helping a poor woman of whose favors he had once been proud, and under whose roof he had found refuge in danger?

This woman, famous at the time of the Directoire for her connection with one of the five kings of the day, married, under his powerful patronage, a contractor, who made millions, and then was ruined by Napoleon in 1802. This man, named Husson, was driven mad by his sudden fall from opulence to poverty; he threw himself into the Seine, leaving his handsome wife expecting a child. Moreau, who was on very intimate terms with Madame Husson, was at the time under sentence of death, so he could not marry the widow, and was in fact obliged to leave France for a time. Madame Husson, only two-and-twenty, in her utter poverty, married an official named Clapart, a young man of twenty-seven—a man of promise, it was said. Heaven preserve women from handsome men of promise! In those days officials rose rapidly from humble beginnings, for the Emperor had an eye for capable men. But Clapart, vulgarly handsome indeed, had no brains. Believing Madame Husson to be very rich, he had affected a great passion; he was simply a burden to her, never able, either then or later, to satisfy the habits she had acquired in her days of opulence. Clapart filled—badly enough—a small place in the Exchequer Office at a salary of not more than eighteen hundred francs a year.

When Moreau came back to be with the Comte de Sérizy and heard of Madame Husson's desperate plight, he succeeded, before his own marriage, in getting her a place as woman of the bedchamber in attendance on MADAME, the Emperor's mother. But in spite of such powerful patronage, Clapart could never get on; his incapacity was too immediately obvious.

In 1815 the brilliant Aspasia of the Directory, ruined by the Emperor's overthrow, was left with nothing to live on but the salary of twelve hundred francs attached to a clerkship in the Municipal Offices, which the Comte de Sérizy's influence secured for Clapart. Moreau, now the only friend of a woman whom he had known as the possessor of millions, obtained for Oscar Husson a half-scholarship held by the Municipality of Paris in the Collège Henri IV., and he sent to the Rue de la Cerisaie, by Pierrotin, all he could decently offer to the impoverished lady.

Oscar was his mother's one hope, her very life. The only fault to be found with the poor woman was her excessive fondness for this boy—his stepfather's utter aversion. Oscar was, unluckily, gifted with a depth of silliness which his mother could never suspect, in spite of Clapart's ironical remarks. This silliness—or, to be accurate, this bumptiousness—disturbed Monsieur Moreau so greatly that he had begged Madame Clapart to send the lad to him for a month that he might judge for himself what line of life he would prove fit for. The steward had some thought of introducing Oscar one day to the Count as his successor.

But, to give God and the Devil their due, it may here be observed as an excuse for Oscar's preposterous conceit, that he had been born under the roof of the Emperor's mother; in his earliest years his eyes had been dazzled by Imperial splendor. His impressible imagination had no doubt retained the memory of those magnificent spectacles, and an image of that golden time of festivities, with a dream of seeing them again. The boastfulness common to schoolboys, all possessed by desire to shine at the expense of their fellows, had in him been exaggerated by those memories of his childhood; and at home perhaps his mother was rather too apt to recall with complacency the days when she had been a queen of Paris under the Directory. Oscar, who had just finished his studies, had, no doubt, often been obliged to assert himself as superior to the humiliations which the pupils who pay are always ready to inflict on the "charity boys" when the scholars are not physically strong enough to impress them with their superiority.

This mixture of departed splendor and faded beauty, of affection resigned to poverty, of hope founded on this son, and maternal blindness, with the heroic endurance of suffering, made this mother one of the sublime figures which in Paris deserve the notice of the observer.

Pierrotin, who, of course, could not know how truly Moreau was attached to this woman, and she, on her part, to the man who had protected her in 1797, and was now her only friend, would not mention to her the suspicion that had dawned in his brain as to the danger which threatened Moreau. The manservant's ominous speech, "We have all enough to do to take care of ourselves," recurred to his mind with the instinct of obedience to those whom he designated as "first in the ranks." Also, at this moment Pierrotin felt as many darts stinging his brain as there are five-franc pieces in a thousand francs. A journey of seven leagues seemed, no doubt, quite an undertaking to this poor mother, who in all her fine lady existence had hardly ever been beyond the barrier; for Pierrotin's replies, "Yes, madame; no, madame——" again and again, plainly showed that the man was only anxious to escape from her too numerous and useless instructions.

"You will put the luggage where it cannot get wet if the weather should change?"

"I have a tarpaulin," said Pierrotin; "and you see, madame, it is carefully packed away."

"Oscar, do not stay more than a fortnight, even if you are pressed," Madame Clapart went on, coming back to her son. "Do what you will, Madame Moreau will never take to you; besides, you must get home by the end of September. We are going to Belleville, you know, to your uncle Cardot's."

"Yes, mamma."

"Above all," she added in a low tone, "never talk about servants. Always remember that Madame Moreau was a lady's maid——"

"Yes, mamma."

Oscar, like all young people whose conceit is touchy, seemed much put out by these admonitions delivered in the gateway of the *Silver Lion*.

"Well, good-bye, mamma; we shall soon be off, the horse is put in."

The mother, forgetting that she was in the open street, hugged her Oscar, and taking a nice little roll out of her bag—

"Here," said she, "you were forgetting your bread and chocolate. Once more, my dear boy, do not eat anything at the inns; you have to pay ten times the value for the smallest morsel."

Oscar wished his mother further as she stuffed the roll and the chocolate into his pocket.

There were two witnesses to the scene, two young men a few years older than the newly fledged school-boy, better dressed than he, and come without their mothers, their demeanor, dress, and manner proclaiming the entire independence which is the end of every lad's desire while still under direct maternal government. To Oscar, at this moment, these two young fellows epitomized the World.

"*Mamma!* says he," cried one of the strangers, with a laugh.

The words reached Oscar's ears, and in an impulse of intense irritation he shouted out:

"Good-bye, mother!"

It must be owned that Madame Clapart spoke rather too loud, and seemed to admit the passers-by to bear witness to her affectionate care.

"What on earth ails you, Oscar?" said the poor woman, much hurt. "I do not understand you," she added severely, fancying she could thus inspire him with respect—a common mistake with women who spoil their children. "Listen, dear Oscar," she went on, resuming her coaxing gentleness, "you have a propensity for talking to everybody, telling everything you know and everything you don't know—out of brag and a young man's foolish self-conceit. I beg you once more to bridle your tongue. You have not seen enough of life, my dearest treasure, to gauge the people you may meet, and there is nothing more dangerous than talking at random in a public conveyance. In a diligence well-bred persons keep silence."

The two young men, who had, no doubt, walked to the end of the yard and back, now made the sound of their boots heard once more under the gateway; they might have heard this little lecture; and so, to be quit of his mother, Oscar took heroic measures, showing how much self-esteem can stimulate the inventive powers.

"Mamma," said he, "you are standing in a thorough draught, you will catch cold. Besides, I must take my place."

The lad had touched some tender chord, for his mother clasped him in her arms as if he were starting on some long voyage, and saw him into the chaise with tears in her eyes.

"Do not forget to give five francs to the servants," said she. "And write to me at least three times in the course of the fortnight. Behave discreetly, and remember all my instructions. You have enough linen to need none washed. And, above all, remember all Monsieur Moreau's kindness; listen to him as to a father, and follow his advice."

As he got into the chaise Oscar displayed a pair of blue stockings as his trousers slipped up, and the new seat to his trousers as his coat-tails parted. And the smile on the faces of the two young men, who did not fail to see these evidences of honorable poverty, was a fresh blow to Oscar's self-esteem.

"Oscar's place is No. 1," said Madame Clapart to Pierrotin. "Settle yourself into a corner," she went on, still gazing at her son with tender affection.

Oh! how much Oscar regretted his mother's beauty, spoilt by misfortune and sorrow, and the poverty and self-sacrifice that hindered her from being nicely dressed. One of the youngsters—the one who wore boots and spurs—nudged the other with his elbow to point out Oscar's mother, and the other twirled his moustache with an air, as much as to say, "A neat figure!"

"How am I to get rid of my mother?" thought Oscar, looking quite anxious.

"What is the matter?" said Madame Clapart.

Oscar pretended not to hear, the wretch! And perhaps, under the circumstances, Madame Clapart showed want of tact; but an absorbing passion is so selfish!

"Georges, do you like traveling with children?" asked one of the young men of his friend.

"Yes, if they are weaned, and are called Oscar, and have chocolate to eat, my dear Amaury."

These remarks were exchanged in an undertone, leaving Oscar free to hear or not to hear them. His manner would show the young man what he might venture on with the lad to amuse himself in the course of the journey. Oscar would not hear. He looked round to see whether his mother, who weighed on him like a nightmare, was still waiting; but, indeed, he knew she was too fond of him to have deserted him yet. He not only involuntarily compared his traveling companion's dress with his own, but he also felt that his mother's costume counted for something as provoking the young men's mocking smile.

"If only they would go!" thought he.

Alas! Amaury had just said to Georges, as he struck the wheel of the chaise with his cane:

"And you are prepared to trust your future career on board this frail vessel?"

"Needs must!" replied Georges in a fateful tone.

Oscar heaved a sigh as he noted the youth's hat, cocked cavalierly over one ear to show a fine head of fair hair elaborately curled, while he, by his stepfather's orders, wore his black hair in a brush above his forehead, cut quite short like a soldier's. The vain boy's face was round and chubby, bright with the color of vigorous health; that of "Georges" was long, delicate, and pale. This young man had a broad brow, and his chest filled out a shawl-pattern waistcoat. As Oscar admired his tightly-fitting iron-gray trousers, and his overcoat, sitting closely to the figure, with Brandenburg braiding and oval buttons, he felt as if the romantic stranger, blessed with so many advantages, were making an unfair display of his superiority, just as an ugly woman is offended by the mere sight of a beauty. The ring of his spurred boot-heels, which the young man accentuated rather too much for Oscar's liking, went to the boy's heart. In short, Oscar was as uncomfortable in his clothes, home-made perhaps out of his stepfather's old ones, as the other enviable youth was satisfied in his.

"That fellow must have ten francs at least in his pocket," thought Oscar.

The stranger happening to turn round, what were Oscar's feelings when he discerned a gold chain about his neck—with a gold watch, no doubt, at the end of it.

Living in the Rue de la Cerisaie since 1815, taken to and from school on his holidays by his stepfather Clapart, Oscar had never had any standard of comparison but his mother's poverty-stricken household. Kept very strictly, by Moreau's advice, he rarely went to the play, and then aspired no higher than to the *Ambigu Comique,* where little elegance met his gaze, even if the absorbed attention a boy devotes to the stage had allowed him to study the house. His stepfather still wore his watch in a fob in the fashion of the Empire, with a heavy gold chain hanging over his stomach, and ending in a bunch of miscellaneous objects—seals, and a watch-key with a flat round top, in which was set a landscape in mosaic. Oscar, who looked on this out-of-date splendor as the *ne plus ultra* of luxury, was quite bewildered by this revelation of superior and less ponderous elegance. The young man also made an insolent display of a pair of good gloves, and seemed bent on blinding Oscar by his graceful handling of a smart cane with a gold knob.

Oscar had just reached the final stage of boyhood in which trifles are the cause of great joys and great anguish, when a real misfortune seems preferable to a ridiculous costume; and vanity, having no great interests in life to absorb it, centres in frivolities, and dress, and the anxiety to be thought a man. The youth magnifies himself, and his self-assertion is all the more marked because it turns on trifles; still, though he envies a well-dressed noodle, he can be also fired with enthusiasm for talent, and admire a man of genius. His faults, when they are not rooted in his heart, only show the exuberance of vitality and a lavish imagination. When a boy of nineteen, an only son, austerely brought up at home as a result of the poverty that weighs so cruelly on a clerk with twelve hundred francs' salary, but worshiped by a mother, who for his sake endures the bitterest privations—when such a boy is dazzled by a youth of two-and-twenty, envies him his frogged coat lined with silk, his sham cashmere waistcoat, and a tie slipped through a vulgar ring, is not this a mere peccadillo such as may be seen in every class of life in the inferior who envies his betters?

Even a man of genius yields to this primitive passion. Did not Rousseau of Geneva envy Venture and Bacle?

But Oscar went on from the peccadillo to the real fault; he felt humiliated; he owed his traveling companion a grudge;

and a secret desire surged up in his heart to show him that he was as good a man as he.

The two young bucks walked to and fro, from the gateway to the stables and back, going out to the street; and as they turned on their heel, they each time looked at Oscar ensconced in his corner. Oscar, convinced that whenever they laughed it was at him, affected profound indifference. He began to hum the tune of a song then in fashion among the Liberals, *"C'est la faute à Voltaire, c'est la faute à Rousseau."* (It is all the fault of Voltaire and Rousseau.) This assumption, no doubt, made them take him for some underling lawyer's clerk.

"Why, perhaps he sings in the chorus at the Opera!" said Amaury.

Exasperated this time, Oscar bounded in his seat; raising the back curtain, he said to Pierrotin:

"When are we to be off?"

"Directly," said the man, who had his whip in his hand, but his eyes fixed on the Rue d'Enghien.

The scene was now enlivened by the arrival of a young man escorted by a perfect pickle of a boy, who appeared with a porter at their heels hauling a barrow by a strap. The young man spoke confidentially to Pierrotin, who wagged his head and hailed his stableman. The man hurried up to help unload the barrow, which contained, besides two trunks, pails, brushes, and boxes of strange shape, a mass of packets and utensils, which the younger of the two newcomers who had climbed to the box-seat stowed and packed away with such expedition that Oscar, smiling at his mother, who was now watching him from the other side of the street, failed to see any of the paraphernalia which might have explained to him in what profession his traveling companions were employed. This boy, about sixteen years of age, wore a holland blouse, with a patent leather belt; his cap, knowingly stuck on one side, proclaimed him a merry youth, as did the picturesque disorder of his curly brown hair tumbling about his shoulders. A black silk tie marked a black line on a very white neck, and seemed to heighten the brightness of his gray eyes. The rest-

less vivacity of a sunburnt, rosy face, the shape of his full
lips, his prominent ears, and his turn-up nose—every feature
of his face showed the bantering wit of a Figaro and the recklessness of youth, while the quickness of his gestures and
saucy glances revealed a keen intelligence, early developed by
the practice of a profession taken up in boyhood. This boy,
whom art or nature had already made a man, seemed indifferent to the question of dress, as though he were conscious of
some intrinsic moral worth; for he looked at his unpolished
boots as if he thought them rather a joke, and at his plain
drill trousers to note the stains on them, but rather to study
the effect than to hide them.

"I have acquired a fine tone!" said he, giving himself a
shake, and addressing his companion.

The expression of the senior showed some authority over
this youngster, in whom experienced eyes would at once
have discerned the jolly art student, known in French studio
slang as a *rapin*.

"Behave, Mistigris!" replied the master, calling him no
doubt by a nickname bestowed on him in the studio.

The elder traveler was a slight and pallid young fellow,
with immensely thick black hair in quite fantastic disorder;
but this abundant hair seemed naturally necessary to a very
large head with a powerful forehead that spoke of precocious
intelligence. His curiously puckered face, too peculiar to
be called ugly, was as hollow as though this singular young
man were suffering either from some chronic malady or from
the privations of extreme poverty—which is indeed a terrible
chronic malady—or from sorrows too recent to have been forgotten.

His clothes, almost in keeping with those of Mistigris in
proportion to his age and dignity, consisted of a much worn
coat of a dull green color, shabby, but quite clean and well
brushed, a black waistcoat buttoned to the neck, as the coat
was too, only just showing a red handkerchief round his
throat. Black trousers, as shabby as the coat, hung loosely
round his lean legs. His boots were muddy, showing that

he had come far, and on foot. With one swift glance the artist took in the depths of the hostelry of the *Silver Lion,* the stables, the tones of color, and every detail, and he looked at Mistigris, who had imitated him, with an ironical twinkle.

"Rather nice!" said Mistigris.

"Yes, very nice," replied the other.

"We are still too early," said Mistigris. "Couldn't we snatch a toothful? My stomach, like nature, abhors a vacuum!"

"Have we time to get a cup of coffee?" said the artist, in a pleasant voice, to Pierrotin.

"Well, don't be long," said Pierrotin.

"We have a quarter of an hour," added Mistigris, thus revealing the genius for inference, which is characteristic of the Paris art student.

The couple disappeared. Just then nine o'clock struck in the inn kitchen. Georges thought it only fair and reasonable to appeal to Pierrotin.

"I say, my good friend, when you are the proud possessor of such a shandrydan as this," and he rapped the wheel with his cane, "you should at least make a merit of punctuality. The deuce is in it! we do not ride in that machine for our pleasure, and business must be devilish pressing before we trust our precious selves in it! And that old hack you call Rougeot will certainly not pick up lost time!"

"We will harness on Bichette while those two gentlemen are drinking their coffee," replied Pierrotin. "Go on, you," he added to the stableman, "and see if old Léger means to come with us——"

"Where is your old Léger?" asked Georges.

"Just opposite at Number 50; he couldn't find room in the Beaumont coach," said Pierrotin to his man, paying no heed to Georges, and going off himself in search of Bichette.

Georges shook hands with his friend and got into the chaise, after tossing in a large portfolio, with an air of much importance; this he placed under the cushion. He took the opposite corner to Oscar.

"This 'old Léger' bothers me,' said he.

"They cannot deprive us of our places," said Oscar. "Mine is No. 1."

"And mine No. 2," replied Georges.

Just as Pierrotin reappeared, leading Bichette, the stableman returned, having in tow a huge man weighing nearly seventeen stone at least.

Old Léger was of the class of farmer who, with an enormous stomach and broad shoulders, wears a powdered queue and a light coat of blue linen. His white gaiters were tightly strapped above the knee over corduroy breeches, and finished off with silver buckles. His hobnailed shoes weighed each a couple of pounds. In his hand he carried a little knotted red switch, very shiny, and with a heavy knob, secured round his wrist by a leather cord.

"And is it you who are known as old Léger?" (Farmer *Light*), said Georges gravely as the farmer tried to lift his foot to the step of the chaise.

"At your service," said the farmer, showing him a face rather like that of Louis XVIII., with a fat, red jowl, while above it rose a nose which in any other face would have seemed enormous. His twinkling eyes were deep set in rolls of fat.

"Come, lend a hand, my boy," said he to Pierrotin.

The farmer was hoisted in by the driver and the stableman to a shout of "Yo, heave ho!" from Georges.

"Oh! I am not going far; I am only going to la Cave!" said Farmer *Light,* answering a jest with good humor. In France everybody understands a joke.

"Get into the corner," said Pierrotin. "There will be six of you."

"And your other horse?" asked Georges. "Is it as fabulous as the third horse of a post-chaise?"

"There it is, master," said Pierrotin, pointing to the little mare that had come up without calling.

"He calls that insect a horse!" said Georges, astonished.

"Oh, she is a good one to go, is that little mare," said the farmer, who had taken his seat.—"Morning, gentlemen.—Are we going to weigh anchor, Pierrotin?"

"Two of my travelers are getting a cup of coffee," said the driver.

The young man with the hollow cheeks and his follower now reappeared.

"Come, let us get off," was now the universal cry.

"We are off—we are off!" replied Pierrotin. "Let her go," he added to his man, who kicked away the stones that scotched the wheels.

Pierrotin took hold of Rougeot's bridle with an encouraging *"Tclk, tclk,"* to warn the two steeds to pull themselves together; and, torpid as they evidently were, they started the vehicle, which Pierrotin brought to a standstill in front of the gate of the *Silver Lion*. After this purely preliminary manœuvre, he again looked down the Rue d'Enghien, and vanished, leaving the conveyance in the care of the stableman.

"Well! Is your governor subject to these attacks?" Mistigris asked of the man.

"He is gone to fetch his oats away from the stable," replied the Auvergnat, who was up to all the arts in use to pacify the impatience to travelers.

"After all," said Mistigris, *"time is a great plaster."*

At that time there was in the Paris studios a mania for distorting proverbs. It was considered a triumph to hit on some change of letters or some rhyming word which should suggest an absurd meaning, or even make it absolute nonsense.[*]

"And Paris was not gilt in a play," replied his comrade.

Pierrotin now returned, accompanied by the Comte de Sérizy, round the corner of the Rue de l'Echiquier; they had no doubt had a short conversation.

"Père Léger, would you mind giving your place up to Monsieur le Comte? It will trim the chaise better."

"And we shall not be off for an hour yet if you go on like this," said Georges. "You will have to take out that infernal bar we have had such plaguey trouble to fit in, and everybody will have to get out for the last comer. Each of us has a right

[*] To translate these not always funny jests is impossible. I have generally tried for no more than an equivalent rendering.—*Translator*.

to the place he booked. What number is this gentleman's?—Come, call them over. Have you a way-bill? Do you keep a book? Which is Monsieur le Comte's place?—Count of what?"

"Monsieur le Comte," said Pierrotin, visibly disturbed, "you will not be comfortable."

"Can't you count, man?" said Mistigris. "Short counts make tall friends."

"Mistigris, behave!" said his master quite seriously.

Monsieur de Sérizy was supposed by his fellow-travelers to be some respectable citizen called Lecomte.

"Do not disturb anybody," said the Count to Pierrotin; "I will sit in front by you."

"Now, Mistigris," said the young artist, "remember the respect due to age. You don't know how dreadfully old you may live to be. *Manners take the van.* Give your place up to the gentleman."

Mistigris opened the apron of the chaise, and jumped out as nimbly as a frog into the water.

"You cannot sit as *rabbit,* august old man!" said he to Monsieur de Sérizy.

"Mistigris, *Tarts are the end of man,*" said his master.

"Thank you, monsieur," said the Count to the artist, by whose side he now took his seat. And the statesman looked with a sagacious eye at the possessors of the back seat, in a way that deeply aggrieved Oscar and Georges.

"We are an hour and a quarter behind time," remarked Oscar.

"People who want a chaise to themselves should book all the places," added Georges.

The Comte de Sérizy, quite sure now that he was not recognized, made no reply, but sat with the expression of a good-natured tradesman.

"And if you had been late, you would have liked us to wait for you, I suppose?" said the farmer to the two young fellows.

Pierrotin was looking out towards the Porte Saint-Denis,

and paused for a moment before mounting to the hard box-seat, where Mistigris was kicking his heels.

"If you are still waiting for somebody, I am not the last," remarked the Count.

"That is sound reasoning," said Mistigris.

Georges and Oscar laughed very rudely.

"The old gentleman is not strikingly original," said Georges to Oscar, who was enchanted with this apparent alliance.

When Pierrotin had settled himself in his place, he again looked back, but failed to discern in the crowd the two travelers who were wanting to fill up his cargo.

"By the Mass, but a couple more passengers would not come amiss," said he.

"Look here, I have not paid; I shall get out," said Georges in alarm.

"Why, whom do you expect, Pierrotin?" said Léger.

Pierrotin cried "Gee!" in a particular tone, which Rougeot and Bichette knew to mean business at last, and they trotted off towards the hill at a brisk pace, which, however, soon grew slack.

The Count had a very red face, quite scarlet indeed, with an inflamed spot here and there, and set off all the more by his perfectly white hair. By any but quite young men this complexion would have been understood as the inflammatory effect on the blood of incessant work. And, indeed, these angry pimples so much disfigured his really noble face, that only close inspection could discern in his greenish eyes all the acumen of the judge, the subtlety of the statesman, and the learning of the legislator. His face was somewhat flat; the nose especially looked as if it had been flattened. His hat hid the breadth and beauty of his brow; and, in fact, there was some justification for the laughter of these heedless lads, in the strange contrast between hair as white as silver and thick, bushy eyebrows still quite black. The Count, who wore a long, blue overcoat, buttoned to the chin in military fashion, had a white handkerchief round his neck, cotton-wool in his ears, and a high shirt collar, showing a square white corner on each cheek. His black trousers covered his boots, of which the tip scarcely showed; he had no ribbon at his buttonhole, and his hands were hidden by his doeskin gloves. Certainly there was nothing in this man which could betray to the lads that he was a peer of France, and one of the most useful men living to his country.

Old Père Léger had never seen the Count, who, on the other hand, knew him only by name. Though the Count, as he got into the chaise, cast about him the inquiring glance which had so much annoyed Oscar and Georges, it was because he was looking for his notary's clerk, intending to impress on him the need for the greatest secrecy in case he should have been compelled to travel, like himself, by Pierrotin's conveyance. But he was reassured by Oscar's appearance and by that of the old farmer, and, above all, by the air of aping the military, with his moustache and his style generally, which stamped Georges an adventurer; and he concluded that his note had reached Maître Alexandre Crottat in good time.

"Père Léger," said Pierrotin as they came to the steep hill in the Faubourg Saint-Denis, at the Rue de la Fidélité, "suppose we were to walk a bit, heh?" On hearing the name, the Count observed:

"I will go out too; we must ease the horses."

"Oh! If you go on at this rate, we shall do fourteen leagues in a fortnight!" exclaimed Georges.

"Well, is it any fault of mine," said Pierrotin, "if a passenger wishes to get out?"

"I will give you ten louis if you keep my secret as I bid you," said the Count, taking Pierrotin by the arm.

"Oh, ho! My thousand francs!" thought Pierrotin, after giving Monsieur de Sérizy a wink, conveying, "Trust me!"

Oscar and Georges remained in the chaise.

"Look here, Pierrotin—since Pierrotin you are," cried Georges, when the travelers had got into the chaise again at the top of the hill, "if you are going no faster than this, say so. I will pay my fare to Saint-Denis, and hire a nag there, for I have important business on hand, which will suffer from delay."

"Oh! he will get on, never fear," replied the farmer. "And the road is not a wide one."

"I am never more than half an hour late," answered Pierrotin.

"Well, well, you are not carting the Pope, I suppose," said Georges, "so hurry up a little."

"You ought not to show any favor," said Mistigris; "and if you are afraid of jolting this gentleman"—and he indicated the Count—"that is not fair."

"All men are equal in the eye of the *Coucou*," said Georges, "as all Frenchmen are in the eye of the Charter."

"Be quite easy," said old Léger, "we shall be at la Chapelle yet before noon." La Chapelle is a village close to the Barrière Saint-Denis.

Those who have traveled know that persons thrown together in a public conveyance do not immediately amalgamate; unless under exceptional circumstances, they do not converse till they are well on their way. This silent interval is spent partly in reciprocal examination, and partly in finding each his own place and taking possession of it. The soul, as much as the body, needs to find its balance. When each severally supposes that he has made an accurate guess at his companion's age, profession, and temper, the most talkative first opens a conversation, which is taken up all the more eagerly, because all feel the need for cheering the way and dispelling the dulness.

This at least, is what happens in a French coach. In other countries manners are different. The English pride themselves on never opening their lips; a German is dull in a coach; Italians are too cautious to chat; the Spaniards have almost ceased to have any coaches; and the Russians have no roads. So it is only in the ponderous French diligence that the passengers amuse each other, in the gay and gossiping nation where each one is eager to laugh and display his humor, where everything is enlivened by raillery, from the misery of the poorest to the solid interests of the upper middle-class. The police do little to check the license of speech, and the gallery of the Chambers has made discussion fashionable.

When a youngster of two-and-twenty, like the young gentleman who was known so far by the name of Georges, has a ready wit, he is strongly tempted, especially in such circumstances as these, to be reckless in the use of it. In the first place, Georges was not slow to come to the conclusion that he was the superior man of the party. He decided that the Count was a manufacturer of the second class, setting him down as a cutler; the shabby looking youth attended by Mistigris he thought but a greenhorn, Oscar a perfect simpleton, and the farmer a capital butt for a practical joke. Having thus taken the measure of all his traveling companions, he determined to amuse himself at their expense.

"Now," thought he, as the *coucou* rolled down the hill from la Chapelle towards the plain of Saint-Denis, "shall I pass myself off as Étienne, or as Béranger?—No, these bumpkins have never heard of either.—A Carbonaro? The Devil! I might be nabbed.—One of Marshal Ney's sons? Pooh, what could I make of that? Tell them the story of my father's death? That would hardly be funny.—Suppose I were to have come back from the Government colony in America? They might take me for a spy, and regard me with suspicion. —I will be a Russian Prince in disguise; I will cram them with fine stories about the Emperor Alexander!—Or if I pretended to be Cousin, the Professor of Philosophy? How I could mystify them! No, that limp creature with the towzled hair looks as if he might have kicked his heels at lecture at the Sorbonne.—Oh, why didn't I think sooner of trotting them out? I can imitate an Englishman so well, I might have been Lord Byron traveling *incog.*—Hang it! I have missed my chance.—The executioner's son? Not a bad way of clearing a space at breakfast.—Oh! I know! I will have been in command of the troops under Ali, the Pasha of Janina."

While he was lost in these meditations, the chaise was

making its way through the clouds of dust which constantly blow up from the side paths of this much-trodden road.

"What a dust!" said Mistigris.

"King Henri is dead," retorted his comrade. "If you said it smelt of vanilla now, you would hit on a new idea!"

"You think that funny," said Mistigris. "Well, but it does now and then remind me of vanilla."

"In the East——" Georges began, meaning to concoct a story.

"In the least——" said Mistigris' master, taking up Georges.

"In the East, I said, from whence I have just returned," Georges repeated, "the dust smells very sweet. But here it smells of nothing unless it is wafted up from such a manure-heap as this."

"You have just returned from the East?" said Mistigris, with a sly twinkle.

"And, you see, Mistigwis, the gentleman is so tired that what he now wequires is west," drawled his master.

"You are not much sunburnt," said Mistigris.

"Oh! I am but just out of bed after three months' illness, caused, the doctors say, by an attack of suppressed plague."

"You have had the plague?" cried the Count, with a look of horror.—"Pierrotin, put me out."

"Get on, Pierrotin," said Mistigris.—"You hear that the plague was suppressed," he went on, addressing Monsieur de Sérizy. "It was the sort of plague that goes down in the course of conversation."

"The plague of which one merely says, 'Plague take it!'" cried the artist.

"Or plague take the man!" added Mistigris.

"Mistigris," said his master, "I shall put you out to walk if you get into mischief.—So you have been in the East, monsieur?" he went on, turning to Georges.

"Yes, monsieur. First in Egypt and then in Greece, where I served under Ali Pasha of Janina, with whom I had a desperate row.—The climate is too much for most men; and the excitements of all kinds that are part of an Oriental life wrecked my liver."

"Oh, ho! a soldier?" said the burly farmer. "Why, how old are you?"

"I am nine-and-twenty," said Georges, and all his fellow-travelers looked at him. "At eighteen I served as a private in the famous campaign of 1813; but I only was present at the battle of Hanau, where I won the rank of sergeant-major. In France, at Montereau, I was made sub-lieutenant, and I was decorated by—no spies here?—by the Emperor."

"And you do not wear the Cross of your Order?" said Oscar.

"A Cross given by the present set? Thank you for nothing. Besides, who that is anybody wears his decorations when traveling? Look at monsieur," he went on, indicating the Comte de Sérizy, "I will bet you anything you please——"

"Betting anything you please is the same thing in France as not betting at all," said Mistigris' master.

"I will bet you anything you please," Georges repeated pompously, "that he is covered with stars."

"I have, in fact," said Monsieur de Sérizy, with a laugh, "the Grand Cross of the Legion of Honor, the Grand Cross of Saint-Andrew of Russia, of the Eagle of Prussia, of the Order of the Annunciada of Sardinia, and of the Golden Fleece."

"Is that all?" said Mistigris. "And it all rides in a public chaise?"

"He is going it, is the brick-red man!" said Georges in a whisper to Oscar. "What did I tell you?" he remarked aloud. —"I make no secret of it, I am devoted to the Emperor!"

"I served under him," said the Count.

"And what a man! Wasn't he?" cried Georges.

"A man to whom I am under great obligations," replied the Count, with a well-affected air of stupidity.

"For your crosses?" said Mistigris.

"And what quantities of snuff he took!" replied Monsieur de Sérizy.

"Yes, he took it loose in his waistcoat pockets."

"So I have been told," said the farmer, with a look of incredulity.

"And not only that, but he chewed and smoked," Georges went on. "I saw him smoking in the oddest way at Waterloo when Marshal Soult lifted him up bodily and flung him into his traveling carriage, just as he had seized a musket and wanted to charge the English!"

"So you were at Waterloo?" said Oscar, opening his eyes very wide.

"Yes, young man, I went through the campaign of 1815. At Mont Saint-Jean I was made captain, and I retired on the Loire when we were disbanded. But, on my honor, I was sick of France, and I could not stay. No, I should have got myself into some scrape. So I went off with two or three others of the same sort, Selves, Besson, and some more, who are in Egypt to this day in the service of Mohammed Pasha, and a queer fellow he is, I can tell you! He was a tobacconist at la Cavalle, and is on the high way to be a reigning prince. You have seen him in Horace Vernet's picture of the *Massacre of the Mamelukes.* Such a handsome man!—I never would abjure the faith of my fathers and adopt Islam; all the more because the ceremony involves a surgical operation for which I had no liking. Besides, no one respects a renegade. If they had offered me a hundred thousand francs a year, then, indeed —and yet, no.—The Pasha made me a present of a thousand *talari.*"

"How much is that?" asked Oscar, who was all ears.

"Oh, no great matter. The talaro is much the same as a five-franc piece. And, on my honor, I did not earn enough to pay for the vices I learned in that thundering vile country—if you can call it a country. I cannot live now without smoking my narghileh twice a day, and it is very expensive——"

"And what is Egypt like?" asked Monsieur de Sérizy.

"Egypt is all sand," replied Georges, quite undaunted. "There is nothing green but the Nile valley. Draw a green strip on a sheet of yellow paper, and there you have Egypt.—

The Egyptians, the fellaheen, have, I may remark, one great advantage over us; there are no gendarmes. You may go from one end of Egypt to the other, and you will not find one."

"I suppose there are a good many Egyptians there," said Mistigris.

"Not so many as you would think," answered Georges. "There are more Abyssinians, Giaours, Vechabites, Bedouins, and Copts.—However, all these creatures are so very far from amusing that I was only too glad to embark on a Genoese polacra, bound for the Ionian Islands to take up powder and ammunition for Ali of Tebelen. As you know, the English sell powder and ammunition to all nations, to the Turks and the Greeks; they would sell them to the Devil if the Devil had money. So from Zante we were to luff up to the coast of Greece.

"And, I tell you, take me as you see me, the name of Georges is famous in those parts. I am the grandson of that famous Czerni-Georges who made war on the Porte; but instead of breaking it down, he was unluckily smashed up. His son took refuge in the house of the French Consul at Smyrna, and came to Paris in 1792, where he died before I, his seventh child, was born. Our treasure was stolen from us by a friend of my grandfather's, so we were ruined. My mother lived by selling her diamonds one by one, till in 1799 she married Monsieur Yung, a contractor, and my stepfather. But my mother died; I quarreled with my stepfather, who, between ourselves, is a rascal; he is still living, but we never meet. The wretch left us all seven to our fate without a word, nor bit nor sup. And that is how, in 1813, in sheer despair, I went off as a conscript.—You cannot imagine with what joy Ali of Tebelen hailed the grandson of Czerni-Georges. Here I call myself simply Georges.—The Pasha gave me a seraglio——"

"You had a seraglio?" said Oscar.

"Were you a Pasha with many tails?" asked Mistigris.

"How is it that you don't know that there is but one Sultan who can create pashas?" said Georges, "and my friend

Tebelen—for we were friends, like two Bourbons—was a rebel against the Padischah.—You know—or you don't know—that the Grand Signor's correct title is Padischah, and not the Grand Turk or the Sultan.

"Do not suppose that a seraglio is any great matter. You might just as well have a flock of goats. Their women are great fools, and I like the grisettes of the *Chaumière* at Mont Parnasse a thousand times better."

"And they are much nearer," said the Comte de Sérizy.

"These women of the seraglio never know a word of French, and language is indispensable to an understanding. Ali gave me five lawful wives and ten slave girls. At Janina that was a mere nothing. In the East, you see, it is very bad style to have wives; you have them, but as we here have our Voltaire and our Rousseau; who ever looks into his Voltaire or his Rousseau? Nobody.—And yet it is quite the right thing to be jealous. You may tie a woman up in a sack and throw her into the water on a mere suspicion by an article of their Code."

"Did you throw any in?"

"I? What! a Frenchman! I was devoted to them."

Whereupon Georges twirled up his moustache, and assumed a pensive air.

By this time they were at Saint-Denis, and Pierrotin drew up at the door of the inn where the famous cheese-cakes are sold, and where all travelers call. The Count, really puzzled by the mixture of truth and nonsense in Georges' rhodomontade, jumped into the carriage again, looked under the cushion for the portfolio which Pierrotin had told him that this mysterious youth had bestowed there, and saw on it in gilt letters the words, "Maître Crottat, Notaire." The Count at once took the liberty of opening the case, fearing, with good reason, that if he did not, farmer Léger might be possessed with similar curiosity; and taking out the deed relating to the Moulineaux farm, he folded it up, put it in the side pocket of his coat, and came back to join his fellow-travelers.

"This Georges is neither more nor less than Crottat's junior clerk. I will congratulate his master, who ought to have sent his head-clerk."

From the respectful attention of the farmer and Oscar, Georges perceived that in them at least he had two ardent admirers. Of course, he put on lordly airs; he treated them to cheese-cakes and a glass of Alicante, and then did the same to Mistigris and his master, asking them their names on the strength of this munificence.

"Oh, monsieur," said the elder, "I am not the proud owner of so illustrious a name as yours, and I have not come home from Asia." The Count, who had made haste to get back to the vast inn kitchen, so as to excite no suspicions, came in time to hear the end of the reply.—"I am simply a poor painter just returned from Rome, where I went at the expense of the Government after winning the Grand Prix five years ago. My name is Schinner."

"Hallo, master, may I offer you a glass of Alicante and some cheese-cakes?" cried Georges to the Count.

"Thank you, no," said the Count. "I never come out till I have had my cup of coffee."

"And you never eat anything between meals? How *Marais, Place Royale,* and *Ile Saint-Louis!*" exclaimed Georges. "When he crammed us just now about his Orders, I fancied him better fun than he is," he went on in a low voice to the painter; "but we will get him on to that subject again—the little tallow-chandler.—Come, boy," said he to Oscar, "drink the glass that was poured out for the grocer, it will make your moustache grow."

Oscar, anxious to play the man, drank the second glass of wine, and ate three more cheese-cakes.

"Very good wine it is!" said old Léger, smacking his tongue.

"And all the better," remarked Georges, "because it comes from Bercy. I have been to Alicante, and, I tell you, this is no more like the wine of that country than my arm is like a windmill. Our manufactured wines are far better than the natural products.—Come, Pierrotin, have a glass. What a pity it is that your horses cannot each drink one; we should get on faster!"

A START IN LIFE

"Oh, that is unnecessary, as I have a gray horse already," said Pierrotin (*gris,* which means gray, meaning also *screwed*).

Oscar, as he heard the vulgar pun, thought Pierrotin a marvel of wit.

"Off!" cried Pierrotin, cracking his whip as soon as the passengers had once more packed themselves into the vehicle.

It was by this time eleven o'clock. The weather, which had been rather dull, now cleared; the wind swept away the clouds; the blue sky shone out here and there; and by the time Pierrotin's chaise was fairly started on the ribbon of road between Saint-Denis and Pierrefitte, the sun had finally drunk up the last filmy haze that hung like a diaphanous veil over the views from this famous suburb.

"Well, and why did you throw over your friend the Pasha?" said the farmer to Georges.

"He was a very queer customer," replied Georges, with an air of hiding many mysteries. "Only think, he put me in command of his cavalry! Very well——"

"That," thought poor Oscar, "is why he wears spurs."

"At that time, Ali of Tebelen wanted to rid himself of Chosrew Pasha, another queer fish.—Chaureff you call him here, but in Turkey they call him Cosserev. You must have read in the papers at the time that old Ali had beaten Chosrew, and pretty soundly too. Well, but for me, Ali would have been done for some days sooner. I led the right wing, and I saw Chosrew, the old sneak, just charging the centre—oh, yes, I can tell you, as straight and steady a move as if he had been Murat.—Good! I took my time, and I charged at full speed, cutting Chosrew's column in two parts, for he had pushed through our centre, and had no cover. You understand——

"After it was all over Ali fairly hugged me."

"Is that the custom in the East?" said the Comte de Sérizy, with a touch of irony.

"Yes, monsieur, as it is everywhere," answered the painter.

"We drove Chosrew back over thirty leagues of country—

like a hunt, I tell you," Georges went on. "Splendid horsemen are the Turks. Ali gave me yataghans, guns, and swords.—'Take as many as you like.'—When we got back to the capital, that incredible creature made proposals to me that did not suit my views at all. He wanted to adopt me as his favorite, his heir. But I had had enough of the life; for, after all, Ali of Tebelen was a rebel against the Porte, and I thought it wiser to clear out. But I must do Monsieur de Tebelen justice, he loaded me with presents; diamonds, ten thousand talari, a thousand pieces of gold, a fair Greek girl for a page, a little Arnaute maid for company, and an Arab horse. Well, there! Ali, the Pasha of Janina, is an unappreciated man; he lacks a historian.—Nowhere but in the East do you meet with these iron souls who, for twenty years, strain every nerve, only to be able to take a revenge one fine morning.

"In the first place, he had the grandest white beard you ever saw, and a hard, stern face———"

"But what became of your treasure?" asked the farmer.

"Ah! there you are! Those people have no State funds nor Bank of France; so I packed my money-bags on board a Greek tartane, which was captured by the Capitan-Pasha himself. Then I myself, as you see me, was within an ace of being impaled at Smyrna. Yes, on my honor, but for Monsieur de Rivière, the Ambassador, who happened to be on the spot, I should have been executed as an ally of Ali Pasha's. I saved my head, or I could not speak so plainly; but as for the ten thousand talari, the thousand pieces of gold, and the weapons, oh! that was all swallowed down by that greedy-guts the Capitan-Pasha. My position was all the more ticklish because the Capitan-Pasha was Chosrew himself. After the dressing he had had, the scamp hàd got this post, which is that of High Admiral in France."

"But he had been in the cavalry, as I understood?" said old Léger, who had been listening attentively to this long story.

"That shows how little the East is understood in the Department of Seine-et-Oise!" exclaimed Georges. "Monsieur, the Turks are like that.—You are a farmer, the Padischah makes you a Field-Marshal; if you do not fulfil your duties to his satisfaction, so much the worse for you. Off with your head! That is his way of dismissing you. A gardener is made préfet, and a prime minister is a private once more. The Ottomans know no laws of promotion or hierarchy.—Chosrew, who had been a horseman, was now a sailor. The Padischah Mohammed had instructed him to fall on Ali by sea; and he had, in fact, mastered him, but only by the help of the English, who got the best of the booty, the thieves! They laid hands on the treasure.

"This Chosrew, who had not forgotten the riding-lesson I had given him, recognized me at once. As you may suppose, I was settled—oh! done for!—if it had not occurred to me to appeal, as a Frenchman and a Troubadour, to Monsieur de Rivière. The Ambassador, delighted to assert himself, demanded my release. The Turks have this great merit, they are as ready to let you go as to cut off your head; they are indifferent to everything. The French consul, a charming man, and a friend of Chosrew's, got him to restore two thousand talari, and his name, I may say, is graven on my heart——"

"And his name——?" asked Monsieur de Sérizy.

He could not forbear a look of surprise when Georges, in fact, mentioned the name of one of our most distinguished Consuls-General, who was at Smyrna at the time.

"I was present, as it fell out, at the execution of the Commandant of Smyrna, the Padischah having ordered Chosrew to put him to death—one of the most curious things I ever saw, though I have seen many. I will tell you all about it by and by at breakfast.

"From Smyrna I went to Spain, on hearing there was a revolution there. I went straight to Mina, who took me for an aide-de-camp, and gave me the rank of Colonel. So I fought for the Constitutional party, which is going to the dogs, for we shall walk into Spain one of these days."

"And you a French officer!" said the Comte de Sérizy severely. "You are trusting very rashly to the discretion of your hearers."

"There are no spies among them," said Georges.

"And does it not occur to you, Colonel Georges," said the Count, "that at this very time a conspiracy is being inquired into by the Chamber of Peers, which makes the Government very strict in its dealings with soldiers who bear arms against France, or who aid in intrigues abroad tending to the overthrow of any legitimate sovereign?"

At this ominous remark, the painter reddened up to his ears, and glanced at Mistigris, who was speechless.

"Well, and what then?" asked old Léger.

"Why, if I by chance were a magistrate, would it not be my duty to call on the gendarmes of the Brigade at Pierrefitte to arrest Mina's aide-de-camp," said the Count, "and to summons all who are in this chaise as witnesses?"

This speech silenced Georges all the more effectually because the vehicle was just passing the Gendarmerie Station, where the white flag was, to use a classical phrase, floating on the breeze.

"You have too many Orders to be guilty of such mean conduct," said Oscar.

"We will play him a trick yet," whispered Georges to Oscar.

"Colonel," said Léger, very much discomfited by the Count's outburst, and anxious to change the subject, "in the countries where you have traveled, what is the farming like? What are their crops in rotation?"

"In the first place, my good friend, you must understand that the people are too busy smoking weeds to burn them on the land——"

The Count could not help smiling, and his smile reassured the narrator.

"And they have a way of cultivating the land which you will think strange. They do not cultivate it all; that is their system. The Turks and Greeks eat onions or rice; they collect opium from their poppies, which yields a large revenue, and tobacco grows almost wild—their famous Latakia. Then there are dates, bunches of sugar-plums, that grow without any trouble. It is a country of endless resources and trade. Quantities of carpets are made at Smyrna, and not dear."

"Ay," said the farmer, "but if the carpets are made of wool, wool comes from sheep; and to have sheep they must have fields, farms, and farming——"

"There must, no doubt, be something of the kind," replied Georges. "But rice, in the first place, grows in water; and then I have always been near the coast, and have only seen the country devastated by war. Besides, I have a perfect horror of statistics."

"And the taxes?" said the farmer.

"Ah! the taxes are heavy. The people are robbed of everything, and allowed to keep the rest. The Pasha of Egypt, struck by the merits of this system, was organizing the Administration on that basis when I left."

"But how?" said old Léger, who was utterly puzzled.

"How?" echoed Georges. "There are collectors who seize the crops, leaving the peasants just enough to live on. And by that system there is no trouble with papers and red tape, the plague of France.—There you are!"

"But what right have they to do it?" asked the farmer.

"It is the land of despotism, that's all. Did you never hear Montesquieu's fine definition of Despotism—'Like the savage, it cuts the tree down to gather the fruit.'"

"And that is what they want to bring us back to!" cried Mistigris. "But a burnt rat dreads the mire."

"And it is what we shall come to," exclaimed the Comte de Sérizy. "Those who hold land will be wise to sell it. Monsieur Schinner must have seen how such things are done in Italy."

"*Corpo di Bacco!* The Pope is not behind his times. But they are used to it there. The Italians are such good people! So long as they are allowed to do a little highway murdering of travelers, they are quite content."

"But you, too, do not wear the ribbon of the Legion of

Honor that was given you in 1819," remarked the Count. "Is the fashion universal?"

Mistigris and the false Schinner reddened up to their hair.

"Oh, with me it is different," replied Schinner. "I do not wish to be recognized. Do not betray me, monsieur. I mean to pass for a quite unimportant painter; in fact, a mere decorator. I am going to a gentleman's house where I am anxious to excite no suspicion."

"Oh, ho!" said the Count, "a lady! a love affair!—How happy you are to be young!"

Oscar, who was bursting in his skin with envy at being nobody and having nothing to say, looked from Colonel Czerni-Georges to Schinner the great artist, wondering whether he could not make something of himself. But what could he be, a boy of nineteen, packed off to spend a fortnight or three weeks in the country with the steward of Presles? The Alicante had gone to his head, and his conceit was making the blood boil in his veins. Thus, when the sham Schinner seemed to hint at some romantic adventure of which the joys must be equal to the danger, he gazed at him with eyes flashing with rage and envy.

"Ah!" said the Count, with a look half of envy and half of incredulity, "you must love a woman very much to make such sacrifices for her sake."

"What sacrifices?" asked Mistigris.

"Don't you know, my little friend, that a ceiling painted by so great a master is covered with gold in payment?" replied the Count. "Why, if the Civil List pays you thirty thousand francs for those of the two rooms in the Louvre," he went on, turning to Schinner, "you would certainly charge a humble individual, a *bourgeois,* as you call us in your studios, twenty thousand for a ceiling, while an unknown decorator would hardly get two thousand francs."

"The money loss is not the worst of it," replied Mistigris. "You must consider that it will be a masterpiece, and that he must not sign it for fear of compromising *her.*"

"Ah! I would gladly restore all my orders to the sovereigns

of Europe to be loved as a young man must be, to be moved to such devotion!" cried Monsieur de Sérizy.

"Ay, there you are," said Mistigris. "A man who is young is beloved of many women; and, as the saying goes, there is safety in grumblers."

"And what does Madame Schinner say to it?" asked the Count, "for you married for love the charming Adélaïde de Rouville, the niece of old Admiral Kergarouët, who got you the work at the Louvre, I believe, through the interest of his nephew the Comte de Fontaine."

"Is a painter ever a married man when he is traveling?" asked Mistigris.

"That, then, is Studio morality?" exclaimed the Count in an idiotic way.

"Is the morality of the Courts where you got your Orders any better?" said Schinner, who had recovered his presence of mind, which had deserted him for a moment when he heard that the Count was so well informed as to the commission given to the real Schinner.

"I never asked for one," replied the Count. "I flatter myself that they were all honestly earned."

"And it becomes you like a pig in dress-boots," said Mistigris.

Monsieur de Sérizy would not betray himself; he put on an air of stupid good-nature as he looked out over the valley of Groslay, into which they diverged where the roads fork, taking the road to Saint-Brice, and leaving that to Chantilly on their right.

"Ay, take that!" said Oscar between his teeth.

"And is Rome as fine as it is said to be?" Georges asked of the painter.

"Rome is fine only to those who love it; you must have a passion for it to be happy there; but, as a town, I prefer Venice, though I was near being assassinated there."

"My word! But for me," said Mistigris, "your goose would have been cooked! It was that rascal Lord Byron who played you that trick. That devil of an Englishman was as mad as a hatter!"

"Hold your tongue," said Schinner. "I won't have anything known of my affair with Lord Byron."

"But you must confess," said Mistigris, "that you were very glad that I had learned to 'box' in our French fashion?"

Now and again Pierrotin and the Count exchanged significant glances, which would have disturbed men a little more worldly-wise than these five fellow-travelers.

"Lords and pashas, and ceilings worth thirty thousand francs! Bless me!" cried the l'Isle-Adam carrier, "I have crowned heads on board to-day. What handsome tips I shall get!"

"To say nothing of the places being paid for," said Mistigris slily.

"It comes in the nick of time," Pierrotin went on. "For, you know, my fine new coach, Père Léger, for which I paid two thousand francs on account—well, those swindling coach-builders, to whom I am to pay two thousand five hundred francs to-morrow, would not take fifteen hundred francs down and a bill for a thousand at two months.—The vultures insist on it all in ready money. Fancy being as hard as that on a man who has traveled this road for eight years, the father of a family, and putting him in danger of losing everything, money and coach both, for lack of a wretched sum of a thousand francs!—Gee up, Bichette.—They would not dare do it to one of the big companies, I lay a wager."

"Bless me! No thong, no crupper!" said the student.

"You have only eight hundred francs to seek," replied the Count, understanding that this speech addressed to the farmer was a sort of bill drawn on himself.

"That's true," said Pierrotin. "Come up, Rougeot!"

"You must have seen some fine-painted ceilings at Venice," said the Count, speaking to Schinner.

"I was too desperately in love to pay any attention to what at the time seemed to me mere trifles," replied Schinner. "And yet I might have been cured of love-affairs; for in the

Venetian States themselves, in Dalmatia, I had just had a sharp lesson."

"Can you tell the tale?" asked Georges. "I know Dalmatia."

"Well, then, if you have been there, you know, of course, that up in that corner of the Adriatic they are all old pirates, outlaws, and corsairs retired from business, when they have escaped hanging, all——"

"Uscoques, in short," said Georges.

On hearing this, the right name, the Count, whom Napoleon had sent into the provinces of Illyria, looked sharply round, so much was he astonished.

"It was in the town where the Maraschino is made," said Schinner, seeming to try to remember a name.

"Zara," said Georges. "Yes, I have been there; it is on the coast."

"You have hit it," said the painter. "I went there to see the country, for I have a passion for landscape. Twenty times have I made up my mind to try landscape painting, which no one understands, in my opinion, but Mistigris, who will one of these days be a Hobbema, Ruysdael, Claude Lorraine, Poussin, and all the tribe in one."

"Well," exclaimed the Count, "if he is but one of them, he will do."

"If you interrupt so often, we shall never know where we are."

"Besides, our friend here is not speaking to you," added Georges to the Count.

"It is not good manners to interrupt," said Mistigris sententiously. "However, we did the same; and we should all be the losers if we didn't diversify the conversation by an exchange of reflections. All Frenchmen are equal in a public chaise, as the grandson of Czerni-Georges told us.—So pray go on, delightful old man, more of your bunkum. It is quite the correct thing in the best society; and you know the saying, Do in Turkey as the Turkeys do."

"I had heard wonders of Dalmatia," Schinner went on. "So off I went, leaving Mistigris at the inn at Venice."

"At the *locanda*," said Mistigris; "put in the local color."

"Zara is, as I have been told, a vile hole——"

"Yes," said Georges; "but it is fortified."

"I should say so!" replied Schinner, "and the fortifications are an important feature in my story. At Zara there are a great many apothecaries, and I lodged with one of them. In foreign countries the principal business of every native is to let lodgings, his trade is purely accessory.

"In the evening, when I had changed my shirt, I went out on my balcony. Now on the opposite balcony I perceived a woman—oh! But a woman! A Greek; that says everything, the loveliest creature in all the town. Almond eyes, eyelids that came down over them like blinds, and lashes like paintbrushes; an oval face that might have turned Raphael's brain, a complexion of exquisite hue, melting tones, a skin of velvet, —hands—oh!"

"And not moulded in butter like those of David's school," said Mistigris.

"You insist on talking like a painter!" cried Georges.

"There, you see! drive nature out with a pitchfork and it comes back in a paint-box," replied Mistigris.

"And her costume—a genuine Greek costume," Schinner went on. "As you may suppose, I was in flames. I questioned my Diafoirus, and he informed me that my fair neighbor's name was Zéna. I changed my shirt. To marry Zéna, her husband, an old villain, had paid her parents three hundred thousand francs, the girl's beauty was so famous; and she really was the loveliest creature in all Dalmatia, Illyria, and the Adriatic.—In that part of the world you buy your wife, and without having seen her——"

"I will not go there," said old Léger.

"My sleep, some nights, is illuminated by Zéna's eyes," said Schinner. "Her adoring young husband was sixty-seven. Good! But he was as jealous—not as a tiger, for they say a tiger is as jealous as a Dalmatian, and my man was worse than a Dalmatian; he was equal to three Dalmatians and a half. He was an Uscoque, a turkey-cock, a high cockalorum game-cock!"

"In short, the worthy hero of a cock-and-bull story," said Mistigris.

"Good for you!" replied Georges, laughing.

"After being a corsair, and perhaps a pirate, my man thought no more of spitting a Christian than I do of spitting out of window," Schinner went on. "A pretty lookout for me. And rich—rolling in millions, the old villain! And as ugly as a pirate may be, for some Pasha had wanted his ears, and he had dropped an eye somewhere on his travels. But my Uscoque made good use of the one he had, and you may take my word for it when I tell you he had eyes all round his head. 'Never does he let his wife out of his sight,' said my little Diafoirus.—'If she should require your services, I would take your place in disguise,' said I. 'It is a trick that is very successful in our stage-plays.'—It would take too long to describe the most delightful period of my life, three days, to wit, that I spent at my window ogling Zéna, and putting on a clean shirt every morning. The situation was all the more ticklish and exciting because the least gesture bore some dangerous meaning. Finally, Zéna, no doubt, came to the conclusion that in all the world none but a foreigner, a Frenchman, and an artist would be capable of making eyes at her in the midst of the perils that surrounded him; so, as she execrated her hideous pirate, she responded to my gaze with glances that were enough to lift a man into the vault of Paradise without any need of pulleys. I was screwed up higher and higher! I was tuned to the pitch of Don Quixote. At last I exclaimed, 'Well, the old wretch may kill me, but here goes!'—Not a landscape did I study; I was studying my corsair's lair. At night, having put on my most highly scented clean shirt, I crossed the street and I went in——"

"Into the house?" said Oscar.

"Into the house?" said Georges.

"Into the house," repeated Schinner.

"Well! you are as bold as brass!" cried the farmer. "I wouldn't have gone, that's all I can say——"

"With all the more reason that you would have stuck in the door," replied Schinner. "Well, I went in," he continued, "and I felt two hands which took hold of mine. I said nothing; for those hands, as smooth as the skin of an onion, impressed silence on me. A whisper in my ear said in Venetian, 'He is asleep.' Then, being sure that no one would meet us, Zéna and I went out on the ramparts for an airing, but escorted, if you please, by an old duenna as ugly as sin, who stuck to us like a shadow; and I could not induce Madame la Pirate to dismiss this ridiculous attendant.

"Next evening we did the same; I wanted to send the old woman home; Zéna refused. As my fair one spoke Greek, and I spoke Venetian, we could come to no understanding— we parted in anger. Said I to myself, as I changed my shirt, 'Next time surely there will be no old woman, and we can make friends again, each in our mother tongue.'—Well, and it was the old woman that saved me, as you shall hear.—It was so fine that, to divert suspicion, I went out to look about me, after we had made it up, of course. After walking round the ramparts, I was coming quietly home with my hands in my pockets when I saw the street packed full of people. Such a crowd!—as if there was an execution. This crowd rushed at me. I was arrested, handcuffed, and led off in charge of the police. No, you cannot imagine, and I hope you may never know, what it is to be supposed to be a murderer by a frenzied mob, throwing stones at you, yelling after you from top to bottom of the high street of a country town, and pursuing you with threats of death! Every eye is a flame of fire, abuse is on every lip, these firebrands of loathing flare up above a hideous cry of 'Kill him! down with the murderer!'—a sort of bass in the background."

"So your Dalmatians yelled in French?" said the Count "You describe the scene as if it had happened yesterday."

Schinner was for the moment dumfounded.

"The mob speaks the same language everywhere," said **Mistigris** the politician.

"Finally," Schinner went on again, "when I was in the local Court of Justice and in the presence of the judges of that country, I was informed that the diabolical corsair was dead, poisoned by Zéna.—How I wished I could put on a clean shirt!

"On my soul, I knew nothing about this melodrama. It would seem that the fair Greek was wont to add a little opium—poppies are so plentiful there, as monsieur has told you—to her pirate's grog to secure a few minutes' liberty to take a walk, and the night before the poor woman had made a mistake in the dose. It was the damned corsair's money that made the trouble for my Zéna; but she accounted for everything so simply, that I was released at once on the strength of the old woman's affidavit, with an order from the Mayor of the town and the Austrian Commissioner of Police to remove myself to Rome. Zéna, who allowed the heirs and the officers of the law to help themselves liberally to the Uscoque's wealth, was let off, I was told, with two years' seclusion in a convent, where she still is.—I will go back and paint her portrait, for in a few years everything will be forgotten.—And these are the follies of eighteen!"

"Yes, and you left me without a sou in the *locanda* at Venice," said Mistigris. "I made my way from Venice to Rome, to see if I could find you, by daubing portraits at five francs a head, and never got paid; but it was a jolly time! Happiness, they say, does not dwell under gilt hoofs."

"You may imagine the reflections that choked me with bile in a Dalmatian prison, thrown there without a protector, having to answer to the Dalmatian Austrians, and threatened with the loss of my head for having twice taken a walk with a woman who insisted on being followed by her housekeeper. That is what I call bad luck!" cried Schinner.

"What," said Oscar guilelessly, "did that happen to you?"

"Why not to this gentleman, since it had already happened during the French occupation of Illyria to one of our most distinguished artillery officers?" said the Count with meaning.

"And did you believe the artillery man?" asked Mistigris slily.

"And is that all?" asked Oscar.

"Well," said Mistigris, "he cannot tell you that he had his head cut off. Those who live last live longest."

"And are there any farms out there?" asked old Léger. "What do they grow there?"

"There is the Maraschino crop," said Mistigris. "A plant that grows just as high as your lips and yields the liqueur of that name."

"Ah!" said Léger.

"I was only three days in the town and a fortnight in prison," replied Schinner. "I saw nothing, not even the fields where they grow the Maraschino."

"They are making game of you," said Georges to the farmer. "Maraschino grows in cases."

Pierrotin's chaise was now on the way down one of the steep sides of the valley of Saint-Brice, towards the inn in the middle of that large village, where he was to wait an hour to let the horses take breath, eat their oats, and get a drink. It was now about half-past one.

"Hallo! It is farmer Léger!" cried the innkeeper, as the vehicle drew up at his door. "Do you take breakfast?"

"Once every day," replied the burly customer. "We can eat a snack."

"Order breakfast for us," said Georges, carrying his cane as if he were shouldering a musket, in a cavalier style that bewitched Oscar.

Oscar felt a pang of frenzy when he saw this reckless adventurer take a fancy straw cigar-case out of his side pocket, and from it a beautiful tan-colored cigar, which he smoked in the doorway while waiting for the meal.

"Do you smoke?" said Georges to Oscar.

"Sometimes," said the schoolboy, puffing out his little chest and assuming a dashing style.

Georges held out the open cigar-case to Oscar and to Schinner.

"The devil!" said the great painter. "Ten-sous cigars!"

"The remains of what I brought from Spain," said the adventurer. "Are you going to have breakfast?"

"No," said the artist. "They will wait for me at the château. Besides, I had some food before starting."

"And you," said Georges to Oscar.

"I have had breakfast," said Oscar.

Oscar would have given ten years of his life to have boots and trouser-straps. He stood sneezing, and choking, and spitting, and sucking up the smoke with ill-disguised grimaces.

"You don't know how to smoke," said Schinner. "Look here," and Schinner, without moving a muscle, drew in the smoke of his cigar and blew it out through his nose without the slightest effort. Then again he kept the smoke in his throat, took the cigar out of his mouth, and exhaled it gracefully.

"There, young man," said the painter.

"And this, young man, is another way," said Georges, imitating Schinner, but swallowing the smoke so that none returned.

"And my parents fancy that I am educated," thought poor Oscar, trying to smoke with a grace. But he felt so mortally sick that he allowed Mistigris to bone his cigar and to say, as he puffed at it with conspicuous satisfaction:

"I suppose you have nothing catching."

But Oscar wished he were only strong enough to hit Mistigris.

"Why," said he, pointing to Colonel Georges, "eight francs for Alicante and cheese-cakes, forty sous in cigars, and his breakfast, which will cost——"

"Ten francs at least," said Mistigris. "But so it is, little dishes make long bills."

"Well, Père Léger, we can crack a bottle of Bordeaux apiece?" said Georges to the farmer.

"His breakfast will cost him twenty francs," cried Oscar. "Why, that comes to more than thirty francs!"

Crushed by the sense of his inferiority, Oscar sat down on

the corner-stone lost in a reverie, which hindered his observing that his trousers, hitched up as he sat, showed the line of union between an old stocking-leg and a new foot to it, a masterpiece of his mother's skill.

"Our understandings are twins, if not our souls," said Mistigris, pulling one leg of his trousers a little way up to show a similar effect. "But a baker's children are always worst bread."

The jest made Monsieur de Sérizy smile as he stood with folded arms under the gateway behind the two lads. Heedless as they were, the solemn statesman envied them their faults; he liked their bounce, and admired the quickness of their fun.

"Well, can you get les Moulineaux? for you went to Paris to fetch the money," said the innkeeper to old Léger, having just shown him a nag for sale in his stables. "It will be a fine joke to screw a bit out of the Comte de Sérizy, a peer of France and a State Minister."

The wily old courtier betrayed nothing in his face, but he looked round to watch the farmer.

"His goose is cooked!" replied Léger in a low voice.

"So much the better; I love to see your bigwigs done.—And if you want a score or so thousand francs, I will lend you the money. But François, the driver of Touchards' six o'clock coach, told me as he went through that Monsieur Margueron is invited to dine with the Comte de Sérizy himself to-day at Presles."

"That is His Excellency's plan, but we have our little notions too," replied the farmer.

"Ah, but the Count will find a place for Monsieur Margueron's son, and you have no places to give away," said the innkeeper.

"No, but if the Count has the Ministers on his side, I have King Louis XVIII. on mine," said Léger in the innkeeper's ear, "and forty thousand of his effigies handed over to Master Moreau will enable me to buy les Moulineaux for two hundred and sixty thousand francs before Monsieur de Sérizy can step in, and he will be glad enough to take it off my hands for three hundred and sixty thousand rather than have the lands valued lot by lot."

"Not a bad turn, master," said his friend.

"How is that for a stroke of business?" said the farmer.

"And, after all, the farm lands are worth it to him," said the innkeeper.

"Les Moulineaux pays six thousand francs a year in kind, and I mean to renew the lease at seven thousand five hundred for eighteen years. So as he invests at more than two and a half per cent, Monsieur le Comte won't be robbed.

"Not to commit Monsieur Moreau, I am to be proposed to the Count by him as a tenant; he will seem to be taking care of his master's interests by finding him nearly three per cent for his money and a farmer who will pay regularly——"

"And what will Moreau get out of the job altogether?"

"Well, if the Count makes him a present of ten thousand francs, he will clear fifty thousand on the transaction; but he will have earned them fairly."

"And, after all, what does the Count care for Presles? He is so rich," said the innkeeper. "I have never set eyes on him myself."

"Nor I neither," said the farmer. "But he is coming at last to live there; he would not otherwise be laying out two hundred thousand francs on redecorating the rooms. It is as fine as the King's palace."

"Well, then," replied the other, "it is high time that Moreau should feather his nest."

"Yes, yes; for when once the Master and Mis'ess are on the spot, they will not keep their eyes in their pockets."

Though the conversation was carried on in a low tone, the Count had kept his ears open.

"Here I have all the evidence I was going in search of," thought he, looking at the burly farmer as he went back into the kitchen. "But perhaps it is no more than a scheme as yet. Perhaps Moreau has not closed with the offer——!" So averse was he to believe that the land-steward was capable of mixing himself up in such a plot.

Pierrotin now came out to give his horses water. The Count supposed that the driver would breakfast with the innkeeper and Léger, and what he had overheard made him fear the least betrayal.

"The whole posse are in league," thought he; "it serves them right to thwart their scheming.—Pierrotin," said he in a low voice as he went up to the driver, "I promised you ten louis to keep my secret; but if you will take care not to let out my name—and I shall know whether you have mentioned it, or given the least clue to it, to any living soul, even at l'Isle-Adam—to-morrow morning, as you pass the château, I will give you the thousand francs to pay for your new coach.—And for greater safety," added he, slapping Pierrotin's back, "do without your breakfast; stay outside with your horses."

Pierrotin had turned pale with joy.

"I understand, Monsieur le Comte, trust me. It is old Père Léger——"

"It concerns every living soul," replied the Count.

"Be easy.—Come, hurry up," said Pierrotin, half opening the kitchen door, "we are late already. Listen, Père Léger, there is the hill before us, you know; I am not hungry; I will go on slowly, and you will easily catch me up.—A walk will do you good."

"The man is in a devil of a hurry!" said the innkeeper. "Won't you come and join us? The Colonel is standing wine at fifty sous, and a bottle of champagne."

"No, I can't. I have a fish on board to be delivered at Stors by three o'clock for a big dinner, and such customers don't see a joke any more than the fish."

"All right," said Léger to the innkeeper; "put the horse you want me to buy in the shafts of your gig, and you can drive us on to pick up Pierrotin. Then we can breakfast in peace, and I shall see what the nag can do. Three of us can very well ride in your trap."

To the Count's great satisfaction, Pierrotin himself brought out his horses. Schinner and Mistigris had walked forward.

Pierrotin picked up the two artists half-way between Saint-

Brice and Poncelles; and just as he reached the top of the hill, whence they had a view of Écouen, the belfry of le Mesnil, and the woods which encircle that beautiful landscape, the sound of a galloping horse drawing a gig that rattled and jingled announced the pursuit of Père Léger and Mina's Colonel, who settled themselves into the chaise again.

As Pierrotin zigzagged down the hill into Moisselles, Georges, who had never ceased expatiating to old Léger on the beauty of the innkeeper's wife at Saint-Brice, exclaimed:

"I say, this is not amiss by way of landscape, Great Painter?"

"It ought not to astonish you, who have seen Spain and the East."

"And I have two of the Spanish cigars left. If nobody objects, will you finish them off, Schinner? The little man had enough with a mouthful or two."

Old Léger and the Count kept silence, which was taken for consent.

Oscar, annoyed at being spoken of as "a little man," retorted while the others were lighting their cigars:

"Though I have not been Mina's aide-de-camp, monsieur, and have not been in the East, I may go there yet. The career for which my parents intend me will, I hope, relieve me of the necessity of riding in a public chaise when I am as old as you are. When once I am a person of importance, and get a place, I will stay in it——"

"*Et cetera punctum!*" said Mistigris, imitating the sort of hoarse crow which made Oscar's speech even more ridiculous; for the poor boy was at the age when the beard begins to grow and the voice to break. "After all," added Mistigris, "extremes bleat."

"My word!" said Schinner, "the horses can scarcely drag such a weight of dignity."

"So your parents intend to start you in a career," said Georges very seriously. "And what may it be?"

"In diplomacy," said Oscar.

Three shouts of laughter went forth like three rockets from

Mistigris, Schinner, and the old farmer. Even the Count could not help smiling. Georges kept his countenance.

"By Allah! But there is nothing to laugh at," said the Colonel. "Only, young man," he went on, addressing Oscar, "it struck me that your respectable mother is not for the moment in a social position wholly beseeming an ambassadress —She had a most venerable straw bag, and a patch on her shoe."

"My mother, monsieur!" said Oscar, fuming with indignation. "It was our housekeeper."

"'Our' is most aristocratic!" cried the Count, interrupting Oscar.

"The King says *our*," replied Oscar haughtily.

A look from Georges checked a general burst of laughter; it conveyed to the painter and to Mistigris the desirability of dealing judiciously with Oscar, so as to make the most of this mine of amusement.

"The gentleman is right," said the painter to the Count, designating Oscar. "Gentlefolks talk of *our* house; only second-rate people talk of my house. Everybody has a mania for seeming to have what he has not. For a man loaded with decorations——"

"Then monsieur also is a decorator?" asked Mistigris.

"You know nothing of Court language.—I beg the favor of your protection, your Excellency," added Schinner, turnto Oscar.

"I must congratulate myself," said the Count, "on having traveled with three men who are or will be famous—a painter who is already illustrious, a future general, and a young diplomatist who will some day reunite Belgium to France."

But Oscar, having so basely denied his mother, and furious at perceiving that his companions were making game of him, determined to convince their incredulity at any cost.

"All is not gold that glitters!" said he, flashing lightnings from his eyes.

"You've got it wrong," cried Mistigris. "All is not told that titters. You will not go far in diplomacy if you do not know your proverbs better than that."

A START IN LIFE

"If I do not know my proverbs, I know my way."

"It must be leading you a long way," said Georges, "for your family housekeeper gave you provisions enough for a sea voyage—biscuits, chocolate——"

"A particular roll and some chocolate, yes, monsieur," returned Oscar. "My stomach is much too delicate to digest the cagmag you get at an inn."

"'Cagmag' is as delicate as your digestion," retorted Georges.

"'Cagmag' is good!" said the great painter.

"The word is in use in the best circles," said Mistigris; "I use it myself at the coffee-house of the *Poule Noire*."

"Your tutor was, no doubt, some famous professor—Monsieur Andrieux of the Academy, or Monsieur Royer-Collard?" asked Schinner.

"My tutor was the Abbé Loraux, now the Vicar of St. Sulpice," replied Oscar, remembering the name of the confessor of the school.

"You did very wisely to have a private tutor," said Mistigris, "for the fountain—of learning—brought forth a mouse; and you will do something for your Abbé, of course?"

"Certainly; he will be a bishop some day."

"Through your family interest?" asked Georges quite gravely.

"We may perhaps contribute to his due promotion, for the Abbé Frayssinous often comes to our house."

"Oh, do you know the Abbé Frayssinous?" asked the Count.

"He is under obligations to my father," replied Oscar.

"And you are on your way to your estates no doubt?" said Georges.

"No, monsieur; but I have no objection to saying where I am going. I am on my way to the château of Presles, the Comte de Sérizy's."

"The devil you are! To Presles?" cried Shinner, turning crimson.

"Then you know Monseigneur the Comte de Sérizy?" asked Georges.

Farmer Léger turned so as to look at Oscar with a bewildered gaze, exclaiming:

"And Monsieur le Comte is at Presles?"

"So it would seem, as I am going there," replied Oscar.

"Then you have often seen the Count?" asked Monsieur de Sérizy.

"As plainly as I see you. I am great friends with his son, who is about my age, nineteen; and we ride together almost every day."

"Kings have been known to harry beggar-maids," said Mistigris sapiently.

A wink from Pierrotin had relieved the farmer's alarm.

"On my honor," said the Count to Oscar, "I am delighted to find myself in the company of a young gentleman who can speak with authority of that nobleman. I am anxious to secure his favor in a somewhat important business in which his help will cost him nothing. It is a little claim against the American Government. I should be glad to learn something as to the sort of man he is."

"Oh, if you hope to succeed," replied Oscar, with an assumption of competence, "do not apply to him, but to his wife; he is madly in love with her, no one knows that better than I, and his wife cannot endure him."

"Why," asked Georges.

"The Count has some skin disease that makes him hideous, and Doctor Alibert has tried in vain to cure it. Monsieur de Sérizy would give half of his immense fortune to have a chest like mine," said Oscar, opening his shirt and showing a clean pink skin like a child's. "He lives alone, secluded in his house. You need a good introduction to see him at all. In the first place, he gets up very early in the morning, and works from three till eight, after eight he follows various treatments, sulphur baths or vapor baths. They stew him in a sort of iron tank, for he is always hoping to be cured."

"If he is so intimate with the King, why is he not 'touched' by him?" asked Georges.

"Then the lady keeps her husband in hot water," said Mistigris.

"The Count has promised thirty thousand francs to a famous Scotch physician who is prescribing for him now," Oscar went on.

"Then his wife can hardly be blamed for giving herself the best——" Schinner began, but he did not finish his sentence.

"To be sure," said Oscar. "The poor man is so shriveled up, so decrepit, you would think he was eighty. He is as dry as parchment, and to add to his misfortune, he feels his position——"

"And feels it hot, I should think," remarked the farmer facetiously.

"Monsieur, he worships his wife, and dares not blame her," replied Oscar. "He performs the most ridiculous scenes with her, you would die of laughing—exactly like Arnolphe in Molière's play."

The Count, in blank dismay, looked at Pierrotin, who seeing him apparently unmoved, concluded that Madame Clapart's son was inventing a pack of slander.

"So, monsieur, if you wish to succeed," said Oscar to the Count, "apply to the Marquis d'Aiglemont. If you have madame's venerable adorer on your side, you will at one stroke secure both the lady and her husband."

"That is what we call killing two-thirds with one bone," said Mistigris.

"Dear me!" said the painter, "have you seen the Count undressed? Are you his valet?"

"His valet!" cried Oscar.

"By the Mass! A man does not say such things about his friends in a public conveyance," added Mistigris. "Discretion, my young friend, is the mother of inattention. I simply don't hear you."

"It is certainly a case of tell me whom you know, and I will tell you whom you hate," exclaimed Schinner.

"But you must learn, Great Painter," said Georges pompously, "that no man can speak ill of those he does not know. The boy has proved at any rate that he knows his Sérizy by heart. Now, if he had only talked of Madame, it might have been supposed that he was on terms——"

"Not another word about the Comtesse de Sérizy, young men!" cried the Count. "Her brother, the Marquis de Ronquerolles, is a friend of mine, and the man who is so rash as to cast a doubt on the Countess' honor will answer to me for his speech."

"Monsieur is right," said the artist, "there should be no humbug about women."

"God, Honor, and the Ladies! I saw a melodrama of that name," said Mistigris.

"Though I do not know Mina, I know the Keeper of the Seals," said the Count, looking at Georges. "And though I do not display my Orders," he added, turning to the painter, "I can hinder their being given to those who do not deserve them. In short, I know so many people, that I know Monsieur Grindot, the architect of Presles.—Stop, Pierrotin; I am going to get out."

Pierrotin drove on to the village of Moisselles, and there, at a little country inn, the travelers alighted. This bit of road was passed in utter silence.

"Where on earth is that little rascal going?" asked the Count, leading Pierrotin into the inn-yard.

"To stay with your steward. He is the son of a poor lady who lives in the Rue de la Cerisaie, and to whom I often carry fruit and game and poultry—a certain Madame Husson."

"Who is that gentleman?" old Léger asked Pierrotin when the Count had turned away.

"I don't know," said Pierrotin. "He never rode with me before; but he may be the Prince who owns the château of Maffliers. He has just told me where to set him down on the road; he is not going so far as l'Isle-Adam."

"Pierrotin fancies he is the owner of Maffliers," said the farmer to Georges, getting back into the chaise.

At this stage the three young fellows, looking as silly as pilferers caught in the act, did not dare meet each other's eye, and seemed lost in reflections on the upshot of their fictions.

"That is what I call a great lie and little wool," observed Mistigris.

"You see, I know the Count," said Oscar.

"Possibly, but you will never be an ambassador," replied Georges. "If you must talk in a public carriage, learn to talk like me and tell nothing."

"The mother of mischief is no more than a midge's sting," said Mistigris, conclusively.

The Count now got into the chaise, and Pierrotin drove on; perfect silence reigned.

"Well, my good friends," said the Count, as they reached the wood of Carreau, "we are all as mute as if we were going to execution."

"A man should know that silence is a bold 'un," said Mistigris with an air.

"It is a fine day," remarked Georges.

"What place is that?" asked Oscar, pointing to the château of Franconville, which shows so finely on the slope of the great forest of Saint-Martin.

"What!" said the Count, "you who have been so often to Presles, do not know Franconville when you see it?"

"Monsieur knows more of men than of houses," said Mistigris.

"A sucking diplomatist may sometimes be oblivious," exclaimed Georges.

"Remember my name!" cried Oscar in a fury, "it is Oscar Husson, and in ten years' time I shall be famous."

After this speech, pronounced with great bravado, Oscar huddled himself into his corner.

"Husson de—what?" asked Mistigris.

"A great family," replied the Count. "The Hussons de la Cerisaie. The gentleman was born at the foot of the Imperial throne."

Oscar blushed to the roots of his hair in an agony of alarm. They were about to descend the steep hill by la Cave, at the bottom of which, in a narrow valley, on the skirt of the forest of Saint-Martin, stands the splendid château of Presles.

"Gentlemen," said Monsieur de Sérizy, "I wish you well in your several careers. You, Monsieur le Colonel, make your peace with the King of France; the Czerni-Georges must be on good terms with the Bourbons.—I have no forecast for you, my dear Monsieur Schinner; your fame is already made, and you have won it nobly by splendid work. But you are such a dangerous man that I, who have a wife, should not dare to offer you a commission under my roof.—As to Monsieur Husson, he needs no interest; he is the master of statesmen's secrets, and can make them tremble.—Monsieur Léger is going to steal a march on the Comte de Sérizy; I only hope that he may hold his own.—Put me down here, Pierrotin, and you can take me up at the same spot to-morrow!" added the Count, who got out, leaving his fellow-travelers quite confounded.

"When you take to your heels you can't take too much," remarked Mistigris, seeing how nimbly the traveler vanished in a sunken path.

"Oh, he must be the Count who has taken Franconville; he is going that way," said Père Léger.

"If ever again I try to humbug in a public carriage I will call myself out," said the false Schinner. "It is partly your fault too, Mistigris," said he, giving his boy a rap on his cap.

"Oh, ho! I—who only followed you to Venice," replied Mistigris. "But play a dog a bad game and slang him."

"Do you know," said Georges to Oscar, "that if by any chance that was the Comte de Sérizy, I should be sorry to find myself in your skin, although it is so free from disease."

Oscar, reminded by these words of his mother's advice, turned pale, and was quite sobered.

"Here you are, gentlemen," said Pierrotin, pulling up at a handsome gate.

"What, already?" exclaimed the painter, Georges, and Oscar all in a breath.

"That's a stiff one!" cried Pierrotin. "Do you mean to say, gentlemen, that neither of you has ever been here before? —There stands the château of Presles!"

"All right," said Georges, recovering himself. "I am going on to the farm of les Moulineaux," he added, not choosing to tell his fellow-travelers that he was bound for the house.

"Then you are coming with me," said Léger.

"How is that?"

"I am the farmer at les Moulineaux. And what do you want of me, Colonel?"

"A taste of your butter," said Georges, pulling out his portfolio.

"Pierrotin, drop my things at the steward's," said Oscar; "I am going straight to the house." And he plunged into a cross-path without knowing whither it led.

"Hallo! Mr. Ambassador," cried Pierrotin, "you are going into the forest. If you want to get to the château, go in by the side gate."

Thus compelled to go in, Oscar made his way into the spacious courtyard with a huge stone-edged flower-bed in the middle, and stone posts all round with chains between. While Père Léger stood watching Oscar, Georges, thunderstruck at hearing the burly farmer describe himself as the owner of les Moulineaux, vanished so nimbly that when the fat man looked round for his Colonel, he could not find him.

At Pierrotin's request the gate was opened, and he went in with much dignity to deposit the Great Schinner's multifarious properties at the lodge. Oscar was in dismay at seeing Mistigris and the artist, the witnesses of his brag, really admitted to the château.

In ten minutes Pierrotin had unloaded the chaise of the painter's paraphernalia, Oscar Husson's luggage, and the neat leather portmanteau, which he mysteriously confided to the lodge-keeper. Then he turned his machine, cracking his whip energetically, and went on his way to the woods of l'Isle-Adam, his face still wearing the artful expression of a peasant summing up his profits.

Nothing was wanting to his satisfaction. On the morrow he would have his thousand francs.

Oscar, with his tail between his legs, so to speak, wandered round the great court, waiting to see what would become of his traveling companions, when he presently saw Monsieur Moreau come out of the large entrance-hall, known as the guardroom, on to the front steps. The land-steward, who wore a long blue riding-coat down to his heels, had on nankin-colored breeches and hunting-boots, and carried a crop in his hand.

"Well, my boy, so here you are? And how is the dear mother?" said he, shaking hands with Oscar. "Good-morning, gentlemen; you, no doubt, are the painters promised us by Monsieur Grindot the architect?" said he to the artists.

He whistled twice, using the end of his riding-whip, and the lodge-keeper came forward.

"Take these gentlemen to their rooms—Nos. 14 and 15; Madame Moreau will give you the keys. Light fires this evening if necessary, and carry up their things.—I am instructed by Monsieur le Comte to ask you to dine with me," he added, addressing the artists. "At five, as in Paris. If you are sportsmen, you can be well amused. I have permission to shoot and fish, and we have twelve thousand acres of shooting outside our own grounds."

Oscar, the painter, and Mistigris, one as much disconcerted as the other, exchanged glances. Still, Mistigris, faithful to his instincts, exclaimed:

"Pooh, never throw the candle after the shade! On we go!"

Little Husson followed the steward, who led the way, walking quickly across the park.

"Jacques," said he to one of his sons, "go and tell your mother that young Husson has arrived, and say that I am obliged to go over to les Moulineaux for a few minutes."

Moreau, now about fifty years of age, a dark man of medium height, had a stern expression. His bilious complexion, highly colored nevertheless by a country life, suggested, at first sight, a character very unlike what his really was. Everything contributed to the illusion. His hair was turning gray, his blue eyes and a large aquiline nose gave him a sinister expression, all the more so because his eyes were too close together; still, his full lips, the shape of his face, and the good-humor of his address, would, to a keen observer, have been indication of kindliness. His very decided manner and abrupt way of speech impressed Oscar immensely with a sense of his penetration, arising from his real affection for the boy. Brought up by his mother to look up to the steward as a great man, Oscar always felt small in Moreau's presence; and now, finding himself at Presles, he felt an oppressive uneasiness, as if he had some ill to fear from this fatherly friend, who was his only protector.

"Why, my dear Oscar, you do not look glad to be here," said the steward. "But you will have plenty to amuse you; you can learn to ride, to shoot, and hunt."

"I know nothing of such things," said Oscar dully.

"But I have asked you here on purpose to teach you."

"Mamma told me not to stay more than a fortnight, because Madame Moreau——"

"Oh, well, we shall see," replied Moreau, almost offended by Oscar's doubts of his conjugal influence.

Moreau's youngest son, a lad of fifteen, active and brisk, now came running up.

"Here," said his father, "take your new companion to your mother."

And the steward himself went off by the shortest path to a keeper's hut between the park and the wood.

The handsome lodge, given by the Count as his land-steward's residence, had been built some years before the Revolution by the owner of the famous estate of Cassan or Bergeret, a farmer-general of enormous wealth, who made himself as notorious for extravagance as Bodard, Pâris, and Bouret, laying out gardens, diverting rivers, building hermitages, Chinese temples, and other costly magnificence.

This house, in the middle of a large garden, of which one wall divided it from the outbuildings of Presles, had formerly had its entrance on the village High Street. Monsieur de Sérizy's father, when he purchased the property, had only to pull down the dividing wall and build up the front gate to make this plot and house part of the outbuildings. Then, by pulling down another wall, he added to his park all the garden land that the former owner had purchased to complete his ring fence.

The lodge, built of freestone, was in the Louis XV. style, with linen-pattern panels under the windows, like those on the colonnades of the Place Louis XV., in stiff, angular folds; it consisted, on the ground floor, of a fine drawing-room opening into a bedroom, and of a dining-room, with a billiard-room adjoining. These two suites, parallel to each other, were divided by a sort of ante-room or hall, and the stairs. The hall was decorated by the doors of the drawing-room and dining-room, both handsomely ornamental. The kitchen was under the dining-room, for there was a flight of ten outside steps.

Madame Moreau had taken the first floor for her own, and had transformed what had been the best bedroom into a boudoir; this boudoir, and the drawing-room below, handsomely fitted up with the best pickings of the old furniture from the château, would certainly have done no discredit to the mansion of a lady of fashion. The drawing room, hung with blue-and-white damask, the spoils of a state bed, and with old gilt-wood furniture upholstered with the same silk, displayed ample curtains to the doors and windows. Some pictures that had formerly been panels, with flower-stands, a few modern tables, and handsome lamps, besides an antique hanging chandelier of cut glass, gave the room a very dignified effect. The carpet was old Persian.

The boudoir was altogether modern and fitted to Madame Moreau's taste, in imitation of a tent, with blue silk ropes on a light gray ground. There was the usual divan with pillows and cushions for the feet, and the flower-stands, carefully cherished by the head-gardener, were a joy to the eye with their pyramids of flowers.

The dining-room and billiard-room were fitted with mahogany. All round the house the steward's lady had planned a flower-garden, beautifully kept, and beyond it lay the park. Clumps of foreign shrubs shut out the stables, and to give admission from the road to her visitors she had opened a gate where the old entrance had been built up.

Thus, the dependent position filled by the Moreaus was cleverly glossed over; and they were the better able to figure as rich folks managing a friend's estate for their pleasure, because neither the Count nor the Countess ever came to quash their pretensions; and the liberality of Monsieur de Sérizy's concessions allowed of their living in abundance, the luxury of country homes. Dairy produce, eggs, poultry, game, fruit, forage, flowers, wood, and vegetables—the steward and his wife had all of these in profusion, and bought literally nothing but butcher's meat and the wine and foreign produce necessary to their lordly extravagance. The poultry-wife made the bread; and, in fact, for the last few years, Moreau had paid his butcher's bill with the pigs of the farm, keeping only as much pork as he needed.

One day the Countess, always very generous to her former lady's maid, made Madame Moreau a present, as a souvenir perhaps, of a little traveling chaise of a past fashion, which Moreau had furbished up, and in which his wife drove out behind a pair of good horses, useful at other times in the grounds. Besides this pair, the steward had his saddle-horse. He ploughed part of the park land, and raised grain enough to feed the beasts and servants; he cut three hundred tons more or less of good hay, accounting for no more than one hundred, encroaching on the license vaguely granted by the Count; and instead of using his share of the produce on the premises, he sold it. He kept his poultry-farm, his pigeons, and his cows on the crops from the park-land; but then the manure from his stables was used in the Count's garden. Each of these pilfering acts had an excuse ready.

Madame Moreau's house-servant was the daughter of one of the gardeners, and waited on her and cooked; she was helped in the housework by a girl, who also attended to the poultry and dairy. Moreau had engaged an invalided soldier named Brochon to look after the horses and do the dirty work.

At Nerville, at Chauvry, at Beaumont, at Maffliers, at Préroles, at Nointel, the steward's pretty wife was everywhere received by persons who did not, or affected not to know her original position in life. And Moreau could confer obligations. He could use his master's interest in matters which are of immense importance in the depths of the country though trivial in Paris. After securing for friends the appointments of Justice of the Peace at Beaumont and at l'Isle-Adam, he had, in the course of the same year, saved an Inspector of Forest-lands from dismissal, and obtained the Cross of the Legion of Honor for the quartermaster at Beaumont. So there was never a festivity among the more respectable neighbors without Monsieur and Madame Moreau being invited. The Curé and the Mayor of Presles were to be seen every evening at their house. A man can hardly help being a good fellow when he has made himself so comfortable.

So Madame la Régisseuse—a pretty woman, and full of airs, like every grand lady's servant who, when she marries, apes her mistress—introduced the latest fashions, wore the most expensive shoes, and never walked out but in fine weather. Though her husband gave her no more than five hundred francs a year for dress, this in the country is a very large sum, especially when judiciously spent; and his "lady," fair, bright, and fresh-looking, at the age of thirty-six, and still slight, neat, and attractive in spite of her three children, still played the girl, and gave herself the airs of a princess. If, as she drove past in her open chaise on her way to Beaumont, some stranger happened to inquire, "Who is that?" Madame Moreau was furious if a native of the place replied, "She is the steward's wife at Presles." She aimed at being taken for the mistress of the château.

She amused herself with patronizing the villagers, as a great lady might have done. Her husband's power with the Count, proved in so many ways, hindered the townsfolk from laughing at Madame Moreau, who was a person of importance in the eyes of the peasantry.

Estelle, however—her name was Estelle—did not interfere in the management, any more than a stockbroker's wife interferes in dealings on the Bourse; she even relied on her husband for the administration of the house and of their income. Quite confident of her own powers of pleasing, she was miles away from imagining that this delightful life, which had gone on for seventeen years, could ever be in danger; however, on hearing that the Count had resolved on restoring the splendid château of Presles, she understood that all her enjoyments were imperiled, and she had persuaded her husband to come to terms with Léger, so as to have a retreat at l'Isle-Adam. She could not have borne to find herself in an almost servile position in the presence of her former mistress, who would undoubtedly laugh at her on finding her established at the lodge in a style that aped the lady of fashion.

The origin of the deep-seated enmity between the Reyberts and the Moreaus lay in a stab inflicted on Madame Moreau by Madame de Reybert in revenge for a pin-prick that the steward's wife had dared to give on the first arrival of the Reyberts, lest her supremacy should be infringed on by the lady *née* de Corroy. Madame de Reybert had mentioned, and perhaps for the first time informed the neighborhood, of Madame Moreau's original calling. The words *lady's maid* flew from lip to lip. All those who envied the Moreaus—and they must have been many—at Beaumont, at l'Isle-Adam, at Maffliers, at Champagne, at Nerville, at Chauvry, at Baillet, at Moisselles, made such pregnant comments that more than one spark from this conflagration fell into the Moreaus' home. For four years, now, the Reyberts, excommunicated by their pretty rival, had become the object of so much hostile animadversion from her partisans, that their position would have been untenable but for the thought of vengeance which had sustained them to this day.

The Moreaus, who were very good friends with Grindot the architect, had been told by him of the arrival ere long of a painter commissioned to finish the decorative panels at the château, Schinner having executed the more important pieces. This great painter recommended the artist we have seen traveling with Mistigris, to paint the borders, arabesques, and other accessory decorations. Hence, for two days past, Madame Moreau had been preparing her war-paint and sitting expectant. An artist who was to board with her for some weeks was worthy of some outlay. Schinner and his wife had been quartered in the château, where, by the Count's orders, they had been entertained like my lord himself. Grindot, who boarded with the Moreaus, had treated the great artist with so much respect, that neither the steward nor his wife had ventured on any familiarity. And, indeed, the richest and most noble landowners in the district had vied with each other in entertaining Schinner and his wife. So now Madame Moreau, much pleased at the prospect of turning the tables, promised herself that she would sound the trumpet before the artist who was to be her guest, and make him out a match in talent for Schinner.

Although on the two previous days she had achieved very coquettish toilets, the steward's pretty wife had husbanded her resources too well not to have reserved the most bewitching till the Saturday, never doubting that on that day at any rate the artist would arrive to dinner. She had shod herself in bronze kid with fine thread stockings. A dress of finely striped pink-and-white muslin, a pink belt with a chased gold buckle, a cross and heart round her neck, and wristlets of black velvet on her bare arms—Madame de Sérizy had fine arms, and was fond of displaying them—gave Madame Moreau the style of a fashionable Parisian. She put on a very handsome Leghorn hat, graced with a bunch of moss roses made by Nattier, and under its broad shade her fair hair flowed in glossy curls.

Having ordered a first-rate dinner and carefully inspected the rooms, she went out at an hour which brought her to the large flower-bed in the court of the château, like the lady of the house, just when the coach would pass. Over her head she held an elegant pink silk parasol lined with white and trimmed with fringe. On seeing Pierrotin hand over to the lodge-keeper the artist's extraordinary-looking luggage, and perceiving no owner, Estelle had returned home lamenting the waste of another carefully arranged dress. And, like most people who have dressed for an occasion, she felt quite incapable of any occupation but that of doing nothing in her drawing-room while waiting for the passing of the Beaumont coach which should come through an hour after Pierrotin's, though it did not start from Paris till one o'clock; thus she was waiting at home while the two young artists were dressing for dinner. In fact, the young painter and Mistigris were so overcome by the description of lovely Madame Moreau given them by the gardener whom they had questioned, that it was obvious to them both that they must get themselves into their best "toggery." So they donned their very best before presenting themselves at the steward's house, whither they were conducted by Jacques Moreau, the eldest of the children, a stalwart youth, dressed in the English fashion, in a round jacket with a turned-down collar, and as happy during the holidays as a fish in water, here on the estate where his mother reigned supreme.

"Mamma," said he, "here are the two artists come from Monsieur Schinner."

Madame Moreau, very agreeably surprised, rose, bid her son set chairs, and displayed all her graces.

"Mamma, little Husson is with father; I am to go to fetch him," whispered the boy in her ear.

"There is no hurry, you can stop and amuse him," said the mother.

The mere words "there is no hurry" showed the two artists how entirely unimportant was their traveling companion, but the tone also betrayed the indifference of a stepmother for her stepchild. In fact, Madame Moreau, who, for seventeen years of married life, could not fail to be aware of her husband's attachment to Madame Clapart and young Husson, hated the mother and son in so overt a manner that it is easy to understand why Moreau had never till now ventured to invite Oscar to Presles.

"We are enjoined, my husband and I," said she to the two artists, "to do the honors of the château. We are fond of art, and more especially of artists," said she, with a simper, "and I beg you to consider yourselves quite at home there. In the country, you see, there is no ceremony; liberty is indispensable, otherwise life is too insipid. We have had Monsieur Schinner here already——"

Mistigris gave his companion a mischievous wink.

"You know him, of course," said Estelle, after a pause.

"Who does not know him, madame?" replied the painter.

"He is as well known as the parish birch," added Mistigris.

"Monsieur Grindot mentioned your name," said Madame Moreau, "but really I——"

"Joseph Bridau, madame," replied the artist, extremely puzzled as to what this woman could be.

Mistigris was beginning to fume inwardly at this fair lady's patronizing tone; still, he waited, as Bridau did too, for some movement, some chance word to enlighten them, one of those expressions of assumed fine-ladyism, which painters, those born and cruel observers of folly—the perennial food of their pencil—seize on in an instant. In the first place, Estelle's large hands and feet, those of a peasant from the district of Saint-Lô, struck them at once; and before long one or two lady's-maid's phrases, modes of speech that gave the lie to the elegance of her dress, betrayed their prey into the hands of the artist and his apprentice. They exchanged a look which pledged them both to take Estelle quite seriously as a pastime during their stay.

"You are so fond of art, perhaps you cultivate it with success, madame?" said Joseph Bridau.

"No. Though my education was not neglected, it was purely commercial. But I have such a marked and delicate feeling for art, that Monsieur Schinner always begged me, when he had finished a piece, to give him my opinion."

"Just as Molière consulted Laforêt," said Mistigris.

Not knowing that Laforêt was a servant-girl, Madame Moreau responded with a graceful droop, showing that in her ignorance she regarded this speech as a compliment.

"How is it that he did not propose just to knock off your head?" said Bridau. "Painters are generally on the lookout for handsome women."

"What is your meaning, pray?" said Madame Moreau, on whose face dawned the wrath of an offended queen.

"In studio slang, to knock a thing off is to sketch it," said Mistigris, in an ingratiating tone, "and all we ask is to have handsome heads to sketch. And we sometimes say in admiration that a woman's beauty has knocked us over."

"Ah, I did not know the origin of the phrase!" replied she, with a look of languishing sweetness at Mistigris.

"My pupil, Monsieur Léon de Lora," said Bridau, "has a great talent for likeness. He would be only too happy, fair being, to leave you a *souvenir* of his skill by painting your charming face."

And Bridau signaled to Mistigris, as much as to say, "Come, drive it home, she really is not amiss!"

Taking this hint, Léon de Lora moved to the sofa by Estelle's side, and took her hand, which she left in his.

"Oh! if only as a surprise to your husband, madame, you could give me a few sittings in secret, I would try to excel myself. You are so lovely, so young, so charming! A man devoid of talent might become a genius with you for his model! In your eyes he would find——"

"And we would represent your sweet children in our arabesques," said Joseph, interrupting Mistigris.

"I would rather have them in my own drawing-room; but that would be asking too much," said she, looking coquettishly at Bridau.

"Beauty, madame, is a queen whom painters worship, and who has every right to command them."

"They are quite charming," thought Madame Moreau.— "Do you like driving out in the evening, after dinner, in an open carriage, in the woods?"

"Oh! oh! oh! oh!" cried Mistigris, in ecstatic tones at each added detail. "Why, Presles will be an earthly paradise."

"With a fair-haired Eve, a young and bewitching woman," added Bridau.

Just as Madame Moreau was preening herself, and soaring into the seventh heaven, she was brought down again like a kite by a tug at the cord.

"Madame!" exclaimed the maid, bouncing in like a cannon ball.

"Bless me, Rosalie, what can justify you in coming in like this without being called?"

Rosalie did not trouble her head about this apostrophe, but said in her mistress' ear:

"Monsieur le Comte is here."

"Did he ask for me?" said the steward's wife.

"No, madame—but—he wants his portmanteau and the key of his room."

"Let him have them then," said she, with a cross shrug to disguise her uneasiness.

"Mamma, here is Oscar Husson!" cried her youngest son, bringing in Oscar, who, as red as a poppy, dared not come forward as he saw the two painters in different dress.

"So here you are at last, boy," said Estelle coldly. "You are going to dress, I hope?" she went on, after looking at him from head to foot with great contempt. "I suppose your mother has not brought you up to dine in company in such clothes as those."

"Oh, no," said the ruthless Mistigris, "a coming diplomatist must surely have a seat—to his trousers! A coat to dine saves wine."

"A coming diplomatist?" cried Madame Moreau.

The tears rose to poor Oscar's eyes as he looked from Joseph to Léon.

"Only a jest by the way," replied Joseph, who wished to help Oscar in his straits.

"The boy wanted to make fun as we did, and he tried to humbug," said the merciless Mistigris. "And now he finds himself the ass with a lion's grin."

"Madame," said Rosalie, coming back to the drawing-room door, "his Excellency has ordered dinner for eight persons at six o'clock; what is to be done?"

While Estelle and her maid were holding counsel, the artists and Oscar gazed at each other, their eyes big with terrible apprehensions.

"His Excellency—Who?" said Joseph Bridau.

"Why, Monsieur le Comte de Sérizy," replied little Moreau.

"Was it he, by chance, in the coucou?" said Léon de Lora.

"Oh!" exclaimed Oscar, "the Comte de Sérizy would surely never travel but in a coach and four."

"How did he come, madame—the Comte de Sérizy?" the painter asked of Madame Moreau when she came back very much upset.

"I have no idea," said she. "I cannot account for his coming, nor guess what he has come for.—And Moreau is out!"

"His Excellency begs you will go over to the château, Monsieur Schinner," said a gardener coming to the door, "and he begs you will give him the pleasure of your company at dinner, as well as Monsieur Mistigris."

"Our goose is cooked!" said the lad with a laugh. "The man we took for a country worthy in Pierrotin's chaise was the Count. So true is it that what you seek you never bind."

Oscar was almost turning to a pillar of salt; for on hearing this, his throat felt as salt as the sea.

"And you! Who told him all about his wife's adorers and his skin disease?" said Mistigris to Oscar.

"What do you mean?" cried the steward's wife, looking at the two artists, who went off laughing at Oscar's face.

Oscar stood speechless, thunderstruck; hearing nothing, though Madame Moreau was questioning him and shaking him violently by one of his arms, which she had seized and clutched tightly; but she was obliged to leave him where he was without having extracted a reply, for Rosalie called her again to give out linen and silver-plate, and to request her to attend in person to the numerous orders given by the Count. The house-servants, the gardeners, everybody on the place, were rushing to and fro in such confusion as may be imagined.

The master had in fact dropped on the household like a shell from a mortar. From above la Cave the Count had made his way by a path familiar to him to the gamekeeper's hut, and reached it before Moreau. The gamekeeper was amazed to see his real master.

"Is Moreau here, I see his horse waiting?" asked Monsieur de Sérizy.

"No, monseigneur; but as he is going over to les Moulineaux before dinner, he left his horse here while he ran across to give some orders at the house."

The gamekeeper had no idea of the effect of this reply, which, under existing circumstances, was, in the eyes of a clear-sighted man, tantamount to assurance.

"If you value your place," said the Count to the keeper, "ride as fast as you can pelt to Beaumont on this horse, and deliver to Monsieur Margueron a note I will give you."

The Count went into the man's lodge, wrote a line, folded it in such a manner that it could not be opened without detection, and gave it to the man as soon as he was in the saddle.

"Not a word to any living soul," said he. "And you, madame," he added to the keeper's wife, "if Moreau is surprised at not finding his horse, tell him that I took it."

And the Count went off across the park, through the gate which was opened for him at his nod.

Inured though a man may be to the turmoil of political life, with its excitement and vicissitudes, the soul of a man who, at the Count's age, is still firm enough to love, is also young enough to feel a betrayal. It was so hard to believe that Moreau was deceiving him, that at Saint-Brice Monsieur de Sérizy had supposed him to be not so much in league with Léger and the notary as, in fact, led away by them. And so, standing in the inn gateway, as he heard Père Léger talking to the innkeeper, he intended to forgive his land-steward after a severe reproof.

And then, strange to say, the dishonesty of his trusted agent had seemed no more than an episode when Oscar had blurted out the noble infirmities of the intrepid traveler, the Minister of Napoleon. Secrets so strictly kept could only have been revealed by Moreau, who had no doubt spoken contemptuously of his benefactor to Madame de Sérizy's maid, or to the erewhile Aspasia of the Directoire.

As he made his way down the cross-road to the château, the peer of France, the great minister, had shed bitter tears, weeping as a boy weeps. They were his last tears that he shed! Every human feeling at once was so cruelly, so mercilessly attacked, that this self-controlled man rushed on across his park like a hunted animal.

When Moreau asked for his horse, and the keeper's wife replied:

"Monsieur le Comte has just taken it."

"Who—Monsieur le Comte?" cried he.

"Monsieur le Comte de Sérizy, the master," said she. "Perhaps he is at the château," added she, to get rid of the steward, who, quite bewildered by this occurrence, went off towards the house.

But he presently returned to question the keeper's wife, for it had struck him that there was some serious motive for his master's secret arrival and unwonted conduct. The woman, terrified at finding herself in a vise, as it were, between the Count and the steward, had shut herself into her lodge, quite determined only to open the door to her husband. Moreau, more and more uneasy, hurried across to the gatekeeper's lodge, where he was told that the Count was dressing. Rosalie, whom he met, announced: "Seven people to dine at the Count's table."

Moreau next went home, where he found the poultry-girl in hot discussion with an odd-looking young man.

"Monsieur le Comte told us, 'Mina's aide-de-camp and a colonel,'" the girl insisted.

"I am not a colonel," replied Georges.

"Well, but is your name Georges?"

"What is the matter?" asked the steward, intervening.

"Monsieur, my name is Georges Marest; I am the son of a rich hardware dealer, wholesale, in the Rue Saint-Martin, and I have come on business to Monsieur le Comte de Sérizy from Maître Crottat, his notary—I am his second clerk."

"And I can only repeat, sir, what monsieur said to me—'A gentleman will come,' says he, 'a Colonel Czerni-Georges, aide-de-camp to Mina, who traveled down in Pierrotin's chaise. If he asks for me, show him into the drawing-room.'"

"There is no joking with his Excellency," said the steward. "You had better go in, monsieur.—But how is it that his Excellency came down without announcing his purpose? And how does he know that you traveled by Pierrotin's chaise?"

"It is perfectly clear," said the clerk, "that the Count is the gentleman who, but for the civility of a young man, would have had to ride on the front seat of Pierrotin's coucou."

"On the front seat of Pierrotin's coucou?" cried the steward and the farm-girl.

"I am quite sure of it from what this girl tells me," said Georges Marest.

"But how——?" the steward began.

"Ah, there you are!" cried Georges. "To humbug the other travelers, I told them a heap of cock-and-bull stories about Egypt, Greece, and Spain. I had spurs on, and I gave myself out as a colonel in the cavalry—a mere joke."

"And what was the gentleman like, whom you believe to be the Count?" asked Moreau.

"Why, he has a face the color of brick," said Georges, "with perfectly white hair and black eyebrows."

"That is the man!"

"I am done for!" said Georges Marest.

"Why?"

"I made fun of his Orders."

"Pooh, he is a thorough good fellow; you will have amused him. Come to the château forthwith," said Moreau. "I am going up to the Count.—Where did he leave you?"

"At the top of the hill."

"I can make neither head nor tail of it!" cried Moreau.

"After all, I poked fun at him, but I did not insult him," said the clerk to himself.

"And what are you here for?" asked the steward.

"I have brought the deed of sale of the farm-lands of les Moulineaux, ready made out.

A START IN LIFE

"Good heavens!" exclaimed Moreau. "I don't understand!"

Moreau felt his heart beat painfully when, after knocking two raps on his master's door, he heard in reply:

"Is that you, Monsieur Moreau?"

"Yes, monseigneur."

"Come in."

The Count was dressed in white trousers and thin boots, a white waistcoat, and a black coat on which glittered, on the right-hand side, the star of the Grand Cross of the Legion of Honor, and on the left, from a button-hole, hung that of the Golden Fleece from a gold chain; the blue ribbon was conspicuous across his waistcoat. He had dressed his hair himself, and had no doubt got himself up to do the honors of Presles to Margueron, and, perhaps, to impress that worthy with the atmosphere of grandeur.

"Well, monsieur," said the Count, who remained sitting, but allowed Moreau to stand, "so we cannot come to terms with Margueron?"

"At the present moment he wants too much for his farm."

"But why should he not come over here to talk about it?" said the Count in an absent-minded way.

"He is ill, monseigneur——"

"Are you sure?"

"I went over there——"

"Monsieur," said the Count, assuming a stern expression that was terrible, "what would you do to a man whom you had allowed to see you dress a wound you wished to keep secret, and who went off to make game of it with a street trollop?"

"I should give him a sound thrashing."

"And if, in addition to this, you discovered that he was cheating your confidence and robbing you?"

"I should try to catch him out and send him to the hulks."

"Listen, Monsieur Moreau. You have, I suppose, discussed my health with Madame Clapart and made fun at her house of my devotion to my wife, for little Husson was giving to the passengers in a public conveyance a vast deal of information with reference to my cures, in my presence, this very morning, and in what words! God knows! He dared to slander my wife.

"Again, I heard from Farmer Léger's own lips, as he returned from Paris in Pierrotin's chaise, of the plan concocted by the notary of Beaumont with him, and with you, with reference to les Moulineaux. If you have been at all to see Margueron, it was to instruct him to sham illness; he is so little ill that I expect him to dinner, and he is coming.—Well, monsieur, as to your having made a fortune of two hundred and fifty thousand francs in seventeen years—I forgive you. I understand it. If you had but asked me for what you took from me, or what others offered you, I would have given it to you; you have a family to provide for. Even with your want of delicacy you have treated me better than another might have done, that I believe——

"But that you, who know all that I have done for my country, for France, you who have seen me sit up a hundred nights and more to work for the Emperor, or toiling eighteen hours a day for three months on end; that you, who know my worship of Madame de Sérizy, should have gossiped about it before a boy, have betrayed my secrets to the mockery of a Madame Husson——"

"Monseigneur!"

"It is unpardonable. To damage a man's interest is nothing, but to strike at his heart!—Ah! you do not know what you have done!"

The Count covered his face with his hands and was silent for a moment.

"I leave you in possession of what you have," he went on, "and I will forget you.—As a point of dignity, of honor, we will part without quarreling, for, at this moment, I can remember what your father did for mine.

"You must come to terms—good terms—with Monsieur de Reybert, your successor. Be calm, as I am. Do not make yourself a spectacle for fools. Above all, no bluster and no haggling. Though you have forfeited my confidence, try to preserve the decorum of wealth.—As to the little wretch who has half killed me, he is not to sleep at Presles. Send him to the inn; I cannot answer for what I might do if he crossed my path."

"I do not deserve such leniency, monseigneur," said Moreau, with tears in his eyes. "If I had been utterly dishonest I should have five hundred thousand francs; and indeed I will gladly account for every franc in detail!—But permit me to assure you, monseigneur, that when I spoke of you to Madame Clapart it was never in derision. On the contrary, it was to deplore your condition and to ask her whether she did not know of some remedy, unfamiliar to the medical profession, which the common people use.—I have spoken of you in the boy's presence when he was asleep—but he heard me, it would seem!—and always in terms of the deepest affection and respect. Unfortunately, a blunder is sometimes punished as a crime. Still, while I bow to the decisions of your just anger, I would have you to know what really happened. Yes, it was heart to heart that I spoke of you to Madame Clapart. And only ask my wife; never have I mentioned these matters to her——"

"That will do," said the Count, whose conviction was complete. "We are not children; the past is irrevocable. . . . Go and set your affairs and mine in order. You may remain in the lodge till the month of October. Monsieur and Madame de Reybert will live in the château. Above all, try to live with them as gentlemen should—hating each other, but keeping up appearances."

The Count and Moreau went downstairs, Moreau as white as the Count's hair, Monsieur de Sérizy calm and dignified.

While this scene was going forward, the Beaumont coach, leaving Paris at one o'clock, had stopped at the gate of Presles' to set down Maître Crottat, who, in obedience to the Count's orders, was shown into the drawing-room to wait for him; there he found his clerk excessively crestfallen, in company with the two painters, all three conspicuously uncomfortable.

Monsieur de Reybert, a man of fifty, with a very surly expression, had brought with him old Margueron and the notary from Beaumont, who held a bundle of leases and title-deeds.

When this assembled party saw the Count appear in full court costume, Georges Marest had a spasm in the stomach, and Joseph Bridau felt a qualm; but Mistigris, who was himself in his Sunday clothes, and who indeed had no crime on his conscience, said loud enough to be heard:

"Well, he looks much nicer now."

"You little rascal," said the Count, drawing him towards him by one ear, "so we both deal in decorations!—Do you recognize your work, my dear Schinner?" he went on, pointing to the ceiling.

"Monseigneur," said the artist, "I was so foolish as to assume so famous a name out of bravado; but to-day's experience makes it incumbent on me to do something good and win glory for that of Joseph Bridau."

"You took my part," said the Count eagerly, "and I hope you will do me the pleasure of dining with me—you and your witty Mistigris."

"You do not know what you are exposing yourself to," said the audacious youngster; "an empty stomach knows no peers."

"Bridau," said the Count, struck by a sudden reminiscence, "are you related to one of the greatest workers under the Empire, a brigadier in command who died a victim to his zeal?"

"I am his son, monseigneur," said Joseph, bowing.

"Then you are welcome here," replied the Count, taking the artist's hand in both his own; "I knew your father, and you may depend on me as on—an American uncle," said Monsieur de Sérizy, smiling. "But you are too young to have a pupil—to whom does Mistigris belong?"

"To my friend Schinner, who has lent him to me," replied Joseph. "Mistigris' name is Léon de Lora. Monseigneur, if you remember my father, will you condescend to bear in mind his other son, who stands accused of conspiring against the State, and is on his trial before the Supreme Court——"

"To be sure," said the Count. "I will bear it in mind, believe me.—As to Prince Czerni-Georges, Ali Pasha's ally, and Mina's aide-de-camp——" said the Count, turning to Georges.

"He?—my second clerk?" cried Crottat.

"You are under a mistake, Maître Crottat," said Monsieur de Sérizy, very severely. "A clerk who hopes ever to become a notary does not leave important documents in a diligence at the mercy of his fellow-travelers! A clerk who hopes to become a notary does not spend twenty francs between Paris and Moisselles! A clerk who hopes to become a notary does not expose himself to arrest as a deserter——"

"Monseigneur," said Georges Marest, "I may have amused myself by playing a practical joke on a party of travelers, but——"

"Do not interrupt his Excellency," said his master, giving him a violent nudge in the ribs.

"A notary ought to develop early the gifts of discretion, prudence, and discernment, and not mistake a Minister of State for a candlemaker."

"I accept sentence for my errors," said Georges, "but I did not leave my papers at the mercy——"

"You are at this moment committing the error of giving the lie to a Minister of State, a peer of France, a gentleman, an old man—and a client.—Look for your deed of sale."

The clerk turned over the papers in his portfolio.

"Do not make a mess of your papers," said the Count, taking the document out of his pocket. "Here is the deed you are seeking."

Crottat turned it over three times, so much was he amazed at receiving it from the hands of his noble client.

"What, sir!"—he at last began, addressing Georges.

"If I had not taken it," the Count went on, "Père Léger—who is not such a fool as you fancy him from his questions as to agriculture, since they might have taught you that a man should always be thinking of his business—Père Léger might have got hold of it and discovered my plans.—You also will give me the pleasure of your company at dinner, but on condition of telling us the history of the Moslem's execution at

Smyrna, and of finishing the memoirs of some client which you read, no doubt, before publication."

"A trouncing for bouncing," said Léon de Lora, in a low voice to Joseph Bridau.

"Gentlemen," said the Count to the notary from Beaumont, to Crottat, Margueron, and Reybert, "come into the other room. We will not sit down to dinner till we have concluded our bargain; for, as my friend Mistigris says, we must know when to *creep* silent."

"Well, he is a thoroughly good fellow," said Léon de Lora to Georges Marest.

"Yes; but if he is a good fellow, my governor is not, and he will request me to play my tricks elsewhere."

"Well, you like traveling," said Bridau.

"What a dressing that boy will get from Monsieur and Madame Moreau!" cried Léon de Lora.

"The little idiot!" said Georges. "But for him the Count would have thought it all very good fun. Well, well, it is a useful lesson, and if I am caught chattering in a coach again——"

"Oh, it is a stupid thing to do," said Joseph Bridau.

"And vulgar too," said Mistigris. "Keep your tongue to clean your teeth."

While the business of the farm was being discussed between Monsieur Margueron and the Comte de Sérizy, with the assistance of three notaries, and in the presence of Monsieur de Reybert, Moreau was slowly making his way home. He went in without looking about him, and sat down on a sofa in the drawing-room, while Oscar Husson crept into a corner out of sight, so terrified was he by the steward's white face.

"Well, my dear," said Estelle, coming in, fairly tired out by all she had had to do, "what is the matter?"

"My dear, we are ruined, lost beyond redemption. I am no longer land-steward of Presles! The Count has withdrawn his confidence."

"And what has caused——?"

"Old Léger, who was in Pierrotin's chaise, let out all about the farm of les Moulineaux; but it is not that which has cut me off for ever from his favor——"

"What, then?"

"Oscar spoke ill of the Countess, and talked of monseigneur's ailments——"

"Oscar?" cried Madame Moreau. "You are punished by your own act! A pretty viper you have nursed in your bosom! How often have I told you——"

"That will do," said Moreau hoarsely.

At this instant Estelle and her husband detected Oscar huddled in a corner. Moreau pounced on the luckless boy like a kite on its prey, seized him by the collar of his olive-green coat, and dragged him into the daylight of a window.

"Speak! What did you say to monseigneur in the coach? What devil loosened your tongue, when you always stand moonstruck if I ask you a question? What did you do it for?" said the steward with terrific violence.

Oscar, too much scared for tears, kept silence, as motionless as a statue.

"Come and ask his Excellency's pardon!" said Moreau.

"As if his Excellency cared about a vermin like him!" shrieked Estelle in a fury.

"Come—come to the château!" Moreau repeated.

Oscar collapsed, a lifeless heap on the floor.

"Will you come, I say?" said Moreau, his rage increasing every moment.

"No, no; have pity!" cried Oscar, who could not face a punishment worse than death.

Moreau took the boy by the collar and dragged him like a corpse across the courtyard, which rang with the boy's cries and sobs; he hauled him up the steps and flung him howling, and as rigid as a post, in the drawing-room at the feet of the Count, who, having settled for the purchase of les Moulineaux, was just passing into the dining-room with his friends.

"On your knees, on your knees, wretched boy. Ask pardon of the man who has fed your mind by getting you a scholarship at college," cried Moreau.

Oscar lay with his face on the ground, foaming with rage. Everybody was startled. Moreau, quite beside himself, was purple in the face from the rush of blood to his head.

"This boy is mere vanity," said the Count, after waiting in vain for Oscar's apology. "Pride can humble itself, for there is dignity in some self-humiliation.—I am afraid you will never make anything of this fellow."

And the Minister passed on.

Moreau led Oscar away and back to his own house.

While the horses were being harnessed to the traveling chaise, he wrote the following letter to Madame Clapart:—

"Oscar, my dear, has brought me to ruin. In the course of his journey in Pierrotin's chaise this morning he spoke of the flirtations of Madame la Comtesse to his Excellency himself, who was traveling incognito, and told the Count his own secrets as to the skin disease brought on by long nights of hard work in his various high offices.—After dismissing me from my place, the Count desired me not to allow Oscar to sleep at Presles, but to send him home. In obedience to his orders, I am having my horses put to my wife's carriage, and Brochon, my groom, will take the little wretch home.

"My wife and I are in a state of despair, which you may imagine, but which I cannot attempt to describe. I will go to see you in a few days, for I must make my plans. I have three children; I must think of the future, and I do not yet know what to decide on, for I am determined to show the Count the value of seventeen years of the life of such a man as I. I have two hundred and sixty thousand francs, and I mean to acquire such a fortune as will allow me to be, some day, not much less than his Excellency's equal. At this instant I feel that I could remove mountains and conquer insurmountable difficulties. What a lever is such a humiliating scene!——

"Whose blood can Oscar have in his veins? I cannot compliment you on your son; his behavior is that of an owl. At this moment of writing he has not yet uttered a word in reply to my questions and my wife's. Is he becoming idiotic, or is he idiotic already? My dear friend, did you not give him due injunctions before he started? How much misfortune you would have spared me by coming with him, as I begged you. If you were afraid of Estelle, you could have stayed at Moisselles. However, it is all over now. Farewell till we meet, soon.—Your faithful friend and servant,

"MOREAU."

At eight o'clock that evening Madame Clapart had come in from a little walk with her husband, and sat knitting stockings for Oscar by the light of a single dip. Monsieur Clapart was expecting a friend named Poiret, who sometimes came in for a game of dominoes, for he never trusted himself to spend an evening in a café. In spite of temperance, enforced on him by his narrow means, Clapart could not have answered for his abstinence when in the midst of food and drink, and surrounded by other men, whose laughter might have nettled him.

"I am afraid Poiret may have been and gone," said he to his wife.

"The lodge-keeper would have told us, my dear," replied his wife.

"She may have forgotten."

"Why should she forget?"

"It would not be the first time she has forgotten things that concern us; God knows, anything is good enough for people who have no servants!"

"Well, well," said the poor woman, to change the subject and escape her husband's pin-stabs. "Oscar is at Presles by this time; he will be very happy in that beautiful place, that fine park——"

"Oh yes, expect great things!" retorted Clapart. "He will make hay there with a vengeance!"

"Will you never cease to be spiteful to that poor boy? What harm has he done you? Dear Heaven! if ever we are in easy circumstances we shall owe it to him perhaps, for he has a good heart."

"Our bones will be gelatine long before that boy succeeds in the world!" said Clapart. "And he will have altered very considerably!—Why, you don't know your own boy; he is a braggart, a liar, lazy, incapable——"

"Supposing you were to go to fetch Poiret," said the hapless mother, struck to the heart by the diatribe she had brought down on her own head.

"A boy who never took a prize at school!" added Clapart.

In the eyes of the commoner sort, bringing home prizes from school is positive proof of future success in life.

"Did you ever take a prize?" retorted his wife. "And Oscar got the fourth *accessit* in philosophy?"

This speech reduced Clapart to silence for a moment.

"And besides," he presently went on, "Madame Moreau must love him as she loves a nail—you know where; she will try to set her husband against him.—Oscar steward at Presles! Why, he must understand land-surveying and agriculture——"

"He can learn."

"He! Never! I bet you that if he got a place there he would not be in it a week before he had done something clumsy, and was packed off by the Comte de Sérizy——"

"Good heavens! How can you be so vicious about the future prospects of a poor boy, full of good points, as sweet as an angel, and incapable of doing an ill turn to any living soul?"

At this moment the cracking of a post-boy's whip and the clatter of a chaise at top speed, with the hoofs of horses pulled up sharply at the outer gate, had roused the whole street. Clapart, hearing every window flung open, went out on the landing.

"Oscar, sent back by post!" cried he in a tone in which his satisfaction gave way to genuine alarm.

"Good God! what can have happened?" said the poor mother, trembling as a leaf is shaken by an autumn wind.

Brochon came upstairs, followed by Oscar and Poiret.

"Good heavens, what has happened?" repeated she, appealing to the groom.

"I don't know, but Monsieur Moreau is no longer steward of Presles, and they say it is your son's doing, and monseigneur has ordered him home again.—However, here is a letter from poor Monsieur Moreau, who is so altered, madame, it is dreadful to see."

"Clapart, a glass of wine for the post-boy, and one for monsieur," said his wife, who dropped into an armchair and read the terrible letter. "Oscar," she went on, dragging herself to her bed, "you want to kill your mother!—After all I said to you this morning——" But Madame Clapart did not finish her sentence; she fainted with misery.

Oscar remained standing, speechless. Madame Clapart, as she recovered her senses, heard her husband saying to the boy as he shook him by the arm:

"Will you speak?"

"Go to bed at once, sir," said she to her son. "And leave him in peace, Monsieur Clapart; do not drive him out of his wits, for he is dreadfully altered!"

Oscar did not hear his mother's remark; he had made for bed the instant he was told.

Those who have any recollection of their own boyhood will not be surprised to hear that, after a day so full of events and agitations, Oscar slept the sleep of the just in spite of the enormity of his sins. Nay, next day he did not find the whole face of nature so much changed as he expected, and was astonished to find that he was hungry, after regarding himself the day before as unworthy to live. He had suffered only in mind, and at that age mental impressions succeed each other so rapidly that each wipes out the last, however deep it may have seemed.

Hence corporal punishment, though philanthropists have made a strong stand against it of late years, is in some cases necessary for children; also, it is perfectly natural, for Nature herself has no other means but the infliction of pain to produce a lasting impression of her lessons. If to give weight to the shame, unhappily too transient, which had overwhelmed Oscar, the steward had given him a sound thrashing, the lesson might have been effectual. The discernment needed for the proper infliction of such corrections is the chief argument against their use; for Nature never makes a mistake, while the teacher must often blunder.

Madame Clapart took care to send her husband out next morning to have her son to herself. She was in a pitiable condition. Her eyes red with weeping, her face worn by a sleepless night, her voice broken; everything in her seemed to sue for mercy by the signs of such grief as she could not have endured a second time. When Oscar entered the room, she beckoned to him to sit down by her, and in a mild but feeling voice reminded him of all the kindness done them by the steward of Presles. She explained to Oscar that for the last six years especially she had lived on Moreau's ingenious charity. Monsieur Clapart's appointment, which they owed, no less than Oscar's scholarship, to the Comte de Sérizy, he would some day cease to hold. Clapart could not claim a pension, not having served long enough either in the Treasury or the city to ask for one. And when Monsieur Clapart should be shelved, what was to become of them?

"I," she said, "by becoming a sick-nurse or taking a place as housekeeper in some gentleman's house, could make my living and keep Monsieur Clapart; but what would become of you? You have no fortune, and you must work for your living. There are but four openings for lads like you—trade, the civil service, the liberal professions, and military service. A young man who has no capital must contribute faithful service and brains; but great discretion is needed in business, and your behavior yesterday makes your success very doubtful. For an official career you have to begin, for years perhaps, as a supernumerary, and need interest to back you; and you have alienated the only protector we ever had—a man high in power. And besides, even if you were blest with the exceptional gifts which enable a young man to rise rapidly, either in business or in an official position, where are we to find the money for food and clothing while you are learning your work?"

And here his mother, like all women, went off into wordy lamentations. What could she do now that she was deprived of the gifts of produce which Moreau was able to send her while managing Presles? Oscar had overthrown his best friend.

Next to trade and office work, of which her son need not even think, came the legal profession as a notary, a pleader, an attorney, or an usher. But then he must study law for three years at least, and pay heavy fees for his admission, his examinations, his *theses,* and diploma; the number of competitors was so great, that superior talent was indispensable, and how was he to live? That was the constantly recurring question.

"Oscar," she said in conclusion, "all my pride, all my life were centered in you. I could bear to look forward to an old age of poverty, for I kept my eyes on you; I saw you entering on a prosperous career, and succeeding in it. That hope has given me courage to endure the privations I have gone through during the last six years to keep you at school, for it has cost seven or eight hundred francs a year besides the half-scholarship. Now that my hopes are crushed, I dread to think of your future fate. I must not spend a sou of Monsieur Clapart's salary on my own son.

"What do you propose to do. You are not a good enough mathematician to pass into a specialist college; and, besides, where could I find the three thousand francs a year for your training?—This is life, my dear child! Well, you are eighteen, and a strong lad—enlist as a soldier; it is the only way you can make a living."

Oscar as yet knew nothing of life. Like all boys who have been brought up in ignorance of the poverty at home, he had no idea of the need to work for his living; the word *trade* conveyed no idea to his mind; and the words *Government office* did not mean much, for he knew nothing of the work. He listened with a look of submission, which he tried to make penitential, but his mother's remonstrances were lost in air. However, at the idea of being a soldier, and on seeing the tears in his mother's eyes, the boy too was ready to weep. As soon as Madame Clapart saw the drops on her boy's cheeks, she was quite disarmed; and, like all mothers in a similar position, she fell back on the generalities which wind up this sort of attack, in which they suffer all their own sorrows and their children's at the same time.

"Come, Oscar, promise me to be more cautious for the future, not to blurt out whatever comes uppermost, to moderate your absurd conceit——" and so on.

Oscar was ready to promise all his mother asked, and pressing him gently to her heart, Madame Clapart ended by embracing him to comfort him for the scolding he had had.

"Now," said she, "you will listen to your mother and follow her advice, for a mother can give her son none but good advice.—We will go and see your uncle Cardot. He is our last hope. Cardot owed a great deal to your father, who, by allowing him to marry his sister, with what was then an immense marriage portion, enabled him to make a large fortune in silk. I fancy he would place you with Monsieur Camusot, his son-in-law and successor in the Rue des Bourdonnais.

"Still, your uncle Cardot has four children of his own. He made over his shop, the *Cocon d'Or,* to his eldest daughter, Madame Camusot. Though Cardot has millions, there are the four children, by two wives, and he hardly knows of our existence. Marianne, his second girl, married Monsieur Protez, of Protez and Chiffreville. He paid four hundred thousand francs to put his eldest son in business as a notary; and he has just invested for his second son Joseph as a partner in the business of Matifat, drug-importers. Thus your uncle Cardot may very well not choose to be troubled about you, whom he sees but four times a year. He has never been to call on me here; but he could come to see me when I was in *Madame Mère's* household, to be allowed to supply silks to their Imperial Highnesses, and the Emperor, and the Grandees at Court.— And now the Camusots are *Ultras!* Camusot's eldest son, by his first wife, married the daughter of a gentleman usher to the King! Well, when the world stoops it grows hunchbacked. And, after all, it is a good business; the *Cocon d'Or* has the custom of the Court under the Bourbons as it had under the Emperor.

"To-morrow we will go to see your uncle Cardot, and I hope you will contrive to behave; for, as I tell you, in him is our last hope."

Monsieur Jean Jérôme Séverin Cardot had lost his second wife six years since—Mademoiselle Husson, on whom, in the days of his glory, the contractor had bestowed a marriage portion of a hundred thousand francs in hard cash. Cardot, the head-clerk of the *Cocon d'Or,* one of the old-established Paris houses, had bought the business in 1793 when its owners were ruined by the *maximum,* and Mademoiselle Husson's money to back him had enabled him to make an almost colossal fortune in ten years. To provide handsomely for his children, he had very ingeniously invested three hundred thousand francs in annuities for himself and his wife, which brought him in thirty thousand francs a year. The rest of his capital he divided into three portions of four hundred thousand francs for his younger children, and the shop was taken as representing that sum by Camusot when he married the eldest girl. Thus the old fellow, now nearly seventy, could dispose of his thirty thousand francs a year without damaging his children's interests; they were all well married, and no avaricious hopes could interfere with their filial affection.

Uncle Cardot lived at Belleville in one of the first houses just above la Courtille. He rented a first floor, whence there was a fine view over the Seine valley, an apartment for which he paid a thousand francs a year, facing south, with the exclusive enjoyment of a large garden; thus he never troubled himself about the three or four other families inhabiting the spacious country house. Secure, by a long lease, of ending his days there, he lived rather shabbily, waited on by his old cook and by a maid who had been attached to his late wife, both of whom looked forward to an annuity of some six hundred francs at his death, and consequently did not rob him. These two women took incredible care of their master, and with all the more devotion since no one could be less fractious or fidgety than he.

The rooms, furnished by the late Madame Cardot, had remained unaltered for six years, and the old man was quite content; he did not spend a thousand crowns a year there, for he dined out in Paris five days a week, and came home at midnight in a private fly that he took at the Barrière de la Courtille. They had hardly anything to do beyond providing him with breakfast. The old man breakfasted at eleven o'clock, then he dressed and scented himself and went to Paris. A man usually gives notice when he means to dine out; Monsieur Cardot gave notice when he was to dine at home.

This little old gentleman, plump, rosy, square, and hearty, was always as neat as a pin, as the saying goes, that is to say, always in black silk stockings, corded silk knee-breeches, a white marcella waistcoat, dazzlingly white linen, and a dark blue coat; he wore violet silk gloves, gold buckles to his shoes, and breeches, a touch of powder on his hair, and a small queue tied with black ribbon. His face was noticeable for the thick, bushy eyebrows, beneath which sparkled his gray eyes, and a large squarely-cut nose that made him look like some venerable prebendary. This countenance did not belie the man. Old Cardot was, in fact, one of the race of frisky *Gérontes* who are disappearing day by day, and who played the part of Turcaret in all the romances and comedies of the eighteenth century. Uncle Cardot would speak to a woman as "Lady fair"; he would take home any woman in a coach who had no other protector; he was "theirs to command," to use his own expression, with a chivalrous flourish. His calm face and snowy hair were the adjuncts of an old age wholly devoted to pleasure. Among men he boldly professed Epicureanism, and allowed himself rather a broad style of jokes. He had made no objection when his son-in-law Camusot attached himself to Coralie, the fascinating actress, for he was, in secret, the Mæcenas of Mademoiselle Florentine, *première danseuse* at the Gaîté theatre

Still, nothing appeared on the surface, or in his evident conduct, to tell tales of these opinions and this mode of life. Uncle Cardot, grave and polite, was supposed to be almost cold, such a display did he make of the proprieties, and even a bigot would have called him a hypocrite. This worthy gentleman particularly detested the priesthood, he was one of the large body of silly people who subscribe to the *Constitutionnel*, and was much exercised about the refusal of rights of burial. He adored Voltaire, though his preference as a matter of taste was for Piron, Verdé, and Collé. Of course, he admired Béranger, of whom he spoke ingeniously as the *high priest of the religion of Lisette*. His daughters, Madame Camusot and Madame Protez, and his two sons would indeed have been knocked flat, to use a vulgar phrase, if any one had told them what their father meant by singing *"La Mère Godichon."*

This shrewd old man had never told his children of his annuity; and they, seeing him live so poorly, all believed that he had stripped himself of his fortune for them, and overwhelmed him with care and affection. And he would sometimes say to his sons, "Do not lose your money, for I have none to leave you." Camusot, who was a man after his own heart, and whom he liked well enough to allow him to join his little parties, was the only one who knew of his annuity of thirty thousand francs. Camusot highly applauded the old fellow's philosophy, thinking that after providing so liberally for his children and doing his duty so thoroughly, he had a right to end his days jovially.

"You see, my dear fellow," the old master of the *Cocon d'Or* would say to his son-in-law, "I might have married again, no doubt, and a young wife would have had children.—Oh, yes, I should have had children, I was at an age when men always have children.—Well, Florentine does not cost me so much as a wife, she never bores me, she will not plague me with children, and will not make a hole in your fortune." And Camusot discovered in old Cardot an admirable feeling for the Family, regarding him as a perfect father-in-law. "He succeeds," he would say, "in reconciling the interests of his children with the pleasures it is natural to indulge in in old age after having gone through all anxieties of business."

Neither the Cardots, nor the Camusots, nor the Protez suspected what the existence was of their old aunt Madame Clapart. Their communications had always been restricted to sending formal letters on the occasions of a death or a marriage, and visiting cards on New Year's Day. Madame Clapart was too proud to sacrifice her feelings for anything but her Oscar's interests, and acted under the influence of her regard for Moreau, the only person who had remained faithful to her in misfortune. She had never wearied old Cardot by her presence or her importunities, but she had clung to him as to a hope. She called on him once a quarter, and talked to him of Oscar Husson, the nephew of the late respected Madame Cardot, taking the lad to see Uncle Cardot three times a year, in the holidays. On each occasion the old man took Oscar to dine at the *Cadran bleu* (the Blue Dial), and to the Gaîté in the evening, taking him home afterwards to the Rue de la Cerisaie. On one occasion, after giving him a new suit of clothes, he had made him a present of the silver mug and spoon and fork required as part of every schoolboy's equipment.

Oscar's mother had tried to convince the old man that Oscar was very fond of him, and she was always talking of the silver mug and spoon and the beautiful suit, of which nothing now survived but the waistcoat. But these little insinuating attentions did Oscar more harm than good with so cunning an old fox as Uncle Cardot. Old Cardot had not been devoted to his late lamented, a bony red-haired woman; also he knew the circumstances of the deceased Husson's marriage to Oscar's mother; and without looking down on her in any way, he knew that Oscar had been born after his father's death, so his poor nephew seemed an absolute alien to the Cardot family. Unable to foresee disaster, Oscar's mother had not made up for this lack of natural ties between the boy and his uncle, and had not succeeded in implanting in the old merchant any liking for her boy in his earliest youth. Like all women who are absorbed in the one idea of motherhood, Madame Clapart could not put herself in Uncle Cardot's place; she thought he ought to be deeply interested in such a charming boy, whose name, too, was that of the late Madame Cardot.

"Monsieur, here is the mother of your nephew Oscar," said the maid to Monsieur Cardot, who was airing himself in the garden before breakfast, after being shaved and having his head dressed by the barber.

"Good-morning, lady fair," said the old silk-merchant, bowing to Madame Clapart, while he wrapped his white quilted dressing-gown across him. "Ah, ha! your youngster is growing apace," he added, pulling Oscar by the ear.

"He has finished his schooling, and he was very sorry that his dear uncle was not present at the distribution of prizes at the Collège Henri IV., for he was named. The name of Husson, of which, let us hope, he may prove worthy, was honorably mentioned."

"The deuce it was!" said the little man, stopping short. He was walking with Madame Clapart and Oscar on a terrace where there were orange-trees, myrtles, and pomegranate shrubs. "And what did he get?"

"The fourth *accessit* in philosophy," said the mother triumphantly.

"Oh, ho. He has some way to go yet to make up for lost time," cried Uncle Cardot. "To end with an *accessit*—is not the treasure of Peru.—You will breakfast with me?" said he.

"We are at your commands," replied Madame Clapart. "Oh, my dear Monsieur Cardot, what a comfort it is to a father and mother when their children make a good start in life. From that point of view, as indeed from every other," she put in, correcting herself, "you are one of the happiest fathers I know. In the hands of your admirable son-in-law and your amiable daughter, the *Cocon d'Or* is still the best shop of the kind in Paris. Your eldest son has been for years as a notary at the head of the best known business in Paris, and he married a rich woman. Your youngest is a partner in a first-rate druggist's business. And you have the sweetest grandchildren! You are the head of four flourishing families.—Oscar, leave us; go and walk round the garden, and do not touch the flowers."

"Why, he is eighteen!" exclaimed Uncle Cardot, smiling at this injunction, "as though Oscar was a child!"

"Alas! indeed he is, my dear Monsieur Cardot; and after bringing him up to that age neither crooked nor bandy, sound in mind and body, after sacrificing everything to give him an education, it would be hard indeed not to see him start in the way to fortune."

"Well, Monsieur Moreau, who got you his half-scholarship at the Collège Henri IV., will start him in the right road," said Uncle Cardot, hiding his hypocrisy under an affectation of bluntness.

"Monsieur Moreau may die," said she. "Besides, he has quarreled beyond remedy with Monsieur le Comte de Sérizy, his patron."

"The decue he has! Listen, madame, I see what you are coming to——"

"No, monsieur," said Oscar's mother, cutting the old man short; while he, out of respect for a "lady fair," controlled the impulse of annoyance at being interrupted. "Alas! you can know nothing of the anguish of a mother who for seven years has been obliged to take six hundred francs a year out of her husband's salary of eighteen hundred. Yes, monsieur, that is our whole income. So what can I do for my Oscar! Monsieur Clapart so intensely hates the poor boy, that I really cannot keep him at home. What can a poor woman do under such circumstances but come to consult the only relative her boy has under heaven?"

"You did quite right," replied Monsieur Cardot, "you never said anything of all this before——"

"Indeed, monsieur," replied Madame Clapart with pride, "you are the last person to whom I would confess the depth of my poverty. It is all my own fault; I married a man whose incapacity is beyond belief. Oh! I am a most miserable woman."

"Listen, madame," said the little old man gravely. "Do not cry. I cannot tell you how much it pains me to see a fair lady in tears. After all, your boy's name is Husson; and if the dear departed were alive, she would do something for the sake of her father's and brother's name——"

"She truly loved her brother!" cried Oscar's mother.

"But all my fortune is divided among my children, who have nothing further to expect from me," the old man went on. "I divided the two million francs I had among them; I wished to see them happy in my lifetime. I kept nothing for myself but an annuity, and at my time of life a man clings to his habits.—Do you know what you must do with this youngster?" said he, calling back Oscar, and taking him by the arm. "Put him to study law, I will pay for his matriculation and preliminary fees. Place him with an attorney; let him learn all the tricks of the trade; if he does well, and gets on and likes the work, and if I am still alive, each of my children will, when the time comes, lend him a quarter of the sum necessary to purchase a connection; I will stand surety for him. From now till then you have only to feed and clothe him; he will know some hard times, no doubt, but he will learn what life is. Why, why! I set out from Lyons with two double louis given me by my grandmother; I came to Paris on foot—and here I am! Short commons are good for the health.—Young man, with discretion, honesty, and hard work success is certain. It is a great pleasure to make your own fortune; and when a man has kept his teeth, he eats what he likes in his old age, singing *La Mère Godichon* every now and then, as I do. —Mark my words: Honesty, hard work, and discretion."

"You hear, Oscar," said his mother. "Your uncle has put in four words the sum-total of all my teaching, and you ought to stamp the last on your mind in letters of fire."

"Oh, it is there!" replied Oscar.

"Well, then, thank your uncle; do you not understand that he is providing for you in the future? You may be an attorney in Paris."

"He does not appreciate the splendor of his destiny," said the old man, seeing Oscar's bewildered face. "He has but just left school.—Listen to me: I am not given to wasting words," his uncle went on. "Remember that at your age honesty is only secured by resisting temptations, and in a great city like Paris you meet them at every turn. Live in a garret under your mother's roof; go straight to your lecture, and from that to your office; work away morning, noon, and night, and study at home; be a second clerk by the time you are two-and-twenty, and a head-clerk at four-and-twenty. Get learning, and you are a made man. And then if you should not like that line of work, you might go into my son's office as a notary and succeed him.—So work, patience, honesty, and discretion—these are your watchwords."

"And God grant you may live another thirty years to see your fifth child realize all our expectations!" cried Madame Clapart, taking the old man's hand and pressing it with a dignity worthy of her young days.

"Come, breakfast," said the kind old man, leading Oscar in by the ear.

During the meal Uncle Cardot watched his nephew on the sly, and soon discovered that he knew nothing of life.

"Send him to see me now and then," said he, as he took leave of her, with a nod to indicate Oscar. "I will lick him into shape."

This visit soothed the poor woman's worst grief, for she had not looked for such a happy result. For a fortnight she took Oscar out walking, watched over him almost tyrannically, and thus time went on till the end of October.

One morning Oscar saw the terrible steward walk in to find the wretched party in the Rue de la Cerisaie breakfasting off a salad of herring and lettuce, with a cup of milk to wash it down.

"We have settled in Paris, but we do not live as we did at Presles," said Moreau, who intended thus to make Madame Clapart aware of the change in their circumstances, brought about by Oscar's misdemeanor. "But I shall not often be in town. I have gone into partnership with old Léger and old Margueron of Beaumont. We are land agents, and we began by buying the estate of Persan. I am the head of the firm, which has got together a million of francs, for I have borrowed on my property. When I find an opening, Père Léger and I go into the matter, and my partners each take a quarter and I half of the profits, for I have all the trouble; I shall always be on the road.

"My wife lives in Paris very quietly, in the Faubourg du Roule. When we have fairly started in business, and shall only be risking the interest on our money, if we are satisfied with Oscar, we may perhaps give him work."

"Well, after all, my friend, my unlucky boy's blunder will no doubt turn out to be the cause of your making a fine fortune, for you really were wasting your talents and energy at Presles." Madame Clapart then told the story of her visit to Uncle Cardot, to show Moreau that she and her son might be no further expense to them.

"The old man is quite right," said the ex-steward. "Oscar must be kept to his work with a hand of iron, and he will no doubt make a notary or an attorney. But we must not wander from the line traced out for him.—Ah! I know the man you want. The custom of an estate agent is valuable. I have been told of an attorney who has bought a practice without any connection. He is a young man; but as stiff as an iron bar, a tremendous worker, a perfect horse for energy and go; his name is Desroches. I will offer him all our business on condition of his taking Oscar in hand. I will offer him a premium of nine hundred francs, of which I will pay three hundred; thus your son will cost you only six hundred, and I will recommend him strongly to his master. If the boy is ever to become a man, it will be under that iron rule, for he will come out a notary, a pleader, or an attorney."

"Come, Oscar, thank Monsieur Moreau for his kindness; you stand there like a mummy. It is not every youth who blunders that is lucky enough to find friends to take an interest in him after being injured by him——"

"The best way to make matters up with me," said Moreau, taking Oscar's hand, "is to work steadily and behave well."

Ten days after this Oscar was introduced by Monsieur Moreau to Maître Desroches, attorney, lately established in the Rue de Béthisy, in spacious rooms at the end of a narrow court, at a relatively low rent. Desroches, a young man of six-and-twenty, the son of poor parents, austerely brought up by an excessively severe father, had himself known what it was to be in Oscar's position; he therefore took an interest in him, but only in the way of which he was himself capable, with all the hardness of his character. The manner of this tall, lean young lawyer, with a dull complexion, and his hair cut short all over his head, sharp in his speech, keen-eyed, and gloomy though hasty, terrified poor Oscar.

"We work day and night here," said the lawyer from the depths of his chair, and from behind a long table, on which papers were piled in alps. "Monsieur Moreau, we will not kill him, but he will have to go our pace.—Monsieur Godeschal!" he called out.

Although it was Sunday, the head-clerk appeared with a pen in his hand.

"Monsieur Godeschal, this is the articled pupil of whom I spoke, and in whom Monsieur Moreau takes the greatest interest; he will dine with us, and sleep in the little attic next to your room. You must allow him exactly time enough to get to the law-schools and back, so that he has not five minutes to lose; see that he learns the Code, and does well at lecture; that is to say, give him law books to read up when he has done his school work. In short, he is to be under your immediate direction, and I will keep an eye on him. We want to turn him out what you are yourself—a capital head-clerk by the time he is ready to be sworn in as an attorney.—Go with Godeschal, my little friend; he will show you your room, and you can move into it."

"You see Godeschal?" Desroches went on, addressing Moreau. "He is a youngster without a sou, like myself; he is Mariette's brother, and she is saving for him, so that he may buy a connection ten years hence.—All my clerks are youngsters, who have nothing to depend on but their ten fingers to make their fortune. And my five clerks and I work like any dozen of other men. In ten years I shall have the finest practice in Paris. We take a passionate interest here in our business and our clients, and that is beginning to be known. I got Godeschal from my greater brother in law, Derville; with him he was second clerk, and only for a fortnight; but we had made friends in that huge office.

"I give Godeschal a thousand francs a year, with board and lodging. The fellow is worth it to me; he is indefatigable! I like that boy! He managed to live on six hundred francs a year, as I did when I was a clerk. What I absolutely insist on is stainless honesty, and the man who can practice it in poverty *is* a man. The slightest failing on that score, and a clerk of mine goes!"

"Come, the boy is in a good school," said Moreau.

For two whole years Oscar lived in the Rue de Béthisy, in a den of the law; for if ever this old-fashioned term could be applied to a lawyer's office, it was to this of Desroches. Under this minute and strict supervision, he was kept so rigidly to hours and to work, that his life in the heart of Paris was like that of a monk.

At five in the morning, in all weathers, Godeschal woke. He went down to the office with Oscar, to save a fire, and they always found the "chief" up and at work. Oscar did the errands and prepared his school-work—studies on an enormous scale. Godeschal, and often the chief himself, showed their pupil what authors to compare, and the difficulties to be met. Oscar never was allowed to pass from one chapter of the Code to the next till he had thoroughly mastered it, and had satisfied both Desroches and Godeschal, who put him through preliminary examinations, far longer and harder than those of the law schools.

On his return from the schools, where he did not spend much time, he resumed his seat in the office and worked again; sometimes he went into the Courts, and he was at the bidding of the merciless Godeschal till dinner-time. Dinner, which he shared with his masters, consisted of a large dish of meat, a dish of vegetables, and a salad; for dessert there was a bit of Gruyère cheese. After dinner, Godeschal and Oscar went back to the office, and worked there till the evening.

Once a month Oscar went to breakfast with his Uncle Cardot, and he spent the Sundays with his mother. Moreau from time to time, if he came to the office on business, would take the boy to dine at the Palais-Royal, and treat him to the play. Oscar had been so thoroughly snubbed by Godeschal and Desroches on the subject of his craving after fashion, that he had ceased to think about dress.

"A good clerk," said Godeschal, "should have two black coats—one old and one new—black trousers, black stockings and shoes. Boots cost too much. You may have boots when you are an attorney. A clerk ought not to spend more than seven hundred francs in all. He should wear good, strong shirts of stout linen.—Oh, when you start from zero to make a fortune, you must know how to limit yourself to what is strictly needful. Look at Monsieur Desroches! He did as we are doing, and you see he has succeeded."

Godeschal practised what he preached. Professing the strictest principles of honor, reticence, and honesty, he acted on them without any display, as simply as he walked and breathed. It was the natural working of his soul, as walking and breathing are the working of certain organs.

Eighteen months after Oscar's arrival, the second clerk had made, for the second time, a small mistake in the accounts of his little cash-box. Godeschal addressed him in the presence of all the clerks:

"My dear Gaudet, leave on your own account, that it may not be said that the chief turned you out. You are either inaccurate or careless, and neither of those faults is of any use here. The chief shall not know, and that is the best I can do for an old fellow-clerk."

Thus, at the age of twenty, Oscar was third clerk in Maître Desroches' office. Though he earned no salary yet, he was fed and lodged, for he did the work of a second clerk. Desroches employed two managing clerks, and the second clerk was overdone with work. By the time he had got through his second year at the schools, Oscar, who knew more than many a man who has taken out his license, did the work of the Courts very intelligently, and occasionally pleaded in chambers. In fact, Desroches and Godeschal were satisfied.

Still, though he had become almost sensible, he betrayed a love of pleasure and a desire to shine, which were only subdued by the stern discipline and incessant toil of the life he led. The estate agent, satisfied with the boy's progress, then relaxed his strictness; and when, in the month of July 1825, Oscar passed his final examination, Moreau gave him enough money to buy some good clothes. Madame Clapart, very happy and proud of her son, prepared a magnificent outfit for the qualified attorney, the second clerk, as he was soon to be. In poor families a gift always takes the form of something useful.

When the Courts re-opened in the month of November, Oscar took the second clerk's room and his place, with a salary of eight hundred francs, board and lodging. And Uncle Cardot, who came privately to make inquiries about his nephew of Desroches, promised Madame Clapart that he would put Oscar in a position to buy a connection if he went on as he had begun.

In spite of such seeming wisdom, Oscar Husson was torn by many yearnings in the bottom of his soul. Sometimes he felt as if he must fly from a life so entirely opposed to his taste and character; a galley slave, he thought, was happier than he. Galled by his iron collar, he was sometimes tempted to run away when he compared himself with some well-dressed youth he met in the street. Now and then an impulse of folly with regard to women would surge up in him; and his resignation was only a part of his disgust of life. Kept steady by Godeschal's example, he was dragged rather than led by his will to follow so thorny a path.

Godeschal, who watched Oscar, made it his rule not to put his ward in the way of temptation. The boy had usually no money, or so little that he could not run into excesses. During the last year the worthy Godeschal had five or six times taken Oscar out for some "lark," paying the cost, for he perceived that the cord round this tethered kid's neck must be loosened; and these excesses, as the austere head-clerk termed them, helped Oscar to endure life. He found little to amuse him at his uncle's house, and still less at his mother's, for she lived even more frugally than Desroches.

Moreau could not, like Godeschal, make himself familiar with Oscar, and it is probable that this true protector made Godeschal his deputy in initiating the poor boy into the many mysteries of life. Oscar, thus learning discretion, could at last appreciate the enormity of the blunder he had committed during his ill-starred journey in the *coucou;* still, as the greater part of his fancies were so far suppressed, the follies of youth might yet lead him astray. However, as by degrees he acquired knowledge of the world and its ways, his reason developed; and so long as Godeschal did not lose sight of him, Moreau hoped to train Madame Clapart's son to a good end.

"How is he going on?" the estate agent asked on his return from a journey which had kept him away from Paris for some months.

"Still much too vain," replied Godeschal. "You give him good clothes and fine linen, he wears shirt-frills like a stockbroker, and my gentleman goes walking in the Tuileries on Sundays in search of adventures. What can I say? He is young.—He teases me to introduce him to my sister, in whose house he would meet a famous crew!—actresses, dancers, dandies, men who are eating themselves out of house and home.—He is not cut out for an attorney, I fear. Still, he does not speak badly; he might become a pleader. He could argue a case from a well-prepared brief."

In November 1825, when Oscar Husson was made second clerk, and was preparing his *thesis* for taking out his license, a new fourth clerk came to Desroches' office to fill up the gap made by Oscar's promotion.

This fourth clerk, whose name was Frédéric Marest, was

intended for the higher walks of the law, and was now ending his third year at the schools. From information received by the inquiring minds of the office, he was a handsome fellow of three-and-twenty, who had inherited about twelve thousand francs a year at the death of a bachelor uncle, and the son of a Madame Marest, the widow of a rich timber merchant. The future judge, filled with the laudable desire to know his business in its minutest details, placed himself under Desroches, intending to study procedure, so as to be fit to take the place of a managing clerk in two years' time. His purpose was to go through his first stages as a pleader in Paris, so as to be fully prepared for an appointment, which, as a young man of wealth, he would certainly get. To see himself a public prosecutor, at the age of thirty, was the height of his ambition.

Though Frédéric Marest was the first cousin of Georges Marest, the practical joker of the journey to Presles, as young Husson knew this youth only by his first name, as Georges, the name of Frédéric Marest had no suggestions for him.

"Gentlemen," said Godeschal at breakfast, addressing all his underlings, "I have to announce the advent of a new student in law; and as he is very rich, we shall, I hope, make him pay his footing handsomely."

"Bring out the Book," cried Oscar to the youngest clerk, "and let us be serious, pray."

The boy clambered like a squirrel along the pigeon-holes to reach a volume lying on the top shelf, so as to collect all the dust.

"It is finely colored!" said the lad, holding it up.

We must now explain the perennial pleasantry which at that time gave rise to the existence of such a book in almost every lawyer's office. An old saying of the eighteenth century—"Clerks only breakfast, farmers generally dine, and lords sup"—is still true, as regards the faculty of law, of every man who has spent two or three years studying procedure under an attorney, or the technicalities of a notary's business under some master of that branch. In the life of a lawyer's clerk work is so unremitting, that pleasure is enjoyed all the more keenly for its rarity, and a practical joke especially is relished with rapture. This, indeed, is what explains up to a certain point Georges Marest's behavior in Pierrotin's chaise. The gloomiest of law-clerks is always a prey to the craving for farcical buffoonery. The instinct with which a practical joke or an occasion for fooling is jumped at and utilized among law-clerks is marvelous to behold, and is found in no other class but among artists. The studio and the lawyer's office are, in this respect, better than the stage.

Desroches, having started in an office without a connection, had, as it were, founded a new dynasty. This "Restoration" had interrupted the traditions of the office with regard to the footing of the newcomer. Desroches, indeed, settling in quarters where stamped paper had never yet been seen, had put in new tables, and clean new file-boxes of white mill-board edged with blue. His staff consisted of clerks who had come from other offices with no connection between them, and thrown together by surprise as it were.

But Godeschal, who had learned his fence under Derville, was not the man to allow the precious tradition of the *Bienvenue* to be lost. The *Bienvenue,* or welcome, is the breakfast which every new pupil must give to the "old boys" of the office to which he is articled. Now, just at the time when Oscar joined the office, in the first six months of Desroches' career, one winter afternoon when work was got through earlier than usual, and the clerks were warming themselves before going home, Godeschal hit upon the notion of concocting a sham register of the *fasti* and High Festivals of the Minions of the Law, a relic of great antiquity, saved from the storms of the Revolution, and handed down from the office of the great Bordin, Attorney to the Châtelet, and the immediate predecessor of Sauvagnest, the attorney from whom Desroches had taken the office. The first thing was to find in some stationer's old stock a ledger with paper bearing an eighteenth century watermark, and properly bound in parchment, in which to enter the decrees of the Council. Having discovered such a volume, it was tossed in the dust, in the ash-pan, in the fireplace, in the kitchen; it was even left in what the clerks called the consulting-room; and it had acquired a tint of mildew that would have enchanted a book-worm, the cracks of primeval antiquity, and corners so worn that the mice might have nibbled them off. The edges were rubbed with infinite skill. The book being thus perfected, here are a few passages which will explain to the dullest the uses to which Desroches' clerks devoted it, the first sixty pages being filled with sham reports of cases.

"In the name of the Father and of the Son and of the Holy Ghost. So be it.

"Whereas, on this day the Festival of our Lady Saint Geneviève, patron saint of this good city of Paris, under whose protection the scribes and scriveners of this office have dwelt since the year of our Lord 1525, we, the undersigned clerks and scriveners of this office of Master Jerosme-Sebastien Bordin, successor here to the deceased Guerbet, who in his lifetime served as attorney to the Châtelet, have recognized the need for us to replace the register and archives of installations of clerks in this glorious office, being ourselves distinguished members of the Faculty of the Law, which former register is now filled with the roll and record of our well-beloved predecessors, and we have besought the keeper of the Palace archives to bestow it with those of other offices, and we have all attended High Mass in the parish church of Saint-Séverin to solemnize the opening of this our new register.

"In token whereof, we here sign and affix our names.

"MALIN, Head-Clerk.

"GREVIN, Second Clerk.

"ATHANASE FERET, Clerk.

"JACQUES HUET, Clerk.

"REGINALD DE SAINT-JEAN-D'ANGELY, Clerk.

"BEDEAU, Office Boy and Gutter-Jumper.

"In the year of our Lord 1787.

"Having attended Mass, we went in a body to la Courtille,

and had a great breakfast, which lasted until seven in the morning."

This was a miracle of caligraphy. An expert could have sworn that the writing dated from the eighteenth century. Then follow twenty-seven reports in full of "Welcome" breakfasts, the last dating from the fatal year 1792.

After a gap of fourteen years, the register re-opened in 1806 with the appointment of Bordin to be attorney to the lower Court of the Seine. And this was the record of the re-constitution of the Kingdom of Basoche (the legal profession generally) :—

"God in His clemency has granted that in the midst of the storms which have devastated France, now a great Empire, the precious archives of the most illustrious office of Master Bordin should be preserved. And we, the undersigned clerks of the most honorable and most worshipful Master Bordin, do not hesitate to ascribe this their marvelous escape, when so many other title-deeds, charters, and letters patent have vanished, to the protection of Saint Geneviève, the patron saint of this office, as likewise to the reverence paid by the last of the attorneys of the old block to all ancient use and custom. And whereas we know not what share to ascribe to the Lady Saint Geneviève and what to Master Bordin in the working of this miracle, we have resolved to go to the Church of Saint Étienne-du-Mont, there to attend a mass to be said at the altar of that saintly shepherdess who sendeth us so many lambs to fleece, and to invite our chief and master to breakfast, in the hope that he may bear the charge thereof. And to this we set our hand.

"OIGNARD, Head-Clerk.
"POIDEVIN, Second Clerk.
"PROUST, Clerk.
"BRIGNOLET, Clerk.
"DERVILLE, Clerk.
"AUGUSTEN CORET, Office Boy.
"At the office, this 10th day of November 1806."

"At three o'clock of the afternoon of the next day, the undersigned, being the clerks of this office, record their gratitude to their very worshipful chief, who hath feasted them at the shop of one Rolland, a cook in the Rue du Hasard, on good wines of three districts, Bordeaux, Champagne, and Burgundy, and on meats of good savor, from four o'clock of the afternoon until half-past seven, with coffee, liqueurs, and ices galore. Yet hath the presence of the worshipful master hindered us from the singing of *laudes* in clerkly modes, nor hath any clerk overstepped the limits of pleasing levity, inasmuch as our worthy, worshipful, and generous master had promised to take up his clerks to see Talma in *Britannicus* at the Théâtre Français. Long may he flourish! May heaven shed blessings on our worshipful master! May he get a good price for this his glorious office! May rich clients come to his heart's desire! May his bills of cost be paid in gold on the nail! May all our future masters be like him! May he be ever beloved of his clerks, even when he is no more!"

Next came thirty-three reports in due form of the receptions of clerks who had joined the office, distinguished by various handwritings in different shades of ink, distinct phraseology, and different signatures, and containing such laudatory accounts of the good cheer and wines as seemed to prove that the reports were drawn up on the spot and *inter pocula*.

Finally, in the month of June, 1822, at the time when Desroches himself had taken the oaths, there was this page of business-like prose:—

"I, the undersigned François Claude Marie Godeschal, being called by Maître Desroches to fulfil the difficult duties of head-clerk in an office where there are as yet no clients, having heard from Maître Derville, whose chambers I have quitted, of the existence of certain famous archives of Basochian banquets and Festivals famous in the Courts, I besought our worshipful master to require them of his predecessor; for it was important to recover that document, which bore the date A. D. 1786, and was the sequel to the archives, deposited with those of the Courts of Law, of which the existence was certified by MM. Terrasse and Duclos, keepers of the said archives, going back to the year 1525, and giving historical details of the highest value as to the manners and cookery of the law-clerks in those days.

"This having been granted, the office was put in possession as at this time of these evidences of the worship constantly paid by our predecessors to the *Dive Bouteille* and to good cheer.

"Whereupon, for the edification of those that come after us, and to continue the sequence of time and cup, I have invited MM. Doublet, second clerk; Vassal, third clerk; Hérisson and Grandemain, assistant clerks; Dumets, office boy, to breakfast on Sunday next at the *Cheval Rouge* on the Quai Saint-Bernard, where we will celebrate the recovery of this volume containing the charter of our guzzlings.

"On this day, Sunday, June 27th, one dozen bottles of various wines were drunk and found excellent. Noteworthy, likewise, were two melons, pies *au jus romanum,* a fillet of beef, and a toast *Agaricibus.* Mademoiselle Mariette, the illustrious sister of the head-clerk, and leading lady at the Royal Academy of Music and Dancing, having given to the clerks of this office stalls for that evening's performance, she is hereby to be remembered for her act of generosity. And it is furthermore resolved that the said clerks shall proceed in a body to return thanks to that noble damsel, and to assure her that on the occasion of her first lawsuit, if the Devil involves her in one, she shall pay no more than the bare costs; to which all set their hand.

"Godeschal was proclaimed the pride of his profession, and the best of good fellows. May the man who treats others so handsomely soon be treating for a business of his own!"

The document was spattered with wine-spots and with blots and flourishes like fireworks.

To give a complete idea of the stamp of truth impressed on

this great work, it will suffice to extract the report of the reception supposed to have been provided by Oscar:—

"To-day, Monday, the 25th day of November 1822, after a meeting held yesterday in the Rue de la Cerisaie, hard by the Arsenal, at the house of Madame Clapart, the mother of the new pupil, by name Oscar Husson, we, the undersigned, declare that the breakfast far surpassed our expectations. It included radishes (red and black), gherkins, anchovies, butter, and olives as introductory *hors-d' œuvres;* of a noble rich broth that bore witness to a mother's care, inasmuch as we recognized in it a delicious flavor of fowl; and by the courtesy of the founder of the feast we were, in fact, informed that the trimmings of a handsome cold dish prepared by Madame Clapart had been judiciously added to the stock concocted at home with such care as is known only in private kitchens.

"*Item,* the aforementioned cold fowl, surrounded by a sea of jelly, the work of the aforenamed mother.

"*Item,* an ox-tongue, *aux tomates,* on which we proved ourselves by no means au-tomata.

"*Item,* a stew of pigeons of such flavor as led us to believe that angels had watched over the pot.

"*Item,* a dish of macaroni flanked by cups of chocolate custard.

"*Item,* dessert, consisting of eleven dishes, among which, in spite of the intoxication resulting from sixteen bottles of excellent wine, we discerned the flavor of an exquisitely and superlatively delicious preserve of peaches.

"The wines of Roussillon and of the Côte du Rhône quite outdid those of Champagne and Burgundy. A bottle of Maraschino, and one of Kirsch, finally, and in spite of delicious coffee, brought us to such a pitch of œnological rapture, that one of us—namely, Master Hérisson—found himself in the Bois de Boulogne when he believed he was still on the Boulevard du Temple; and that Jacquinaut, the gutter-jumper, aged fourteen, spoke to citizens' wives of fifty-seven, taking them for women on the street; to which all set their hand.

"Now, in the statutes of our Order there is a law strictly observed, which is, that those who aspire to the benefits and honors of the profession of the law shall restrict the magnificence of their 'welcome' to the due proportion with their fortune, inasmuch as it is a matter of public notoriety that no man with a private income serves Themis, and that all clerks' are kept short of cash by their fond parents; wherefore, it is with great admiration that we here record the munificence of Madame Clapart, widow after her first marriage of Monsieur Husson, the new licentiate's father, and declare that it was worthy of the cheers we gave her at the dessert; to which all set their hand."

This rigmarole had already taken in three newcomers, and three real breakfasts were duly recorded in this imposing volume.

On the day when a neophyte first made his appearance in the office, the boy always laid the archives on the desk in front of his seat, and the clerks chuckled as they watched the face of the new student while he read these grotesque passages. Each in turn, *inter pocula,* had been initiated into the secret of this practical joke, and the revelation, as may be supposed, filled them with the hope of mystifying other clerks in the future.

So, now, my readers can imagine the countenances of the four clerks and the boy, when Oscar, now in his turn the practical joker, uttered the words, "Bring out the Book."

Ten minutes later, a handsome young man came in, well grown and pleasant looking, asked for Monsieur Desroches, and gave his name at once to Godeschal.

"I am Frédéric Marest," said he, "and have come to fill the place of third clerk here."

"Monsieur Husson," said Godeschal, "show the gentleman his seat, and induct him into our ways of work."

Next morning the new clerk found the Book lying on his writing-pad; but after reading the first pages, he only laughed, gave no invitation, and put the book aside on his desk.

"Gentlemen," said he, as he was leaving at five o'clock, "I have a cousin who is managing-clerk to Maître Léopold Hannequin, the notary, and I will consult him as to what I should do to pay my footing."

"This looks badly," cried Godeschal. "Our sucking magistrate is no greenhorn."

"Oh! we will lead him a life!" said Oscar.

Next afternoon, at about two o'clock, Oscar saw a visitor come in, and recognized in Hannequin's head-clerk Georges Marest.

"Why, here is Ali Pasha's friend!" said he, in an airy tone.

"What? you here, my lord, the Ambassador?" retorted Georges, remembering Oscar.

"Oh, ho! then you are old acquaintances?" said Godeschal to Georges.

"I believe you! We played the fool in company," said Georges, "above two years ago.—Yes, I left Crottat to go to Hannequin in consequence of that very affair."

"What affair?" asked Godeschal.

"Oh, a mere nothing," replied Georges, with a wink at Oscar. "We tried to make game of a Peer of France, and it was he who made us look foolish.—And now, I hear you want to draw my cousin."

"We do not draw anything," said Oscar with dignity. "Here is our charter." And he held out the famous volume at a page where sentence of excommunication was recorded against a refractory student, who had been fairly driven out of the office for stinginess in 1788.

"Still, I seem to smell game," said Georges, "for here is the trail," and he pointed to the farcical archives. "However, my cousin and I can afford it, and we will give you a feast such as you never had, and which will stimulate your imagination when recording it here.—To-morrow, Sunday, at the *Rocher de Cancale,* two o'clock. And I will take you afterwards to spend the evening with Madame la Marquise de las Florentinas y Cabirolos, where we will gamble, and you will meet the élite of fashion. And so, gentlemen of the lower Court," he went on, with the arrogance of a notary, "let us have your best behavior, and carry your wine like gentlemen of the Regency."

"Hurrah!" cried the clerks like one man. "Bravo!—*Very well!*—*Vivat!*—Long live the Marests!——"

"*Pontins,*" added the boy (Les Marais Pontins—the Pontine Marshes).

"What is up?" asked Desroches, coming out of his private room. "Ah! you are here, Georges," said he to the visitor. "I know you, you are leading my clerks into mischief." And he went back into his own room, calling Oscar.

"Here," said he, opening his cash-box, "are five hundred francs; go to the Palace of Justice and get the judgment in the case of Vandenesse *vs.* Vandenesse out of the copying-clerk's office; it must be sent in this evening if possible. I promised Simon a refresher of twenty francs; wait for the copy if it is not ready, and do not let yourself be put off. Derville is quite capable of putting a drag on our wheels if it will serve his client.—Count Félix de Vandenesse is more influential than his brother the Ambassador, our client. So keep your eyes open, and if the least difficulty arises, come to me at once."

Oscar set out, determined to distinguish himself in this little skirmish, the first job that had come to him since his promotion.

When Georges and Oscar were both gone, Godeschal tried to pump the new clerk as to what jest might lie, as he felt sure, under the name of the Marquise de las Florentinas y Cabirolos; but Frédéric carried on his cousin's joke with the coolness and gravity of a judge, and by his replies and his manner contrived to convey to all the clerks that the Marquise de las Florentinas was the widow of a Spanish grandee, whom his cousin was courting. Born in Mexico, and the daughter of a Creole, this wealthy young widow was remarkable for the free-and-easy demeanor characteristic of the women of the Tropics.

"'She likes to laugh, She likes to drink, She likes to sing as we do,'" said he, quoting a famous song by Béranger. "And Georges," he went on, "is very rich; he inherited a fortune from his father, who was a widower, and who left him eighteen thousand francs a year, which, with twelve thousand left to each of us by an uncle, make an income of thirty thousand francs. And he hopes to be Marquis de las Florentinas, for the young widow bears her title in her own right, and can confer it on her husband."

Though the clerks remained very doubtful as to the Marquise, the prospect of a breakfast at the *Rocher de Cancale*, and of a fashionable soirée, filled them with joy. They reserved their opinion as to the Spanish lady, to judge her without appeal after having seen her.

The Marquise de las Florentinas was, in fact, neither more nor less than Mademoiselle Agathe Florentine Cabirolle, leading *danseuse* at the Gaîté Theatre, at whose house Uncle Cardot "sang *La Mère Godichon*." Within a year of the very reparable loss of the late Madame Cardot, the fortunate merchant met Florentine one evening coming out of Coulon's dancing school. Dazzled by the beauty of this flower of the ballet—Florentine was then but thirteen—the retired shopkeeper followed her to the Rue Pastourelle, where he had the satisfaction of learning that the future divinity of the dance owed her existence to a humble doorkeeper. The mother and daughter, transplanted within a fortnight to the Rue de Crussol, there found themselves in modest but easy circumstances. So it was to this "Patron of the Arts," to use a time-honored phrase, that the stage was indebted for the budding artist.

The generous Mæcenas almost turned their simple brains by giving them mahogany furniture, curtains, carpets, and a well-fitted kitchen; he enabled them to keep a servant, and allowed them two hundred and fifty francs a month. Old Cardot, with his *ailes de pigeon*. to them seemed an angel, and was treated as a benefactor should be. This was the golden age of the old man's passion.

For three years the singer of *La Mère Godichon* was so judicious as to keep Mademoiselle Cabirolle and her mother in this unpretentious house, close to the theatre; then, for love of the Terpsichorean art, he placed his protégée under Vestris. And, in 1820, he was so happy as to see Florentine dance her first steps in the ballet of a spectacular melodrama called "The Ruins of Babylon." Florentine was now sixteen.

Soon after this first appearance Uncle Cardot was "an old hunks," in the young lady's estimation; however, as he had tact enough to understand that a dancer at the Gaîté Theatre must keep up a position, and raised her monthly allowance to five hundred francs a month, if he was no longer an angel, he was at least a friend for life, a second father. This was the age of silver.

Between 1820 and 1823 Florentine went through the experience which must come to every ballet-dancer of nineteen or twenty. Her friends were the famous opera-singers Mariette and Tullia; Florine, and poor Coralie, so early snatched from Art, Love, and Camusot. And as little uncle Cardot himself was now five years older, he had drifted into the indulgence of that half-fatherly affection which old men feel for the young talents they have trained, and whose successes are theirs. Besides, how and where should a man of sixty-eight have formed such another attachment as this with Florentine, who knew his ways, and at whose house he could sing *La Mère Godichon* with his friends? So the little man found himself under a half matrimonial yoke of irresistible weight. This was the age of brass.

In the course of the five years of the ages of gold and of silver, Cardot had saved ninety thousand francs. The old man had had much experience; he foresaw that by the time he was seventy Florentine would be of age; she would probably come out on the Opera stage, and, of course, expect the luxury and splendor of a leading lady. Only a few days before the evening now to be described, Cardot had spent forty-five thousand francs in establishing his Florentine in a suitable style, and had taken for her the apartment where the now dead Coralie had been the joy of Camusot. In Paris, apartments and houses, like streets, have a destiny.

Glorying in magnificent plate, the leading lady of the Gaîté gave handsome dinners, spent three hundred francs a month on dress, never went out but in a private fly, and kept a maid, a cook, and a page. What she aimed at indeed was a command to dance at the opera. The *Cocon d'Or* laid its handsomest products at the feet of its former master to please Mademoiselle Cabirolle, known as Florentine, just as, three years since, it had gratified every wish of Coralie's; but still without the knowledge of uncle Cardot's daughter, for the father and his son-in-law had always agreed that decorum must be respected at home. Madame Camusot knew nothing of her husband's extravagance or her father's habits.

Now, after being the master for seven years, Cardot felt himself in tow of a pilot whose power of caprice was unlimited. But the unhappy old fellow was in love. Florentine alone must close his eyes, and he meant to leave her a hundred thousand francs. The age of iron had begun.

Georges Marest, handsome, young, and rich, with thirty thousand francs a year, was paying court to Florentine. Every dancer is by way of loving somebody as her protector loves her, and having a young man to escort her out walking or driving, and arrange excursions into the country. And, however disinterested, the affections of a leading lady are always a luxury, costing the happy object of her choice some little trifle. Dinners at the best restaurants, boxes at the play, carriages for driving in the environs of Paris, and choice wines lavishly consumed—for ballet-dancers live now like the athletes of antiquity.

Georges, in short, amused himself as young men do who suddenly find themselves independent of paternal discipline; and his uncle's death, almost doubling his income, enlarged his ideas. So long as he had but the eighteen thousand francs a year left him by his parents he intended to be a notary; but, as his cousin remarked to Desroches' clerks, a man would be a noodle to start in a profession with as much money as others have when they give it up. So the retiring law-clerk was celebrating his first day of freedom by this breakfast, which was also to pay his cousin's footing.

Frédéric, more prudent than Georges, persisted in his legal career.

As a fine young fellow like Georges might very well marry a rich creole, and the Marquis de las Florentinas y Cabirolos might very well in the decline of life—as Frédéric hinted to his new companions—have preferred to marry for beauty rather than for noble birth, the clerks of Desroches' office—all belonging to impecunious families, and having no acquaintance with the fashionable world—got themselves up in their Sunday clothes, all impatience to see the Mexican Marquesa de las Florentinas y Cabirolos.

"What good luck," said Oscar to Godeschal as he dressed in the morning, "that I should have just ordered a new coat, waistcoat, and trousers, and a pair of boots, and that my precious mother should have given me a new outfit on my promotion to be second clerk. I have six fine shirts with frills out of the dozen she gave me. We will make a good show! Oh! if only one of us could carry off the Marquise from that Georges Marest!"

"A pretty thing for a clerk in Maître Desroches' office!" cried Godeschal. "Will you never be cured of your vanity—brat!"

"Oh, monsieur," said Madame Clapart, who had just come in to bring her son some ties, and heard the managing clerk's remarks, "would to God that Oscar would follow your good advice! It is what I am always saying to him, 'Imitate Monsieur Godeschal, take his advice,' is what I say."

"He is getting on, madame," said Godeschal, "but he must not often be so clumsy as he was yesterday, or he will lose his place in the master's good graces. Maître Desroches cannot stand a man who is beaten. He sent your son on his first errand yesterday, to fetch away the copy of the judgment delivered in a will case, which two brothers, men of high rank, are fighting against each other, and Oscar allowed himself to be circumvented. The master was furious. It was all I could do to set things straight by going at six this morning to find the copying-clerk, and I made him promise to let me have the judgment in black and white by seven to-morrow morning."

"Oh, Godeschal," cried Oscar, going up to his superior and grasping his hand, "you are a true friend!"

"Yes, monsieur," said Madame Clapart, "it is a happy thing for a mother to feel that her son has such a friend as you, and you may believe that my gratitude will end only with my life. Oscar, beware of this Georges Marest; he has already been the cause of your first misfortune in life."

"How was that?" asked Godeschal.

The too-confiding mother briefly told the head-clerk the story of poor Oscar's adventure in Pierrotin's chaise.

"And I am certain," added Godeschal, "that the humbug has planned some trick on us this evening. I shall not go to the Marquise de las Florentinas. My sister needs my help in drawing up a fresh engagement, so I shall leave you at dessert. But be on your guard, Oscar. Perhaps they will make you gamble, and Desroches' office must not make a poor mouth. Here, you can stake for us both; here are a hundred francs," said the kind fellow, giving the money to Oscar, whose purse had been drained by the tailor and bootmaker. "Be careful; do not dream of playing beyond the hundred francs; do not let play or wine go to your head. By the Mass! even a second clerk has a position to respect; he must not play on promissory paper, nor overstep a due limit in anything. When a man is second clerk he must remember that he will presently be an attorney. So not to drink, not to play high, and to be moderate in all things, must be your rule of conduct. Above all, be in by midnight, for you must be at the Courts by seven to fetch away the copy of that judgment. There is no law against some fun, but business holds the first place."

"Do you hear, Oscar?" said Madame Clapart. "And see

how indulgent Monsieur Godeschal is, and how he combines the enjoyments of youth with the demands of duty."

Madame Clapart, seeing the tailor and bootmaker waiting for Oscar, remained behind a moment with Godeschal to return the hundred francs he had just lent the boy.

"A mother's blessing be on you, monsieur, and on all you do," said she.

The mother had the supreme delight of seeing her boy well dressed; she had bought him a gold watch, purchased out of her savings, as a reward for his good conduct.

"You are on the list for the conscription next week," said she, "and as it was necessary to be prepared in case your number should be drawn, I went to see your uncle Cardot; he is delighted at your being so high up at the age of twenty, and at your success in the examinations at the law schools, so he has promised to find the money for a substitute. Do you not yourself feel some satisfaction in finding good conduct so well rewarded? If you still have to put up with some privations, think of the joy of being able to purchase a connection in only five years! And remember too, dear boy, how happy you make your mother."

Oscar's face, thinned down a little by hard study, had developed into a countenance to which habits of business had given a look of gravity. He had done growing, and had a beard; in short, from a boy he had become a man. His mother could not but admire him, and she kissed him fondly, saying:

"Yes, enjoy yourself, but remember Monsieur Godeschal's advice.—By the way, I was forgetting: here is a present from our friend Moreau—a pocketbook."

"The very thing I want, for the chief gave me five hundred francs to pay for that confounded judgment in Vandenesse, and I did not want to leave them in my room."

"Are you carrying the money about with you?" said his mother in alarm. "Supposing you were to lose such a sum of money! Would you not do better to leave it with Monsieur Godeschal?"

"Godeschal!" cried Oscar, thinking his mother's idea admirable.

But Godeschal, like all clerks on Sunday, had his day to himself from ten o'clock, and was already gone.

When his mother had left, Oscar went out to lounge on the Boulevards till it was time for the breakfast. How could he help airing those resplendent clothes, that he wore with such pride, and the satisfaction that every man will understand who began life in narrow circumstances? A neat double-breasted blue cashmere waistcoat, black kerseymere trousers made with pleats, a well-fitting black coat, and a cane with a silver-gilt knob, bought out of his little savings, were the occasion of very natural pleasure to the poor boy, who remembered the clothes he had worn on the occasion of that journey to Presles, and the effect produced on his mind by Georges.

Oscar looked forward to a day of perfect bliss; he was to see the world of fashion for the first time that evening! And it must be admitted that to a lawyer's clerk starved of pleasure, who had for long been craving for a debauch, the sudden play of the senses was enough to obliterate the wise counsels of Godeschal and his mother. To the shame of the young be it said, good advice and warnings are never to seek. Apart from the morning's lecture, Oscar felt an instinctive dislike of Georges; he was humiliated in the presence of a man who had witnessed the scene in the drawing-room at Presles, when Moreau had dragged him to the Count's feet.

The moral sphere has its laws; and we are always punished if we ignore them. One, especially, the very beasts obey invariably and without delay. It is that which bids us fly from any one who has once injured us, voluntarily or involuntarily, intentionally or no. The being who has brought woe or discomfort on us is always odious. Whatever his rank, however near be the ties of affection, we must part. He is the emissary of our evil genius. Though Christian theory is opposed to such conduct, obedience to this inexorable law is essentially social and preservative. James II.'s daughter, who sat on her father's throne, must have inflicted more than one wound on him before her usurpation. Judas must certainly have given

Jesus some mortal thrust or ever he betrayed Him. There is within us a second sight, a mind's eye, which foresees disasters; and the repugnance we feel to the fateful being is the consequence of this prophetic sense. Though religion may command us to resist it, distrust remains and its voice should be listened to.

Could Oscar, at the age of twenty, be so prudent? Alas! When, at two o'clock, Oscar went into the room of the *Rocher de Cancale,* where he found three guests besides his fellow-clerks—to wit, an old dragoon captain named Giroudeau; Finot, a journalist who might enable Florentine to get an engagement at the opera; and du Bruel, an author and friend of Tullia's, one of Mariette's rivals at the opera,—the junior felt his hostility melt away under the first hand-shaking, the first flow of talk among young men, as they sat at a table handsomely laid for twelve. And indeed Georges was charming to Oscar.

"You are," said he, "following a diplomatic career, but in private concerns; for what is the difference between an ambassador and an attorney? Merely that which divides a nation from an individual. Ambassadors are the attorneys of a people.—If I can ever be of any use to you, depend on me."

"My word! I may tell you now," said Oscar, "you were the cause of a terrible catastrophe for me."

"Pooh!" said Georges, after listening to the history of the lad's tribulations. "It was Monsieur de Sérizy who behaved badly. His wife?—I would not have her at a gift. And although the Count is Minister of State and Peer of France, I would not be in his red skin! He is a small-minded man, and I can afford to despise him now."

Oscar listened with pleasure to Georges' ironies on the Comte de Sérizy, for they seemed to diminish the gravity of his own fault, and he threw himself into the young man's spirit as he predicted that overthrow of the nobility of which the citizen class then had visions, to be realized in 1830.

They sat down at half-past three; dessert was not on the table before eight. Each course of dishes lasted two hours.

None but law-clerks can eat so steadily! Digestions of eighteen and twenty are inexplicable to the medical faculty. The wine was worthy of Borrel, who had at that time succeeded the illustrious Balaine, the creator of the very best restaurant in Paris—and that is to say in the world—for refined and perfect cookery.

A full report of this Belshazzar's feast was drawn up at dessert, beginning with—*Inter pocula aurea restauranti, qui vulgo dicitur Rupes Cancali:* and from this introduction the rapturous record may be imagined which was added to this Golden Book of the High Festivals of the Law.

Godeschal disappeared after signing his name, leaving the eleven feasters, prompted by the old captain of the Imperial Dragoons, to devote themselves to the wine, the liqueurs, and the toasts, over a dessert of pyramids of sweets and fruits like the pyramids of Thebes. By half-past ten the "boy" of the office was in a state which necessitated his removal; Georges packed him into a cab, gave the driver his mother's address, and paid his fare. Then the ten remaining guests, as drunk as Pitt and Dundas, talked of going on foot by the Boulevards, the night being very fine, as far as the residence of the Marquise, where, at a little before midnight, they would find a brilliant company. The whole party longed to fill their lungs with fresh air; but excepting Georges, Giroudeau, Finot, and du Bruel, all accustomed to Parisian orgies, no one could walk. So Georges sent for three open carriages from a job-master's stables, and took the whole party for an airing on the outer Boulevards for an hour, from Montmartre to the Barrière du Trône, and back by Bercy, the quays, and the Boulevards to the Rue de Vendôme.

The youngsters were still floating in the paradise of fancy to which intoxication transports boys, when their entertainer led them into Florentine's rooms. Here sat a dazzling assembly of the queens of the stage, who, at a hint, no doubt, from Frédéric, amused themselves by aping the manners of fine ladies. Ices were handed round, the chandeliers blazed with wax lights. Tullia's footman, with those of Madame lu Val-Noble and Florine, all in gaudy livery, carried round sweetmeats on silver trays. The hangings, choice products of the looms of Lyons, and looped with gold cord, dazzled the eye. The flowers on the carpet suggested a garden-bed. Costly toys and curiosities glittered on all sides. At first, and in the obfuscated state to which Georges had brought them, the clerks, and Oscar in particular, believed in the genuineness of the Marquesa de las Florentinas y Cabirolos.

On four tables set out for play, gold pieces lay in glittering heaps. In the drawing-room the women were playing at Vingt-et-un, Nathan, the famous author, holding the deal. Thus, after being carried tipsy and half-asleep along the dimly-lighted Boulevards, the clerks woke to find themselves in Armida's Palace. Oscar, on being introduced by Georges to the sham Marquise, stood dumfounded, not recognizing the ballet-dancer from the Gaîté in an elegant dress cut aristocratically low at the neck and richly trimmed with lace—a woman looking like a vignette in a keepsake, who received them with an air and manners that had no parallel in the experience or the imagination of a youth so strictly bred as he had been. After he had admired all the splendor of the rooms, the beautiful women who displayed themselves and who had vied with each other in dress for this occasion—the inauguration of all this magnificence,—Florentine took Oscar by the hand and led him to the table where Vingt-et-un was going on.

"Come, let me introduce you to the handsome Marquise d'Anglade, one of my friends——"

And she took the hapless Oscar up to pretty Fanny Beaupré, who, for the last two years, had filled poor Coralie's place in Camusot's affections. The young actress had just achieved a reputation in the part of a Marquise in a melodrama at the Porte-Saint-Martin, called *la Famille d'Anglade,* one of the successes of the day.

"Here, my dear," said Florentine, "allow me to introduce to you a charming youth who can be your partner in the game."

"Oh! that will be very nice!" replied the actress, with a fascinating smile, as she looked Oscar down from head to foot. "I am losing. We will go shares, if you like."

"I am at your orders, Madame la Marquise," said Oscar, taking a seat by her side.

"You shall stake," said she, "and I will play. You will bring me luck. There, that is my last hundred francs——" And the sham Marquise took out a purse of which the rings were studded with diamonds, and produced five gold pieces. Oscar brought out his hundred francs in five-franc pieces, already shamefaced at mingling the ignoble silver cart-wheels with the gold coin. In ten rounds the actress had lost the two hundred francs.

"Come! this is stupid!" she exclaimed. "I will take the deal. We will still be partners?" she asked of Oscar.

Fanny Beaupré rose, and the lad, who, like her, was now the centre of attention to the whole table, dared not withdraw, saying that the devil alone was lodged in his purse. He was speechless, his tongue felt heavy and stuck to his palate.

"Lend me five hundred francs," said the actress to the dancer.

Florentine brought her five hundred francs, which she borrowed of Georges, who had just won at écarté eight times running.

"Nathan has won twelve hundred francs," said the actress to the clerk. "The dealer always wins; do not let us be made fools of," she whispered in his ear.

Every man of feeling, of imagination, of spirit will understand that poor Oscar could not help opening his pocketbook and taking out the five hundred franc note. He looked at Nathan, the famous writer, who, in partnership with Florine, staked high against the dealer.

"Now then, boy, sweep it in!" cried Fanny Beaupré, signing to Oscar to take up two hundred francs that Florine and Nathan had lost.

The actress did not spare the losers her banter and jests. She enlivened the game by remarks of a character which Oscar thought strange; but delight stifled these reflections, for the first two deals brought in winnings of two thousand francs. Oscar longed to be suddenly taken ill and to fly, leaving his partner to her fate, but honor forbade it. Three more deals had carried away the profits. Oscar felt the cold sweat down his spine; he was quite sobered now. The last two rounds absorbed a thousand francs staked by the partners; Oscar felt thirsty, and drank off three glasses of iced punch.

The actress led him into an adjoining room, talking nonsense to divert him; but the sense of his error so completely overwhelmed Oscar, to whom Desroches' face appeared like a vision in a dream, that he sank on to a splendid ottoman in a dark corner and hid his face in his handkerchief. He was fairly crying. Florentine detected him in this attitude, too sincere not to strike an actress; she hurried up to Oscar, pulled away the handkerchief, and seeing his tears led him into a boudoir.

"What is the matter, my boy?" said she.

To this voice, these words, this tone, Oscar, recognizing the motherliness of a courtesan's kindness, replied:

"I have lost five hundred francs that my master gave me to pay to-morrow morning for a judgment; there is nothing for it but to throw myself into the river; I am disgraced."

"How can you be so silly?" cried Florentine. "Stay where you are, I will bring you a thousand francs. Try to recover it all, but only risk five hundred francs, so as to keep your chief's money. Georges plays a first-rate game at écarté; bet on him."

Oscar, in his dreadful position, accepted the offer of the mistress of the house.

"Ah!" thought he, "none but a Marquise would be capable of such an action. Beautiful, noble, and immensely rich! Georges is a lucky dog!"

He received a thousand francs in gold from the hands of Florentine, and went to bet on the man who had played him this trick. The punters were pleased at the arrival of a new man, for they all, with the instinct of gamblers, went over to the side of Giroudeau, the old Imperial officer.

"Gentlemen," said Georges, "you will be punished for your defection, for I am in luck.—Come, Oscar; we will do for them."

But Georges and his backer lost five games running. Having thrown away his thousand francs, Oscar, carried away by the gambling fever, insisted on holding the cards. As a result of the luck that often favors a beginner, he won; but Georges puzzled him with advice; he told him how to discard, and frequently snatched his hand from him, so that the conflict of two wills, two minds, spoiled the run of luck. In short, by three in the morning, after many turns of fortune and unhoped-for recoveries, still drinking punch, Oscar found himself possessed of no more than a hundred francs. He rose from the table, his brain heavy and dizzy, walked a few steps, and dropped on to a sofa in the boudoir, his eyes sealed in leaden slumbers.

"Mariette," said Fanny Beaupré to Godeschal's sister, who had come in at about two in the morning, "will you dine here to-morrow? My Camusot will be here and Père Cardot; we will make them mad."

"How?" cried Florentine. "My old man has not sent me word."

"He will be here this morning to tell you that he proposes to sing *la Mère Godichon*," replied Fanny Beaupré. "He must give a house-warming too, poor man."

"The devil take him and his orgies!" exclaimed Florentine. "He and his son-in-law are worse than magistrates or managers.—After all, Mariette, you dine well here," she went on. "Cardot orders everything from Chevet. Bring your Duc de Maufrigneuse; we will have fun, and make them dance."

Oscar, who caught the names of Cardot and Camusot, made an effort to rouse himself; but he could only mutter a word or two which were not heard, and fell back on the silk cushion.

"You are provided, I see," said Fanny Beaupré to Florentine, with a laugh.

"Ah! poor boy, he is drunk with punch and despair. He

has lost some money his master had intrusted to him for some office business. He was going to kill himself, so I lent him a thousand francs, of which those robbers Finot and Giroudeau have fleeced him. Poor innocent!"

"But we must wake him," said Mariette. "My brother will stand no nonsense, nor his master either."

"Well, wake him if you can, and get him away," said Florentine, going back into the drawing-room to take leave of those who were not gone.

The party then took to dancing—character dances, as they were called; and at daybreak Florentine went to bed very tired, having forgotten Oscar, whom nobody, in fact, remembered, and who was still sleeping soundly.

At about eleven o'clock a terrible sound awoke the lad, who recognized his uncle Cardot's voice, and thought he might get out of the scrape by pretending still to be asleep, so he hid his face in the handsome yellow velvet cushions in which he had passed the night.

"Really, my little Florentine," the old man was saying, "it is neither good nor nice of you. You were dancing last night in the *Ruines,* and then spent the night in an orgy. Why, it is simply destruction to your freshness, not to say that it is really ungrateful of you to inaugurate this splendid apartment without me, with strangers, without my knowing it—who knows what may have happened!"

"You old monster!" cried Florentine. "Have you not a key to come in whenever you like? We danced till half-past five, and you are so cruel as to wake me at eleven."

"Half-past eleven, Titine," said the old man humbly. "I got up early to order a dinner from Chevet worthy of an Archbishop.—How they have spoilt the carpets! Whom had you here?"

"You ought to make no complaints, for Fanny Beaupré told me that you and Camusot were coming, so I have asked the others to meet you—Tullia, du Bruel, Mariette, the Duc de Maufrigneuse, Florine, and Nathan. And you will have the five loveliest women who ever stood behind the footlights, and we will dance you a *pas de Zéphire*."

"It is killing work to lead such a life!" cried old Cardot. "What a heap of broken glasses, what destruction! The anteroom is a scene of horror!"

At this moment the amiable old man stood speechless and fascinated, like a bird under the gaze of a reptile. He caught sight of the outline of a young figure clothed in black cloth.

"Heyday! Mademoiselle Cabirolle!" said he at last.

"Well, what now?" said she.

The girl's eyes followed the direction of Père Cardot's gaze, and when she saw the youth still there, she burst into a fit of crazy laughter, which not only struck the old man dumb, but compelled Oscar to look round. Florentine pulled him up by the arm, and half choked with laughing as she saw the hangdog look of the uncle and nephew.

"You here, nephew?"

"Oh ho! He is your nephew?" cried Florentine, laughing more than ever. "You never mentioned this nephew of yours. —Then Mariette did not take you home?" said she to Oscar, who sat petrified. "What is to become of the poor boy?"

"Whatever he pleases!" replied old Cardot drily, and turning to the door to go away.

"One minute, Papa Cardot; you will have to help your nephew out of the mess he has got into by my fault, for he has gambled away his master's money, five hundred francs, besides a thousand francs of mine which I lent him to get it back again."

"Wretched boy, have you lost fifteen hundred francs at play —at your age?"

"Oh! uncle, uncle!" cried the unhappy Oscar, cast by these words into the depths of horror at his position. He fell on his knees at his uncle's feet with clasped hands. "It is twelve o'clock; I am lost, disgraced. Monsieur Desroches will show no mercy—there was an important business, a matter on which he prides himself—I was to have gone this morning to fetch away the copy of the judgment in Vandenesse *vs.* Vandenesse!

What has happened?—What has become of me?—Save me for my father's sake—for my aunt's.—Come with me to Maître Desroches and explain; find some excuse——"

The words came out in gasps, between sobs and tears that might have softened the Sphinx in the desert of Luxor.

"Now, old skinflint," cried the dancer in tears, "can you leave your own nephew to disgrace, the son of the man to whom you owe your fortune, since he is Oscar Husson? Save him, I say, or Titine refuses to own you as her milord!"

"But how came he here?" asked the old man.

"What! so as to forget the hour when he should have gone the errand he speaks of? Don't you see, he got drunk and dropped there, dead-tired and sleepy? Georges and his cousin Frédéric treated Desroches' clerks yesterday at the *Rocher de Cancale.*"

Cardot looked at her, still doubtful.

"Come, now, old baboon, if it were anything more should I not have hidden him more effectually?" cried she.

"Here, then, take the five hundred francs, you scamp!" said Cardot to his nephew. "That is all you will ever have of me. Go and make matters up with your master if you can.—I will repay the thousand francs mademoiselle lent you, but never let me hear your name again."

Oscar fled, not wishing to hear more; but when he was in the street he did not know where to go.

The chance which ruins men, and the chance that serves them, seemed to be playing against each other on equal terms for Oscar that dreadful morning; but he was destined to fail with a master who, when he made up his mind, never changed it.

Mariette, on returning home, horrified at what might befall her brother's charge, wrote a line to Godeschal, enclosing a five-hundred-franc note, and telling her brother of Oscar's drunken bout and disasters. The good woman, ere she went to sleep, instructed her maid to take this letter to Desroches' chambers before seven. Godeschal, on his part, waking at six, found no Oscar. He at once guessed what had happened. He took five hundred francs out of his savings and hurried off to the copying-clerk to fetch the judgment, so as to lay it before Desroches for signature in his office at eight. Desroches, who always rose at four, came to his room at seven o'clock. Mariette's maid, not finding her mistress' brother in his attic, went down to the office and was there met by Desroches, to whom she very naturally gave the note.

"Is it a matter of business?" asked the lawyer. "I am Maître Desroches."

"You can see, monsieur," said the woman.

Desroches opened the letter and read it. On finding the five-hundred-franc note he went back into his own room, furious with his second clerk. Then at half-past seven he heard Godeschal dictating a report on the judgment to another clerk, and a few minutes later Godeschal came into the room in triumph.

"Was it Oscar Husson who went to Simon this morning?" asked Desroches.

"Yes, monsieur," replied Godeschal.

"Who gave him the money?" said the lawyer.

"You," said Godeschal, "on Saturday."

"It rains five-hundred-franc notes, it would seem!" cried Desroches. "Look here, Godeschal, you are a good fellow, but that little wretch Husson does not deserve your generosity. I hate a fool, but yet more I hate people who will go wrong in spite of the care of those who are kind to them." He gave Godeschal Mariette's note and the five hundred francs she had sent. "Forgive me for opening it, but the maid said it was a matter of business.—You must get rid of Oscar."

"What trouble I have had with that poor little ne'er-do-well!" said Godeschal. "That scoundrel Georges Marest is his evil genius; he must avoid him like the plague, for I do not know what might happen if they met a third time."

"How is that?" asked Desroches, and Godeschal sketched the story of the practical joking on the journey to Presles.

"To be sure," said the lawyer. "I remember Joseph Bridau

told me something about that at the time. It was to that meeting that we owed the Comte de Sérizy's interest in Bridau's brother."

At this moment Moreau came in, for this suit over the Vandenesse property was an important affair to him. The Marquis wanted to sell the Vandenesse estate in lots, and his brother opposed such a proceeding.

Thus the land-agent was the recipient of the justifiable complaints and sinister prophecies fulminated by Desroches as against his second clerk; and the unhappy boy's most friendly protector was forced to the conclusion that Oscar's vanity was incorrigible.

"Make a pleader of him," said Desroches; "he only has to pass his final; in that branch of the law his faults may prove to be useful qualities, for conceit spurs the tongue of half of our advocates."

As it happened, Clapart was at this time out of health, and nursed by his wife, a painful and thankless task. The man worried the poor soul, who had hitherto never known how odious the nagging and spiteful taunts can be in which a half-imbecile creature gives vent to his irritation when poverty drives him into a sort of cunning rage. Delighted to have a sharp dagger that he could drive home to her motherly heart, he had suspected the fears for the future which were suggested to the hapless woman by Oscar's conduct and faults. In fact, when a mother has received such a blow as she had felt from the adventure at Presles she lives in perpetual alarms; and by the way in which Madame Clapart cried up Oscar whenever he achieved a success, Clapart understood all her secret fears and would stir them up on the slightest pretext.

"Well, well, Oscar is getting on better than I expected of him. I always said his journey to Presles was only a blunder due to inexperience. Where is the young man who never made a mistake? Poor boy, he is heroic in his endurance of the privations he would never have known if his father had lived. God grant he may control his passions!" and so on.

So, while so many disasters were crowding on each other in

the Rue de Vendôme and the Rue de Béthisy, Clapart, sitting by the fire wrapped in a shabby dressing-gown, was watching his wife, who was busy cooking over the bedroom fire some broth, Clapart's herb tea, and her own breakfast.

"Good heavens! I wish I knew how things fell out yesterday. Oscar was to breakfast at the Rocher de Cancale, and spend the evening with some Marquise——"

"Oh! don't be in a hurry; sooner or later murder will out," retorted her husband. "Do you believe in the Marquise? Go on; a boy who has his five senses and a love of extravagances—as Oscar has, after all—can find Marquises in Spain costing their weight in gold! He will come home some day loaded with debt——"

"You don't know how to be cruel enough, and to drive me to despair!" exclaimed Madame Clapart. "You complained that my son ate up all your salary, and he never cost you a sou. For two years you have not had a fault to find with Oscar, and now he is second clerk, his uncle and Monsieur Moreau provide him with everything, and he has eight hundred francs a year of his own earning. If we have bread in our old age, we shall owe it to that dear boy. You really are too unjust."

"You consider my foresight an injustice?" said the sick man sourly.

There came at this moment a sharp ring at the bell. Madame Clapart ran to open the door, and then remained in the outer room, talking to Moreau, who had come himself to soften the blow that the news of Oscar's levity must be to his poor mother.

"What! He lost his master's money?" cried Madame Clapart in tears.

"Aha! what did I tell you?" said Clapart, who appeared like a spectre in the doorway of the drawing-room, to which he had shuffled across under the prompting of curiosity.

"But what is to be done with him?" said his wife, whose distress left her insensible to this stab.

"Well, if he bore my name," said Moreau, "I should calmly

allow him to be drawn for the conscription, and if he should be called to serve, I would not pay for a substitute. This is the second time that sheer vanity has brought him into mischief. Well, vanity may lead him to some brilliant action, which will win him promotion as a soldier. Six years' service will at any rate add a little weight to his feather-brain, and as he has only his final examination to pass, he will not do so badly if he finds himself a pleader at six-and-twenty, if he chooses to go to the bar after paying the blood-tax, as they say. This time, at any rate, he will have had his punishment, he will gain experience and acquire habits of subordination. He will have served his apprenticeship to life before serving it in the Law Courts."

"If that is the sentence you would pronounce on a son," said Madame Clapart, "I see that a father's heart is very unlike a mother's.—My poor Oscar—a soldier——?"

"Would you rather see him jump head foremost into the Seine after doing something to disgrace himself? He can never now be an attorney; do you think he is fitted yet to be an advocate? While waiting till he reaches years of discretion, what will he become? A thorough scamp; military discipline will at any rate preserve him from that."

"Could he not go into another office? His uncle Cardot would certainly pay for a substitute—and Oscar will dedicate his thesis to him——"

The clatter of a cab, in which was piled all Oscar's personal property, announced the wretched lad's return, and in a few minutes he made his appearance.

"So here you are, Master Joli-Cœur!" cried Clapart.

Oscar kissed his mother, and held out a hand to Monsieur Moreau, which that gentleman would not take. Oscar answered this contempt with a look to which indignation lent a firmness new to the bystanders.

"Listen, Monsieur Clapart," said the boy, so suddenly grown to be a man; "you worry my poor mother beyond endurance, and you have a right to do so; she is your wife—for her sins. But it is different with me. In a few months I shall be of age, and you have no power over me even while I am a minor. I have never asked you for anything. Thanks to this gentleman, I have never cost you one sou, and I owe you no sort of gratitude; so, have the goodness to leave me in peace."

Clapart, startled by this apostrophe, went back to his armchair by the fire. The reasoning of the lawyer's clerk and the suppressed fury of a young man of twenty, who had just had a sharp lecture from his friend Godeschal, had reduced the sick man's imbecility to silence, once and for all.

"An error into which you would have been led quite as easily as I, at my age," said Oscar to Moreau, "made me commit a fault which Desroches thinks serious, but which is really trivial enough; I am far more vexed with myself for having taken Florentine, of the Gaîté theatre, for a Marquise, and actresses for women of rank, than for having lost fifteen hundred francs at a little orgy where everybody, even Godeschal, was somewhat screwed. This time, at any rate, I have hurt no one but myself. I am thoroughly cured.—If you will help me, Monsieur Moreau, I swear to you that in the course of the six years during which I must remain a clerk before I can practice——"

"Stop a bit!" said Moreau. "I have three children; I can make no promises."

"Well, well," said Madame Clapart, with a reproachful look at Moreau, "your uncle Cardot——"

"No more uncle Cardot for me," replied Oscar, and he related the adventure of the Rue de Vendôme.

Madame Clapart, feeling her knees give way under the weight of her body, dropped on one of the dining-room chairs as if a thunderbolt had fallen.

"Every possible misfortune at once!" said she, and fainted away.

Moreau lifted the poor woman in his arms, and carried her to her bed. Oscar stood motionless and speechless.

"There is nothing for you but to serve as a soldier," said the estate-agent, coming back again. "That idiot Clapart will not last three months longer, it seems to me; your mother will not have a sou in the world; ought I not rather to keep for her the little money I can spare? This was what I could not say to you in her presence. As a soldier, you will earn your bread, and you may meditate on what life is to the penniless."

"I might draw a lucky number," said Oscar.

"And if you do?—Your mother has been a very good mother to you. She gave you an education, she started you in a good way; you have lost it; what could you do now? Without money, a man is helpless, as you now know, and you are not the man to begin all over again by pulling off your coat and putting on a workman's or artisan's blouse. And then your mother worships you.—Do you want to kill her? For she would die of seeing you fallen so low."

Oscar sat down, and could no longer control his tears, which flowed freely. He understood now a form of appeal which had been perfectly incomprehensible at the time of his first error.

"Penniless folks ought to be perfect!" said Moreau to himself, not appreciating how deeply true this cruel verdict was.

"My fate will soon be decided," said Oscar; "the numbers are drawn the day after to-morrow. Between this and then I will come to some decision."

Moreau, deeply grieved in spite of his austerity, left the family in the Rue de la Cerisaie to their despair.

Three days after Oscar drew Number 27. To help the poor lad, the ex-steward of Presles found courage enough to go to the Comte de Sérizy and beg his interest to get Oscar into the cavalry. As it happened, the Count's son, having come out well at his last examination on leaving the École Polytechnique, had been passed by favor, with the rank of sub-lieutenant, into the cavalry regiment commanded by the Duc de Maufrigneuse. And so, in the midst of his fall, Oscar had the small piece of luck of being enlisted in this fine regiment at the Comte de Sérizy's recommendation, with the promise of promotion to be quartermaster in a year's time.

Thus chance placed the lawyer's clerk under the command of Monsieur de Sérizy's son.

After some days of pining, Madame Clapart, who was deeply stricken by all these misfortunes, gave herself up to the remorse which is apt to come over mothers whose conduct has not been blameless, and who, as they grow old, are led to repent. She thought of herself as one accursed. She ascribed the miseries of her second marriage and all her son's ill-fortune to the vengeance of God, who was punishing her in expiation of the sins and pleasures of her youth. This idea soon became a conviction. The poor soul went to confession, for the first time in forty years, to the Vicar of the Church of Saint-Paul, the Abbé Gaudron, who plunged her into the practices of religion.

But a spirit so crushed and so loving as Madame Clapart's could not fail to become simply pious. The Aspasia of the Directory yearned to atone for her sins that she might bring the blessing of God down on the head of her beloved Oscar, and before long she had given herself up to the most earnest practices of devotion and works of piety. She believed that she had earned the favor of Heaven when she had succeeded in saving Monsieur Clapart, who, thanks to her care, lived to torment her; but she persisted in seeing in the tyranny of this half-witted old man the trials inflicted by Him who loves while He chastens us.

Oscar's conduct meanwhile was so satisfactory that in 1830 he was first quartermaster of the company under the Vicomte de Sérizy, equivalent in rank to a sub-lieutenant of the line, as the Duc de Maufrigneuse's regiment was attached to the King's guards. Oscar Husson was now five-and-twenty. As the regiments of Guards were always quartered in Paris, or within thirty leagues of the capital, he could see his mother from time to time and confide his sorrows to her, for he was clear-sighted enough to perceive that he could never rise to be an officer. At that time cavalry officers were almost always chosen from among the younger sons of the nobility, and men without the distinguishing *de* got on but slowly. Oscar's whole ambition was to get out of the guards and enter some cavalry regiment of the line as a sub-lieutenant; and in the month of February 1830 Madame Clapart, through the interest of the Abbé Gaudron, now at the head of his parish, gained the favor of the Dauphiness, which secured Oscar's promotion.

Although the ambitious young soldier professed ardent devotion to the Bourbons, he was at heart a liberal. In the struggle, in 1830, he took the side of the people. This defection, which proved to be important by reason of the way in which it acted, drew public attention to Oscar Husson. In the moment of triumph, in the month of August, Oscar, promoted to be lieutenant, received the Cross of the Legion of Honor, and succeeded in obtaining the post of aide-de-camp to la Fayette, who made him captain in 1832. When this devotee to "the best of all Republics" was deprived of his command of the National Guard, Oscar Husson, whose devotion to the new royal family was almost fanaticism, was sent as major with a regiment to Africa on the occasion of the first expedition undertaken by the Prince. The Vicomte de Sérizy was now lieutenant-colonel of that regiment. At the fight at the Macta, where the Arabs remained masters of the field, Monsieur de Sérizy was left wounded under his dead horse. Oscar addressed his company.

"It is riding to our death," said he, "but we cannot desert our Colonel."

He was the first to charge the enemy, and his men, quite electrified, followed. The Arabs, in the shock of surprise at this furious and unexpected attack, allowed Oscar to pick up his Colonel, whom he took on his horse and rode off at a pelting gallop, though in this act, carried out in the midst of furious fighting, he had two cuts from a yataghan on the left arm.

Oscar's valiant conduct was rewarded by the Cross of an Officer of the Legion of Honor, and promotion to the rank of lieutenant-colonel. He nursed the Vicomte de Sérizy with devoted affection; the Comtesse de Sérizy joined her son and carried him to Toulon, where, as all the world knows, he died of his wounds. Madame de Sérizy did not part her son from the man who, after rescuing him from the Arabs, had cared for him with such unfailing devotion.

Oscar himself was so severely wounded that the surgeons called in by the Countess to attend her son pronounced amputation necessary. The Count forgave Oscar his follies on the occasion of the journey to Presles, and even regarded himself as the young man's debtor when he had buried his only surviving son in the chapel of the Château de Sérizy.

A long time after the battle of the Macta, an old lady dressed in black, leaning on the arm of a man of thirty-four, at once recognizable as a retired officer by the loss of one arm and the rosette of the Legion of Honor at his button-hole, was to be seen at eight o'clock one morning, waiting under the gateway of the Silver Lion, Rue du Faubourg Saint-Denis, till the diligence should be ready to start.

Pierrotin, the manager of the coach services of the Valley of the Oise, passing by Saint-Leu-Taverny and l'Isle-Adam, as far as Beaumont, would hardly have recognized in this bronzed officer that little Oscar Husson whom he had once driven to Presles. Madame Clapart, a widow at last, was quite as unrecognizable as her son. Clapart, one of the victims of Fieschi's machine, had done his wife a better turn by the manner of his death than he had ever done her in his life. Of course, Clapart, the idler, the lounger, had taken up a place on *his* Boulevard to see *his* legion reviewed. Thus the poor bigot had found her name down for a pension of fifteen hundred francs a year by the decree which indemnified the victims of this infernal machine.

The vehicle, to which four dappled gray horses were now being harnessed—steeds worthy of the *Messageries royales*,— was in four divisions, the *coupé*, the *interieur*, the *rotonde* behind, and the *imperiale* at top. It was identically the same as the diligences called *Gondoles*, which, in our day, still main-tain a rivalry on the Versailles road with two lines of railway. Strong and light, well painted and clean, lined with good blue cloth, furnished with blinds of arabesque design and red morocco cushions, the *Hirondelle de l'Oise* could carry nineteen travelers. Pierrotin, though he was by this time fifty-six, was little changed. He still wore a blouse over his black coat, and still smoked his short pipe, as he watched two porters in stable-livery piling numerous packages on the roof of his coach.

"Have you taken seats?" he asked of Madame Clapart and Oscar, looking at them as if he were searching his memory for some association of ideas.

"Yes, two inside places, name of Bellejambe, my servant," said Oscar. "He was to take them when he left the house last evening."

"Oh, then monsieur is the new collector at Beaumont," said Pierrotin. "You are going down to take the place of Monsieur Margueron's nephew?"

"Yes," replied Oscar, pressing his mother's arm as a hint to her to say nothing. For now he in his turn wished to remain unknown for a time.

At this instant Oscar was startled by recognizing Georges' voice calling from the street:

"Have you a seat left, Pierrotin?"

"It strikes me that you might say Monsieur Pierrotin without breaking your jaw," said the coach-owner angrily.

But for the tone of his voice Oscar could never have recognized the practical joker who had twice brought him such ill-luck. Georges, almost bald, had but three or four locks of hair left above his ears, and carefully combed up to disguise his bald crown as far as possible. A development of fat in the wrong place, a bulbous stomach, had spoiled the elegant figure of the once handsome young man. Almost vulgar in shape and mien, Georges showed the traces of disaster in love, and of a life of constant debauchery, in a spotty red complexion, and thickened, vinous features. His eyes had lost the sparkle and eagerness of youth, which can only be preserved by decorous and studious habits.

Georges, dressed with evident indifference to his appearance, wore a pair of trousers with straps, but shabby, and of a style that demanded patent leather boots; the boots he wore, thick and badly polished, were at least three-quarters of a year old, which is in Paris as much as three years anywhere else. A shabby waistcoat, a tie elaborately knotted, though it was but an old bandanna, betrayed the covert penury to which a decayed dandy may be reduced. To crown all, at this early hour of the day Georges wore a dress-coat instead of a morning-coat, the symptom of positive poverty. This coat, which must have danced at many a ball, had fallen, like its owner, from the opulence it once represented, to the duties of daily scrub. The seams of the black cloth showed white ridges, the collar was greasy, and wear had pinked out the cuffs into a dog's tooth edge. Still, Georges was bold enough to invite attention by wearing lemon-colored gloves—rather dirty, to be sure, and on one finger the outline of a large ring was visible in black.

Round his tie, of which the ends were slipped through a pretentious gold ring, twined a brown silk chain in imitation of hair, ending no doubt in a watch. His hat, though stuck on with an air, showed more evidently than all these other symptoms the poverty of a man who never has sixteen francs to spend at the hatter's when he lives from hand to mouth. Florentine's *ci-devant* lover flourished a cane with a chased handle, silver-gilt, but horribly dinted. His blue trousers, tartan waistcoat, sky-blue tie, and red-striped cotton shirt, bore witness, in spite of so much squalor, to such a passion for show that the contrast was not merely laughable, but a lesson.

"And this is Georges?" said Oscar to himself. "A man I left in possession of thirty thousand francs a year!"

"Has Monsieur *de* Pierrotin still a vacant seat in his *coupé?*" asked Georges ironically.

"No, my *coupé* is taken by a peer of France, Monsieur Moreau's son-in-law, Monsieur le Baron de Canalis, with his wife and his mother-in-law. I have only a seat in the body of the coach."

"The deuce! It would seem that under every form of government peers of France travel in Pierrotin's conveyances! I will take the seat in the *intérieur*," said Georges, with a reminiscence of the journey with Monsieur de Sérizy.

He turned to stare at Oscar and the widow, but recognized neither mother nor son. Oscar was deeply tanned by the African sun; he had a very thick moustache and whiskers; his hollow cheeks and marked features were in harmony with his military deportment. The officer's rosette, the loss of an arm, the plain dark dress, would all have been enough to mislead Georges' memory, if indeed he remembered his former victim. As to Madame Clapart, whom he had scarcely seen on the former occasion, ten years spent in pious exercises of the severest kind had absolutely transformed her. No one could have imagined that this sort of Gray Sister hid one of the Aspasias of 1797.

A huge old man, plainly but very comfortably dressed, in whom Oscar recognized old Léger, came up slowly and heavily; he nodded familiarly to Pierrotin, who seemed to regard him with the respect due in all countries to millionaires.

"Heh! why, it is Père Léger! more ponderous than ever!" cried Georges.

"Whom have I the honor of addressing?" asked the farmer very drily.

"What! Don't you remember Colonel Georges, Ali Pasha's friend? We traveled this road together, once upon a time, with the Comte de Sérizy, who preserved his incognito."

One of the commonest follies of persons who have come down in the world is insisting on recognizing people, and on being recognized.

"You are very much changed," said the old land-agent, now worth two millions of francs.

"Everything changes," said Georges. "Look at the Silver Lion inn, and at Pierrotin's coach, and see if they are the same as they were fourteen years since."

"Pierrotin is now owner of all the coaches that serve the

Oise Valley, and has very good vehicles," said Monsieur Léger. "He is a citizen now of Beaumont, and keeps an inn there where his coaches put up; he has a wife and daughter who know their business——"

An old man of about seventy came out of the inn and joined the group of travelers who were waiting to be told to get in.

"Come along, Papa Reybert!" said Léger. "We have no one to wait for now but your great man."

"Here he is," said the land-steward of Presles, turning to Joseph Bridau.

Neither Oscar nor Georges would have recognized the famous painter, for his face was the strangely worn countenance now so well known, and his manner was marked by the confidence born of success. His black overcoat displayed the ribbon of the Legion of Honor. His dress, which was careful in all points, showed that he was on his way to some country fête.

At this moment a clerk with a paper in his hand bustled out of an office constructed at one end of the old kitchen of the Silver Lion, and stood in front of the still unoccupied *coupé*.

"Monsieur and Madame de Canalis, three places!" he called out, then coming to the *intérieur,* he said, "Monsieur Bellejambe, two places; Monsieur Reybert, three; monsieur—your name?" added he to Georges.

"Georges Marest," replied the fallen hero in an undertone.

The clerk then went to the *rotonde* (the omnibus at the back of the old French diligence), round which stood a little crowds of nurses, country folks, and small shopkeepers, taking leave of each other. After packing the six travelers, the clerk called the names of four youths who clambered up on to the seat on the *imperiale,* and then said, "Right behind!" as the signal for starting.

Pierrotin took his place by the driver, a young man in a blouse, who in his turn said, "Get' up," to his horses.

The coach, set in motion by four horses purchased at Roye, was pulled up the hill of the Faubourg Saint-Denis at a gentle trot, but having once gained the level above Saint-Laurent, it spun along like a mail-coach as far as Saint-Denis in forty minutes. They did not stop at the inn famous for cheese-cakes, but turned off to the left of Saint-Denis, down the valley of Montmorency.

It was here, as they turned, that Georges broke the silence which had been kept so far by the travelers who were studying each other.

"We keep rather better time than we did fifteen years ago," said he, taking out a silver watch. "Heh! Père Léger?"

"People are so condescending as to address me as Monsieur Léger," retorted the millionaire.

"Why, this is our blusterer of my first journey to Presles," exclaimed Joseph Bridau. "Well, and have you been fighting new campaigns in Asia, Africa, and America?" asked the great painter.

"By Jupiter! I helped in the Revolution of July, and that was enough, for it ruined me."

"Oho! you helped in the Revolution of July, did you?" said Bridau. "I am not surprised, for I never could believe what I was told, that it made itself."

"How strangely meetings come about," said Monsieur Léger, turning to Reybert. "Here, Papa Reybert, you see the notary's clerk to whom you owe indirectly your place as steward of the estates of Sérizy."

"But we miss Mistigris, now so famous as Léon de Lora," said Joseph Bridau, "and the little fellow who was such a fool as to tell the Count all about his skin complaints—which he has cured at last—and his wife, from whom he has parted to die in peace."

"Monsieur le Comte is missing too," said Reybert.

"Oh!" said Bridau sadly, "I am afraid that the last expedition he will ever make will be to l'Isle-Adam, to be present at my wedding."

"He still drives out in the park," remarked old Reybert.

"Does his wife come often to see him?" asked Léger.

"Once a month," replied Reybert. "She still prefers Paris; she arranged the marriage of her favorite niece, Mademoiselle du Rouvre, to a very rich young Pole, Count Laginski, in September last——"

"And who will inherit Monsieur de Sérizy's property?" asked Madame Clapart.

"His wife.—She will bury him," replied Georges. "The Countess is still handsome for a woman of fifty-four, still very elegant, and at a distance quite illusory——"

"Elusive, you mean? She will always elude you," Léger put in, wishing, perhaps, to turn the tables on the man who had mystified him.

"I respect her," said Georges in reply.—"But, by the way, what became of that steward who was so abruptly dismissed in those days?"

"Moreau?" said Léger. "He is deputy now for Seine-et-Oise."

"Oh, the famous *centre* Moreau (of l'Oise)?" said Georges.

"Yes," replied Léger. *"Monsieur* Moreau (of l'Oise). He helped rather more than you in the Revolution of July, and he has lately bought the splendid estate of Pointel, between Presles and Beaumont."

"What, close to the place he managed, and so near his old master! That is in very bad taste," cried Georges.

"Do not talk so loud," said Monsieur de Reybert, "for Madame Moreau and her daughter, the Baronne de Canalis, and her son-in-law, the late minister, are in the coupé."

"What fortune did he give her that the great orator would marry his daughter?"

"Well, somewhere about two millions," said Léger.

"He had a pretty taste in millions," said Georges, smiling, and in an undertone, "He began feathering his nest at Presles ——"

"Say no more about Monsieur Moreau," exclaimed Oscar. "It seems to me that you might have learned to hold your tongue in a public conveyance!"

Joseph Bridau looked for a few seconds at the one-armed officer, and then said:

"Monsieur is not an ambassador, but his rosette shows that

he has risen in the world; and nobly too, for my brother and General Giroudeau have often mentioned you in their despatches——"

"Oscar Husson!" exclaimed Georges. "On my honor, but for your voice, I should never have recognized you."

"Ah! is this the gentleman who so bravely carried off the Vicomte Jules de Sérizy from the Arabs?" asked Reybert, "and to whom Monsieur le Comte has given the collectorship at Beaumont pending his appointment to Pontoise?"

"Yes, monsieur," said Oscar.

"Well, then," said the painter, "I hope, monsieur, that you will do me the pleasure of being present at my marriage, at l'Isle-Adam."

"Whom are you marrying?" asked Oscar.

"Mademoiselle Léger, Monsieur de Reybert's granddaughter. Monsieur le Comte de Sérizy was good enough to arrange the matter for me. I owe him much as an artist, and he was anxious to establish my fortune before his death—I had scarcely thought of it——"

"Then Père Léger married?" said Georges.

"My daughter," said Monsieur de Reybert, "and without any money."

"And he has children?"

"One daughter. Quite enough for a widower who had no other children," said Père Léger. "And, like my partner Moreau, I shall have a famous man for my son-in-law."

"So you still live at l'Isle-Adam?" said Georges to Monsieur Léger, almost respectfully.

"Yes; I purchased Cassan."

"Well, I am happy in having chosen this particular day for doing the Oise Valley," said Georges, "for you may do me a service, gentlemen."

"In what way?" asked Léger.

"Well, thus," said Georges. "I am employed by the Society of *l'Espérance,* which has just been incorporated, and its by-laws approved by letters patent from the King. This institution is, in ten years, to give marriage portions to girls, and annuities to old people; it will pay for the education of children; in short, it takes care of everybody——"

"So I should think!" said old Léger, laughing. "In short, you are an insurance agent."

"No, monsieur, I am Inspector-General, instructed to establish agencies and correspondents with the Company throughout France; I am acting only till the agents are appointed; for it is a delicate and difficult matter to find honest men——"

"But how did you lose your thirty thousand francs a year?" asked Oscar.

"As you lost your arm!" the ex-notary's clerk replied sharply to the ex-attorney's clerk.

"Then you invested your fortune in some brilliant deed?" said Oscar, with somewhat bitter irony.

"By Jupiter! my investments are a sore subject. I have more deeds than enough."

They had reached Saint-Leu-Taverny, where the travelers got out while they changed horses. Oscar admired the briskness with which Pierrotin unbuckled the straps of the swingbar, while his driver took out the leaders.

"Poor Pierrotin!" thought he. "Like me, he has not risen much in life. Georges has sunk into poverty. All the others, by speculation and skill, have made fortunes. Do we breakfast here, Pierrotin?" he asked, clapping the man on the shoulder.

"I am not the driver," said Pierrotin.

"What are you, then?" asked Colonel Husson.

"I am the owner," replied Pierrotin.

"Well, well, do not quarrel with an old friend," said Oscar, pointing to his mother, but still with a patronizing air; "do you not remember Madame Clapart?"

It was the more graceful of Oscar to name his mother to Pierrotin, because at this moment Madame Moreau (de l'Oise) had got out of the *coupé* and looked scornfully at Oscar and his mother as she heard the name.

"On my honor, madame, I should never have known you; nor you either, monsieur. You get it hot in Africa, it would seem?"

The disdainful pity Oscar had felt for Pierrotin was the last blunder into which vanity betrayed the hero of this Scene; and for that he was punished, though not too severely. On this wise: Two months after he had settled at Beaumont-sur-Oise, Oscar paid his court to Mademoiselle Georgette Pierrotin, whose fortune amounted to a hundred and fifty thousand francs, and by the end of the winter of 1838 he married the daughter of the owner of the Oise Valley coach service.

The results of the journey to Presles had given Oscar discretion, the evening at Florentine's had disciplined his honesty, the hardships of a military life had taught him the value of social distinctions and submission to fate. He was prudent, capable, and consequently happy. The Comte de Sérizy, before his death, obtained for Oscar the place of Revenue Collector at Pontoise. The influence of Monsieur Moreau (de l'Oise), of the Comtesse de Sérizy, and of Monsieur le Baron de Canalis, who, sooner or later, will again have a seat in the Ministry, will secure Monsieur Husson's promotion to the post of Receiver-General, and the Camusots now recognize him as a relation.

Oscar is a commonplace man, gentle, unpretentious, and modest; faithful—like the Government he serves—to the happy medium in all things. He invites neither envy nor scorn. In short, he is the modern French citizen.

PARIS, *February 1842.*

A SECOND HOME

*To Madame la Comtesse Louise de Turheim as a token of
remembrance and affectionate respect.*

The Rue du Tourniquet-Saint-Jean, formerly one of the darkest and most tortuous of the streets about the Hôtel de Ville, zigzagged round the little gardens of the Paris Préfecture, and ended at the Rue Martroi, exactly at the angle of an old wall now pulled down. Here stood the turnstile to which the street owed its name; it was not removed till 1823, when the Municipality built a ballroom on the garden plot adjoining the Hôtel de Ville, for the fête given in honor of the Duc d'Angoulême on his return from Spain.

The widest part of the Rue du Tourniquet was the end opening into the Rue de la Tixeranderie, and even there it was less than six feet across. Hence in rainy weather the gutter water was soon deep at the foot of the old houses, sweeping down with it the dust and refuse deposited at the corner-stones by the residents. As the dust-carts could not pass through, the inhabitants trusted to storms to wash their always miry alley; for how could it be clean? When the summer sun shed its perpendicular rays on Paris like a sheet of gold, but as piercing as the point of a sword, it lighted up the blackness of this street for a few minutes without drying the permanent damp that rose from the ground-floor to the first story of these dark and silent tenements.

The residents, who lighted their lamps at five o'clock in the month of June, in winter never put them out. To this day the enterprising wayfarer who should approach the Marais along the quays, past the end of the Rue du Chaume, the Rues de l'Homme Armé, des Billettes, and des Deux-Portes, all leading to the Rue du Tourniquet, might think he had passed through cellars all the way.

Almost all the streets of old Paris, of which ancient chronicles laud the magnificence, were like this damp and gloomy labyrinth, where antiquaries still find historical curiosities to admire. For instance, on the house then forming the corner where the Rue du Tourniquet joined the Rue de la Tixeranderie, the clamps might still be seen of two strong iron rings fixed to the wall, the relics of the chains put up every night by the watch to secure public safety.

This house, remarkable for its antiquity, had been constructed in a way that bore witness to the unhealthiness of these old dwellings; for, to preserve the ground-floor from damp, the arches of the cellars rose about two feet above the soil, and the house was entered up three outside steps. The door was crowned by a closed arch, of which the keystone bore a female head and some time-eaten arabesques. Three windows, their sills about five feet from the ground, belonged to a small set of rooms looking out on the Rue du Tourniquet, whence they derived their light. These windows were protected by strong iron bars, very wide apart, and ending below in an outward curve like the bars of a baker's window.

If any passer-by during the day were curious enough to peep into the two rooms forming this little dwelling, he could see nothing; for only under the sun of July could he discern, in the second room, two beds hung with green serge, placed side by side under the paneling of an old-fashioned alcove; but in the afternoon, by about three o'clock, when the candles were lighted, through the pane of the first room an old woman might be seen sitting on a stool by the fireplace, where she nursed the fire in a brazier, to simmer a stew, such as porters' wives are expert in. A few kitchen utensils, hung up against the wall, were visible in the twilight.

At that hour an old table on trestles, but bare of linen, was laid with pewter-spoons, and the dish concocted by the old woman. Three wretched chairs were all the furniture of this room, which was at once the kitchen and the dining-room.

Over the chimney-shelf were a piece of looking-glass, a tinder-box, three glasses, some matches, and a large, cracked white jug. Still, the floor, the utensils, the fireplace, all gave a pleasant sense of the perfect cleanliness and thrift that pervaded the dull and gloomy home.

The old woman's pale, withered face was quite in harmony with the darkness of the street and the mustiness of the place. As she sat there, motionless, in her chair, it might have been thought that she was as inseparable from the house as a snail from its brown shell; her face, alert with a vague expression of mischief, was framed in a flat cap made of net, which barely covered her white hair; her fine, gray eyes were as quiet as the street, and the many wrinkles in her face might be compared to the cracks in the walls. Whether she had been born to poverty, or had fallen from some past splendor, she now seemed to have been long resigned to her melancholy existence.

From sunrise till dark, excepting when she was getting a meal ready, or, with a basket on her arm, was out purchasing provisions, the old woman sat in the adjoining room by the further window, opposite a young girl. At any hour of the day the passer-by could see the needlewoman seated in an old, red velvet chair, bending over an embroidery frame, and stitching indefatigably.

Her mother had a green pillow on her knee, and busied herself with hand-made net; but her fingers could move the bobbins but slowly; her sight was feeble, for on her nose there rested a pair of those antiquated spectacles which keep their place on the nostrils by the grip of a spring. By night these two hardworking women set a lamp between them; and the light, concentrated by two globe-shaped bottles of water, showed the elder the fine network made by the threads on her pillow, and the younger the most delicate details of the pattern she was embroidering. The outward bend of the window bars had allowed the girl to rest a box of earth on the window-sill, in which grew some sweet peas, nasturtiums, a sickly little honeysuckle, and some convolvulus that twined its frail stems up the iron bars. These etiolated plants produced a few pale flowers, and added a touch of indescribable sadness and sweetness to the picture offered by this window, in which the two figures were appropriately framed.

The most selfish soul who chanced to see this domestic scene would carry away with him a perfect image of the life led in Paris by the working class of women, for the embroideress evidently lived by her needle. Many, as they passed through the turnstile, found themselves wondering how a girl could preserve her color, living in such a cellar. A student of lively imagination, going that way to cross to the Quartier-Latin, would compare this obscure and vegetative life to that of the ivy that clung to these chill walls, to that of the peasants born to labor, who are born, toil, and die unknown to the world they have helped to feed. A house-owner, after studying the house with the eye of a valuer, would have said, "What will become of those two women if embroidery should go out of fashion?" Among the men who, having some appointment at the Hôtel de Ville or the Palais de Justice, were obliged to go through this street at fixed hours, either on their way to business or on their return home, there may have been some charitable soul. Some widower or Adonis of forty, brought so often into the secrets of these sad lives, may perhaps have reckoned on the poverty of this mother and daughter, and have hoped to become the master at no great cost of the innocent work-woman, whose nimble and dimpled fingers, youthful figure, and white skin—a charm due, no doubt, to living in this sunless street— had excited his admiration. Perhaps, again, some honest clerk, with twelve hundred francs a year, seeing every day the diligence the girl gave to her needle, and appreciating the purity of her life, was only waiting for improved prospects to unite one humble life with another, one form of toil to another, and to bring at any rate a man's arm and a calm affection, pale-hued like the flowers in the window, to uphold this home.

Vague hope certainly gave life to the mother's dim, gray eyes. Every morning, after the most frugal breakfast, she took up her pillow, though chiefly for the look of the thing, for she would lay her spectacles on a little mahogany work-table as old as herself, and look out of window from about half-past eight till ten at the regular passers in the street; she caught their glances, remarked on their gait, their dress, their countenance, and almost seemed to be offering her daughter, her gossiping eyes so evidently tried to attract some magnetic sympathy by manœuvres worthy of the stage. It was evident that this little review was as good as a play to her, and perhaps her single amusement.

The daughter rarely looked up. Modesty, or a painful consciousness of poverty, seemed to keep her eyes riveted to the work-frame; and only some exclamation of surprise from her mother moved her to show her small features. Then a clerk in a new coat, or who unexpectedly appeared with a woman on his arm, might catch sight of the girl's slightly upturned nose, her rosy mouth, and gray eyes, always bright and lively in spite of her fatiguing toil. Her late hours had left a trace on her face by a pale circle marked under each eye on the fresh rosiness of her cheeks. The poor child looked as if she were made for love and cheerfulness—for love, which had drawn two perfect arches above her eyelids, and had given her such a mass of chestnut hair, that she might have hidden under it as under a tent, impenetrable to the lover's eye—for cheerfulness, which gave quivering animation to her nostrils, which carved two dimples in her rosy cheeks, and made her quick to forget her troubles; cheerfulness, the blossom of hope, which gave her strength to look out without shuddering on the barren path of life.

The girl's hair was always carefully dressed. After the manner of Paris needlewomen, her toilet seemed to her quite complete when she had brushed her hair smooth and tucked up the little short curls that played on each temple in contrast with the whiteness of her skin. The growth of it on the back of her neck was so pretty, and the brown line, so clearly traced, gave such a pleasing idea of her youth and charm, that the observer, seeing her bent over her work, and unmoved by any sound, was inclined to think of her as a coquette. Such inviting promise had excited the interest of more than one young man, who turned round in the vain hope of seeing that modest countenance.

"Caroline, there is a new face that passes regularly by, and not one of the old ones is to compare with it."

These words, spoken in a low voice by her mother one August morning in 1815, had vanquished the young needle-woman's indifference, and she looked out on the street; but in vain, the stranger was gone.

"Where has he flown to?" said she.

"He will come back no doubt at four; I shall see him coming, and will touch your foot with mine. I am sure he will come back; he has been through the street regularly for the last three days; but his hours vary. The first day he came by at six o'clock, the day before yesterday it was four, yesterday as early as three. I remember seeing him occasionally some time ago. He is some clerk in the Préfet's office who has moved to the Marais.—Why!" she exclaimed, after glancing down the street, "our gentleman of the brown coat has taken to wearing a wig; how much it alters him!"

The gentleman of the brown coat was, it would seem, the individual who commonly closed the daily procession, for the old woman put on her spectacles and took up her work with a sigh, glancing at her daughter with so strange a look that Lavater himself would have found it difficult to interpret. Admiration, gratitude, a sort of hope for better days, were mingled with pride at having such a pretty daughter.

At about four in the afternoon the old lady pushed her foot against Caroline's, and the girl looked up quickly enough to see the new actor, whose regular advent would thenceforth lend variety to the scene. He was tall and thin, and wore black, a man of about forty, with a certain solemnity of demeanor; as his piercing hazel eye met the old woman's dull gaze, he made her quake, for she felt as though he had the gift of reading hearts, or much practice in it, and his presence must surely be as icy as the air of this dank street. Was the dull, sallow complexion of that ominous face due to excess of work, or the result of delicate health?

The old woman supplied twenty different answers to this question; but Caroline, next day, discerned the lines of long mental suffering on that brow that was so prompt to frown. The rather hollow cheeks of the Unknown bore the stamp of the seal which sorrow sets on its victims as if to grant them the consolation of common recognition and brotherly union for resistance. Though the girl's expression was at first one of lively but innocent curiosity, it assumed a look of gentle sympathy as the stranger receded from view, like the last relation following in a funeral train.

The heat of the weather was so great, and the gentleman was so absent-minded, that he had taken off his hat and forgotten to put it on again as he went down the squalid street. Caroline could see the stern look given to his countenance by the way the hair was brushed from his forehead. The strong impression, devoid of charm, made on the girl by this man's appearance was totally unlike any sensation produced by the other passengers who used the street; for the first time in her life she was moved to pity for some one else than herself and her mother; she made no reply to the absurd conjectures that supplied material for the old woman's provoking volubility, and drew her long needle in silence through the web of stretched net; she only regretted not having seen the stranger more closely, and looked forward to the morrow to form a definite opinion of him.

It was the first time, indeed, that a man passing down the street had ever given rise to much thought in her mind. She generally had nothing but a smile in response to her mother's hypotheses, for the old woman looked on every passer-by as a possible protector for her daughter. And if such suggestions, so crudely presented, gave rise to no evil thoughts in Caroline's mind, her indifference must be ascribed to the persistent and unfortunately inevitable toil in which the energies of her sweet youth were being spent, and which would infallibly mar the clearness of her eyes or steal from her fresh cheeks the bloom that still colored them.

For two months or more the "Black Gentleman"—the name they had given him—was erratic in his movements; he did not always come down the Rue du Tourniquet; the old woman sometimes saw him in the evening when he had not passed in the morning, and he did not come by at such regular hours as the clerks who served Madame Crochard instead of a clock; moreover, excepting on the first occasion, when his look had given the old mother a sense of alarm, his eyes had never once dwelt on the weird picture of these two female gnomes. With the exception of two carriage-gates and a dark ironmonger's shop, there were in the Rue du Tourniquet only barred windows, giving light to the staircases of the neighboring houses; thus the stranger's lack of curiosity was not to be accounted for by the presence of dangerous rivals; and Madame Crochard was greatly piqued to see her "Black Gentleman" always lost in thought, his eyes fixed on the ground, or straight before him, as though he hoped to read the future in the fog of the Rue du Tourniquet. However, one morning, about the middle of September, Caroline Crochard's roguish face stood out so brightly against the dark background of the room, looking so fresh among the belated flowers and faded leaves that twined round the window-bars, the daily scene was gay with such contrasts of light and shade, of pink and white blending with the light material on which the pretty needlewoman was working, and with the red and brown hues of the chairs, that the stranger gazed very attentively at the effects of this living picture. In point of fact, the old woman, provoked by her "Black Gentleman's" indifference, had made such a clatter with her bobbins that the gloomy and pensive passer-by was perhaps prompted to look up by the unusual noise.

The stranger merely exchanged glances with Caroline, swift indeed, but enough to effect a certain contact between their souls, and both were aware that they would think of each other. When the stranger came by again, at four in the afternoon, Caroline recognized the sound of his step on the echoing pavement; they looked steadily at each other, and with evident purpose; his eyes had an expression of kindliness which made him smile, and Caroline colored; the old mother noted them both with satisfaction. Ever after that memorable afternoon, the Gentleman in Black went by twice a day, with rare exceptions, which both the women observed. They concluded from the irregularity of the hours of his homecoming that he was not released so early, nor so precisely punctual as a subordinate official.

All through the first three winter months, twice a day, Caroline and the stranger thus saw each other for so long as it took him to traverse the piece of road that lay along the length of the door and three windows of the house. Day after day this brief interview had a hue of friendly sympathy which at last had acquired a sort of fraternal kindness. Caroline and the stranger seemed to understand each other from the first; and then, by dint of scrutinizing each other's faces, they learned to know them well. Ere long it came to be, as it were, a visit that the Unknown owed to Caroline; if by any chance her Gentleman in Black went by without bestowing on her the half-smile of his expressive lips, or the cordial glance of his brown eyes, something was missing to her all day. She felt as an old man does to whom the daily study of a newspaper is such an indispensable pleasure that on the day after any great holiday he wanders about quite lost, and seeking, as much out of vagueness as for want of patience, the sheet by which he cheats an hour of life.

But these brief meetings had the charm of intimate friendliness, quite as much for the stranger as for Caroline. The girl could no more hide a vexation, a grief, or some slight ailment from the keen eye of her appreciative friend than he could conceal anxiety from hers.

"He must have had some trouble yesterday," was the thought that constantly arose in the embroideress' mind as she saw some change in the features of the "Black Gentleman."

"Oh, he has been working too hard!" was a reflection due to another shade of expression which Caroline could discern.

The stranger, on his part, could guess when the girl had spent Sunday in finishing a dress, and he felt an interest in the pattern. As quarter-day came near he could see that her pretty face was clouded by anxiety, and he could guess when Caroline had sat up late at work; but above all, he noted how the gloomy thoughts that dimmed the cheerful and delicate features of her young face gradually vanished by degrees as their acquaintance ripened. When winter had killed the climbers and plants of her window garden, and the window was kept closed, it was not without a smile of gentle amusement that the stranger observed the concentration of the light within, just at the level of Caroline's head. The very small fire and the frosty red of the two women's faces betrayed the poverty of their home; but if ever his own countenance expressed regretful compassion, the girl proudly met it with assumed cheerfulness.

Meanwhile the feelings that had arisen in their hearts remained buried there, no incident occurring to reveal to either of them how deep and strong they were in the other; they had never even heard the sound of each other's voice. These mute friends were even on their guard against any nearer acquaintance, as though it meant disaster. Each seemed to fear lest it should bring on the other some grief more serious than those they felt tempted to share. Was it shyness or friendship that checked them? Was it a dread of meeting with selfishness, or the odious distrust which sunders all the residents within the walls of a populous city? Did the voice of conscience warn them of approaching danger? It would be impossible to explain the instinct which made them as much enemies as friends, at once indifferent and attached, drawn to each other by impulse, and severed by circumstance. Each perhaps hoped to preserve a cherished illusion. It might almost have been thought that the stranger feared lest he should hear some vulgar word from those lips as fresh and pure as a flower, and that Caroline felt herself unworthy of the mysterious personage who was evidently possessed of power and wealth.

As to Madame Crochard, that tender mother, almost angry at her daughter's persistent lack of decisiveness, now showed a sulky face to the "Black Gentleman," on whom she had hitherto smiled with a sort of benevolent servility. Never before had she complained so bitterly of being compelled, at her age, to do the cooking; never had her catarrh and her rheumatism wrung so many groans from her; finally, she could not, this winter, promise so many ells of net as Caroline had hitherto been able to count on.

Under these circumstances, and towards the end of December, at the time when bread was dearest, and that dearth of corn was beginning to be felt which made the year 1816 so hard on the poor, the stranger observed on the features of the girl whose name was still unknown to him, the painful traces of a secret sorrow which his kindest smiles could not dispel. Before long he saw in Caroline's eyes the dimness attributable to long hours at night. One night, towards the end of the month, the Gentleman in Black passed down the Rue du Tourniquet at the quite unwonted hour of one in the morning. The perfect silence allowed of his hearing before passing the house the lachrymose voice of the old mother, and Caroline's even sadder tones, mingling with the swish of a shower of sleet. He crept along as slowly as he could; and then, at the risk of being taken up by the police, he stood still below the window to hear the mother and daughter, while watching them through the largest of the holes in the yellow muslin curtains, which were eaten away by wear as a cabbage leaf is riddled by caterpillars. The inquisitive stranger saw a sheet of paper on the table that stood between the two work-frames, and on which stood the lamp and the globes filled with water. He at once identified it as a writ. Madame Crochard was weeping, and Caroline's voice was thick, and had lost its sweet, caressing tone.

"Why be so heartbroken, mother? Monsieur Molineux will not sell us up or turn us out before I have finished this dress; only two nights more and I shall take it home to Madame Roguin."

"And supposing she keeps you waiting as usual?—And will the money for the gown pay the baker too?"

The spectator of this scene had long practice in reading faces; he fancied he could discern that the mother's grief was as false as the daughter's was genuine; he turned away, and presently came beck. When he next peeped through the hole in the curtain, Madame Crochard was in bed. The young needlewoman, bending over her frame, was embroidering with indefatigable diligence; on the table, with the writ, lay a triangular hunch of bread, placed there, no doubt, to sustain her in the night and to remind her of the reward of her industry. The stranger was tremulous with pity and sympathy; he threw his purse in through a cracked pane so that it should fall at the girl's feet; and then, without waiting to enjoy her surprise, he escaped, his cheeks tingling.

Next morning the shy and melancholy stranger went past with a look of deep preoccupation, but he could not escape Caroline's gratitude; she had opened her window and affected to be digging in the square window-box buried in snow, a pretext of which the clumsy ingenuity plainly told her benefactor that she had been resolved not to see him only through the pane. Her eyes were full of tears as she bowed her head, as much as to say to her benefactor, "I can only repay you from my heart."

But the Gentleman in Black affected not to understand the meaning of this sincere gratitude. In the evening, as he came by, Caroline was busy mending the window with a sheet of paper, and she smiled at him, showing her row of pearly teeth like a promise. Thenceforth the Stranger went another way, and was no more seen in the Rue du Tourniquet.

It was one day early in the following May that, as Caroline was giving the roots of the honeysuckle a glass of water, one Saturday morning, she caught sight of a narrow strip of cloudless blue between the black lines of houses, and said to her mother:

"Mamma, we must go to-morrow for a trip to Montmorency!"

She had scarcely uttered the words, in a tone of glee, when the Gentleman in Black came by, sadder and more dejected than ever. Caroline's innocent and ingratiating glance might have been taken for an invitation. And, in fact, on the following day, when Madame Crochard, dressed in a pelisse of claret-colored merinos, a silk bonnet, and striped shawl of an imitation Indian pattern, came out to choose seats in a chaise at the corner of the Rue du Faubourg Saint-Denis and the Rue d'Enghien, there she found her Unknown standing like a man waiting for his wife. A smile of pleasure lighted up the Stranger's face when his eye fell on Caroline, her neat feet shod in plum-colored prunella gaiters, and her white dress tossed by a breeze that would have been fatal to an ill-made woman, but which displayed her graceful form. Her face, shaded by a rice-straw bonnet lined with pink silk, seemed to beam with a reflection from heaven; her broad, plum-colored belt set off a waist he could have spanned; her hair, parted in two brown bands over a forehead as white as snow, gave her an expression of innocence which no other feature contradicted. Enjoyment seemed to have made Caroline as light as the straw of her hat; but when she saw the Gentleman in Black, radiant hope suddenly eclipsed her bright dress and her beauty. The Stranger, who appeared to be in doubt, had not perhaps made up his mind to be the girl's escort for the day till this revelation of the delight she felt on seeing him. He at once hired a vehicle with a fairly good horse, to drive to Saint-Leu-Taverny, and he offered Madame Crochard and her daughter seats by his side. The mother accepted without ado; but presently, when they were already on the way to Saint-Denis, she was by way of having scruples, and made a few civil speeches as to the possible inconvenience two women might cause their companion.

"Perhaps, monsieur, you wished to drive alone to Saint-Leu-Taverny," said she, with affected simplicity.

Before long she complained of the heat, and especially of her cough, which, she said, had hindered her from closing her eyes all night; and by the time the carriage had reached Saint-

Denis, Madame Crochard seemed to be fast asleep. Her snores, indeed, seemed, to the Gentleman in Black, rather doubtfully genuine, and he frowned as he looked at the old woman with a very suspicious eye.

"Oh, she is fast asleep," said Caroline guilelessly; "she never ceased coughing all night. She must be very tired."

Her companion made no reply, but he looked at the girl with a smile that seemed to say:

"Poor child, you little know your mother!"

However, in spite of his distrust, as the chaise made its way down the long avenue of poplars leading to Eaubonne, the Stranger thought that Madame Crochard was really asleep; perhaps he did not care to inquire how far her slumbers were genuine or feigned. Whether it were that the brilliant sky, the pure country air, and the heady fragrance of the first green shoots of the poplars, the catkins of willow, and the flowers of the blackthorn had inclined his heart to open like all the nature around him; or that any longer restraint was too oppressive while Caroline's sparkling eyes responded to his own, the Gentleman in Black entered on a conversation with his young companion, as aimless as the swaying of the branches in the wind, as devious as the flitting of the butterflies in the azure air, as illogical as the melodious murmur of the fields, and, like it, full of mysterious love. At that season is not the rural country as tremulous as a bride that has donned her marriage robe; does it not invite the coldest soul to be happy? What heart could remain unthawed, and what lips could keep its secret, on leaving the gloomy streets of the Marais for the first time since the previous autumn, and entering the smiling and picturesque valley of Montmorency; on seeing it in the morning light, its endless horizons receding from view; and then lifting a charmed gaze to eyes which expressed no less infinitude mingled with love?

The Stranger discovered that Caroline was sprightly rather than witty, affectionate, but ill educated; but while her laugh was giddy, her words promised genuine feeling. When, in response to her companion's shrewd questioning, the girl spoke with the heartfelt effusiveness of which the lower classes are lavish, not guarding it with reticence like people of the world, the Black Gentleman's face brightened, and seemed to renew its youth. His countenance by degrees lost the sadness that lent sternness to his features, and little by little they gained a look of handsome youthfulness which made Caroline proud and happy. The pretty needlewoman guessed that her new friend had been long weaned from tenderness and love, and no longer believed in the devotion of woman. Finally, some unexpected sally in Caroline's light prattle lifted the last veil that concealed the real youth and genuine character of the Stranger's physiognomy; he seemed to bid farewell forever to the ideas that haunted him, and showed the natural liveliness that lay beneath the solemnity of his expression.

Their conversation had insensibly become so intimate, that by the time when the carriage stopped at the first houses of the straggling village of Saint-Leu, Caroline was calling the gentleman Monsieur Roger. Then for the first time the old mother awoke.

"Caroline, she has heard everything!" said Roger suspiciously in the girl's ear.

Caroline's reply was an exquisite smile of disbelief, which dissipated the dark cloud that his fear of some plot on the old woman's part had brought to this suspicious mortal's brow. Madame Crochard was amazed at nothing, approved of everything, followed her daughter and Monsieur Roger into the park, where the two young people had agreed to wander through the smiling meadows and fragrant copses made famous by the taste of Queen Hortense.

"Good heavens! how lovely!" exclaimed Caroline when standing on the green ridge where the forest of Montmorency begins, she saw lying at her feet the wide valley with its combes sheltering scattered villages, its horizon of blue hills, its church towers, its meadows and fields, whence a murmur came up, to die on her ear like the swell of the ocean. The three wanderers made their way by the bank of an artificial stream and came to the Swiss valley, where stands a châlet that had more than once given shelter to Hortense and Napoleon. When Caroline had seated herself with pious reverence on the mossy wooden bench where kings and princesses and the Emperor had rested, Madame Crochard expressed a wish to have a nearer view of a bridge that hung across between two rocks at some little distance, and bent her steps towards that rural curiosity, leaving her daughter in Monsieur Roger's care, though, telling them that she would not go out of sight.

"What, poor child!" cried Roger, "have you never longed for wealth and the pleasures of luxury? Have you never wished that you might wear the beautiful dresses you embroider?"

"It would not be the truth, Monsieur Roger, if I were to tell you that I never think how happy people must be who are rich. Oh yes! I often fancy, especially when I am going to sleep, how glad I should be to see my poor mother no longer compelled to go out, whatever the weather, to buy our little provisions, at her age. I should like her to have a servant who, every morning before she was up, would bring her up her coffee, nicely sweetened with white sugar. And she loves reading novels, poor dear soul! Well, and I would rather see her wearing out her eyes over her favorite books than over twisting her bobbins from morning till night. And again, she ought to have a little good wine. In short, I should like to see her comfortable—she is so good."

"Then she has shown you great kindness?"

"Oh yes," said the girl, in a tone of conviction. Then, after a short pause, during which the two young people stood watching Madame Crochard, who had got to the middle of the rustic bridge, and was shaking her finger at them, Caroline went on:

"Oh yes, she has been so good to me. What care she took of me when I was little! She sold her last silver forks to apprentice me to the old maid who taught me to embroider.— And my poor father! What did she not go through to make him end his days in happiness!" The girl shivered at the remembrance, and hid her face in her hands.—"Well! come! let us forget past sorrows!" she added, trying to rally her high spirits. She blushed as she saw that Roger too was moved, but she dared not look at him.

"What was your father?" he asked.

"He was an opera-dancer before the Revolution," said she, with an air of perfect simplicity, "and my mother sang in the chorus. My father, who was leader of the figures on the stage, happened to be present at the siege of the Bastille. He was recognized by some of the assailants, who asked him whether he could not lead a real attack, since he was used to leading such enterprises on the boards. My father was brave; he accepted the post, led the insurgents, and was rewarded by the nomination to the rank of captain in the army of Sambre-et-Meuse, where he distinguished himself so far as to rise rapidly to be a colonel. But at Lutzen he was so badly wounded that, after a year's sufferings, he died in Paris.—The Bourbons returned; my mother could obtain no pension, and we fell into such abject misery that we were compelled to work for our living. For some time past she has been ailing, poor dear, and I have never known her so little resigned; she complains a good deal, and, indeed, I cannot wonder, for she has known the pleasures of an easy life. For my part, I cannot pine for delights I have never known, I have but one thing to wish for."

"And that is?" said Roger eagerly, as if roused from a dream.

"That women may long continue to wear embroidered net dresses, so that I may never lack work."

The frankness of this confession interested the young man, who looked with less hostile eyes on Madame Crochard as she slowly made her way back to them.

"Well, children, have you had a long talk?" said she, with a half-laughing, half-indulgent air. "When I think, Monsieur Roger, that the 'little Corporal' has sat where you are sitting," she went on after a pause. "Poor man! how my husband worshiped him! Ah! Crochard did well to die, for he could not have borne to think of him where *they* have sent him!"

Roger put his finger to his lips, and the good woman went on very gravely, with a shake of her head:

"All right, mouth shut and tongue still! But," added she, unhooking a bit of her bodice, and showing a ribbon and cross tied round her neck by a piece of black ribbon, "they shall never hinder me from wearing what *he* gave to my poor Crochard, and I will have it buried with me."

On hearing this speech, which at that time was regarded as seditious, Roger interrupted the old lady by rising suddenly, and they returned to the village through the park walks. The young man left them for a few minutes while he went to order a meal at the best eating-house in Taverny; then, returning to fetch them, he led the way through the alleys cut in the forest.

The dinner was cheerful. Roger was no longer the melancholy shade that was wont to pass along the Rue du Tourniquet; he was not the "Black Gentleman," but rather a confiding young man ready to take life as it came, like the two hard-working women who, on the morrow, might lack bread; he seemed alive to all the joys of youth, his smile was quite affectionate and childlike.

When, at five o'clock, this happy meal was ended with a few glasses of champagne, Roger was the first to propose that they should join the village ball under the chestnuts, where he and Caroline danced together. Their hands met with sympathetic pressure, their hearts beat with the same hopes; and under the blue sky and the slanting, rosy beams of sunset, their eyes sparkled with fires which, to them, made the glory of the heavens pale. How strange is the power of an idea, of a desire! To these two nothing seemed impossible. In such magic moments, when enjoyment sheds its reflections on the future, the soul foresees nothing but happiness. This sweet day had created memories for these two to which nothing could be compared in all their past existence. Would the source prove to be more beautiful than the river, the desire more enchanting than its gratification, the thing hoped for more delightful than the thing possessed?

"So the day is already at an end!" On hearing this exclamation from her unknown friend when the dance was over,

Caroline looked at him compassionately, as his face assumed once more a faint shade of sadness.

"Why should you not be as happy in Paris as you are here?" she asked. "Is happiness to be found only at Saint-Leu? It seems to me that I can henceforth never be unhappy anywhere."

Roger was struck by these words, spoken with the glad unrestraint that always carries a woman further than she intended, just as prudery often lends her greater cruelty than she feels. For the first time since that glance, which had, in a way, been the beginning of their friendship, Caroline and Roger had the same idea; though they did not express it, they felt it at the same instant, as a result of a common impression like that of a comforting fire cheering both under the frost of winter; then, as if frightened by each other's silence, they made their way to the spot where the carriage was waiting. But before getting into it, they playfully took hands and ran together down the dark avenue in front of Madame Crochard. When they could no longer see the white net cap, which showed as a speck through the leaves where the old woman was—"Caroline!" said Roger in a tremulous voice, and with a beating heart.

The girl was startled, and drew back a few steps, understanding the invitation this question conveyed; however, she held out her hand, which was passionately kissed, but which she hastily withdrew, for by standing on tiptoe she could see her mother.

Madame Crochard affected blindness, as if, with a reminiscence of her old parts, she was only required to figure as a supernumerary.

The adventures of these two young people were not continued in the Rue du Tourniquet. To see Roger and Caroline once more, we must leap into the heart of modern Paris, where, in some of the newly-built houses, there are apartments that seem made on purpose for newly-married couples to spend their honeymoon in. There the paper and paint are as fresh as the bride and bridegroom, and the decorations are in blossom like their love; everything is in harmony with youthful notions and ardent wishes.

Half-way down the Rue Taitbout, in a house whose stone walls were still white, where the columns of the hall and the doorway were as yet spotless, and the inner walls shone with the neat painting which our recent intimacy with English ways had brought into fashion, there was, on the second floor, a small set of rooms fitted by the architect as though he had known what their use would be. A simple airy ante-room, with a stucco dado, formed an entrance into a drawing-room and dining-room. Out of the drawing-room opened a pretty bedroom, with a bathroom beyond. Every chimney-shelf had over it a fine mirror elegantly framed. The doors were crowded with arabesques in good taste, and the cornices were in the best style. Any amateur would have discerned there the sense of distinction and decorative fitness which mark the work of modern French architects.

For above a month Caroline had been at home in this apartment, furnished by an upholsterer who submitted to an artist's guidance. A short description of the principal room will suffice to give an idea of the wonders it offered to Caroline's delighted eyes when Roger installed her there. Hangings of gray stuff trimmed with green silk adorned the walls of her bedroom; the seats, covered with light-colored woolen sateen, were of easy and comfortable shapes, and in the latest fashion; a chest of drawers of some simple wood, inlaid with lines of a darker hue, contained the treasures of the toilet; a writing-table to match served for inditing love-letters on scented paper; the bed, with antique draperies, could not fail to suggest thoughts of love by its soft hangings of elegant muslin; the window-curtains, of drab silk with green fringe, were always half drawn to subdue the light; a bronze clock represented Love crowning Psyche; and a carpet of Gothic design on a red ground set off the other accessories of this delightful retreat. There was a small dressing-table in front of a long glass, and here the ex-needlewoman sat, out of patience with Plaisir, the famous hairdresser.

"Do you think you will have done to-day?" said she.

"Your hair is so long and so thick, madame," replied Plaisir.

Caroline could not help smiling. The man's flattery had no doubt revived in her mind the memory of the passionate praises lavished by her lover on the beauty of her hair, which he delighted in.

The hairdresser having done, a waiting-maid came and held counsel with her as to the dress in which Roger would like best to see her. It was in the beginning of September 1816, and the weather was cold; she chose a green *grenadine* trimmed with chinchilla. As soon as she was dressed, Caroline flew into the drawing-room and opened a window, out of which she stepped on to the elegant balcony, that adorned the front of the house; there she stood, with her arms crossed, in a charming attitude, not to show herself to the admiration of the passers-by and see them turn to gaze at her, but to be able to look out on the Boulevard at the bottom of the Rue Taitbout. This side view, really very comparable to the peephole made by actors in the drop-scene of a theatre, enabled her to catch a glimpse of numbers of elegant carriages, and a crowd of persons, swept past with the rapidity of *Ombres Chinoises*. Not knowing whether Roger would arrive in a carriage or on foot, the needlewoman from the Rue du Tourniquet looked by turns at the foot-passengers, and at the tilburies—light cabs introduced into Paris by the English.

Expressions of refractoriness and of love passed by turns over her youthful face when, after waiting for a quarter of an hour, neither her keen eye nor her heart had announced the arrival of him whom she knew to be due. What disdain, what indifference were shown in her beautiful features for all the other creatures who were bustling like ants below her feet. Her gray eyes, sparkling with fun, now positively flamed. Given over to her passion, she avoided admiration with as much care as the proudest devote to encouraging it when they drive about Paris, certainly feeling no care as to whether her fair countenance leaning over the balcony, or her little foot between the bars, and the picture of her bright eyes and delicious turned-up nose would be effaced or no from the minds of the passers-by who admired them; she saw but one face, and had but one idea. When the spotted head of a certain bay horse happened to cross the narrow strip between the two rows of houses, Caroline gave a little shiver and stood on tiptoe in hope of recognizing the white traces and the color of the tilbury. It was he!

Roger turned the corner of the street, saw the balcony, whipped the horse, which came up at a gallop, and stopped at the bronze-green door that he knew as well as his master did. The door of the apartment was opened at once by the maid, who had heard her mistress' exclamation of delight. Roger rushed up to the drawing-room, clasped Caroline in his arms, and embraced her with the effusive feeling natural when two beings who love each other rarely meet. He led her, or rather they went by a common impulse, their arms about each other, into the quiet and fragrant bedroom; a settee stood ready for them to sit by the fire, and for a moment they looked at each other in silence, expressing their happiness only by their clasped hands, and communicating their thoughts in a fond gaze.

"Yes, it is he!" she said at last. "Yes, it is you. Do you know, I have not seen you for three long days, an age!—But what is the matter? You are unhappy."

"My poor Caroline——"

"There, you see! 'poor Caroline'——"

"No, no, do not laugh, my darling; we cannot go to the Feydeau Theatre together this evening."

Caroline put on a little pout, but it vanished immediately.

"How absurd I am! How can I think of going to the play when I see you? Is not the sight of you the only spectacle I care for?" she cried, pushing her fingers through Roger's hair.

"I am obliged to go to the Attorney-General's. We have a knotty case in hand. He met me in the great hall at the Palais; and as I am to plead, he asked me to dine with him.

But, my dearest, you can go to the theatre with your mother, and I will join you if the meeting breaks up early."

"To the theatre without you!" cried she in a tone of amazement; "enjoy any pleasure you do not share! O my Roger! you do not deserve a kiss," she added, throwing her arms round his neck with an artless and impassioned impulse.

"Caroline, I must go home and dress. The Marais is some way off, and I still have some business to finish."

"Take care what you are saying, monsieur," said she, interrupting him. "My mother says that when a man begins to talk about his busines, he is ceasing to love."

"Caroline! Am I not here? Have I not stolen this hour from my pitiless——"

"Hush!" said she, laying a finger on his mouth. "Don't you see that I am in jest."

They had now come back to the drawing-room, and Roger's eye fell on an object brought home that morning by the cabinetmaker. Caroline's old rosewood embroidery-frame, by which she and her mother had earned their bread when they lived in the Rue du Tourniquet-Saint-Jean, had been refitted and polished, and a net dress, of elaborate design, was already stretched upon it.

"Well, then, my dear, I shall do some work this evening. As I stitch, I shall fancy myself gone back to those early days when you used to pass by me without a word, but not without a glance; the days when the remembrance of your look kept me awake all night. O my dear old frame—the best piece of furniture in my room, though you did not give it me!—You cannot think," said she, seating herself on Roger's knees; for he, overcome by irresistible feelings, had dropped into a chair. "Listen.—All I can earn by my work I mean to give to the poor. You have made me rich. How I love that pretty home at Bellefeuille, less because of what it is than because you gave it me! But tell me, Roger, I should like to call myself Caroline de Bellefeuille—can I? You must know: is it legal or permissible?

As she saw a little affirmative grimace—for Roger hated

the name of Crochard—Caroline jumped for glee, and clapped her hands.

"I feel," said she, "as if I should more especially belong to you. Usually a woman gives up her own name and takes her husband's——" An idea forced itself upon her and made her blush. She took Roger's hand and led him to the open piano.—"Listen," said she, "I can play my sonata now like an angel!" and her fingers were already running over the ivory keys, when she felt herself seized round the waist.

"Caroline, I ought to be far from hence!"

"You insist on going? Well, go," said she, with a pretty pout, but she smiled as she looked at the clock and exclaimed joyfully, "At any rate, I have detained you a quarter of an hour!"

"Good-bye, Mademoiselle de Bellefeuille," said he, with the gentle irony of love.

She kissed him and saw her lover to the door; when the sound of his steps had died away on the stairs she ran out on to the balcony to see him get into the tilbury, to see him gather up the reins, to catch a parting look, hear the crack of his whip and the sound of his wheels on the stones, watch the handsome horse, the master's hat, the tiger's gold lace, and at last to stand gazing long after the dark corner of the street had eclipsed this vision.

Five years after Mademoiselle Caroline de Bellefeuille had taken up her abode in the pretty house in the Rue Taitbout, we again look in on one of those home-scenes which tighten the bonds of affection between two persons who truly love. In the middle of the blue drawing-room, in front of the window opening to the balcony, a little boy of four was making a tremendous noise as he whipped the rocking-horse, whose two curved supports for the legs did not move fast enough to please him; his pretty face, framed in fair curls that fell over his white collar, smiled up like a cherub's at his mother when she said to him from the depths of an easy-chair, "Not so much noise, Charles; you will wake your little sister."

A SECOND HOME

The inquisitive boy suddenly got off his horse, and treading on tiptoe as if he were afraid of the sound of his feet on the carpet, came up with one finger between his little teeth, and standing in one of those childish attitudes that are so graceful because they are so perfectly natural, raised the muslin veil that hid the rosy face of a little girl sleeping on her mother's knee.

"Is Eugénie asleep, then?" said he, quite astonished. "Why is she asleep when we are awake?" he added, looking up with large, liquid black eyes.

"That only God can know," replied Caroline with a smile.

The mother and boy gazed at the infant, only that morning baptized.

Caroline, now about four-and-twenty, showed the ripe beauty which had expanded under the influence of cloudless happiness and constant enjoyment. In her the Woman was complete.

Delighted to obey her dear Roger's every wish, she had acquired the accomplishments she had lacked; she played the piano fairly well, and sang sweetly. Ignorant of the customs of a world that would have treated her as an outcast, and which she would not have cared for even if it had welcomed her—for a happy woman does not care for the world—she had not caught the elegance of manner or learned the art of conversation, abounding in words and devoid of ideas, which is current in fashionable drawing-rooms; on the other hand, she worked hard to gain the knowledge indispensable to a mother whose chief ambition is to bring up her children well. Never to lose sight of her boy, to give him from the cradle that training of every minute which impresses on the young a love of all that is good and beautiful, to shelter him from every evil influence and fulfil both the painful duties of a nurse and the tender offices of a mother,—these were her chief pleasures.

The coy and gentle being had from the first day so fully resigned herself never to step beyond the enchanted sphere where she found all her happiness, that, after six years of the tenderest intimacy, she still knew her lover only by the name of Roger. A print of the picture of Psyche lighting her lamp to gaze on Love in spite of his prohibition, hung in her room, and constantly reminded her of the conditions of her happiness. Through all these six years her humble pleasures had never importuned Roger by a single indiscreet ambition, and his heart was a treasure-house of kindness. Never had she longed for diamonds or fine clothes, and had again and again refused the luxury of a carriage which he had offered her. To look out from her balcony for Roger's cab, to go with him to the play or make excursions with him, on fine days in the environs of Paris, to long for him, to see him, and then to long again,—these made up the history of her life, poor in incidents but rich in happiness.

As she rocked the infant, now a few months old, on her knee, singing the while, she allowed herself to recall the memories of the past. She lingered more especially on the months of September, when Roger was accustomed to take her to Bellefeuille and spend the delightful days which seem to combine the charms of every season. Nature is equally prodigal of flowers and fruit, the evenings are mild, the mornings bright, and a blaze of summer often returns after a spell of autumn gloom. During the early days of their love, Caroline had ascribed the even mind and gentle temper, of which Roger gave her so many proofs, to the rarity of their always longed-for meetings, and to their mode of life, which did not compel them to be constantly together, as a husband and wife must be. But now she could remember with rapture that, tortured by foolish fears, she had watched him with trembling during their first stay on this little estate in the Gatinais. Vain suspiciousness of love! Each of these months of happiness had passed like a dream in the midst of joys which never rang false. She had always seen that kind creature with a tender smile on his lips, a smile that seemed to mirror her own.

As she called up these vivid pictures, her eyes filled with tears; she thought she could not love him enough, and was tempted to regard her ambiguous position as a sort of tax levied by Fate on her love. Finally, invincible curiosity led her to wonder for the thousandth time what events they could be that led so tender a heart as Roger's to find his pleasure in clandestine and illicit happiness. She invented a thousand romances on purpose really to avoid recognizing the true reason, which she had long suspected but tried not to believe in. She rose, and carrying the baby in her arms, went into the dining-room to superintend the preparations for dinner.

It was the 6th of May 1822, the anniversary of the excursion to the Park of Saint-Leu, which had been the turning-point of her life; each year it had been marked by heartfelt rejoicing. Caroline chose the linen to be used, and arranged the dessert. Having attended with joy to these details, which touched Roger, she placed the infant in her pretty cot and went out on to the balcony, whence she presently saw the carriage which her friend, as he grew to riper years, now used instead of the smart tilbury of his youth. After submitting to the first fire of Caroline's embraces and the kisses of the little rogue who addressed him as papa, Roger went to the cradle, looked at his little sleeping daughter, kissed her forehead, and then took out of his pocket a document covered with black writing.

"Caroline," said he, "here is the marriage portion of Mademoiselle Eugénie de Bellefeuille."

The mother gratefully took the paper, a deed of gift of securities in the State funds.

"But why," said she, "have you given Eugénie three thousand francs a year, and Charles no more than fifteen hundred?"

"Charles, my love, will be a man," replied he. "Fifteen hundred francs are enough for him. With so much for certain, a man of courage is above poverty. And if by chance your son should turn out a nonentity, I do not wish him to be able to play the fool. If he is ambitious, this small income will give him a taste for work.—Eugénie is a girl; she must have a little fortune."

The father then turned to play with his boy, whose effusive affection showed the independence and freedom in which he was brought up. No sort of shyness between the father and child interfered with the charm which rewards a parent for his devotion; and the cheerfulness of the little family was as sweet as it was genuine. In the evening a magic-lantern displayed its illusions and mysterious pictures on a white sheet to Charles' great surprise, and more than once the innocent child's heavenly rapture made Caroline and Roger laugh heartily.

Later, when the little boy was in bed, the baby woke and craved its limpid nourishment. By the light of a lamp, in the chimney corner, Roger enjoyed the scene of peace and comfort, and gave himself up to the happiness of contemplating the sweet picture of the child clinging to Caroline's white bosom as she sat, as fresh as a newly opened lily, while her hair fell in long brown curls that almost hid her neck. The lamplight enhanced the grace of the young mother, shedding over her, her dress, and the infant, the picturesque effects of strong light and shadow.

The calm and silent woman's face struck Roger as a thousand times sweeter than ever, and he gazed tenderly at the rosy, pouting lips from which no harsh word had ever been heard. The very same thought was legible in Caroline's eyes as she gave a sidelong look at Roger, either to enjoy the effect she was producing on him, or to see what the end of the evening was to be. He, understanding the meaning of this cunning glance, said with assumed regret, "I must be going. I have a serious case to be finished, and I am expected at home. Duty before all things—don't you think so, my darling?"

Caroline looked him in the face with an expression at once sad and sweet, with the resignation which does not, however, disguise the pangs of a sacrifice.

"Good-bye, then," said she. "Go, for if you stay **an hour longer I cannot** so lightly bear to set you free."

"My dearest," said he with a smile, "I have three days' holiday, and am supposed to be twenty leagues away from Paris."

A few days after this anniversary of the 6th of May, Mademoiselle de Bellefeuille hurried off one morning to the Rue Saint-Louis, in the Marais, only hoping she might not arrive too late at a house where she commonly went once a week. An express messenger had just come to inform her that her mother, Madame Crochard, was sinking under a complication of disorders produced by constant catarrh and rheumatism.

While the hackney coach-driver was flogging up his horses at Caroline's urgent request, supported by the promise of a handsome present, the timid old women, who had been Madame Crochard's friends during her later years, had brought a priest into the neat and comfortable second-floor rooms occupied by the old widow. Madame Crochard's maid did not know that the pretty lady at whose house her mistress so often dined was her daughter, and she was one of the first to suggest the services of a confessor, in the hope that this priest might be at least as useful to herself as to the sick woman. Between two games of boston, or out walking in the Jardin Turc, the old beldames with whom the widow gossiped all day had succeeded in rousing in their friend's stony heart some scruples as to her former life, some visions of the future, some fears of hell, and some hopes of forgiveness if she should return in sincerity to a religious life. So on this solemn morning three ancient females had settled themselves in the drawing-room where Madame Crochard was "at home" every Tuesday. Each in turn left her armchair to go to the poor old woman's bedside and to sit with her, giving her the false hopes with which people delude the dying.

At the same time, when the end was drawing near, when the physician called in the day before would no longer answer for her life, the three dames took counsel together as to whether it would not be well to send word to Mademoiselle de Bellefeuille. Françoise having been duly informed, it was decided that a commissionaire should go to the Rue Taitbout to inform the young relation whose influence was so disquieting to the four women; still, they hoped that the Auvergnat would be too late in bringing back the person who so certainly held the first place in the widow Crochard's affections. The widow, evidently in the enjoyment of a thousand crowns a year, would not have been so fondly cherished by this feminine trio, but that neither of them, nor Françoise herself, knew of her having any heir. The wealth enjoyed by Mademoiselle de Bellefeuille, whom Madame Crochard, in obedience to the traditions of the older opera, never allowed herself to speak of by the affectionate name of daughter, almost justified the four women in their scheme of dividing among themselves the old woman's "pickings."

Presently the one of these three sibyls who kept guard over the sick woman came shaking her head at the other anxious two, and said:

"It is time we should be sending for the Abbé Fontanon. In another two hours she will neither have the wit nor the strength to write a line."

Thereupon the toothless old cook went off, and returned with a man wearing a black gown. A low forehead showed a small mind in this priest, whose features were mean; his flabby, fat cheeks and double chin betrayed the easy-going egotist; his powdered hair gave him a pleasant look, till he raised his small, brown eyes, prominent under a flat forehead, and not unworthy to glitter under the brows of a Tartar.

"Monsieur l'Abbé," said Françoise, "I thank you for all your advice; but believe me, I have taken the greatest care of the dear soul."

But the servant, with her dragging step and woe-begone look, was silent when she saw that the door of the apartment was open, and that the most insinuating of the three dowagers was standing on the landing to be the first to speak with the confessor. When the priest had politely faced the honeyed and bigoted broadside of words fired off from the widow's three friends, he went into the sickroom to sit by Madame Crochard.

Decency, and some sense of reserve, compelled the three women and old Françoise to remain in the sitting-room, and to make such grimaces of grief as are possible in perfection only to such wrinkled faces.

"Oh, is it not ill-luck!" cried Françoise, heaving a sigh. "This is the fourth mistress I have buried. The first left me a hundred francs a year, the second a sum of fifty crowns, and the third a thousand crowns down. After thirty years' service, that is all I have to call my own."

The woman took advantage of her freedom to come and go, to slip into a cupboard, whence she could hear the priest.

"I see with pleasure, daughter," said Fontanon, "that you have pious sentiments; you have a sacred relic round your neck."

Madame Crochard, with a feeble vagueness which seemed to show that she had not all her wits about her, pulled out the Imperial Cross of the Legion of Honor. The priest started back at seeing the Emperor's head; he went up to the penitent again, and she spoke to him, but in such a low tone that for some minutes Françoise could hear nothing.

"Woe upon me!" cried the old woman suddenly. "Do not desert me. What, Monsieur l'Abbé, do you think I shall be called to account for my daughter's soul?"

The Abbé spoke too low, and the partition was too thick for Françoise to hear the reply.

"Alas!" sobbed the woman, "the wretch has left me nothing that I can bequeath. When he robbed me of my dear Caroline, he parted us, and only allowed me three thousand francs a year, of which the capital belongs to my daughter."

"Madame has a daughter, and nothing to live on but an annuity," shrieked Françoise, bursting into the drawing-room.

The three old crones looked at each other in dismay. One of them, whose nose and chin nearly met with an expresion that betrayed a superior type of hypocrisy and cunning, winked her eyes; and as soon as Françoise's back was turned, she gave her friends a nod, as much as to say, "That slut is too knowing by half; her name has figured in three wills already."

So the three old dames sat on.

However, the Abbé presently came out, and at a word from him the witches scuttered down the stairs at his heels, leaving Françoise alone with her mistress. Madame Crochard, whose sufferings increased in severity, rang, but in vain, for this woman, who only called out, "Coming, coming—in a minute!" The doors of cupboards and wardrobes were slamming as though Françoise were hunting high and low for a lost lottery ticket.

Just as this crisis was at a climax, Mademoiselle de Bellefeuille came to stand by her mother's bed, lavishing tender words on her.

"O my dear mother, how criminal I have been! You are ill, and I did not know it; my heart did not warn me. However, here I am——"

"Caroline——"

"What is it?"

"They fetched a priest——"

"But send for a doctor, bless me!" cried Mademoiselle de Bellefeuille. "Françoise, a doctor! How is it that those ladies never sent for a doctor?"

"They sent for a priest——" repeated the old woman with a gasp.

"She is so ill—and no soothing draught, nothing on her table!"

The mother made a vague sign, which Caroline's watchful eye understood, for she was silent to let her mother speak.

"They brought a priest—to hear my confession, as they said. —Beware, Caroline!" cried the old woman with an effort, "the priest made me tell him your benefactor's name."

"But who can have told you, poor mother?"

The old woman died, trying to look knowingly cunning. If Mademoiselle de Bellefeuille had noted her mother's face, she might have seen what no one ever will see—Death laughing.

A SECOND HOME

To enter into the interests that lay beneath this introduction to my tale, we must for a moment forget the actors in it, and look back at certain previous incidents, of which the last was closely concerned with the death of Madame Crochard. The two parts will then form a whole—a story which, by a law peculiar to life in Paris, was made up of two distinct sets of actions.

Toward the close of the month of November 1805, a young barrister, aged about six-and-twenty, was going down the stairs of the hotel where the High Chancellor of the Empire resided, at about three o'clock one morning. Having reached the courtyard in full evening dress, under a keen frost, he could not help giving vent to an exclamation of dismay—qualified, however, by the spirit which rarely deserts a Frenchman—at seeing no hackney coach waiting outside the gates, and hearing no noises such as arise from the wooden shoes or harsh voices of the hackney-coachmen of Paris. The occasional pawing of the horses of the Chief Justice's carriage—the young man having left him still playing *bouillote* with Cambacérès—alone rang out in the paved court, which was scarcely lighted by the carriage lamps. Suddenly the young lawyer felt a friendly hand on his shoulder, and turning round, found himself face to face with the Judge, to whom he bowed. As the footman let down the steps of his carriage, the old gentleman, who had served the Convention, suspected the junior's dilemma.

"All cats are gray in the dark," said he good-humoredly. "The Chief Justice cannot compromise himself by putting a pleader in the right way! Especially," he went on, "when the pleader is the nephew of an old colleague, one of the lights of the grand Council of State which gave to France the Napoleonic Code."

At a gesture from the chief magistrate of France under the Empire, the foot-passenger got into the carriage.

"Where do you live?" asked the great man, before the foot man who awaited his orders had closed the door.

"Quai des Augustins, monseigneur."

The horses started, and the young man found himself alone with the Minister, to whom he had vainly tried to speak before and after the sumptuous dinner given by Cambacérès; in fact, the great man had evidently avoided him throughout the evening.

"Well, Monsieur *de* Granville, you are on the high road!"

"So long as I sit by your Excellency's side——"

"Nay, I am not jesting," said the Minister. "You were called two years since, and your defence in the case of Simeuse and Hauteserre has raised you high in your profession."

"I had supposed that my interest in those unfortunate émigrés had done me no good."

"You are still very young," said the great man gravely. "But the High Chancellor," he went on, after a pause, "was greatly pleased with you this evening. Get a judgeship in the lower courts; we want men. The nephew of a man in whom Cambacérès and I take great interest must not remain in the background for lack of encouragement. Your uncle helped us to tide over a very stormy season, and services of that kind are not to be forgotten." The Minister sat silent for a few minutes. "Before long," he went on, "I shall have three vacancies open in the Lower Courts and in the Imperial Court in Paris. Come to see me, and take the place you prefer. Till then work hard, but do not be seen at my receptions. In the first place, I am overwhelmed with work; and besides that, your rivals may suspect your purpose and do you harm with the patron. Cambacérès and I, by not speaking a word to you this evening, have averted the accusation of favoritism."

As the great man ceased speaking, the carriage drew up on the Quai des Augustins; the young lawyer thanked his generous patron for the two lifts he had conferred on him, and then knocked at his door pretty loudly, for the bitter wind blew cold about his calves. At last the old lodgekeeper pulled up the latch; and as the young man passed his window, called out in a hoarse voice, "Monsieur Granville, here is a letter for you."

The young man took the letter, and in spite of the cold, tried to identify the writing by the gleam of a dull lamp fast dying out. "From my father!" he exclaimed, as he took his bedroom candle, which the porter at last had lighted. And he ran up to his room to read the following epistle:—

"Set off by the next mail; and if you can get here soon enough, your fortune is made. Mademoiselle Angélique Bontems has lost her sister; she is now an only child; and, as we know, she does not hate you. Madame Bontems can now leave her about forty thousand francs a year, besides whatever she may give her when she marries. I have prepared the way.

"Our friends will wonder to see a family of old nobility allying itself to the Bontems; old Bontems was a red republican of the deepest dye, owning large quantities of the nationalized land, that he bought for a mere song. But he held nothing but convent lands, and the monks will not come back; and then, as you have already so far derogated as to become a lawyer, I cannot see why we should shrink from a further concession to the prevalent ideas. The girl will have three hundred thousand francs; I can give you a hundred thousand; your mother's property must be worth fifty thousand crowns, more or less; so if you choose to take a judgeship, my dear son, you are quite in a position to become a senator as much as any other man. My brother-in-law the Councillor of State will not indeed lend you a helping-hand; still, as he is not married, his property will some day be yours, and if you are not senator by your own efforts, you will get it through him. Then you will be perched high enough to look on at events. Farewell. Yours affectionately."

So young Granville went to bed full of schemes, each fairer than the last. Under the powerful protection of the High Chancellor, the Chief Justice, and his mother's brother—one of the originators of the Code—he was about to make a start in a coveted position before the highest court of the Empire, and he already saw himself a member of the bench whence Napoleon selected the chief functionaries of the realm. He could also promise himself a fortune handsome enough to keep up his rank, for which the slender income of five thousand francs from an estate left him by his mother would be quite insufficient.

To crown his ambitious dreams with a vision of happiness, he called up the guileless face of Mademoiselle Angélique Bontems, the companion of his childhood. Until he came to boyhood his father and mother had made no objection to his intimacy with their neighbor's pretty little daughter; but when, during his brief holiday visits to Bayeux, his parents, who prided themselves on their good birth, saw what friends the young people were, they forbade his ever thinking of her. Thus for ten years past Granville had only had occasional glimpses of the girl, whom he still sometimes thought of as "his little wife." And in those brief moments when they met free from the active watchfulness of their families, they had scarcely exchanged a few vague civilities at the church door or in the street. Their happiest days had been those when, brought together by one of those country festivities known in Normandy as *Assemblées*, they could steal a glance at each other from afar.

In the course of the last vacation Granville had twice seen Angélique, and her downcast eyes and drooping attitude had led him to suppose that she was crushed by some unknown tyranny.

He was off by seven next morning to the coach office in the Rue Notre-Dame-des-Victoires, and was so lucky as to find a vacant seat in the diligence then starting for Caen.

It was not without deep emotion that the young lawyer saw once more the spires of the cathedral at Bayeux. As yet no hope of his life had been cheated, and his heart swelled with the generous feelings that expand in the youthful soul.

After the too lengthy feast of welcome prepared by his father, who awaited him with some friends, the impatient youth was conducted to a house, long familiar to him, standing in the Rue Teinture. His heart beat high when his father—still known in the town of Bayeux as the Comte de Granville—knocked loudly at a carriage gate off which the green paint was dropping in scales. It was about four in the afternoon. A young maid-servant, in a cotton cap, dropped a short courtesy to the two gentlemen, and said that the ladies would soon be home from vespers.

The Count and his son were shown into a low room used as a drawing-room, but more like a convent parlor. Polished panels of dark walnut made it gloomy enough, and around it some old-fashioned chairs covered with worsted work and stiff armchairs were symmetrically arranged. The stone chimney-shelf had no ornament but a discolored mirror, and on each side of it were the twisted branches of a pair of candle-brackets, such as were made at the time of the Peace of Utrecht. Against a panel opposite, young Granville saw an enormous crucifix of ebony and ivory surrounded by a wreath of box that had been blessed. Though there were three windows to the room, looking out on a country-town garden, laid out in formal square beds edged with box, the room was so dark that it was difficult to discern, on the wall opposite the windows, three pictures of sacred subjects painted by a skilled hand, and purchased, no doubt, during the Revolution by old Bontems, who, as governor of the district, had never neglected his opportunities. From the carefully polished floor to the green checked holland curtains everything shone with conventual cleanliness.

The young man's heart felt an involuntary chill in this silent retreat where Angélique dwelt. The habit of frequenting the glittering Paris drawing-rooms, and the constant whirl of society, had effaced from his memory the dull and peaceful surroundings of a country life, and the contrast was so startling as to give him a sort of internal shiver. To have just left a party at the house of Cambacérès, where life was so large, where minds could expand, where the splendor of the Imperial Court was so vividly reflected, and to be dropped suddenly into a sphere of squalidly narrow ideas—was it not like a leap from Italy into Greenland?—"Living here is not life!" said he to himself, as he looked round the Methodistical room. The old Count, seeing his son's dismay, went up to him, and taking his hand, led him to a window, where there was still a gleam of daylight, and while the maid was lighting the yellow tapers in the candle branches he tried to clear away the clouds that the dreary place had brought to his brow.

"Listen, my boy," said he. "Old Bontems' widow is a frenzied bigot. 'When the devil is old——' you know! I see that the place goes against the grain. Well, this is the whole truth; the old woman is priest-ridden; they have persuaded her that it was high time to make sure of heaven, and the better to secure Saint Peter and his keys she pays beforehand. She goes to Mass every day, attends every service, takes the Communion every Sunday God has made, and amuses herself by restoring chapels. She has given so many ornaments, and albs, and chasubles, she has crowned the canopy with so many feathers, that on the occasion of the last Corpus Christi procession as great a crowd came together as to see a man hanged, just to stare at the priests in their splendid dresses and all the vessels regilt. This house too is a sort of Holy Land. It was I who hindered her from giving those three pictures to the Church—a Domenichino, a Correggio, and an Andrea del Sarto—worth a good deal of money."

"But Angélique?" asked the young man.

"If you do not marry her, Angélique is done for," said the Count. "Our holy apostles counsel her to live a virgin martyr. I have had the utmost difficulty in stirring up her little heart, since she has been the only child, by talking to her of you; but, as you will easily understand, as soon as she is married you will carry her off to Paris. There, festivities, married life, the theatres, and the rush of Parisian society, will soon make her forget confessionals, and fasting, and hair shirts, and Masses, which are the exclusive nourishment of such creatures."

"But the fifty thousand francs a year derived from Church property? Will not all that return——"

"That is the point!" exclaimed the Count, with a cunning glance. "In consideration of this marriage—for Madame Bontems' vanity is not a little flattered by the notion of grafting the Bontems on to the genealogical tree of the Granvilles—the aforenamed mother agrees to settle her fortune absolutely on the girl, reserving only a life-interest. The priesthood, therefore, are set against the marriage; but I have had the banns published, everything is ready, and in a week you will be out of the clutches of the mother and her Abbés. You will have the prettiest girl in Bayeux, a good little soul who will give you no trouble, because she has sound principles. She has been mortified, as they say in their jargon, by fasting and prayer——and," he added in a low voice, "by her mother."

A modest tap at the door silenced the Count, who expected to see the two ladies appear. A little page came in, evidently in a great hurry; but, abashed by the presence of the two gentlemen, he beckoned to a housekeeper, who followed him. Dressed in a blue cloth jacket with short tails, and blue-and-white striped trousers, his hair cut short all round, the boy's expression was that of a chorister, so strongly was it stamped with the compulsory propriety that marks every member of a bigoted household.

"Mademoiselle Gatienne," said he, "do you know where the books are for the offices of the Virgin? The ladies of the Congregation of the Sacred Heart are going in procession this evening round the church."

Gatienne went in search of the books.

"Will they go on much longer, my little man?" asked the Count.

"Oh, half an hour at most."

"Let us go to look on," said the father to his son. "There will be some pretty women there, and a visit to the Cathedral can do us no harm."

The young lawyer followed him with a doubtful expression.

"What is the matter?" said the Count.

"The matter, father, is that I am sure I am right."

"But you have said nothing."

"No; but I have been thinking that you have still ten thousand francs a year left of your original fortune. You will leave them to me—as long a time hence as possible, I hope. But if you are ready to give me a hundred thousand francs to make a foolish match, you will surely allow me to ask you for only fifty thousand to save me from such a misfortune, and enjoy as a bachelor a fortune equal to what your Mademoiselle Bontems would bring me."

"Are you crazy?"

"No, father. These are the facts. The Chief Justice promised me yesterday that I should have a seat on the Bench. Fifty thousand francs added to what I have, and to the pay of my appointment, will give me an income of twelve thousand francs a year. And I then shall most certainly have a chance of marrying a fortune, better than this alliance, which will be poor in happiness if rich in goods."

"It is very clear," said his father, "that you were not brought up under the old *régime*. Does a man of our rank ever allow his wife to be in his way?"

"But, my dear father, in these days marriage is———"

"Bless me!" cried the Count, interrupting his son, "then what my old *émigré* friends tell me is true, I suppose. The Revolution has left us habits devoid of pleasure, and has infected all the young men with vulgar principles. You, like my Jacobin brother-in-law, will harangue me, I suppose, on the Nation, Public Morals, and Disinterestedness!—Good Heavens! But for the Emperor's sisters, where should we be?"

The still hale old man, whom the peasants on the estate persisted in calling the Signeur de Granville, ended his speech as they entered the Cathedral porch. In spite of the sanctity of the place, and even as he dipped his fingers in the holy water, he hummed an air from the opera of *Rose et Colas,* and then led the way down the side aisles, stopping by each pillar to survey the rows of heads, all in lines like ranks of soldiers on parade.

The special service of the Sacred Heart was about to begin. The ladies affiliated to that congregation were in front near the choir, so the Count and his son made their way to that part of the nave, and stood leaning against one of the columns where there was least light, whence they could command a view of this mass of faces, looking like a meadow full of flowers. Suddenly, close to young Granville, a voice, sweeter than it seemed possible to ascribe to a human being, broke into song, like the first nightingale when winter is past. Though it mingled with the voices of a thousand other women and the notes of the organ, that voice stirred his nerves as though they vibrated to the too full and too piercing sounds of a harmonium. The Parisian turned round, and, seeing a young figure, though, the head being bent, her face was entirely concealed by a large white bonnet, concluded that the voice was hers. He fancied that he recognized Angélique in spite of a brown merino pelisse that wrapped her, and he nudged his father's elbow.

"Yes, there she is," said the Count, after looking where his son pointed, and then, by an expressive glance, he directed his attention to the pale face of an elderly woman who had already detected the strangers, though her false eyes, deep set in dark circles, did not seem to have strayed from the prayer-book she held.

Angélique raised her face, gazing at the altar as if to inhale the heavy scent of the incense that came wafted in clouds over the two women. And then, in the doubtful light that the tapers shed down the nave, with that of a central lamp and of some lights round the pillars, the young man beheld a face which shook his determination. A white watered-silk bonnet closely framed features of perfect regularity, the oval being completed by the satin ribbon tie that fastened it under her dimpled chin. Over her forehead, very sweet though low, hair of a pale gold color parted in two bands and fell over her cheeks, like the shadow of leaves on a flower. The arches of her eyebrows were drawn with the accuracy we admire in the best Chinese paintings. Her nose, almost aquiline in profile, was exceptionally firmly cut, and her lips were like two rosy lines lovingly traced with a delicate brush. Her eyes, of a light blue, were expressive of innocence.

Though Granville discerned a sort of rigid reserve in this girlish face, he could ascribe it to the devotion in which Angélique was rapt. The solemn words of prayer, visible in the cold, came from between rows of pearls, like a fragrant mist, as it were. The young man involuntarily bent over her a little to breathe this diviner air. This movement attracted the girl's notice; her gaze, raised to the altar, was diverted to Granville, whom she could see but dimly in the gloom; but she recognized him as the companion of her youth, and a memory more vivid than prayer brought a supernatural glow to her face; she blushed. The young lawyer was thrilled with joy at seeing the hopes of another life overpowered by those of love, and the glory of the sanctuary eclipsed by earthly reminiscences; but his triumph was brief. Angélique dropped her veil, assumed a calm demeanor, and went on singing without letting her voice betray the least emotion.

Granville was a prey to one single wish, and every thought of prudence vanished. By the time the service was ended, his impatience was so great that he could not leave the ladies to go home alone, but came at once to make his bow to "his little wife." They bashfully greeted each other in the Cathedral porch in the presence of the congregation. Madame Bontems was tremulous with pride as she took the Comte de Granville's arm, though he, forced to offer it in the presence of all the world, was vexed enough with his son for his ill-advised impatience.

For about a fortnight, between the official announcement of the intended marriage of the Vicomte de Granville to Mademoiselle Bontems and the solemn day of the wedding, he came assiduously to visit his lady-love in the dismal drawing-room, to which he became accustomed. His long calls were devoted to watching Angélique's character; for his prudence, happily, had made itself heard again the day after their first meeting. He always found her seated at a little table of some West Indian wood, and engaged in marking the linen of her trousseau. Angélique never spoke first on the subject of religion. If the young lawyer amused himself with fingering the handsome rosary that she kept in a little green velvet bag, if he laughed as he looked at a relic such as usually is attached to this means of grace, Angélique would gently take the rosary out of his hands and replace it in the bag without a word, putting it away at once. When, now and then, Granville was so bold as to make mischievous remarks as to certain religious practices, the pretty girl listened to him with the obstinate smile of assurance.

"You must either believe nothing, or believe everything the Church teaches," she would say. "Would you wish to have a woman without a religion as the mother of your children?— No.—What man may dare judge as between disbelievers and God? And how can I then blame what the Church allows?"

Angélique appeared to be animated by such fervent charity, the young man saw her look at him with such perfect conviction, that he sometimes felt tempted to embrace her religious views; her firm belief that she was in the only right road aroused doubts in his mind, which she tried to turn to account.

But then Granville committed the fatal blunder of mistaking the enchantment of desire for that of love. Angélique was so happy in reconciling the voice of her heart with that of duty, by giving way to a liking that had grown up with her from childhood, that the deluded man could not discern which of the two spoke the louder. Are not all young men ready to trust the promise of a pretty face and to infer beauty of soul from beauty of feature? An indefinable impulse leads them to believe that moral perfection must co-exist with physical perfection. If Angélique had not been at liberty to give vent to her sentiments, they would soon have dried up in her heart like a plant watered with some deadly acid. How should a lover be aware of bigotry so well hidden?

This was the course of young Granville's feelings during

that fortnight, devoured by him like a book of which the end is absorbing. Angélique, carefully watched by him, seemed the gentlest of creatures, and he even caught himself feeling grateful to Madame Bontems, who, by implanting so deeply the principles of religion, had in some degree inured her to meet the troubles of life.

On the day named for signing the inevitable contract, Madame Bontems made her son-in-law pledge himself solemnly to respect her daughter's religious practices, to allow her entire liberty of conscience, to permit her to go to communion, to church, to confession as often as she pleased, and never to control her choice of priestly advisers. At this critical moment Angélique looked at her future husband with such pure and innocent eyes, that Granville did not hesitate to give his word. A smile puckered the lips of the Abbé Fontanon, a pale man, who directed the consciences of this household. Mademoiselle Bontems, by a slight nod, seemed to promise that she would never take an unfair advantage of this freedom. As to the old Count, he gently whistled the tune of an old song, *Va-t-en voir s'ils viennent* ("Go and see if they are coming on!")

A few days after the wedding festivities, of which so much is thought in the provinces, Granville and his wife went to Paris, whither the young man was recalled by his appointment as public prosecutor to the Supreme Court of the Seine circuit.

When the young couple set out to find a residence, Angélique used the influence that the honeymoon gives to every wife in persuading her husband to take a large apartment in the ground-floor of a house at the corner of the Vieille Rue du Temple and the Rue Neuve Saint-François. Her chief reason for this choice was that the house was close to the Rue d'Orleans, where there was a church, and not far from a small chapel in the Rue Saint-Louis.

"A good housewife provides for everything," said her husband, laughing.

Angélique pointed out to him that this part of Paris, known as the Marais, was within easy reach of the Palais de Justice, and that the lawyers they knew lived in the neighborhood. A fairly large garden made the apartment particularly advantageous to a young couple; the children—if Heaven should send them any—could play in the open air; the courtyard was spacious, and there were good stables.

The lawyer wished to live in the Chaussée d'Antin, where everything is fresh and bright, where the fashions may be seen while still new, where a well-dressed crowd throngs the Boulevards, and the distance is less to the theatres or places of amusement; but he was obliged to give way to the coaxing ways of a young wife, who asked this as his first favor; so, to please her, he settled in the Marais. Granville's duties required him to work hard—all the more, because they were new to him—so he devoted himself in the first place to furnishing his private study and arranging his books. He was soon established in a room crammed with papers, and left the decoration of the house to his wife. He was all the better pleased to plunge Angélique into the bustle of buying furniture and fittings, the source of so much pleasure and of so many associations to most young women, because he was rather ashamed of depriving her of his company more often than the usages of early married life require. As soon as his work was fairly under way, he gladly allowed his wife to tempt him out of his study to consider the effect of furniture or hangings, which he had before only seen piecemeal or unfinished.

If the old adage is true that says a woman may be judged of from her front door, her rooms must express her mind with even greater fidelity. Madame de Granville had perhaps stamped the various things she had ordered with the seal of her own character; the young lawyer was certainly startled by the cold, arid solemnity that reigned in these rooms; he found nothing to charm his taste; everything was discordant, nothing gratified the eye. The rigid mannerism that prevailed in the sitting-room at Bayeux had invaded his home; the broad panels were hollowed in circles, and decorated with those arabesques of which the long, monotonous mouldings are in such bad taste. Anxious to find excuses for his wife, the young husband began again, looking first at the long and lofty ante-room through which the apartment was entered. The color of the panels, as ordered by his wife, was too heavy, and the very dark green velvet used to cover the benches added to the gloom of this entrance—not, to be sure, an important room, but giving a first impression—just as we measure a man's intelligence by his first address. An ante-room is a kind of preface which announces what is to follow, but promises nothing.

The young husband wondered whether his wife could really have chosen the lamp of an antique pattern, which hung in the centre of this bare hall, the pavement of black and white marble, and the paper in imitation of blocks of stone, with green moss on them in places. A handsome, but not new, barometer hung on the middle of one of the walls, as if to accentuate the void. At the sight of it all, he looked round at his wife; he saw her so much pleased by the red braid binding to the cotton curtains, so satisfied with the barometer and the strictly decent statue that ornamented a large Gothic stove, that he had not the barbarous courage to overthrow such deep convictions. Instead of blaming his wife, Granville blamed himself, accusing himself of having failed in his duty of guiding the first steps in Paris of a girl brought up at Bayeux.

From this specimen, what might not be expected of the other rooms? What was to be looked for from a woman who took fright at the bare legs of a Caryatid, and who would not look at a chandelier or a candle-stick if she saw on it the nude outlines of an Egyptian bust? At this date the school of David was at the height of its glory; all the art of France bore the stamp of his correct design and his love of antique types, which indeed gave his pictures the character of colored sculpture. But none of these devices of Imperial luxury found civic rights under Madame de Granville's roof. The spacious, square drawing-room remained as it had been left from the time of Louis XV., in white and tarnished gold, lavishly adorned by the architect with checkered lattice-work and the hideous garlands due to the uninventive designers of the time. Still, if harmony at least had prevailed, if the furniture of modern mahogany had but assumed the twisted forms of which Boucher's corrupt taste first set the fashion, Angélique's room would only have suggested the fantastic contrast of a young couple in the nineteenth century living as though they were in the eighteenth; but a number of details were in ridiculous discord. The consoles, the clocks, the candelabra, were decorated with the military trophies which the wars of the Empire commended to the affections of the Parisians; and the Greek helmets, the Roman crossed daggers, and the shields so dear to military enthusiasm that they were introduced on furniture of the most peaceful uses, had no fitness side by side with the delicate and profuse arabesques that delighted Madame de Pompadour.

Bigotry tends to an indescribably tiresome kind of humility which does not exclude pride. Whether from modesty or by choice, Madame de Granville seemed to have a horror of light and cheerful colors; perhaps, too, she imagined that brown and purple beseemed the dignity of a magistrate. How could a girl accustomed to an austere life have admitted the luxurious divans that may suggest evil thoughts, the elegant and tempting boudoirs where naughtiness may be imagined?

The poor husband was in despair. From the tone in which he approved, only seconding the praises she bestowed on herself, Angélique understood that nothing really pleased him; and she expressed so much regret at her want of success, that Granville, who was very much in love, regarded her disappointment as a proof of her affection instead of resentment for an offence to her self-conceit. After all, could he expect a girl just snatched from the humdrum of country notions, with no experience of the niceties and grace of Paris life, to know or do any better? Rather would he believe that his wife's choice had been overruled by the tradesmen than allow himself to own the truth. If he had been less in love, he would have understood that the dealers, always quick to discern their customers' ideas, had blessed Heaven for sending them a tasteless little bigot, who would take their old-fashioned goods off their hands. So he comforted the pretty provincial.

"Happiness, dear Angélique, does not depend on a more or less elegant piece of furniture; it depends on the wife's sweetness, gentleness, and love."

"Why, it is my duty to love you," said Angélique mildly, "and I can have no more delightful duty to carry out."

Nature has implanted in the heart of woman so great a desire to please, so deep a craving for love, that, even in a youthful bigot, the ideas of salvation and a future existence must give way to the happiness of early married life. And, in fact, from the month of April, when they were married, till the beginning of winter, the husband and wife lived in perfect union. Love and hard work have the grace of making a man tolerably indifferent to external matters. Being obliged to spend half the day in court fighting for the gravest interests of men's lives or fortunes, Granville was less alive than another might have been to certain facts in his household.

If, on a Friday, he found none but Lenten fare, and by chance asked for a dish of meat without getting it, his wife, forbidden by the Gospel to tell a lie, could still, by such subterfuges as are permissible in the interests of religion, cloak what was premeditated purpose under some pretext of her own carelessness or the scarcity in the market. She would often exculpate herself at the expense of the cook, and even go so far as to scold him. At that time young lawyers did not, as they do now, keep the fasts of the Church, the four rogation seasons, and the vigils of festivals; so Granville was not at first aware of the regular recurrence of these Lenten meals, which his wife took care should be made dainty by the addition of teal, moor-hen, and fish-pies, that their amphibious meat or high seasoning might cheat his palate. Thus the young man unconsciously lived in strict orthodoxy, and worked out his salvation without knowing it.

On week-days he did not know whether his wife went to Mass or no. On Sundays, with very natural amiability, he accompanied her to church to make up to her, as it were, for sometimes giving up vespers in favor of his company; he could not at first fully enter into the strictness of his wife's religious views. The theatres being impossible in summer by reason of the heat, Granville had not even the opportunity of the great success of a piece to give rise to the serious question of playgoing. And, in short, at the early stage of an union to which a man has been led by a young girl's beauty, he can hardly be exacting as to his amusements. Youth is greedy rather than dainty, and possession has a charm in itself. How should he be keen to note coldness, dignity, and reserve in the woman to whom he ascribes the excitement he himself feels, and lends the glow of the fire that burns within him? He must have attained a certain conjugal calm before he discovers that a bigot sits waiting for love with her arms folded.

Granville, therefore, believed himself happy till a fatal event brought its influence to bear on his married life. In the month of November 1808 the Canon of Bayeux Cathedral, who had been the keeper of Madame Bontems' conscience and her daughter's, came to Paris, spurred by the ambition to be at the head of a church in the capital—a position which he regarded perhaps as the stepping-stone to a bishopric. On resuming his former control of this wandering lamb, he was horrified to find her already so much deteriorated by the air of Paris, and strove to reclaim her to his chilly fold. Frightened by the exhortations of this priest, a man of about eight-and-thirty, who brought with him, into the circle of the enlightened and tolerant Paris clergy, the bitter provincial catholicism and the inflexible bigotry which fetter timid souls with endless exactions, Madame de Granville did penance and returned from her Jansenist errors.

It would be tiresome to describe minutely all the circumstances which insensibly brought disaster on this household; it will be enough to relate the simple facts without giving them in strict order of time.

The first misunderstanding between the young couple was, however, a serious one.

When Granville took his wife into society she never declined solemn functions, such as dinners, concerts, or parties given by the Judges superior to her husband in the legal profession; but for a long time she constantly excused herself on the plea of a sick headache when they were invited to a ball. One day Granville, out of patience with these assumed indispositions, destroyed a note of invitation to a ball at the house of a Councillor of State, and gave his wife only a verbal invitation. Then, on the evening, her health being quite above suspicion, he took her to a magnificent entertainment.

"My dear," said he, on their return home, seeing her wear an offensive air of depression, "your position as a wife, the rank you hold in society, and the fortune you enjoy, impose on you certain duties of which no divine law can relieve you. Are you not your husband's pride? You are required to go to balls when I go, and to appear in a becoming manner."

"And what is there, my dear, so disastrous in my dress?"

"It is your manner, my dear. When a young man comes up to speak to you, you look so serious that a spiteful person might believe you doubtful of your own virtue. You seem to fear lest a smile should undo you. You really look as if you were asking forgiveness of God for the sins that may be committed around you. The world, my dearest, is not a convent.—But, as you have mentioned your dress, I may confess to you that it is no less a duty to conform to the customs and fashions of Society."

"Do you wish that I should display my shape like those indecent women who wear gowns so low that impudent eyes can stare at their bare shoulders and their——"

"There is a difference, my dear," said her husband, interrupting her, "between uncovering your whole bust and giving some grace to your dress. You wear three rows of net frills that cover your throat up to your chin. You look as if you had desired your dressmaker to destroy the graceful line of your shoulders and bosom with as much care as a coquette would devote to obtaining from hers a bodice that might emphasize her covered form. Your bust is wrapped in so many folds, that every one was laughing at your affectation of prudery. You would be really grieved if I were to repeat the ill-natured remarks made on your appearance."

"Those who admire such obscenity will not have to bear the burthen if we sin," said the lady tartly.

"And you did not dance?" asked Granville.

"I shall never dance," she replied.

"If I tell you that you ought to dance!" said her husband sharply. "Yes, you ought to follow the fashions, to wear flowers in your hair, and diamonds. Remember, my dear, that rich people—and we are rich—are obliged to keep up luxury in the State. Is it not far better to encourage manufacturers than to distribute money in the form of alms through the medium of the clergy?"

"You talk as a statesman!" said Angélique.

"And you as a priest," he retorted.

The discussion was bitter. Madame de Granville's answers, though spoken very sweetly and in a voice as clear as a church bell, showed an obstinacy that betrayed priestly influence. When she appealed to the rights secured to her by Granville's promise, she added that her director specially forbade her going to balls; then her husband pointed out to her that the priest was overstepping the regulations of the Church.

This odious theological dispute was renewed with great violence and acerbity on both sides when Granville proposed to take his wife to the play. Finally, the lawyer, whose sole aim was to defeat the pernicious influence exerted over his wife by her old confessor, placed the question on such a footing that Madame de Granville, in a spirit of defiance, referred it by writing to the Court of Rome, asking in so many words whether a woman could wear low gowns and go to the play and to balls without compromising her salvation.

The reply of the venerable Pope Pius VII. came at once, strongly condemning the wife's recalcitrancy and blaming the priest. This letter, a chapter on conjugal duties, might have been dictated by the spirit of Fénelon, whose grace and tenderness pervaded every line.

"A wife is right to go wherever her husband may take her. Even if she sins by his command, she will not be ultimately held answerable." These two sentences of the Pope's homily only made Madame de Granville and her director accuse him of irreligion.

But before this letter had arrived, Granville had discovered the strict observance of fast days that his wife forced upon him, and gave his servants orders to serve him with meat every day in the year. However much annoyed his wife might be by these commands, Granville, who cared not a straw for such indulgence or abstinence, persisted with manly determination.

Is it not an offence to the weakest creature that can think at all to be compelled to do, by the will of another, anything that he would otherwise have done simply of his own accord? Of all forms of tyranny, the most odious is that which constantly robs the soul of the merit of its thoughts and deeds. It has to abdicate without having reigned. The word we are readiest to speak, the feelings we most love to express, die when we are commanded to utter them.

Ere long the young man ceased to invite his friends, to give parties or dinners; the house might have been shrouded in crape. A house where the mistress is a bigot has an atmosphere of its own. The servants, who are, of course, under her immediate control, are chosen among a class who call themselves pious, and who have an unmistakable physiognomy. Just as the jolliest fellow alive, when he joins the *gendarmerie*, has the countenance of a gendarme, so those who give themselves over to the practices of devotion acquire a uniform expression; the habit of lowering their eyes and preserving a sanctimonious mien clothes them in a livery of hypocrisy which rogues can affect to perfection.

And besides, bigots constitute a sort of republic; they all know each other; the servants they recommend and hand on from one to another are a race apart, and preserved by them, as horse-breeders will admit no animal into their stables that has not a pedigree. The more the impious—as they are thought—come to understand a household of bigots, the more they perceive that everything is stamped with an indescribable squalor; they find there, at the same time, an appearance of avarice and mystery, as in a miser's home, and the dank scent of cold incense which gives a chill to the stale atmosphere of a chapel. This methodical meanness, this narrowness of thought, which is visible in every detail, can only be expressed by one word—Bigotry. In these sinister and pitiless houses Bigotry is written on the furniture, the prints, the pictures; speech is bigoted, the silence is bigoted, the faces are those of bigots. The transformation of men and things into bigotry is an inexplicable mystery, but the fact is evident. Everybody can see that bigots do not walk, do not sit, do not speak, as men of the world walk, sit, and speak. Under their roof every one is ill at ease, no one laughs, stiffness and formality infect everything, from the mistress' cap down to her pincushion; eyes are not honest, the folks move like shadows, and the lady of the house seems perched on a throne of ice.

One morning poor Granville discerned with grief and pain that all the symptoms of bigotry had invaded his home. There are in the world different spheres in which the same effects are seen though produced by dissimilar causes. Dulness hedges such miserable homes round with walls of brass, enclosing the horrors of the desert and the infinite void. The home is not so much a tomb as that far worse thing—a convent. In the centre of this icy sphere the lawyer could study his wife dispassionately. He observed, not without keen regret, the narrow-mindedness that stood confessed in the very way that her hair grew, low on the forehead, which was slightly depressed; he discovered in the perfect regularity of her features a certain set rigidity which before long made him hate the assumed sweetness that had bewitched him. Intuition told him that one day of disaster those thin lips might say, "My dear, it is for your good!"

Madame de Granville's complexion was acquiring a dull pallor and an austere expression that were a kill-joy to all who came near her. Was this change wrought by the ascetic habits of a pharisaism which is not piety any more than avarice is economy? It would be hard to say. Beauty without expression is perhaps an imposture. This imperturbable set smile that the young wife always wore when she looked at Granville seemed to be a sort of Jesuitical formula of happiness, by which she thought to satisfy all the requirements of married life. Her charity was an offence, her soulless beauty was monstrous to those who knew her; the mildness of her speech was an irritation: she acted, not on feeling, but on duty.

There are faults which may yield in a wife to the stern lessons of experience, or to a husband's warnings; but nothing can counteract false ideas of religion. An eternity of happiness to be won, set in the scale against worldly enjoyment, triumphs over everything and makes every pang endurable. Is it not the apotheosis of egotism, of Self beyond the grave? Thus even the Pope was censured at the tribunal of the priest and the young devotee. To be always in the right is a feeling which absorbs every other in these tyrannous souls.

For some time past a secret struggle had been going on between the ideas of the husband and wife, and the young man was soon weary of a battle to which there could be no end. What man, what temper, can endure the sight of a hypocritically affectionate face and categorical resistance to his slightest wishes? What is to be done with a wife who takes advantage of his passion to protect her coldness, who seems determined on being blandly inexorable, prepares herself ecstatically to play the martyr, and looks on her husband as a scourge from God, a means of flagellation that may spare her the fires of purgatory? What picture can give an idea of these women who make virtue hateful by defying the gentle precepts of that faith which Saint John epitomized in the words, "Love one another"?

If there was a bonnet to be found in a milliner's shop that was condemned to remain in the window, or to be packed off to the colonies, Granville was certain to see it on his wife's head; if a material of bad color or hideous design were to be found, she would select it. These hapless bigots are heartbreaking in their notions of dress. Want of taste is a defect inseparable from false pietism.

And so, in the home-life that needs the fullest sympathy, Granville had no true companionship. He went out alone to parties and the theatres. Nothing in his house appealed to him. A huge Crucifix that hung between his bed and Angélique's seemed figurative of his destiny. Does it not represent a murdered Divinity, a Man-God, done to death in all the prime of life and beauty? The ivory of that cross was less cold than Angélique crucifying her husband under the plea of virtue. This it was that lay at the root of their woes; the young wife saw nothing but duty where she should have given love. Here, one Ash Wednesday, rose the pale and spectral form of Fasting in Lent, of Total Abstinence, commanded in a severe tone—and Granville did not deem it advisable to write in his turn to the Pope and take the opinion of the Consistory on the proper way of observing Lent, the Ember days, and the eve of great festivals.

His misfortune was too great! He could not even complain, for what could he say? He had a pretty young wife attached to her duties, virtuous—nay, a model of all the virtues. She had a child every year, nursed them herself, and brought them up in the highest principles. Being charitable, Angélique was promoted to rank as an angel. The old women who constituted the circle in which she moved—for at that time it was not yet "the thing" for young women to be religious as a matter of fashion—all admired Madame de Granville's piety, and regarded her, not indeed as a virgin, but as a martyr. They blamed not the wife's scruples, but the barbarous philoprogenitiveness of the husband.

Granville, by insensible degrees, overdone with work, bereft of conjugal consolations, and weary of a world in which he wandered alone, by the time he was two-and-thirty had sunk into the Slough of Despond. He hated life. Having too lofty a notion of the responsibilities imposed on him by his position to set the example of a dissipated life, he tried to deaden feeling by hard study, and began a great book on Law.

But he was not allowed to enjoy the monastic peace he had hoped for. When the celestial Angélique saw him desert worldly society to work at home with such regularity, she tried to convert him. It had been a real sorrow to her to know that her husband's opinions were not strictly Christian; and she sometimes wept as she reflected that if her husband should die it would be in a state of final impenitence, so that she could not hope to snatch him from the eternal fires of Hell. Thus Granville was the mark for the mean ideas, the vacuous arguments, the narrow views by which his wife—fancying she had achieved the first victory—tried to gain a second by bringing him back within the pale of the Church.

This was the last straw. What can be more intolerable than the blind struggle in which the obstinacy of a bigot tries to meet the acumen of a lawyer? What more terrible to endure than the acrimonious pin-pricks to which a passionate soul prefers a dagger-thrust? Granville neglected his home. Everything there was unendurable. His children, broken by their mother's frigid despotism, dared not go with him to the play; indeed, Granville could never give them any pleasure without bringing down punishment from their terrible mother. His loving nature was weaned to indifference, to a selfishness worse than death. His boys, indeed, he saved from this hell by sending them to school at an early age, and insisting on his right to train them. He rarely interfered between his wife and her daughters; but he was resolved that they should marry as soon as they were old enough.

Even if he had wished to take violent measures, he could have found no justification; his wife, backed by a formidable army of dowagers, would have had him condemned by the whole world. Thus Granville had no choice but to live in complete isolation; but, crushed under the tyranny of misery, he could not himself bear to see how altered he was by grief and toil. And he dreaded any connection or intimacy with women of the world, having no hope of finding any consolation.

The improving history of this melancholy household gave rise to no events worthy of record during the fifteen years between 1806 and 1825. Madame de Granville was exactly the same after losing her husband's affection as she had been during the time when she called herself happy. She paid for Masses, beseeching God and the Saints to enlighten her as to what the faults were which displeased her husband, and to show her the way to restore the erring sheep; but the more fervent her prayers, the less was Granville to be seen at home.

For about five years now, having achieved a high position as a judge, Granville had occupied the *entresol* of the house to avoid living with the Comtesse de Granville. Every morning a little scene took place, which, if evil tongues are to be believed, is repeated in many households as the result of incompatibility of temper, of moral or physical malady, or of antagonisms leading to such disaster as is recorded in this history. At about eight in the morning a housekeeper, bearing no small resemblance to a nun, rang at the Comte de Granville's door. Admitted to the room next to the Judge's study, she always repeated the same message to the footman, and always in the same tone:

"Madame would be glad to know whether Monsieur le Comte has had a good night, and if she is to have the pleasure of his company at breakfast."

"Monsieur presents his compliments to Madame la Comtesse," the valet would say, after speaking with his master, "and begs her to hold him excused; important business compels him to be in court this morning."

A minute later the woman reappeared and asked on madame's behalf whether she would have the pleasure of seeing Monsieur le Comte before he went out.

"He is gone," was always the reply, though often his carriage was still waiting.

This little dialogue by proxy became a daily ceremonial. Granville's servant, a favorite with his master, and the cause of more than one quarrel over his irreligious and dissipated conduct, would even go into his master's room, as a matter of form, when the Count was not there, and come back with the same formula in reply.

The aggrieved wife was always on the watch for her husband's return, and standing on the steps so as to meet him like an embodiment of remorse. The petty aggressiveness which lies at the root of the monastic temper was the foundation of Madame de Granville's; she was now five-and-thirty, and looked forty. When the Count was compelled by decency to speak to his wife or to dine at home, she was only too well pleased to inflict her company upon him, with her acid-sweet remarks and the intolerable dulness of her narrow-minded circle, and she tried to put him in the wrong before the servants and her charitable friends.

When, at this time, the post of President in a provincial court was offered to the Comte de Granville, who was in high favor, he begged to be allowed to remain in Paris. This refusal, of which the Keeper of the Seals alone knew the reasons, gave rise to extraordinary conjectures on the part of the Countess' intimate friends and of her director. Granville, a rich man with a hundred thousand francs a year, belonged to one of the first families of Normandy. His appointment to be Presiding Judge would have been the stepping-stone to a peer's seat; whence this strange lack of ambition? Why had he given up his great book on Law? What was the meaning of the dissipation which for nearly six years had made him a stranger to his home, his family, his study, to all he ought to hold dear? The Countess' confessor, who based his hopes of a bishopric quite as much on the families he governed as on the services he rendered to an association of which he was an ardent propagator, was much disappointed by Granville's refusal, and tried to insinuate calumnious explanations: "If Monsieur le Comte had such an objection to provincial life, it was perhaps because he dreaded finding himself under the necessity of leading a regular life, compelled to set an example of moral conduct, and to live with the Countess, from whom nothing could have alienated him but some illicit connection; for how could a woman so pure as Madame de Granville ever tolerate the disorderly life into which her husband had drifted?" The sanctimonious women accepted as facts these hints, which unluckily were not merely hypothetical, and Madame de Granville was stricken as by a thunderbolt.

Angélique, knowing nothing of the world, of love and its follies, was so far from conceiving of any conditions of married life unlike those that had alienated her husband as possible, that she believed him to be incapable of the errors which are crimes in the eyes of any wife. When the Count ceased to demand anything of her, she imagined that the tranquillity he now seemed to enjoy was in the course of nature; and, as she had really given to him all the love which her heart was capable of feeling for a man, while the priest's conjectures were the utter destruction of the illusions she had hitherto cherished, she defended her husband; at the same time, she could not eradicate the suspicion that had been so ingeniously sown in her soul.

These alarms wrought such havoc in her feeble brain that they made her ill; she was worn by low fever. These incidents took place during Lent 1822; she would not pretermit her austerities, and fell into a decline that put her life in danger. Granville's indifference was added torture; his care and attention were such as a nephew feels himself bound to give to some old uncle.

Though the Countess had given up her persistent nagging and remonstrances, and tried to receive her husband with affectionate words, the sharpness of the bigot showed through, and one speech would often undo the work of a week.

Towards the end of May, the warm breath of spring, and more nourishing diet than her Lenten fare, restored Madame de Granville to a little strength. One morning, on coming home from Mass, she sat down on a stone bench in the little garden, where the sun's kisses reminded her of the early days of her married life, and she looked back across the years to see wherein she might have failed in her duty as a wife and mother. She was broken in upon by the Abbé Fontanon in an almost indescribable state of excitement.

"Has any misfortune befallen you, Father?" she asked with filial solicitude.

"Ah! I only wish," cried the Normandy priest, "that all the woes inflicted on you by the hand of God were dealt out to me; but, my admirable friend, there are trials to which you can but bow."

"Can any worse punishments await me than those with which Providence crushes me by making my husband the instrument of His wrath?"

"You must prepare yourself, daughter, to yet worse mischief than we and your pious friends had ever conceived of."

"Then I may thank God," said the Countess, "for vouchsafing to use you as the messenger of His will, and thus, as ever, setting the treasures of mercy by the side of the scourges of His wrath, just as in bygone days He showed a spring to Hagar when He had driven her into the desert."

"He measures your sufferings by the strength of your resignation and the weight of your sins."

"Speak; I am ready to hear!" As she said it she cast her eyes up to heaven. "Speak, Monseiur Fontanon."

"For seven years Monsieur Granville has lived in sin with a concubine, by whom he has two children; and on this adulterous connection he has spent more than five hundred thousand francs, which ought to have been the property of his legitimate family."

"I must see it to believe it!" cried the Countess.

"Far be it from you!" exclaimed the Abbé. "You must forgive, my daughter, and wait in patience and prayer till God enlightens your husband; unless, indeed, you choose to adopt against him the means offered you by human laws."

The long conversation that ensued between the priest and his penitent resulted in an extraordinary change in the Countess; she abruptly dismissed him, called her servants, who were alarmed at her flushed face and crazy energy. She ordered her carriage—countermanded it—changed her mind twenty times in the hour; but at last, at about three o'clock, as if she had come to some great determination, she went out, leaving the whole household in amazement at such a sudden transformation.

"Is the Count coming home to dinner?" she asked of his servant, to whom she never would speak.

"No, madame."

"Did you go with him to the Courts this morning?"

"Yes, madame."

"And to-day is Monday?"

"Yes, madame."

"Then do the Courts sit on Mondays nowadays?"

"Devil take you!" cried the man, as his mistress drove off after saying to the coachman:

"Rue Taitbout."

Mademoiselle de Bellefeuille was weeping: Roger, sitting by her side, held one of her hands between his own. He was silent, looking by turns at little Charles—who, not understanding his mother's grief, stood speechless at the sight of her tears—at the cot where Eugénie lay sleeping, and Caroline's face, on which grief had the effect of rain falling across the beams of cheerful sunshine.

"Yes, my darling," said Roger, after a long silence, "that is the great secret: I am married. But some day I hope we may form but one family. My wife has been given over ever since last March. I do not wish her dead; still, if it should please God to take her to Himself, I believe she will be happier in Paradise than in a world to whose griefs and pleasures she is equally indifferent."

"How I hate that woman! How could she bear to make you unhappy? And yet it is to that unhappiness that I owe my happiness!"

Her tears suddenly ceased.

"Caroline, let us hope," cried Roger. "Do not be frightened by anything that priest may have said to you. Though my wife's confessor is a man to be feared for his power in the congregation, if he should try to blight our happiness I would find means——"

"What could you do?"

"We would go to Italy; I would fly——"

A shriek that rang out from the adjoining room made Roger start and Mademoiselle de Bellefeuille quake; but she rushed into the drawing-room, and there found Madame de Granville in a dead faint. When the Countess recovered her senses, she sighed deeply on finding herself supported by the Count and her rival, whom she instinctively pushed away with a gesture of contempt. Mademoiselle de Bellefeuille rose to withdraw.

"You are at home, madame," said Granville, taking Caroline by the arm. "Stay."

The Judge took up his wife in his arms, carried her to the carriage, and got into it with her.

"Who is it that has brought you to the point of wishing me dead, of resolving to fly?" asked the Countess, looking at her husband with grief mingled with indignation. "Was I not young? you thought me pretty—what fault have you to find with me? Have I been false to you? Have not I been a virtuous and well-conducted wife? My heart has cherished no image but yours, my ears have listened to no other voice. What duty have I failed in? What have I ever denied you?"

"Happiness, madame," said the Count severely. "You know, madame, that there are two ways of serving God. Some Christians imagine that by going to church at fixed hours to say a *Paternoster,* by attending Mass regularly and avoiding sin, they may win heaven—but they, madame, will go to hell; they have not loved God for Himself, they have not worshiped Him as He chooses to be worshiped, they have made no sacrifice. Though mild in seeming, they are hard on their neighbors; they see the law, the letter, not the spirit.—This is how you have treated me, your earthly husband; you have sacrificed my happiness to your salvation; you were always absorbed in prayer when I came to you in gladness of heart; you wept when you should have cheered my toil; you have never tried to satisfy any demands I have made on you."

"And if they were wicked," cried the Countess hotly, "was I to lose my soul to please you?"

"It is a sacrifice which another, a more loving woman, has dared to make," said Granville coldly.

"Dear God!" she cried, bursting into tears, "Thou hearest! Has he been worthy of the prayers and penance I have lived in, wearing myself out to atone for his sins and my own?—Of what avail is virtue?"

"To win Heaven, my dear. A woman cannot be at the same time the wife of a man and the spouse of Christ. That would be bigamy; she must choose between a husband and a nunnery. For the sake of future advantage you have stripped your soul of all the love, all the devotion, which God commands that you should have for me, you have cherished no feeling but hatred——"

"Have I not loved you?" she put in.

"No, madame."

"Then what is love?" the Countess involuntarily inquired.

"Love, my dear," replied Granville, with a sort of ironical surprise, "you are incapable of understanding it. The cold sky of Normandy is not that of Spain. This difference of climate is no doubt the secret of our disaster.—To yield to our caprices, to guess them, to find pleasure in pain, to sacrifice the world's opinion, your pride, your religion even, and still regard these offerings as mere grains of incense burnt in honor of the idol—that is love——"

"The love of ballet-girls!" cried the Countess in horror. "Such flames cannot last, and must soon leave nothing but ashes and cinders, regret or despair. A wife ought, in my opinion, to bring you true friendship, equable warmth——"

"You speak of warmth as negroes speak of ice," retorted the Count, with a sardonic smile. "Consider that the humblest daisy has more charms than the proudest and most gorgeous of the red hawthorns that attract us in spring by their strong scent and brilliant color.—At the same time," he went on, "I will do you justice. You have kept so precisely in the straight path of imaginary duty prescribed by law, that only to make you understand wherein you have failed towards me, I should be obliged to enter into details which would offend your dignity, and instruct you in matters which would seem to you to undermine all morality."

"And you dare to speak of morality when you have but just left the house where you have dissipated your children's fortune in debaucheries?" cried the Countess, maddened by her husband's reticence.

"There, madame, I must correct you," said the Count, coolly interrupting his wife. "Though Mademoiselle de Bellefeuille is rich, it is at nobody's expense. My uncle was master of his fortune, and had several heirs. In his lifetime, and out of pure friendship, regarding her as his niece, he gave her the little estate of Bellefeuille. As for anything else, I owe it to his liberality——"

"Such conduct is only worthy of a Jacobin!" said the sanctimonious Angélique.

"Madame, you are forgetting that your own father was one of the Jacobins whom you scorn so uncharitably," said the Count severely. "Citizen Bontems was signing death-warrants at a time when my uncle was doing France good service."

Madame de Granville was silenced. But after a short pause, the remembrance of what she had just seen reawakened in her soul the jealousy which nothing can kill in a woman's heart, and she murmured, as if to herself—"How can a woman thus destroy her own soul and that of others?"

"Bless me, madame," replied the Count, tired of this dialogue, "you yourself may some day have to answer that question." The Countess was scared. "You perhaps will be held excused by the merciful Judge, who will weigh our sins," he went on, "in consideration of the conviction with which you have worked out my misery. I do not hate you—I hate those who have perverted your heart and your reason. You have prayed for me, just as Mademoiselle de Bellefeuille has given me her heart and crowned my life with love. You should have been my mistress and the prayerful saint by turns.—Do me the justice to confess that I am no reprobate, no debauchee.

My life was cleanly. Alas! after seven years of wretchedness, the craving for happiness led me by an imperceptible descent to love another woman and make a second home. And do not imagine that I am singular; there are in this city thousands of husbands, all led by various causes to live this twofold life."

"Great God!" cried the Countess. "How heavy is the cross Thou hast laid on me to bear! If the husband Thou hast given me here below in Thy wrath can only be made happy through my death, take me to Thyself!"

"If you had always breathed such admirable sentiments and such devotion, we should be happy yet," said the Count coldly.

"Indeed," cried Angélique, melting into a flood of tears, "forgive me if I have done any wrong. Yes, monsieur, I am ready to obey you in all things, feeling sure that you will desire nothing but what is just and natural; henceforth I will be all you can wish your wife to be."

"If your purpose, madame, is to compel me to say that I no longer love you, I shall find the cruel courage to tell you so. Can I command my heart? Can I wipe out in an instant the traces of fifteen years of suffering?—I have ceased to love.— These words contain a mystery as deep as lies the words *I love*. Esteem, respect, friendship may be won, lost, regained; but as to love—I might school myself for a thousand years, and it would not blossom again, especially for a woman too old to respond to it."

"I hope, Monsieur le Comte, I sincerely hope, that such words may not be spoken to you some day by the woman you love, and in such a tone and accent——"

"Will you put on a dress *à la Grecque* this evening, and come to the Opera?"

The shudder with which the Countess received the suggestion was a mute reply.

Early in December 1833, a man, whose perfectly white hair and worn features seemed to show that he was aged by grief rather than by years, was walking at midnight along the Rue Gaillon. Having reached a house of modest appearance, and only two stories high, he paused to look up at one of the attic windows that pierced the roof at regular intervals. A dim light scarcely showed through the humble panes, some of which had been repaired with paper. The man below was watching the wavering glimmer with the vague curiosity of a Paris idler, when a young man came out of the house. As the light of the street lamp fell full on the face of the first comer, it will not seem surprising that, in spite of the darkness, this young man went towards the passer-by, though with the hesitancy that is usual when we have any fear of making a mistake in recognizing an acquaintance.

"What, is it you," cried he, "Monsieur le Président? Alone at this hour, and so far from the Rue Saint-Lazare. Allow me to have the honor of giving you my arm.—The pavement is so greasy this morning, that if we do not hold each other up," he added, to soothe the elder man's susceptibilities, "we shall find it hard to escape a tumble."

"But, my dear sir, I am no more than fifty-five, unfortunately for me," replied the Comte de Granville. "A physician of your celebrity must know that at that age a man is still hale and strong."

"Then you are in waiting on a lady, I suppose," replied Horace Bianchon. "You are not, I imagine, in the habit of going about Paris on foot. When a man keeps such fine horses——"

"Still, when I am not visiting in the evening, I commonly return from the Courts or the club on foot," replied the Count.

"And with large sums of money about you, perhaps!" cried the doctor. "It is a positive invitation to the assassin's knife."

"I am not afraid of that," said Granville, with melancholy indifference.

"But, at least, do not stand about," said the doctor, leading the Count towards the boulevard. "A little more and I shall believe that you are bent on robbing me of your last illness, and dying by some other hand than mine."

"You caught me playing the spy," said the Count. "Whether on foot or in a carriage, and at whatever hour of the night I may come by, I have for some time past observed at a window on the third floor of your house the shadow of a person who seems to work with heroic constancy."

The Count paused as if he felt some sudden pain. "And I take as great an interest in that garret," he went on, "as a citizen of Paris must feel in the finishing of the Palais Royal."

"Well," said Horace Bianchon eagerly, "I can tell you ——"

"Tell me nothing," replied Granville, cutting the doctor short. "I would not give a centime to know whether the shadow that moves across that shabby blind is that of a man or a woman, nor whether the inhabitant of that attic is happy or miserable. Though I was surprised to see no one at work there this evening, and though I stopped to look, it was solely for the pleasure of indulging in conjectures as numerous and as idiotic as those of idlers who see a building left half finished. For nine years, my young——" the Count hesitated to use a word; then he waved his hand, exclaiming—"No, I will not say friend—I hate everything that savors of sentiment.—Well, for nine years past I have ceased to wonder that old men amuse themselves with growing flowers and planting trees; the events of life have taught them disbelief in all human affection; and I grew old within a few days. I will no longer attach myself to any creature but to unreasoning animals, or plants, or superficial things. I think more of Taglioni's grace than of all human feeling. I abhor life and the world in which I live alone. Nothing, nothing," he went on, in a tone that startled the younger man, "no, nothing can move or interest me."

"But you have children?"

"My children!" he repeated bitterly. "Yes—well, is not my eldest daughter the Comtesse de Vandenesse? The other will, through her sister's connections, make some good match.

As to my sons, have they not succeeded? The Viscount was public prosecutor at Limoges, and is now President of the Court at Orléans; the younger is public prosecutor in Paris.— My children have their own cares, their own anxieties and business to attend to. If of all those hearts one had been devoted to me, if one had tried by entire affection to fill up the void I have here," and he struck his breast, "well, that one would have failed in life, have sacrificed it to me. And why should he? Why? To bring sunshine into my few remaining years—and would he have succeeded? Might I not have accepted such generosity as a debt? But, doctor," and the Count smiled with deep irony, "it is not for nothing that we teach them arithmetic and how to count. At this moment perhaps they are waiting for my money."

"O Monsieur le Comte, how could such an idea enter your head—you who are kind, friendly, and humane! Indeed, if I were not myself a living proof of the benevolence you exercise so liberally and so nobly——"

"To please myself," replied the Count. "I pay for a sensation, as I would to-morrow pay a pile of gold to recover the most childish illusion that would but make my heart glow.— I help my fellow-creatures for my own sake, just as I gamble; and I look for gratitude from none. I should see you die without blinking; and I beg of you to feel the same with regard to me. I tell you, young man, the events of life have swept over my heart like the lavas of Vesuvius over Herculaneum. The town is there—dead."

"Those who have brought a soul as warm and as living as yours was to such a pitch of indifference are indeed guilty!"

"Say no more," said the Count, with a shudder of aversion.

"You have a malady which you ought to allow me to treat," said Bianchon in a tone of deep emotion.

"What, do you know of a cure for death?" cried the Count irritably.

"I undertake, Monsieur le Comte, to revive the heart you believe to be frozen."

"Are you a match for Talma, then?" asked the Count satirically.

"No, Monsieur le Comte. But Nature is as far above Talma as Talma is superior to me.—Listen: the garret you are interested in is inhabited by a woman of about thirty, and in her love is carried to fanaticism. The object of her adoration is a young man of pleasing appearance, but endowed by some malignant fairy with every conceivable vice. This fellow is a gambler, and it is hard to say which he is most addicted to— wine or women; he has, to my knowledge, committed acts deserving punishment by law. Well, and to him this unhappy woman sacrificed a life of ease, a man who worshiped her, and the father of her children.—But what is wrong, Monsieur le Comte?"

"Nothing. Go on."

"She has allowed him to squander a perfect fortune; she would, I believe, give him the world if she had it; she works night and day; and many a time she has, without a murmur, seen the wretch she adores rob her even of the money saved to buy the clothes the children need, and their food for the morrow. Only three days ago she sold her hair, the finest hair I ever saw; he came in, she could not hide the gold piece quickly enough, and he asked her for it. For a smile, for a kiss, she gave up the price of a fortnight's life and peace. Is it not dreadful, and yet sublime?—But work is wearing her cheeks hollow. Her children's crying has broken her heart; she is ill, and at this moment moaning on her wretched bed. This evening they had nothing to eat; the children have not strength to cry, they were silent when I went up."

Horace Bianchon stood still. Just then the Comte de Granville, in spite of himself, as it were, had put his hand into his waistcoat pocket.

"I can guess, my young friend, how it is that she is yet alive if you attend her," said the elder man.

"O poor soul!" cried the doctor, "who could refuse to help her? I only wish I were richer, for I hope to cure her of her passion."

"But how can you expect me to pity a form of misery of which the joys to me would seem cheaply purchased with my whole fortune!" exclaimed the Count, taking his hand out of his pocket empty of the notes which Bianchon had supposed his patron to be feeling for. "That woman feels, she is alive! Would not Louis XV. have given his kingdom to rise from the grave and have three days of youth and life! And is not that the history of thousands of dead men, thousands of sick men, thousands of old men?"

"Poor Caroline!" cried Bianchon.

As he heard the name the Count shuddered, and grasped the doctor's arm with the grip of an iron vise, as it seemed to Bianchon.

"Her name is Caroline Crochard?" asked the President, in a voice that was evidently broken.

"Then you know her?" said the doctor, astonished.

"And the wretch's name is Solvet.—Ay, you have kept your word!" exclaimed Granville; "you have roused my heart to the most terrible pain it can suffer till it is dust. That emotion, too, is a gift from hell, and I always know how to pay those debts."

By this time the Count and the doctor had reached the corner of the Rue de la Chaussée d'Antin. One of those nightbirds who wander round with a basket on their back and crook in hand, and were, during the Revolution, facetiously called the Committee of Research, was standing by the curbstone where the two men now stopped. This scavenger had a shriveled face worthy of those immortalized by Charlet in his caricatures of the sweepers of Paris.

"Do you ever pick up a thousand-franc note?"

"Now and then, master."

"And you restore them?"

"It depends on the reward offered."

"You're the man for me," cried the Count, giving the man a thousand-franc note. "Take this, but, remember, I give it you on condition of your spending it at the wineshop, of your getting drunk, fighting, beating your wife, blacking your friends' eyes. That will give work to the watch, the surgeon, the druggist—perhaps to the police, the public prosecutor, the

"You're the man for me," said the Count

judge, and the prison warders. Do not try to do anything else, or the devil will be revenged on you sooner or later."

A draughtsman would need at once the pencil of Charlet and of Callot, the brush of Teniers and of Rembrandt, to give a true notion of this night-scene.

"Now I have squared accounts with hell, and had some pleasure for my money," said the Count in a deep voice, pointing out the indescribable physiognomy of the gaping scavenger to the doctor, who stood stupefied. "As for Caroline Crochard!—she may die of hunger and thirst, hearing the heart-rending shrieks of her starving children, and convinced of the baseness of the man she loves. I will not give a sou to rescue her; and because you have helped her, I will see you no more——"

The Count left Bianchon standing like a statue, and walked as briskly as a young man to the Rue Saint-Lazare, soon reaching the little house where he resided, and where, to his surprise, he found a carriage waiting at the door.

"Monsieur, your son, the attorney-general, came about an hour since," said the man-servant, "and is waiting for you in your bedroom."

Granville signed to the man to leave him.

"What motive can be strong enough to require you to infringe the order I have given my children never to come to me unless I send for them?" asked the Count of his son as he went into the room.

"Father," replied the younger man in a tremulous voice, and with great respect, "I venture to hope that you will forgive me when you have heard me."

"Your reply is proper," said the Count. "Sit down," and he pointed to a chair. "But whether I walk up and down, or take a seat, speak without heeding me."

"Father," the son went on, "this afternoon, at four o'clock, a very young man who was arrested in the house of a friend of mine, whom he had robbed to a considerable extent, appealed to you.—He says he is your son."

"His name?" asked the Count hoarsely.

"Charles Crochard."

"That will do," said the father, with an imperious wave of the hand.

Granville paced the room in solemn silence, and his son took care not to break it.

"My son," he began, and the words were pronounced in a voice so mild and fatherly, that the young lawyer started, "Charles Crochard spoke the truth.—I am glad you came to me to-night, my good Eugène," he added. "Here is a considerable sum of money"—and he gave him a bundle of banknotes—"you can make any use of them you think proper in this matter. I trust you implicitly, and approve beforehand whatever arrangements you may make, either in the present or for the future.—Eugène, my dear son, kiss me. We part perhaps for the last time. I shall to-morrow crave my dismissal from the King, and I am going to Italy.

"Though a father owes no account of his life to his children, he is bound to bequeath to them the experience Fate sells him so dearly—is it not a part of their inheritance?—When you marry," the Count went on, with a little involuntary shudder, "do not undertake it lightly; that act is the most important of all those which society requires of us. Remember to study at your leisure the character of the woman who is to be your partner; but consult me too, I will judge of her myself. A lack of union between husband and wife, from whatever cause, leads to terrible misfortune; sooner or later we are always punished for contravening the social law.—But I will write to you on this subject from Florence. A father who has the honor of presiding over a supreme court of justice must not have to blush in the presence of his son. Good-bye."

PARIS, *February* 1830—*January* 1842.

MODESTE MIGNON

AND OTHER STORIES

INTRODUCTION

Modeste Mignon occupies a very peculiar place in Balzac's works—a place, indeed, which, though for the form's sake more than anything else the author has connected it with the rest of the *Comédie* by some repetition of personages, is almost entirely isolated. I think it has puzzled some devoted Balzacians—so much so, that I have seen it omitted even from lists of his works suitable to "the young person," in which it surely should have had an eminent place. As it is distinctly late—it was written in 1844, and nothing of combined magnitude and first-class importance succeeded it except *Les Parents Pauvres*—it may not impossibly serve as a basis for the expectation that if Balzac, after his re-establishment in Paris as a wealthy personage, had received a new lease of life and vigor instead of a sentence of death, we might have had from him a series of works as different from anything that he had composed before as *Modeste Mignon* is from her sisters.

In saying this, I do not mean to put the book itself in the very first class of its author's work. It is too much of an experiment for that—of an experiment as far as the heroine is concerned, the boldness and novelty of which is likely to be underestimated by almost any reader, unless he be a literary student who pays strict attention to times and seasons. Even in England (though Charlotte Brontë was planning her at this very time) the wilful unconventional heroine was something of a novelty; and when it is remembered how infinitely stricter was the standard of the French *ingénue*, until quite recently, than it ever, even in the depths of the eighteenth century, was in England, the audacity of the conception of Modeste may be at least generally appreciated. And it is specially important to observe that though the author puts in Charles Mignon's mouth a vindication of the French process of tying a girl hand and foot and handing her over to the best bidder as a husband, instead of allowing her to choose for herself, Modeste's audacity in pursuing the opposite method is crowned with complete success, if not with success of exactly the kind that she anticipated. Except the case of Savinien de Portenduère and Ursule Mirouët, hers is, so far as I can remember, the only example in the whole *Comédie* of a love-marriage which, as we are told, was wholly successful, without even vacillations on the wife's part or relapses on the husband's. It is true that, with a slight touch of cowardice or concession, Balzac has made Modeste half a German; but this is a very venial bowing in the porch, not the chancel, of the House of Rimmon.

Whether the young lady is as entirely successful and as entirely charming as she is undeniably audacious in conception, is not a point for equally positive pronouncement. Just as it was probably necessary for Balzac, in order not to outrage the feelings of his readers too much, to put that Teutonic strain in Modeste, so he had, in all probability, to exhibit her as capricious, and almost unamiable, in order to attain the fitness of things in connection with so terrible a young person. It is certain that even those who by no means rejoice in pattern heroines, even those who "like them rather wicked," may sometimes think Modeste nasty in her behavior to her family, to Butscha, and, perhaps, to her future husband. She is, for instance, quite wrong about the whip,

INTRODUCTION

which she might have refused altogether, but could not with decency accept from one person and refuse from another. But what has just been said will cover this and other petulances and outbursts. So "shoking" a young person (it is very cheerful and interesting to think how much more exactly that favorite *vox nihili* of French speech expresses French than English sentiment) could not but behave "shokingly."

Most of the minor characters are good: Butscha, a difficult and, in any case, slightly improbable personage, is, in his own way, very good indeed. It was probably necessary for Balzac, in turning the usual scheme of the French novel upside down, to provide a rather timid hero for such a masterful heroine; and it must be admitted that Ernest de la Brière is a rather preternaturally good young man. Still, he is not mawkish; and except that he should not have given Modeste quite such a valuable present, he behaves more like a gentleman in the full English sense than any other of Balzac's heroes.

The very full, very elaborate, and very unfavorable portrait of Canalis offers again much scope for difference of mere taste and opinion, without the possibility of laying down a conclusion very positively. Even if tradition were not unanimous on the subject, it would be quite certain that Canalis is a direct presentment of Lamartine, from whom he is so ostentatiously dissociated. And there can, of course, be no two opinions as to the presentment being very distinctly unfavorable—much more so than the earlier introductions of this same Canalis, which are either complimentary or colorless for the most part, though his vanity is sometimes hinted at. I do not know whether Balzac had any private quarrel with the poet, or whether Lamartine's increasing leanings towards Republicanism exasperated the always monarchical novelist. But it is certain that Canalis cuts rather a bad figure here—that Lamartine was actually supposed to have married for money—and that the whole thing has more of the nature of a personal attack than anything else in Balzac, except the outbreak against Sainte-Beuve in *Un Prince de la Bohème*.

Perhaps it should be added that the practice of correspondence between incognitas and men of letters, not unknown in any country, has been rather frequent and famous in France. The chief example is, of course, that interchange of communications between Mérimée and Mlle. Jenny Dacquin, which had such important results for literature, and such not unimportant ones for the parties concerned. Balzac himself rejoiced in a Modeste called Louise, whom, however, he seems never to have seen; and there is little doubt that Lamartine the actual was attacked, as the fictitious Canalis boasts that he was, by scores of such persons. The chief instance I can think of in which such a correspondence led to matrimony was that of Southey and his second wife Caroline Bowles.

The history of *Modeste Mignon* is short and simple. It was first given to the public in the spring and summer of 1844 by the *Journal des Débats,* and before the end of the year it appeared in four volumes, published by Roux and Cassanet. It had here seventy-five chapter divisions, with headings. In 1845, scarcely a twelve-month after its first appearance, it took its place in the *Comédie.*

Le Messe de l'Athée, by the common consent of competent judges, takes rank with the novelist's very best work. Its extreme brevity makes it almost impossible for the author to indulge in those digressions from which he never could entirely free himself when he allowed himself much room. We do not hear more of the inward character of Desplein than is necessary to make us appreciate the touching history which is the centre of the anecdote; the thing in general could not be presented at greater advantage than it is. Nor in itself could it be much, if at all, better. As usual, it is more or less of a personal confession. Balzac, it must always be remembered, was himself pretty definitely "on the side of the angels." As a Frenchman, as a man with a strong eighteenth-century tincture in him, as a student of Rabelais, as one not too much given to regard nature and fate through rose-colored spectacles, as a product of more or less godless education (for his school-days came before the neo-catholic revival), and in many other ways, he was not exactly an orthodox person. But he had no ideas foreign to orthodoxy; and neither in his novels, nor in his letters, nor elsewhere, would it be possible to find a private expression of unbelief. And such a story as this is worth a bookseller's warehouse full of tracts, coming as it does from Honoré de Balzac.

Le Messe de l'Athée appeared first in the *Chronique de Paris* for January 4, 1836; next year joined the other *Etudes Philosophiques;* and in 1844 the *Vie Privée* and the *Comédie.*

G. S.

No special connection is apparent between *L'Enfant Maudit* and any of the other stories going to make up the *Comédie.* Incidents as well as personages are isolated, while even the style belongs to another period—the earlier or transitional, when Balzac was good, apparently, for nothing better than the *Œuvres de Jeunesse*. One of two theories must explain its position: Either it was written earlier than the first date it bears, 1831; or it marks a temporary retrogression—rare as such instances are—to the unfinished and amateurish style of the apprentice. While the story is not good in workmanship, no fault can be found with it on the score of morals. A frankness almost brutal characterizes the overture; proprieties are thrown to the winds—a trait Balzac held in common with other French authors—yet, when we remember the novelist's manifest intention to portray life as it is, none but the prude can disapprove. The principal fault of the story, aside from its nightmarishness, lies in the tremendous overbalancing of its characters. Against the fragile figures of the Countess and Étienne and Gabrielle—all seemingly cast in the same delicate mould—the terrible Count looms too vividly. In one place only does this too great and too constant menace heighten the effect of the story: the simple scenes of love-making stand forth sharply like a gleam of sunlight athwart an ominous sky.

L'Enfant Maudit carries two dates, 1831-1836. This may be explained by the complicated manner of its appearance. The *Revue des Deux Mondes* for January 1831 contained the first part only, not bearing its present caption, and in three chapters. The second part, originally called *La Perle Brisée*, was first published in the *Chronique de Paris*, October 1836. In 1837 it was made an *Etude Philosophique;* ten years thereafter it was included in a volume with *Madame de la Chanterie*, without, however, disturbing its present and previously established headings to the two parts.

MODESTE MIGNON

To a Polish Lady

Daughter of an enslaved land, an angel in your love, a demon in your imagination, a child in faith, an old man in experience, a man in brain, a woman in heart, a giant in hope, a mother in suffering, a poet in your dreams, and Beauty itself withal—this work, in which your love and your fancy, your faith, your experience, your suffering, your hopes, and your dreams, are like chains by which hangs a web less lovely than the poetry cherished in your soul—the poetry whose expression when it lights up your countenance is, to those who admire you, what the characters of a lost language are to the learned—this work is yours. DE BALZAC.

IN the beginning of October 1829, Monsieur Simon-Babylas Latournelle, a notary, was walking up the hill from le Havre to Ingouville arm in arm with his son, and accompanied by his wife. By her, like a page, came the notary's head-clerk, a little hunchback named Jean Butscha. When these four persons—of whom two at least mounted by the same way every evening—reached the turn in the zigzag road (like what the Italians call a Cornice), the notary looked about him to see whether any one might overhear him from some garden terrace above or below, and as an additional precaution he spoke low.

"Exupère," said he to his son, "try to carry out in an intelligent manner, without guessing at the meaning, a little manœuvre I will explain to you; and even if you have a suspicion, I desire you will fling it into the Styx which every notary or law-student ought to keep handy for other people's secrets. After paying your respects, homage, and devoir to Madame and Mademoiselle Mignon, to Monsieur and Madame Dumay, and to Monsieur Gobenheim, if he is at the Chalet, when silence is restored, Monsieur Dumay will take you aside; look attentively—I allow you—at Mademoiselle Modeste all the time he is talking to you. My worthy friend will ask you to go out for a walk and return in about an hour, at about nine o'clock, with a hurried air; try to seem quite out of breath, then whisper in his ear, but loud enough for Mademoiselle Modeste to hear: 'The young man is coming!' "

Exupère was to start for Paris on the following day to begin his law studies. It was this prospect of departure which had led Latournelle to propose to his friend Dumay that his son should play the assistant in the important conspiracy which may be suspected from his instructions.

"Is Mademoiselle Modeste suspected of carrying on an intrigue?" asked Butscha timidly of his mistress.

"Hsh—Butscha!" replied Madame Latournelle, taking her husband's arm.

Madame Latournelle, the daughter of the Registrar of the lower Court, considers herself justified by her birth in describing her family as *parliamentary*. These pretensions account for the efforts made by the lady, whose face is rather too red and rough, to assume the majesty of the tribunal whose verdicts are recorded by her father. She takes snuff, holds herself as stiff as a post, gives herself airs of importance, and looks exactly like a mummy that has been galvanized into life for a moment. She tries to give her sharp voice an aristocratic tone, but she no more succeeds in that than in concealing her defective education. Her social value is indisputable when you look at the caps she wears, bristling with flowers, the false fronts plastered on her temples, and the gowns she chooses. How could the shops get rid of such goods if it were not for such as Madame Latournelle?

This worthy woman's absurdities might have passed almost unremarked, for she was essentially charitable and pious, but that Nature, which sometimes has its little jest by turning these grotesque creations, gave her the figure of a drum-major so as to display the devices of her provincial mind. She has never been out of le Havre, she believes in the infallibility of le Havre, she buys everything at le Havre, and gets her dresses there; she speaks of herself as Norman to the finger tips, she reverences her father, and adores her husband. Little Latournelle was bold enough to marry this woman when she had attained the post-matrimonial age of thirty-three, and they contrived to have a son. As he might anywhere have won the sixty thousand francs which the Registrar had to settle, his unusual courage was set down to a wish to avoid the irruption of the Minotaur, against which his personal attractions would hardly have guaranteed him if he had been so rash as to set his house on fire by bringing home a pretty young wife. The notary had, in fact, simply discerned the good qualities of Mademoiselle Agnès—her name was Agnès—and remarked how soon a wife's beauty is a thing of the past to her husband. As to the insignificant youth to whom the Registrar gave his Norman name at the font, Madame Latournelle was so much astonished to find herself a mother at the age of thirty-five years and seven months, that she would even now find milk to suckle him withal if he needed it—the only hyperbole which can give a notion of her maternal mania.

"How handsome my boy is!" she would say to her little friend Modeste Mignon, without any ulterior motive, as she looked at him on their way to church, her beautiful Exupère leading the way.

"He is like you," Modeste Mignon would reply, as she might have said, "What bad weather!"

This sketch of the woman, a mere accessory figure, seems necessary when it is said that Madame Latournelle had for three years past been the chaperon of the young girl for whom the notary and his friend Dumay were laying one of those snares which, in the *Physiologie du Mariage,* I have called mouse-traps.

As for Latournelle, imagine a good little man, as wily as the purest honesty will allow, but whom every stranger would take for a rogue at first sight of the singular face, to which every one at le Havre is accustomed. Weak eyes, always red, compel the worthy lawyer to wear green spectacles to protect them. Each eyebrow, thinly marked with down, projects' about a line beyond the brown tortoise-shell rim of the glasses, thus making a sort of double arch. If you never happen to have noticed in some passer-by the effect of these two semi-circles, one above the other, and divided by a hollow, you cannot conceive how puzzling such a face may be; especially when this face is pale and haggard, and ends in a point like that of Mephistopheles, which painters have taken from the cat, and this is what Babylas Latournelle is like. Above those vile green spectacles rises a bald skull, with a wig all the more obviously artificial because it seems endowed with motion, and is so indiscreet as to show a few white hairs straggling below it all round, while it never sits straight on the forehead. As we look at this estimable Norman, dressed in black like a beetle, on two legs like pins, and know him to be the most honest soul living, we wonder, but cannot discover, what is the reason of such contradictory physiognomies.

Jean Butscha, a poor, abandoned foundling, of whom the Registrar Labrosse and his daughter had taken charge, had risen to be head-clerk by sheer hard work, and was lodged and fed by his master, who gave him nine hundred francs a year. With no appearance of youth, and almost a dwarf, he had made Modeste his idol; he would have given his life for her. This poor creature, his eyes, like two slow matches under thickened eyelids, marked by the smallpox, crushed by a mass of wooly hair, encumbered by his huge hands, had lived under the gaze of pity from the age of seven. Is not this enough to account for him in every way? Silent, reserved, exemplary in his conduct, and religious, he wandered through the vast expanse marked on the map of the realm of Love, as Love without Hope, the barren and sublime wilderness of Longing. Modeste had nicknamed this grotesque clerk "The Mysterious

Dwarf." This led Butscha to read Walter Scott's romance, and he said to Modeste:

"Would you like to have a rose from your Mysterious Dwarf in case of danger?"

Modeste hurled the soul of her adorer down into its mud hovel again by one of the terrible looks which young women fling at men whom they do not like. Butscha had called himself *le clerc obscur* (the obscure clerk), not knowing that the pun dated back to the origin of coats-of-arms; but he, like his master's wife, had never been away from le Havre.

It is perhaps necessary, for the benefit of those who do not know that town, to give a word of explanation as to whither the Latournelle family were bound, the head-clerk evidently being included. Ingouville is to le Havre what Montmartre is to Paris, a high hill with the town spread at its foot; with this difference, however—that the sea and the Seine surround the town and the hill; that le Havre is permanently limited by enclosing fortifications; and finally, that the mouth of the river, the port and the docks, form a scene quite unlike that offered by the fifty thousand houses of Paris.

At the foot of Montmartre an ocean of slates displays its rigid blue waves; at Ingouville you look down on what might be moving roofs stirred by the wind. This high ground, which, from Rouen to the sea, follows the course of the river, leaving a wider or narrower margin between itself and the water, contains treasures of picturesque beauty with its towns, its ravines, its valleys, and its meadows, and rose to immense value at Ingouville after 1818, from which year dates the prosperity of le Havre. This hamlet became the Auteuil, the Ville-d'Avray, the Montmorency of the merchants, who built themselves terraced villas on this amphitheatre, to breathe the sea air sweetened by the flowers of their magnificent gardens. These bold speculators rest there from the fatigues of the counting-house, and the atmosphere of the closely packed houses, with no space between them—often not even a courtyard, the inevitable result of the growth of the population, the unyielding belt of the ramparts and the expansion of the docks.

And, indeed, how dreary is the heart of the town, how glad is Ingouville! The law of social development has made the suburb of Graville sprout into life like a mushroom; it is larger now than le Havre itself, clinging to the foot of the slope like a serpent. Ingouville, on the ridge, has but one street; and, as in all such places, the houses looking over the Seine have an immense advantage over those on the opposite side of the road, from which the view is shut out, though they stand like spectators, on tiptoe, to peep over the roofs. Here, however, as everywhere else, compromises have been exacted. Some of the houses perched on the top occupy a superior position, or enjoy a right of view which compels their neighbor to keep his buildings below a certain height. Then the broken rocky soil has cuttings here and there for roads leading up the amphitheatre, and through these dips, some of the plots get a glimpse of the town, the river, or the sea. Though it is not precipitous, the high ground ends rather suddenly in a cliff; from the top of the street, which zigzags up the steep slope, coombes are visible where villages are planted: Saint-Adresse, two or three Saints-who-knows-who, and coves where the sea roars. This side of Ingouville, almost deserted, is in striking contrast to the handsome villas that overlook the Seine valley. Are the gales a foe to vegetation? Do the merchants shrink from the expense of gardening on so steep a slope? Be this as it may, the traveler by steamboat is startled at finding the coast so bare and rugged to the west of Ingouville—a beggar in rags next to a rich man sumptuously clothed and perfumed.

In 1829, one of the last houses towards the sea—now, no doubt, in the middle of Ingouville—was called, perhaps is still called, the Chalet. It had been originally a gatekeeper's lodge, with a plot of garden in front. The owner of the villa to which it belonged—a house with a paddock, gardens, an aviary, hothouses, and meadows—had a fancy to bring this lodge into harmony with the splendor of his residence, and had it rebuilt in the style of an English cottage. He divided it by a low wall from his lawn, graced with flowers, borders, and the terrace of the villa, and planted a hedge close to the wall to screen it. Behind this cottage, called the Chalet in spite of all he could do, lie the kitchen garden and orchards. This Chalet—a chalet without cows or dairy—has no fence from the road but a paling, of which the wood has become invisible under a luxuriant hedge.

Now, on the other side of the road, the opposite house has a similar paling and hedge. Being built under special conditions, it allows the town to be seen from the Chalet.

This little house was the despair of Monsieur Vilquin, the owner of the villa. And this is why. The creator of this residence, where every detail loudly proclaimed, "Here millions are displayed!" had extended his grounds into the country solely, as he said, not to have his gardeners in his pocket. As soon as it was finished, the Chalet could only be inhabited by a friend.

Monsieur Mignon, the first owner, was greatly attached to his cashier, and this story will prove that Dumay fully returned the feeling; he therefore offered him this little home. Dumay, a stickler for formalities, made his master sign a lease for twelve years at three hundred francs a year; and Monsieur Mignon signed it willingly, saying, "Consider, my dear Dumay, you are binding yourself to live with me for twelve years."

In consequence of events to be here related, the estates of Monsieur Mignon, formerly the richest merchant in le Havre, were sold to Vilquin, one of his opponents on 'Change. In his delight at taking possession of the famous Villa Mignon, the purchaser forgot to ask for this lease to be cancelled. Dumay, not to hinder the sale, would at that time have signed anything Vilquin might have required; but when once the sale was completed, he stuck to his lease as to a revenge. He stayed in Vilquin's pocket, in the heart of the Vilquin family, watching Vilquin, annoying Vilquin, in short, Vilquin's gadfly. Every morning, at his window, Vilquin felt a surge of violent vexation as he saw this gem of domestic architecture, this Chalet which had cost sixty thousand francs, and which blazed like a ruby in the sunshine.

An almost exact comparison! The architect had built the cottage of the finest red bricks, pointed with white. The window frames are painted bright green, and the timbers a yellow-brown. The roof projects several feet. A pretty fretwork balcony adorns the first floor, and a veranda stands out like a glass cage from the middle of the front. The ground-floor consists of a pretty drawing-room and a dining-room, divided by the bottom landing of the stairs, which are of wood designed and decorated with elegant simplicity. The kitchen is at the back of the dining-room, and behind the drawing-room is a small room which, at this time, was used by Monsieur and Madame Dumay as their bedroom. On the first floor the architect has planned two large bedrooms, each with a dressing-room, the veranda served as a sitting-room; and above these, in the roof, which looks like two cards leaning against each other, are two servants' rooms, each with a dormer window, attics, but fairly spacious.

Vilquin had the meanness to build a wall on the side next the kitchen garden and orchard. Since this act of vengeance, the few square yards secured to the Chalet by the lease are like a Paris garden. The outbuildings, constructed and painted to match the Chalet, back against the neighboring grounds.

The interior of this pleasant residence harmonizes with the exterior. The drawing-room, floored with polished iron-wood, is decorated with a marvelous imitation of Chinese lacquer. Myriad-colored birds, and impossibly green foliage, in fantastic Chinese drawing, stand out against a black background, in panels with gilt frames. The dining-room is completely fitted with pine-wood carved and fretted, as in the high-class peasants' houses in Russia. The little ante-room, formed by the landing, and the staircase are painted like old oak, to represent Gothic decoration. The bedrooms, hung with chintz, are attractive by their costly simplicity. That in which the cashier and his wife slept is wainscoted, like the cabin of a steamship. These shipowners' vagaries account for Vilquin's fury. This ill-starred purchaser wanted to lodge his son-in-law and his daughter in the Cottage. This plan, being known to Dumay, may subsequently explain his Breton obstinacy.

The entrance to the Chalet is through a trellised iron gate, with lance-heads, standing some inches above the paling and the hedge. The little garden, of the same width as the pompous lawn beyond, was just now full of flowers—roses, dahlias, and the choicest and rarest products of the hothouse flora; for another subject of grievance to Vilquin was that the pretty little hothouse, Madame's hothouse as it was called, belongs to the Chalet, and divides the Chalet from the Villa—or connects them, if you like to say so. Dumay indemnified himself for the cares of his place by caring for the conservatory, and its exotic blossoms were one of Modeste's chief pleasures. The billiard-room of Vilquin's villa, a sort of passage room, was formerly connected with this conservatory by a large turret-shaped aviary, but after the wall was built which blocked out the view of the orchard, Dumay bricked up the door.

"Wall for wall!" said he.

"You and Dumay have both gone to the wall!" Vilquin's acquaintance on 'Change threw in his teeth; and every day the envied speculator was hailed with some new jest.

In 1827 Vilquin offered Dumay six thousand francs a year and ten thousand francs in compensation if he would cancel the lease; the cashier refused, though he had but a thousand crowns laid by with Gobenheim, a former clerk of his master's. Dumay is indeed a Breton whom fate has planted out in Normandy. Imagine the hatred for his tenants worked up in Vilquin, a Norman with a fortune of three million francs. What high treason to wealth to dare prove to the rich the impotence of gold! Vilquin, whose desperation made him the talk of le Havre, had first offered Dumay the absolute freehold of another pretty house, but Dumay again refused. The town was beginning to wonder at this obstinacy, though many found a reason for it in the statement, "Dumay is a Breton."

In fact, the cashier thought that Madame and Mademoiselle

Mignon would be too uncomfortable anywhere else. His two idols dwelt here in a temple worthy of them, and at least had the benefit of this sumptuous cottage, where a dethroned king might have kept up the majesty of his surroundings, a kind of decorum which is often lacking to those who have fallen. The reader will not be sorry perhaps to have made acquaintance with Modeste's home and habitual companions; for, at her age, persons and things influence the future as much as character does, if indeed the character does not derive from them certain ineffaceable impressions.

By the Latournelles' manner as they went into the Chalet, a stranger might have guessed that they came there every evening.

"Already here, sir?" said the notary, on finding in the drawing-room a young banker of the town, Gobenheim, a relation of Gobenheim-Keller, the head of the great Paris house. This young fellow, who was lividly pale—one of those fair men with black eyes, in whose fixed gaze there is something fascinating—who was as sober in speech as in habits, dressed in black, strongly built, though as thin as a consumptive patient, was a constant visitor to his former master's family and the cashier's house, far less from affection than from interest; whist was played there at two sous a point, and evening dress was not insisted on; he took nothing but a few glasses of *eau sucrée,* and need offer no civilities in return. By his apparent devotion to the Mignons he got credit for a good heart; and it excused him from going into society in le Havre, from useless expenditure, and disturbing the arrangements of his domestic life. This youthful devotee of the Golden Calf went to bed every evening at half-past ten, and rose at five in the morning. Also, being certain of secrecy in Latournelle and Butscha, Gobenheim could analyze in their presence various knotty questions, benefit by the notary's gratuitous advice, and reduce the gossip on 'Change to its true value. This sucking gold-eater (Gobe-or, a witticism of Butscha's) was of the nature of the substances known to chemistry as absorbents. Ever since disaster had overwhelmed the houe of Mignon, to which he had been apprenticed by the Kellers to learn the higher branches of maritime trade, no one at the Chalet had ever asked him to do a single thing, not even a simple commission; his answer was known beforehand. This youth looked at Modeste as he might have examined a penny lithograph.

"He is one of the pistons of the huge machine called Trade," said poor Butscha, whose wit betrayed itself by little ironies, timidly uttered.

The four Latournelles greeted, with the utmost deference, an old lady dressed in black, who did not rise from the armchair in which she sat, for both her eyes were covered with the yellow film produced by cataract. Madame Mignon may be painted in a sentence. She attracted attention at once by the august expression of those mothers whose blameless life is a challenge to the strokes of fate, though fate has taken them as a mark for its shafts, who form the large class of Niobes. Her white wig, well curled and well put on, became her cold white face, like those of the burgomasters' wives painted by Mirevelt. The extreme neatness of her dress—velvet boots, a lace collar, a shawl put on straight—bore witness to Modeste's tender care for her mother.

When a minute's silence—as predicted by the notary—reigned in the pretty room, Modeste, seated by her mother, for whom she was embroidering a kerchief, was for a moment the centre of all eyes. This inquisitiveness, concealed under the commonplace questions always asked by callers, even those who meet every day, might have betrayed the little domestic plot against the girl, even to an indifferent person; but Gobenheim, more than indifferent, noticed nothing; he lighted the candles on the card-table. Dumay's attitude made the situation a terrible one for Butscha, for the Latournelles, and, above all, for Madame Dumay, who knew that her husband was capable of shooting Modeste's lover as if he were a mad dog. After dinner, the cashier had gone out for a walk, taking with him two magnificent Pyrenean dogs, whom he suspected of treason, and had, therefore, left with a farmer, formerly a tenant of Monsieur Mignon's; then, a few minutes before the Latournelles had come in, he had brought his pistols from their place by his bed, and had laid them on the chimney-shelf, without letting Modeste see it. The young girl paid no attention to all these arrangements—strange, to say the least of it.

Though short, thick-set, and battered, with a low voice, and an air of listening to his own words, this Breton, formerly a lieutenant in the Guard, has determination and presence of mind so plainly stamped on his features, that, in twenty years, no man in the army had ever tried to make game of him. His eyes, small and calmly blue, are like two specks of steel. His manners, the expression of his face, his mode of speech, his gait, all suit his short name of Dumay. His strength, which is well known, secures him against any offence. He can kill a man with a blow of his fist; and, in fact, achieved this doughty deed at Botzen, where he found himself in the rear of his company, without any weapon, and face to face with a Saxon.

At this moment, the man's set but gentle countenance was sublimely tragical; his lips, as pale as his face, betrayed convulsive fury subdued by Breton determination; his brow was damp with slight perspiration, visible to all, and understood to be a cold moisture. The notary knew that the upshot of all this might be a scene in an assize court. In fact, the cashier was playing a game for Modeste's sake, where honor, fidelity, and feelings of far more importance than any social ties, were at stake; and it was the outcome of one of those compacts of which, in the event of fatal issues, none but God can be the judge. Most dramas lie in the ideas we form of things. The events which seem to us dramatic are only such as our soul turns to tragedy or comedy, as our own nature tends.

Madame Latournelle and Madame Dumay, charged with keeping watch over Modeste, both had an indescribable artificial manner, a quaver in their voice, which the object of their suspicions did not notice, she seemed so much absorbed by her work. Modeste laid each strand of cotton with an accuracy

that might be the envy of any embroiderer. Her face showed
the pleasure she derived from the satin stitch petal that put
the finish to a flower. The hunchback, sitting between Madame Latournelle and Gobenheim, was swallowing tears and
wondering how he could get round to Modeste, and whisper
two words of warning in her ear. Madame Latournelle, by
placing herself in front of Madame Mignon, had cut off
Modeste, with the diabolical ingenuity of a pious prude. Madame Mignon, silent, blind, and whiter than her usual pallor,
plainly betrayed her knowledge of the ordeal to which the
girl was to be subjected. Now, at the last moment, perhaps
she disapproved of the stratagem, though deeming it necessary.
Hence her silence. She was weeping in her heart. Exupère, the
trigger of the trap, knew nothing whatever of the piece in which
chance had cast him for a part. Gobenheim was as indifferent as Modeste herself seemed to be—a consequence of his
nature.

To a spectator in the secret, the contrast between the utter
ignorance of one-half of the party, and the tremulous tension
of the others, would have been thrilling. In these days, more
than ever, novel-writers deal largely in such effects; and they
are in their rights, for nature has at all times outdone their
skill. In this case, as you will see, social nature—which is
nature within nature—was allowing itself the pleasure of
making fact more interesting than romance, just as torrents
produce effects forbidden to painters, and achieve marvels by
arranging or polishing stones so that architects and sculptors
are amazed.

It was eight o'clock. At this season of the year it is the
hour of the last gleam of twilight. That evening the sky was
cloudless, the mild air caressed the earth, flowers breathed
their fragrance, the grinding gravel could be heard under the
feet of persons returning from their walk. The sea shone
like a mirror.

There was so little wind that the candles on the table
burned with a steady flame though the windows were half
open. The room, the evening, the house—what a setting for

the portrait of this young creature, who at the moment was being studied by her friends with the deep attention of an artist gazing at *Margherita Doni,* one of the glories of the Pitti palace. Was Modeste, a flower enshrined like that of Catullus, worthy of all these precautions?—You have seen the cage: this is the bird.

At the age of twenty, slender and delicately made, like one of the Sirens invented by English painters to grace a Book of Beauty, Modeste, like her mother before her, bears the engaging expression of a grace little appreciated in France, where it is called sentimentality, though among the Germans it is the poetry of the heart suffusing the surface, and displayed in affectation by simpletons, in exquisite manners by sensible girls. Her most conspicuous feature was her pale gold hair, which classed her with the women called, no doubt in memory of Eve, *blondes celestes,* heavenly fair, whose sheeny skin looks like silk paper laid over the flesh, shivering in the winter or reveling in the sunshine of a look, and making the hand envious of the eye. Under this hair, as light as marabout feathers, and worn in ringlets, the brow, so purely formed that it might have been drawn by compasses, is reserved and calm to placidity, though bright with thought; but when or where could a smoother one be found, or more transparently frank? It seems to have a lustre like pearl. Her eyes, of grayish blue, as clear as those of a child, have all a child's mischief and innocence, in harmony with the arch of eyebrows scarcely outlined, as lightly touched in as those painted in Chinese faces. This playful innocence is accentuated by nacreous tones, with blue veins round the eyes and on the temples, a peculiarity of those delicate complexions. Her face, of the oval so often seen in Raphael's Madonnas, is distinguished by the cool, maidenly flush of her cheeks, as tender as a China rose, on which the long lashes of her transparent eyelids cast a play of light and shade. Her throat, bent over her work, and slender to fragility, suggests the sweeping lines dear to Leonardo. A few freckles, like the patches of the past century, show that Modeste is a daughter

Modeste Mignon

of earth, and not one of the creations seen in dreams by the Italian School of Angelico. Lips, full but finely curved, and somewhat satirical in expression, betray a love of pleasure. Her shape, pliant without being frail, would not scare away motherhood, like that of girls who seek to triumph through the unhealthy pressure of stays. Buckram, steel, and stay-lace never improved or formed such serpentine lines of elegance, resembling those of a young poplar swayed by the wind. A pearl-gray dress, long in the waist, and trimmed with cherry-colored gimp, accentuated the pure bust and covered the shoulders, still somewhat thin, over a deep muslin tucker, which betrayed only the outline of the curves where the bosom joins the shoulders. At the sight of this countenance, at once vague and intelligent, with a singular touch of determination given to it by a straight nose with rosy nostrils and firmly-cut outlines—a countenance where the poetry of an almost mystical brow was belied by the voluptuous curve of the mouth—where, in the changing depths of the eyes, candor seemed to fight for the mastery with the most accomplished irony—an observer might have thought that this young girl, whose quick ear caught every sound, whose nose was open to the fragrance of the blue flower of the ideal, must be the arena of a struggle between the poetry that plays round the daily rising of the sun and the labors of the day, between fancy and reality. Modeste was both curious and modest, knowing her fate, and purely chaste, the virgin of Spain rather than of Raphael.

She raised her head on hearing Dumay say to Exupère, "Come here, young man," and seeing them talk together in a corner of the room, she fancied it was about some commission for Paris. She looked at the friends who surrounded her as if astonished at their silence, and exclaimed with a perfectly natural air:

"Well, are you not going to play?" pointing to the green table that Madame Latournelle called the altar.

"Let us begin," said Dumay, after dismissing Exupère.

"Sit there, Butscha!" said Madame Latournelle, placing

the table between the clerk and the group formed by **Madame Mignon** and her daughter.

"And you—come here," said Dumay to his wife, desiring her to stay near him.

Madame Dumay, a little American of six-and-thirty, secretly wiped away her tears; she was devoted to Modeste, and dreaded a catastrophe.

"You are not lively this evening," said Modeste.

"We are playing," said Gobenheim, sorting his hand.

However interesting the situation may seem, it will be far more so when Dumay's position with regard to Modeste is explained. If the brevity of the style makes the narrative dry, this will be forgiven for the sake of hastening to the end of this scene, and of the need, which rules all dramas, for setting forth the argument.

Dumay—Anne-François-Bernard—born at Vannes, went as a soldier in 1799, joining the army of Italy. His father, a president of the Revolutionary Tribunal, had distinguished himself by so much vigor that the country was too hot to hold the son when his father, a second-rate lawyer, perished on the scaffold after the 9th of Thermidor. His mother died of grief; and Anne, having sold everything he possessed, went off to Italy at the age of twenty-two, just as our armies were defeated. In the department of the Var he met a young man who, for similar reasons, was also in search of glory, thinking the battlefield less dangerous than Provence.

Charles Mignon, the last survivor of the family to whom Paris owes the street and the hôtel built by Cardinal Mignon, had for his father a crafty man, who wished to save his estate of la Bastie, a nice little fief under the Counts of Provence, from the clutches of the Revolution. Like all nervous people in those days, the Comte de la Bastie, now Citizen Mignon, thought it healthier to cut off other heads than to lose his own. This supposed terrorist vanished on the 9th of Thermidor, and was thenceforth placed on the list of *émigrés*. The fief of la Bastie was sold. The pepper-caster towers of the dishonored château were razed to the ground. Finally, Citizen Mignon himself, discovered at Orange, was killed with his wife and children, with the exception of Charles Mignon, whom he had sent in search of a refuge in the department of the Hautes-Alpes. Charles, stopped by these shocking tidings, awaited quieter times in a valley of Mont Genèvre. There he lived till 1799 on a few louis his father had put into his hand at parting. At last, when he was three-and-twenty, with no fortune but his handsome person—the southern beauty which, in its perfection, is a glorious thing, the type of Antinoüs, Hadrian's famous favorite—he resolved to stake his Provençal daring on the red field of war, regarding his courage as a vocation, as did many another. On his way to headquarters at Nice he met the Breton.

The two infantrymen, thrown together by the similarity of their destiny and the contrast of their nature, drank of the torrent from the same cup, divided their allowance of biscuit, and were sergeants by the time peace was signed after the battle of Marengo.

When war broke out again, Charles Mignon got leave to be transferred to the cavalry, and then lost sight of his comrade. The last of the Mignons of la Bastie was, in 1812, an officer of the Legion of Honor, and Major of a cavalry regiment, hoping to be reinstated as Comte de la Bastie and made Colonel by the Emperor. Then, taken prisoner by the Russians, he was sent with many more to Siberia. His traveling companion was a poor lieutenant, in whom he recognized Anne Dumay, with no decoration, brave indeed, but hapless, like the millions of rank-and-file with worsted epaulettes, the web of men on which Napoleon painted the picture of his Empire. In Siberia, to pass the time, the lieutenant-colonel taught his comrade arithmetic and writing, for education had seemed unimportant to his Scævola parent. Charles found in his first traveling companion one of those rare hearts to whom he could pour out all his griefs while confiding all his joys.

The Provençal had, ere this, met the fate which awaits every handsome young fellow. In 1804, at Frankfort-on-the-Main,

he was adored by Bettina Wallenrod, the only daughter of a
banker, and married her with all the more enthusiasm because
she was rich, one of the beauties of the town, and he was still
only a lieutenant with no fortune but the most uncertain prospects of a soldier of that time. Old Wallenrod, a decayed
German baron—bankers are always barons—was enchanted
to think that the handsome lieutenant was the sole representative of the Mignons of la Bastie, and approved the affections
of the fair Bettina, whom a painter—for there was a painter
then at Frankfort—had taken for his model of an ideal figure
of Germany. Wallenrod, who already thought of his grandsons as Comtes de la Bastie-Wallenrod, invested in the French
funds a sufficient sum to secure to his daughter thirty thousand francs a year. This dower made a very small hole in
his coffers, seeing how small a capital was required. The Empire, following a practice not uncommon among debtors, rarely
paid the half-yearly dividends. Charles, indeed, was somewhat alarmed at this investment, for he had not so much faith
in the Imperial Eagle as the German baron had. The phenomenon of belief, or of admiration, which is only a transient
form of belief, can hardly exist in illicit companionship with
the idol. An engineer dreads the machine which the traveler
admires, and Napoleon's officers were the stokers of his locomotive when they were not the fuel. Baron von Wallenrod-Tustall-Bartenstild then promised to help the young people.
Charles loved Bettina Wallenrod as much as she loved him,
and that is saying a great deal; but when a Provençal is fired,
anything seems natural to him in the matter of feeling. How
could he help worshiping a golden-haired woman who had
stepped out of a picture by Albert Dürer, an angel of good
temper, with a fortune famous in Frankfort?

So Charles had four children, of whom only two daughters
were alive at the time when he poured out his sorrows on the
Breton's heart. Without knowing them, Dumay was fond
of these two little girls, the effect of the sympathy so well
understood by Charlet, who shows us the soldier as fatherly
to every child. The elder, named Bettina Caroline, was born

in 1805; the second, Marie Modeste, in 1808. The unhappy lieutenant-colonel, having had no news of those he loved, came back on foot in 1814, with the lieutenant for his companion, all across Russia and Prussia. The two friends, for whom any difference of rank had ceased to exist, arrived at Frankfort just as Napoleon landed at Cannes. Charles found his wife at Frankfort, but in mourning; she had had the grief of losing the father who adored her, and who longed always to see her smiling, even by his deathbed. Old Wallenrod did not survive the overthrow of the Empire. At the age of seventy-two he had speculated largely in cotton, believing still in Napoleon's genius, and not knowing that genius is as often the slave of events as their master.

The last of the Wallenrods, the true Wallenrod-Tustall-Bartenstild, had bought almost as many bales of cotton as the Emperor had sacrificed men during his tremendous campaign in France.

"I am tying in cotton" (I am dying in clover), said this father to his daughter, for he was of the Goriot species, trying to beguile her of her grief, which terrified him, "and I tie owing noting to noboty,"—and the Franco-German died struggling with the French language his daughter loved.

Charles Mignon, happy to have saved his wife and daughters from this double shipwreck, now returned to Paris, where the Emperor made him Lieutenant-Colonel of the Cuirassiers of the Guard, and Commander of the Legion of Honor. The Colonel at last was General and Count, after Napoleon's first success; but his dream was drowned in torrents of blood at Waterloo. He was slightly wounded, and retired to the Loire, leaving Tours before the troops were disbanded.

In the spring of 1816 Charles realized the capital of his thirty thousand francs a year, which gave him about four hundred thousand francs, and decided on going to make his fortune in America, leaving a country where persecution already pressed hardly on Napoleon's soldiers. He went from Paris to le Havre, accompanied by Dumay, whose life he had saved in one of the frequent chances of war, by taking him behind him on his horse in the confusion that ended the day of Waterloo. Dumay shared the Colonel's opinions and despondency. Charles, to whom the Breton clung like a dog, for the poor infantryman worshiped the two little girls, thought that Dumay's habits of obedience and discipline, his honesty and his attachment, would make him a servant not less faithful than useful. He therefore proposed to him to take service under him in private life. Dumay was very happy to find himself adopted into a family with whom he hoped to live like mistletoe on an oak.

While waiting an opportunity of sailing, choosing among the ships, and meditating on the chances offered in the various ports of their destination, the Colonel heard rumors of the splendid fortunes that the peace held in store for le Havre. While listening to a discussion between two of the natives, he saw a means of making his fortune, and set up forthwith as a shipowner, a banker, and a country gentleman. He invested two hundred thousand francs in land and houses, and freighted a ship for New York with a cargo of French silks bought at Lyons at a low figure. Dumay sailed on the vessel as his agent. While the Colonel was settling himself with his family in the handsomest house in the Rue Royale, and studying the science of banking with all the energy and prodigious acumen of a Provençal, Dumay made two fortunes, for he returned with a cargo of cotton bought for a mere song. This transaction produced an enormous capital for Mignon's business. He then purchased the villa at Ingouville, and rewarded Dumay by giving him a small house in the Rue Royale.

The worthy Breton had brought back with him from New York with his bales a pretty little wife, who had been chiefly attracted by his nationality as a Frenchman. Miss Grummer owned about four thousand dollars, twenty thousand francs, which Dumay invested in his Colonel's business. Dumay, now the *alter ego* of the shipowner, very soon learned bookkeeping, the science which, to use his phrase, distinguished the sergeant-majors of trade. This guileless soldier, whom fortune had neglected for twenty years, thought himself the happiest man in the world when he saw himself master of a house—which his employer's munificence furnished very prettily—of twelve hundred francs a year of interest on his capital, and of three thousand six hundred francs in salary. Never in his dreams had Lieutenant Dumay hoped for such prosperity; but he was even happier in feeling himself the hub of the richest merchant's house in le Havre.

Madame Dumay had the sorrow of losing all her children at their birth, and the disasters of her last confinement left her no hope of having any; she therefore attached herself to the two Mignon girls as affectionately as Dumay, who would not have loved his own children so well. Madame Dumay, the child of agriculturists, accustomed to a thrifty life, found two thousand four hundred francs enough for herself and her housekeeping. Thus, year by year, Dumay put two thousand and some hundred francs into the Mignon concern. When the master made up the annual balance, he added to the cashier's credit a bonus in proportion to the business done. In 1824 the sum to the cashier's account amounted to fifty-eight thousand francs. Then it was that Charles Mignon, Comte de la Bastie, a title that was never mentioned, crowned his cashier's joy by giving him a lease of the Chalet, where we now find Modeste and her mother.

Madame Mignon's deplorable condition had its cause in the catastrophe to which Charles' absence was due, for her husband had left her a still handsome woman. It had taken three years of sorrow to destroy the gentle German lady, but it was one of those sorrows which are like a worm lying at the heart of a fine fruit. The sum-total of her woes is easily stated: Two children who died young had stamped a double *ci-gît* on a soul which could never forget. Charles' captivity in Siberia had been to this loving heart a daily death. The disasters of the great Wallenrod house, and the unhappy banker's death on his empty money-bags, coming in the midst of Bettina's suspense about her husband, was a final blow. The joy of seeing him again almost killed this German floweret. Then came the second overthrow of the Empire, and their plans for emigration had been like relapses of the same fit of fever.

At last ten years of constant prosperity, the amusements of her home-life, the handsomest house in le Havre, the dinners, balls, and entertainments given by the successful merchant, the magnificence of the Villa Mignon, the immense respect and high esteem enjoyed by her husband, with the undivided affection of this man, who responded to perfect love by love equally perfect,—all these had reconciled the poor woman to life.

Then, at the moment when all her doubts were at rest, and she looked forward to a calm evening after her stormy day, a mysterious disaster, buried in the heart of the double household, and presently to be related, came like a summons from misfortune. In 1826, in the midst of a party, when all the town was ready to return Charles Mignon as its deputy, three letters, from New York, London, and Paris, came like three hammer-strokes on the glass house of Prosperity. In ten minutes ruin swooped down with vulture's wings on this unheard-of good fortune like the frost on the Grande Armée in 1812. In one night which he spent with Dumay over the books, Charles Mignon was prepared for the worst. Everything he possessed, not excepting the furniture, would avail to pay everybody.

"Le Havre," said the Colonel to the Lieutenant, "shall never see me in the mud. Dumay, I will take your sixty thousand francs at six per cent——"

"At three, Colonel."

"At nothing, then," said Charles peremptorily. "I make you my partner in my new enterprise. The *Modeste,* which is no longer mine, sails to-morrow; the captain takes me with him. You—I place you in charge of my wife and daughter. I shall never write. No news is good news."

Dumay, still but a lieutenant, had not asked his Colonel by a word what his purpose was.

"I suspect," said he to Latournelle with a knowing air, "that the Colonel has laid his plans."

On the following morning, at break of day, he saw his master safe on board the good ship *Modeste,* bound for Constantinople. Standing on the vessel's poop, the Breton said to the Provençal:

"What are your last orders, Colonel?"

"That no man ever goes near the Chalet!" cried the father, with difficulty restraining a tear. "Dumay, guard my last child as a bull-dog might. Death to any one who may try to tempt my second daughter! Fear nothing, not even the scaffold. I would meet you there!"

"Colonel, do your business in peace. I understand. You will find Mademoiselle Modeste as you leave her, or I shall be dead! You know me, and you know our two Pyrenean dogs. No one shall get at your daughter. Forgive me for using so many words."

The two soldiers embraced as men who had learned to appreciate each other in the heart of Siberia.

The same day the *Courrier du Havre* published this terrible, simple, vigorous, and honest leading paragraph:—

"The house of Charles Mignon has suspended payment, but the undersigned liquidators pledge themselves to pay all the outstanding debts. Bearers of bills at date can at once discount them. The value of the landed estate will completely cover current accounts.

"This notice is issued for the honor of the house, and to prevent any shock to general credit on the Havre Exchange.

"Monsieur Charles Mignon sailed this morning in the *Modeste* for Asia Minor, having left a power of attorney to enable us to realize every form of property, even landed estate.

> "Dumay, liquidator for the banking account.
> "Latournelle, notary, liquidator for the houses and land in town and country.
> "Gobenheim, liquidator for commercial bills."

Latournelle owed his prosperity to Monsieur Mignon's kindness; he had, in 1817, lent the notary a hundred thousand francs to buy the best business in le Havre. The poor lawyer, without any pecuniary resources, was by that time forty years old; he had been a head-clerk for ten years, and looked forward to being a clerk for the rest of his days. He was the only man in le Havre whose devotion could compare with Dumay's, for Gobenheim took advantage of this bankruptcy to carry on Mignon's connection and business, which enabled him to start his little banking concern. While universal regret was expressed on 'Change, on the Quays, and in every home; while praises of a blameless, honorable, and beneficent man were on every lip, Latournelle and Dumay, as silent and as busy as emmets, were selling, realizing, paying, and settling up. Vilquin gave himself airs of generosity, and bought the villa, the town-house, and a farm, and Latournelle took advantage of this first impulse to extract a good price from Vilquin.

Every one wanted to call on Madame and Mademoiselle Mignon, but they had obeyed Charles and taken refuge at the Chalet the very morning of his departure, of which at the first moment they knew nothing. Not to be shaken in his purpose by their grief, the courageous banker had kissed his wife and daughter in their sleep. Three hundred cards were left at the door. A fortnight later the most complete oblivion, as Charles had prophesied, showed the two women the wisdom and dignity of the step enjoined on them.

Dumay appointed representatives of his master at New York, London, and Paris. He followed up the liquidation of the three banking houses to which Mignon's ruin was due, and between 1826 and 1828 recovered five hundred thousand francs, the eighth part of Charles' fortune. In obedience to the orders drawn up the night before his departure, Dumay forwarded this sum at the beginning of 1828, through the house of Mongenod at New York, to be placed to Monsieur Mignon's credit. All this was done with military punctuality, excepting with regard to the retention of thirty thousand francs for the personal needs of Madame and Mademoiselle Mignon. This, which Charles had ordered, Dumay did not carry out. The Breton sold his house in the town for twenty thousand francs, and gave this to Madame Mignon, reflecting that the more money his Colonel could command, the sooner he would return.

"For lack of thirty thousand francs a man sometimes is lost," said he to Latournelle, who bought the house at his friend's price; and there the inhabitants of the Chalet could always find rooms.

This, to the famous house of Mignon, le Havre, was the outcome of the crisis which, in 1825-26, upset the principal centres of commerce, and caused—if you remember that hurricane—the ruin of several Paris bankers, one of them the President of the Chamber of Commerce. It is intelligible that this tremendous overthrow, closing a civic reign of ten years, might have been a deathblow to Bettina Wallenrod, who once more found herself parted from her husband, knowing nothing of his fate, apparently as full of peril and adventure as Siberian exile; but the trouble that was really bringing her to the grave was to these visible griefs what an ill-starred child is to the commonplace troubles of a family—a child that gnaws and devours its home. The fatal stone that had struck this mother's heart was a tombstone in the little cemetery of Ingouville, on which may be read:

BETTINA CAROLINE MIGNON
AGED TWO-AND-TWENTY
PRAY FOR HER!
1827.

This inscription is for the girl who lies there what many an epitaph is for the dead—a table of contents to an unknown book. Here is the book in its terrible epitome, and it may explain the pledge demanded and given in the parting words of the colonel and subaltern.

A young man, extremely handsome, named Georges d'Estourny, came to le Havre on the common pretext of seeing the sea, and he saw Caroline Mignon. A man of some pretence to fashion, and from Paris, never lacks some introductions; he was therefore invited by the intervention of a friend of the Mignons to an entertainment at Ingouville. He fell very much in love with Caroline and her fortune, and schemed for a happy issue. At the end of three months he had played every trick of the seducer, and run away with Caroline. The father of a family who has two daughters ought no more to admit a young man to his house without knowing him than he should allow books or newspapers to lie about without having read them. The innocence of a girl is like milk which is turned by a thunder-clap, by an evil smell, by a hot day, or even by a breath.

When he read his eldest daughter's farewell letter, Charles Mignon made Madame Dumay set out instantly for Paris. The family alleged the need for a change of air suddenly prescribed by the family doctor, who lent himself to this necessary pretext; but this could not keep the town from gossiping about her absence.

"What, such a strong girl, with the complexion of a Spaniard, and hair like jet!—She, consumptive!"

"Yes—so they say. She did something imprudent——"

"Ah, ha!" cried some Vilquin.

"She came in from a ride bathed in perspiration and drank iced water, at least so Dr. Troussenard says."

By the time Madame Dumay returned, the troubles of the Mignons were an exhausted subject; no one thought anything more of Caroline's absence or the reappearance of the cashier's wife.

At the beginning of 1827 the newspapers were full of the trial of Georges d'Estourny, who was proved guilty of constant cheating at play. This young pirate vanished abroad without thinking any more about Mademoiselle Mignon, whose money value was destroyed by the bankruptcy at le Havre. Before long Caroline knew that she was deserted, and her father a ruined man. She came home in a fearful state of mortal illness, and died a few days afterwards at the Chalet. Her death, at any rate, saved her reputation. The malady spoken of by Monsieur Mignon at the time of his daughter's elopement was very generally believed in, and the medical orders which had sent her off, it was said, to Nice.

To the very last the mother hoped to save her child. Bettina was her darling, as Modeste was her father's. There was something touching in this preference: Bettina was the image of Charles, as Modeste was of her mother. They perpetuated their love in their children. Caroline, a Provençal, inherited from her father the beautiful blue-black hair, like a raven's wing, which we admire in the daughters of the south, the hazel, almond-shaped eye as bright as a star, the olive complexion with the golden glow of a velvety fruit, the arched foot, the Spanish bust that swells beneath the bodice. And the father and mother were alike proud of the charming contrast of the two sisters.

"A demon and an angel!" people used to say, without ill meaning, though it was prophetic.

After spending a month in tears in her room, where she insisted on staying and seeing no one, the poor German lady came forth with her eyes seriously injured. Before she lost her sight she went, in spite of all her friends, to look at Caroline's tomb. This last image remained bright in her darkness, as the red spectre of the last object we have seen remains when we shut our eyes in bright daylight. After this terrible and twofold disaster, Dumay, though he could not be more devoted, was more anxious than ever about Modeste, now an only child, though her father knew it not. Madame Dumay, who was crazy about Modeste, like all women who have no children, overpowered her with her deputy motherhood, but without disobeying her husband's orders. Dumay was distrustful of female friendships. His injunctions were absolute.

"If ever any man, of whatever age or rank, speaks to Modeste," said Dumay, "if he looks at her, casts sheep's eyes at her, he is a dead man. I will blow his brains out and surrender myself to the Public Prosecutor. My death may save her. If you do not wish to see me cut my throat, fill my place unfailingly when I am in town."

For three years Dumay had examined his pistols every night. He seemed to have included in his oath the two Pyrenean dogs, remarkably intelligent beasts; one slept in the house, the other was sentinel in a kennel that he never came out of, and he never barked; but the minute when those dogs should set their teeth in an intruder would be a terrible one for him.

The life may now be imagined which the mother and daughter led at the Chalet. Monsieur and Madame Latournelle, frequently accompanied by Gobenheim, came almost every evening to visit their friends and play a rubber. Conversation would turn on business at le Havre, on the trivial events of country town life. They left between nine and ten. Modeste went to put her mother to bed; they said their prayers together, they talked over their hopes, they spoke of the dearly loved traveler. After kissing her mother, Modeste went to her own room at about ten o'clock. Next morning Modeste dressed her mother with the same care, the same prayers, the same little chat. To Modeste's honor, from the day when her mother's terrible infirmity deprived her of one of her senses, she made herself her waiting-maid, and always with the same solicitude at every hour, without wearying of it, or finding it monotonous. Her affection was supreme, and always ready, with a sweetness rare in young girls, and that was highly appreciated by those who saw her tenderness. And so, Modeste was, in the eyes of the Latournelles and of Monsieur and Madame Dumay, the jewel I have described. Between breakfast and dinner, on sunny days, Madame Mignon and Madame Dumay took a little walk as far as the shore, Modeste assisting, for the blind woman needed the support of two arms.

A month before the scene in which this digression falls as a parenthesis, Madame Mignon had held council with her only friends, Madame Latournelle, the notary, and Dumay, while Madame Dumay was giving Modeste the little diversion of a long walk.

"Listen, my friends," said the blind woman, "my daughter is in love. I feel it; I see it. A strange change has come over her, and I cannot think how you have failed to observe it . . ."

"Bless my stars!" the Lieutenant exclaimed.

"Do not interrupt me, Dumay. For the last two months Modeste has dressed herself with care as if she were going to meet some one. She has become excessively particular about her shoes; she wants her foot to look nice, and scolds Madame Gobain the shoemaker. Some days the poor child sits gloomy and watchful, as if she expected somebody; her voice is short and sharp, as though by questioning her I broke in on her expectancy, her secret hopes; and then, if that somebody has been——"

"Bless my stars!"

"Sit down, Dumay," said the lady. "Well, then Modeste is gay. Oh! you do not see that she is gay; you cannot discern these shades, too subtle for eyes to see that have all nature to look at. Her cheerfulness betrays itself in the tones of her voice, accents which I can detect and account for. Modeste, instead of sitting still and dreaming, expends her light activity in flighty movement. In short, she is happy! There is a tone of thanksgiving even in the ideas she utters. Oh, my friends, I have learned to know happiness as well as grief. By the kiss my poor Modeste gives me I can guess what is going on in her mind; whether she has had what she was expecting, or is uneasy. There are many shades in kisses, even in those of a young girl—for Modeste is innocence itself, but it is not ignorant innocence. Though I am blind, my affection is clairvoyant, and I implore you— watch my daughter."

On this, Dumay, quite ferocious, the notary as a man who is bent on solving a riddle, Madame Latournelle as a duenna who has been cheated, and Madame Dumay, who shared her husband's fears,—all constituted themselves spies over Modeste. Modeste was never alone for a moment. Dumay spent whole nights under the windows, wrapped in a cloak like a jealous Spaniard; still, armed as he was with military sagacity, he could find no accusing clue. Unless she were in love with the nightingales in Vilquin's Park, or some goblin prince, Modeste could have seen no one, could neither have received nor given a signal. Madame Dumay, who never went to bed till she had seen Modeste asleep, hovered about the roads on the high ground near the Chalet with a vigilance equal to her husband's. Under the eyes of these four Argus, the blameless child, whose smallest actions were reported and analyzed, was so absolutely acquitted of any criminal proceedings, that the friends suspected Madame Mignon of a craze, a monomania. It devolved on Madame Latournelle, who herself took Modeste to church and home again, to tell the mother that she was under a mistake.

"Modeste," said she, "is a very enthusiastic young person; she has passions for this one's poetry and that one's prose. You could not see what an impression was made on her by that executioner's piece (a phrase of Butscha's, who lent wit without any return to his benefactress), called *le Dernier Jour d'un condamné;* but she seemed to me beside herself with her admiration of that Monsieur Hugo. I cannot think where that sort of people (Victor Hugo, Lamartine, and Byron were what Madame Latournelle meant by *that sort*) go to find their ideas. The little thing talked to me about *Childe Harold;* I did not choose to have the worst of it; I was fool enough to set to work to read it that I might be able to argue with her. I don't know whether it is to be set down to the translation, but my heart heaved, my eyes were dizzy. I could not get on with it. It is full of howling comparisons, of rocks that faint away, of the lavas of war!

"Of course, as it is an Englishman on his travels, one must expect something queer, but this is really too much! You fancy you are in Spain, and he carries you up into the clouds above the Alps; he makes the torrents and the stars speak; and then there are too many virgins! You get sick of them.

In short, after Napoleon's campaigns we have had enough
of flaming shot and sounding brass which roll on from page
to page. Modeste tells me that all this pathos comes
from the translator, and I ought to read the English. But
I am not going to learn English for Lord Byron when I
would not learn it for Exupère! I much prefer the romances
of Ducray-Duménil to these English romances! I am too
thoroughly Norman to fall in love with everything that comes
from abroad, and especially from England——"

Madame Mignon, notwithstanding her perpetual mourning,
could not help smiling at the idea of Madame Latournelle
reading *Childe Harold*. The stern lady accepted this smile
as approbation of her doctrines.

"And so, my dear Madame Mignon, you mistake Modeste's
imaginings, the result of her reading, for love affairs. She is
twenty. At that age a girl loves herself. She dresses to see
herself dressed. Why, I used to make my little sister, who is
dead now, put on a man's hat, and we played at gentleman
and lady. . . . You, at Frankfort, had a happy girlhood,
but let us be just: Modeste here has no amusements. In
spite of our readiness to meet her lightest wishes, she knows
that she is guarded, and the life she leads has little pleasure
to offer a girl who could not, as she can, find something to
divert her in books. Take my word for it, she loves no one
but you. Think yourself lucky that she falls in love with
nobody but Lord Byron's corsairs, Walter Scott's romantic
heroes, or your Germans, Count Egmont, Werther, Schiller,
and all the other *ers*."

"Well, madame?" said Dumay respectfully, alarmed by
Madame Mignon's silence.

"Modeste is not merely ready for love; she loves somebody,"
said the mother obstinately.

"Madame, my life is at stake, and you will no doubt allow
me—not for my own sake, but for my poor wife's and for the
Colonel's, and all our sakes—to try to find out which is mistaken—the watch-dog or the mother."

"It is you, Dumay! Oh, if I could but look my daughter
in the face!" said the poor blind woman.

"But who is there that she can love?" replied Madame Latournelle. "As for us—I can answer for my Exupère."

"It cannot be Gobenheim, whom we hardly see for nine hours out of the week since the Colonel went away. Besides, he is not thinking of Modeste—that crown-piece made man! His uncle, Gobenheim-Keller, told him, 'Get rich enough to marry a Keller!' With that for a programme, there is no fear that he will even know of what sex Modeste is. Those are all the men we see here. I do not count Butscha, poor little hunchback. I love him; he is your Dumay, madame," he said to the notary's wife. "Butscha knows very well that if he glanced at Modeste it would cost him a combing *à la mode de Vannes*.—Not a soul ever comes near us. Madame Latournelle, who since—since your misfortune, comes to take Modeste to church and bring her home again, has watched her carefully these last days during the Mass, and has seen nothing suspicious about her. And then, if I must tell you everything, I myself have raked the paths round the house for the last month, and I have always found them in the morning with no footmarks."

"Rakes are not costly nor difficult to use," said the German lady.

"And the dogs?" asked Dumay.

"Lovers can find sops for them," replied Madame Mignon.

"I could blow out my own brains if you are right, for I should be done for," cried Dumay.

"And why, Dumay?"

"Madame, I could not meet the Colonel's eye if he were not to find his daughter, especially now that she is his only child; and as pure, as virtuous as she was when he said to me on board the ship, 'Do not let the fear of the scaffold stop you, Dumay, when Modeste's honor is at stake.'"

"I know you both—how like you!" said Madame Mignon, much moved.

"I will wager my eternal salvation that Modeste is as innocent as she was in her cradle," said Madame Dumay.

"Oh, I will know all about it," replied Dumay, "if Madame la Comtesse will allow me to try a plan, for old soldiers are knowing in stratagems."

"I allow you to do anything that may clear up the matter without injuring our last surviving child."

"And what will you do, Anne," said his wife, "to find out a young girl's secret when it is so closely kept?"

"All of you obey me exactly," said the Lieutenant, "for you must all help."

This brief account, which, if elaborately worked up, would have furnished forth a complete picture of domestic life—how many families will recognize in it the events of their own home!—is enough to give a clue to the importance of the little details previously given of the persons and circumstances of this evening, when the Lieutenant had undertaken to cope with a young girl, and to drag from the recesses of her heart a passion detected by her blind mother.

An hour went by in ominous calm, broken only by the hieroglyphical phrases of the whist players: "Spade!—Trump!—Cut!—Have we the honors?—Two trebles!—Eight all!—Who deals?"—phrases representing in these days the great emotions of the aristocracy of Europe. Modeste stitched, without any surprise at her mother's taciturnity. Madame Mignon's pocket-handkerchief slipped off her lap on to the floor; Butscha flew to pick it up. He was close to Modeste, and as he rose said in her ear, "Be on your guard!"

Modeste raised astonished eyes, and their light, pointed darts as it seemed, filled the hunchback with ineffable joy.

"She loves no one," said the poor fellow to himself, and he rubbed his hands hard enough to flay them.

At this moment Exupère flew through the garden and into the house, rushing into the drawing-room like a whirlwind, and said in Dumay's ear, "Here is the young man!"

Dumay rose, seized his pistols, and went out.

"Good God! Supposing he kills him!" cried Madame Dumay, who burst into tears.

"But what is going on?" asked Modeste, looking at her friends with an air of perfect candor, and without any alarm.

"Something about a young man who prowls round the Chalet!" cried Madame Latournelle.

"What then?" said Modeste. "Why should Dumay kill him?"

"*Sancta simplicitas!*" said Butscha, looking at his master as proudly as Alexander gazes at Babylon in Lebrun's picture.

"Where are you going, Modeste?" asked her mother, as her daughter was leaving the room.

"To get everything ready for you to go to bed, mamma," replied Modeste, in a voice as clear as the notes of a harmonica.

"You have had all your trouble for nothing," said Butscha to Dumay when he came in.

"Modeste is as saintly as the Virgin on our altar!" cried Madame Latournelle.

"Ah, good Heavens! Such agitation is too much for me," said the cashier. "And yet I am a strong man."

"I would give twenty-five sous to understand one word of what you are at this evening," said Gobenheim; "you all seem to me to have gone mad."

"And yet a treasure is at stake," said Butscha, standing on tiptoe to speak into Gobenheim's ear.

"Unfortunately, I am almost positive of the truth of what I say," repeated the mother.

"Then it now lies with you, madame," said Dumay quietly, "to prove that we are wrong."

When he found that nothing was involved but Modeste's reputation, Gobenheim took his hat, bowed, and went away, carrying off ten sous, and regarding a fresh rubber as hopeless.

"Exupère, and you, Butscha, leave us," said Madame Latournelle. "Go down to the town. You will be in time to see one piece; I will treat you to the play."

As soon as Madame Mignon was left with her four friends, Madame Latournelle glanced at Dumay, who, being a Breton, understood the mother's persistency, and then at her husband fidgeting with the cards, and thought herself justified in speaking.

"Come, Madame Mignon, tell us what decisive evidence has struck your ear?"

"Oh, my dear friend, if you were a musician, you, like me, would have heard Modeste's tone when she sings of love."

The piano belonging to the two sisters was one of the few feminine luxuries among the furniture brought from the town-house to the Chalet. Modeste had mitigated some tedium by studying without a master. She was a born musician, and played to cheer her mother. She sang with natural grace the German airs her mother taught her. From this instruction and this endeavor had resulted the phenomenon, not uncommon in natures prompted by a vocation, that Modeste unconsciously composed purely melodic strains, as such composition is possible without a knowledge of harmony. Melody is to music what imagery and feeling are to poetry, a flower that may blossom spontaneously. All nations have had popular melodies before the introduction of harmony. Botany came after flowers. Thus Modeste, without having learned anything of the technique of painting beyond what she had gathered from seeing her sister work in watercolors, could stand enchanted before a picture by Raphael, Titian, Rubens, Murillo, Rembrandt, Albert Dürer, or Holbein, that is to say, the highest ideal of each nation. Now, for about a month, Modeste had more especially burst into nightingale songs, into new strains so poetical as to arouse her mother's attention, surprised as she was to find Modeste bent on composition and trying airs to unfamiliar words.

"If your suspicions have no other foundation," said Latournelle to Madame Mignon, "I pity your sensitiveness."

"When a young girl sings in Brittany," said Dumay, now grave again, "the lover is very near."

"I will let you overhear Modeste improvising," said the mother, "and you will see!——"

"Poor child!" said Madame Dumay. "If she could but know of our anxiety, she would be in despair; and she would tell us the truth, especially if she knew all it meant to Dumay."

"To-morrow, my friends, I will question Modeste," said Madame Mignon; "and perhaps I shall achieve more by affection than you have gained by ruse."

Was the comedy of the "Ill-guarded Daughter" being enacted here, as it is everywhere and at all times, while these worthy Bartolos, these spies, these vigilant watch-dogs failed to scent, to guess, to detect the lover, the conspiracy, the smoke of the fire?

This was not the consequence of any defiance between a prisoner and her jailers, between the tyranny of the dungeon and the liberty of the captive, but merely the eternal repetition of the first drama played as the curtain rose on the new Creation: Eve in Paradise. Which, in this case, was right—the mother or the watch-dog?

None of the persons about Modeste understood the girl's heart—for, be assured, the soul and the face were in unison. Modeste had transplanted her life into a world of which the existence is as completely denied in our days as the New World of Christopher Columbus was denied in the sixteenth century. Fortunately, she could be silent, or she would have been thought mad.

We must first explain the influence that past events had had on the girl. Two especially had formed her character, as they had awakened her intelligence. Monsieur and Madame Mignon, startled by the disaster that had come upon Bettina, had, before their bankruptcy, resolved on seeing Modeste married, and their choice fell on the son of a wealthy banker, a native of Hamburg, who had settled at le Havre in 1815, and who was under some obligations to them. This young man—Francisque Althor—the dandy of le Havre, handsome in the style which captivates the philistine, what the English call a heavy-weight—florid healthy coloring, firm flesh, and square shoulders—threw over his bride elect, at the news of their disaster, so completely that he had never since set eyes on Modeste, or on Madame Mignon, or on the Dumays. Latournelle having made so bold as to speak to the father, Jacob Althor, on the subject, the old German had shrugged his shoulders, and replied, "I do not know what you mean."

This reply, repeated to Modeste to give her experience, was a lesson she understood all the better because Latournelle and Dumay made voluminous comments on this base desertion. Charles Mignon's two daughters, spoiled children as they were, rode, had their own horses and servants, and enjoyed fatal liberty. Modeste, finding herself in command of a recognized lover, had allowed Francisque to kiss her hand, and put his arm round her to help her to mount; she had accepted flowers, and the trifling gifts of affection which are the burden of paying court to a young lady; she worked him a purse, believing in bonds of that kind, so strong to noble souls, but mere cobwebs to the Gobenheims, Vilquins, and Althors.

In the course of the spring, after Madame Mignon and her daughter had moved into the Chalet, Francisque Althor went to dine with the Vilquins. On catching sight of Modeste beyond the wall of the lawn, he looked away. Six weeks after he married Mademoiselle Vilquin—the eldest. Then Modeste learned that she, handsome, young, and well born, had for three months been simply Mademoiselle Million. So Modeste's poverty, which was of course known, was a sentinel which guarded the ways to the Chalet quite as well as the Dumays' prudence and the Latournelles' vigilance. Mademoiselle Mignon was never mentioned but with insulting pity: "Poor girl! what will become of her? She will die an old maid."—"What a hard lot! After seeing all the world at her feet, and having a chance of marrying Althor, to find that no one will have anything to say to her?"—"Such a life of luxury, my dear! and to have sunk to penury!"

Nor were these insults spoken in private and only guessed

by Modeste; more than once she heard them uttered by the young men and girls of the town when walking at Ingouville, who, knowing that Madame and Mademoiselle Mignon lived at the Chalet, discussed them audibly as they went past the pretty little house. Some of the Vilquins' friends wondered that these ladies could bear to live so near the home of their former splendor. Modeste, sitting behind closed shutters, often heard such impertinence as this: "I cannot think how they can live there!" one would say to another, walking round the garden, perhaps to help the Vilquins to be rid of their tenants. "What do they live on?—What can they do there? —The old woman is gone blind!—Is Mademoiselle Mignon still pretty?—Ah, she has no horses now. How dashing she used to be!"

As she heard this savage nonsense spoken by envy, foul-mouthed and surly, and tilting at the past, many girls would have felt the blood rise to their very brow; others would have wept, some would have felt a surge of rage; but Modeste smiled as we smile at a theatre, hearing actors speak. Her pride could not descend to the level which such words, rising from below, could reach.

The other event was even more serious than this mercenary desertion. Bettina-Caroline had died in her sister's arms; Modeste had nursed her with the devotion of a woman, with the inquisitiveness of a maiden imagination. The two girls, in the watches of the night, had exchanged many a confidence. What dramatic interest hung round Bettina in the eyes of her innocent sister! Bettina knew passion only as misfortune; she was dying because she had loved. Between two girls every man, wretch though he be, is a lover. Passion is the one thing really absolute in human life; it will always have its own. Georges d'Estourny, a gambler, dissipated and guilty, always dwelt in the memory of these two young things as the Parisian dandy of the Havre parties, the cynosure of every woman—Bettina believed that she had snatched him from Madame Vilquin's flirtations—and, to crown all, Bettina's successful lover. In a young girl her worship is stronger than social reprobation. In Bettina's mind, justice had erred; how should she have condemned a young man by whom she had been loved for six months, loved with passion in the mysterious retreat where Georges hid her in Paris, that he might preserve his liberty? Thus, Bettina, in her death, had inoculated her sister with love.

The sisters had often discussed the great drama of passion, to which imagination lends added importance; and the dead girl had taken Modeste's purity with her to her grave, leaving her not perhaps all-knowing, but, at any rate, all-curious. At the same time, remorse had often set sharp pangs in Bettina's heart, and she lavished warnings on her sister. In the midst of her revelations, she never failed to preach obedience in Modeste, absolute obedience to her family. On the eve of her death, she implored her sister to remember the pillow she had soaked with her tears, and never to imitate the conduct her sufferings could scarcely expiate. Bettina accused herself of having brought the lightning down on those dear to her; she died in despair at not receiving her father's forgiveness. In spite of the consolations of religion, which was softened by such deep repentance, Bettina's last words, in a heartrending cry, were, "Father! Father!"

"Never give your heart but with your hand," said she to Modeste, an hour before her death; "and, above all, accept no attentions without my mother's consent or papa's."

These words, touching in their simple truth, and spoken in the hour of death, found an echo in Modeste's mind, all the more because Bettina made her take a solemn vow. The poor girl, with prophetic insight, drew from under her pillow a ring on which she had had engraved *Pense à Bettina, 1827*—"Remember Bettina"—instead of a motto, sending it by the hand of her faithful servant Françoise Cochet, to be done in the town. A few minutes before she breathed her last sigh, she placed this ring on her sister's finger, begging her to wear it till she should be married. Thus, between these two girls there had been a strange succession of acute remorse and artless descriptions of that brief summer which had been so soon followed by the autumn winds of desertion, while tears, regrets, and memories were constantly overruled by a dread of evil.

And yet this drama of the young creature seduced, and returning to die of a dreadful disorder under the roof of elegant poverty, the meanness of the Vilquins' son-in-law, and her mother's blindness, resulting from her griefs, only account for the surface of Modeste's character, with which the Dumays and the Latournelles had to be content, for no devotion can fill the mother's place. This monotonous life in the pretty Chalet, among the beautiful flowers grown by Dumay; these habits, as regular as the working of a clock; this provincial propriety; these rubbers at cards by which she sat knitting; this silence, only broken by the moaning of the sea at the equinoxes; this monastic peace covered the stormiest kind of life—the life of ideas, the life of the spiritual world.

We sometimes wonder at the lapses of young girls, but that is when they have no blind mother to sound with her stick the depths of the maiden heart undermined by the caverns of fancy.

The Dumays were asleep when Modeste opened her window, imagining that a man might pass by— the man of her dreams, the knight who would take her on a pillion, defying Dumay's pistols. In her dejection after her sister's death, Modeste had plunged into such constant reading as was enough to make her idiotic. Having been brought up to speak two languages, she was mistress of German as well as of French; then she and Caroline had learned English of Madame Dumay. Modeste, who, in such matters, found little supervision from her uncultivated companions, fed her soul on the masterpieces of modern English, German, and French literature—Lord Byron, Goethe, Schiller, Walter Scott, Hugo, Lamartine, Crabbe, Moore, the great works of the seventeenth and eighteenth centuries, history and the theatre, romance from Rabelais to Manon Lescaut, from Montaigne's *Essays* to Diderot, from the *Fabliaux* to *la Nouvelle Héloïse,* the thoughts of three countries furnished her brain with a medley of images. And her mind was beautiful in its cold guilelessness, its repressed virginal instincts, from which sprang forth, flashing, armed, sincere, and powerful, an intense admiration for genius. To Modeste, a new book was a great event; she was so happy over a great work as to alarm Madame Latournelle, as we have seen, and saddened when it failed to take her heart by storm.

But no gleam of this lurid flame ever appeared on the surface; it escaped the eye of Lieutenant Dumay and his wife as well as of the Latournelles; but the ear of the blind mother could not fail to hear its crackling. The deep contempt which Modeste thenceforth conceived for all ordinary men soon gave her countenance an indescribably proud and shy expression which qualified its German simplicity, but which agrees with one detail of her face; her hair, growing in a point in the middle of her forehead, seems to continue the slight furrow made by thought between her brows, and makes this shy look perhaps a little too wild.

This sweet girl's voice—before his departure Charles Mignon used to call her his little "Solomon's slipper," she was so clever—had acquired delightful flexibility of accent from her study of three languages. This advantage is yet further enhanced by a suave fresh quality which goes to the heart as well as to the ear. Though her mother could not see the hope of high destiny stamped on her daughter's brow, she could study the changes of her soul's development in the tones of that amorous voice.

After this period of ravenous reading, there came to Modeste a phase of the singular faculty possessed by a lively imagination; of living as an actor in an existence pictured as in a dream; of representing things wished for with a vividness so keen, that it verges on reality; of enjoying them in fancy, of devouring time even, seeing herself married, grown old, attending her own funeral, like Charles V.—in short, of playing out the drama of life, and at need that of death too.

As for Modeste, she played the drama of love. She imagined herself adored to the height of her wishes, and passing through every social phase. As the heroine of some dark romance, she loved either the executioner or some villain who died on the scaffold, or else, like her sister, some penniless fop, whose misdemeanors were the affair of the police court. She pictured herself as a courtesan, and laughed men to scorn in the midst of perpetual festivities, like Ninon. By turns, she led the life of an adventuress or of a popular actress, going through the vicissitudes of a Gil Blas, or the triumphs of Pasta, Malibran, Florine. Satiated with horrors, she would come back to real life. She married a notary, she ate the dry bread of respectability, she saw herself in Madame Latournelle. She accepted a laborious life, facing the worries of accumulating a fortune; then she began to romance again; she was loved for her beauty; the son of a peer of France, artistic and eccentric, read her heart, and discerned the star which the genius of a Staël had set on her brow. At last her father returned a millionaire. Justified by experience, she subjected her lovers to tests, preserving her own freedom; she owned a splendid château, servants, carriages, everything that luxury has most curious to bestow; and she mystified her lovers till she was forty, when she accepted an offer.

This edition of the *Arabian Nights,* of which there was but one copy, lasted nearly a year, and brought Modeste to satiety of invention. She too often held life in the hollow of her hand; she could say to herself very philosophically, and too seriously, too bitterly, too often, "Well; and then?" not to sink now to her waist in those depths of disgust, into which men of genius fall who are too eager to escape by the vast labor of the task to which they have devoted themselves. But for her rich nature and her youth, Modeste would have retired to a cloister. This satiety flung the girl, still soaked in Catholic feeling, into a love of goodness, and of the infinitude of heaven. She conceived of charity as the occupation of her life; still she groped in forlorn gloom as she found there no aliment for the fancy that gnawed at her heart like a malignant insect in the cup of a flower. She calmly stitched at baby clothes for poor women; and she listened absently to

Monsieur Latournelle grumbling at Monsieur Dumay for trumping a thirteenth, of forcing him to play his last trump. Faith led Modeste into a strange path. She fancied that by becoming irreproachable in the Catholic sense, she might achieve such a pitch of sanctity that God would hear her and grant her desires.

"Faith, as Jesus Christ says, can remove mountains; the Saviour made His apostle walk on the Lake of Tiberias; while I only ask of God to send me a husband," thought she. "That is much easier than going for a walk on the sea."

She fasted all through Lent, and did not commit the smallest sin; then she promised herself that on coming out of church on a certain day she would meet a handsome young man, worthy of her, whom her mother would approve, and who would follow her, madly in love. On the day she had fixed for God to send her this angel without fail, she was persistently followed by a horrible beggar; it poured with rain, and there was not one young man out of doors. She went down to the quay to see the English come on shore, but every Englishman had an English damsel almost as handsome as herself, and Modeste could not see anything like a Childe Harold who had lost his way. At that stage tears rose to her eyes as she sat, like Marius, on the ruins of her imaginings. One day when she made an appointment with God for the third time, she believed that the elect of her dreams had come into the church, and she dragged Madame Latournelle to look behind every pillar, imagining that he was hiding out of delicacy. Thenceforth she concluded that God had no power. She often made conversations with this imaginary lover, inventing question and answer, and giving him a very pretty wit.

Thus it was her heart's excessive ambition, buried in romance, which gave Modeste the discretion so much admired by the good people who watched over her; they might have brought her many a Francisque Althor or Vilquin *fils,* she would not have stooped to such boors. She required simply and purely a man of genius; talent she thought little of, as a barrister is nothing to a girl who is set on an ambassador. She wished for riches only to cast them at her idol's feet. The golden background against which the figures of her dreams stood out was less precious than her heart overflowing with a woman's delicacy; for her ruling idea was to give wealth and happiness to a Tasso, a Milton, a Jean-Jacques Rousseau, a Murat, a Christopher Columbus. Vulgar sorrows appealed but little to this soul, which longed to extinguish the stake of such martyrs unrecognized during their lifetime. Modeste thirsted for unconfessed suffering, the great anguish of the mind.

Sometimes she imagined the balm, she elaborated the tenderness, the music, the thousand devices by which she would have soothed the fierce misanthropy of Jean-Jacques. Again she fancied herself the wife of Lord Byron, and almost entered into his scorn of realities, while making herself as fantastic as the poetry of Manfred, and into his doubts while making him a Catholic. Modeste accused all the women of the seventeenth century as guilty of Molière's melancholy.

"How is it," she wondered, "that some living, wealthy, and beautiful woman does not rush forth to meet every man of genius, to make herself his slave like Lara, the mysterious page?"

As you see, she had quite understood the English poet's wail, as sung by Gulnare. She greatly admired the conduct of the young English girl who came to propose to the younger Crébillon, who married her. The story of Sterne and Eliza Draper was a joy to her for some months; as the imaginary heroine of a similar romance, she studied the sublime part of Eliza again and again. The exquisite feeling so gracefully expressed in those letters filled her eyes with the tears which, it is said, never rose to those of the wittiest of English writers.

Modeste thus lived for some time by her sympathy, not merely with the works, but with the personal character of her favorite authors. Goldsmith, the author of *Obermann*, Charles Nodier, Maturin—the poorest, the most unhappy were her gods; she understood their sufferings, she entered into their squalor, blending with heaven-sent visions; she poured on them the treasures of her heart; she pictured herself clearly as supplying the comforts of life to these artists, martyrs to their gifts. This noble compassion, this intuitive knowledge of the difficulties of work, this worship for talent, is one of the rarest vagaries that ever beat its wings in a woman's soul. At first it is like a secret between her and God, for there is nothing dazzling in it, nothing to flatter her vanity—that potent auxiliary of all actions in France.

From this third phase of her ideas there was born in Modeste a violent desire to study one of these anomalous lives to the very heart of it, to know the springs of thought, the secret sorrows of genius, and what it craves, and what it is. And so, in her, the rashness of phantasy, the wanderings of her soul in a void, her excursions into the darkness of the future, the impatience of her undeveloped love to centre in an object, the nobleness of her notions of life, her determination to suffer in some lofty sphere rather than to paddle in the slough of provincial life as her mother had done, the vow she had made to herself never to go wrong, to respect her parents' home and never bring to it anything but joy,—all this world of feeling at last took shape: Modeste purposed to be the wife of a poet, an artist, a man, in short, superior to the crowd; but she meant to choose him, and to subject him to a thorough study, before giving him her heart, her life, her immense tenderness freed from the trammels of passion.

She began by reveling in this pretty romance. Perfect tranquillity possessed her soul. Her countenance was gradually colored by it. She became the lovely and sublime image of Germany that you have seen, the glory of the Chalet, the pride of Madame Latournelle and the Dumays. Then Modeste lived a double life. She humbly and lovingly fulfilled all the trivial tasks of daily life at the Chalet, using them as a check to hold in the poem of her ideal existence, like the Carthusians, who order their material life by rule and occupy their time to allow the soul to develop itself in prayer.

All great intellects subject themselves to some mechanical employment to obtain control of thought. Spinoza ground lenses, Bayle counted the tiles in a roof, Montesquieu worked in his garden. The body being thus under control, the spirit spreads its wings in perfect security. So Madame Mignon, who read her daughter's soul, was right. Modeste was in love; she loved with that Platonic sentiment which is so rare, so little understood—the first illusion of girlhood, the subtlest of feelings, the heart's daintiest morsel. She drank deep draughts from the cup of the unknown, the impossible, the visionary. She delighted in the Blue Bird of the Maiden's Paradise, which sings far away, on which none may lay hands, which lets itself be seen, while the shot of no gun can ever touch it; its magical colors, like the sparkling of gems, dazzle the eye, but it is never more seen when once reality appears—the hideous Harpy bringing witnesses and the *Maire* in her train. To have all the poetry of love without the presence of the lover! How exquisite an orgy! What a fair chimera of all colors and every plumage!

This was the trifling foolish accident which sealed the girl's fate.

Modeste saw on a bookseller's counter a lithographed portrait of de Canalis, one of her favorites. You know what libels these sketches are, the outcome of an odious kind of speculation which falls upon the persons of celebrated men, as if their face were public property. So Canalis, caught in a Byronic attitude, offered to public admiration his disordered hair, his bare throat, and the excessively high forehead proper to every bard. Victor Hugo's brow will lead to as many heads being shaved as there were sucking field-marshals who rushed to die on the strength of Napoleon's glory.

Modeste was struck by this head, made sublime by commercial requirements; and on the day when she bought the portrait, one of the finest books by Arthès had just come out. Though it may sound to her discredit, it must be confessed that she long hesitated between the illustrious poet and the illustrious prose writer. But were these two great men unmarried? Modeste began by securing the co-operation of

Françoise Cochet, the girl whom poor Bettina-Caroline had taken with her from le Havre and brought back again. She lived in the town, and Madame Mignon and Madame Dumay would employ her for a day's work in preference to any other. Modeste had this somewhat homely creature up into her room; she swore that she would never cause her parents the smallest grief, nor exceed the limits imposed on a young lady; she promised Françoise that in the future, on her father's return, the poor girl should have an easy life, on condition of her keeping absolute secrecy as to the service required of her. What was it?—A mere trifle, a perfectly innocent thing. All that Modeste asked of her accomplice was that she should post certain letters and fetch the replies, addressed to Françoise Cochet.

The bargain concluded, Modeste wrote a polite note to Dauriat, the publisher of Canalis' poems, in which she asked him, in the interests of the great poet, whether Canalis were married, begging him to address the answer to Mademoiselle Françoise, *post restante,* au Havre. Dauriat, who, of course, could not take such a letter seriously, sent a reply concocted in his private room by five or six journalists, each in turn adding his jest.

"MADEMOISELLE,—Canalis (Baron de), Constant-Cyr-Melchior, member of the French Academy, born in 1800 at Canalis, Corrèze; stands five feet four, is in good condition, vaccinated, thoroughbred, has served his term under the conscription, enjoys perfect health, has a small landed estate in Corrèze, and wishes to marry, but looks for great wealth.

"His arms are, party per pale gules a broad axe or, and sable a shell argent; surmounted by a baron's coronet; supporters, two larches proper. The motto *Or et fer* (gold and iron) has never proved auriferous.

"The first Canalis, who went to the Holy Land in the first crusade, is mentioned in the Chronicles of Auvergne as carrying no weapon but an axe, by reason of the complete indigence in which he lived, and which has ever since weighed on his posterity. Hence, no doubt, the blazon. The axe brought him nothing but an empty shell. This noble baron became famous, having discomfited many infidels, and he died at Jerusalem, without either gold or iron, as bare as a worm, on the road to Ascalon, the ambulance service having not yet been called into existence.

"The castle of Canalis—the land yields a few chestnuts—consists of two dismantled towers joined by a wall, remarkable for its superior growth of ivy, and it pays twenty-two francs to the revenue.

"The publisher, undersigned, begs to remark that he pays Monsieur de Canalis ten thousand francs per volume for his poetry. He does not give his empty shells for nothing.

"The Bard of the Corrèze lives at Rue de Paradis-Poissonnière, No. 29, which is a suitable situation for a poet of the Seraphic School. Worms (*les vers*) are a bait for gudgeon. Letters must be prepaid.

"Certain noble dames of the Faubourg Saint-Germain often, it is said, make their way to Paradise and patronize the divinity. King Charles X. thinks so highly of this great poet as to believe him capable of becoming a statesman. He has recently made him an officer of the Legion of Honor, and, which is more to the purpose, Master of Appeals, attached to the Ministry for Foreign Affairs. These functions in no way keep the great man from drawing a pension of three thousand francs from the fund devoted to the encouragement of art and letters. This pecuniary success causes, in the publishing world, an eighth plague which Egypt was spared—a plague of worms (*les vers*) !

"The last edition of the works of Canalis, printed on handmade paper, large 8vo, with vignettes by Bixiou, Joseph Bridau, Schinner, Sommervieux, and others, printed by Didot, is in five volumes, price nine francs, post paid."

This letter fell like a paving-stone on a tulip. A poet as Master of Appeals, in the immediate circle of a Minister, drawing a pension, aiming at the red rosette, adored of the ladies of the Faubourg Saint-Germain! Was this at all like the threadbare poet wandering on the quays, melancholy and dreamy, overwrought by work, and climbing up to his garret again loaded with poetic inspiration? At the same time, Modeste saw through the jest of the envious publisher, which conveyed, "I made Canalis! I made Nathan!" Then she re-read Canalis' verses, very catching verses, full of hypocrisy, and which require a few words of analysis if only to explain her infatuation.

Canalis is distinguished from Lamartine, the chief of the Seraphic School, by a sort of sick-nurse blarney, a perfidious sweetness, and exquisite correctness. If the chief, with his sublime outcry, may be called an eagle, Canalis, all rose and white, is a flamingo. In him women discern the friend they yearn for, a discreet confidant, their interpreter, the being who understands them, and who explains them to themselves.

The broad margins with which Dauriat had graced his last edition were covered with confessions scribbled in pencil by Modeste, who sympathized with this dreamy and tender soul. Canalis has not life in his gift; he does not breathe it into his creations; but he knows how to soothe vague sufferings such as Modeste was a victim to. He speaks to girls in their own language, lulling the pain of the most recent wounds, and silencing groans, and even sobs. His talent does not consist in preaching loftily to the sufferer, in giving her the medicine of strong emotions; he is content to say in a musical voice which commands belief: "I am unhappy, as you are; I understand you fully; come with me, we will weep together on the bank of this stream, under the willows!" And they go! and listen to his verse, as vacuous and as sonorous as the song of a nurse putting a baby to sleep! Canalis—like Nodier in this—bewitches you by an artlessness, which in the prose writer is natural but in the poet elaborately studied, by his archness, his smile, his fallen flowers, his childlike philosophy. He mimics the language of early days well enough to carry you back to the fair field of illusion.

To an eagle we are pitiless; we insist on the quality of the diamond, flawless perfection; but from Canalis we are satisfied with the orphan's mite; everything may be forgiven him. He seems such a good fellow, human above everything. These seraphic airs succeed with him, as those of a woman will always succeed if she acts simplicity well—the startled, youthful, martyred, suffering angel.

Modeste, summing up her impressions, felt that she trusted that soul, that countenance, as attractive as Bernardin de Saint-Pierre's. She paid no heed to the publisher. And so, at the beginning of the month of August, she wrote the following letter to this Dorat of the sacristy, who even now is regarded as one of the stars of the modern Pleiades.

I.

To Monsieur de Canalis.

"Many times ere now, monsieur, I have intended to write to you—and why? You can guess: to tell you how much I delight in your talent. Yes, I feel a longing to express to you the admiration of a poor country-bred girl, very solitary in her nook, whose sole joy is in reading your poetry. From *René* I came to you. Melancholy tends to reverie. How many other women must have paid you the homage of their secret thoughts! What chance have I of being of the elect in such a crowd? What interest can this paper have, though full of my soul, above all the perfumed letters which beset you? I introduce myself with more to perplex you than any other woman. I intend to remain unknown, and yet ask your entire confidence, as if you had known me a long time.

"Answer me, be kind to me. I do not pledge myself to tell my name some day, still I do not positively say no. . . . What more can I add to this letter? Regard it, monsieur, as a great effort, and allow me to offer you my hand—oh, a very friendly hand—that of your servant,

"O. D'Este-M.

"If you do me the favor of replying, address your letter, I beg, to Mademoiselle F. Cochet, Poste Restante, le Havre."

Now every damsel, whether romantic or no, can imagine Modeste's impatience during the next few days! The air was full of tongues of flame; the trees looked like plumage; she did not feel her body; she floated above nature! The earth vanished under her tread. Wondering at the powers of the post office, she followed her little sheet of paper through space; she was glad, as we are glad at twenty at the first exercise of our will. She was bewitched, possessed, as people were in the Middle Ages. She pictured to herself the poet's lodgings, his room; she saw him opening the letter, and she made a million guesses.

Having sketched his poetry, it is necessary here to give an outline of the man. Canalis is small and thin, with an aristocratic figure; dark, gifted with a foolish face and a rather insignificant head, that of a man who has more vanity than pride. He loves luxury, display, and splendor. Fortune is a necessity to him more than to other men. No less proud of his birth than of his talent, he has swamped his ancestors by too great personal pretensions. After all, the Canalis are neither Navarreins, nor Cadignans, nor Grandlieus, nor Nègrepelisses; however, nature has done much to support his pretensions. He has the eyes of Oriental lustre that we look for in a poet, a very pretty refinement of manner, a thrilling voice; but a mannerism that is natural to him almost nullifies these advantages. He is an actor in perfect good faith. He displays a very elegant foot—it is an acquired habit. He has a declamatory style of talk, but it is his own. His affectation is theatrical, but it has become a second nature. These faults, as we must call them, are in harmony with an unfailing generosity which may be termed carpet-knightliness in contrast to chivalry. Canalis has not faith enough to be a Don Quixote, but he is too high-minded not to take invariably the nobler side in any question. His poetry, which comes out in a military eruption on every possible occasion, is a great disadvantage to the poet, who is not indeed lacking in wit, but whose talent hinders his wit from developing. He is the slave of his reputation; he aims at seeming superior to it.

Hence, as frequently happens, the man is completely out of tune with the products of his mind. The author of these insinuating, artless poems, full of tender sentiment, of these calm verses as clear as lake ice, of this caressing womanish poetry, is an ambitious little man, buttoned tightly into his coat, with the air of a diplomate, dreaming of political influence, stinking of the aristocrat, scented and conceited, thirsting for a fortune that he may have an income equal to his ambitions, and already spoiled by success under two aspects—the crown of bays and the crown of myrtle. A salary of eight thousand francs, a pension of three thousand, two thousand from the Académie, a thousand crowns of inherited income—a good deal reduced by the agricultural requirements of the Canalis estate, and the ten thousand francs he gets from his poems one year with another—twenty-five thousand francs a year in all.

To Modeste's hero this income was all the more precarious because he spent, on an average, five or six thousand francs a year more than he received, but hitherto the King's privy purse and the secret funds of the Ministry had made up the deficit. He had composed a hymn for the coronation, for which he had been rewarded with a service of plate; he refused a sum of money, saying that the Canalis owed their homage to the King of France. The *Roi Chevalier* smiled, and ordered from Odiot a costly version of the lines from *Zaïre*.

> What! Rhymester, did you ever hope to vie
> With Charles the Tenth in generosity?

Canalis had drained himself dry, to use a picturesque vulgarism; he knew that he was incapable of inventing a fresh form of poetry; his lyre has not seven strings, it has but one;

and so long had he played on it, that the public left him now
no choice but to use it to hang himself, or to be silent. De
Marsay, who could not endure Canalis, had uttered a sarcasm
of which the poisoned dart had pierced the poet's conceit
to the quick.

"Canalis," he had said, "strikes me as being just like the
man of whom Frederic the Great spoke after a battle, as the
trumpeter who had never ceased blowing the same note
through his penny pipe!"

Canalis was anxious to become a political personage, and
as a beginning made capital of a journey he had taken to
Madrid when the Duc de Chaulieu was ambassador, accompanying him as *attaché*—but to the Duchess, as the jest went in
fashionable drawing-rooms. How often has a jest sealed a
man's fate! Colla, the erewhile President of the Cisalpine
Republic, and the greatest advocate in Piémont, is told by a
friend, at the age of forty, that he knows nothing of botany;
he is nettled, he becomes a Jussieu, cultivates flowers, invents
new ones, and publishes, in Latin, the *Flora of Piémont,* the
work of ten years!

"Well, after all, Canning and Chateaubriand were statesmen," said the extinguished poet, "and in me de Marsay shall
find his master!"

Canalis would have liked to write an important political
work; but he was afraid of getting into trouble with French
prose, a cruelly exacting medium to those who have acquired
the habit of taking four Alexandrine lines to express one
idea. Of all the poets of the day, only three—Victor Hugo,
Théophile Gautier, and de Vigny—have been able to conquer
the double glory of a poet and a prose-writer, which was also
achieved by Voltaire, Molière, and Rabelais. It is one of
the rarest triumphs in French literature, and distinguishes
a poet far above his fellows. Our poet of the Faubourg Saint-
Germain was therefore very wise to try to find shelter for
his chariot under the guardian roof of a Government office.

When he was made Master of Appeals, he felt the need of
a secretary, a friend who might fill his place on many oc-

casions, cook his affairs with publishers, see to his fame in the newspapers, and, at a pinch, support him in politics—in short, would be his satellite. Several men, famous in art, science, or letters, have one or two such followers in Paris, a captain in the Guards, or a Court Chamberlain, who live in the beams of their sunshine, a sort of aides-de-camp intrusted with delicate tasks, allowing themselves to be compromised at need, working round the idol's pedestal, not quite his equals and not quite his superiors, men bold in puffery, the first in every breach, covering his retreats, looking after his business, and devoted to him so long as their illusions last, or till their claims are satisfied. Some at last perceive that their Great Man is ungrateful; others feel that they are being made use of; many weary of the work; and few indeed are satisfied by the mild interchange of sentiment, the only reward to be looked for from an intimacy with a superior man, and which satisfied Ali, raised by Mahomet to his own level. Many, deluded by their self-conceit, think themselves as clever as their Great Man. Devotion is rare, especially without reward and without hope, as Modeste conceived of it.

Nevertheless, a Menneval is occasionally to be met with; and, in Paris more than anywhere, men love to live in the shade and to work in silence, Benedictines who have lost their way in a world which has no monastery for them. These valiant lambs bear in their deeds and in their private lives the poetry which writers put into words. They are poets at heart, in their secluded meditations, in their tenderness, as others are poets on paper, in the fields of intellect, and at so much a verse, like Lord Byron—like all those who live, alas! by ink, which in these days is the water of Hippocrene, for which the Government is to blame.

It was a young consulting referendary of the Court of Exchequer who constituted himself the poet's secretary; he was attracted by the poet's fame, and the future prospects of this vaunted political genius, and led by the advice of Madame d'Espard, who thus played the Duchesse de Chaulieu's cards for her; and Canalis made much of him, as a speculator does of his first shareholder. The beginnings of this alliance had quite an air of friendship. The younger man had already gone through a course of the same kind with one of the Ministers who fell in 1827; but the Minister had taken care to find him a place in the Exchequer.

Ernest de la Brière, at that time seven-and-twenty, decorated with the Legion of Honor, with nothing in the world but the emoluments of his office, had the habit of business, and after hanging about the private room of the Prime Minister for four years, he knew a good deal. He was gentle, amiable, with an almost maidenly soul, full of good feeling, and he hated to be seen in the foreground. He loved his country, he yearned to be of use, but brilliancy dazzled him. If he had had his choice, the place of secretary to a Napoleon would have been more to his mind than that of Prime Minister.

Ernest, having become the friend of Canalis, did great things for him, but in eighteen months he became aware of the shallowness of a nature which was poetical merely in its literary expression. The truth of the homely proverb, "The cowl does not make the monk," is especially applicable in literature. It is most rare to find a talent and character in harmony. A man's faculties are not the sum-total of the man. This discord, of which the manifestations are startling, is the outcome of an unexplored—a perhaps unexplorable—mystery. The brain and its products of every kind—since in the arts the hand of man carries out his brain—form a world apart that flourishes under the skull, perfectly independent of the feelings, of what are called the virtues of a citizen, of the head of a family, of a private householder. And yet this is not final; nothing in man is final. It is certain that a debauchee will exhaust his talents in orgies, and a drunkard drown it in his libations, while a good man can never acquire talent by wholesome decency; but it is also almost proved that Virgil, the poet of love, never loved a Dido; and that Rousseau, the pattern citizen, had pride enough to furnish forth a whole aristocracy. Nevertheless, Michael Angelo and Raphael showed the happy concord of talent and character. Hence talent is in men, as far as the individual is concerned, what beauty is in women—a promise. Let us give twofold admiration to the man whose heart and character are equally perfect with his talent.

Ernest, when he detected under the poet an ambitious egoist—the worst species of egoist, for some are amiable—felt a singular diffidence about leaving him. Honest souls do not easily break their bonds, especially those they have voluntarily accepted. The secretary, then, was on very good terms with the poet when Modeste's letter was flying through the mail, but on the good terms of constant self-effacement. La Brière felt he owed Canalis something for the frankness with which he had revealed himself. And indeed, in this man, who will be accounted great so long as he lives, and made much of, like Marmontel, his defects are the seamy side of brilliant qualities. But for his vanity, his pretentious conceit, he might not have been gifted with that sonorous verbiage which is a necessary instrument in the political life of the day. His shallowness is part of his rectitude and loyalty; his ostentation is paired with liberality. Society profits by the results; the motives may be left to God.

Still, when Modeste's letter arrived, Ernest had no illusions left as to Canalis. The two friends had just breakfasted, and were chatting in the poet's study; he was at that time living in ground-floor rooms looking out on a garden, beyond a courtyard.

"Ah!" cried Canalis, "I was saying the other day to Madame de Chaulieu that I must cast forth some new poem; admiration is running low, for it is some time since I have had any anonymous letters——"

"An unknown lady?"

"Unknown! A d'Este, and from le Havre! It is evidently an assumed name!"

And Canalis handed the letter to la Brière. This poem, this veiled enthusiasm, in short, Modeste's very heart, was recklessly exposed by the gesture of a coxcomb.

"It is a grand thing," said the young accountant, "thus to

attract the chastest feelings, to compel a helpless woman to shake off the habits forced upon her by education, by nature, by society, to break through conventionalities. . . . What privileges genius commands! A letter like this in my hand, written by a girl, a genuine girl, without reservation, with enthusiasm . . ."

"Well?" said Canalis.

"Well, if you had suffered as much as Tasso, you ought to find it reward enough!" exclaimed la Brière.

"So we tell ourselves at the first or at the second letter," said Canalis. "But at the thirtieth! . . . but when we have discovered that the young enthusiast is an old hand! . . . but when at the end of the radiant path traveled over by the poet's imagination we have seen some English old maid sitting on a milestone and holding out her hand! . . . but when the angel—by post—turns into a poor creature, moderately good-looking, in search of a husband! . . . Well, then, the effervescence subsides."

"I am beginning to think," said la Brière, smiling, "that glory has something poisonous in it, like certain gorgeous flowers."

"Besides, my dear fellow," Canalis went on, "all these women, even when they are sincere, have an ideal to which we rarely correspond. They never tell themselves that a poet is a man, and a tolerably vain one, as I am accused of being; it never occurs to them that he is rough-ridden by a sort of feverish excitement which makes him disagreeable and uncertain. They want him to be always great, always splendid; they never dream that talent is a disease; that Nathan lives on Florine; that d'Arthez is too fat; that Joseph Bridau is too thin; that Béranger can go on foot; that the divinity may foam at the mouth. A Lucien de Rubempré, a verse-writer, and a pretty fellow, is a Phenix. So why go out of your way to receive bad compliments and sit under the cold showerbath of a disillusioned woman's helpless stare?"

"Then the true poet," said la Brière, "ought to remain hidden, like God, in the centre of his universe, and be visible only in his creations!"

"Then glory would be too dearly paid for," replied Canalis. "There is some good in life, I tell you," said he, taking a cup of tea. "When a woman of birth and beauty loves a poet, she does not hide herself in the gallery or the stage-box of a theatre, like a duchess smitten by an actor; she feels strong enough and sufficiently protected by her beauty, by her fortune, by her name, to say, as in every epic poem, 'I am the nymph Calypso, and I love Telemachus.' Mystification is the resource of small minds. For some time now I have never answered such masqueraders——"

"Oh! how I could love a woman who had come to me!" cried la Brière, restraining a tear. "It may be said in reply, my dear Canalis, that it is never a poor creature that rises to the level of a celebrated man; she is too suspicious, too vain, too much afraid. It is always a star, a——"

"A Princess," said Canalis, with a shout of laughter, "who condescends to him, I suppose?—My dear fellow, such a thing happens once in a century. Such a passion is like the plant that flowers once in a hundred years.—Princesses who are young, rich, and handsome have too much else to do; they are enclosed, like all rare plants, within a hedge of silly men, well born and well bred, and as empty as an elder-stem. My dream, alas! the crystal of my dream hung with garlands of flowers all the way hither from la Corrèze, and with what fervor!—But no more of that!—it is in fragments, at my feet, long since.—No, no, every anonymous letter is a beggar! And what demands they make. Write to this young person, assuming her to be young and pretty, and you will see! You will have your hands full. One cannot in reason love every woman. Apollo, or at any rate, the Apollo Belvedere, is a consumptive dandy who must save his strength."

"But when a woman comes to you like this," argued Ernest, "her excuse must lie in her certainty that she can eclipse the most adored mistress in tenderness, in beauty—and then a little curiosity——"

"Ah!" said Canalis, "my too youthful Ernest, you must allow me to be faithful to the fair Duchess, who is all my joy!"

"You are right—too right," replied Ernest.

Nevertheless, the young secretary read and re-read Modeste's letter, trying to guess the mind behind it.

"But there is nothing extravagant in it, no appeal to your genius, only to your heart," he said to Canalis. "This perfume of modesty and the exchange proposed would tempt me——"

"Sign it yourself; answer her, and follow up the adventure to the end; it is a poor bargain that I offer you," exclaimed Canalis, with a smile. "Go on; you will have something to tell me in three months' time, if it lasts three months . . ."

Four days after Modeste received the following letter, written on handsome paper, under a double cover, and sealed with the arms of Canalis.

II.

To Mademoiselle O. d'Este-M.

"MADEMOISELLE,—Admiration for great works—admitting that mine may be great—implies a certain holy simplicity which is a defence against irony and a justification, in the eyes of every tribunal, of the step you have taken in writing to me. Above all, I must thank you for the pleasure which such a testimonial never fails to give, even when undeserved, for the writer of verse and the poet alike secretly believe themselves worthy of them, self-love is a form of matter so far from repellent of praise. The best proof of friendship that I can give to an unknown lady in return for this balm, which heals the stings of criticism, is surely to share with her the harvest of my experience, at the risk of scaring away her living illusions.

"Mademoiselle, the noblest palm a young girl can bear is that of a saintly, pure, and blameless life. Are you alone in the world? That is a sufficient answer. But if you have a family, a father or a mother, consider all the sorrows that a letter like yours may entail—written to a poet whom you do not know. Not every writer is an angel; they have their faults. Some are fickle, reckless, conceited, ambitious, dissipated; and imposing as innocence must be, chivalrous as a French poet may be, you might find more than one degenerate bard willing to encourage your affection only to betray it. Then your letter would not be interpreted as I read it. He would find a meaning in it which you have not put there, and which in your innocence you do not even suspect. Many authors, many natures!

"I am extremely flattered by your having thought me worthy to understand you; but if you had addressed yourself to an insincere talent, to a cynic whose writings were melancholy while his life was a continual carnival, you might have found at the end of your sublime imprudence some bad man, a dangler behind the scenes, or wine-shop hero! You, under the arbor of clematis where you dream over poetry, cannot smell the stale cigar smoke which depoetizes the manuscript; just as when you go to a ball, dressed in the dazzling products of the jeweler's skill, you never think of the sinewy arms, the toilers in their shirt-sleeves, the wretched workshops whence spring these radiant flowers of handicraft.

"Go further. What is there in the solitary life of reverie that you lead—by the seashore, no doubt—to interest a poet whose task it is to divine everything, since he must describe everything? Our young girls here are so highly accomplished, that no daughter of Eve can vie with them! What reality was ever so good as a dream? And you now, you, a young girl brought up to be the duteous mother of a family, what would you gain by an initiation into the terrible excitement of a poet's life in this appalling capital, to be defined only as a hell we love.

"If you took up your pen, prompted by the wish to enliven your monotonous existence as an inquisitive girl, has not this a semblance of depravity? What meaning am I to attribute to your letter? Are you one of a caste of reprobates, seeking a friend at a distance? Are you cursed with ugliness, and do you feel you have a noble soul with none to trust? Alas!— a sad conclusion—you have either gone too far, or not far enough. Either let it end here, or, if you persist, tell me more than in the letter you have already written.

"But, mademoiselle, if you are young, if you have a family, if you feel that you bear in your heart a heavenly spikenard, to be shed, as the Magdalen shed hers on Christ's feet, suffer yourself to be appreciated by some man who is worthy of you, and become what every good girl should be— an admirable wife, the virtuous mother of children. A poet is the poorest conquest any young woman can aspire to; he has too much vanity, too many salient angles which must run counter to the legitimate vanity of a wife, and bruise the tenderness which has no experience of life. The poet's wife should love him for long before marrying him; she must resign herself to be as charitable and as indulgent as the angels, to all the virtues of motherhood. These qualities, mademoiselle, exist only as a germ in a young girl.

"Listen to the whole truth; do I not owe it you in return for your intoxicating flattery? Though it may be glorious to marry a great celebrity, a woman soon discovers that a man, however superior, is but a man like all others. He then the less fulfils her hopes, because miracles are expected of him. A famous poet is then in the predicament of a woman whose overpraised beauty makes us say, 'I had pictured her as handsomer'; she does not answer to the requirements of the portrait sketched by the same fairy to whom I owe your letter— Imagination!

"Again, great qualities of mind develop and flourish only in an invisible sphere; the poet's wife sees only the unpleasant side of it; she sees the jewels made instead of wearing them. If the brilliancy of an exceptional position is what fascinates you, I warn you, its pleasures are soon exhausted. You would be provoked to find so much that is rough in a situation which from afar looks so smooth, so much ice on a glittering height! And then, as women never have set foot in the world of difficulty, they presently cease to value what they once admired, when they fancy that they have understood the workmanship at a glance.

"I will conclude with a last reflection, which you will do wrong to mis-read as an entreaty in disguise; it is the advice of a friend. A communion of souls cannot be complete excepting between two persons who are prepared to conceal nothing. Could you show yourself as you really are to a stranger? I pause before the consequences of such a notion.

"Accept, mademoiselle, all the respect we owe to every woman, even to those who are unknown, and who wear a mask."

To think that she had carried this letter between her skin and her stays, under the scorching busk, for a whole day! . . . that she had postponed reading it till an hour when everybody was asleep, till midnight, after waiting for the solemn hour in the pangs of a fiery imagination! . . . that she had blessed the poet, had read in fancy a thousand letters, had conceived of everything excepting this drop of cold water shed on the most diaphanous visions of fancy, and destroying them as prussic acid destroys life! . . . It was enough to make her hide her face—as Modeste did—under her sheets though she was alone, and put out the candle, and weep.

All this happened in the early days of July. Modeste presently got up, paced her room, and then opened the window. She wanted air. The scent of flowers came up to her with the peculiar freshness of night-perfumes. The sea, lighted up by the moon, twinkled like a mirror. A nightingale was singing in the Vilquins' park.

"Ah! there is the poet!" said Modeste to herself, her anger dying out.

The bitterest reflections crowded on her mind. She was stung to the quick; she wanted to read the letter again. She relighted the candle, and studied this careful production, till at last she heard the early voices of real life.

"He is in the right, and I am in the wrong," thought she. "But how could I expect to find one of Molière's old men under the star-spangled robe of a poet?"

When a woman or a girl is caught red-handed, she feels intense hatred of the witness, the first cause, or the object of her folly. And so Modeste, genuine, natural, and coy, felt her heart swell with a dreadful longing to trample on this essence of rectitude, and throw him over into some abyss of contradiction, to pay him back this stunning blow.

The pure-hearted child, whose head alone had been corrupted by her reading, by her sister's long agony, and by the perilous meditations of her solitude, was roused by a sunbeam falling on her face. She had lain for three hours tacking about on the immense ocean of doubt. Such nights are never forgotten.

Modeste went at once to her little lacquer table, her father's gift, and wrote a letter dictated by the infernal spirit of revenge which disports itself at the bottom of a young girl's heart.

III.

To Monsieur de Canalis.

"MONSIEUR,—You are certainly a great poet, but you are something better—an honest man. After showing so much frank loyalty to a young girl on the verge of an abyss, have you enough to reply without the least hypocrisy or evasion to this question:

"Would you have written the letter I have received in answer to mine—would your ideas, your language, have been the same if some one had whispered in your ear, what may be true: 'Mademoiselle O. d'Este-M. has six millions of francs, and does not want to have a simpleton for her master'?

"For one moment admit this hypothesis for a fact. Be as honest with me as with yourself; fear nothing, I am superior to my twenty years, nothing that is genuine can injure you in my estimation. When I shall have read that confession, if indeed you vouchsafe to make it to me, you shall have an answer to your first letter.

"After admiring your talent, which is often sublime, allow me to do homage to your delicacy and rectitude, which compel me to sign myself

"Your humble servant,
"O. D'ESTE-M."

When this note was placed in la Brière's hands, he went out to walk on the Boulevards, tossed in his soul like a light bark in a tempest when the wind blows every minute from a different point of the compass. One of the young men of whom we meet so many—a true Parisian, would have summed up the case in these words, "An old hand!" But to a young fellow whose soul is lofty and refined, this sort of implied oath, this appeal to veracity, had the power to arouse the three judges that lurk at the bottom of every conscience. And Honor, Truth, and Justice, rising erect, cried aloud.

"Ah! my dear Ernest," said Truth, "you certainly would not have written a lecture to a rich heiress. No, no, my boy, you would have set off, nose on for le Havre, to find out whether the young lady were handsome, and you would have been much aggrieved by the preference given to genius. And if you could only have tripped your friend up, and have made yourself acceptable in his place, Mademoiselle d'Este would have been divine!"—"What," said Justice, "you pity yourselves, you men of brains or wit, and without cash, when you see rich girls married to men whom you would not employ as porters; you run amuck against the sordidness of the age, which is eager to wed money with money, and never to unite some young fellow full of talent to a rich and highborn beauty; now here is one who rebels against the spirit of the time, and the poet retorts with a blow on her heart!"—"Rich or poor, young or old, handsome or plain, this girl is in the right, she has brains, she casts the poet into the mire of self-interest," cried Honor. "She deserves a sincere, noble, and honest reply, and, above all, the true expression of your thought! Examine yourself. Sound your heart, and purge it of its meannesses! What would Molière's Alceste say?"— And la Brière, starting from the Boulevard Poissonnière, lost in meditation, walked so slowly, that at the end of an hour he had but just reached the Boulevard des Capucines. He returned by the quays to the Exchequer, at that time situated near the Sainte-Chapelle. Instead of verifying accounts, he sat under the spell of his perplexities.

"She has not six millions, that is clear," said he to himself; "but that is not the question . . ."

Six days later Modeste received the following letter:

IV.

To Mademoiselle O. d'Este-M.

"MADEMOISELLE,—You are not a d'Este. That is an assumed name to conceal your own. Are such revelations as you request due to a person who is false as to her identity? Attend; I will answer your question by asking another, Are you of illustrious parentage? of noble birth? of a family of townsfolk?

"Morality indeed cannot change; it is one; but its obligations vary in different spheres. As the sun sheds a different light on different aspects, producing the variety we admire, morality makes social duty conform to rank and position. What is a peccadillo in the soldier, is a crime in the general, and *vice versa*. The proprieties are not the same for a peasant girl who reaps the field, for a workwoman at fifteen sous a day, for the daughter of a small shopkeeper, for a young girl of the middle class, for the child of a rich commercial house, for the heiress of a noble family, for a daughter of the race of Este. A king must not stoop to pick up a gold coin, and a workman must turn back to look for a piece of ten sous he has dropped, though both alike ought to observe the laws of economy. A d'Este owning six millions of francs may wear a broad-brimmed hat and feathers, flourish a riding whip, mount an Arab horse, and come as an Amazon in gold lace, followed by a groom, to say to a poet, 'I love poetry, and desire to expiate the wrongs done by Leonora to Tasso,' while the daughter of a merchant would be simply ridiculous in imitating her.

"To what social class do you belong? Answer truly, and I will as truly reply to the question you ask me.

"Not being so happy as to know you, though already bound to you by a sort of poetical communication, I do not like to offer you any vulgar homage. It is already a triumph of mischief for you perhaps to have perplexed a man whose books are published."

The young accountant was not lacking in skill of fence which a man of honor may allow himself. By return of post he received this reply:

V.

To Monsieur de Canalis.

"You are more and more cautious, my dear poet. My father is a count. The most distinguished member of our family was a cardinal, in the days when cardinals were the equals of kings. At the present day our race, almost extinct, ends in me; but I have the necessary quarterings to admit me to any Court or any Chapter. In short, we are a match for the Canalis. Excuse my not forwarding our coat-of-arms.

"Try to write as sincerely as I do. I await your reply to know whether I may still subscribe myself, as now,
"Your servant,
"O. d'Este-M."

"What advantage the young person takes of her position!" exclaimed la Brière. "But is she truthful?"

It is not for nothing that a man has been for four years a Minister's private secretary; that he has lived in Paris and watched its intrigues; and the purest soul is always more or less intoxicated by the heady atmosphere of the Empress city. La Brière, rejoicing that he was not Canalis, secured a place in the mail-coach for le Havre, after writing a letter in which he promised a reply by a certain day, excusing the delay by the importance of the confession required of him, and the business of his office. He took the precaution of obtaining from the Director-General of the Mails a line enjoining silence and compliance on the head of the office at le Havre. He could thus wait to see Françoise Cochet arrive at the office, and quietly follow her home. Guided by her, he mounted the hill of Ingouville, and saw Modeste Mignon at the window of the Chalet.

"Well, Françoise?" asked the girl.

"Yes, mademoiselle, I have got one."

Ernest, struck by this celestially fair type of beauty, turned on his heel, and inquired of a passer-by the name of the owner of that splendid residence.

"That?" asked the native, pointing to the great house.

"Yes, my good fellow."

"Oh, that belongs to Monsieur Vilquin, the richest shipowner of the place, a man who does not know how much he has."

"I know of no Cardinal Vilquin in history," said the accountant to himself, as he went down the town again, to return to Paris.

Of course, he questioned the postmaster as to the Vilquin family. He learned that the Vilquins owned an immense fortune; that Monsieur Vilquin had a son and two daughters, one of them married to young Monsieur Althor. Prudence saved la Brière from showing any adverse interest in the Vilquins; the postmaster was already looking at him with suspicion.

"Is there no one at the house just now besides the family?" he asked.

"Just at present the Hérouville family are there. There is some talk of a marriage between the young Duke and the second Mademoiselle Vilquin."

"There was a famous Cardinal d'Hérouville," thought la Brière, "in the time of the Valois; and, under Henri IV., the terrible Marshal, who was created Duke."

Ernest returned, having seen enough of Modeste to dream of her; to believe that, rich or poor, if she had a noble soul, he would gladly make her Madame la Brière, and he determined to carry on the correspondence.

Do your utmost, hapless Frenchwoman, to remain unknown, to weave the very least little romance in the midst of a civilization which takes note on public squares of the hour when every hackney cab comes and goes, which counts every letter and stamps them twice at the exact hours when they are posted and when they are delivered, which numbers the houses, which registers each floor on the schedule of taxes, after making a list of the windows and doors, which ere long will have every acre of land, down to the smallest holdings and its most trifling details, laid down on the broad sheets of a survey—a giant's task, by command of a giant! Try, rash maidens, to evade—not, indeed, the eye of the police, but the ceaseless gossip which, in the poorest hamlet, scrutinizes your most trivial acts, counts the dishes at the Préfet's dessert, and sees the melon rind outside the door of the small annuitant, which tries to hear the chink of gold when Economy adds it to her treasury, and every evening, over the fire, sums up the incomes of the village, of the town, of the department.

Modeste, by a commonplace mistake, had escaped the most innocent espionage, for which Ernest already blamed himself. But what Parisian could endure to be the dupe of a little country girl? Never be duped! This odious maxim is a solvent for all man's noble sentiments. From the letter he wrote, where every lash of the scourge of conscience has left its mark, the reader may easily imagine the conflict of feelings to which the honest youth was a prey.

A few days later, Modeste, sitting at her window on a fine summer day, read the following pages:

VI.

To Mademoiselle O. d'Este-M.

"MADEMOISELLE,—Without hypocrisy, yes, if I had been sure that you had an immense fortune, I should have acted quite differently. Why? I have sought the reason, and it is this. There is in us an inborn feeling, developed, too, to an extreme by society, which urges us to seek and to seize happiness. Most men confound happiness with the means to happiness, and in their eyes fortune is its chief element. I should therefore have endeavored to please you, spurred by the social instinct that has in all ages made wealth a religion. At least, I think so. The wisdom which substitutes good sense for impulse is not to be looked for in a man who is still young; and when the prey is in sight, the animal instinct lurking in the heart of man urges him on. Thus, instead of a lecture, I should have sent you compliments and flattery.

"Should I have respected myself? I doubt it. Mademoiselle, in such a case, success brings absolution; but as to happiness, that is another matter. Should I not distrust my wife if I won her thus? Most certainly. Your action would, sooner or later, have resumed its true character; your husband, however great you might deem him, would at last have reproached you for having humiliated him; and you, sooner or later, might have learned to despise him. An ordinary man cuts the Gordian knot of a marriage for money with the sword of tyranny. A strong man forgives. The poet bewails himself. This, mademoiselle, is the answer given by my honesty.

"Now, attend to me well. Yours is the triumph of having made me reflect deeply, both on you, whom I know not enough, and on myself, whom I know but little. You have had the skill to stir up the evil thoughts that grovel at the bottom of every heart; but in me the outcome has been a generous something, and I hail you with my most grateful blessings, as, at sea, we hail a lighthouse warning us of rocks where we might have been wrecked.

"And now for my confession, for I would not lose your esteem nor my own for the price of all the treasures on earth. I was bent on knowing who you were. I have just come back from le Havre, where I saw Françoise Cochet, followed her to Ingouville, and saw you in your magnificent villa. You are as lovely as a poet's dream of woman; but I know not whether you are Mademoiselle Vilquin hidden under Mademoiselle d'Hérouville, or Mademoiselle d'Hérouville hidden under Mademoiselle Vilquin. Though all is fair in war, I blushed at playing the spy, and I paused in my investigations. You piqued my curiosity; owe me no grudge for having been so womanly, is it not a poet's privilege? Now I have opened my heart to you; I have let you read it; you may believe in the sincerity of what I am about to add. Brief as was the glimpse I had of you, it was enough to modify my opinion. You are a poet and a poem even before being a woman. Yes, there is in you something more precious than beauty; you are the ideal of art, of fancy.

"The step you took, blamable in a young girl fated to a commonplace existence, is different in one gifted with such a character as I suppose you to have. Among the vast number of beings flung by chance into social life to make up a generation, there are exceptions. If your letter is the outcome of long poetical musing on the lot which the law reserves for women; if, carried away by the vocation of a superior and cultivated mind, you have wished to know something of the intimate life of a man to whom you concede the chance endowment of genius, in order to create a friendship with a soul akin to your own, exempt from vulgar conditions, and evading all the limitations of your sex—you are indeed an exception! The law which is good to measure the actions of the crowd is then very narrow to qualify your determination. But then the words of my first letter recur in all their meaning, 'You have done too much or not enough.'

"Once more accept my thanks for the service you have done me in compelling me to probe my heart; for you have cured me of the error, common enough in France, of regarding marriage as a means to fortune. In the midst of the disturbance of my conscience a sacred voice has spoken. I have solemnly sworn to myself to make my own fortune, that my choice of a wife may never be determined by mercenary motives. Finally, I have blamed and repressed the unbecoming curiosity you aroused in me. You have not six millions. It would be impossible at le Havre that a young lady possessed of such a fortune should remain unknown, and you would have been betrayed by the pack of those aristocratic families which I see in pursuit of heiresses here in Paris, and which has sent the King's chief equerry on a visit to your Vilquins. So the sentiments I express are put forward as a positive rule, apart from all romance or statement of fact.

"Now, prove to me that you have one of those souls which we allow to disobey the common law, and you will grant in your mind that this second letter is in the right as well as the first. You are destined to a middle-class life; obey the iron law that holds society together. You are a superior woman, and I admire you; but if you are bent on yielding to the instinct you ought to repress, I pity you; these are the conditions of the social state. The admirable moral of the domestic epic *Clarissa Harlowe* is that the victim's love, though legitimate and sincere, leads to her ruin, because it has its rise and progress in defiance of her family. The family, silly and cruel as it is, is in its rights as against Lovelace. The family is society.

"Believe me, for a girl, as for a wife, her glory will always consist in restraining her ardent whims within the strictest limits of propriety. If I had a daughter who might become a Madame de Staël, I would wish that she might die at fifteen. Can you think, without the acutest regret, of your own child exhibited on the stage of celebrity and parading to win the applause of the mob? However high a woman may have raised herself in the secret poetry of her dreams, she must sacrifice her superiority on the altar of family life. Her soaring moods, her genius, her aspirations towards the lofty and the sublime, all the poem of a girl's soul belongs to the man she accepts, the children she may bear. I discern in you a secret ambition to enlarge the narrow circle of life to which every woman is condemned, and to bring passion and love into your marriage. Ah! it is a beautiful dream; it is not impossible; it is difficult; but it has been realized to bring incompatible souls—forgive me a word which has become ridiculous—to desperation.

"If you look for a sort of Platonic regard, it can only lead you to despair in the future. If your letter was a sport, play no more. And so this little romance ends, does it not? It will not have been altogether barren of fruit; my honesty has taken up arms; and you, on your part, have learned something certain about social life. Turn your gaze on real life, and throw the transient enthusiasm to which literature has given birth into the virtues of your sex. Farewell, mademoiselle; do me the honor of granting me your esteem. Since seeing you—or her whom I believe to be you—your letter has seemed to me quite natural; so fair a flower would instinctively turn towards the sun of poetry. So love poetry still, as you doubtless love flowers and music, the sumptuous grandeur of the sea, the beauties of Nature—all as ornaments of the soul; but remember all I have had the honor of telling you about poets. Be sure you do not marry an ass; seek with care for the mate God has created for you. There are, take my word for it, many clever men capable of appreciating you and of making you happy. If I were rich, and you were poor, I would some day lay my fortune and my heart at your feet, for I believe you have a soul full of riches and of loyalty; and I would intrust you with my life and honor in the fullest confidence. Once more farewell, fair daughter of fair Eve."

On reading this letter—at one gulp, like a drink of cold water in a desert—the mountain weighing on Modeste's heart was lifted; then, perceiving the mistakes she had made in carrying out her scheme, she corrected them at once by making some wrappers for Françoise, on which she wrote her own address at Ingouville, desiring her to come no more to the Chalet. Thenceforth Françoise was to go home, place each letter as it came from Paris in one of these wrappers, and privily repost it in the town. Modeste promised herself always to meet the postman, standing at the front door at the hour when he should pass.

As to the feelings excited in Modeste by this reply, in which poor la Brière's noble heart throbbed under the brilliant mask of Canalis, they were as infinite as the waves which rolled up to die one after another on the shore, while, with her eyes fixed on the ocean, she gave herself up to the joy of having harpooned an angel's soul, so to speak, in the sea of Paris, of having discerned that in a really superior man the heart may sometimes be on a par with genius, and of having been well advised by the voice of presentiment. A mastering interest would henceforth inspire her life. The enclosure of her pretty home, the wires of her cage were broken. Thought could soar on widespread wings.

"Oh, dear father," she cried, looking across to the horizon, "make us very rich!"

Her answer, which Ernest de la Brière read five days later, will tell more than any comments can.

VII.

To Monsieur de Canalis.

"MY FRIEND,—Let me call you so—you have enchanted me, and I would not have you other than you are in this letter— the first; oh, let it not be the last! Who but a poet could ever have so perfectly excused and understood a girl?

"I wish to speak to you with the same sincerity as that which dictated the opening lines of your letter.

"In the first place, happily, you do not know me. I can tell you, gladly, that I am neither that frightful Mademoiselle Vilquin, nor that most noble and most faded Mademoiselle d'Hérouville, who hovers between thirty and fifty, and cannot make up her mind to a creditable age. Cardinal d'Hérouville flourished in Church history before the cardinal who is our only pride, for I do not count lieutenant-generals, or abbés who write small volumes of too big verse, as celebrities.

"Also, I do not live in the Vilquins' gorgeous villa; thank God, not the millionth part of a drop of their blood, chilled in many a counting-house, flows in my veins. I am by birth partly German, partly a child of Southern France; in my brain lurks Teutonic sentiment, and in my blood the energy of the Provençal. I am of noble birth both on my father's and my mother's side; through my mother I have connections on every page of the *Almanach de Gotha*. But I have taken every precaution; it is not in the power of any man, not even of the police, to lift my disguise. I shall remain shrouded, unknown. As to myself and my belongings, *mes propres,* as they say in Normandy, be quite easy; I am at least as good-looking as the little person—happy, though she knows it not— on whom your eyes fell; and I do not think myself a pauper, though I am not attended in my walks by ten sons of peers! I have even seen the contemptible farce played in my behoof of the heiress adored for her millions.

"Finally, make no attempt to find me, not even to win a bet. Alas! though free, I am guarded; in the first place, by myself, and then by very brave folks, who would not hesitate to stick a knife in your heart if you tried to penetrate this retreat. I say this, not to incite your courage or your curiosity; I believe no such sentiments are needed to arouse your interest in me, or to secure your attachment.

"I now proceed to reply to the second and greatly enlarged edition of your sermon.

"Shall I make a confession? When I found you so suspicious, taking me for a *Corinne*—how her improvisations have bored me!—I said to myself that many a tenth Muse had, ere now, led you by the tow-line of curiosity into her inmost vales, and proposed to you to taste the fruits of her schoolgirl Parnassus. . . . Be quite easy, my friend; though I love poetry, I have no copies of verses in my blotting-book; my stockings are, and will remain, perfectly white. You will not be bored by any 'trifles' in one or two volumes. In short, if I should ever say to you 'Come,' you know now that you will not find an old maid, ugly and penniless. . . .

"Oh! my friend, if you could only know how much I regret that you should have come to le Havre! You have altered the aspect of what you call my romance. God alone can weigh in His Almighty hands the treasure I had in store for a man great enough, confiding and clear-sighted enough, to set out on the strength of my letters, after having made his way step by step through all the recesses of my heart, and to come to our first meeting with the guilelessness of a child! I dreamed of such innocence in a genius; you have marred that treasure. I forgive you; you live in Paris; and, as you say, a poet is a man.

"Will you, therefore, take me to be a silly schoolgirl, cherishing the enchanted garden of illusions? Nay, do not amuse yourself with throwing stones at the broken windows of a long ruined castle. You, a man of wit, how is it that you never guessed that Mademoiselle d'Este had already read herself the lecture contained in your first letter? No, my dear poet, my first note was a pebble flung by a boy loitering along the highway, who thinks it fun to startle a landowner reading his tax-paper under shelter of his fruit-trees; or, rather, was the line carefully fixed by a fisherman from the top of a rock by the seashore, in hope of a miraculous draught.

"All you say so beautifully about family ties has my approbation. The man I shall love, and of whom I shall think myself worthy, shall have my heart and my life with my parents' consent. I would neither distress nor startle them; I am certain of overruling them, and they have no prejudices. Again, I am strong enough to defy the illusions of my fancy. I have built a stronghold with my own hands, and have allowed it to be fortified by the unbounded devotion of those who watch over me as a treasure—not that I am not strong enough to defend myself in open fight; for, may I tell you, fate has clothed me in well-tempered armor on which is stamped the word DISDAIN. I have the deepest horror of everything which suggests self-interest, of all that is not entirely noble, pure, and disinterested. Without being romantic, I worship the beautiful and the ideal; though I have been romantic, all to myself, in my dreams. And so I could recognize the truth —true even to platitude—of what you wrote me as to social life.

"For the present, we are only, and can only be, friends.— Why seek a friend among the unknown? you will ask. Your person is unknown to me; but your mind and heart are known to me; I like them, and I am conscious of infinite feelings in my soul, which demand a man of genius as their only confidant. I do not want the poem of my heart to be wasted; it shall be as beautiful for you as it would have been for God alone. What a precious thing is a trusty comrade to whom we may say what we will! Can you reject the unspoiled blossoms of a genuine girl? They will fly to you as gnats fly to the sunbeams. I am sure that your intellect has never before won you such a success—the confidences of a young girl. Listen to her prattle, accept the songs she has hitherto sung only for herself.

"By and by, if our souls are really akin, if on trial our characters agree, some day an old white-haired retainer will await you, standing by the roadside, and conduct you to a chalet, a villa, a castle, a palace—I do not yet know of what type that temple of Hymen may be—brown and gold, the colors of Austria, which marriage has made so powerful—nor whether such a conclusion may be possible; but confess that it is poetical, and that Mademoiselle d'Este has good ideas. Does she not leave you free? Does she come on jealous tiptoe to glance round Paris drawing-rooms? Does she lay on you the task of some high emprise, the chains which paladins of old voluntarily hung on their arm? What she asks of you is a really spiritual and mystical alliance.

"Come, come to my heart whenever you are unhappy, wounded, weary. Tell me everything, conceal nothing; I shall have balm for all your sorrows. I, my friend, am but twenty; but my mind is fifty, and I have unhappily known through another, my second self, the horrors and ecstasies of passion. I know all that the human heart can possibly contain of meanness and infamy, and yet I am the most honest girl living. No; I have no illusions left; but I have something better—faith and religion. There, I have played first in our game of confidences.

"Whoever my husband may be, if he is my own choice, he may sleep in peace; he might sail for the Indies, and on his return he would find me finishing the tapestry begun at his departure; no eyes would have looked into mine, no man's voice would have tainted the air in my ear; in every stitch he might find a line of the poem of which he was the hero. Even if I should have been taken in by a fair and false exterior, that man would have every flower of my thought, every refinement of my tenderness, all the wordless sacrifices of proud and never suppliant resignation. Yes, I have vowed to myself never even to go out with my husband when he does not want me; I will be the divinity of his hearth. This is my human religion.—But why should I not test and choose the man to whom I shall be what life is to the body? Does a man ever find life an inconvenience? What is a wife who annoys her husband? Not life, but a sickness. By life, I mean the perfect health which makes every hour an enjoyment.

"To return to your letter, which will always be dear to me. Yes, jesting apart, it really contains what I had hoped for— the expression of prosaic sentiments, which are as necessary to family life as air is to the lungs, and without which happiness is out of the question. What I hoped for in my friend was, that he should act as an honest man, think as a poet, love as women love; and this is now, beyond a doubt, no longer a chimera.

"Farewell, my friend. At present I am poor. That is one of the reasons which make me cling to my mask, my incognito, my impenetrable fortress.

"I read your last poem in the *Revue,* and with what delight, after having mastered the austere and secret loftiness of your soul!

"Will it aggrieve you greatly to be told that a girl beseeches God fervently in your behalf, that she makes you her one thought, and that you have no rival in her heart but her father and mother? Can there be any reason why you should reject these pages that are full of you, that are written for you, that none but you will read? Repay me in kind. I am as yet so little a woman, that your effusions, so long as they are genuine and full, will suffice for the happiness of your

"O. D'ESTE-M."

"Great Heavens! am I in love with her already!" exclaimed the young referendary, when he discovered that he had been sitting for an hour with this letter in his hand after having read it. "What must I do next? She believes she is writing to our great poet. Ought I to carry on the deception? Is she a woman of forty, or a girl of twenty?"

Ernest was fascinated by the abyss of the unknown. The unknown is dark infinitude, and nothing is more enthralling. From that murky vastness flash fires which rend it from time to time, and light up visions like those of Martin. In a life as full as that of Canalis, an adventure of this kind is swept away like a cornflower among the boulders of a torrent; in that of a young referendary awaiting the reinstatement in power of the party of which his patron was the representative, and who, as a precaution, was dry-nursing Canalis for parliament, this pretty girl—his imagination persistently believed her to be the fair-haired damsel he had seen—was bound to find a place in his heart, and commit all the ravages caused by a romance when it breaks into a humdrum existence, like a wolf into a farmyard. So Ernest thought a great deal about his unknown correspondent, and he replied by the following letter—an elaborate and pretentious letter, but already betraying some passion by its tone of annoyance.

VIII.

To Mademoiselle O. d'Este-M.

"MADEMOISELLE,—Is it quite fair in you to come and establish yourself in a poor poet's heart with the admitted purpose of leaving him to his fate if he should not be to your mind, and bequeathing to him perennial regrets after showing him, for a few minutes, an image of perfection were it but assumed, or, at least, a first promise of happiness?

"I was wanting in foresight when I requested the letter in which you have begun the display of your elegant assortment of ideas. A man may well fall in love with a stranger who can unite so much daring with so much originality, such fancy with such feeling. Who but would long to know you after reading these first confidences? It is only by a really great effort that I preserve my balance when I think of you, for in you are combined all things that can disturb a man's heart and brain. So I take advantage of the remains of coolness I am able to preserve to put the case humbly before you.

"Do you believe, mademoiselle, that letters which are more or less truthful in relation to life as it really is, and more or less insincere, since the letters we may write to each other must be the expression of the moment when we send them forth, and not the general outcome of our characters—do you believe, I ask, that however fine they may be, these letters can ever take the place of the expression of ourselves we should give through the practical evidence of daily life? Each man is twofold: There is the invisible life of the spirit, which letters may satisfy, and the mechanical life, to which we attach, alas! more importance than you, at your age, can imagine. These two existences ought both to agree with the ideal you cherish, and this, it may be said, very rarely happens.

"The pure, spontaneous, disinterested homage of a solitary soul, at once well-informed and chaste, is one of those heavenly flowers whose color and fragrance are a consolation for every grief, every wound, every mortification entailed by a literary life in Paris; and I thank you with a fervor equal to your own; but after this poetical exchange of my woes in return for the pearls of your charity, what can you expect? I have neither the genius nor the splendid position of Lord Byron; above all, I have not the halo of his artificial damnation and his imaginary social grievances; but what would you have hoped for from him in similar circumstances? His friendship, no doubt. Well, he, who ought only to have been proud, was eaten up by an offensive and sickly vanity which discouraged friendship. I, who am a thousand times less great than he—may not I too have such discords of nature as make life unpleasing, and turn friendship into the most difficult burden? What will you get in return for your dreams? The vexations of a life which will not be wholly yours.

"The bargain is a mad one, for this reason: The poetry of your dreams is but a plagiarism. A young German girl, not half-German like you, but wholly German, in the intoxication of her twenty years, adored Goethe; she made him her friend, her religion, her god, knowing that he was married. Frau Goethe, a good German soul, a poet's wife, lent herself to this worship with very shrewd complacency—which failed to cure Bettina! But what was the end? The ecstatic married some substantial worthy German. Between ourselves, let us confess that a girl who should have made herself the handmaid of a genius, who should have raised herself to his level by understanding him, and have adored him piously till her death—as one of those divine figures might have done that painters have represented on the doors of their mystical shrines—and who, when Germany should lose Goethe, would have retired to some wilderness never more to see mankind—as Lord Bolingbroke's lady did—let us confess that this girl would have lived for ever in the poet's glory as Mary Magdalen does in the blood-stained triumph of the Saviour.

"If this is sublime, what do you say to the converse of it?

"Being neither Lord Byron nor Goethe, but merely the writer of a few approved poems, I cannot claim the honors of worship. I have little in me of the martyr. I have a heart, but I am also ambitious, for I have to make my fortune, and I am yet young. See me as I am. The King's favor and the patronage of his Ministers afford me a decent maintenance; I have all the habits of a very commonplace man. I go to evening parties exactly like the first fool you meet; but my carriage-wheels do not run, as the present times require, on ground made solid under me by securities in the State funds.

"Though I am not rich, I have not, on the other hand, the distinction conferred by a garret, by neglected work, by glory in penury, on certain men of greater merit than mine; for instance, on d'Arthez.

"What prosaic fifth act will you not find for the enchanted fancy of your young enthusiasm? Let it rest here. If I have been so happy as to seem to you an earthly wonder, you will have been to me something radiant and supernal, like a star that blazes and vanishes. Let nothing tarnish this episode in our lives. By remaining as we are, I may love you, going through one of those mad passions which break down every obstacle and light fires in the heart, which are alarming by their violence out of all proportion to their duration; and, supposing that I should succeed in pleasing you, we must end in the vulgarest way—marriage, housekeeping, and children! Oh, Bélise and Henriette Chrysale in one, can that be? So, farewell."

IX.

To Monsieur de Canalis.

"My Friend,—Your letter gave me as much pain as pleasure. Perhaps we may soon find it all pleasure to read each other's letters. Understand me. We speak to God, we ask of Him many things; He remains speechless. Now I want to have from you the answers God never gives us. Cannot such a friendship as that of Mademoiselle de Gournay and Montaigne be repeated? Have you not known the household of Sismonde de Sismondi, at Geneva, the most touching home-life ever seen, and of which I have been told—something like that of the Marchese and Marchesa di Pescara, happy even in their old age? Good heavens! is it impossible that there should be two harps, which, though at a distance, respond to each other as in a symphony, and vibrate so as to produce delicious harmony? Man alone, in all creation, is at once the harp, the musician, and the hearer.

"Do you see me fretting after the manner of ordinary women? Do not I know that you go into society and see the handsomest and cleverest women in Paris? Can I not imagine that one of those sirens might embrace you in her cold scales, and that it is she who has sent the answer that grieves me by its prosaic reflections? There is, my friend, something more beautiful than these flowers of Parisian blandishment; there is a flower that grows at the height of those Alpine peaks called men of genius; the pride of humanity, which they fructify by shedding on it the clouds they collect with their heads in the skies; that flower I intend to cultivate and to make it open, for its wild, sweet perfumes will never fail us; they are perennial.

"Do me the honor to believe that in me there is nothing common. If I had been Bettina—for I know to whom you allude—I would never have been Frau von Arnim; and if I had been one of Lord Byron's loves, I should at this moment be in a convent. You have touched me in a sensitive spot.

"You do not know me; you will know me. I feel in myself a sublime something which may be spoken of without vanity. God has implanted in my soul the root of that hybrid plant I have mentioned as native to Alpine heights, and I will not stick it in a flower-pot at my window to see it perish. No, that gorgeous and unique blossom, full of intoxicating fragrance, shall not be dragged through the vulgarities of life; it is yours—yours without a glance having blighted it, yours for ever! Yes, dear one, yours are all my thoughts, even the most secret, the most mad; yours is the heart of a girl without reserve; yours an infinite affection. If I do not like you personally, I shall not marry.

"I can live the life of the heart, the life of your mind, of your feelings; they please me, and I shall always be, as I am now, your friend. There is beauty of nature in you, and that is enough for me. There lies my life. Do not disdain a pretty young handmaiden who, for her part, does not shrink from the idea of being some day the poet's old housekeeper, in some sort his housewife, in some sort his common-sense, in some sort his wealth. This devoted maid, so precious in your lives, is pure, disinterested Friendship, to whom everything is revealed; who listens sometimes with a shake of the head, and who sits late, spinning by the light of the lamp, to be at hand when the poet comes home, soaked by the rain or out of sorts. This is my destiny if I am never to be a happy and faithfully attached wife: I can smile on one as on the other.

"And do not suppose that France will be deeply aggrieved if Mademoiselle d'Este does not give her two or three children, or refuses even to be a Madame Vilquin, or the like? I, for my part, shall never be an old maid. I shall make myself a motherhood by beneficence, and by secretly sharing the existence of a great man, to whom I shall dedicate all my thoughts and all my earthly efforts. I have the utmost horror of the commonplace. If I should be free and rich—and I know I am young and handsome—I will never become the property of some simpleton under the excuse of his being the son of a peer of France; nor of some good-looking man, who would be the woman of the two; nor of any man who would make me blush twenty times a day at the thought that I was his. Be quite easy on that score.

"My father adores my wishes too much ever to contravene them. If my poet likes me, if I like him, the glorious palace of our love will be built so high that it will be absolutely inaccessible to misfortune. I am an eaglet; you will see it in my eye. I will not repeat what I have already told you, but I put it into fewer words when I assure you that I shall be of all women the most glad to be as completely the captive of love, as I am at this moment of my father's will.

"Come, my friend, let us reduce to the truth of romance what has come upon us by my free-will.

"A girl of lively imagination shut up in a turret is dying to run about in a park which only her eyes can explore; she invents a way of opening her bars, she springs out of window, climbs the park wall, and goes off to sport at her neighbor's. It is the eternal comedy! . . . Well, that girl is my soul, the neighboring park is your genius. Is it not most natural? Was a neighbor ever heard of who complained of his trellis being damaged by pretty feet?

"So much for the poet; but must the ultra-reasonable hero of Molière's comedies have reasons? Here are plenty. My dear Géronte, marriages are commonly made in direct opposition to common-sense. A family makes inquiries as to a young man. If this Léandre, provided by a friendly gossip, or picked up in a ballroom, has robbed no one, if he has no visible stain, if he has as much money as is expected, if he has come from college or has had a legal training, thus satisfying the usual ideas of education, he is allowed to call on a young lady, dressed to receive him from the moment when she gets up, instructed by her mother to be careful of what she says, and enjoined to keep anything of her soul or heart from being read in her countenance by assuming a set smile, like a dancer finishing a pirouette; she is armed with the most positive instructions as to the perils of showing her true character, and advised not to appear too distressingly knowing. The parents, when all the points of interest are satisfactorily settled between them, are simple-minded enough to recommend the young people to know all they can of each other during the few moments when they are alone, when they talk together, when they walk out—without any kind of freedom, for they know that they are tied already. Under such conditions a man dresses his mind as carefully as his person, and the girl on her side does the same. This miserable farce, carried on with gifts of flowers and jewels and places at the play, is what is called courting a girl.

"This is what I rebel against, and I mean to make legal marriage the outcome of a long marriage of souls. In all a girl's life this is the only moment when she needs reflection, insight, and experience. Her liberty and happiness are at stake, and you place neither the dice nor the box in her hands; she bets on the game; she is but a looker-on. I have the right, the will, and the power to work out my own woe, and I will use them—as my mother did when, guided by instinct, she married the most generous, devoted, and loving of men, who bewitched her one evening by his beauty. I know you to be single, a poet, and handsome. You may be sure that I never should have chosen for my confidant one of your brethren in Apollo who was married. If my mother was attracted by a handsome face, which is perhaps the genius of form, why should not I be attracted by mind and form combined? Shall I know you better after studying you by correspondence than after beginning by the vulgar method of so many months of courting? 'That is the question,' saith Hamlet.

"My plan, my dear Chrysale, has at least the advantage of not compromising our persons. I know that love has its illusions, and every illusion has its morrow. Therein lies the reason why so many lovers part who believed themselves bound for life. The true test lies in suffering and in happiness. When, after standing this double test of life, two beings have shown all their faults and good qualities, and have learned each other's characters, they may go to the tomb hand in hand; but, my dear Argante, who tells you that our little drama has no future before it? . . . And, at any rate, shall we not have had the pleasure of our correspondence?

"I await your commands, monseigneur, and remain, with all my heart, yours obediently,

"O. D'ESTE-M."

X.

To Mademoiselle O. d'Este-M.

"You are a demon! I love you. Is that what you want, extraordinary girl? Perhaps you only wish to divert your leisure in the country by looking on at the follies of which a poet is capable? That would be a very wicked thing. Your two letters betray just enough of mischief to suggest the doubt to a Parisian. But I am no longer master of myself; my life and future hang on the answer you may send me. Tell me whether the certain possession of an unbounded affection given to you, in defiance of social conventionalities, can touch you; if you will allow me to visit you. There will still be ample room for doubt and agony of mind in the question whether I shall be personally agreeable to you. If your answer is favorable, I alter my life, and bid adieu to many vexations which we are so foolish as to call happiness.

"Happiness, my dear, beautiful, unknown one, is what you have dreamed it; a perfect fusion of feelings, an absolute harmony of souls, a keen sense of ideal beauty—so far as God vouchsafes it to us here below—stamped on the common actions of a life whose round we are bound to follow; above all constancy of heart, far more precious than what we call fidelity. Can anything be called a sacrifice when the end is the supremest good, the dream of poets and of maidens, the poem to which on entering life—as soon as the spirit tries its wings—every lofty mind looks up with longing, brooding eyes, only to see it dashed to pieces against a stumbling-stone as hard as it is vulgar; for almost every man sees the foot of reality set down at once on that mysterious egg which hardly ever hatches out?

"I will not as yet tell you of myself, of my past, of my character, nor of an affection—almost motherly on one side, and on mine almost filial—in which you have already wrought a change with results in my life that may explain the word sacrifice. You have made me forgetful, not to say ungrateful. Is that enough to satisfy you? Oh! speak! Say one word, and I shall love you till my eyes are closed in death, as Pescara loved his wife, as Romeo loved his Juliet, and faithfully. Our life—mine, at any rate—will be that untroubled happiness of which Dante speaks as being the atmosphere of his 'Paradiso' —a poem infinitely superior to his 'Inferno.'

"Strange to say, it is not myself, but you, whom I doubt in the long meditations in which I have allowed myself—like you, perhaps—to follow the chimerical course of a dream-life. Yes, dear one, I feel in me the strength to love thus, to go on my way to the tomb gently, slowly, always smiling, arm in arm with the woman I love, without a cloud on the fair weather of my soul. Yes, I have courage enough to look forward to our old age together, to see us both with white hair, like the venerable historian of Italy, still inspired by the same affection, but changed by the spirit of each season.

"You see, I can no longer be no more than your friend. Though Chrysale, Oronte, and Argante, you say, have come to life again in me, I am not yet so senile as to drink of a cup held by the fair hands of a veiled woman without feeling a fierce desire to tear away the domino, the mask, and to see her face. Either write no more, or give me hope. I must have a glimpse of you, or throw up the game. Must I say farewell? Will you allow me to sign myself,

"YOUR FRIEND?"

XI.

To Monsieur de Canalis.

"What flattery! How quickly has grave Anselme turned into a dashing Léandre! To what am I to ascribe such a change? Is it to the black I have scribbled on white, to the ideas which are to the flowers of my soul what a rose drawn in black-lead pencil is to the roses of the garden? Or to the remembrance of the girl you took for me, who is to my real self what a waiting-maid is to her mistress? Have we exchanged parts? Am I reason, and are you folly?

"A truce to this nonsense. Your letter made me acquainted with intoxicating joys of soul, the first I have not owed to family feelings. What, a poet has asked, are the ties of blood which weigh so heavily on ordinary souls in comparison with those which Heaven forges for us of mysterious sympathies? Let me thank you—no, there are no thanks for such things. Blessings on you for the happiness you have given me; may you be happy with the gladness you poured into my soul.

"You have explained to me some apparent injustice in social life. There is something brilliant in glory, something masculine which becomes men alone, and God has prohibited women from wearing this halo, while giving us love and tenderness with which to refresh the brows on which its awful light rests. I feel my mission, or rather, you have confirmed me in it.

"Sometimes, my friend, I have risen in the morning in a frame of inconceivable sweetness. A sort of peace, tender and divine, gave me a sense as of Heaven. My first thought was like a blessing. I used to call these mornings my German *levers,* to distinguish them from my southern sunsets, full of heroic deeds of battles, of Roman festivals, and of ardent verse. Well, after having read the letter into which you breathed a fever of impatience, I felt in my heart the lightness of one of those heavenly awakenings, when I loved air and nature, and felt myself destined to die for some one I loved. One of your poems, 'Le Chant d'une jeune fille,' describes these delicious hours when gladness is sweet, when prayer is a necessity, and it is my favorite piece. Shall I put all my flattery into one line: I think you worthy to be me!

"Your letter, though short, allowed me to read your heart. Yes, I could guess your tumultuous impulses, your excited curiosity, your plans, all the faggots carried (by whom) for the pyre of your heart. But I do not yet know enough of you to comply with your request. Understand, dear one, it is mystery which allows me the freedom that betrays the depths of my soul. When once we have met, farewell to our knowledge of each other.

"Shall we make a bargain? Was the first we made a bad one for you? You gained my esteem by it. And admiration supported by esteem is a great thing, my friend. First write me a sketch of your life in a few words; then tell me about your life in Paris, day by day, without any disguise, as if you were chatting to an old friend: well, then, after that I will carry our friendship a step further. I will see you, my friend, that I promise you; and it is a great deal.

"All this, dear, I warn you, is neither an intrigue nor an adventure; it cannot result in any kind of 'affair' of gallantry, as you men say among yourselves. My life is involved in it, and moreover—a thing which sometimes causes me terrible remorse as to the thoughts I send flying to you in flocks—not less involved is the life of a father and mother I adore, whom I must satisfy in my choice, and who in my friend must find a son.

"How far can you lordly souls, to whom God has given the wings of angels, but not always their perfections, yield to the Family and its petty needs? A text I have pondered over already! Although before going forth to you I said in my heart, 'Be bold!' it has not quaked the less on the road, and I have never deceived myself either as to the roughness of the way or the difficulties of the mountain I had to climb. I have followed it all out in long meditations. Do I not know that men as eminent as you are have known the love they have inspired quite as well as that they have felt; that they have had more than one romance; and that you, above all, while cherishing those thoroughbred chimeras which a woman will buy at any cost, have gone through more final than first chapters? And yet I could say to myself, 'Be bold!' because I have studied the geography of the high peaks of Humanity that you accuse of coldness—studied them more than you think. Did you not say of Byron and Goethe that they were two colossal masses of egoism and poetry? Ah, my friend, you there fall into the error of superficial minds; but it was perhaps generosity on your part, false modesty, or the hope of evading me.

"The vulgar may be allowed, but you may not, to regard the results of hard work as a development of the individual. Neither Lord Byron, nor Goethe, nor Walter Scott, nor Cuvier, nor any inventor belongs to himself; they are all the slaves of an idea; and this mysterious power is more jealous than a woman, it absorbs them, it makes them or kills them for its own advantage. The visible outcome of this concealed life resembles egoism in its effects; but how dare we say that a man who has sold himself for the delight, the instruction, or the greatness of his age, is an egoist? Is a mother accused of selfishness when she sacrifices everything for her child? Well, the detractors of genius do not discern its teeming maternity, that is all.

"The poet's life is so perpetual a sacrifice that he needs a gigantic organization to enable him to enjoy the pleasures of an ordinary life. Hence, if, like Molière, he insists on living the life of feelings while giving them expression in their most acute crises, what disasters come upon him! for to me the comic side of Molière, as overlaying his private life, is really horrible. The magnanimity of genius seems to me almost divine, and I have classed you with that noble family of egoists so called. Oh! if I had found shallowness, self-interest, and ambition where, as it is, I admire all the flowers of the soul that I love best, you cannot know what slow suffering would have consumed me. I found disappointment sitting at the portal of my sixteenth year; what should I have done if at twenty I had found fame a liar, and the man, who in his writings had expressed so many of the sentiments buried in my heart, incapable of understanding that heart when disclosed to him alone?

"Do you know, my friend, what would have become of me? I am going to admit you to the very depths of my soul. Well, I should have said to my father, 'Bring me any son-in-law to your mind; I give up all free-will; get me married to please yourself!'—and the man might have been a notary, a banker, avaricious, stupid, provincial, as tiresome as a rainy day, as vulgar as a parish voter; he might have been a manufacturer or some brave but brainless soldier—he would have found in me his most resigned and attentive slave. But then—dreadful suicide at every instant!—my soul would never have unfolded in the life-giving beams of the sun it worships. Not a murmur should ever have revealed to my father, my mother, or my children the suicide of the being who is at this moment shaking its prison-bars, flashing lightnings from my eyes, flying to you on outspread pinions, perching like a Polyhymnia in the corner of your study, breathing its atmosphere, and gazing at everything with a mildly inquisitive eye. Sometimes in the fields, where my husband might have taken me, I should have escaped a little way from my babes, and, seeing a lovely morning, would secretly have shed a few very bitter tears. Finally, in my heart, and in the corner of a drawer, I should have stored a little comfort for every girl betrayed by love, poor poetical souls dragged into torments by a smiling face!

"But I believe in you, my friend. This faith purifies the most fantastic notions of my secret ambition, and sometimes —see how frank I can be—I long to be in the middle of the story we have just begun, so assured am I of my feelings, such strength for love do I feel in my heart, such constancy founded on reason, such heroism to fulfil the duty I am creating for myself in case love should ever turn to duty.

"If it were given to you to follow me to the splendid seclusion where I picture our happiness, if you could know my schemes, you might utter some terrible sentence about madness, and I should perhaps be cruelly punished for sending so much poetry to a poet. Yes, I want to be a living spring, to be as inexhaustible as a beautiful country during the twenty years which nature allows us to shine in. I will keep satiety at a distance by refinements and variety. I will be brave for my love as other women are for the world. I will vary happiness, lend wit to tenderness, and piquancy to faithfulness. I am ambitious; I will kill my past rivals, dispel superficial troubles by the sweetness, the proud self-devotion of a wife, and, for a whole lifetime, give such care to the nest as a bird gives for only a few days. This immense dower ought, and could, only be offered to a great man before being dropped into the mire of vulgar conventionality.

"Now, do you still think my first letter a mistake? A gust of some mysterious will flung me towards you, as a tempest may carry a rose-bush to the heart of a stately willow. And in the letter I keep here—next my heart—you have exclaimed like your ancestor when he set out for the crusades, 'It is God's will!'

"You will be saying, 'How she chatters!' All those about me say, 'Mademoiselle is very silent!'

"O. D'ESTE-M."

These letters seemed very original to those persons to whose kindness the author of the *Comédie Humaine* is beholden for them; but their admiration for this duel between two minds crossing their pens, while their faces were hidden by the strictest incognito, may not be generally shared. Of a hundred spectators, eighty perhaps will be tired of this assault of arms. So the respect due to the majority—even to a possible majority—in every country enjoying a constitutional government, advises the suppression of eleven more letters exchanged by Ernest and Modeste during the month of September; if a flattering majority should clamor for them, let us hope that it may one day afford me the means of restoring them here.

Tempted on by a wit as audacious as the heart beneath

seemed to be adorable, the poor private secretary's really heroic feelings gave themselves the rein in those letters, which each reader's imagination may conceive of as finer than they really are, when picturing this harmony of two unfettered souls. Ernest, indeed, lived only on these dear scraps of paper, as a miser lives on those sent forth by the bank; while in Modeste a deep attachment had grown up in the place of the pleasure of bringing excitement into a life of celebrity, and being, in spite of distance, its chief element. Ernest's affection completed Canalis' glory. Alas! it often takes two men to make one perfect lover, just as in literature a type can only be produced by a compound of the peculiarities of several different characters. How often has a woman said in a drawing-room after some intimate talk: "That man would be my ideal as to his soul, but I feel that I love that other who is no more than a fancy of my senses!"

The last letter written by Modeste, which here follows, gives us a glimpse of the *Isle of Pheasants,* whither the divagations of this correspondence was conducting our lovers.

XII.

To Monsieur de Canalis.

"Be at le Havre on Sunday; go into the church after the one o'clock service, walk round it two or three times, go out without speaking to anyone, without asking anybody a question; wear a white rose in your button-hole. Then return to Paris, you will there find an answer. This answer will not be such as you expect, for I must tell you, the future is not yet in my hands. But should I not be really mad to say *yes* without having seen you? When I have seen you, I can say *no* without offence. I am sure to remain unrecognized."

This was the letter Modeste had sent off the very day before that on which the futile struggle between herself and Dumay had taken place. So she was happy in looking forward with yearning impatience to Sunday, when her eyes would prove her intuitions, her heart, to be right or wrong—one of the most solemn moments in a woman's life, made, too, as romantic as the most enthusiastic girl could desire by three months of communion soul to soul.

Everybody, excepting her mother, had taken this torpor of expectancy for the placidity of innocence. However stringent the laws of family life and religious bonds, there are still Julies d'Étanges and Clarissas—souls which, like a brimming cup, overflow under the divine touch. Was not Modeste splendid in the fierce energy she brought to bear on repressing her exuberant youth, and remaining concealed? Let us confess that the memory of her sister was more potent than any social limitations; she had sheathed her will in iron that she might not fail her father or her family. But what a turbulent upheaval! and how could a mother fail to perceive it?

On the following day Modeste and Madame Dumay led Madame Mignon out into the noonday sun to her bench among the flowers. The blind woman turned her pale withered face towards the ocean, inhaled the scent of the sea, and took Modeste's hand in her own, for the girl was sitting by her mother. Even as she was about to question her child, the mother hesitated between forgiveness and remonstrance, for she knew that this was love, and to her, as to the false Canalis, Modeste seemed exceptional.

"If only your father may be here in time! If he delays much longer, he will find you alone of those he loved! Promise me once more, Modeste, never to leave him," she said, with motherly persuasiveness.

Modeste raised her mother's hands to her lips, and kissed them softly, as she replied:

"Need I tell you so again?"

"Ah, my child; you see, I myself left my father to go to my husband! And my father was alone too; I was his only child. . . . Is that what God is punishing me for, I wonder?—All I ask you is to marry in agreement with your father's choice, to keep a place for him in your heart, not to sacrifice him to your happiness; to keep him in the bosom of your family. Before I lost my sight I made a note of my wishes; he will carry them out; I have enjoined on him to keep the whole of his fortune, not that I have a thought of distrusting you, but can one ever be sure about a son-in-law? I, my child, was I prudent? A flash of an eye settled my whole life. Beauty, the most deceitful of shows, spoke the truth to me; but if it should ever be the same with you, poor child, swear to me that if appearances should carry you away, as they did your mother, you would leave it to your father to make inquiries as to the character, the heart, and the previous life of the man of your choice, if you make a choice."

"I will never marry without my father's consent," replied Modeste.

On hearing this answer, her mother sat in complete silence, and her half-dead countenance showed that she was pondering on it, as blind people ponder, meditating on her daughter's tone in speaking of it.

"You see, my child," said Madame Mignon, after a long silence, "the thing is this: If Caroline's wrong-doing is killing me by inches, your father would never survive yours; I know him; he would blow his brains out; there would be neither life nor happiness on earth for him . . ."

Modeste walked away a few steps, and returned in a minute.

"Why did you leave me?" asked Madame Mignon.

"You made me cry, mamma," said Modeste.

"Well, my angel, kiss me then. You love no one here? You have no one paying attentions to you?"

"No, mamma," said the little Jesuit.

"Can you swear to that?"

"Really, truly!" cried Modeste.

Madame Mignon said no more; she still doubted.

"In short, if you should choose a husband, your father would know all about it?"

"I promised that to my sister and to you, mother. What sin do you suppose I could commit when every minute I read on my finger, *Remember Bettina!*—Poor little sister!"

At the moment when the words, "Poor little sister!" were

followed by an interval of silence between Modeste and her mother, from whose darkened eyes fell tears which Modeste could not check even by falling at Madame Mignon's knees and crying, "Forgive me; forgive me, mamma!"—at that very moment the worthy Dumay was mounting the hill of Ingouville at a rapid pace, an abnormal incident in the cashier's life.

Three letters had once brought them ruin; one had brought fortune back to them. That morning Dumay had received, by the hand of a captain just returned from the China seas, the first news he had had of his patron and only friend.

*To Monsieur Dumay, formerly cashier to the
firm of Mignon.*

"MY DEAR DUMAY,—Barring misadventure by sea, I shall follow closely on the vessel by which I am forwarding this letter; I would not leave the ship to which I am accustomed. I told you, No news was to be good news; but the first words of this letter will rejoice you, for those words are, I have at least seven millions of francs! I am bringing a large part of it in indigo, a third in good bills on London and Paris, another third in bright gold. The money you sent me enabled me to make the sum I had determined on—two millions for each of the girls, and comfort for myself.

"I have been dealing wholesale in opium for the Canton houses, all ten times as rich as I am. You have no notion in Europe of what the rich China merchants are. I traveled from Asia Minor, where I could buy opium cheap, to Canton, where I sold it in bulk to the firms that deal in it.

"My last voyage was to the Malay Archipelago, where I could buy indigo of the first quality with the proceeds of the opium trade. Perhaps I may find that I have five or six hundred thousand francs more, as I am valuing my indigo only at cost price.

"I have been quite well all the time; never an ailment. That is the reward of traveling for one's children! At the beginning of the second year I was able to purchase the *Mignon,* a nice brig of seven hundred tons burden, built of teak, and lined with the same, and copper-bottomed; fitted throughout to suit my convenience. This, too, is worth something. The seafaring life, the constant change needed in my trading, and hard work, as being in a way my own captain on the high seas, have all kept me in excellent health.

"To speak of all this is to speak of my two girls and my dear wife! I hope that on hearing of my ruin the wretch who robbed me of my Bettina may have deserted her, and the wandering lamb have returned to the cottage. She, no doubt, will need a larger dower.

"My three women and my good Dumay—you have all four been constantly in my thoughts during these three years. Dumay, you are a rich man. Your share, besides my own fortune, amounts to five hundred and sixty thousand francs, which I am forwarding to you by a draft, payable to yourself only, by the firm of Mongenod, who are advised from New York. A few months more and I shall see you all again —well, I hope.

"Now, my dear Dumay, I write to you only, because I wish you to keep the secret of my fortune, and I leave it to you to prepare my dear ones for the joy of my return. I have had enough of trade, and I mean to leave le Havre.

"The choice of my sons-in-law is a very serious matter. It is my intention to repurchase the estate and château of la Bastie, to endow it with an entailed settlement of a hundred thousand francs a year at least, and to petition the King to confer my name and titles on one of my sons-in-law. You, my dear Dumay, know the misfortune that befell us in consequence of the fatal splendor given by wealth. By that I wrecked the honor of one of my daughters. I carried back to Java the most wretched of fathers—an unhappy Dutch merchant with nine millions of francs, whose two daughters had been both carried off by villains! We wept together like two children. So I will not have the amount of my fortune known.

"I shall not land at le Havre, but at Marseilles. My mate is a Provençal, an old retainer of my family, whom I have enabled to make a little fortune. Castagnould will have my instructions to repurchase la Bastie, and I shall dispose of my indigo through the firm of Mongenod. I shall place my money in the Bank of France, and come home to you, professing to have made no more than about a million of francs in merchandise. My daughters will be reputed to have two hundred thousand francs apiece. Then my great business will be to decide which of my sons-in-law may be worthy to succeed to my name, my arms, and my titles, and to live with us; but they must both be, as you and I are, absolutely steady, firm, loyal, and honest men.

"I have never doubted you, old boy, for a single instant. I have felt sure that my dear and admirable wife, with yours and yourself, will have drawn an impassable fence round my daughter, and that I may press a kiss full of hope on the pure brow of the angel that remains to me. Bettina-Caroline, if you have been able to screen her fault, will have a fortune. After trying war and trade, we will now go in for agriculture, and you must be our steward. Will that suit you?

"And so, old friend, you are master of your line of conduct to the family, to tell them, or to say nothing of my success. I trust to your judgment; you are to say just what you think right. In four years there may have been many changes of character. I make you the judge; I so greatly fear my wife's tender weakness with her daughters.

"Farewell, my dear old Dumay. Tell my wife and daughters that I have never failed to embrace them in my heart every day, morning and evening. The second draft, for forty thousand francs, payable, like the other, to you alone, is for my wife and daughters to go on with.

"Your master and friend,
"CHARLES MIGNON."

"Your father is coming home," said Madame Mignon to her daughter.

"What makes you think that, mamma?" asked Modeste.

"Nothing could make Dumay run but having that news to bring us."

Modeste, lost in her own thoughts, had not seen nor heard Dumay.

"Victory!" shouted the Lieutenant from the gate. "Madame, the Colonel has never been ill, and he is coming home. . . . He is coming on the *Mignon,* a good ship of his own, which, with the cargo he describes to me, must be worth eight or nine hundred thousand francs. But he urgently begs you will say nothing about it; the disaster to our poor lost child has eaten deeply into his heart."

"He has made room in it for a grave then," said Madame Mignon.

"And he ascribes this disaster—as seems to me most probable—to the greed which a large fortune excites in young men. My poor Colonel hopes to find the lost lamb among us here.—Let us rejoice among ourselves, and say nothing to anybody, not even to Latournelle if possible.—Mademoiselle," he added to Modeste apart, "write a letter to your father to tell him of the loss in the family and its terrible consequences, so as to prepare him for the dreadful sight that awaits him; I will undertake that he shall get the letter before arriving at le Havre, for he will be obliged to come through Paris; write fully, you have plenty of time; I will take the letter on Monday; on Monday, no doubt, I shall have to go to Paris——"

Modeste was now afraid lest Dumay and Canalis should meet; she was eager to go up to her room and write to put off the assignation.

"Tell me, mademoiselle," Dumay went on in the humblest tone, but standing in her path, "that your father will find his daughter without a feeling in her heart but that which was in it when he left—of love for her mother."

"I have sworn to my sister and my mother—I have sworn to myself to be my father's comfort, his joy, and his pride, and—I—will be," replied Modeste, with a haughty and scornful glance at Dumay. "Do not mar my joy at knowing that my father will soon be amongst us again by any offensive suspicions. A young girl's heart cannot be hindered from beating; you do not wish me to be a mummy? I belong to my family; but my heart is my own. If I love any one, my father and mother shall be told of it. Are you satisfied, monsieur?"

"Thank you, mademoiselle," replied Dumay. "You have restored me to life. But you might at least have called me Dumay, even when giving me a slap in the face!"

"Swear to me," said her mother, "that you have never exchanged a word or a glance with any young man."

"I can swear it," said Modeste, smiling, and looking at Dumay, who was studying her, with a mischievous smile like a girl's playing off some joke.

"Can she really be so false!" exclaimed Dumay, when Modeste had gone into the house.

"My daughter Modeste may have her faults," said the mother, "but she is incapable of a lie."

"Well, then, let us make ourselves easy," replied the lieutenant, "and be satisfied that misfortune has closed its account with us."

"God grant it!" said Madame Mignon. "You will see him, Dumay; I can only hear him. . . . There is much sadness in my joy."

Modeste, meanwhile, though happy in the thought of her father's return, was, like Pierrette, distressed to see all her eggs broken. She had hoped for a larger fortune than Dumay had spoken of. She was ambitious for her poet, and wished for at least half of the six millions of which she had written in her second letter. Thus absorbed by her double happiness, and annoyed by the grievance of her comparative poverty, she sat down to her piano, the confidant of so many girls, who tell it their anger, and their wishes, expressing them in their way of playing.

Dumay was talking to his wife, walking to and fro below her window, confiding to her the secret of their good fortune, and questioning her as to her hopes, wishes, and intentions. Madame Dumay, like her husband, had no family but the Mignon family. The husband and wife decided on living in Provence, if the Count should go to Provence, and to leave their money to any child of Modeste's that might need it.

"Listen to Modeste," said Madame Mignon to them; "only a girl in love could compose such a melody without any knowledge of music."

Homes may burn, fortunes may collapse, fathers may come back from their travels, Empires may fall, cholera may ravage the town—a girl's love pursues its flight as nature keeps her course, or that horrible acid discovered by chemistry which might pierce through the earth if it were not absorbed in the centre.

This is the ballad Modeste had improvised to some verses which must be quoted here, though they are to be found in the second volume of poems published by Dauriat; for, to adapt them to the air, the young composer had broken the rhythm by some changes which might puzzle the admirers of a poet who is sometimes too precise.

And here, too, since modern typography allows of it, is Modeste's music, to which her exquisite expression lent the charm we admire in the greatest singers—a charm that no printing, were it phonetic or hieroglyphic, could ever represent.

A MAIDEN'S SONG.

MODESTE MIGNON

Come a- wake, my heart, for the soar-ing lark.......... Wings her up-ward flight as she chants her lay. Sleep no more, my heart, for the vi - o - let Breathes her

in - cense to God at break of day, Ev - 'ry
blos - som re - fresh'd, and soft - ly un - clos - ing,
O - pens an eye to be - hold it - self...... fair. In each
chal - ice a gem, a dew - drop re - pos - ing,
3
3

Mir - rors its hues Ere it dies in the air. We
feel in the breeze that the an - gel of flow - ers Has
kiss'd ev - 'ry rose as he pass'd in the night, Has
guard - ed their beau - ty through all the dark hours, Their

first smile is his in the sweet morn - ing light.
Then a - wake, my heart, for the soar - ing lark
Wings her ear - ly flight, and chants her lay.
3
Night and sleep be - gone! my heart, the vi - o - let

MODESTE MIGNON

To God her in - cense breathes at break of day.

Night and sleep be - gone! my heart, the vi - o - let To

God her in - cense breathes at break of day.

"It is pretty," said Madame Dumay. "Modeste is very musical; that is all."

"She has the very devil in her!" exclaimed the cashier, for the mother's dread had entered into his soul and made his blood run cold.

"She is in love," said Madame Mignon.

By her success in communicating her conviction as to Modeste's secret passion, on the irrefragable evidence of that melody, Madame Mignon chilled the cashier's joy over his patron's return and success. The worthy Breton went off to the town to do his day's business at Gobenheim's; then, before going home to dinner, he called on the Latournelles to mention his fears, and once more to request their help and co-operation.

"Yes, my good friend," said Dumay on the threshold, as he took leave of the notary, "I am of madame's opinion. She is in love, sure enough; beyond that the devil only knows! . . . I am disgraced!"

"Do not worry yourself, Dumay," said the little notary. "We certainly, among us all, must be a match for that little lady. Sooner or later every girl who is in love does something rash which betrays her secret; we will talk it over this evening."

So all these persons, devoted to the Mignon family, were still a prey to the same anxiety as had tormented them before the experiment that the old soldier had expected to be decisive. The futility of all these struggles so spurred Dumay's conscience that he would not go to Paris to fetch his fortune before he had discovered the clue to this enigma. All these hearts, caring far more for sentiment than for self-interest, understood that unless he found this daughter innocently pure, the Colonel might die of grief on finding Bettina dead and his wife blind. The unhappy Dumay's despair made so deep an impression on the Latournelles, that they forgot their loss of Exupère, whom they had sent off to Paris that morning. During the dinner hour, when the three were alone, Monsieur and Madame Latournelle and Butscha turned the matter over under every aspect, and considered every conceivable hypothesis.

"If Modeste were in love with any one at le Havre, she would have quaked last night," said Madame Latournelle, "so her lover must be elsewhere."

"She swore this morning to her mother, in Dumay's presence, that she had not exchanged a glance or a word with a living soul," said the notary.

"Then she loves as I do!" said Butscha.

"And how do you love, my poor boy?" asked Madame Latournelle.

"Madame," replied the little hunchback, "I love all to myself, from afar, almost as far as from hence to the stars."

"And how do you get there, you great goose?" said Madame Latournelle, smiling at him.

"Ah, madame, what you take to be a hump is the sheath for my wings."

"Then this explains your seal!" exclaimed the lawyer.

The clerk's seal was a star, with the motto, *Fulgens, sequar* —Shine, and I will follow you—the device of the house of Chastillonest.

"A beautiful creature may be as diffident as the most hideous," said Butscha, as if talking to himself. "Modeste is quite clever enough to have feared lest she should be loved only for her beauty."

Hunchbacks are wonderful creatures, and due entirely to civilization; for, in the scheme of nature, weak or deformed beings ought to perish. A curvature or twist of the spinal column gives to these men, who seem to be Nature's outcasts, a flashing look, in which is concentrated a greater quantity of nervous fluids than other men can command, in the very centre where they are elaborated and act, and whence they are sent forth like a light to vivify their inmost being. Certain forces are the result, detected occasionally by magnetism, but most frequently lost in the waste places of the spiritual world. Try to find a hunchback who is not gifted in some remarkable way, either with a cheerful wit, superlative malignity, or sublime kindliness. These beings, privileged beings though they know it not, live within themselves as Butscha did, when they have not exhausted their splendidly concentrated powers in the battle they have fought to conquer obstacles and remain alive.

In this way we may explain the superstitious and popular traditions, which we owe to the belief in gnomes, in frightful dwarfs, in misshapen fairies—the whole race of bottles, as Rabelais has it, that contain rare balsams and elixirs.

Thus Butscha almost read Modeste; and with the eagerness of a hopeless lover, of a slave ever ready to die like the soldiers who, deserted and alone amid Russian snows, still shouted *"Vive l'Empereur!"* he dreamed of discovering her secret for himself alone.

As his chief and Madame Latournelle walked up to the Chalet, he followed them with a very anxious mien, for it was imperative that he should conceal from every watchful eye, from every listening ear, the snare in which he meant to entrap the girl. There should be a flashing glance, a start detected, as when a surgeon lays his finger on a hidden injury.

That evening Gobenheim did not join them; Butscha was Monsieur Dumay's partner against Monsieur and Madame Latournelle. At about nine o'clock, while Modeste was absent preparing her mother's room, Madame Mignon and her friends could talk openly; but the poor clerk, stricken by the conviction which had come on him too, seemed as far away from the discussion as Gobenheim had been the night before.

"Why, Butscha, what ails you?" exclaimed Madame Latournelle, astonished at him. "One might think you had lost all your relations!"

A tear started to the poor fellow's eye—a foundling, deserted by a Swedish sailor, and his mother dead of grief in the workhouse!

"I have no one in the world but you," he replied in husky tones; "and your compassion is too pious ever to be withdrawn from me, for I will never cease to deserve your kindness."

The answer struck an equally sensitive chord in those present, that of delicacy.

"We all love you, Monsieur Butscha," said Madame Mignon with emotion.

"I have six hundred thousand francs of my own!" cried the worthy Dumay. "You shall be a notary at le Havre, and Latournelle's successor."

The American, for her part, had taken the poor hunchback's hand and pressed it.

"You have six hundred thousand francs!" cried Latournelle, pricking up his ears at this speech, "and you let these ladies stay here! And Modeste has no horse! And she no longer has lessons in music, in painting, in——"

"Oh, he has only had the money a few hours," exclaimed the American wife.

"Hush!" said Madame Mignon. While this was going on, the dignified Madame Latournelle had recovered herself. She turned to Butscha.

"My dear boy," said she, "you have so much affection around you, that I never considered the particular bearing of a common phrase as applied to you; but you may thank me for my blunder, since it has shown you what friends you have earned by your beautiful nature."

"Then you have some news of Monsieur Mignon?" asked the notary.

"He is coming home," said Madame Mignon; "but we must keep it secret.—When my husband hears how Butscha has clung to us, and that he has shown us the warmest and most disinterested friendship when the world turned its back on us, he will not leave you to provide for him entirely, Dumay. And so, my friend," she added, trying to turn towards Butscha, "you may proceed at once to deal with Latournelle——"

"He is of full age, five-and-twenty," said Latournelle. "And, on my part, it is paying off a debt, my dear fellow, if I give you the refusal of my practice."

Butscha kissed Madame Mignon's hand, wetting it with his tears, and showed a tearful face when Modeste opened the drawing-room door.

"Who has been distressing my mysterious dwarf?" she asked.

"Oh, mademoiselle, do we children nursed in sorrow ever shed tears of grief? I have just received such marks of attachment, that I was moved with tenderness for all those in whom I liked to believe I had found relations. I am to be a notary; I may grow rich. Ah, ha! Poor Butscha may some day be rich Butscha. You do not know what audacity exists in this abortion!" he exclaimed.

The hunchback struck himself hard on his cavernous breast, and placed himself in front of the fireplace after giving Modeste a look that stole like a gleam from under his heavy, drooping eyelids; for in this unforeseen conjuncture he had found his chance of sounding his sovereign lady's heart.

For an instant Dumay fancied that the clerk had dared aspire to Modeste; he exchanged looks with his friends which were understood by all, and which made them gaze at the little hunchback with a sort of dread mingled with curiosity.

"I—I too—have my dreams," Butscha went on, not taking his eyes off Modeste.

The girl looked down instinctively, in a way which was a revelation to the clerk. "You love romances; allow me, in the midst of my joy, to confide my secret to you, and you will tell me if the end of the romance I have dreamed of for my life is possible. . . . If not, of what use is fortune. To me, more than any one else, money is happiness, since to me happiness means the enriching of the one I love! You who know so many things, mademoiselle, tell me whether a man can be loved independently of his person—handsome or ugly, and for his soul alone."

Modeste looked up at Butscha. It was a terrible, questioning look, for at this moment Modeste shared Dumay's suspicions. "When I am rich, I shall look out for some poor but beautiful girl, a foundling like myself, who has suffered much, and is very unhappy; I will write to her, comfort her, be her good genius; she shall read my heart, my soul; she shall have all my wealth, in both kinds—my gold, offered with great delicacy, and my mind, beautified by all the graces which the misfortune of birth has denied to my grotesque form! And I will remain hidden, like a cause which science seeks. God perhaps is not beautiful.—The girl will naturally be curious and want to see me; but I shall tell her that I am a monster of ugliness, I will describe myself as hideous——"

At this, Modeste looked hard in his face. If she had said, "What do you know of my love affairs?" it could not have been more explicit.

"If I am so happy as to be loved for the poetry of my soul! —if, some day, I might seem to that woman to be only slightly deformed, confess that I shall be happier than the handsomest of men, than even a man of genius beloved by such a heavenly creature as you are——"

The blush that mounted to Modeste's face betrayed almost the whole of the girl's secret to the hunchback.

"Well, now, if a man can enrich the girl he loves, and charm her heart irrespective of his person, is that the way to be loved?—This has been the poor hunchback's dream— yesterday's dream; for to-day your adorable mother has given me the clue to my future treasure by promising to facilitate my acquiring an office and connection. Still, before becoming a Gobenheim, I must know whether such a horrible transformation will achieve its end. What do you think, mademoiselle, on your part?"

Modeste was so taken by surprise, that she did not observe Butscha's appeal to her judgment. The lover's snare was better contrived than the soldier's; for the poor girl, quite bewildered, stood speechless.

"Poor Butscha!" said Madame Latournelle to her husband, "is he going mad?"

"You want to play the fairy tale of Beauty and the Beast," said Modeste at last, "and you forget that the Beast is turned into Prince Charming."

"Do you think so?" said the dwarf. "Now I have always imagined that transformation to symbolize the phenomenon of the soul becoming visible and eclipsing the body by its radiant glory. If I should never be loved, I shall remain invisible, that is all!—You and yours, madame," said he to his mistress, "instead of having a dwarf at your command, will have a life and fortune."

Butscha returned to his seat, and said to the three players, affecting perfect calmness:

"Who deals?"

But to himself he was saying with grief, "She wants to be loved for her own sake; she is corresponding with some sham great man, and how far has she gone?"

"My dear mamma, it has struck a quarter to ten," said Modeste to her mother.

Madame Mignon bid her friends good-night, and went to bed.

Those who insist on loving in secret may be watched over by Pyrenean dogs, mothers, Dumays, Latournelles—they are in no danger from these; but a lover! It is diamond cut diamond, fire against fire, wit against wit, a perfect equation, of which the terms are equal and interchangeable.

On Sunday morning Butscha was beforehand with Madame Latournelle, who always went to escort Modeste to mass, and stayed cruising about outside the Chalet, waiting for the postman.

"Have you a letter for Mademoiselle Modeste this morning?" he asked of that humble functionary as he approached.

"No, monsieur, no——"

"We have been good customers of the Government for some time past!" exclaimed the clerk.

"I believe you!" replied the postman.

Modeste from her room saw and heard this little interview; she posted herself at her window at this hour, behind the Venetian shutter, to watch for the postman.

She went down and out into the little garden, where, in a husky voice, she called out, "Monsieur Butscha."

"Here am I, mademoiselle," said the hunchback, coming to the little gate, which Modeste herself opened.

"Will you tell me whether you include among your titles to the affection of a woman the disgraceful espionage you choose to exercise?" asked the girl, trying to overwhelm her slave by her gaze and queenly attitude.

"Yes, mademoiselle," he proudly replied. "I had never imagined," he added in a low voice, "that a worm could do good service to a star! But so it is. Would you rather have your heart read by your mother, Monsieur Dumay, and Madame Latournelle, than by a poor creature, almost an outcast from life, who is yours as much as one of the flowers you cut to gratify you for a moment? They all know that you love; I alone know how. Take me as you would take a watch-dog; I will obey you, I will protect you, I will never bark, and I will have no opinions about you. All I ask is that you will let me be of some use to you. Your father placed a Dumay in your menagerie; try a Butscha, and you will find it quite another story! A poor Butscha, who asks for nothing, not even for a bone."

"Well, I will take you on trial," said Modeste, who only wished to be rid of so sharp a guardian. "Go at once to all the hotels at Graville and le Havre, and ask if a M. Arthur has arrived from England——"

"Listen, mademoiselle," said Butscha respectfully, but interrupting Modeste, "I will just go for a walk on the beach, and that will be all that is necessary, for you do not wish me to go to church, that is all."

Modeste looked at the hunchback in blank astonishment.

"Yes, mademoiselle, though you have wrapped your face in wadding and a handkerchief, you have no cold; though you have a double veil to your hat, it is only to see without being seen."

"What endows you with so much penetration?" cried Modeste, reddening.

"Why, mademoiselle, you have no stays on! A cold would not require you to disguise your figure by putting on several petticoats, to hide your hands in old gloves, and your pretty feet in hideous boots, to dress yourself anyhow, to——"

"That will do," said she. "But, now, how am I sure that you will obey me?"

"My master wanted to go to Sainte-Adresse, and was rather put out; but as he is really very kind, he would not deprive me of my Sunday. Well, I will propose to him that we should go——"

"Go then, and I shall trust to you——"

"Are you sure you will not want me at le Havre?"

"Quite.—Listen, mysterious dwarf, and look up," she said, pointing to a cloudless sky. "Can you see the track left by the bird that flew across just now? Well, my actions, as pure as that pure air, leave no more trace than that. Reassure Dumay and the Latournelles, reassure my mother; and be sure that this hand" (and she held out to him a slender little hand with upturned finger-tips, transparent to the light) "will never be given away, never even warmed by the kiss of what is called a lover, before my father's return."

"And why do you want me to keep away from church today?"

"Do you cross-question me, after all I have done you the honor to tell you and require of you?"

Butscha bowed without replying, and hastened home, enraptured at thus entering the service of his anonymous mistress.

An hour later Monsieur and Madame Latournelle came to fetch Modeste, who complained of a dreadful toothache.

"I really had not strength to dress," said she.

"Well, then, stay at home," said the notary's wife.

"No, no. I will go and pray for my father's safe return," replied Modeste; "and I thought that if I wrapped up well, it would do me more good than harm to go out."

So Mademoiselle Mignon set out alone with Latournelle. She would not take his arm for fear of being questioned as to the internal tremor that agitated her at the idea of so soon seeing her great poet. One look, the first, was about to decide her future existence.

Is there in the life of man a more exquisite moment than that of the first promised meeting? Can the feelings that lie buried in his heart, and that then burst into life, ever be known again? Can he ever again feel the pleasure that he finds, as did Ernest de la Brière, in choosing his best razors, his finest shirts, spotless collars, and impeccable clothes? We deify everything that is associated with that supreme hour. We imagine poems in our hearts, secret poems as beautiful as the woman's, and on the day when each reads the other's soul all is over! Is it not the same with these things as with the blossom of those wild fruits, at once sharp and sweet, lost in forest depths, the delight of the sun, no doubt; or, as Canalis says in "The Maiden's Song," the gladness of the plant itself which the Angel of Flowers has allowed to see its own beauty?

This leads to the reflection that la Brière, a modest soul, like many another penurious being for whom life begins with toil and money difficulties, had never yet been loved. He had arrived at le Havre the night before, and had at once gone to bed, like a coquette, to efface every trace of his journey; and he had now, after taking a bath, just completed a carefully advantageous toilet. This, perhaps, is the place for giving a full-length portrait of him, if only to justify the last letter Modeste was ever to write to him.

Born of a good family at Toulouse, distantly connected with that Minister who took him under his patronage, Ernest has the well-bred air which comes of an education begun from the cradle; the habit of business has given it solidity without effort, for pedantry is the rock on which precocious gravity is commonly wrecked. Of medium height, his face is attractively refined and gentle; his complexion warm, though colorless, was at that time set off by a slender moustache and a small imperial, a *virgule à la Mazarin*. But for these manly witnesses, he would, perhaps, have looked too much like a girl dressed up, so delicate is the cut of his face and lips, so natural is it to attribute to a woman teeth of transparent enamel and almost artificial evenness. Add to these feminine characteristics a voice as sweet as his looks, as gentle as his turquoise blue eyes, with Oriental lids, and you will perfectly understand how it was that the Minister had nicknamed his young private secretary Mademoiselle de la Brière. His broad, smooth forehead, framed under thick black hair, has a dreamy look that does not contradict the expression of his countenance, which is wholly melancholy. The prominence of the eyebrows, though delicately arched, overshadows the eyes, and adds to this look of melancholy by the sadness—a physical sadness, so to speak—that the eyelids give when they half close the eyes. This secret bashfulness, to which we give the name of modesty, characterizes his features and person. The whole result will, perhaps, be better understood if we add that the theory of perfect drawing demands greater length in the shape of the head, more space between the chin, which ends abruptly, and the forehead, on which the hair grows too low. Thus the face looks flattened. Work had already graven a furrow between the eyebrows, which were thick, and too nearly met, like those of all jealous natures. Though la Brière was as yet slight, his figure was one of those which, developing late, are unexpectedly stout at the age of thirty.

The young man might very well have typified, to those who are familiar with French history, the royal and mysterious personality of Louis XIII., with his melancholy diffidence for no known reason, pallid under his crown, loving the fatigue of hunting, and hating work; so timid with his mistress as to respect her virtue, so indifferent to his friend as to leave him to be beheaded; explicable only by his remorse at having avenged his father on his mother—either a Catholic Hamlet or the victim of some incurable malady. But the canker-worm which paled the King's cheek and unnerved his strength, was as yet, in Ernest, no more than simple distrust of himself, the shyness of a man to whom no woman had ever said, "How I love you!" and, above all, wasted self-sacrifice. After hearing the knell of a monarchy in the fall of a minister, the poor boy had found in Canalis a rock hidden under tempting mosses; he was seeking a despotism to worship; and this uneasiness, that of a dog in search of a master, gave him the expression of the king who found his. These clouds and feelings, this "pale cast" over his whole person, made his face far more attractive than the young secretary himself imagined, annoyed as he was sometimes to find himself classed by women as a *beau ténébreux*— gloomily handsome; a style gone quite out of fashion at a time when every man would gladly keep the clarions of advertisement for his own exclusive use.

So Ernest the diffident had sought the adornment of the most fashionable clothes. For this interview, when everything would depend on first sight, he donned black trousers and carefully polished boots, a sulphur-colored waistcoat, revealing an excessively fine shirt fastened with opal studs, a black necktie, and a short blue coat, which looked as if it had been glued to his back and waist by some new process; his rosette graced the button-hole. He wore smart kid gloves of the color of Florentine bronze, and held in his left hand a light cane and his hat, with a certain Louis-quatorze air; thus showing, as the sacred place demanded, his carefully combed hair, on which the light shed satin-like reflections. Standing sentry under the porch from the very beginning of the service, he studied the church while watching all the Christians, more especially those in petticoats, who came to dip their fingers in the holy water.

As Modeste came in, an inner voice cried out, "'Tis he!"

That coat and figure, so essentially Parisian, the rosette, the gloves, the walking-stick, the scented hair—none of these things were native to le Havre. And when la Brière turned to look at the notary's tall and showy wife, the little notary himself and the bundle—a word dedicated to this sense by women—under which Modeste had concealed herself, though she was fully prepared, the poor child was stricken to the heart by the aspect of this romantic countenance, in the bright daylight from the open door. She could not be mistaken; a small white rose almost hid the rosette. Would Ernest recognize his unknown fair hidden under an old hat and a double veil? Modeste was so fearful of the clairvoyance of love that she walked with an elderly shuffle.

"Wife," said Latournelle, as he went to his place, "that man does not belong to le Havre."

"So many strangers come through," replied the lady.

"But do strangers ever think of coming to see our church, which is not more than two centuries old?"

Ernest remained in the porch all through the service without seeing any woman who realized his hopes. Modeste, on her part, could not control her trembling till near the end. She was agitated by joys which she alone could have described. At last she heard on the pavement the step of a gentleman, for, Mass being over, Ernest was walking round the church, where no one remained but the *dilettanti* of prayer, who became to him the object of anxious and piercing scrutiny. He remarked the excessive trembling of the prayer-book held by the veiled lady as he passed her; and as she was the only one who hid her face, he conceived some suspicions, confirmed by Modeste's dress, which he studied with the care of an inquisitive lover.

When Madame Latournelle left the church, he followed her at a decent distance, and saw her, with Modeste, go into the house in the Rue Royale, where Mademoiselle Mignon usually waited till the hour of vespers. Ernest studied the house, decorated with escutcheons, and asked of a passer-by the name of the owner, who was mentioned almost with pride as Monsieur Latournelle, the first notary of le Havre.

As he lounged down the Rue Royale, trying to catch a glimpse of the interior of the house, Modeste could see her lover; she then declared herself to be too ill to attend vespers, and Madame Latournelle kept her company. So poor Ernest had his cruise for his pains. He dared not go to loiter about Ingouville; he made it a point of honor to obey, and returned to Paris after writing a letter while waiting for the coach, and posting it for Françoise Cochet to receive next morning with the postmark of le Havre.

Monsieur and Madame Latournelle dined at the Chalet every Sunday, taking Modeste home after vespers. As soon as the young lady felt better, they all went up to Ingouville, followed by Butscha. Modeste, quite happy, now dressed herself beautifully. As she went down to dinner she forgot all about her disguise of the morning and her cold, and sang:

> Night and sleep begone! My heart, the violet
> To God her incense breathes at break of day!

Butscha felt a thrill as he beheld Modeste, she seemed to him so completely changed; for the wings of love fluttered, as it were, on her shoulders, she looked like a sylph, and her cheeks glowed with the divine hue of happiness.

"Whose words are those which you have set to such a pretty air?" Madame Mignon asked her daughter.

"They are by Canalis, mamma," she replied, turning in an instant to the finest crimson, from her neck to the roots of her hair.

"Canalis!" exclaimed the dwarf, who learned from Modeste's tone and blush all of her secret that he as yet knew not. "He, the great poet, does he write ballads?"

"They are some simple lines," replied she, "to which I have ventured to adapt some reminiscences of German airs."

"No, no, my child," said Madame Mignon; "that music is your own, my dear!"

Modeste, feeling herself grow hotter and hotter, went out into the garden, taking Butscha with her.

"You can do me a great service," said she, in an undertone. "Dumay is affecting discretion to my mother and me as to the amount of the fortune my father is bringing home, and I want to know the truth. Has not Dumay, at different times, sent papa five hundred and something thousand francs? My father is not the man to stay abroad four years simply to double his capital. Now a ship is coming in that is all his own, and the share he offers Dumay amounts to nearly six hundred thousand francs."

"We need not question Dumay," said Butscha. "Your father had lost, as you know, four millions of francs before his departure, these he has no doubt recovered; he would certainly have given Dumay ten per cent of his profits; so, from the fortune the worthy Breton confesses to, my chief and I calculate that the Colonel's must amount to six or seven millions——"

"Oh, father!" cried Modeste, crossing her arms, and raising her eyes to heaven, "you have given me a second life!"

"Oh, mademoiselle, you love a poet! A man of that stamp is more or less of a Narcissus. Will he love you as he ought? A craftsman in words, always absorbed in fitting sentences together, is very fatiguing. A poet, mademoiselle, is not poetry—no more than the seed is the flower."

"Butscha, I never saw such a handsome man!"

"Beauty, mademoiselle, is a veil which often serves to hide many imperfections."

"He has the most angelic heart that heaven——"

"God grant you may be right," said the dwarf, clasping his hands. "May you be happy! That man, like yourself, will have a slave in Jean Butscha. I shall then no longer be a notary; I shall give myself up to study—to science——"

"And why?"

"Well, mademoiselle, to bring up your children, if you will condescend to allow me to be their tutor. . . . Oh! if you would accept a piece of advice! Look here, let me go to work my own way. I could ferret out this man's life and habits, could discover if he is kind, if he is violent or gentle, if he will show you the respect you deserve, if he is capable of loving you perfectly, preferring you to all else, even to his own talent——"

"What can it matter if I love him?" said she simply.

"To be sure, that is true," cried the hunchback.

At this moment Madame Mignon was saying to her friends:

"My daughter has this day seen the man she loves."

"Can it be that sulphur-colored waistcoat that puzzled you so much, Latournelle?" cried the notary's wife. "That young man had a pretty white rosebud in his button-hole——"

"Ah!" said the mother, "a token to be known by!"

"He wore the rosette of the Legion of Honor," Madame Latournelle went on. "He is a charming youth! But we are all wrong; Modeste never raised her veil, she was huddled up like a pauper, and——"

"And she said she was ill," added the notary. "But she has thrown off her mufflers, and is perfectly well now!"

"It is incomprehensible!" said Dumay.

"Alas! it is as clear as day," said the notary.

"My child," said Madame Mignon to Modeste, who came in, followed by Butscha, "did you happen to see in church this morning a well-dressed little man with a white rose in his button-hole, and the rosette——"

"I saw him," Butscha hastily put in, seeing by the attention of the whole party what a trap Modeste might fall into. "It was Grindot, the famous architect, with whom the town is treating for the restoration of the church. He came from Paris, and I found him this morning examining the outside as I set out for Sainte-Adresse."

"Oh! he is an architect! He puzzled me greatly," said Modeste, to whom Butscha had secured time to recover herself.

Dumay looked askance at Butscha. Modeste, put on her guard, assumed an impenetrable demeanor. Dumay's suspicions were excited to the highest pitch, and he resolved to go next day to the Mairie and ascertain whether the expected architect had in fact been at le Havre. Butscha, on his part, very uneasy as to Modeste's ultimate fate, decided on starting for Paris to set a watch over Canalis.

Gobenheim arrived in time to play a rubber, and his presence repressed the ferment of feeling. Modeste awaited her mother's bedtime almost with impatience; she wanted to write, and this is the letter her love dictated to her when she thought that every one was asleep.

XIII.

To Monsieur de Canalis.

"Oh, my best-beloved friend, what vile libels are your portraits displayed in the print-sellers' windows! And I who was happy with that detestable lithograph! I am quite shy of loving such a handsome man. No, I cannot conceive that Paris women can be so stupid as not to see, one and all, that you are the fulfilment of their dreams. You neglected! You loveless!—I do not believe a word you have said about your obscure and laborious life, your devotion to an idol till now vainly sought for. You have been too well loved, monsieur; your brow, as pale and smooth as a magnolia petal, plainly shows it, and I shall be wretched.

"What am I now?—Ah! why have you called me forth to life? In one instant I felt that I had shed my ponderous chrysalis! My soul burst the crystal which held it captive; it rushed through my veins. In short, the cold silence of things suddenly ceased to me; everything in nature spoke to me. The old church to me was luminous; its vault, glittering with gold and azure, like that of an Italian church, sparkled above my head. The melodious strains, sung by angels to martyrs to make them forget their anguish, sounded through the organ! The hideous pavement of le Havre seemed like a flowery path. I recognized the sea as an old friend, whose language, full of sympathy, I had never known well enough. I saw how the roses in my garden and greenhouse had long worshiped me, and whispered to me to love! They all smiled on me on my return from church; and, to crown all, I heard your name of Melchior murmured by the flower-bells; I saw it written on the clouds! Yes, I am indeed alive, thanks to you—poet more beautiful than that cold and prim Lord Byron, whose face is as dull as the English climate. Wedded to you by one only of your Oriental glances which pierced my black veil, you transfused your blood into my veins, and it fired me from head to foot. Ah, we do not feel life like that when our mothers bring us into the world? A blow dealt to you would fall on me at the same instant, and my existence henceforth can only be accounted for by your mind. I know now the purpose of the divine harmony of music; it was invented by the angels to express love.

"To be a genius and handsome too, my Melchior, is too much. A man should have a choice at his birth. But when I think of the treasures of tenderness and affection you have lavished on me, especially during this last month, I wonder whether I am dreaming! Nay, you must be hiding some mystery. What woman could give you up without dying of it? Yes, jealousy has entered my heart with such love as I could not believe in! Could I imagine such a conflagration?

"A new and inconceivable vagary! I now wish you were ugly! What follies I committed when I got home! Every yellow dahlia reminded me of your pretty waistcoat, every white rose was a friend, and I greeted them with a look which was yours, as I am wholly! The color of the gentleman's well-fitting gloves—everything, to the sound of his step on the flagstones—everything is so exactly represented by my memory that, sixty years hence, I shall still see the smallest details of this high day, the particular color of the atmosphere, and the gleam of the sunbeam reflected from a pillar; I shall hear the prayer which your advent broke into; I shall breathe the incense from the altar; and I shall fancy that I feel above our heads the hands of the priest who was giving us the final benediction just as you went past. That good Abbé Marcellin has married us already. The superhuman joy of experiencing this world of new and unexpected emotions can only be equaled by the joy I feel in telling you of them, in rendering up all my happiness to him who pours it into my soul with the unstinting bounty of the sun. So no more veils, my beloved! Come, oh, come back soon! I will unmask with joy.

"You have, no doubt, heard of the firm of Mignon of le Havre? Well, in consequence of an irreparable loss, I am the sole heiress of the family. Do not scorn us, you who are descended from one of the heroes of Auvergne. The arms of Mignon de la Bastie will not dishonor those of Canalis. They are *gules, a bend sable charged with three besants, in each quarter a patriarchal cross or,* surmounted by a cardinal's hat, and the cord and tassels as mantling. My dear, I will be faithful to our motto, *Una fides, unus Dominus!* The true faith, and one Lord.

"Perhaps, my friend, you will think there is some irony in my name after all I have here confessed. It is Modeste. Thus, I did not altogether cheat you in signing 'O. d'Este-M.' Nor did I deceive you in speaking of my fortune; it will, I believe, amount to the sum which has made you so virtuous. And I know so surely that to you money is so unimportant a consideration, that I can write of it unaffectedly. At the same time, you must let me tell you how glad I am to be able to endow our happiness with the freedom of action and movement that wealth gives, the power of saying, 'Let us go——' when the fancy takes us to see a foreign land, of flying off in a comfortable carriage, seated side by side, without a care about money; and happy, too, to give you the right of saying to the King, 'I have such a fortune as you require in your peers!'

"In this, Modeste Mignon can be of some service to you, and her money will find noble uses. As to your humble servant, you have seen her once, at her window in a wrapper. —Yes, the fair-haired daughter of Eve was your unknown correspondent; but how little does the Modeste of to-day resemble her whom you then saw! She was wrapped in a shroud, and this other—have I not told you so?—has derived from you the life of life. Pure and permitted love, a love that my father, now at last returning from his travels and with riches, will sanction, has uplifted me with its childlike but powerful hand from the depths of the tomb where I was sleeping. You awoke me as the sun awakes the flowers. The glance of her you love is not now that of the bold-faced little Modeste! Oh, no; it is bashful, it has glimpses of happiness, and veils itself under chaste eyelids. My fear now is that I cannot deserve my lot. The King has appeared in his glory; my liege has now a mere vassal, who implores his forgiveness for taking such liberties, as the thimble-rigger with loaded dice did after cheating the Chevalier de Grammont.

"Yes, beloved poet, I will be your 'Mignon,' but a happier Mignon than Goethe's, for you will leave me to dwell in my native land, won't you?—in your heart.

"As I write this bridal wish, a nightingale in the Vilquins' park has just answered for you. Oh! let me quickly hear that the nightingale, with his long-drawn note, so pure, so clear, so full, inundating my heart with love and gladness, like an Annunciation, has not lied.

"My father will pass through Paris on his way from Marseilles. The house of Mongenod, his correspondents, will know his address; go to see him, my dearest Melchior, tell him that you love me, and do not try to tell him how much I love you; let that be a secret always between us and God! I, dear adored one, will tell my mother everything. She, a daughter of Wallenrod Tustall-Bartenstild, will justify me by her caresses; she will be made happy by our secret and romantic poem, at once human and divine! You have the daughter's pledge; now obtain the consent of the Comte de la Bastie, the father of your own

"MODESTE.

"*P. S.*—Above all, do not come to le Havre without having

obtained my father's permission; and, if you love me, you will be able to discover him on his way through Paris."

"What are you doing at this time of night, Mademoiselle Modeste?" asked Dumay.

"I am writing to my father," she replied to the old soldier. "Did you not tell me that you were starting to-morrow?"

Dumay had no answer to this, and went to bed, while Modeste wrote a long letter to her father.

Next day Françoise Cochet, alarmed at seeing the Havre postmark, came up to the Chalet to deliver to her young mistress the following letter, and carry away that which Modeste had written.

To Mademoiselle O. d'Este-M.

"My heart warns me that you were the woman, so carefully veiled and disguised, placed between Monsieur and Madame Latournelle, who have but one child, a son. Ah, dearly loved one! if you are of humble rank, devoid of position, distinction, or even fortune, you cannot imagine what my joy would be. You must know me by this time; why not tell me the whole truth? I am no poet excepting through love, in my heart, and for you. Oh, what immense affection I must have to stay here, in this Hôtel de Normandie, and not walk up to Ingouville, that I can see from my windows? Will you love me as I love you? To have to leave le Havre for Paris in such uncertainty! Is not that being punished for loving as if I had committed a crime?—I have obeyed you blindly.

"Ah! let me soon have a letter; for, if you are mysterious, I have returned mystery for mystery, and I must at last throw off the mask of my incognito, and tell you how little I am a poet, abdicating the glory you have lent me."

This letter greatly disturbed Modeste; she could not withdraw her own, which Françoise had already posted by the time she read the last lines once more, puzzled as to their meaning; but she went up to her room, and wrote an answer, asking for explanations.

During these little incidents, others, equally small, were happening in the town, and were destined to make Modeste forget her uneasiness. Dumay, having gone early to le Havre, at once knew that no architect had arrived there the night before last. Furious at the lie told him by Butscha, which revealed a complicity which he would know the meaning of, he hurried from the Mairie to the Latournelles.

"Where is your Master Butscha?" asked he of his friend the notary, on not finding the clerk in the office.

"Butscha, my dear fellow? He is on the road to Paris, whisked away by the steamboat. Early this morning, on the quay, he met a sailor, who told him that his father, the Swedish sailor, has come into some money. Butscha's father went to India, it would seem, and served some prince, a Mahratta, and he is now in Paris——"

"A pack of lies! Shameful! Monstrous! Oh, I will find that damned hunchback; I am going to Paris, and on purpose for that!" cried Dumay. "Butscha is deceiving us! He knows something about Modeste, and has never told us. If he dares meddle in the matter—— He shall never be a notary; I will cast him back on his mother, in the mire, in the——"

"Come, my friend, never hang a man without trying him," replied Latournelle, terrified at Dumay's exasperation.

After explaining on what his suspicions were founded, Dumay begged Madame Latournelle to stay at the Chalet with Modeste during his absence.

"You will find the Colonel in Paris," said the notary. "In the shipping news this morning, in the *Commerce* newspaper, under the heading of Marseilles.—Here, look!" he said, handing him the sheet, 'The *Bettina-Mignon,* Captain Mignon, arrived October 16th,' and to-day is the 17th. At this moment all le Havre knows of the master's return."

Dumay requested Gobenheim to dispense henceforth with his services; he then returned at once to the Chalet, going in at the moment when Modeste had just closed her letters to her father and to Canalis. The two letters were exactly alike in shape and thickness, differing only in the address. Modeste thought she had laid that to her father over that to her Melchior, and had done just the reverse. This mistake, so common in the trifles of life, led to the discovery of her secret by her mother and Dumay.

The lieutenant was talking eagerly to Madame Mignon in the drawing-room, confiding to her the fresh fears to which Modeste's duplicity and Butscha's connivance had given rise.

"I tell you, madame," he exclaimed, "he is a viper we have warmed on our hearth; there is not room for a soul in these fag-ends of humanity."

Modeste had slipped the letter to her father into her pocket, fancying that it was the letter to her lover, and went down with that addressed to Canalis in her hand, hearing Dumay speak of starting immediately for Paris.

"What is wrong with my poor Mysterious Dwarf, and why are you talking so loud?" said she at the door of the drawing-room.

"Butscha, mademoiselle, set out for Paris this morning, and you, no doubt, can say why!—It must be to carry on some intrigue with the so-called little architect in a sulphur-colored waistcoat, who, unluckily for the hunchback's falsehood, has not yet been to le Havre."

Modeste was startled; she guessed that the dwarf had gone off to make his own inquiries as to the poet's manners and customs; she turned pale, and sat down.

"I will be after him; I will find him!" said Dumay. "That, no doubt, is the letter for your father?" he added, holding out his hand. "I will send it to Mongenod's—if only my Colonel and I do not cross on the way."

Modeste gave him the letter. Little Dumay, who could read without spectacles, mechanically read the address:

"Monsieur le Baron de Canalis, Rue de Paradis-Poissonnière, No. 29!" he exclaimed. "What is the meaning of this?"

"Ah! my child, then he is the man you love!" cried Madame Mignon. "The verses you set to music are by him——"

"And it is his portrait that you have upstairs in a frame!" added Dumay.

"Give me back that letter, Monsieur Dumay," said Modeste, drawing herself up, like a lioness defending her cubs.

"Here it is, mademoiselle," he replied. Modeste slipped the letter into her bosom, and held out to Dumay that addressed to her father.

"I know you to be capable of anything, Dumay," said she; "but if you move a single step towards Monsieur de Canalis, I will take one out of this house, and never come back!"

"You will kill your mother!" replied Dumay, who went to call his wife.

The poor mother had fainted away, stricken to the heart by Modeste's threatening speech.

"Good-bye, wife," said the Breton, embracing the little American. "Save the mother; I am going to save the daughter."

He left Modeste and Madame Dumay with Madame Mignon, made his preparations in a few minutes, and went down to le Havre. An hour later he set off by post with the swiftness which passion or interest alone can give to the wheels.

Madame Mignon soon revived under her daughter's care, and went up to her room, leaning on Modeste's arm; the only reproach she uttered when they were alone was to say, "Unhappy child! what have you done? Why hide anything from me? Am I so stern?"

"Why, of course, I was going to tell you everything," replied the girl in tears.

She told her mother the whole story; she read her all the letters and replies; she plucked the rose of her poem to pieces, petal by petal, to lay in the heart of the kind German lady; this took up half the day. When her confession was ended, and she saw something like a smile on the lips of the too indulgent blind woman, she threw herself into her arms with tears.

"Oh, mother!" cried she, in the midst of her sobs, "you whose heart is of gold, and all poetry, and like some choice vessel moulded by God to contain the one pure and heavenly love that can fill a whole life!—you whom I long to imitate by loving nothing on earth but my husband—you must know how bitter are these tears which I shed at this moment, which fall wet on your hands.—The butterfly with iridescent wings, that beautiful second soul which your daughter has cherished with maternal care—my love, my sacred love, that inspired and living mystery, has fallen into vulgar hands that will tear its wings and its veil under the cruel pretext of enlightening me, of inquiring whether genius is as correct as a banker, if my Melchior is capable of amassing dividends, if he has some love affair to be unearthed, if he is not guilty in vulgar eyes of some youthful episode, which to our love is what a cloud is to the sun. What are they going to do?— Here, feel my hand; I am in a fever! They will kill him!"

Modeste, seized by a deadly shivering fit, was obliged to go to bed, alarming her mother, Madame Latournelle, and Madame Dumay, who nursed her while the Lieutenant was traveling to Paris, whither the logic of events transfers our tale for the moment.

Men who are truly modest, like Ernest de la Brière, and especially those who, though knowing their own value, are neither loved nor appreciated, will understand the infinite rapture in which the young secretary reveled as he read Modeste's letter. After discovering the wit and greatness of his mind, his young and guileless but wily mistress thought him handsome. This is the supremest flattery. Why? Because Beauty is no doubt the Master's signature on the work into which He has infused His soul; it is the divinity made manifest; and to see it where it does not exist, to create it by the power of an enchanted eye, is—is it not?—the crowning magic of love.

And the poor young fellow could exclaim to himself with the ecstasy of an applauded author:

"At last I am loved!"

When once a woman, a courtesan, or an innocent girl has let the words escape her, "How handsome you are!" even if it be untrue, if the man allows the subtle poison of the words to enter his brain, he is thenceforth tied by eternal bonds to the bewitching liar, to the truthful or deluded woman; she is his world; he thirsts for this testimony; he would never weary of it, not even if he were a prince.

Ernest proudly paced his room; he stood in front of the mirror—three-quarter face, in profile; he tried to criticise his own features, but a diabolical, insinuating voice said to him, "Modeste is right!" and he came back to the letter and read it again. He saw the heavenly fair one, he talked to her! Then, in the midst of his rapture, came the overwhelming thought, "She believes me to be Canalis, and she is a millionaire!"

All his happiness fell with a crash, as a man falls when, walking in his sleep, he has reached the ridge of a roof, and hearing a voice, steps forward, and is dashed to pieces on the stones.

"But for the halo of glory, I should be ugly!" cried he. "What a horrible predicament I have got myself into!"

La Brière was too thoroughly the man of his letters, too entirely the pure and noble soul he had shown in them, to hesitate at the voice of honor. He at once resolved to go and confess everything to Modeste's father if he were in Paris, and to inform Canalis fully of the outcome of their very Parisian practical joke. To this sensitive young fellow the vastness of Modeste's fortune was a casting reason. Above all, he would not be suspected of having used the stimulation of this correspondence, though on his side so perfectly sincere, for filching a fortune. Tears stood in his eyes as he walked from his rooms in the Rue Chantereine to Mongenod the banker's, whose prosperity, connections, and prospects were partly the work of the Minister to whom he himself was indebted.

At the time when la Brière was closeted with the head of the house of Mongenod, and acquiring all the information he needed in his strange position, such a scene was taking place in Canalis' house as Dumay's hasty departure might have led us to expect.

Dumay, like a true soldier of the Imperial School, whose blood had been boiling all through his journey, conceived of a poet as an irresponsible fellow, a man who fooled in rhyme, living in a garret, dressed in black cloth white at all the seams, whose boots sometimes had soles, whose linen was anonymous, who always looked as if he had just dropped from the clouds, when he was not scribbling as intently as Butscha. But the ferment that muttered in his brain and heart received a sort of cold shower-bath when he reached the poet's handsome residence, saw a man cleaning a carriage in the courtyard, found himself in a splendid dining-room with another servant dressed like a banker, to whom the groom had referred him, and who looked him from head to foot as he said that Monsieur le Baron could not see any one.

"Monsieur le Baron has a meeting to-day," he added, "at the Council of State."

"I am right?" asked Dumay; "this is the house of Monsieur de Canalis, who writes poetry?"

"Monsieur le Baron de Canalis," said the footman, "is no doubt the great poet you mean; but is also Master of Appeals to the State Council, and attached to the Foreign Office."

Dumay, who had come to box a rhymester's ears, to use his own contemptuous expression, had found a State functionary. The drawing-room where he was kept waiting, remarkable for its magnificence, presented to his contemplation the row of crosses that glittered on Canalis' evening coat, left by the servant over the back of a chair. Presently he was attracted by the sheen and workmanship of a silver gilt cup, and the words, "The gift of MADAME," struck his eye. Opposite this, on a bracket, was a Sèvres vase, over which was engraved, "Given by Madame la Dauphine." These silent warnings restored Dumay to his common sense, while the man-servant was asking his master whether he could receive a stranger, who had come from le Havre on purpose to see him—his name Dumay.

"What is he like?" asked Canalis.

"Has a good hat, and the red ribbon."

At a nod of assent, the man went out, and returned announcing:

"Monsieur Dumay."

When he heard his own name, when he stood before Canalis in a study as costly as it was elegant, his feet on a carpet quite as good as the best in the Mignons' old house, when he met the glance prepared by the poet, who was playing with the tassels of a sumptuous dressing-gown, Dumay was so absolutely dumfounded that he left the great man to speak first.

"To what, monsieur, do I owe the honor of this visit?"

"Monsieur," Dumay began, still standing.

"If you have much to say, pray be seated," said Canalis, interrupting him; and the poet sank back into his large easy-chair, and crossed his legs, raising the upper one to rock his foot on a level with his eye, while staring hard at Dumay, who, to use his own soldier's phrase, felt like a dummy.

"I am listening, monsieur," said the poet. "My time is precious; I am due at the office——"

"Monsieur," said Dumay, "I will be brief. You have bewitched—how I know not—a young lady at le Havre—handsome, rich, the last and only hope of two noble families, and I have come to ask you your intentions."

Canalis, who for the last three months had been absorbed by serious matters, who aimed at promotion to the grade of Commander of the Legion of Honor, and to be Minister to a German Court, had totally forgotten the letter from le Havre.

"I?" cried he.

"You," replied Dumay.

"Monsieur," said Canalis, smiling, "I know no more what you mean than if you were talking Hebrew. I bewitch a young girl?—I, who——?" A lordly smile curled the poet's lip. "Come, monsieur. I am not a boy that I should amuse myself by stealing poor wild fruit when I have ample orchards open to me, where the finest peaches in the world ripen. All

Paris knows where my affections are placed. That there should be at le Havre a young lady suffering from some admiration, of which I am wholly unworthy, for the verses I have written, my dear sir, would not astonish me! Nothing is commoner. Look there! You see that handsome ebony-box inlaid with mother-of-pearl, and fitted with iron wrought as fine as lace. That coffer belonged to Pope Leo X.; it was given to me by the Duchesse de Chaulieu, who had it from the King of Spain.—I have devoted it to the preservation of all the letters I receive from every part of Europe, written by unknown women and girls. Oh! I have the greatest respect for those posies of flowers culled from the very soul, and sent to me in a moment of enthusiasm that is indeed worthy of all respect. Yes, to me the impulse of a heart is a noble and beautiful thing!—Others, mocking spirits, screw up such notes to light their cigars, or give them to their wives for curl-papers; I—who am a bachelor, monsieur—have too much delicate feeling not to treasure these artless and disinterested offerings in a kind of tabernacle; indeed, I hoard them with no little reverence, and when I am dying I will see them burnt under my eyes. So much the worse for those who think me ridiculous! What is to be said? I am grateful by nature, and these testimonials help me to endure the criticisms and annoyances of a literary life. When I receive in my spine the broadside of an enemy in ambush behind a newspaper, I look at that chest and say to myself, 'There are, here and there, a few souls whose wounds have been healed, or beguiled or staunched by me——' "

The rhodomontade, pronounced with the cleverness of a great actor, petrified the little cashier, whose eyes dilated while his astonishment amused the great poet.

"To you," the peacock went on, still spreading his tail, "out of respect for a position I can sympathize with, I can but propose that you should open that treasury, and look there for your young lady; but I never forget names. I know what I am saying, and you are mistaken . . ."

"And this is what happens to a poor girl in this gulf called

Paris!" cried Dumay. "The idol of her parents, the delight of her friends, the hope, the darling of them all; the pride of her family, for whom six persons have made a rampart against disaster of their hearts and their fortunes."

Dumay paused, and then went on:

"Well, monsieur, you are a great poet, and I am but a poor soldier. For fifteen years, while I served my country in the ranks, I felt the wind of many a bullet in my face, I crossed Siberia, where I was kept a prisoner, the Russians flung me on a truck like a bale of goods, I have endured everything; I have seen no end of my comrades die—— And you, monsieur, have sent such a chill through my bones as I never felt before!"

Dumay believed that he had touched the poet; he had flattered him—an almost impossible achievement, for the ambitious man had by this time forgotten the first phial of precious balm that Praise had broken on his head.

"You see, my brave friend," said the poet solemnly, as he laid his hand on Dumay's shoulder, feeling it a strange thing that he should be able to make a soldier of the Empire shiver, "this girl is everything to you—— But to society, what is she? Nothing. If at this moment the most important mandarin in China is closing his eyes and putting the Empire into mourning, does that grieve you deeply? In India the English are killing thousands of men as good as we are; and at this moment, as I speak, the most charming woman is there being burnt—but you have had coffee for breakfast all the same? Indeed, at this minute, here in Paris, you may find several mothers of families lying on straw and bringing a child into the world without a rag to wrap it in!—And here is some delicious tea in a cup that cost five louis, and I am writing verses to make the ladies of Paris exclaim, *'Charming, charming! divine, exquisite! it goes to the heart!'*

"Social nature, like Mother Nature herself, is great at forgetting. Ten years hence you will be amazed at the step you have taken. You are in a city where we die, and marry, and worship each other at an assignation; where a girl suffocates herself, while a man of genius and his cargo of ideas full of humanitarian benefits go to the bottom, side by side, often under the same roof, and knowing nothing of each other.— And you come and expect us to swoon with anguish at this commonplace question, 'Is a certain young person at le Havre this or that, or is she not?'—Oh, you really are——"

"And you call yourself a poet!" cried Dumay. "But do you really feel nothing of what you depict?"

"If we felt all the misery or joy that we describe, we should be worn out in a few months, like old shoes," said the poet, smiling. "Listen, you shall not have come from le Havre to Paris, and to me, Canalis, without having anything to take back with you. Soldier!"—and Canalis had the figure and gesture of an Homeric hero—"learn this from the poet, 'Every noble feeling in each of us is a poem so essentially individual that our best friend, our self, takes no interest in it. It is a treasure belonging to each alone——' "

"Forgive me for interrupting you," said Dumay, who gazed at Canalis with horror, "but you have been to le Havre?"

"I spent a night and day there in the spring of 1824 on my way to London."

"You are a man of honor," Dumay went on. "Can you give me your word of honor that you do not know Mademoiselle Modeste Mignon?"

"This is the first time I ever heard her name," replied Canalis.

"Oh, monsieur," cried Dumay, "into what dark intrigue am I about to plunge? May I count on you to help me in my inquiries? For some one, I am certain, has been making use of your name. You ought to have received a letter yesterday from le Havre."

"I have received nothing! You may be sure, monsieur, that I will do all that lies in my power to be of service to you."

Dumay took leave, his heart full of anxiety, believing that hideous little Butscha had hidden himself in the semblance of the great poet to captivate Modeste; while Butscha, on the contrary, as keen and clever as a prince who avenges himself, sharper than a spy, was making inquisition into the poet's life and actions, escaping detection by his insignificance like an insect working its way into the young wood of a tree.

The Breton had but just left when la Brière came into his friend's room. Canalis naturally mentioned the visit of this man from le Havre.

"Hah!" said Ernest, "Modeste Mignon! I have come on purpose to speak about that affair."

"Bless me!" cried Canalis, "do you mean to say I have made a conquest by proxy?"

"Why, yes, that is the turning-point of the drama. My friend, I am loved by the sweetest girl in the world, beautiful enough to shine among the beauties of Paris, with a heart and education worthy of Clarissa Harlowe; she has seen me, she likes my looks—and she believes me to be the great poet Canalis.

"Nor is this all: Modeste Mignon is of good birth, and Mongenod has just told me that her father, the Comte de la Bastie, must have a fortune of something like six millions of francs. This father has come home within three days, and I have just begged him to arrange an interview with me, at two o'clock—through Mongenod, who in his note mentioned that it concerned his daughter's happiness.—You will understand that before meeting the father I was bound to tell you everything."

"Among all the blossoms that open to the sunshine of fame," said Canalis with emphasis, "there is one glorious plant which, like the orange, bears its golden fruit amid the thousand united perfumes of wit and beauty! one elegant shrub, one true passion, one perfect happiness—and it has evaded me!" Canalis kept his eyes on the carpet that Ernest might not read them. "How," he went on after a pause, to recover his presence of mind, "how is it possible, among the intoxicating scents of these fancy-paper notes, and these phrases that mount to the brain, to detect the genuine heart—the girl, the woman, in whom true love is hidden under the livery of flattery, who loves us for ourselves, and who offers us happiness? No one could do it but an angel or a demon, and I am only an ambitious Master of Appeals!

"Ah, my dear fellow, fame transforms us into a butt, a target for a thousand arrows. One of us owed his marriage to a copy of hydraulic verses; and I, even more ingratiating, more the ladies' man than he, shall have missed my chance— for you love this poor girl?" said he, looking at la Brière.

"Oh!" cried la Brière.

"Well, then, be happy, Ernest," said the poet, taking his friend's arm and leaning on it. "As it turns out, I shall not have been ungrateful to you! You are handsomely rewarded for your devotion, for I will be generously helpful to your happiness."

Canalis was furious, but he could not behave otherwise, so he took the benefit of his ill-luck by using it as a pedestal. A tear rose to the young secretary's eye; he threw his arms round Canalis and embraced him.

"Oh, Canalis, I did not half know you!"

"What did you expect? It takes time to travel round the world," replied the poet with emphatic irony.

"Consider," said la Brière, "that immense fortune——"

"Well, my friend, will it not be in good hands?" cried Canalis, pointing his effusiveness by a charming gesture.

"Melchior," said la Brière, "I am yours in life and death."

He wrung the poet's hands, and went away hastily; he was eager to see Monsieur Mignon.

At this hour the Comte de la Bastie was suffering all the sorrows that had been lurking for him as their prey. He had learned from his daughter's letter the facts of Bettina-Caroline's death and her mother's blindness; and Dumay had just told him the story of the terrible imbroglio of Modeste's love affair.

"Leave me to myself," he said to his faithful friend.

When the Lieutenant had closed the door, the unhappy father threw himself on a couch and lay there, his head in his hands, shedding the few thin tears that lie under the eyelids of a man of fifty-six without falling, wetting them, but drying quickly and rising again, the last dews of the autumn of human life.

"To have children you love and a wife you adore, is to have many hearts and offer them all to the dagger!" cried he, starting to his feet with a furious bound, and pacing the room. "To be a father is to give oneself over to misfortune, bound hand and foot. If I meet that fellow d'Estourny I will kill him. Daughters! Who would have daughters? One gets hold of a scoundrel; and the other, my Modeste, of what? A coward, who deludes her under the gilt-paper armor of a poet. If only it were Canalis! There would be no great harm done. But this Scapin of a lover!—I will throttle him with my own hands!" said he to himself, with an involuntary gesture of energetic atrocity. "And what then," he thought, "if my child should die of grief."

Mechanically he looked out of the window of the Hotel des Princes, and came back to sit down on the divan, where he remained motionless. The fatigue of six voyages to the Indies, the anxieties of investments, the dangers he had met and escaped, care and sorrow had silvered Charles Mignon's hair. His fine military face, clean in outline, was bronzed by the sun of Malaysia, China, and Asia Minor, and had assumed an imposing expression, which grief at this moment made sublime.

"And Mongenod tells me I can perfectly trust the young man who is to come to speak to me about my daughter!——"

Ernest de la Brière was just then announced by one of the servants whom the Comte de la Bastie had attached to him in the course of these four years, and had picked out from the crowd of men under him.

"You come, monsieur, with an introduction from my friend Mongenod?" said he.

"Yes," replied Ernest, gazing timidly at a face as gloomy as Othello's. "My name is Ernest de la Brière, connected, monsieur, with the family of the late Prime Minister; I was his private secretary when he was in office. At his fall, His

Excellency was good enough to place me in the Court of Exchequer, where I am now first-class Referendary, and where I may rise to be a Master——"

"And what has all this to do with Mademoiselle de la Bastie?" asked Charles Mignon.

"Monsieur, I love her, and it is my unhoped-for happiness to be loved by her. . . . Listen, monsieur," said Ernest, interrupting a terrible movement on the part of the angry father, "I have the strangest confession to make to you, the most ignominious for a man of honor. And the worst punishment of my conduct, which perhaps was natural, is not this revelation to you—I dread the daughter even more than the father."

Ernest then told the prologue of this domestic drama, quite simply, and with the dignity of sincerity; he did not omit the twenty and odd letters they had exchanged—he had brought them with him—nor the interview he had just had with Canalis. When the father had read all these letters, the poor lover, pale and suppliant, quaked before the fiery looks of the Provençal.

"Well, monsieur," said Mignon, "in all this there is only one mistake, but it is all-important. My daughter has not six millions of francs; her fortune at most is two hundred thousand francs in settlement, and very doubtful expectations."

"Oh, monsieur!" cried Ernest, throwing his arms round Charles Mignon, and hugging him, "you relieve me of a load that oppressed me. Now, perhaps, nothing will come in the way of my happiness!—I have interest; I shall soon be Master of the Exchequer. If she had but ten thousand francs, if I had to accept nominal settlements, Mademoiselle Mignon would still be the wife of my choice; and to make her happy, as happy as you have made yours, to be a true son to you—yes, monsieur, for my father is dead—this is the deepest wish of my heart."

Charles Mignon drew back three steps, and fixed on la Brière a look that sank into the young man's eyes, as a poniard goes into its sheath; then he stood silent, reading in those fascinated eyes and on that eager countenance the most perfect candor and the purest truthfulness.

"Is fate at last wearied out?" said he to himself in an undertone. "Can I have found a paragon son-in-law in this youth?" He walked up and down the room in great excitement.

"Well, monsieur," he said at length, "you owe implicit obedience to the sentence you have come to ask, for otherwise you would at this moment be acting a mere farce."

"Indeed, monsieur——"

"Listen to me," said the father, nailing la Brière to the spot by a look. "I will be neither severe, nor hard, nor unjust. You must take the disadvantages with the advantages of the false position in which you have placed yourself. My daughter imagines that she is in love with one of the great poets of our day, whose fame chiefly has fascinated her. Well, then, ought not I, as her father, to enable her to choose between the celebrity which has seemed a lighthouse to her, and the humble reality thrown to her by chance in the irony it so often allows itself? Must she not be free to choose between you and Canalis? I trust to your honor to be silent as to what I have just told you concerning the state of my affairs. You and your friend, the Baron de Canalis, must come to spend the last fortnight of this month of October at le Havre. My house will be open to you both; my daughter will have the opportunity of knowing you. Remember, you yourself are to bring your rival, and to allow him to believe all the fables that may be current as to the Comte de la Bastie's millions. I shall be at le Havre by to-morrow, and shall expect you three days later. Good-morning, monsieur."

Poor la Brière very slowly made his way back to Canalis. At that moment the poet, face to face with himself, could give himself up to the torrent of reflections that flow from that "second thought" which Talleyrand so highly praised. The first thought is the impulse of nature, the second that of society.

"A girl with six millions of francs! And my eyes failed to

discern the glitter of that gold through the darkness! With such a fortune as that, I can be a peer of France, count, ambassador!—I have answered the most ordinary women, simpletons, intriguing girls who only wanted an autograph! And I rebelled against these *bal masqué* wiles on the very day when heaven sent me a chosen soul, an angel with wings of gold!— Pooh! I will write a sublime poem, and the chance will come again! What luck for that little la Brière, who spread his tail in my sunbeams!—And what plagiary. I am the model, and he is to be the statue! This is playing the fable of 'Bertrand and Raton.'—Six millions, and an angel, a Mignon de la Bastie!—An aristocratic angel, who loves poetry and the poet!—And I meanwhile display my muscles as a strong man, perform athletics, like Alcides, to astonish this champion of physical strength by moral force—this brave soldier full of fine feeling, this young girl's friend, who will tell her I have a soul of iron. I am playing Napoleon, when I ought to show myself as a seraph!—I shall have won a friend perhaps, and have paid dear for him; but friendship is a fine thing. Six millions—that is the price of a friend; a man cannot have many at that figure!"

At this last point of exclamation la Brière came into his friend's room; he was depressed.

"Well, what is the matter?" said Canalis.

"The father insists that his daughter shall be enabled to choose between the two Canalis——"

"Poor boy!" said the poet, laughing. "A clever man is that father!"

"I have pledged my honor to take you to le Havre," said la Brière, dolefully.

"My dear boy," said Canalis, "if your honor is at stake, you may depend upon me. I will ask for a month's leave of absence."

"Oh, Modeste is lovely!" cried la Brière in despair, "and you will easily extinguish me! Still, I was amazed to find good fortune coming my way; I said to myself, it is all a mistake!"

"Pooh! We shall see," said Canalis with ruthless cheerfulness.

That evening, after dinner, Charles Mignon and his cashier were flying, at the cost of three francs a stage to the postilion, from Paris to le Havre. The father had completely allayed his watch-dog's alarms as to Modeste's love affairs, had released him from his responsibilities, and reassured him as to Butscha's proceedings.

"Everything is for the best, my good old friend," said Charles, who had made inquiries of Mongenod as to Canalis and la Brière. "We have two players for one part," he added, laughing.

At the same time, he enjoined absolute silence on his old comrade as to the comedy about to be played at the Chalet, and his gentle revenge, or, if you will, the lesson to be given by a father to his child. From Paris to le Havre was one long dialogue between the friends, by which the Colonel learned the smallest events that had happened in his family during the past four years; and Charles told Dumay that Desplein, the great surgeon, was to come before the end of the month to examine the Countess' eyes, and decide whether it would be possible to remove the cataract and restore her sight.

A few minutes before the breakfast hour at the Chalet, the cracking of a whip, by a postilion counting on a large gratuity, announced the return of the two soldiers. Only the joy of a father coming home to his family after a long absence would give rise to such a detonation, and all the women were standing at the little gate.

There are so many fathers, and so many children—more fathers perhaps than children—who can enter into the excitement of such a meeting, that literature is never required to depict it; happily! for the finest words, and poetry itself, are inadequate to such emotions. Perhaps, indeed, the sweeter emotions have no literary side.

Not a word was spoken that day that could disturb the happiness of the Mignon family. There was a truce between the father, the mother, and the daughter as to the mysterious love affair which had paled Modeste's cheek. She was up to-day for the first time. The Colonel, with the delicate tenderness that characterizes a true soldier, sat all the time by his wife's side, her hand constantly held in his, and he watched Modeste, never tired of admiring her refined, elegant, and poetic beauty. Is it not by such small things that we know a man of true feeling?

Modeste, fearful of troubling the melancholy happiness of her father and mother, came from time to time to kiss the traveler's brow, and by kissing him so often, seemed to wish to kiss him for two.

"Ah, darling child! I understand you," said her father, pressing Modeste's hand at a moment when she was smothering him with affection.

"Hush!" said Modeste in his ear, pointing to her mother.

Dumay's rather perfidious silence left Modeste very uneasy as to the results of his journey to Paris; she now and then stole a look at the Lieutenant, but could not penetrate that tough skin. The Colonel, as a prudent father, wished to study his only daughter's nature, and, above all, to consult his wife, before proceeding to a discussion on which the happiness of the whole family would depend.

"To-morrow, my dearest child, rise early," said he at night, "and if it is fine, we will go for a walk together on the seashore. We have to talk over your poems, Mademoiselle de la Bastie."

These words, spoken with a smile that was reflected on Dumay's lips, were all Modeste could know; still, this was enough to allay her anxiety and to make her too curious to get to sleep till late, so busy was her fancy.

Next morning Modeste was dressed and ready before the Colonel.

"You know everything, my dear father," said she, as soon as they had started on their way to the sea.

"I know everything—and a good many things that you do not know," replied he.

Thereupon the father and daughter walked some few steps in silence.

"Now tell me, my child, how a daughter so worshiped by her mother could take so decisive a step as to write to a man unknown to her without asking that mother's advice?"

"Well, papa, because mamma would not have allowed it."

"And do you think, my child, that it was right? Though you have inevitably been left to bring yourself up, how is it that your reason or your insight—if modesty failed you—did not tell you that to act in such a way was to throw yourself at a man's head? Can it be that my daughter, my only child, lacks pride and delicacy? Oh! Modeste, you gave your father two hours of hell's torments in Paris; for, in point of fact, your conduct, morally, has been the same as Bettina's, without having the excuse of seduction; you have been a coquette in cold blood, and that is love without heart, the worst vice of the French woman."

"I—without pride?" said Modeste in tears. "But he has never seen me!"

"*He* knows your name."

"I never let him know it till the moment when our eyes had set the seal to three months of correspondence, during which our souls had spoken to each other!"

"Yes, my dear mistaken angel, you have brought a kind of reason to bear on this madness which has compromised your happiness and your family."

"Well, after all, papa, happiness is the justification of such boldness," said she, with a touch of temper.

"Ah! Then it is merely boldness?" cried her father.

"Such boldness as my mother allowed herself," she answered hastily.

"Refractory child! Your mother, after meeting me at a ball, told her father, who adored her, that same evening that she believed she could be happy with me.—Now, be candid, Modeste; is there any resemblance between love, at first sight it is true, but under a father's eye, and the mad act of writing to an unknown man?"

"An unknown man? Nay, papa, one of our greatest poets, whose character and life are under the light of day, exposed to gossip and calumny; a man clothed in glory, to whom, my dear father, I was but a dramatic, literary personage—a girl of Shakespeare's—till the moment when I felt I must know whether the man were as attractive as his soul is beautiful."

"Bless me, my poor child, you are dreaming of poetry in connection with marriage. But if, in all ages, girls have been cloistered in the family; if God and social law have placed them under the stern yoke of paternal sanction, it is precisely and on purpose to spare them the misfortunes to which the poetry that fascinates you must lead while it dazzles you, and which you therefore cannot estimate at its true worth. Poetry is one of the graces of life; it is not the whole of life."

"Papa, it is an action for ever undecided before the tribunal of facts, for there is a constant struggle between our hearts and the family authority."

"Woe to the girl who should find happiness by means of such resistance!" said the Colonel gravely. "In 1813 one of my fellow-officers, the Marquis d'Aiglemont, married his cousin against her father's warnings, and the household paid dearly for the obstinacy that a girl could mistake for love. —In these matters the family is supreme."

"My *fiancé* has told me all that," said she. "He assumed the part of *Orgon* for some time, and had the courage to run down the personal character of poets."

"I have read the correspondence," said her father, with a meaning smile that made Modeste uneasy. "And I may, on that point, remark that your last letter would hardly be allowable in a girl who had been seduced—in a Julie d'Étanges. Good God! what mischief comes of romances!"

"If they were never written, my dear father, we should still enact them. It is better to read them. There are fewer romantic adventures now than in the time of Louis XIV. and Louis XV., when fewer novels were published.—Besides, if you have read our letters, you must have perceived that I have found you for a son-in-law the most respectful son, the most angelic nature, the strictest honesty, and that we love each other at least as much as you and mamma did. . . . Well, I will admit that the affair has not been conducted exactly as etiquette requires. I made a mistake, if you like——"

"I have read your letters," repeated her father, interrupting her, "so I know how he justified you in your own eyes for a step which might perhaps be excusable in a woman who knows life, who is carried away by passion, but which in a girl of twenty is a monstrous fault——"

"A fault in common people's eyes, in those of narrow-minded Gobenheims, who measure out life with a T square! But do not let us go beyond the artistic and poetic world, paps. —We young girls live between two alternatives: we may show a man that we love him by mincing graces, or we may go to meet him frankly. And is not this last method really great and noble? We French girls are disposed of by our family like merchandise, at three months' date, sometimes much sooner, like Mademoiselle Vilquin; but in England, Switzerland, and Germany they are married more nearly on the system I have adopted. What can you say to that? Am I not half German?"

"Child," exclaimed the Colonel, looking at his daughter, "the superiority of France lies precisely in the common sense, the strict logic to which our splendid language compels the mind. France is the Reason of the world! England and Germany are romantic in this point; but even there the great families follow their customs.—You girls would rather not believe, then, that your parents, who know life, have the charge of your souls and your happiness, and that it is their duty to steer you clear of the rocks! . . . Good God!" he went on, "is this their fault or ours? Ought we to bend our children under a yoke of iron? Must we always be punished for the tenderness which prompts us to make them happy, which, unfortunately, makes them heart of our heart!"

As she heard this ejaculation, spoken almost with tears, Modeste cast a side glance at her father.

"Is it wrong in a girl whose heart is free," said she, "to choose for her husband a man who is not only charming in himself, but who is also a man of genius, of good birth, and in a fine position—a gentleman as gentle as myself?"

"Then you love him?" said the Colonel.

"I tell you, father," said she, laying her head on his breast, "if you do not want to see me die——"

"That is enough," said the Colonel; "your passion is, I see, unchangeable."

"Unchangeable."

"Nothing could move you?"

"Nothing in the world."

"You can conceive of no alteration, no betrayal," her father went on. "You love him for better, for worse, for the sake of his personal charm; and if he should be a d'Estourny, you still would love him?"

"Oh, papa, you do not know your child! Could I love a coward, a man devoid of truth and honor—a gallows-bird!"

"Then supposing you have been deceived?"

"By that charming young fellow, so candid—almost melancholy?—You are laughing at me, or you have not seen him."

"I see; happily your love is not so imperative as you say. I have suggested conditions which might modify your poem.—Well, then, you will admit that fathers are of some use?"

"You wanted to give me a lesson, papa—a sort of object-lesson, it would seem."

"Poor misled girl!" said her father severely; "the lesson is not of my giving; I have nothing to do with it beyond trying to soften the blow."

"Say no more, papa; do not trifle with my very life," said Modeste, turning pale.

"Nay, my child, summon up your courage. It is you who have trifled with life, and life now laughs you to scorn."

Modeste looked at her father in bewilderment.

"Listen; if the young man you love, whom you saw in

church at le Havre four days ago, were a contemptible wretch ——."

"It is not true!" said she. "That pale, dark face, so noble and full of poetry——"

"Is a lie!" said the Colonel, interrupting her. "He is no more Monsieur de Canalis than I am that fisherman hauling up his sail to go out——"

"Do you know what you are killing in me?" said Modeste.

"Be comforted, my child; though fate has made your fault its own punishment, the mischief is not irreparable. The youth you saw, with whom you have exchanged hearts by correspondence, is an honest fellow; he came to me to confess his dilemma. He loves you, and I should not object to him as a son-in-law."

"And if he is not Canalis, who is he?" asked Modeste, in a broken voice.

"His secretary. His name is Ernest de la Brière. He is not of superior birth, but he is one of those average men, with solid virtues and sound morals, whom parents like. And what does it matter to us, after all? You have seen him; nothing can change your feelings; you have chosen him, you know his soul—it is as noble as he is good-looking."

The Comte de la Bastie was checked by a sigh from Modeste. The poor child, perfectly white, her eyes fixed on the sea, and as rigid as the dead, had been struck as by a pistol-shot by the words, *"One of those average men, with solid virtues and sound morals, whom parents like."*

"Deceived!" she said at last.

"As your poor sister was, but less seriously."

"Let us go home, papa," she said, rising from the knoll on which they had been sitting. "Listen, father; I swear before God to obey your wishes, whatever they may be, in the business of marriage."

"Then you have already ceased to love?" asked her father sarcastically.

"I loved a true man without a falsehood on his face, as honest as you yourself, incapable of disguising himself like an actor, of dressing himself up in another man's glory."

"You said that nothing could move you!" said the Colonel ironically.

"Oh, do not make game of me!" cried she, clasping her hands, and looking at her father in an agony of entreaty. "You do not know how you are torturing my heart and my dearest beliefs by your satire——"

"God forbid! I have said the exact truth."

"You are very good, father," she replied, after a pause, with a certain solemnity.

"And he has your letters! Heh?" said Charles Mignon. "If those crazy effusions of your soul had fallen into the hands of one of those poets who, according to Dumay, use them for pipe-lights——"

"Oh, that is going too far."

"So Canalis told him."

"He saw Canalis?"

"Yes," replied the Colonel.

They walked on a little way in silence.

"That, then," said Modeste, when they had gone a few steps, "was why that gentleman spoke so ill of poets and poetry. Why did that little secretary talk of—— But, however," she added, interrupting herself, "were not his virtues, his qualities, his fine sentiments, a mere epistolary make-up? The man who steals another's fame and name may very well——"

"Pick locks, rob the Treasury, murder on the highway," said Charles Mignon, smiling. "That is just like you—you girls, with your uncompromising feelings and your ignorance of life. A man who can deceive a woman has either escaped the scaffold or must end there."

This raillery checked Modeste's effervescence, and again they were both silent.

"My child," the Colonel added, "men in the world—as in nature, for that matter—are bound to try to win your hearts, and you defend them. You have reversed the position. Is that well? In a false position everything is false. Yours, then, was the first wrong step.—No, a man is not a monster because he tries to attract a woman; our rights allow us to be the aggressors, with all the consequences, short of crime and baseness. A man may still have virtues even after throwing over a woman, for this simply means that he has failed to find the treasure he sought in her; while no woman but a queen, an actress, or a woman so far above the man in rank that to him she is like a queen, can take the initiative without incurring much blame.—But a girl! She is false to everything that God has given her, every flower of saintliness, dignity, and sweetness, whatever grace, poetry, or precaution she may infuse into the act."

"To seek the master and find the servant! To play the old farce of Love and Chance on one side only!" she exclaimed, with bitter feeling. "Oh, I shall never hold up my head again!"

"Foolish child! Monsieur Ernest de la Brière is, in my eyes, at least the equal of Monsieur de Canalis; he has been private secretary to a Prime Minister, he is Referendary to the Court of Exchequer, he is a man of heart, he adores you, —but he does not write verses.—No, I confess it, he is not a poet; but he may have a heart full of poetry. However, my poor child," he added, in reply to Modeste's face of disgust, "you will see them both—the false and the real Canalis——"

"Oh, papa!"

"Did you not swear to obey me in everything that concerns the *business* of your marriage? Well, you may choose between them the man you prefer for your husband. You began with a poem, you may end with a page of bucolics by trying to detect the true nature of these gentlemen in some rustic excursions, a shooting or a fishing party."

Modeste bent her head and returned to the Chalet with her father, listening to what he said, and answering in monosyllables. She had fallen humiliated into the depths of a bog, from the Alp where she fancied she had flown up to an eagle's nest. To adopt the poetical phraseology of an author of that period, "After feeling the soles of her feet too tender to tread on the glass sherds of reality, Fancy, which had united every characteristic of woman in that fragile form, from the day-dreams of a modest girl, all strewn with violets, to the unbridled desires of a courtesan, has now led her to the midst of her enchanted gardens, where, hideous surprise! instead of an exquisite blossom, she found growing from the soil the hairy and twisted limbs of the Mandragora."

From the mystic heights of her love, Modeste had dropped on to the dull, flat road, lying between ditches and ploughed lands—the road, in short, that is paved with vulgarity. What girl with an ardent spirit but would be broken by such a fall? At whose feet had she cast her promises?

The Modeste who returned to the Chalet bore no more resemblance to the girl who had gone out two hours before, than the actress in the street resembles the heroine on the stage. She sank into a state of apathy that was painful to behold. The sun was darkened, nature was under a shroud, the flowers had no message for her. Like every girl of a vehement disposition, she drank a little too deep of the cup of disenchantment. She rebelled against reality, without choosing as yet to bend her neck to the yoke of the family and of society; she thought it too heavy, too hard, too oppressive. She would not even listen to the comfort offered by her father and mother, and felt an indescribable savage delight in abandoning herself to her mental sufferings.

"Then poor Butscha was right!" she exclaimed one evening.

This speech shows how far she had traveled in so short a time on the barren plains of Reality, guided by her deep dejection. Grief, when it comes of the upheaval of all our hopes, is an illness; it often ends in death. It would be no mean occupation for modern physiology to investigate the process and means by which a thought can produce the same deadly effects as a poison; how despair can destroy the appetite, injure the pylorus, and change all the functions of the strongest vitality. This was the case with Modeste. In three days she presented an image of morbid melancholy; she sang no more, it was impossible to make her smile; her parents and friends were alarmed. Charles Mignon, uneasy at seeing nothing of the two young men, was thinking of going to fetch them; but on the fourth day Monsieur Latournelle had news of them, and this was how.

Canalis, immensely tempted by such a rich marriage, would neglect no means of outdoing la Brière, while Ernest could not complain of his having violated the laws of friendship. The poet thought that nothing put a lover at a greater disadvantage in a young lady's eyes than figuring in an inferior position; so he proposed, in the most innocent manner possible, that he and la Brière should keep house together, taking a little country place at Ingouville, where they might live for a month under pretext of recruiting their health.

As soon as la Brière had consented to this proposal, at first regarding it as very natural, Canalis insisted on his being his guest, and made all the arrangements himself. He sent his man-servant to le Havre, desiring him to apply to Monsieur Latournelle for the choice of a country cottage at Ingouville, thinking that the notary would certainly talk over the matter with the Mignon family. Ernest and Canalis, it may be supposed, had discussed every detail of their adventure; and la Brière, always prolix, had given his rival a thousand valuable hints.

The servant, understanding his master's intentions, carried them out to admiration; he trumpeted the advent of the great poet, to whom his doctors had ordered some sea-baths to recruit him after the double fatigues of politics and literature. This grand personage required a house of at least so many rooms; for he was bringing his secretary, his cook, two men-servants, and a coachman, not to mention Monsieur Germain Bonnet, his body-servant. The traveling carriage the poet selected and hired for a month was very neat, and could serve for making some excursions; and Germain was in search of two saddle-horses for hire in the neighborhood, as Monsieur le Baron and his secretary were fond of horse-exercise. In the presence of little Latournelle, Germain, as he went over various houses, spoke much of the secretary, and rejected two villas on the ground that Monsieur de la Brière would not be well accommodated.

"Monsieur le Baron," said he, "regards his secretary as his best friend. Oh, I should catch it handsomely if Monsieur de la Brière were not as well served as Monsieur le Baron himself. And, after all, Monsieur de la Brière is Referendary to the Court of Exchequer."

Germain was never seen dressed otherwise than in a suit of black, with good gloves and boots, turned out like a gentleman. Imagine the effect he produced, and the notion that was formed of the great poet from this specimen. A clever man's servant becomes clever too; the master's cleverness presently "runs" and colors the man. Germain did not overact his part; he was straightforward and genial, as Canalis had instructed him to be. Poor la Brière had no suspicion of the injury Germain was doing him, or of the depreciation to which he had exposed himself; for some echoes of public report rose from the lower depths to Modeste's ears. Thus Canalis was bringing his friend in his retinue, in his carriage; and Ernest's simple nature did not allow him to perceive his false position soon enough to remedy it.

The delay which so provoked Charles Mignon was caused by the poet's desire to have his arms painted on the doors of the chaise, and by his orders to the tailor; for Canalis took in the wide world of such trivialities, of which the least may influence a girl.

"Make yourself easy," said Latournelle to the Colonel on the fifth day. "Monsieur de Canalis' man came to a determination this morning. He has taken Madame Amaury's cottage at Sanvic, furnished, for seven hundred francs, and has written to his master that he can start, and will find everything ready on his arrival. So the gentlemen will be here by Sunday. I have also had this note from Butscha. Here —it is not long: 'My dear Master, I cannot get back before Sunday. Between this and then I must get some important information which nearly concerns some one in whom you are interested.'"

The announcement of this arrival did not make Modeste at all less sad; the sense of a fall, of humiliation, still held sway over her, and she was not such a born coquette as her father thought her. There is a charming and permissible kind of flirtation, the coquetry of the soul, which might be called the good breeding of love; and Charles Mignon, when reproving his daughter, had failed to distinguish between the desire to please and the factitious love of the mind, between the craving to love and self-interest. Just like a soldier of the Empire, he saw in the letters he had so hastily read a girl throwing herself at a poet's head; but in many letters—omitted here for the sake of brevity—a connoisseur would have admired the maidenly and graceful reserve which Modeste had immediately substituted for the aggressive and frivolous pertness of her first effusions—a transition very natural in a woman.

On one point her father had been cruelly right. It was her last letter—in which Modeste, carried away by threefold love, had spoken as though their marriage were a decided thing, which really brought her to shame. Still, she thought her father very hard, very cruel, to compel her to receive a man so unworthy of her, towards whom her soul had flown almost unveiled. She had questioned Dumay as to his interview with the poet; she had ingeniously extracted from him every detail, and she could not think Canalis such a barbarian as the lieutenant thought him. She could smile at the fine papal chest containing the letters of the *mille et trois* ladies of this literary Don Giovanni. Again and again she was on the point of saying to her father, "I am not the only girl who writes to him; the cream of womankind send leaves for the poet's crown of bay."

In the course of this week Modeste's character underwent a transformation. This catastrophe—and it was a great one to so poetical a nature—aroused her latent acumen and spirit of mischief, and her suitors were to find her a formidable adversary. For, in fact, in any girl, if her heart is chilled, her head grows clear; she then observes everything with a certain swiftness of judgment and a spirit of mockery, such as Shakespeare has admirably painted in the person of Beatrice in *Much Ado about Nothing*. Modeste was seized by intense disgust of mankind, since the most distinguished of them had deceived her hopes. In love, what a woman mistakes for disgust is simply seeing clearly; but in matters of feeling no woman, especially no young girl, ever sees truly. When she ceases to admire, she contemns. So Modeste, after going through fearful tortures of mind, inevitably put on the armor on which, as she declared, she had stamped the word Contempt; thenceforward she could look on as a disinterested spectator at what she called the Farce of Suitors, although she filled the part of leading lady. More especially was she bent on pertinaciously humiliating Monsieur de la Brière.

"Modeste is saved," said Madame Mignon to her husband with a smile. "She means to be revenged on the false Canalis by trying to fall in love with the true one."

This was, indeed, Modeste's plan. It was so obvious that her mother, to whom she confided her vexation, advised her to treat Monsieur de la Brière with oppressive civility.

"These two young fellows," said Madame Latournelle on the Saturday, "have no suspicion of the troop of spies at their heels, for here are eight of us to keep an eye on them."

"What, my dear—two?" cried little Latournelle; "there are three of them!—Gobenheim is not here yet, so I may speak."

Modeste had looked up, and all the others, following her example, gazed at the notary.

"A third lover, and he is a lover, has put himself on the list——"

"Bless me!" said Charles Mignon.

"But he is no less a person," the notary went on pompously, "than His Lordship Monsieur le Duc d'Hérouville, Marquis de Saint-Séver, Duc de Nivron, Comte de Bayeux, Vicomte d'Essigny, High Equerry of France, and Peer of the Realm, Knight of the Orders of the Spur and of the Golden Fleece, Grandee of Spain, and son of the last Governor of Normandy.

—He saw Mademoiselle Modeste when he was staying with the Vilquins, and he then only regretted—as his notary told me, who arrived yesterday from Bayeux—that she was not rich enough for him, since his father, on his return from exile, had found nothing left but his Château of Hérouville, graced by his sister's presence.—The young Duke is three-and-thirty. I am definitively charged to make overtures, Monsieur le Comte," added Latournelle, turning respectfully to the Colonel.

"Ask Modeste," said her father, "whether she wishes to have another bird in her aviary; for, so far as I am concerned, I am quite willing that this fine gentleman equerry should pay his addresses to her."

Notwithstanding the care with which Charles Mignon avoided seeing anybody, stayed in the Chalet, and never went out but with Modeste, Gobenheim, whom they could hardly cease to receive at the Chalet, had gossiped about Dumay's wealth; for Dumay, a second father to Modeste, had said to Gobenheim when he left his service, "I shall be my Colonel's steward, and all my money, excepting what my wife may keep, will go to my little Modeste's children."

So every one at le Havre had echoed the plain question that Latournelle had asked himself:

"Must not Monsieur Charles Mignon have made an enormous fortune if Dumay's share amounts to six hundred thousand francs, and if Dumay is to be his steward?"

"Monsieur Mignon came home in a ship of his own," said the gossips on 'Change, "loaded with indigo. The freight alone, not to mention the vessel, is worth more than he gives out to be his fortune."

The Colonel would not discharge the servants he had so carefully chosen during his travels, so he was obliged to hire a house for six months in the lower part of Ingouville; he had a body-servant, a cook, and a coachman—both negroes—and a mulatto woman and two mulatto men on whose faithfulness he could rely. The coachman was inquiring for riding horses for mademoiselle and his master, and for carriage horses for the chaise in which the Colonel and the Lieutenant had come home. This traveling carriage, purchased in Paris, was in the latest fashion, and bore the arms of la Bastie with a Count's coronet. All these things, mere trifles in the eyes of a man who had been living, for four years, in the midst of the unbounded luxury of the Indies, of the Hong merchants, and the English at Canton, were the subject of comment to the traders of le Havre and the good folks of Graville and Ingouville. Within five days there was a hubbub of talk which flashed across Normandy like a fired train of gunpowder.

"Monsieur Mignon has come home from China with millions," was said at Rouen, "and it would seem that he has become a Count in the course of his travels."

"But he was Comte de la Bastie before the Revolution," somebody remarked.

"So a Liberal, who for five-and-twenty years was known as Charles Mignon, is now called Monsieur le Comte! What are we coming to?"

Thus, in spite of the reserve of her parents and intimates, Modeste was regarded as the richest heiress in Normandy, and all eyes could now see her merits. The Duc d'Hérouville's aunt and sister, in full drawing-room assembly at Bayeux, confirmed Monsieur Charles Mignon's right to the arms and title of Count conferred on Cardinal Mignon, whose Cardinal's hat and cords were, out of gratitude, assumed in place of a crest and supporters. These ladies had caught sight of Mademoiselle de la Bastie from the Vilquins', and their solicitude for the impoverished head of the house at once scented an opportunity.

"If Mademoiselle de la Bastie is as rich as she is handsome," said the young Duke's aunt, "she will be the best match in the province. And she, at any rate, is of noble birth!"

The last words were a shot at the Vilquins, with whom they could not come to terms after enduring the humiliation of paying them a visit.

Such were the little events which led to the introduction of another actor in this domestic drama, contrary to all the laws of Aristotle and Horace. But the portrait and biography of this personage, so tardy in his appearance, will not detain us long, since he is of the smallest importance. Monsieur le Duc will not fill more space here than he will in history.

His Lordship Monsieur le Duc d'Hérouville, the fruit of the matrimonial autumn of the last Governor of Normandy, was born at Vienna in 1796, during the emigration. The old Marshal, who returned with the King in 1814, died in 1819 without seeing his son married, though he was Duc de Nivron; he had nothing to leave him but the immense Château of Hérouville, with the park, some outlying ground and a farm, all painfully repurchased, and worth about fifteen thousand francs a year. Louis XVIII. gave the young Duke the post of Master of the Horse; and under Charles X. he received the allowance of twelve thousand francs a year granted to impecunious peers.

But what were twenty-seven thousand francs a year for such a family? In Paris, indeed, the young Duke had the use of the Royal carriages, and his official residence at the King's stables in the Rue Saint-Thomas du Louvre; his salary paid the expenses of the winter, and the twenty-seven thousand francs paid those of the summer in Normandy.

Though this great man was still a bachelor, the fault was less his own than that of his aunt, who was not familiar with La Fontaine's fables. Mademoiselle d'Hérouville's pretensions were stupendous, quite out of harmony with the spirit of the age; for great names without money can hardly meet with any wealthy heiresses among the high French nobility, which finds it difficult enough to enrich its sons, ruined by the equal division of property. To find an advantageous match for the young Duc d'Hérouville she should have cultivated the great financial houses, and this haughty daughter of the noble house offended them all by her cutting speeches. During the early years of the Restoration, between 1817 and 1825, while looking out for millions, Mademoiselle d'Hérouville refused Mademoiselle Mongenod, the banker's daughter, with whom Monsieur de Fontaine was content. And now, after various good matches had been marred by her pride, she had just decided that the fortune of the Nucingens had been amassed by too vile means to allow of her lending herself to Madame de Nucingen's ambitious desire to see her daughter a duchess. The King, anxious to restore the splendor of the Hérouvilles, had almost made the match himself, and he publicly taxed Mademoiselle d'Hérouville with folly. Thus the aunt made her nephew ridiculous, and the Duke laid himself open to ridicule.

It is a fact that when the great things of humanity vanish they leave some fragments (*frusteaux,* Rabelais would call them); and the French nobility in our day shows too many fag-ends. In this long study of manners neither the clergy nor the nobility have anything to complain of. Those two great and magnificent social necessaries are well represented; but would it not be false to the proud title of Historian to be other than impartial, to fail to show here the degeneracy of the race—just as you will elsewhere find the study of an émigré, the Comte de Mortsauf (*le Lys dans la Vallée*), and every noblest feature of the noble, in the Marquis d'Espard (*l'Interdiction*).

How was it that a race of brave and strong men, that the house of d'Hérouville, which gave the famous Marshal to the Royal cause, cardinals to the Church, captains to the Valois, and brave men to Louis XIV., ended in a frail creature smaller than Butscha? It is a question we may ask ourselves in many a Paris drawing-room, as we hear one of the great names of France announced, and see a little slender slip of a man come in who seems only to breathe, or a prematurely old fellow, or some eccentric being, in whom the observer seeks, but scarcely finds, a feature in which imagination can see a trace of original greatness. The dissipations of the reign of Louis XV., the orgies of that selfish time, have produced the etiolated generation in which fine manners are the sole survivors of extinct great qualities. Style is the only inheritance preserved by the nobility. Thus, apart from certain exceptions, the defection which left Louis XVI. to perish may be to some extent explained by the miserable heritage of the reign of Madame de Pompadour.

The Master of the Horse, a young man with blue eyes, fair, pale, and slight, had a certain dignity of mind; but his small size, and his aunt's mistake in having led him to be uselessly civil to the Vilquins, made him excessively shy. The d'Hérouvilles had had a narrow escape of dying out in the person of a cripple (*l'Enfant maudit*). But the Grand Marshal—as the family always called the d'Hérouville whom Louis XIII. had created Duke—had married at the age of eighty-two, and, of course, the family had been continued. The young Duke liked women; but he placed them too high, he respected them too much, he adored them, and was not at his ease but with those whom no one respects. This character had led to his living a twofold life. He avenged himself on women of easy life for the worship he paid in the drawing-rooms, or, if you like, the boudoirs, of Saint-Germain. His ways and his tiny figure, his weary face, his blue eyes, with their somewhat ecstatic expression, had added to the ridicule poured on him, most unjustly, for he was full of apprehensiveness and wit; but his wit had no sparkle, and was never seen excepting when he was quite at his ease. Fanny Beaupré, the actress, who was supposed to be his highly paid and most intimate friend, used to say of him, "It is good wine, but so tightly corked up that you break your corkscrews."

The handsome Duchesse de Maufrigneuse, whom the Master of the Horse could only adore, crushed him by a speech which, unluckily, was repeated, as all clever but ill-natured speeches are.

"He reminds me," said she, "of a trinket, beautifully wrought, but which we show more than we use, and always keep in cotton wool."

Even his title of Master of the Horse would, by force of contrast, make good King Charles X. laugh, though the Duc d'Hérouville was a capital horseman. Men, like books, are sometimes valued too late. Modeste had had a glimpse of the

Duke during his fruitless visit to the Vilquins, and as he went by, all these remarks involuntarily recurred to her mind; but in the position in which she now stood, she perceived how valuable the Duc d'Hérouville's suit would be to save her from being at the mercy of a Canalis.

"I do not see," said she to Latournelle, "why the Duc d'Hérouville should not be allowed to call. In spite of our indigence," she added, with a mischievous glance at her father, "I am supposed to be an heiress. I shall have at last to publish a card of the field.—Have you not noticed how Gobenheim's looks have changed in the course of this week? He is in despair because he cannot set down his faithful attendance for whist to the score of mute admiration of me!"

"Hush, my darling! here he is," said Madame Latournelle.

"Old Althor is in despair," said Gobenheim to Monsieur Mignon as he came in.

"What about?" asked the Comte de la Bastie.

"Vilquin is going to fail, they say, and on 'Change here you are said to have several millions——"

"No one knows," said Charles Mignon very drily, "what my obligations in India may amount to, and I do not care to admit the public to my confidence in business matters.—Dumay," he added in his friend's ear, "if Vilquin is in difficulties, we may be able to get the place back for what he gave for it in ready money."

Such was the state of affairs brought about by chance when, on Sunday morning, Canalis and la Brière, preceded by a courier, arrived at Madame Amaury's villa. They were told that the Duc d'Hérouville and his sister had arrived on the previous Tuesday at a hired house in Graville, for the benefit of their health. This competition led to a jest in the town that rents would rise at Ingouville.

"She will make the place a perfect hospital if this goes on!" remarked Mademoiselle Vilquin, disgusted at not becoming a duchess.

The perennial comedy of *The Heiress*, now to be performed at the Chalet, might certainly, from the frame of mind in which it found Modeste, have been, as she had said in jest, a competition, for she was firmly resolved, after the overthrow of her illusions, to give her hand only to the man whose character should prove perfectly satisfactory.

On the morrow of their arrival, the rivals—still bosom friends—prepared to make their first visit to the Chalet that evening. They devoted the whole of Sunday and all Monday morning to unpacking, to taking possession of Madame Amaury's house, and to settling themselves in it for a month. Besides, the poet, justified by his position as Minister's apprentice in allowing himself some craft, had thought of everything; he wished to get the benefit of the excitement that might be caused by his arrival, of which some echoes might reach the Chalet. Canalis, supposed to be much fatigued, did not go out; la Brière went twice to walk past the Chalet, for he loved with a sort of desperation, he had the greatest dread of having repelled Modeste, his future seemed wrapped in thick clouds.

The two friends came down to dinner on that Monday in array for their first visit, the most important of all. La Brière was dressed as he had been in church on that famous Sunday; but he regarded himself as the satellite to a planet, and trusted wholly to the chance of circumstances. Canalis, on his part, had not forgotten his black coat, nor his orders, nor the drawing-room grace perfected by his intimacy with the Duchesse de Chaulieu, his patroness, and with the finest company of the Faubourg Saint-Germain. Canalis had attended to every detail of dandyism, while poor Ernest was prepared to appear in the comparative carelessness of a hopeless man.

As he waited on the two gentlemen at table, Germain could not help smiling at the contrast. At the second course he came in with a diplomatic, or, to be exact, a disturbed air.

"Monsieur le Baron," said he to Canalis in a low voice, "did you know that Monsieur the Master of the Horse is coming to Graville to be cured of the same complaint as you and Monsieur de la Brière?"

"The little Duc d'Hérouville?" cried Canalis.

"Yes, sir."

"Can he have come for Mademoiselle de la Bastie?" asked la Brière, coloring.

"For Mademoiselle Mignon," replied Germain.

"We are done!" cried Canalis, looking at la Brière.

"Ah!" Ernest eagerly replied, "that is the first time you have said *we* since we left Paris. Till this moment you have said *I*."

"You know me!" cried Melchior with a burst of laughter. "Well, we are not in a position to hold our own against an officer of the Household, against the titles of Duke and Peer, nor against the marsh-lands which the Privy Council has just conferred, on the strength of my report, on the House of Hérouville."

"His Highness," said la Brière with mischievous gravity, "offers you a plum of consolation in the person of his sister."

Just at this moment the Comte de la Bastie was announced. The two young men rose to receive him, and la Brière hastened to meet him and introduce Canalis.

"I had to return the visit you paid me in Paris," said Charles Mignon to the young Referendary, "and I knew that by coming here I should have the added pleasure of seeing one of our great living poets."

"Great?—monsieur," the poet replied with a smile; "there can be nothing great henceforth in an age to which the reign of Napoleon was the preface. To begin with, we are a perfect tribe of so-called great poets. And besides, second-rate talent apes genius so well that it has made any great distinction impossible."

"And is that what has driven you into politics?" asked the Comte de la Bastie.

"It is the same in that field too," said Canalis. "There will be no more great statesmen; there will be only men who are more or less in touch with events. Under the system produced by the Charter, monsieur, which regards the schedule of the rates you pay as a patent of nobility, there is nothing substantial but what you went to find in China—a fortune."

Melchior, well pleased with himself, and satisfied with the impression he was making on his future father-in-law, now turned to Germain.

"Give us coffee in the drawing-room," said he, bowing to the merchant to leave the dining-room.

"I must thank you, Monsieur le Comte," said la Brière, "for having spared me the embarrassment of not knowing how I might introduce my friend at your house. To your kind heart you add a happy wit——"

"Oh, such wit as is common to the natives of Provence," said Mignon.

"Ah, you come from Provence?" cried Canalis.

"Forgive my friend," said la Brière; "he has not studied the history of the la Basties as I have."

At the word friend, Canalis shot a deep look at Ernest.

"If your health permits," said the Provençal to the great poet, "I claim the honor of receiving you this evening under my roof. It will be a day to mark, as the ancients have it, *albo notanda lapillo*. Though we are somewhat shy of receiving so great a glory in so small a house, you will gratify my daughter's impatience, for her admiration has led her even to set your verses to music."

"You possess what is better than glory," said Canalis. "You have beauty in your home, if I may believe Ernest."

"Oh, she is a good girl, whom you will find quite provincial," said the father.

"Provincial as she is, she has a suitor in the Duc d'Hérouville," cried Canalis in a hard tone.

"Oh," said Monsieur Mignon, with the deceptive frankness of a southerner, "I leave my daughter free to choose. Dukes, princes, private gentlemen, they are all the same to me, even men of genius. I will pledge myself to nothing; the man my Modeste may prefer will be my son-in-law, or rather my son," and he looked at la Brière. "Madame de la Bastie is a German; she cannot tolerate French etiquette, and I allow myself to be guided by my two women. I would always rather ride inside a carriage than on the box. We can discuss such serious matters in jest, for we have not yet seen the Duc d'Hérouville, and I do not believe in marriages arranged by proxy any more than in suitors forced on girls by their parents."

"That is a declaration equally disheartening and encouraging to two young men who seek in marriage the philosopher's stone of happiness," said Canalis.

"Do not you think it desirable, necessary, and indeed good policy, to stipulate for perfect liberty for the parents, the daughter, and the suitors?" said Charles Mignon.

Canalis, at a glance from la Brière, made no reply, and the conversation continued on indifferent subjects. After walking two or three times round the garden, the father withdrew, begging the two friends to pay their visit.

"That is our dismissal," cried Canalis. "You understood it as I did. After all, in his place I should not hesitate between the Master of the Horse and either of us, charming fellows as we may be."

"I do not think so," said la Brière. "I believe that the worthy officer came simply to gratify his own impatience to see you, and to declare his neutrality while opening his house to us. Modeste, bewitched by your fame, and misled as to my identity, finds herself between Poetry and hard Fact. It is my misfortune to be the hard Fact."

"Germain," said Canalis to the servant who came in to clear away the coffee, "order the carriage round. We will go out in half an hour, and take a drive before going to the Chalet."

The two young men were equally impatient to see Modeste, but la Brière dreaded the meeting, while Canalis looked forward to it with a confidence inspired by conceit. Ernest's impulsive advances to her father, and the flattery by which he had soothed the merchant's aristocratic pride while showing up the poet's awkwardness, made Canalis determine that he would play a part. He resolved that he would display all his powers of attraction, but at the same time affect indifference, seem to disdain Modeste, and so goad the girl's vanity. A disciple of the beautiful Duchesse de Chaulieu, he here showed himself worthy of his reputation as a man who knew women well; though he did not really know them, since no man does who is the happy victim of an exclusive passion. While the luckless Ernest, sunk in a corner of the carriage, was crushed by the terrors of true love and the anticipated wrath, scorn, contempt—all the lightnings of an offended and disappointed girl—and kept gloomy silence, Canalis, not less silent, was preparing himself, like an actor studying an important part in a new play.

Neither of them certainly looked like a happy man.

For Canalis, indeed, the matter was serious. To him the mere fancy for marrying involved the breach of the serious friendship which had bound him for nearly ten years to the Duchesse de Chaulieu. Though he had screened his journey under the common excuse of overwork—in which no woman ever believes, even if it is true—his conscience troubled him somewhat; but to la Brière the word Conscience seemed so Jesuitical that he only shrugged his shoulders when the poet spoke of his scruples.

"Your conscience, my boy, seems to me to mean simply your fear of losing the gratifications of vanity, some solid advantages, and a pleasant habit in sacrificing Madame de Chaulieu's affection; for, if you are successful with Modeste, you will certainly have nothing to regret in the aftermath of a passion so constantly reaped during these eight years past. If you tell me that you are afraid of offending your protectress, should she learn the real reason of your visit here, I can easily believe you. To throw over the Duchess and fail at the Chalet is staking too much! And you mistake the distress of this alternative for remorse!"

"You know nothing about sentiment!" cried Canalis, nettled, as a man always is when he asks for a compliment and hears the truth.

"That is just what a bigamist would say to a dozen jurymen," said la Brière, laughing.

This epigram made a yet more disagreeable impression on Canalis; he thought la Brière much too clever and too free for a secretary.

The arrival of a handsome carriage, with a coachman in Canalis' livery, made all the greater sensation at the Chalet, because the two gentlemen were expected, and all the persons of this tale, excepting only the Duke and Butscha, were assembled there.

"Which is the poet?" asked Madame Latournelle of Dumay, as they stood in the window bay, where she had posted herself on hearing the carriage wheels.

"The one who marches like a drum-major," replied the cashier.

"Ah, hah!" said the lady, studying Melchior, who strutted like a man on whom the world has its eye.

Though rather severe, Dumay's judgment—a simple soul, if ever man was—had hit the mark. Canalis was, morally speaking, a sort of Narcissus; this was the fault of the great lady who flattered him immensely, and spoilt him as women older than their adorers always will flatter and spoil men. A woman past her first youth, who means to attach a man permanently, begins by glorifying his faults, so as to make all rivalry impossible; for her rival cannot at once be in the secret of that subtle flattery to which a man so easily becomes accustomed. Coxcombs are the product of this feminine industry, when they are not coxcombs by nature.

Hence Canalis, caught young by the beautiful Duchess, justified himself for his airs and graces by telling himself that they pleased a woman whose taste was law. Subtle as these shades of feeling are, it is not impossible to render them. Thus Melchior had a real talent for reading aloud, which had been much admired, and too flattering praise had led him into an exaggerated manner, which neither poet nor actor can set bounds to, and which made de Marsay say—always de Marsay —that he did not declaim, but brayed out his verses, so fully would he mouth the vowels as he listened to himself. To use the slang of the stage, he pumped himself out, and made too long pauses. He would examine his audience with a knowing look, and give himself self-satisfied airs, with the aids to emphasis of "sawing the air" and "windmill action"—picturesque phrases, as the catchwords of Art always are. Canalis indeed had imitators, and was the head of a school in this style. This melodramatic emphasis had slightly infected his conversation and given it a declamatory tone, as will have been seen in his interview with Dumay. When once the mind has become foppish, manners show the influence. Canalis had come at last to a sort of rhythmic gait, he invented attitudes, stole looks at himself in the glass, and made his language harmonize with the position he assumed. He thought so much of the effect to be produced, that more than once Blondet, a mocking spirit, had bet he would pull him up short—and had done it—merely by fixing a set gaze on the poet's hair, or boots, or the tail of his coat.

At the end of ten years these antics, which at first had passed under favor of youthful exuberance, had grown stale, and all the more so as Melchior himself seemed somewhat worn. Fashionable life is as fatiguing for men as for women, and perhaps the Duchess' twenty years' seniority weighed on Canalis more than on her; for the world saw her still handsome, without a wrinkle, without rouge, and without heart. Alas! neither men nor women have a friend to warn them at the moment when the fragrance of modesty turns rancid, when a caressing look is like a theatrical trick, when the expressiveness of a face becomes a grimace, when the mechanism of their liveliness shows its rusty skeleton. Genius alone can renew its youth like the serpent, and in grace, as in all else, only the heart never grows stale. Persons of genuine feeling are single-hearted. Now in Canalis, as we know, the heart was dry. He wasted the beauty of his gaze by assuming at inappropriate moments the intensity that deep thought gives to the eyes.

And, then, praise to him was an article of exchange, in

which he wanted to have all the advantage. His way of paying compliments, which charmed superficial persons, to those of more refined taste might seem insultingly commonplace, and the readiness of his flattery betrayed a set purpose. In fact, Melchior lied like a courtier. To the Duc de Chaulieu, who had proved an ineffective speaker when, as Minister for Foreign Affairs, he had been obliged to mount the Tribune, Canalis had unblushingly said, "Your Excellency was sublime!"

Many men like Canalis might have had their affectations eradicated by failure administered in small doses. Trifling, indeed, as such faults are in the gilded drawing-rooms of the Faubourg Saint-Germain—where everyone contributes a quota of absurdities, and this kind of audacity, artificiality, inflation if you will, has a background of excessive luxury and magnificent dress which is perhaps an excuse for it—they are monstrously conspicuous in the depths of the country, where what is thought ridiculous is the very opposite of all this. Canalis, indeed, at once pompous and mannered, could not now metamorphose himself; he had had time to set in the mould into which the Duchess had cast him, and he was, moreover, very Parisian, or, if you prefer it, very French. The Parisian is amazed that everything, everywhere, is not what it is in Paris, and the Frenchman that it is not what it is in France. Good taste consists in accommodating oneself to the manners of other places without losing too much of one's native character, as Alcibiades did—the model of a gentleman. True grace is elastic. It yields to every circumstance, it is in harmony with every social atmosphere, it knows how to walk in the street in a cheap dress, remarkable only for its fitness, instead of parading the feathers and gaudy hues which some vulgar people flaunt.

Now, Canalis, influenced by a woman who loved him for her own sake rather than for his, wanted to be himself a law, and to remain what he was wherever he might go. He believed that he carried his private public with him—a mistake shared by some other great men in Paris.

While the poet made a studied entrance into the little drawing-room, la Brière sneaked in like a dog that is afraid of being beaten.

"Ah, here is my soldier!" said Canalis, on seeing Dumay, after paying Madame Mignon his respects, and bowing to the other women. "Your anxieties are relieved, I hope?" he went on, offering him his hand with a flourish. "But the sight of mademoiselle sufficiently explains their gravity. I spoke only of earthly beings, not of angels."

The hearers by their expression asked for a clue to this riddle.

"Yes, I shall regard it as a triumph," the poet went on, understanding that everybody wanted an explanation, "that I succeeded in alarming one of those men of iron whom Napoleon succeeded in finding to form the piles on which he tried to found an empire too vast to be permanent. Only time can serve to cement such a structure!—But have I any right to boast of my triumph? I had nothing to do with it; it was the triumph of fancy over fact. Your battles, dear Monsieur Dumay; your heroic cavalry charges, Monsieur le Comte; in short, War, was the form assumed by Napoleon's thoughts. And of all these things what remains? The grass that grows over them knows nothing of them, nor will harvests mark the spot; but for history, but for writing, the future might know nothing of this heroic age! Thus your fifteen years of struggle are no more than ideas, and that is what will save the Empire; poets will make a poem of it. A land that can win such battles ought to be able to sing them!"

Canalis paused to collect, by a sweeping glance at their faces, the tribute of admiration due to him from these country folks.

"You cannot doubt, monsieur," said Madame Mignon, "how much I regret being unable to see you, from the way you indemnify me by the pleasure I feel in listening to you."

Modeste, dressed as she had been on the day when this story opens, having made up her mind to think Canalis sublime, sat speechless, and dropped her embroidery, which hung from her fingers at the end of the needleful of cotton.

"Modeste, this is Monsieur de la Brière.—Monsieur Ernest—my daughter," said Charles Mignon, thinking that the secretary was thrown rather too much into the background.

The young lady bowed coldly to Ernest, giving him a look intended to convey to the whole party that she had never seen him before.

"I beg your pardon," said she, without a blush, "the fervent admiration I profess for our greatest poet is, in my friends' eyes, a sufficient excuse for my having seen no one else."

The clear young voice, with a ring in it like the famous tones of Mademoiselle Mars, enchanted the poor Referendary, already dazzled by Modeste's beauty, and in his amazement he spoke a few words which, had they been true, would have been sublime:

"But he is my friend," said he.

"Then you will have forgiven me," she replied.

"He is more than a friend," cried Canalis, taking Ernest by the shoulder, and leaning on him as Alexander leaned on Hephaestion. "We love each other like two brothers——"

Madame Latournelle cut the poet short in the middle of his speech by saying to her husband:

"Surely monsieur is the gentleman we saw in church?"

"Why not?" said Charles Mignon, seeing Ernest color.

Modeste gave no sign, but took up her work again.

"You may be right; I have been twice to le Havre," said la Brière, sitting down by the side of Dumay.

Canalis, bewildered by Modeste's beauty, misunderstood the admiration she expressed, and flattered himself that his efforts had been perfectly successful.

"I should think a man of genius devoid of heart if he had not about him some attached friend," said Modeste, to revive the subject interrupted by Madame Latournelle's awkwardness.

"Mademoiselle, Ernest's devotion is enough to make me

believe that I am good for something," said Canalis. "For my dear Pylades is full of talent; he was quite half of the greatest Minister we have had since the Peace. Though he fills a distinguished position, he consents to be my tutor in politics. He teaches me business, he feeds me with his experience, while he might aspire to the highest office. Oh! he is much superior to me——"

At a gesture from Modeste, Melchior added gracefully:

"The poetry I write he bears in his heart; and if I dare speak so to his face, it is because he is as diffident as a nun."

"Come, come, that will do," said la Brière, who did not know how to look. "My dear fellow, you might be a mother wanting to get her daughter married."

"How can you think, monsieur, of becoming a politician?" said Charles Mignon to Canalis.

"For a poet it is abdication!" said Modeste. "Politics are the stand-by of men without imagination."

"Nay, mademoiselle, in these days the Tribune is the grandest stage in the world; it has taken the place of the lists of chivalry; it will be the meeting-place of every kind of intellect, as of old the army was of every form of courage."

Canalis had mounted his war-horse; for ten minutes he declaimed on the subject of political life:—Poetry was the preface to a statesman. In these days the orator's province was lofty generalization; he was the pastor of ideas. If a poet could show his countrymen the road of the future, did he cease to be himself? He quoted Chateaubriand, asserting that he would some day be more important on his political than on his literary side. The French Chambers would be the guiding light of humanity. Contests by words henceforth had taken the place of fighting on the battlefield. Such or such a sitting had been a second Austerlitz, and the speakers had risen to the dignity of generals; they spent as much of their life, courage, and strength, they wore themselves out as much as generals in war. Was not speech almost the most exhausting expenditure of vital power that man could indulge in, etc., etc.

This long harangue, made up of modern commonplace, but clothed in high-sounding phrases, newly-coined words, and intended to prove that the Baron de Canalis must some day be one of the glories of the Tribune, made a deep impression on the notary, on Gobenheim, on Madame Latournelle, and Madame Mignon. Modeste felt as if she were at the play and fired with enthusiasm for the actor, exactly as Ernest was in her presence; for though the secretary knew all these fine phrases by heart, he was listening to them by the light of the girl's eyes, and falling in love to the verge of madness. To this genuine lover Modeste had eclipsed all the different Modestes he had pictured to himself when reading or answering her letters.

This visit, of which Canalis had fixed the limits beforehand, for he would not give his admirers time to get tired of him, ended by an invitation to dinner on the following Monday.

"We shall no longer be at the Chalet," said the Comte de la Bastie; "it is Dumay's home once more. I am going back to my old house by an agreement for six months, with the right of redemption, which I have just signed with Monsieur Vilquin in my friend Latournelle's office."

"I only hope," said Dumay, "that Vilquin may not be in a position to repay the sum you have lent him on it."

"You will be in a home suitable to your fortune," said Canalis.

"To the fortune I am supposed to have," Charles Mignon put in.

"It would be a pity," said the poet, with a charming bow to Modeste, "that this Madonna should lack a frame worthy of her divine perfections."

This was all that Canalis said about Modeste, for he had affected not to look at her, and to behave like a man who is not at liberty to think of marriage.

"Oh, my dear Madame Mignon, he is immensely clever!" exclaimed the notary's wife, when the gravel was heard crunching under the Parisians' feet.

"Is he rich? that is the question," said Gobenheim.

Modeste stood at the window, not missing a single gesture of the great poet's, and never casting a glance on Ernest de la Brière. When Monsieur Mignon came into the room again, and Modeste, after receiving a parting bow from the two young men as the carriage turned, had resumed her seat, a deep discussion ensued, such as country people indulge in on Paris visitors after a first meeting. Gobenheim reiterated his remark, "Is he rich?" in reply to the trio of praise sung by Madame Latournelle, Modeste, and her mother.

"Rich?" retorted Modeste. "What can it matter? Cannot you see that Monsieur de Canalis is a man destined to fill the highest posts in the Government? He has more than wealth; he has the means of acquiring wealth!"

"He will be an Ambassador or a Minister," said Monsieur Mignon.

"The taxpayers may have to pay for his funeral nevertheless," said little Latournelle.

"Why?" asked Charles Mignon.

"He strikes me as being a man to squander all the fortunes which Mademoiselle Modeste so liberally credits him with the power of earning."

"How can Modeste help being liberal to a man who regards her as a Madonna?" said Dumay, faithful to the aversion Canalis had roused in him.

Gobenheim was preparing the whist-table, with all the more eagerness because since Monsieur Mignon's return Latournelle and Dumay had allowed themselves to play for ten sous a point.

"Now, my little darling," said the father to his daughter in the window recess, "you must own that papa thinks of everything. In a week, if you send orders this evening to the dressmaker you used to employ in Paris and to your other tradesmen, you may display yourself in all the magnificence of an heiress, while I take time to settle into our old house. You shall have a nice pony, so take care to have a habit made—the Master of the Horse deserves that little attention."

"All the more so as we must show our friends the country,"

said Modeste, whose cheeks were recovering the hues of health.

"The secretary," said Madame Mignon, "is not much to speak of."

"He is a little simpleton," said Madame Latournelle. "The poet was attentive to everybody. He remembered to thank Latournelle for finding him a house, by saying to me that he seemed to have consulted a lady's taste. And the other stood there as gloomy as a Spaniard, staring hard, looking as if he could swallow Modeste. If he had looked at me so, I should have been frightened."

"He has a very pleasant voice," Madame Mignon observed.

"He must have come to le Havre to make inquiries about the house of Mignon for the poet's benefit," said Modeste, with a sly look at her father. "He is certainly the man we saw in church."

Madame Dumay and the Latournelles accepted this explanation of Ernest's former journey.

"I tell you what, Ernest," said Canalis when they had gone twenty yards, "I see no one in the Paris world, not a single girl to marry, that can compare with this adorable creature!"

"Oh! it is all settled," replied la Brière, with concentrated bitterness; "she loves you—or, if you choose, she will love you. Your fame half won the battle. In short, you have only to command. You can go there alone next time; Modeste has the deepest contempt for me, and she is right; but I do not see why I should condemn myself to the torture of going to admire, desire, and adore what I never can possess."

After a few condoling speeches, in which Canalis betrayed his satisfaction at having produced a new edition of Cæsar's famous motto, he hinted at his wish to be "off" with the Duchesse de Chaulieu. La Brière, who could not endure the conversation, made an excuse of the loveliness of a rather doubtful night to get out and walk; he flew like a madman to the cliffs, where he stayed till half-past ten, given up to a sort of frenzy, sometimes walking at a great pace and spouting soliloquies, sometimes standing still or sitting down, without observing the uneasiness he was giving to two coastguards on the lookout. After falling in love with Modeste's mental culture and aggressive candor, he now added his adoration of her beauty, that is to say, an unreasoning and inexplicable passion to all the other causes that had brought him ten days ago to church at le Havre.

Then he wandered back to the Chalet, where the Pyrenean dogs barked at him so furiously that he could not allow himself the happiness of gazing at Modeste's windows. In love, all these thing are of no more account than the underpainting covered by the final touches is to the painter; but they are nevertheless the whole of love, as concealed painstaking is the whole of art; the outcome is a great painter and a perfect lover, which the public and the woman worship at last—often too late.

"Well!" cried he aloud, "I will stay, I will endure. I shall see her and love her selfishly, for my own joy! Modeste will be my sun, my life, I shall breathe by her breath, I shall rejoice in her joys, I shall pine over her sorrows, even if she should be the wife of that egoist Canalis——"

"That is something like love, monsieur!" said a voice proceeding from a bush by the wayside. "Bless me! is everybody in love with Mademoiselle de la Bastie?"

Butscha started forth and gazed at la Brière. Ernest sheathed his wrath as he looked at the dwarf in the moonlight, and walked on a few steps without replying.

"Two soldiers serving in the same company should be on better terms than that," said Butscha. "If you are not in love with Canalis, I am not very sweet on him myself."

"He is my friend," said Ernest.

"Oh! then you are the little secretary?" replied the hunchback.

"I would have you to know, monsieur," said la Brière, "that I am no man's secretary. I have the honor to call myself councillor to one of the High Courts of Justice of this realm."

"I have the honor, then, of making my bow to Monsieur

de la Brière," said Butscha. "I have the honor to call myself head clerk to Maître Latournelle, the first notary in le Havre, and I certainly am better off than you are.—Yes—for I have had the happiness of seeing Mademoiselle Modeste de la Bastie almost every afternoon for the last four years, and I propose to live within her ken as one of the King's household lives at the Tuileries. If I were offered the throne of Russia, I should reply, 'I like the sun too well!'—Is not that as much as to say, monsieur, that I care for her more than for myself —with all respect and honor? And do you suppose that the high and mighty Duchesse de Chaulieu will look with a friendly eye on the happiness of Madame de Canalis, when her maid, who is in love with Monsieur Germain, and is already uneasy at that fascinating valet's long absence at le Havre, as she dresses her mistress' hair complains . . ."

"How do you know all this?" said la Brière, interrupting him.

"In the first place, I am a notary's clerk," replied Butscha. "And have you not observed that I have a hump? It is full of ingenuity, monsieur. I made myself cousin to Mademoiselle Philoxène Jacmin, of Honfleur, where my mother was born, also a Jacmin—there are eleven branches of Jacmins at Honfleur.—And so my fair cousin, tempted by the hope of a highly improbable legacy, told me a good many things."

"And the Duchess is vindictive?" said la Brière.

"As vengeful as a queen, said Philoxène. She has not yet forgiven the Duke for being only her husband," replied Butscha. "She hates as she loves. I am thoroughly informed as to her temper, her dress, her tastes, her religion, and her meannesses, for Philoxène stripped her body and soul. I went to the Opera to see Madame de Chaulieu, and I do not regret my ten francs—I am not thinking of the piece. If my hypothetical cousin had not told me that her mistress had seen fifty springs, I should have thought it lavish to give her thirty; she has known no winter, my lady the Duchess!"

"True," said la Brière, "she is a cameo preserved by the onyx.—Canalis would be in great difficulties if the Duchess knew of his plans; and I hope, monsieur, that you will go no further in an espionage so unworthy of an honest man."

"Monsieur," said Butscha proudly, "to me Modeste is the State. I do not spy, I forestall! The Duchesse de Chaulieu will come here if necessary, or will remain quietly where she is if I think it advisable."

"You?"

"I."

"And by what means?" asked la Brière.

"Ah, that is the question," said the little hunchback. He plucked a blade of grass. "This little plant imagines that man builds palaces for its accommodation, and one day it dislodges the most firmly cemented marble, just as the populace, having found a foothold in the structure of the feudal system, overthrew it. The power of the weakest that can creep in everywhere is greater than that of the strong man who relies on his cannon. There are three of us, a Swiss league, who have sworn that Modeste shall be happy, and who would sell our honor for her sake.—Good-night, monsieur. If you love Mademoiselle de la Bastie, forget this conversation, and give me your hand to shake, for you seem to me to have a heart!—I was pining to see the Chalet; I got here just as she put out her candle. I saw you when the dogs gave tongue, I heard you raging; and so I took the liberty of telling you that we serve under the same colors, in the regiment of loyal devotion!"

"Good," replied la Brière, pressing the hunchback's hand. "Then be kind enough to tell me whether Mademoiselle Modeste ever fell in love with a man before her secret correspondence with Canalis?"

"Oh!" cried Butscha, "the mere question is an insult!— And even now who knows whether she is in love? Does she herself know? She has rushed into enthusiasm for the mind, the genius, the spirit of this verse-monger, this vendor of literary pinchbeck; but she will study him—we shall all study him; I will find some means of making his true character peep out from beneath the carapace of the well-mannered man, and we shall see the insignificant head of his ambition and his vanity," said Butscha, rubbing his hands. "Now, unless mademoiselle is mad enough to die of it——"

"Oh, she sat entranced before him as if he were a miracle!" cried la Brière, revealing the secret of his jealousy.

"If he is really a good fellow, and loyal, and loves her, if he is worthy of her," Butscha went on, "if he gives up his Duchess, it is the Duchess I will spread a net for!—There, my dear sir, follow that path, and you will be at home in ten minutes."

But Butscha presently turned back and called to the hapless Ernest, who, as an ardent lover, would have stayed all night to talk of Modeste.

"Monsieur," said Butscha, "I have not yet had the honor of seeing our great poet; I am anxious to study that splendid phenomenon in the exercise of his functions; do me the kindness to come and spend the evening at the Chalet the day after to-morrow; and stay some time, for a man does not completely betray himself in an hour. I shall know, before any one, if he loves, or ever will love, or ever could love Mademoiselle Modeste."

"You are very young to——"

"To be a professor!" said Butscha, interrupting la Brière. "Ah, monsieur, the deformed come into the world a hundred years old. Besides, a sick man, you see, when he has been ill a long time, becomes more knowing than his doctor; he understands the ways of the disease, which is more than a conscientious doctor always does. Well, in the same way, a man who loves a woman while the woman cannot help scorning him for his ugliness or his misshapen person, is at last so qualified in love that he could pass as a seducer, as the sick man at last recovers his health. Folly alone is incurable. —Since the age of six, and I am now five-and-twenty, I have had neither father nor mother; public charity has been my mother, and the King's commissioner my father.—Nay, do not be distressed," he said, in reply to Ernest's expression, "I am less miserable than my position—— Well, since I was six years old, when the insolent eyes of a servant of Madame Latournelle's told me I had no right to wish to love, I have loved and have studied women. I began with ugly ones— it is well to take a bull by the horns. So I took for the first subject of my studies Madame Latournelle herself, who has been really angelic to me. I was perhaps wrong; however, so it was. I distilled her in my alembic, and I at last discovered hidden in a corner of her soul this idea, 'I am not as ugly as people think!'—And in spite of her deep piety, by working on that idea, I could have led her to the brink of the abyss—to leave her there."

"And have you studied Modeste?"

"I thought I had told you," replied the hunchback, "that my life is hers, as France is the King's! Now do you understand my playing the spy in Paris? I alone know all the nobleness and pride, the unselfishness, and unexpected sweetness that lie in the heart and soul of that adorable creature —the indefatigable kindness, the true piety, the light-heartedness, information, refinement, affability——"

Butscha drew out his handkerchief to stop two tears from falling, and la Brière held his hand for some time.

"I shall live in her radiance! It comes from her, and it ends in me, that is how we are united, somewhat as nature is to God by light and the word.—Good-night, monsieur, I never chattered so much in my life; but seeing you below her windows, I guessed that you loved her in my way."

Butscha, without waiting for an answer, left the unhappy lover, on whose heart this conversation had shed a mysterious balm. Ernest determined to make Butscha his friend, never suspecting that the clerk's loquacity was chiefly intended to open communications with Canalis' house. In what a flow and ebb of thoughts, resolutions, and schemes was Ernest lapped before falling asleep; and his friend Canalis was sleeping the sleep of the triumphant, the sweetest slumber there is next to that of the just.

At breakfast the friends agreed to go together to spend the evening of the following day at the Chalet, and be initiated into the mild joys of provincial whist. To get rid of this day they ordered the horses, both warranted to ride and drive, and ventured forth into a country certainly as unknown to them as China; for the least known thing in France to a Frenchman, is France.

As he reflected on his position as a lover rejected and scorned, the secretary made somewhat such a study of himself as he had been led to make by the question Modeste had put to him at the beginning of their correspondence. Though misfortune is supposed to develop virtues, it only does so in virtuous people; for this sort of cleaning up of the conscience takes place only in naturally cleanly persons. La Brière determined to swallow his griefs with Spartan philosophy, to preserve his dignity, and never allow himself to be betrayed into a mean action; while Canalis, fascinated by such an enormous fortune, vowed to himself that he would neglect nothing that might captivate Modeste. Egoism and unselfishness, the watchwords of these two natures, brought them by a moral law, which sometimes has whimsical results, to behave in opposition to their characters. The selfish man meant to act self-sacrifice, the man who was all kindness would take refuge on the Aventine Hill of pride. This phenomenon may also be seen in politics. Men often turn their natures inside out, and not infrequently the public do not know the right side from the wrong.

After dinner they heard from Germain that the Master of the Horse had arrived; he was introduced at the Chalet that evening by Monsieur Latournelle. Mademoiselle d'Hérouville managed to offend the worthy lawyer at once, by sending a message through a footman, desiring him to call at her house, instead of simply sending her nephew to take up the lawyer, who would certainly have talked till his dying day of the visit paid by the Master of the Horse. So when his lordship offered to take him to Ingouville in his carriage, the little notary merely said that he must return home to accompany his wife. Seeing by his sullen manner that there was something wrong, the Duke graciously replied, "If you will allow me, I shall have the honor of going round to fetch Madame Latournelle."

In spite of an emphatic shrug of his despotic aunt's shoulders, the Duke set out with the little notary. Intoxicated with the delight of seeing a magnificent carriage at her door, and men in the royal livery to let down the steps, the lawyer's wife did not know which way to turn for her gloves, her parasol, her bag, and her dignity, when it was announced to her that the Master of the Horse had come to fetch her. As soon as she was in the carriage, while pouring out civilities to the little Duke, she suddenly exclaimed with kindly impulse:

"Oh, and Butscha?"

"Bring Butscha too," said the Duke, smiling.

As the harbor-men, who had collected round the dazzling vehicle, saw these three little men with that tall meagre woman, they looked at each other and laughed.

"If you stuck them together end to end, perhaps you might make a man tall enough for that long May-pole," said a sailor from Bordeaux.

"Have you anything else to take with you, madame," the Duke asked jestingly, as the footman stood waiting for his orders.

"No, monseigneur," replied she, turning scarlet, and looking at her husband as much as to say, "What have I done wrong?"

"His Lordship," said Butscha, "does me too much honor in speaking of me as a thing; a poor clerk like me is a nameless object."

Though he spoke lightly, the Duke colored and made no reply. Grand folks are always in the wrong to bandy jests with those below them. Banter is a game, and a game implies equality. And, indeed, it is to obviate the unpleasant results of such a transient familiarity that, when the game is over, the players have a right not to recognize each other.

The Duke's visit to le Havre was ostensibly for the settlement of an immense undertaking, namely, the reclaiming of a vast tract of land, left dry by the sea between two streams, of which the ownership had just been confirmed to the Hérouville family by the High Court of Appeal. The proposed scheme was no less a matter than the adjustment of sluice gates to two bridges, to drain a tract of mud flats extending for about a kilometre, with a breadth of three or four hundred acres, to embank roads and dig dikes. When the Duc d'Hérouville had explained the nature and position of the land, Charles Mignon observed that he would have to wait till nature had enabled the soil to settle by the consolidation of its still shifting natural constituents.

"Time, which has providentially enriched your estate, Monsieur le Duc, must be left to complete its work," said he, in conclusion. "You will do well to wait another fifty years before setting to work."

"Do not let that be your final opinion, Monsieur le Comte," said the Duke. "Come to Hérouville, see, and judge for yourself."

Charles Mignon replied that some capitalist would need to look into the matter with a cool head; and this remark had given Monsieur d'Hérouville an excuse for calling at the Chalet.

Modeste made a deep impression on him; he begged the favor of a visit from her, saying that his aunt and sister had heard of her, and would be happy to make her acquaintance. On this, Charles Mignon proposed to introduce his daughter to the two ladies, and invited them to dine with him on the day when he should be re-established in his former home; this the Duke accepted. The nobleman's blue ribbon, his title, and, above all, his rapturous glances, had their effect on Modeste; still, she was admirably calm in speech, manner, and dignity. The Duke when he left seemed loath to depart, but he had received an invitation to go to the Chalet every evening, on the pretext that, of course, no courtier of Charles X. could possibly endure an evening without a game of whist.

So, on the following evening, Modeste was to see her three admirers all on the stage at once.

Say what she will, it is certainly flattering to a girl to see several rivals fluttering around her, men of talent, fame, or high birth, all trying to shine and please her, though the logic of the heart will lead her to sacrifice everything to personal predilection. Even if Modeste should lose credit by the admission, she owned, at a later day, that the feelings expressed in her letters had paled before the pleasure of seeing three men, so different, vying with each other—three men, each of whom would have done honor to the most exacting family pride. At the same time, this luxury of vanity gave way before the misanthropical spirit of mischief engendered by the bitter affront which she already thought of merely as a disappointment. So when her father said to her with a smile:

"Well, Modeste, would you like to be a duchess?"

"Ill fortune has made me philosophical," she replied, with a mocking courtesy.

"You are content to be Baroness?" said Butscha.

"Or Viscountess?" replied her father.

"How could that be?" said Modeste quickly.

"Why, if you were to accept Monsieur de la Brière, he would certainly have influence enough with the King to get leave to take my title and bear my arms."

"Oh, if it is a matter of borrowing a disguise, he will make no difficulties!" replied Modeste bitterly.

Butscha did not understand this sarcasm, of which only Monsieur and Madame Mignon and Dumay knew the meaning.

"As soon as marriage is in question, every man assumes a disguise," said Madame Latournelle, "the women set them the example. Ever since I can remember I have heard it said, 'Monsieur this or mademoiselle that is making a very good match'—so the other party must be making a bad one, I suppose?"

"Marriage," said Butscha, "is like an action at law; one side is always left dissatisfied; and if one party deceives the other, half the married couples one sees certainly play the farce at the cost of the other."

"Whence you conclude, Sire Butscha?" asked Modeste.

"That we must always keep our eyes sternly open to the enemy's movements," replied the clerk.

"What did I tell you, my pet?" said Charles Mignon, alluding to his conversation with his daughter on the seashore.

"Men, to get married," said Latournelle, "play as many parts as mothers make their daughters play in order to get them off their hands."

"Then you think stratagem allowable?" said Modeste.

"On both sides," cried Gobenheim. "Then the game is even."

This conversation was carried on in a fragmentary manner, between the deals, and mixed up with the opinions each one allowed himself to express about Monsieur d'Hérouville, who was thought quite good-looking by the little notary, by little Dumay, and by little Butscha.

"I see," said Madame Mignon, with a smile, "that Madame Latournelle and my husband are quite monsters here!"

"Happily for him the Colonel is not excessively tall," replied Butscha, while the lawyer was dealing, "for a tall man who is also intelligent is always a rare exception."

But for this little discussion on the legitimate use of matrimonial wiles, the account of the evening so anxiously expected by Butscha might seem lengthy; but wealth, for which so much secret meanness was committed, may perhaps lend to the minutiæ of private life the interest which is always aroused by the social feeling so frankly set forth by Ernest in his reply to Modeste.

In the course of the next morning Desplein arrived. He stayed only so long as was needful for sending to le Havre for a relay of post-horses, which were at once put in—about an hour. After examining Madame Mignon, he said she would certainly recover her sight, and fixed the date for the operation a month later. This important consultation was held, of course, in the presence of the family party at the Chalet, all anxiously eager to hear the decision of the Prince of

Science. The illustrious member of the Academy of Science asked the blind woman ten short questions, while examining her eyes in the bright light by the window. Modeste, amazed at the value of time to this famous man, noticed that his traveling chaise was full of books, which he intended to read on the way back to Paris, for he had come away on the previous evening, spending the night in sleeping and traveling.

The swiftness and clearness of Desplein's decisions on every answer of Madame Mignon's, his curt speech, his manner, all gave Modeste, for the first time, any clear idea of a man of genius. She felt the enormous gulf between Canalis, a man of second-rate talents, and Desplein, a more than superior mind.

A man of genius has in the consciousness of his talent, and the assurance of his fame, a domain, as it were, where his legitimate pride can move and breathe freely without incommoding other people. Then the incessant conflict with men and things gives him no time to indulge the coquettish conceits in which the heroes of fashion indulge, as they hastily reap the harvest of a passing season, while their vanity and self-love are exacting and irritable, like a sort of custom-house alert to seize a toll on everything that passes within its ken.

Modeste was all the more delighted with the great surgeon because he seemed struck by her extreme beauty—he, under whose hands so many women had passed, and who for years had been scrutinizing them with the lancet and microscope.

"It would really be too bad," said he, with the gallantry which he could so well assume, in contrast to his habitual abruptness, "that a mother should be deprived of seeing such a lovely daughter."

Modeste herself waited on the great surgeon at the simple luncheon he would accept. She, with her father and Dumay, escorted the learned man, for whom so many sick were longing, as far as the chaise which waited for him at the side gate, and there, her eyes beaming with hope, she said once more to Desplein:

"Then dear mamma will really see me?"

"Yes, my pretty Will-o'-the-Wisp, I promise you she shall," he replied, with a smile; "and I am incapable of deceiving you, for I too have a daughter."

The horses whirled him off as he spoke the words, which had an unexpected touch of feeling. Nothing is more bewitching than the unforeseen peculiar to very clever men.

This visit was the event of the day, and it left a track of light in Modeste's soul. The enthusiastic child admired without guile this man whose life was at everybody's command, and in whom the habit of contemplating physical suffering had overcome every appearance of egoism.

In the evening, when Gobenheim, the Latournelles, Canalis, Ernest, and the Duc d'Hérouville had assembled, they congratulated the Mignon family on the good news given them by Desplein. Then, of course, the conversation, led by Modeste, as we know her from her letters, turned on this man whose genius, unfortunately for his glory, could only be appreciated by the most learned men and the Medical Faculty. And Gobenheim uttered this speech, which is in our days the sanctifying anointing of genius in the ears of economists and bankers:

"He makes enormous sums."

"He is said to be very greedy!" replied Canalis.

The praise lavished on Desplein by Modeste annoyed the poet. Vanity behaves like Woman. They both believe that they lose something by praise or affection bestowed on another. Voltaire was jealous of the wit of a man whom Paris admired for two days, just as a duchess takes offence at a glance bestowed on her waiting maid. So great is the avarice of these two feelings, that they feel robbed of a pittance bestowed on the poor.

"And do you think, monsieur," asked Modeste, with a smile, "that a genius should be measured, by the ordinary standard?"

"It would first be necessary, perhaps," said Canalis, "to define a man of genius. One of his prime characteristics is inventiveness—the invention of a type, of a system, of a power. Napoleon was an inventor, apart from his other characteristics of genius. He invented his method of warfare. Walter Scott is an inventor, Linnæus was an inventor, so are Geoffroy Saint-Hilaire and Cuvier. Such men are geniuses above all else. They renew, or expand, or modify science or art. But Desplein is a man whose immense talent consists in applying laws that were previously discovered; in detecting, by natural intuition, the final tendency of every temperament, and the hour marked out by nature for the performance of an operation. He did not, like Hippocrates, lay the foundations of Science itself. He has not discovered a system, like Galen, Broussais, or Rasori. His is the genius of the executant, like Moscheles on the piano, Paganini on the violin, or Farinelli on his own larynx—men who display immense powers, but who do not create music. Between Beethoven and Madame Catalani you will allow that to him should be awarded the crown of genius and suffering; to her a vast heap of five-franc pieces. We can pay our debt to one, while the world must for ever remain in debt to the other! We owe more and more to Molière every day, and we have already overpaid Baron."

"It seems to me that you are giving too large a share to ideas, my dear fellow," said la Brière, in a sweet and gentle voice that was in startling contrast to the poet's peremptory style, for his flexible voice had lost its insinuating tone and assumed the dominant ring of rhetoric. "Genius ought to be estimated chiefly for its utility. Parmentier, Jacquard, and Papin, to whom statues will one day be erected, were also men of genius. They have in a certain direction altered, or will alter, the face of nations. From this point of view Desplein will always appear in the eyes of thinking men accompanied by a whole generation whose tears and sufferings have been alleviated by his mighty hand."

That Ernest should have expressed this opinion was enough to prompt Modeste to contest it.

"In that case, monsieur," said she, "the man who should find means to reap corn without spoiling the straw, by a machine that should do the work of ten laborers, would be a man of genius?"

"Oh yes, my child," said Madame Mignon, "he would be blessed by the poor, whose bread would then be cheaper; and he whom the poor bless is blessed by God."

"That is to give utility the preference over art," said Modeste, with a toss of her head."

"But for utility," said her father, "on what would art be founded? On what basis would it rest, on what would the poet live, and who would give him shelter, who would pay him?"

"Oh, my dear father, that is quite the view of a merchant captain, a Philistine, a counter-jumper. That Gobenheim or Monsieur de la Brière should hold it I can understand; they are interested in the solution of such social problems; but you, whose life has been so romantically useless to your age, since your blood spilt on the soil of Europe, and the terrible sufferings required of you by a Colossus, have not hindered France from losing ten departments which the Republic had conquered,—how can you subscribe to a view so excessively *out of date,* as the Romantics have it? It is easy to see that you have dropped from China."

The disrespect of Modeste's speech was aggravated by the scornful and contemptuous flippancy of the tone in which she intentionally spoke, and which astonished Madame Latournelle, Madame Mignon, and Dumay. Madame Latournelle, though she opened her eyes wide enough, could not see what Modeste was driving at; Butscha, who was as alert as a spy, looked significantly at Monsieur Mignon on seeing his face flush with deep and sudden indignation.

"A little more, mademoiselle, and you would have failed in respect to your father," said the Colonel with a smile, enlightened by Butscha's glance. "That is what comes of spoiling a child."

"I am an only daughter!" she retorted insolently.

"Unique!" said the notary, with emphasis.

"Monsieur," said Modeste to Latournelle, "my father is

very willing that I should educate him. He gave me life, I give him wisdom—he will still be my debtor."

"But there is a way of doing it—and, above all, a time for it," said Madame Mignon.

"But mademoiselle is very right," said Canalis, rising, and placing himself by the chimney-piece in one of the finest postures of his collection of attitudes. "God in His foresight has given man food and clothing, and has not directly endowed him with Art! He has said to man, 'To eat, you must stoop to the earth; to think, you must uplift yourself to Me!' —We need the life of the soul as much as the life of the body. Hence there are two forms of utility—obviously we do not wear books on our feet. From the utilitarian point of view, a canto of an epic is not to compare with a bowl of cheap soup from a charity kitchen. The finest idea in the world cannot take the place of the sail of a ship. An automatic boiler, no doubt, by lifting itself two inches, supplies us with calico thirty sous a yard cheaper; but this machine and the inventions of industry do not breathe the life of the people, and will never tell the future that it has existed; whereas Egyptian art, Mexican art, Greek or Roman art, with their masterpieces, stigmatized as useless, have borne witness to the existence of these nations through a vast space of time in places where great intermediate nations have vanished without leaving even a name-card, for lack of men of genius! Works of genius form the *summum* of a civilization, and presuppose a great use. You, no doubt, would not think a pair of boots better in itself than a drama, nor prefer a windmill to the Church of Saint-Ouen? Well, a nation is moved by the same spirit as an individual, and man's favorite dream is to survive himself morally, as he reproduces himself physically. What survives of a nation is the work of its men of genius.

"At this moment France is a vigorous proof of the truth of this proposition. She is assuredly outdone by England in industry, commerce, and navigation; nevertheless, she leads the world, I believe, by her artists, her gifted men, and the taste of her products. There is not an artist, not a man of mark anywhere, who does not come to Paris to win his patent of mastery. There is at this day no school of painting but in France; and we shall rule by the Book more surely perhaps, and for longer, than by the Sword.

"Under Ernest's system the flowers of luxury would be suppressed—the beauty of woman, music, painting, and poetry. Society would not, indeed, be overthrown; but who would accept life on such terms? All that is useful is horrible and ugly. The kitchen is indispensable in a house, but you take good care never to stay in it; you live in a drawing-room, ornamented, as this is, with perfectly superfluous things. Of what use are those beautiful pictures and all this carved woodwork? Nothing is beautiful but what we feel to be useless. We have called the sixteenth century the age of the Renaissance with admirable accuracy of expression. That century was the dawn of a new world; men will still talk of it when some preceding ages are forgotten, whose sole merit will be that they have existed—like the millions of beings that are of no account in a generation."

"*Guenille, soit! ma guenille m'est chère*"—"A poor thing, but mine own," said the Duc d'Hérouville playfully, during the silence that followed this pompous declamation of prose.

"But," said Butscha, taking up the cudgels against Canalis, "does the art exist which, according to you, is the sphere in which genius should disport itself? Is it not rather a magnificent fiction which social man is madly bent on believing? What need have I for a landscape in Normandy hanging in my room, when I can go and see it so well done by God? We have in our dreams finer poems than the *Iliad*. For a very moderate sum I can find at Valognes, at Carentan, as in Provence, at Arles, Venuses quite as lovely as Titian's. The *Police News* publishes romances, different indeed from Walter Scott's, but with terrible endings, in real blood, and not in ink. Happiness and virtue are far above art and genius!"

"Bravo, Butscha!" cried Madame Latournelle.

"What did he say?" asked Canalis of la Brière, ceasing

to watch Modeste, in whose eyes and attitude he read the delightful evidence of her artless admiration.

The scorn with which he had been treated, and, above all, the girl's disrespectful speech to her father, had so depressed the unhappy la Brière that he made no reply; his gaze, sadly fixed on Modeste, betrayed absorbed meditation. The little clerk's argument was, however, repeated with some wit by the Duc d'Hérouville, who ended by saying that the raptures of Saint Theresa were far superior to the inventions of Lord Byron.

"Oh, Monsieur le Duc," remarked Modeste, "that is wholly personal poetry, while Lord Byron's or Molière's is for the benefit of the world——"

"Then you must make your peace with the Baron," interrupted her father quickly. "Now you are insisting that genius is to be useful, as much so as cotton; but you will, perhaps, think logic as stale and out of date as your poor old father."

Butscha, la Brière, and Madame Latournelle exchanged half-laughing glances, which spurred Modeste on in her career of provocation, all the more because for a moment she was checked.

"Nay, mademoiselle," said Canalis with a smile, "we have not fought nor even contradicted each other. Every work of art, whether in literature, music, painting, sculpture, or architecture, carries with it a positive social utility, like that of any other form of commercial produce. Art is the truest form of commerce; it takes it for granted. A book in these days helps its writer to pocket about ten thousand francs, and its production involves printing, paper-making, type-founding, and the booksellers' trade; that is to say, the occupation of thousands of hands. The performance of a symphony by Beethoven or of an opera by Rossini demands quite as many hands, machines, and forms of industry.

"The cost of a building is a still more tangible answer to the objection. It may, indeed, be said that works of genius rest on a very costly basis, and are necessarily profitable to the working man."

Fairly started on this text, Canalis talked on for some minutes with a lavish use of imagery, and reveling in his own words; but it befell him, as often happens with great talkers, to find himself at the end of his harangue just where he started, and agreeing with la Brière, though he failed to perceive it.

"I discern with pleasure, my dear Baron," said the little Duke slily, "that you will make a great constitutional Minister."

"Oh," said Canalis, with an ostentatious flourish, "what do we prove by all our discussions? The eternal truth of this axiom, 'Everything is true and everything is false.' Moral truths, like living beings, may be placed in an atmosphere where they change their appearance to the point of being unrecognizable?"

"Society lives by condemned things," said the Duc d'Hérouville.

"What flippancy!" said Madame Latournelle in a low voice to her husband.

"He is a poet," said Gobenheim, who overheard her.

Canalis, who had soared ten leagues above his audience, and who was, perhaps, right in his final philosophical dictum, took the sort of chill he read on every face for a symptom of ignorance; but he saw that Modeste understood him, and was content, never discerning how offensive such a monologue is to country folks, whose one idea is to prove to Parisians the vitality, intelligence, and good judgment of the provinces.

"Is it long since you last saw the Duchesse de Chaulieu?" asked the Duke of Canalis, to change the subject.

"I saw her six days ago," replied Canalis.

"And she is well?"

"Perfectly well."

"Remember me to her, pray, when you write."

"I hear she is charming," Modeste remarked to the Duke.

"Monsieur le Baron," said he, "knows more about that than I do."

"She is more than charming," said Canalis, accepting the

Duke's perfidious challenge. "But I am partial, mademoiselle; she has been my friend these ten years. I owe to her all that may be good in me; she has sheltered me from the perils of the world. Besides, the Duc de Chaulieu started me in the way I am going. But for their influence the King and Princesses would often have forgotten a poor poet as I am; my affection, therefore, is always full of gratitude."

And he spoke with tears in his voice.

"How much we all ought to love the woman who has inspired you with such sublime song and such a noble sentiment," said Modeste with feeling. "Can one conceive of a poet without a Muse?"

"He would have no heart," said Canalis; "he would write verse as dry as Voltaire's—who never loved any one but Voltaire."

"When I was in Paris," said Dumay, "did you not do me the honor of assuring me that you felt none of the feelings you expressed?"

"A straight hit, my worthy soldier," replied the poet with a smile; "but you must understand that at the same time it is allowable to have a great deal of heart in the intellectual life as well as in real life. A man may express very fine sentiments without feeling them, or feel them without being able to express them. La Brière, my friend here, loves to distraction," said he generously, as he looked at Modeste. "I, who love at least as much as he does, believe—unless I am under an illusion—that I can give my passion a literary form worthy of its depth.—Still, I will not answer for it, mademoiselle," said he, turning to Modeste with a rather over elaborate grace, "that I shall not be bereft of wits by to-morrow——"

And thus the poet triumphed over every obstacle, burning in honor of his love the sticks they tried to trip him up with, while Modeste was dazzled by this Parisian brilliancy, which was unfamiliar to her, and which lent a glitter to the orator's rhetoric.

"What a mountebank!" said Butscha in a whisper to Latournelle, after listening to a magniloquent tirade on the

Catholic religion, and the happiness of having a pious wife, poured out in response to an observation from Madame Mignon.

Modeste had a bandage over her eyes; the effect of his delivery, and the attention she intentionally devoted to Canalis, prevented her perceiving what Butscha saw and noted—the declamatory tone, the lack of simplicity, rant taking the place of feeling, and all the incoherence which prompted the clerk's rather too severe epithet.

While Monsieur Mignon, Dumay, Butscha, and Latournelle wondered at the poet's want of sequence, overlooking, indeed, the inevitable digressions of conversation, which in France is always very devious, Modeste was admiring the poet's versatility, saying to herself as she led him to follow the tortuous windings of her fancy, "He loves me!"

Butscha, like all the other spectators of this performance, as we must call it, was struck by the chief fault of all egoists, which Canalis shows a little too much, like all men who are accustomed to speechify in drawing-rooms. Whether he knew beforehand what the other speaker meant to say, or merely did not listen, or had the power of listening while thinking of something else, Melchior wore the look of inattention which is as disconcerting to another man's flow of words as it is wounding to his vanity.

Not to attend to what is said is not merely a lack of politeness; it is an expression of contempt. And Canalis carries this habit rather too far, for he often neglects to reply to a remark that requires an answer, and goes off to the subject he is absorbed in without any polite transition. Though this form of impertinence may be accepted without protest from a man of position, it nevertheless creates a leaven of hatred and vengeful feeling at the bottom of men's hearts; in an equal, it may even break up a friendship.

When by any chance Melchior compels himself to listen, he falls into another failing—he only lends himself, he does not give himself up. Nothing in social intercourse pays better than the bestowal of attention. "Blessed are they that hear!"

is not only a precept of the Gospel, it is also an excellent speculation; act on it, and you will be forgiven everything, even vices. Canalis took much upon him in the intention of charming Modeste; but while he was sacrificing himself to her, he was himself all the while with the others.

Modeste, pitiless for the ten persons she was martyrizing, begged Canalis to read them some piece of his verse; she wanted to hear a specimen of that much-praised elocution.

Canalis took the volume offered him by Modeste and cooed —for that is the correct word—the poem that is supposed to be his finest, an imitation of Moore's "Loves of the Angels," entitled "Vitalis," which was received with some yawns by Mesdames Latournelle and Dumay, by Gobenheim, and the cashier.

"If you play whist well, monsieur," said Gobenheim, offering him five cards spread out in a fan, "I have never met with so accomplished a gentleman."

The question made every one laugh, for it was the expression of the common wish.

"I play it well enough to be able to end my days in a country town," replied Canalis. "There has, I dare say, been more of literature and conversation than whist players care to have," he added in an impertinent tone, flinging the book on to the side table.

This incident shows what dangers are incurred by the hero of a salon when, like Canalis, he moves outside his orbit; he is then in the case of an actor who is a favorite with one particular public, but whose talent is wasted when he quits his own stage and ventures on to that of a superior theatre.

The Baron and the Duke were partners; Gobenheim played with Latournelle. Modeste sat down at the great poet's elbow, to the despair of Ernest, who marked on the capricious girl's countenance the progress of Canalis' fascination. La Brière had not known the power of seduction possessed by Melchior, and often denied by nature to genuine souls, who are generally shy. This gift demands a boldness and readiness of spirit which might be called the acrobatic agility of the mind;

it even allows of a little part-playing; but is there not, morally speaking, always something of the actor in a poet? There is, indeed, a wide difference between expressing feelings we do not experience though we can imagine them in all their variety, and pretending to have them when they seem necessary to success on the stage of private life; and yet, if the hypocrisy needful to a man of the world has cankered the poet, he easily transfuses the powers of his talent into the expression of the required sentiment, just as a great man who has buried himself in solitude at last finds his heart overflowing into his brain.

"He is playing for millions," thought la Brière in anguish; "and he will act passion so well that Modeste will believe in it!"

And instead of showing himself more delightful and wittier than his rival, la Brière, like the Duc d'Hérouville, sat gloomy, uneasy, and on the watch; but while the courtier was studying the heiress' vagaries, Ernest was a prey to the misery of black and concentrated jealousy, and had not yet won a single glance from his idol. He presently went into the garden for a few minutes with Butscha.

"It is all over, she is crazy about him," said he. "I am worse than disagreeable—and, after all, she is right! Canalis is delightful, he is witty even in his silence, he has passion in his eyes, poetry in his harangues——"

"Is he an honest man?" asked Butscha.

"Oh yes," replied la Brière. "He is loyal, chivalrous, and under Modeste's influence he is quite capable of getting over the little faults he has acquired under Madame de Chaulieu——"

"You are a good fellow!" exclaimed the little hunchback. "But is he capable of loving—will he love her?"

"I do not know——" replied Ernest. "Has she mentioned me?" he asked after a short silence.

"Yes," said Butscha, and he repeated what Modeste had said about borrowing a disguise.

The young fellow threw himself on a seat and hid his face

in his hands. He could not restrain his tears, and would not let Butscha see them; but the dwarf was the man to guess them.

"What is wrong, monsieur?" said he.

"She is right!" cried la Brière, suddenly sitting up. "I am a wretch."

He told the story of the trick he had been led into by Canalis, explaining to Butscha that he had wished to undeceive Modeste before she had unmasked; and he overflowed in rather childish lamentations over the perversity of his fate. Butscha's sympathy recognized this as love in its most vigorous and youthful artlessness, in its genuine and deep anxiety.

"But why," said he, "do you not make the best of yourself to Mademoiselle Modeste, instead of leaving your rival to prance alone?"

"Ah! you evidently never felt your throat tighten as soon as you tried to speak to her," said la Brière. "Do you not feel a sensation at the roots of your hair, and all over your skin, when she looks at you, even without seeing you?"

"Still you have your wits about you sufficiently to be deeply grieved when she as good as told her father that he was an old woman."

"Monsieur, I love her too truly not to have felt it like a dagger-thrust when I heard her thus belie the perfection I ascribed to her!"

"But Canalis, you see, justified her," replied Butscha.

"If she has more vanity than good feeling, she would not be worth regretting!" said Ernest.

At this moment Modeste came out to breathe the freshness of the starlit night with Canalis, who had been losing at cards, her father, and Madame Dumay. While his daughter walked on with Melchior, Charles Mignon left her and came up to la Brière.

"Your friend ought to have been an advocate, monsieur," said he with a smile, and looking narrowly at the young man.

"Do not be in a hurry to judge a poet with the severity you might exercise on an ordinary man, like me, for instance, Monsieur le Comte," said la Brière. "The poet has his mission. He is destined by nature to see the poetical side of every question, just as he expresses the poetry of everything; thus when you fancy that he is arguing against himself, he is faithful to his calling. He is a painter ready to represent either a Madonna or a courtesan. Molière is alike right in his pictures of old men and young men, and Molière certainly had a sound judgment. These sports of fancy which corrupt second-rate minds have no influence over the character of really great men."

Charles Mignon pressed the young fellow's hand, saying, "At the same time, this versatility might be used by a man to justify himself for actions diametrically antagonistic, especially in politics."

At this moment Canalis was saying in an insinuating voice, in reply to some saucy remark of Modeste's: "Ah, mademoiselle, never believe that the multiplicity of emotions can in any degree diminish strength of feeling. Poets, more than other men, must love with constancy and truth. In the first place, do not be jealous of what is called 'The Muse.' Happy is the wife of a busy man! If you could but hear the lamentations of the wives who are crushed under the idleness of husbands without employment, or to whom wealth gives much leisure, you would know that the chief happiness of a Parisian woman is liberty,—sovereignty in her home. And we poets allow the wife to hold the sceptre, for we cannot possibly condescend to the tyranny exerted by small minds. We have something better to do.—If ever I should marry, which I vow is a very remote disaster in my life, I should wish my wife to enjoy the perfect moral liberty which a mistress always preserves, and which is perhaps the source of all her seductiveness."

Canalis put forth all his spirit and grace in talking of love, marriage, the worship of woman, and arguing with Modeste, till presently Monsieur Mignon, who came to join them, seized a moment's silence to take his daughter by the arm and lead her back to Ernest, whom the worthy Colonel had advised to attempt some explanation.

"Mademoiselle," said Ernest in a broken voice, "I cannot possibly endure to remain here the object of your scorn. I do not defend myself, I make no attempt at justification; I only beg to point out to you that before receiving your flattering letter addressed to the man and not to the poet—your last letter—I desired, and by a letter written at le Havre I intended, to dispel the mistake under which you wrote. All the feelings I have had the honor of expressing to you are sincere. A hope beamed on me when, in Paris, your father told me that he was poor;—but now, if all is lost, if nothing is left to me but eternal regrets, why should I stay where there is nothing for me but torture?—Let me only take away with me one smile from you. It will remain graven on my heart."

"Monsieur," said Modeste, who appeared cold and absent-minded, "I am not the mistress here; but I certainly should deeply regret keeping any one here who should find neither pleasure nor happiness in staying!"

She turned away, and took Madame Dumay's arm to go back into the house. A few minutes later all the personages of this domestic drama, once more united in the drawing-room, were surprised to see Modeste sitting by the Duc d'Hérouville, and flirting with him in the best style of the most wily Parisienne. She watched his play, gave him advice when he asked it, and took opportunities of saying flattering things to him, placing the chance advantage of noble birth on the same level as that of talent or of beauty.

Canalis knew, or fancied he knew, the reason for this caprice: he had tried to pique Modeste by speaking of marriage as a disaster, and seeming to be averse to it; but like all who play with fire, it was he who was burnt. Modeste's pride and disdain alarmed the poet; he came up to her, making a display of jealousy all the more marked because it was assumed. Modeste, as implacable as the angels, relished the pleasure she felt in the exercise of her power, and naturally carried it too far. The Duc d'Hérouville had never been so well treated: a woman smiled on him!

At eleven o'clock, an unheard-of hour at the Chalet, the

three rivals left, the Duke thinking Modeste charming, Canalis regarding her as a coquette, and la Brière heartbroken by her relentlessness.

For a week the heiress still remained to her three admirers just what she had been on that evening, so that the poet seemed to have triumphed, in spite of the whims and freaks which from time to time inspired some hopes in the Duc d'Hérouville. Modeste's irreverence to her father, and the liberties she took with him; her irritability towards her blind mother, as she half-grudgingly did her the little services which formerly had been the delight of her filial affection, seemed to be the outcome of a wayward temper and liveliness tolerated in her childhood. When Modeste went too far she would assert a code of her own, and ascribe her levity and fractiousness to her spirit of independence. She owned to Canalis and the Duke that she hated obedience, and regarded this as an obstacle in the way of marriage, thus sounding her suitors' character after the manner of those who pierce the soil to bring up gold, coal, stone, or water.

"I will never find a husband," said she, the day before that on which the family were to reinstate themselves in the Villa, "who will endure my caprices with such kindness as my father's, which has never failed for an instant, or the indulgence of my adorable mother."

"They know that you love them, mademoiselle," said la Brière.

"Be assured, mademoiselle, that your husband will know the full value of his treasure," added the Duke.

"You have more wit and spirit than are needed to break in a husband," said Canalis, laughing.

Modeste smiled, as Henri IV. may have smiled when, by extracting three answers to an insidious question, he had revealed to some foreign Ambassador the character of his three leading Ministers.

On the day of the dinner, Modeste, led away by her preference for Canalis, walked alone with him for some time up and down the graveled walk leading from the house to the lawn with its flower-beds. It was easy to perceive, from the poet's gestures and the young heiress' demeanor, that she was lending a favorable ear to Canalis, and the two Demoiselles d'Hérouville came out to interrupt a *tête-à-tête* that scandalized them. With the tact natural to women in such cases, they turned the conversation to the subject of the Court, of the high position conferred by an office under the Crown, explaining the difference subsisting between an appointment to the Household and one held under the Crown; they tried, in fact, to intoxicate Modeste by appealing to her pride, and displaying to her one of the highest positions which a woman at that time could hope to attain.

"To have a Duke in your son," cried the old lady, "is a positive distinction. The mere title is a fortune out of reach of reverses, to bequeath to your children."

"To what ill-fortune," said Canalis, very ill-pleased at this interruption to his conversation, "must we attribute the small success that the Master of the Horse has hitherto achieved in the matter in which that title is supposed to be of most service as supporting a man's pretensions?"

The two unmarried ladies shot a look at Canalis as full of venom as a viper's fangs, but were so put out of countenance by Modeste's sarcastic smile that they had not a word in reply.

"The Master of the Horse," said Modeste to Canalis, "has never blamed you for the diffidence you have learned from your fame; why then grudge him his modesty?"

"Also," said the Duke's aunt, "we have not yet met with a wife worthy of my nephew's rank. Some we have seen who had merely the fortune that might suit the position; others who, without the fortune, had indeed the right spirit; and I must confess that we have done well to wait till God should give us the opportunity of making acquaintance with a young lady in whom should be united both the noble soul and the handsome fortune of a Duchesse d'Hérouville!"

"My dear Modeste," said Hélène d'Hérouville, walking

away a few steps with her new friend, "there are a thousand Barons de Canalis in the kingdom, and a hundred poets in Paris who are as good as he; and he is so far from being a great man, that I, a poor girl, fated to take the veil for lack of a dower, would have nothing to say to him!—And you do not know, I dare say, that he is a man who has, for the last ten years, been at the beck and call of the Duchesse de Chaulieu. Really, none but an old woman of sixty could put up with the endless little ailments with which, it is said, the poet is afflicted, the least of which was unendurable in Louis XVI. Still, the Duchess, of course, does not suffer from them as his wife would; he is not so constantly with her as a husband would be——"

And so by one of the manœuvres peculiar to woman against woman, Hélène d'Hérouville whispered in every ear the calumnies which women, jealous of Madame de Chaulieu, propagated concerning the poet. This trivial detail, not rare in the gossip of young girls, shows that the Comte de la Bastie's fortune was already made the object of ardent rivalry.

Within ten days, opinions at the Chalet had varied considerably about the three men who aspired to Modeste's hand. This change, wholly to the disadvantage of Canalis, was founded on considerations calculated to make the hero of any form of fame reflect deeply. When we see the passion with which an autograph is craved, it is impossible to doubt that public curiosity is strongly excited by celebrity. Most provincials, it is evident, have no very exact idea of the manner in which illustrious persons fasten their cravat, walk on the Boulevard, gape at the crows, or eat a cutlet; for, as soon as they see a man wearing the halo of fashion, or resplendent with popularity—more or less transient, no doubt, but always the object of envy—they are ready to exclaim, "Ah! so that is the thing!" or, "Well, that is odd!" or something equally absurd. In a word, the strange charm that is produced by every form of renown, even when justly acquired, has no permanence. To superficial minds, especially to the sarcastic and the envious, it is an impression as swift as a lightning flash, and never repeated. Glory, it would seem, like the sun, is hot and luminous from afar, but, when we get near, it is as cold as the peak of an Alp. Perhaps a man is really great only to his peers; perhaps the defects inherent in the conditions of humanity are more readily lost to their eyes than to those of vulgar admirers. Thus, to be constantly pleasing, a poet would be compelled to display the deceptive graces of those persons who can win forgiveness for their obscurity by amiable manners and agreeable speeches, since, besides genius, the vapid drawing-room virtues and harmless domestic twaddle are exacted from him.

The great poet of the Faubourg Saint-Germain, who refused to yield to this law of society, found that insulting indifference soon took the place of the fascination at first caused by his conversation at evening parties. Cleverness too prodigally displayed produces the same effect on the mind as a shop full of cut glass has on the eyes; this sufficiently explains that Canalis' glitter soon wearied those people who, to use their own words, like something solid. Then, under the necessity of appearing an ordinary man, the poet found many rocks ahead where la Brière could win the good opinion of those who, at first, had thought him sullen. They felt the desire to be revenged on Canalis for his reputation by making more of his friend. The most kindly people are so made. The amiable and unpretentious Referendary shocked nobody's vanity; falling back on him, every one discerned his good heart, his great modesty, the discretion of a strong box, and delightful manners. On political questions the Duc d'Hérouville held Ernest far above Canalis. The poet, as erratic, ambitious, and mutable as Tasso, loved luxury and splendor, and ran into debt; while the young lawyer, even-minded, living prudently, and useful without officiousness, hoped for promotion without asking it, and was saving money meanwhile.

Canalis had indeed justified the good people who were watching him. For the last two or three days he had given way to fits of irritability, of depression, of melancholy, without any apparent cause—the caprices of temper that come of the nervous poetical temperament. These eccentricities —as they are called in a country town—had their cause in the wrong, which each day made worse, that he was doing to the Duchesse de Chaulieu, to whom he knew he ought to write, without being able to make up his mind to do it; they were anxiously noted by the gentle American and worthy Madame Latournelle, and more than once came under discussion between them and Madame Mignon. Canalis, knowing nothing of these discussions, felt their effect. He was no longer listened to with the same attention, the faces round him did not express the rapture of the first days, while Ernest was beginning to be listened to. For the last two days the poet had, therefore, been bent on captivating Modeste, and seized every moment when he could be alone with her to cast over her the tangles of the most impassioned language. Modeste's heightened color plainly showed the two Demoiselles d'Hérouville with what pleasure the heiress heard insinuating conceits charmingly spoken; and, uneasy at the poet's rapid advances, they had recourse to the *ultima ratio* of women in such predicaments—to calumny, which rarely misses its aim when it appeals to vehement physical repulsion.

As he sat down to dinner, the poet saw a cloud on his idol's brow, and read in it Mademoiselle d'Hérouville's perfidy; so he decided that he must offer himself as a husband to Modeste at the first opportunity he should have of speaking to her. As he and the two noble damsels exchanged some subacid, though polite remarks, Gobenheim nudged Butscha, who sat next to him, to look at the poet and the Master of the Horse.

"They will demolish each other," said he in a whisper.

"Canalis has genius enough to demolish himself unaided," said the dwarf.

In the course of the dinner, which was extremely splendid, and served to perfection, the Duke achieved a great triumph over Canalis. Modeste, whose riding-habit had arrived the evening before, talked of the various rides to be taken in the neighborhood. In the course of the conversation that ensued she was led to express a strong wish to see a hunt—a pleasure she had never known. The Duke at once proposed to arrange a hunt for Mademoiselle Mignon's benefit in one of the Crown forest-lands a few leagues from le Havre. Thanks to his connection with the Master of the King's Hounds, the Prince de Cadignan, he had it in his power to show Modeste a scene of royal magnificence, to charm her by showing her the dazzling world of a Court, and making her wish to enter it by marriage. The glances exchanged by the Duke and the two Demoiselles d'Hérouville, which Canalis happened to catch, distinctly said, "The heiress is ours!"— enough to urge the poet, who was reduced to mere personal glitter, to secure some pledge of her affection without loss of time.

Modeste, somewhat scared at having gone further than she intended with the d'Hérouvilles, after dinner, when they were walking in the grounds, went forward a little distance in a rather marked manner, accompanied by Melchior. With a young girl's not illegitimate curiosity, she allowed him to guess the calumnies repeated by Hélène, and on a remonstrance from Canalis she pledged him to secrecy, which he promised.

"These lashes of the tongue," said he, "are fair war in the world of fashion; your simplicity is scared by them; for my part, I can laugh at them—nay, I enjoy them. Those ladies must think his lordship's interests seriously imperiled, or they would not have recourse to them."

Then, profiting by the opportunity given by such a piece of information, Canalis justified himself with so much mocking wit, and passion so ingeniously expressed, while thanking Modeste for her confidence, in which he insisted in seeing a slight strain of love, that she found herself quite as deeply compromised towards the poet as she was towards the Duke. Canalis felt that daring was necessary; he declared himself in plain terms. He paid his vows to Modeste in a style through which his poetic fancy shone like a moon ingeniously staged, with a brilliant picture of herself—beautifully fair, and arrayed to admiration for this family festival. The inspiration so cleverly called up, and encouraged by the complicity of the evening, the grove, the sky, and the earth, led the grasping lover beyond all reason; for he even talked of his disinterestedness, and succeeded by the flowers of his eloquence in giving a new aspect to Diderot's stale theme of *"Five hundred francs and my Sophie,"* or the *"Give me a cottage and your heart!"* of every lover who knows that his father-in-law has a fortune.

"Monsieur," said Modeste, after enjoying the music of this concerto so admirably composed on "a familiar theme," "my parents leave me such freedom as has allowed me to hear you; but you must address yourself to them."

"Well, then," cried Canalis, "only tell me that if I get their consent you will be quite satisfied to obey them."

"I know beforehand," said she, "that my father has some wishes which might offend the legitimate pride of a family as old as yours, for he is bent on transmitting his title and his name to his grandsons."

"Oh, my dear Modeste, what sacrifice would I not make to place my life in the hands of such a guardian angel as you are!"

"You must allow me not to decide my fate for life in one moment," said she, going to join the Demoiselles d'Hérouville.

These two ladies were at that minute flattering little Latournelle's vanity in the hope of securing him to their interests. Mademoiselle d'Hérouville, to whom we must give the family name to distinguish her from her niece Hélène, was conveying to the notary that the place of President of the Court at le Havre, which Charles X. would give to a man recommended by them, was an appointment due to his honesty and talents as a lawyer. Butscha, who was walking with la Brière, in great alarm at Melchior's audacity and rapid progress, found means to speak to Modeste for a few minutes at the bottom of the garden steps as the party went indoors to give themselves up to the vexations of the inevitable rubber.

"Mademoiselle, I hope you do not yet address him as Melchior," said he in an undertone.

"Not far short of it, my Mysterious Dwarf," she replied, with a smile that might have seduced an angel.

"Good God!" cried the clerk, dropping his hands, which almost touched the steps.

"Well, and is not he as good as that odious gloomy Referendary in whom you take so much interest?" cried she, putting on for Ernest a haughty look of scorn, such as young girls alone have the secret of, as though their maidenhood lent them wings to soar so high. "Would your little Monsieur de la Brière take me without a settlement?" she added after a pause.

"Ask your father," replied Butscha, going a few steps on, so as to lead Modeste to a little distance from the windows. "Listen to me, mademoiselle. You know that I who speak to you am ready to lay down not my life only, but my honor for you, at any time, at any moment. So you can believe in me, you can trust me with things you would not perhaps tell your father.—Well, has that sublime Canalis ever spoken to you in the disinterested way that allows you to cast such a taunt at poor Ernest?"

"Yes."

"And you believe him?"

"That, Malignant Clerk," said she, giving him one of the ten or twelve nicknames she had devised for him, "is, as it seems to me, casting a doubt on the strength of my self-respect."

"You can laugh, dear mademoiselle, so it cannot be serious. I can only hope that you are making a fool of him."

"What would you think of me, Monsieur Butscha, if I thought I had any right to mock at either of the gentlemen who do me the honor to wish for me as a wife? I can tell you, Maître Jean, that even when she appears to scorn the most contemptible admiration, a girl is always flattered at having it offered to her."

"Then I flatter you——?" said the clerk, his face lighting up as a town is illuminated on some great occasion.

"You——?" said she. "You give me the most precious kind of friendship, a feeling as disinterested as that of a mother for her child! Do not compare yourself to any one else, for even my father is obliged to yield to me." She paused. "I cannot tell you that I love you, in the sense men give to the word; but what I feel for you is eternal, and can never know any change."

"Well, then," said Butscha, stooping to pick up a pebble that he might leave a kiss and a tear on the tip of Modeste's shoe, "let me watch over you as a dragon watches over a treasure.—The poet spreads before you just now all the filagree of his elaborate phrases, the tinsel of his promises. He sang of love to the sweetest chord of his lyre no doubt? If when this noble lover is fully assured of your having but a small fortune, you should see his demeanor change; if you then find him cold and embarrassed, will you still make him your husband, still honor him with your esteem?"

"Can he be a Francisque Althor?" she asked, with an expression of the deepest disgust.

"Let me have the pleasure of working this transformation scene," said Butscha. "Not only do I intend that it shall be sudden, but I do not despair of restoring your poet to you afterwards, in love once more, of making him blow hot and cold on your heart with as good a grace as when he argues for and against the same thing in the course of a single evening, sometimes without being aware of it——"

"And if you are right," said she, "whom can I trust?"

"The man who truly loves you."

"The little Duke?"

Butscha looked at Modeste. They both walked on a few steps in silence. The girl was impenetrable; she did not wince.

"Mademoiselle, will you allow me to put into words the thoughts that lurk at the bottom of your heart like watermosses in a pool, and that you refuse to explain to yourself even?"

"Why, indeed!" cried Modeste, "is my privy councillor-in-waiting a mirror too?"

"No, but an echo," he replied, with a little bow stamped with the utmost modesty. "The Duke loves you, but he loves you too well. I, a dwarf, have fully understood the exquisite delicacy of your soul. You would hate to be adored like the holy wafer in a monstrance. But being so eminently a woman, you could no more bear to see a man of whom you were always secure perpetually at your feet, than you could endure an egoist like Canalis, who would always care more for himself than for you. . . . Why? I know not. I would I could be a woman, and an old woman, to learn the reason of the programme I can read in your eyes, which is perhaps that of every girl.

"At the same time, your lofty soul craves for adoration. When a man is at your feet you cannot throw yourself at his. 'But you cannot go far in that way,' Voltaire used to say. So the little Duke has, morally speaking, too many genuflexions, and Canalis not enough—not to say none at all. And I can read the mischief hidden in your smile when you are speaking to the Master of the Horse, when he speaks to you and you reply. You would never be unhappy with the Duke; everybody would be pleased if you chose him for your husband; but you would not love him. The coldness of egoism and the excessive fervor of perennial raptures no doubt have a negative effect on the heart of every woman.

"Obviously this is not the perpetual triumph that you would enjoy in the infinite delights of such a marriage as that you dream of, in which you would find a submission to be proud of, great little sacrifices that are gladly unconfessed, successes looked forward to with rapture, and unforeseen magnanimity to which it is a joy to yield; in which a woman finds herself understood even to her deepest secrets, while her love is sometimes a protection to her protector——"

"You are a wizard!" cried Modeste.

"Nor will you meet with that enchanting equality of feeling, that constant sharing of life, and that certainty of giving happiness which makes marriage acceptable, if you marry a Canalis, a man who thinks only of himself, to whom *I* is the only note in the scale, and whose attention has not yet condescended so low as to listen to your father or the Duke. An ambitious man, not of the first class, to whom your dignity and supremacy matter little, who will treat you as a necessary chattel in the house, who insults you already by his indifference on points of honor. Yes, if you allowed yourself to go so far as to slap your mother, Canalis would shut his eyes that he might not see your guilt, so hungry is he for your fortune!

"So, mademoiselle, I was not thinking of the great poet, who is but a little actor, nor of my lord Duke, who would be for you a splendid match, but not a husband——"

"Butscha, my heart is a blank page on which you yourself write what you read," replied Modeste. "You are carried away by your provincial hatred of everything that compels you to look above your head. You cannot forgive the poet for being a political man, for having an eloquent tongue, and a splendid future; you calumniate his purpose——"

"His, mademoiselle! He would turn his back on you within twenty-four hours with the meanness of a Vilquin."

"Well, make him play such a farcical scene, and——"

"Ay, and in every key; in three days—on Wednesday—do not forget. Until then, mademoiselle, amuse yourself by making the musical box play all its airs, that the vile discords of the antiphony may come out all the more clearly."

Modeste gaily returned to the drawing-room, where of all the men present, la Brière alone, seated in the recess of a window—whence, no doubt, he had been looking at his idol— rose at her entrance, as if an usher had shouted, "The Queen!" It was a respectful impulse, full of the eloquence peculiar to action, which surpasses that of the finest speech. Spoken love is not to be compared with love in action—every girl of twenty is fifty as concerns this axiom; this is the seducer's strongest argument.

Instead of looking Modeste in the face, as Canalis did, bowing to her as an act of public homage, the disdained lover watched her with a slow side glance, as humble as Butscha's, almost timid. The young heiress observed this demeanor as she went to place herself by Canalis, in whose game she affected an interest. In the course of the conversation, la Brière learned, from a remark she made to her father, that Modeste intended to begin riding again on the following Wednesday, and she mentioned that she had no riding-whip suitable to match with her handsome new habit. Ernest flashed a glance at the dwarf like a spark of fire, and a few minutes later they were walking together on the terrace.

"It is now nine o'clock," said la Brière. "I am off to Paris as fast as my horse will carry me. I can be there by ten to-morrow morning. My dear Butscha, from you she will accept a gift with pleasure, for she has a great regard for you; let me give her a riding-whip in your name; and, believe me, in return for such an immense favor you have in me not indeed a friend, but a slave!"

"Go; you are happy," said the clerk. "You have money."

"Tell Canalis from me that I shall not be in to-night, and that he must invent some excuse for my absence for two days."

An hour later Ernest had set out on horseback for Paris, where he arrived after twelve hours' riding, his first care being to secure a place in the mail coach for le Havre on the following day. He then went to the three first jewelers in Paris, comparing handles of riding-whips, and seeking what art could produce of the most royal perfection. He found one made by Stidmann for a Russian lady, who, after ordering it, had been unable to pay for it—a fox-hunt wrought in gold, with a ruby at the top, and exorbitantly expensive as compared with a Referendary's stipend; all his savings were swallowed up, amounting to seven thousand francs. Ernest gave a sketch of the arms of la Bastie, allowing twenty hours for them to be engraved instead of those that were on it. This handle, a masterpiece of workmanship, was fitted to an india-rubber whip, and placed in a red morocco case, lined with velvet, with a monogram of two M's on the top.

By Wednesday morning la Brière had returned by the mail, in time to breakfast with Canalis. The poet had explained his secretary's absence by saying that he was busy with some work forwarded from Paris. Butscha who had gone to the coach office to hold out a welcoming hand to Ernest on the arrival of the mail, flew to give this work of art to Françoise Cochet, desiring her to place it on Modeste's dressing-table.

"You are going out riding, no doubt, with Mademoiselle Modeste," said Butscha, on returning to Canalis' villa to inform Ernest, by a side glance, that the whip had safely reached its destination.

"I!" said la Brière. "I am going to bed."

"Well!" exclaimed Canalis, looking at his friend, "I do not understand you at all."

Breakfast was ready, and the poet naturally invited the clerk to sit down with them. Butscha had stayed, intending to get himself invited if necessary by la Brière, seeing on Germain's countenance the success of a hunchback's trick, of which his promise to Modeste may have given a hint.

"Monsieur was very wise to keep Monsieur Latournelle's clerk," said Germain in his master's ear. Canalis and Germain, on a hint from the latter, passed into the drawing-room. "This morning I went out to see some fishing, an expedition to which I was invited the day before yesterday by the owner of a boat I have made acquaintance with."

Germain did not confess that he had had such bad taste as to play billiards in a café in le Havre, where Butscha had surrounded him with a number of his friends in order to be able to work upon him.

"What then?" said Canalis. "Come to the point, and at once."

"Monsieur le Baron, I heard a discussion about Monsieur Mignon, which I did my best to keep going—no one knew who I lived with. I tell you, Monsieur le Baron, everybody in le Havre says that you are running your head against a wall. Mademoiselle de la Bastie's fortune is, like her name, very modest. The ship on which the father came home is not his own; it belongs to some China merchants, with whom he has to settle, and things are said about it that are far from flattering to the Colonel.—Having heard that you and Monsieur le Duc were rivals for Mademoiselle de la Bastie, I take the liberty of mentioning it; for, between you and him, it is better that his lordship should swallow the bait. On my way back I took a turn on the quay, past the theatre, where the merchants walk up and down, and I pushed my way boldly among them. These worthy folks, seeing a well-dressed man, began to talk about the affairs of the town; from one thing to another I led them to speak of Colonel Mignon; and they were so much of the same mind as the fishermen that I felt it my duty to speak. That is why I left you, sir, to get up and dress alone . . ."

"What is to be done?" cried Canalis, feeling that he was too deeply pledged to withdraw from his promises to Modeste.

"You know my attachment to you, sir," said Germain, seeing that the poet was thunderstruck, "and you will not be surprised if I offer a piece of advice. If you can make this clerk drunk, he will let the cat out of the bag, and if he won't open his mouth for two bottles of champagne, he certainly will for the third. It would be a strange thing, too, if monsieur, who will certainly be an ambassador one day, for Philoxène heard Madame la Duchesse say so,—if you, sir, cannot get round a country lawyer's clerk."

At this moment Butscha, the unknown author of this fishing expedition, was begging the Referendary to say nothing about his journey to Paris, and not to interfere with his manœuvres at breakfast. Butscha meant to take advantage of a reaction of feeling unfavorable to Charles Mignon, which had set in at le Havre.

This was the cause of this reaction. Monsieur le Comte de la Bastie had entirely ignored those of his former friends who, during his absence, had neglected his wife and children. On hearing that a dinner was to be given at the Villa Mignon, each one flattered himself he would be among the guests, and expected an invitation; but when it was known that only

Gobenheim, the Latournelles, the Duke, and the two Parisians were to be asked, there was a loud outcry at the merchant's arrogance; his marked avoidance of seeing anybody, and of ever going down to lè Havre, was commented on, and attributed to scorn, on which the whole town avenged itself by casting doubts on Mignon's sudden wealth. By dint of gossip everybody soon ascertained that the money advanced to Vilquin on the Villa had been found by Dumay. This fact gave the most malignant persons grounds for the libelous supposition that Charles had confided to Dumay's known devotion the funds concerning which he anticipated litigation on the part of his so-called partners in Canton. Charles' reticence, for his constant aim was to conceal his wealth, and the gossip of his servants, who had been put on their guard, lent an appearance of truth to these monstrous fables, believed by all who were governed by the spirit of detraction that animates rival traders. In proportion as parochial pride had formerly cried up his immense fortune as one of the makers of le Havre, so now provincial jealousy cast doubt on it.

Butscha, to whom the fishermen of the port owed more than one good turn, desired them to be secret, and to cram their new friend. He was well served. The owner of the boat told Germain that a cousin of his, a sailor, was coming from Marseilles, having just been paid off in consequence of the sale of the brig in which the Colonel had come home. The vessel was being sold by order of one Castagnould, and the cargo—according to the cousin—was worth only three or four hundred thousand francs at most.

"Germain," said Canalis, as the servant was leaving the room, "bring us up some Champagne and some Bordeaux. A member of the legal faculty of Normandy must carry away some memories of a poet's hospitality.—And he has the wit of *le Figaro*," added Canalis, laying his hand on the dwarf's shoulder; "that *petit-journal* brilliancy must be made to sparkle and foam with the wine of Champagne; we will not spare ourselves either, Ernest! Why, it is two years at least since I last got tipsy," he added, turning to la Brière.

"With wine?—That I can quite understand," replied the clerk. "You get tipsy with yourself every day! In the matter of praise, you drink your fill. You are handsome; you are famous during your lifetime; your conversation is on a level with your genius; and you fascinate all the women, even my master's wife. Loved as you are by the most beautiful Sultana Valideh I ever saw—it is true, I have never seen another—you can, if you choose, marry Mademoiselle de la Bastie.—Why, merely with making this inventory of your present advantages, to say nothing of the future—a fine title, a peerage, an embassy!—I am quite fuddled, like the men who bottle wine for other people to drink."

"All this social magnificence is nothing," replied Canalis, "without that which gives them value—a fortune! Here we are men among men; fine sentiments are delightful in stanzas."

"And in certain circum*stanzas*," said Butscha, with a significant smile.

"You, a master of the mystery of settlements," said the poet, smiling at the pun, "must know as well as I do that cottage rhymes to nothing better than pottage."

At table Butscha played with signal success the part of le Rigaudin in *la Maison en loterie,* alarming Ernest, to whom the jests of a lawyer's office were unfamiliar; they are a match for those of the studio. The clerk repeated all the scandal of le Havre, the history of every fortune, of every boudoir, and of all the crimes committed just outside of the pale of the law, what is called sailing as close hauled as possible (in Normandy, *se tirer d'affaire comme on peut*). He spared no one, and his spirits rose with the stream of wine he poured down his throat like storm water through a gutter.

"Do you know, la Brière," said Canalis, filling up Butscha's glass, "that this brave boy would be a first-rate secretary to an Ambassador?"

"And cut out his master!" retorted the dwarf with a look at Canalis, of insolence redeemed by the sparkle of carbonic acid gas. "I have enough spirit of intrigue and little enough gratitude to climb on to your shoulders. A poet supporting an abortion!—Well, it has been seen, and pretty frequently—in libraries. Why, you are staring at me as if I were swallowing swords. Heh! my dear, great genius, you are a very superior man; you know full well that gratitude is a word for idiots; it is to be found in the dictionary, but not in the human heart. I O U is a formula unhonored on the green banks of Parnassus or Pindus. Do you suppose I feel the debt to my master's wife for having brought me up? Why, the whole town has paid it off in esteem, praise, and admiration, the most precious of all coin. I do not see the virtue that is merely an investment for the benefit of one's vanity. Men make a trade of reciprocal services; the word gratitude represents the debit side, that is all.

"As to intrigue, I adore it!—What!" he went on, in reply to a gesture from Canalis, "do you not delight in the faculty which enables a crafty man to get the upper hand of a man of genius, which requires constant observation of the vices and weaknesses of our betters, and a sense of the nick of time for everything? Ask diplomacy whether the triumph of cunning over strength is not the most delightful success there is. If I were your secretary, Monsieur le Baron, you would soon be Prime Minister, because it would be to my interest!—Now, would you like a sample of my little talents of that kind? Hearken! You love Mademoiselle Modeste to distraction, and you are very right. In my opinion, the girl is a genuine Parisienne, for here and there a Parisienne sprouts in the country. Our Modeste would be a wife to push a man. She has that sort of thing," said he, giving his hand a twirl in the air. "You have a formidable rival in the Duke. Now, what will you give me to pack him off within three days?"

"Let us finish this bottle," said the poet, refilling Butscha's glass.

"You will make me drunk!" said the clerk, swallowing down his ninth glass of champagne. "Is there a bed where I may sleep for an hour? My master is as sober as a camel, the old fox, and Madame Latournelle too. They would both be hard upon me, and they would have good reason, while I should have lost mine, and I have some work to do."

Then going back to a former subject without any transition, after the manner of a man when he is screwed, he exclaimed:

"And then, what a memory I have! It is a match for my gratitude."

"Butscha!" exclaimed the poet, "just now you said that you had no gratitude; you are contradicting yourself."

"Not at all," said the clerk. "Forgetting almost always means remembering!—Now, then, on we go! I am made to be a secretary."

"And now will you set to work to get rid of the Duke?" asked Canalis, charmed to find the conversation tending naturally to the subjects he aimed at.

"That—is no concern of yours," said Butscha, with a tremendous hiccup.

Butscha rolled his head on his shoulders, and his eyes from Germain to la Brière, and from la Brière to Canalis, in the manner of a man who feels intoxication creeping over him, and wants to know in what esteem he is held; for in the wreck of drunkenness it may be noted that self-esteem is the last sentiment to float.

"Look here, great poet, you are a jolly fellow, you are. Do you take me for one of your readers, you who sent your friend to Paris to procure information concerning the house of Mignon. I humbug, you humbug, we humbug. Well and good; but do me the honor to believe that I am clear-headed enough always to keep as much conscience as I need in my sphere of life. As head clerk to Maître Latournelle my heart is a padlocked despatch-box, my lips never breathe a word of any paper concerning the clients. I know everything, and I know nothing. And then, passion is no secret: I love Modeste, she is a pupil of mine, she must marry well; and I could get round the Duke if necessary. But you are going to marry——"

"Germain, coffee and liqueurs," said Canalis.

"Liqueurs?" repeated Butscha, holding up a forbidding

hand like a too knowing maiden putting aside some little temptation. "Oh, my poor work! By the way, there is a marriage contract to be drawn up, and my second clerk is as stupid as a matrimonial bargain, and quite capable of p-p-poking a penknife through the bride's personal property. He thinks himself a fine fellow because he measures nearly six feet —the idiot!"

"Here, this is Crème de Thé, a West Indian liqueur," said Canalis.—"You who are Mademoiselle Modeste's adviser——"

"Her adviser?——"

"Well, do you think she loves me?"

"Ye-e-es, more than she loves the Duke," drawled the dwarf, rousing himself from a sort of torpor, which he acted to admiration. "She loves you for your disinterestedness. She told me that for you she felt equal to the greatest sacrifices, to giving up dress, spending only a thousand francs a year, devoting her life to prove to you that in marrying her you would have done a stroke of business. And she is devilish honest (hiccup), I can tell you, and well informed; there is nothing that girl does not know."

"That and three hundred thousand francs," said Canalis.

"Oh! there may be as much as you say," replied the clerk with enthusiasm. "Mignon Papa—and you see he is really a Mignon, a dear papa, that's what I like him for—to marry his only daughter—well, he would strip himself of everything. The Colonel has been accustomed under your Restoration to live on half-pay (hiccup), and he will be quite happy living with Dumay, speculating in a small way at le Havre; he will be sure to give the child his three hundred thousand francs.—Then we must not forget Dumay, who means to leave his fortune to Modeste. Dumay, you know, is a Breton; his birth gives security to the bargain; he never changes his mind, and his fortune is quite equal to his master's. At the same time, since they listen to me at least as much as to you, though I do not talk so much nor so well, I said to them, 'You are putting too much money into your house; if Vilquin leaves it on your hands, there are two hundred thousand francs that will bring you no return. There will be only a hundred thousand francs left to turn over, and that, in my opinion, is not enough.'—At this moment the Colonel and Dumay are talking it over. Take my word for it, Modeste is rich. The people of the town talk nonsense, they are envious. Why, who in the department has such a portion?" said Butscha, holding up his fingers to count. "Two to three hundred thousand francs in hard cash!" said he, folding down his left thumb with the forefinger of his right hand. "That is for one. The freehold of the Villa Mignon," and he doubled down his left forefinger, "for two; Dumay's fortune for three," he added, ticking it off on the middle finger. "Why, little Mother Modeste is a lady with six hundred thousand francs of her own when the two old soldiers shall have gone aloft to take further orders from God A'mighty."

This blunt and artless communication, broken by sips of liqueur, sobered Canalis as much as it seemed to intoxicate Butscha. To the lawyer's clerk, a mere provincial, this fortune was evidently colossal. He let his head drop on the palm of his right hand, and with the elbow majestically resting on the table, he sat blinking and talking to himself: "In twenty years, at the pace the Code is taking us, melting down fortunes by the process of subdivision, an heiress with six hundred thousand francs will be as rare as disinterestedness in a money-lender. You may say that Modeste will spend at least twelve thousand francs a year, the interest of her fortune; but she is a very nice girl—very nice—very nice. She is as you may say—a poet must have imagery—she is an ermine as knowing as a monkey."

"And what did you tell me?" cried Canalis in an undertone to la Brière. "That she had six millions?"

"My dear fellow," said Ernest, "allow me to remark that I could say nothing. I am bound by an oath, and it is perhaps saying more than I ought to tell you——"

"An oath? and to whom?"

"To Monsieur Mignon."

"Why, Ernest! when you know how indispensable fortune is

to me"—Butscha was snoring—"you who know my position, and all I should lose in the Rue de Grenelle by marrying— you would have coolly allowed me to plunge in?" said Canalis, turning pale. "But this is a matter between friends; and our friendship, my boy, is a compact of a far older date than this that the wily Provençal has required of you."

"My dear fellow," said Ernest, "I love Modeste too well to——"

"Idiot, take her!" cried the poet. "So break your oath——"

"Do you solemnly promise, on your honor as a man, to forget what I tell you, and to be just the same to me as though I had never confided to you, come what may?"

"I swear it by the sacred memory of my mother!"

"Well, when I was in Paris, Monsieur Mignon told me that he was very far from having such a colossal fortune as the Mongenods had spoken of. The Colonel intends to give his daughter two hundred thousand francs. But then, Melchior, was the father suspicious? or was he sincere? It is no concern of mine to solve that question. If she should condescend to choose me, Modeste, with nothing, should be my wife."

"A blue-stocking, appallingly learned, who has read everything and knows everything—in theory," cried Canalis, in reply to a protesting gesture of la Brière's; "a spoilt child, brought up in luxury during her early years, and weaned from it for the last five! Oh, my poor friend, pause, consider——"

"Ode and Code!" said Butscha, rousing himself. "You go in for the Ode, and I for the Code; there is only a C between. Code, from coda, a tail! You have treated me handsomely, and I like you—don't have anything to do with the Code.— Listen; a piece of good advice is not a bad return for your wine and your Crème de Thé. Old Mignon is cream too, the cream of good fellows. Well, trot out your horse, he is riding out with his daughter; you can speak frankly to him; ask him about her marriage portion; he will give you a plain answer, and you will see to the bottom of things as sure as I am tipsy, and you are a great man; but then there must be no mistake, we leave le Havre together, I suppose? I am to be your secretary, since this little chap, who thinks I am drunk, and is laughing at me, is going to leave you.—Go ahead. March! —and leave him to marry the girl."

Canalis went to dress.

"Not a word; he is rushing on suicide," said Butscha, as cool as Gobenheim, to la Brière, very quietly; and he telegraphed behind Canalis a signal of scorn familiar to the Paris street boy. "Good-bye, Master," he went on at the top of his voice, "may I go and get forty winks in Madame Amaury's summer-house?"

"Make yourself at home," replied the poet.

The clerk, loudly laughed at by Canalis' three servants, made his way to the summer-house, plunging into flower-beds and baskets with the perverse grace of an insect describing its endless zigzags as it tries to escape through a closed window. He scrambled up into the gazebo, and when the servants had got indoors, he sat down on a wooden bench and gave himself up to the joys of triumph. He had fooled the superior man; not only had he snatched off his mask, but he had seen him untie the strings, and he laughed as an author laughs at his piece, with a full appreciation of the value of this *vis comica*.

"Men are tops!" cried he; "you have only to find the end of the string that is wound round them. Why, any one could make me faint away by simply saying, 'Mademoiselle Modeste has fallen off her horse and broken her leg.'"

A few minutes later, Modeste, wearing a bewitching habit of dark-green kerseymere, a little hat with a green veil, doeskin gloves, and velvet boots, over which the lace frills of her drawers fell gracefully, had mounted her handsomely-saddled pony, and was showing to her father and the Duc d'Hérouville the pretty gift she had just received; she was delighted with it, seeing in it one of those attentions which most flatter a woman.

"Was it you, Monsieur le Duc?" said she, holding out the sparkling end of her whip. "There was a card on it with the words, 'Guess if you can,' and a row of dots. Françoise and Madame Dumay ascribe this charming surprise to Butscha; but my dear Butscha is not rich enough to pay for such fine rubies! And my father, on my saying on Sunday evening that I had no whip, sent for that one from Rouen."

Modeste pointed to a whip in her father's hand with a handle set closely with turquoises, a fashionable novelty then, but now rather common.

"I only wish, mademoiselle—I would give ten years of my life to have the right of offering such a magnificent jewel," replied the Duke politely.

"Ah! then here is the audacious man," cried Modeste, seeing Canalis come up on horseback. "None but a poet can find such exquisite things.—Monsieur," she went on to Melchior, "my father will be angry with you; you are justifying those who blame you for your extravagance."

"Hah!" cried Canalis simply, "then that is what took la Brière from le Havre to Paris as fast as he could ride."

"Your secretary took such a liberty!" said Modeste, turning pale, and flinging the whip to Françoise Cochet with a vehemence expressive of the deepest contempt. "Give me back that whip, father!"

"The poor boy is lying on his bed broken with fatigue!" Melchior went on, as they followed the girl, who had gone off at a gallop. "You are hard, mademoiselle. 'I have this chance alone of reminding her of my existence,' was what he said."

"And could you esteem a woman who was capable of preserving keepsakes from every comer?" said Modeste.

Modeste, who was surprised at receiving no reply from Canalis, ascribed his inattention to the sound of the horse's hoofs.

"How you delight in tormenting those who are in love with you!" said the Duke. "Your pride and dignity so entirely belie your vagaries that I am beginning to suspect that you do yourself injustice by deliberately planning your malicious tricks."

"What! you have just discovered that, Monsieur le Duc?" said she, with a laugh. "You have exactly as much insight as a husband!"

For about a kilometre they rode on in silence. Modeste was surprised at being no longer aware of the flaming glances of Canalis, whose admiration for the beauties of the landscape seemed rather more than was natural. On the preceding evening Modeste had pointed out to the poet a beautiful effect of color in the sunset over the sea, and, finding him as speechless as a mute, had said:

"Well, do not you see it all?"

"I see nothing but your hand," he had replied.

"Does Monsieur de la Brière know how to ride?" Modeste asked, to pique him.

"He is not a very good horseman, but he goes," replied the poet, as cold as Gobenheim had been before the Colonel's return.

As they went along a cross-road, down which Monsieur Mignon turned to go through a pretty valley to a hill overlooking the course of the Seine, Canalis let Modeste and the Duke go forward, slackening his speed so as to bring his horse side by side with the Colonel's.

"Monsieur le Comte," said he, "you are a frank soldier, so you will regard my openness as a claim to your esteem. When an offer of marriage, with all the too barbarous, or, if you will, too civilized discussions to which it gives rise, is made through a third person, everyone suffers. You and I are both men of perfect discretion, and you, like me, are past the age for surprises, so let us speak as man to man.—I will set the example. I am nine-and-twenty, I have no landed estate, I am an ambitious man. That I ardently admire Mademoiselle Modeste you must have seen. Now, in spite of the faults your charming daughter delights in affecting——"

"To say nothing of those she really has," said the Colonel, smiling.

"I should be glad indeed to make her my wife, and I believe I could make her happy. The whole question of my future life turns on the point of fortune. Every girl who is open to marriage must be loved whatever comes of it; at the same time, you are not the man to get rid of your dear Modeste without a portion, and my position would no more allow of my marrying 'for love,' as the phrase is, than of proposing to a girl without a fortune at least equal to my own. My salary, and some sinecures, with what I get from the Academy and my writings, come to about thirty thousand francs a year, a fine income for a bachelor. If my wife and I between us have sixty thousand francs a year, I could continue to live on much the same footing as at present. Have you a million francs to give Mademoiselle Modeste?"

"Oh! monsieur, we are very far from any agreement," said the Colonel jesuitically.

"Well, then, we have said nothing about the matter—only whistled," said Canalis anxiously. "You will be quite satisfied with my conduct, Monsieur le Comte; I shall be one more of the unfortunate men crushed by that charming young lady. Give me your word that you will say nothing of this to anybody, not even to Mademoiselle Modeste; for," he added, by way of consolation, "some change might occur in my position which would allow of my asking her hand without a settlement."

"I swear it," said the Colonel. "You know, monsieur, with what exaggerated language the public, in the provinces as in Paris, talk of fortunes made and lost. Success and failure are alike magnified, and we are never so lucky or so unlucky as report says. In business there is no real security but investment in land when cash transactions are settled. I am awaiting with anxious impatience the reports of my various agents; nothing is as yet concluded—neither the sale of my merchandise and my ship, nor my account with China. I shall not for the next ten months know the amount of my capital. However, in Paris, when talking to Monsieur de la Brière, I guaranteed a settlement on my daughter of two hundred thousand francs in money down. I intend to purchase a landed estate and settle it in tail on my grandchildren, obtaining for them a grant of my titles and coat-of-arms."

After the first words of this speech Canalis had ceased to listen.

The four riders now came out on a wide road and rode abreast up to the plateau, which commands a view of the rich valley of the Seine towards Rouen, while on the other horizon they could still see the line of the sea.

"Butscha was indeed right, God is a great landscape maker," said Canalis, as he looked down on the panorama, unique among those for which the hills above the Seine are justly famous.

"But it is when out hunting, my dear Baron," said the Duke, "when nature is roused by a voice, by a stir in the silence, that the scenery, as we fly past, seems most really sublime with the rapid change of effect."

"The sun has an inexhaustible palette," said Modeste, gazing at the poet in a sort of bewilderment. On her making a remark as to the absence of mind she observed in Canalis, he replied that he was reveling in his own thoughts, an excuse which writers can make in addition to those common to other men.

"Are we really blest when we transfer our life to the centre of the world, and add to it a thousand factitious needs and over-wrought vanities?" said Modeste, as she contemplated the calm and luxuriant champaign which seemed to counsel philosophical quietude.

"Such bucolics, mademoiselle, are always written on tables of gold," said the poet.

"And imagined, perhaps, in a garret," replied the Colonel.

Modeste gave Canalis a piercing look, and saw him flinch; there was a sound of bells in her ears; for a moment everything grew dark before her; then, in a hard, cold tone, she exclaimed:

"Ah! it is Wednesday!"

"It is not with the idea of flattering a merely transient

fancy of yours, mademoiselle," said the Duc d'Hérouville solemnly—for this little scene, so tragical to Modeste, had given him time for thought—"but, I assure you, I am so utterly disgusted with the world, the Court, and Paris life, that, for my part, with a Duchesse d'Hérouville so full of charms and wit as you are, I could pledge myself to live like a philosopher in my château, doing good to those about me, reclaiming my alluvial flats, bringing up my children——"

"This shall be set down to your credit, Duke," said Modeste, looking steadily at the noble gentleman. "You flatter me," she added, "for you do not think me frivolous, and you believe that I have enough resources in myself to live in solitude.—And that perhaps will be my fate," she added, looking at Canalis with a compassionate expression.

"It is the lot of all small fortunes," replied the poet. "Paris requires Babylonian luxury. I sometimes wonder how I have managed to live till now."

"The King is Providence to you and me," said the Duke frankly, "for we both live on His Majesty's bounty. If, since the death of Monsieur le Grand, as Cinq-Mars was called, we had not always held his office in our family, we should have had to sell Hérouville to be demolished by the *Bande Noire*. Believe me, mademoiselle, it is to me a terrible humiliation to mix up financial considerations with the thought of marriage——"

The candor of this avowal, which came from the heart, and the sincerity of this regret, touched Modeste.

"In these days," said the poet, "nobody in France, Monsieur le Duc, is rich enough to commit the folly of marrying a woman for her personal merits, her charm, her character, or her beauty——"

The Colonel looked at Canalis with a strange expression, after studying his daughter, whose face no longer expressed any astonishment.

"Then for a man of honor," he said, "it is a noble use of riches to devote them to repair the ravages that time has wrought on our old historical families."

"Yes, papa," said the girl gravely.

The Colonel asked the Duke and Canalis to dine at the villa, without ceremony, in their riding dress, and set them the example by not changing his for dinner. When, on their return, Modeste went to change her dress, she looked curiously at the trinket that had come from Paris, and that she had so cruelly disdained.

"How exquisitely such work is done nowadays," said she to Françoise Cochet, who was now her maid.

"And that poor young gentleman, mademoiselle, ill of a fever——"

"Who told you so?"

"Monsieur Butscha. He came here just now to bid me say you had no doubt found out that he had kept his word on the day he named."

Modeste went downstairs, dressed with queenly simplicity.

"My dear father," said she, quite audibly, taking the Colonel's arm, "will you go and ask after Monsieur de la Brière, and oblige me by taking back his present. You may put it to him that my small fortune, as well as my own taste, prohibits my using such toys as are fit only for a queen or a courtesan. Besides, I can only accept presents from the man I may hope to marry. Beg our excellent young friend to keep the whip till you find yourself rich enough to buy it of him."

"Then my little girl is full of good sense!" said the Colonel, kissing her on the forehead.

Canalis took advantage of a conversation between the Duc d'Hérouville and Madame Mignon to go out on the terrace, where Modeste presently joined him, urged by curiosity, while he believed it was by her desire to become Madame Canalis. Somewhat alarmed at his own audacity in thus executing what a soldier would call "right about face," though, according to the jurisprudence of ambitious souls, every man in his place would have done the same, and just as suddenly, he tried to find some plausible reasons as he saw the ill-starred Modeste come out to him.

"Dear Modeste," said he, in insinuating tones, "as we are

on such terms of friendship, will you be offended if I point out to you how painful your replies with regard to Monsieur d'Hérouville must be to a man who loves you, and, above all, to a poet, whose soul is a woman, is all nerves, and suffering from the myriad jealousies of a genuine passion. I should be a poor diplomate indeed if I had not understood that your preliminary flirtations, your elaborate recklessness, were the outcome of a plan to study our characters——"

Modeste raised her head with a quick, intelligent, and pretty movement, of a type that may perhaps be traced to certain animals to which instinct gives wonderful grace.

"And so, thrown back on myself, I was no longer deceived by them. I marveled at your subtle wit, in harmony with your character and your countenance. Be satisfied that I never imagined your assumed duplicity to be anything but an outer wrapper, covering the most adorable candor. No, your intelligence, your learning, have left untainted the exquisite innocence we look for in a wife. You are the very wife for a poet, a diplomatist, a thinker, a man fated to live through hazardous moments, and I admire you as much as I feel attached to you. I entreat you, unless you were merely playing with me yesterday when you accepted the pledges of a man whose vanity will turn to pride if he is chosen by you, whose faults will turn to virtues at your divine touch—I beseech you, do not crush the feeling he has indulged till it is a vice!

"Jealousy in me is a solvent, and you have shown me what its violence is; it is fearful; it eats into everything! Oh! it is not the jealousy of Othello!" said he, in reply to a movement on Modeste's part. "No, no! I myself am in question; I am spoilt in this regard. You know of the one affection to which I owe the only form of happiness I have ever known— and that very incomplete (he shook his head).

"Love is depicted as a child by every nation, because it cannot be conceived of but as having all life before it. Well, this love of mine had its term fixed by nature; it was still-born. The most intuitive motherliness discerned and soothed this aching spot in my heart, for a woman who feels—who sees—

that she is dying to the joys of love, has angelic consideration; the duchess has never given me a pang of that kind. In ten years not a word, not a look, has failed of its mark. I attach more importance than ordinary people do to words, thoughts, and looks. To me a glance is an infinite possession, the slightest doubt is a mortal poison, and acts instantaneously: I cease to love. In my opinion—which is opposed to that of the vulgar, who revel in trembling, hoping, waiting—love ought to dwell in absolute assurance, childlike, infinite. To me the enchanting purgatory which women delight in inflicting on us with their caprices is an intolerable form of happiness which I will have nothing to say to; to me, love is heaven or hell. Hell I will not have; I feel that I am strong enough to endure the sempiternal blue of Paradise. I give myself unreservedly, I will have no secrets, no doubts, no delusions, in my future life, and I ask for reciprocity. Perhaps I offend you by doubting you! But, remember, I am speaking only of myself——"

"And a great deal," said Modeste, hurt by all the lancet points of this harangue, in which the Duchesse de Chaulieu was used as a sledge-hammer, "but it can never be too much; I have a habit of admiring you, my dear poet."

"Well, then, can you promise me the dog-like fidelity I offer you? Is it not fine? Is it not what you wish for?"

"But why, my dear poet, do you not look for a wife who is dumb and blind and something of a fool? I am quite prepared to please my husband in all things; but you threaten to deprive a girl of the very happiness you promise her, to snatch it from her at the slightest movement, the slightest word, the slightest look! You cut the bird's wings and want to see it fly! I knew that poets were accused of inconsistency —Oh! quite unjustly," she added, as Canalis protested by a gesture, "for the supposed fault is merely the result of a vulgar misapprehension of the suddenness of their impulses. Still, I had not thought that a man of genius would devise the contradictory conditions of such a game, and then call it life! You insist on impossibilities just to have the pleasure of putting me in the wrong, like those enchanters who in fairy tales set tasks to persecuted damsels whom good fairies rescue——"

"In this case true love will be the fairy," said Canalis, rather drily, seeing that his motive for a separation had been detected by the acute and delicate intelligence which Butscha had put on the scent.

"You, at this moment, my dear poet, are like those parents who inquire as to a girl's fortune before mentioning what their son's will be. You make difficulties with me, not knowing whether you have any right to do so. Love cannot be based on agreements discussed in cold blood. The poor Duke allows himself to be managed with all the submissiveness of Uncle Toby in Sterne's novel, with this difference, that I am not the widow Wadman, though bereaved at this moment of many illusions concerning poetry.—Yes! we hate to believe anything, we girls, that can overthrow our world of fancy!—I had been told all this beforehand!—Oh! you are trying to quarrel with me in a way unworthy of you! I cannot recognize the Melchior of yesterday."

"Because Melchior has detected in you an ambition you still cherish——"

Modeste looked at Canalis from head to foot with an imperial glance.

"But I shall some day be an ambassador and a peer as he is——"

"You take me for a vulgar schoolgirl!" she said, as she went up the steps. But she turned hastily, and added in some confusion, for she felt suffocating:

"That is less insolent than taking me for a fool. The change in your demeanor is due to the nonsense current in le Havre, which Françoise, my maid, has just repeated to me."

"Oh, Modeste, can you believe that?" cried Canalis, with theatrical emphasis. "Then you think that I want to marry you only for your fortune!"

"If I do you this injustice after your edifying remarks on the hills by the Seine, it lies with you to undeceive me, and thenceforth I will be what you would wish me to be," said she, blighting him with her scorn.

"If you think you can catch me in that trap, my lady," said the poet to himself as he followed her, "you fancy me younger than I am. What an ado, to be sure, for a little slut for whose esteem I care no more than for that of the King of Borneo. However, by ascribing to me an ignoble motive she justifies my present attitude. Isn't she cunning?—La Brière will be saddled, like the little fool that he is; and five years hence we shall laugh at him well, she and I."

The coolness produced by this dispute between Modeste and Canalis was obvious to all eyes that evening. Canalis withdrew early, on the pretext of la Brière's illness, leaving the field free to the Master of the Horse. At about eleven Butscha, who had come to escort Madame Latournelle home, said in an undertone to Modeste:

"Was I right?"

"Alas, yes!" said she.

"But have you done as we agreed, and left the door ajar so that he may return?"

"My anger was too much for me," replied Modeste. "Such meanness brought the blood to my head, and I told him my mind."

"Well, so much the better! When you have quarreled so that you cannot speak civilly to each other, even then I undertake to make him so devoted and pressing that you yourself are taken in by him."

"Come, come, Butscha; he is a great poet, a gentleman, and a man of intellect."

"Your father's eight millions will be more than all that."

"Eight millions!" said Modeste.

"My master, who is selling his business, is setting out for Provence to look into Castagnould's investments as your father's agent. The sum-total of the contracts for repurchasing the lands of la Bastie amounts to four millions of francs, and your father has consented to every item. Your settlement is to be two millions, and the Colonel allows one for establishing you in Paris with a house and furniture. Calculate."

"Ah, then I may be Duchesse d'Hérouville," said Modeste, looking at Butscha.

"But for that ridiculous Canalis, you would have kept *his* whip, as sent by me," said Butscha, putting in a word for la Brière.

"Monsieur Butscha, do you really expect me to marry the man you may choose?" said Modeste, laughing.

"That worthy young fellow loves as truly as I do; you loved him yourself for a week, and he is a man of genuine heart," replied the clerk.

"And can he compete with a Crown appointment, do you think? There are but six—the High Almoner, the Chancellor, the Lord Chamberlain, the Master of the Horse, the High Constable, the High Admiral.—But there are no more Lords High Constable."

"But in six months, mademoiselle, the people, composed of an infinite number of malignant Butschas, may blow upon all this grandeur. Besides, what does nobility matter in these days? There are not a thousand real noblemen in France. The d'Hérouvilles are descended from an Usher of the Rod under Robert of Normandy. You will have many a vexation from those two knife-faced old maids.—If you are bent on being a Duchess—well, you belong to Franche Comté, the Pope will have at least as much consideration for you as for the tradespeople, he will sell you a duchy ending in *nia* or *agno*.—Do not trifle with your happiness for the sake of a Crown appointment!"

The reflections indulged in by Canalis during the night were all satisfactory. He could imagine nothing in the world worse than the situation of a married man without a fortune. Still tremulous at the thought of the danger he had been led into by his vanity, which he had pledged, as it were, to Modeste by his desire to triumph over the Duc d'Hérouville, and by his belief in Monsieur Mignon's millions, he began to wonder what the Duchesse de Chaulieu must be thinking of his stay at le Havre, aggravated by five days' cessation from letter-writing, whereas in Paris they wrote each other four or five notes a week.

"And the poor woman is struggling to get me promoted to be Commander of the Legion of Honor, and to the place of Minister to the Grand Duchy of Baden!" cried he.

Forthwith, with the prompt decisiveness which in poets, as in speculators, is the result of a clear intuition of the future, he sat down and wrote the following letter:—

To Madame la Duchesse de Chaulieu.

"MY DEAR ÉLÉONORE,—You are no doubt astonished at having had no news of me, but my stay here is not merely a matter of health; I also have had to do my duty in some degree to our little friend la Brière. The poor boy has fallen desperately in love with a certain Demoiselle Modeste de la Bastie, a little pale-faced, insignificant thread-paper of a girl, who, by the way, has as a vice a mania for literature, and calls herself poetical to justify the whims, the tantrums, and changes of a pretty bad temper. You know Ernest, he is so easily made a fool of, that I would not trust him alone. Mademoiselle de la Bastie set up a strange flirtation with your Melchior; she was very well inclined to be your rival, though she has lean arms and scraggy shoulders, like most young girls, hair more colorless than Madame de Rochefide's, and a very doubtful expression in her little gray eye. I pulled up this Immodeste's advances pretty short—perhaps rather too roughly; but that is the way of an absorbing passion. What do I care for all the women on earth, who, all put together, are not worth you?

"The people with whom we spend our time, who surround this heiress, are *bourgeois* enough to make one sick. Pity me; I spend my evenings with notaries' clerks, their wives, their cashiers, and a provincial money-lender; wide indeed is the gulf between this and the evenings in the Rue de Grenelle. The father's trumped-up fortune—he has just come home from China—has secured us the company of that omnipresent suitor the Master of the Horse, hungrier for millions than ever, since it will cost six or seven, they say, to reclaim and work the much-talked-of alluvion of Hérouville. The King has no idea what a fatal gift he has made to the little Duke. His Grace, who does not suspect how small a fortune his hoped-for father-in-law possesses, is jealous only of me. La Brière is making his way with his idol under cover of his friend, who serves as a screen.

"In spite of Ernest's raptures, I, the poet, think of the substantial; and the information I have gathered as to the gentleman's wealth casts a gloomy hue over our secretary's prospects, for his lady-love has sharp enough teeth to eat a hole in any fortune. Now, if my angel would redeem some of our sins, she would try to find out the truth about this matter, by sending for her banker, Mongenod, and cross-questioning him with the skill that distinguishes her. Monsieur Charles Mignon, formerly a Colonel in the Cavalry of the Imperial Guard, has for seven years been in constant communication with Mongenod's house. They talk here of two hundred thousand francs in settlement at most; and before making an offer in form for the young lady on Ernest's behalf, I should be glad to have positive data. As soon as the good folks are agreed, I return to Paris. I know a way of bringing the business to a satisfactory conclusion for our lover. All that is needed is to secure permission for Monsieur Mignon's son-in-law to take his title of Count, and no man is more likely to obtain such a grant than Ernest, in view of his services, especially when seconded by us three—you, the Duke, and myself. With his tastes, Ernest, who will undoubtedly rise to be a Master of the Exchequer, will be perfectly happy living in Paris if he is certain of twenty-five thousand francs a year, a permanent office, and a wife—poor wretch!

"Oh, my dear! how I long to see the Rue de Grenelle again! A fortnight's absence, when it does not kill love, revives the ardor of its early days, and you know, better perhaps than I, all the reasons that make my love eternal. My bones in the tomb will love you still! Indeed, I cannot hold out! If I am compelled to remain ten days longer, I must go to Paris for a few hours.

"Has the Duke got me rope to hang myself? And you, dear life, shall you have to take the Baden waters this season? The cooing of your *beau ténébreux,* as compared with the accents of happy love—always the same, and true to itself for nearly ten years past—has given me a deep contempt of marriage; I had never seen all this so close to my eyes before. Ah! my dear, what is called wrongdoing is a far closer tie between two souls than the law—is it not?"

This idea served as the text for two pages of reminiscences and of aspirations of too private a nature for publication.

On the day before Canalis posted this letter, Butscha, who wrote under the name of Jean Jacmin to his imaginary cousin Philoxène, had sent off his answer twelve hours in advance of the poet's letter. The Duchess, for the last fortnight extremely alarmed and offended by Melchior's silence, had dictated Philoxène's letter to her cousin; and now, after reading the clerk's reply—somewhat too decisive for the vanity of a lady of fifty—had made minute inquiries as to Colonel Mignon's fortune. Finding herself betrayed, deserted for money, Éléonore gave herself up to a paroxysm of rage, hatred, and cold malignancy. Philoxène, knocking at the door of her mistress' luxurious room, on going in, found her with tears in her eyes, and stood amazed at this unprecedented phenomenon, which she had never before seen during fifteen years of service.

"We expiate the happiness of ten years in ten minutes!" exclaimed the Duchess.

"A letter from le Havre, madame."

Éléonore read Canalis' effusion of prose without observing Philoxène's presence, and the maid's surprise was heightened as she saw the Duchess' face recover its serenity as she read the letter. If you hold out to a drowning man a pole as thick as a walking stick, he will regard it as the king's highway to safety; and so the happy Éléonore believed in the poet's good faith as she perused these sheets in which love and business, lies and truth, elbowed each other.

Just now, when the banker had left her, she had sent for her husband to hinder Melchior's promotion if there were time yet; but a generous regret came over her that rose to a sublime impulse.

"Poor boy!" thought she, "he has not the smallest thought of ill. He loves me as he did the first day; he tells me everything.—Philoxène!" said she, noticing her head maid loitering about, and affecting to arrange the toilet-table.

"Madame la Duchesse?"

"My hand-glass, child."

Éléonore looked at herself, noted the razor-fine lines grooving her forehead, but invisible at a distance; and she sighed, for she believed that in that sigh she was taking leave of love. Then she had a man's thought, above the pettiness of woman —a thought which is sometimes intoxicating; an intoxication which may perhaps account for the clemency of the Semiramis of the North when she made her young and lovely rival Momonoff's wife.

"Since he has not failed me, I will get the millions and the girl for him," thought she, "if this little Mademoiselle Mignon is as plain as he says she is."

Three knocks, delicately rapped out, announced the Duke, for whom his wife herself opened the door.

"Ah! you are better, my dear," cried he, with the assumed gladness that courtiers so well know how to put on, and by which simpletons are taken in.

"My dear Henri," said she, "it is really inconceivable that you should not by this time have secured Melchior's appointment, after sacrificing yourself for the King during your year's ministry, knowing that it would scarcely endure so long!"

The Duke glanced at Philoxène; and the maid, by an almost imperceptible jerk of the head, showed him the letter from le Havre on the dressing-table. "You would be bored to death in Germany, and quarrel with Melchior before your return," said the Duke artlessly.

"Why?"

"Well, would you not always be together?" replied the erewhile Ambassador with comical candor.

"Oh! no," said she; "I mean to get him married."

"If d'Hérouville is to be believed, our dear Canalis has not waited for your good offices," replied the Duke, smiling. "Grandlieu yesterday read me some passages of a letter to him from the Master of the Horse, which was no doubt edited by his aunt to come to your ears; for Mademoiselle d'Hérouville, always on the lookout for a fortune, knows that Grandlieu and I play whist together almost every evening. That good little d'Hérouville invites the Prince de Cadignan to a Royal Hunt in Normandy, begging him to persuade the King to go, so as to turn the damsel's head when she finds herself the object of such a chivalrous procession. In fact, two words from Charles X. would settle everything. D'Hérouville says the girl is incomparably lovely."

"Henri, let us go to le Havre!" cried the Duchess, interrupting her husband.

"But on what excuse?" said he gravely—a man who had been in the intimate confidence of Louis XVIII.

"I never saw a hunt."

"That would be all very well if the King should be there, but to go so far for a hunt would be ridiculous; and he will not go, I have just spoken to him about it."

"MADAME perhaps would go——"

"That is a better plan," said the Duke; "and the Duchesse de Maufrigneuse may help you to get her away from Rosny. Then the King would make no objection to his hounds being taken out.—But do not go to le Havre, my dear," said the Duke, in a paternal tone; "it would make you conspicuous. Look here; this, I think, will be a better plan. Gaspard has his Château of Rosembray on the further side of the forest of Brotonne; why not give him a hint to receive all the party there?"

"Through whom?"

"Why, his wife the Duchess, who attends the Holy Table with Mademoiselle d'Hérouville, might ask Gaspard to do it if the old maid hinted it to her."

"You are the dearest man!" said Éléonore. "I will write two lines to the old lady, and to Diane; for we must have hunting-suits made. The little hat, now I think of it, makes one look very much younger.—Did you win yesterday at the English Embassy?"

"Yes," said the Duke; "I wiped out my score."

"And, above all, Henri, set everything aside till Melchior's two promotions are settled."

After writing a few lines to the fair Diane de Maufrigneuse, and a note to Mademoiselle d'Hérouville, Éléonore flung this reply like the smack of a horse-whip across Canalis' lies:—

To Monsieur le Baron de Canalis.

"MY DEAR POET,—Mademoiselle de la Bastie is beautiful; Mongenod assures me her father has eight millions of francs; I had thought of making her your wife, so I am deeply annoyed by your want of confidence in me. If before you started for le Havre, you aimed at getting la Brière married to her, I cannot imagine your not telling me so plainly before you went. And why pass a fortnight without writing a line to a friend so easily alarmed as I am?

"Your letter came a little late; I had already seen the banker. You are a child, Melchior; you try to be cunning with us. That is not right. Even the Duke is amazed at your behavior; he thinks you not quite gentlemanly—which casts a doubt on the virtue of your lady mother.

"Now, I want to see things for myself. I shall, I believe, have the honor of attending MADAME to the hunt arranged by the Duc d'Hérouville for Mademoiselle de la Bastie. I will contrive that you shall be invited to stay at Rosembray, as the hunt will probably take place at the Duc de Verneuil's.

"Believe me, none the less, my dear poet, your friend for life,   ÉLÉONORE."

"There, Ernest," said Canalis, tossing this letter, which arrived at breakfast time, across the table in la Brière's face.

"That is the two thousandth love-letter I have received from that woman, and there is not one single *tu*. The noble Éléonore never compromised herself further than what you find there.—Get married, and make haste about it! The worst marriage in the world is more tolerable than the lightest of these halters.—Well, I am the veriest Nicodemus that ever dropped from the moon. Modeste has millions; she is lost to me for ever; for no one ever comes back from the poles, where we now are, to the tropics, where we dwelt three days ago! Besides, I have all the more reason to wish for your triumph over the little Duke, because I told the Duchesse de Chaulieu that I came here only for your sake; so now I shall work for you."

"Alas! Melchior, Modeste must need have so superior, so mature a character, and such a noble mind, to resist the spectacle of the Court, and all the splendor so skilfully displayed in her honor and glory by the Duke, that I cannot believe in the existence of such perfection; and yet—if she is still the Modeste of her letters, there may be a hope——"

"You are a happy fellow, young Boniface, to see the world and your lady-love through such green spectacles!" exclaimed Canalis, going out to walk in the garden.

The poet, caught between two falsehoods, could not make up his mind what to do next.

"Play the game by the rules, and you lose!" cried he, as he sat in the summer-house. "Every man of sense would undoubtedly have acted as I did four days ago, and have crept out of the trap in which I found myself. For in such a case you don't wait to untie the knots; you break through everything!—Come, I must be cold, calm, dignified, hurt. Honor will not allow of any other demeanor. English rigidity is the only way to recover Modeste's respect. After all, if I only get out of the scrape by falling back on my old felicity, my ten years' fidelity will be rewarded. Éléonore will find me a suitable match."

The hunt was destined to be the rallying point of all the

passions brought into play by the Colonel's fortune and his
daughter's beauty. There was a sort of truce among the contending parties during the few days needed to prepare this
solemn act of forestry; the drawing-room in the Villa Mignon
had the peaceful appearance of a very united family party.
Canalis, intrenched in his part of a much-injured man, made
a display of courtesy; he put aside his pretentiousness, gave
no more specimens of oratorical talent, and was charming, as
clever men are when they shed their affectations. He discussed
the money-market with Gobenheim, war with the Colonel,
Germany with Madame Mignon, and housekeeping with Madame Latournelle, trying to win them over to la Brière. The
Duc d'Hérouville frequently left the field free to the two
friends, as he was obliged to go to Rosembray to consult the
Duc de Verneuil and superintend the execution of the orders
issued by the Master of the Hounds, the Prince de Cadignan.

Meanwhile, the comic element was not lacking. Modeste
found herself between the disparagement Canalis tried to cast
on the Duke's gallant attentions, and the exaggerated views of
the two demoiselles d'Hérouville, who came every evening.
Canalis pointed out to Modeste that, far from being the
heroine of the day, she would be scarcely noticed. MADAME
would be attended by the Duchesse de Maufrigneuse, the
daughter-in-law of the Master of the Hounds, by the Duchesse
de Chaulieu, and some other ladies of the Court, and among
them a mere girl would produce no sensation. Some
officers would, no doubt, be invited from the garrison at
Rouen, etc. Hélène was never tired of repeating to the girl,
whom she looked upon as her sister-in-law, that she would, of
course, be presented to MADAME; that the Duc de Verneuil
would certainly invite her and her father to stay at Rosembray; that if the Colonel had any favor to ask of the King—
such as a peerage—this would be an unique opportunity, for
they did not despair of getting the King there on the third
day; that she would be surprised at the charming reception
she would meet with from the handsomest women of the
Court, the Duchesses de Chaulieu, de Maufrigneuse, de Lenon-

court-Chaulieu, etc.; Modeste's prejudices against the Faubourg Saint-Germain would disappear—and so forth, and so forth. It was a most amusing little warfare, with its marches and counter-marches and strategy, which the Dumays, the Latournelles, Gobenheim and Butscha looked on at, and enjoyed, saying among themselves all manner of hard things about the nobility, as they watched their elaborate, cruel, and studied meanness.

The assurances of the d'Hérouville faction were justified by an invitation, in the most flattering terms, from the Duc de Verneuil and the Master of the King's Hounds to Monsieur le Comte de la Bastie and his daughter to be present at a Royal Hunt at Rosembray on the 7th, 8th, 9th, and 10th of November.

La Brière, oppressed by gloomy presentiments, reveled in Modeste's presence in that spirit of concentrated avidity whose bitter joys are known only to lovers irrevocably and for ever discarded. The flashes of happiness in his inmost self, mingled with melancholy reflections on the same theme, "She is lost to me!" made the poor youth a pathetic spectacle, all the more touching because his countenance and person were in harmony with this depth of feeling. There is nothing more poetical than such a living elegy that has eyes, that walks, and sighs without rhyming.

Finally, the Duc d'Hérouville came to arrange for Modeste's journey. After crossing the Seine, she was to proceed in the Duke's traveling carriage with his aunt and sister. The Duke was perfect in his courtesy; he invited Canalis and la Brière, telling them, as he told Monsieur Mignon, that they would find hunters at their service.

The Colonel asked his daughter's three lovers to breakfast on the day of the departure. Then Canalis tried to execute a scheme that had ripened in his mind during the last few days—namely, to reconquer Modeste, and to trick the Duchess, the Master of the Horse, and la Brière. A graduate in diplomacy could not remain bogged in such a position as that in which he found himself. La Brière, on his part, had made up his mind to bid Modeste an eternal farewell. Thus each suitor, as he foresaw the conclusion of a struggle that had been going on for three weeks, proposed to put in a last word, like a pleader to the judge before sentence is pronounced.

After dinner the day before, the Colonel took his daughter by the arm and impressed on her the necessity for coming to a decision.

"Our position with the d'Hérouville family would be intolerable at Rosembray. Do you want to be a duchess?" he asked Modeste.

"No, father," she replied.

"Then do you really love Canalis——?"

"Certainly not, papa; a thousand times, no!" said she, with childish irritability.

The Colonel looked at her with a sort of glee.

"Ah! I have not influenced you," cried the kind father. "But I may tell you now that even in Paris I had chosen my son-in-law when, on my impressing on him that I had no fortune, he threw his arms round me, saying that I had lifted a hundredweight from his heart."

"Of whom are you speaking?" asked Modeste, coloring.

"Of the man of solid virtues and sound morals," said he, mockingly repeating the phrase which, on the day after his return, had scattered Modeste's dreams.

"Oh, I am not thinking of him, papa! Leave me free to refuse the Duke myself; I know him, I know how to soothe him——"

"Then your choice is not made?"

"Not yet. I still have to guess a few syllables in the riddle of my future; but after having had a glimpse of the Court, I will tell you all my secret at Rosembray."

"You will join the hunt, will you not?" said the Colonel to Ernest, whom he saw coming down the path where he was walking with Modeste.

"No, Colonel," replied Ernest. "I have come to take leave of you and of mademoiselle. I am going back to Paris."

"You have no curiosity?" said Modeste, interrupting him, and looking at the bashful youth.

"Nothing is needed to keep me," said he, "but the expression of a wish I hardly hope for."

"If that is all, it will give me pleasure, at any rate," said the Colonel, as he went forward to meet Canalis, leaving his daughter alone for a moment with the hapless Ernest.

"Mademoiselle," said the young man, looking up at her with the courage of despair; "I have a petition to make."

"To me?"

"Let me depart forgiven! My life can never be happy; I must endure the remorse of having lost my happiness, by my own fault no doubt; but at least——"

"Before we part for ever," replied Modeste, interrupting him *à la* Canalis, "I want to know one thing only; and though you once assumed a disguise, I do not think that you will now be such a coward as to deceive me——"

At the word "coward" Ernest turned pale.

"You are merciless!" he exclaimed.

"Will you be frank with me?"

"You have the right to ask me such a humiliating question," said he, in a voice made husky by the violent beating of his heart.

"Well, then, did you read my letters out to Monsieur de Canalis?"

"No, mademoiselle; and though I gave them to the Colonel to read, it was only to justify my love, by showing him how my affection had had birth, and how genuine my efforts had been to cure you of your fancy."

"But what put this ignoble masquerading into your head?" she asked, with a kind of impatience.

La Brière related, in all its details, the scene to which Modeste's first letter had given rise, and the challenge which had resulted from Ernest's high opinion in favor of a young lady yearning for glory, as a plant strives for its share of the sunshine.

"Enough," said Modeste, concealing her agitation. "If you have not my heart, monsieur, you have my highest esteem."

This simple speech made la Brière quite dizzy. He felt himself totter, and leaned against a shrub, like a man whose senses are failing him. Modeste, who had walked away, turned her head and hastily came back.

"What is the matter?" she exclaimed, taking him by the hand to save him from falling.

Modeste felt his hand like ice, and saw a face as white as a lily; all the blood had rushed to his heart.

"Forgive me, mademoiselle,—I had fancied myself so despised——"

"Well," said she, with haughty scorn, "I did not say that I loved you."

And she again left la Brière, who, notwithstanding this hard speech, thought he was walking on the upper air. The earth felt soft beneath his feet, the trees seemed decked with flowers, the sky was rosy, and the air blue, as in the temples of Hymen at the close of a fairy drama that ends happily. In such circumstances, women are Janus-like, they see what is going on behind them without turning round; and Modeste saw in her lover's expression the unmistakable symptoms of a love such as Butscha's, which is beyond a doubt the *ne plus ultra* of a woman's desire. And the high value attached by la Brière to her esteem was to Modeste an infinitely sweet experience.

"Mademoiselle," said Canalis, leaving the Colonel, and coming to meet Modeste, "in spite of the small interest you take in my sentiments, it is a point of honor with me to wipe out a stain from which I have too long suffered. Here is what the Duchess wrote to me five days after my arrival here."

He made Modeste read the first few lines of the letter, in which the Duchess said that she had seen Mongenod, and wished that Melchior should marry Modeste; then having torn off the rest, he placed them in her hand.

"I cannot show you the remainder," said he, putting the paper in his pocket; "but I intrust these few lines to your delicacy, that you may be able to verify the handwriting. The girl who could ascribe to me such ignoble sentiments is quite capable of believing in some collusion, some stratagem. This may prove to you how much I care to convince you that the difference between us was not based on the vilest interest on my part. Ah! Modeste," he went on, with tears in his voice, "your poet—Madame de Chaulieu's poet—has not less poetry in his heart than in his mind. You will see the Duchess; suspend your judgment of me till then." And he left Modeste quite disconcerted.

"On my word! They are all angels," said she to herself. "All too fine for marriage! Only the Duke is a human being."

"Mademoiselle Modeste, this hunt makes me very uneasy," said Butscha, appearing on the scene with a parcel under his arm. "I dreamed that your horse ran away with you, so I have been to Rouen to get you a Spanish snaffle; I have been told that a horse can never get it between his teeth. I implore you to use it; I have shown it to the Colonel, who has thanked me more than the thing is worth."

"Poor dear Butscha!" cried Modeste, touched to tears by this motherly care.

Butscha went off skipping like a man who has suddenly heard of the death of an old uncle leaving a fortune.

"My dear father," said Modeste, on returning to the drawing-room, "I should like very much to have that handsome whip; supposing you were to offer to exchange with Monsieur de la Brière—that whip for your picture by Ostade?"

Modeste cast a side glance at Ernest while the Colonel made this proposal, standing in front of the picture—the only thing he possessed as a memorial of the campaigns he had fought in; he had bought it of a citizen of Ratisbon. And seeing the eagerness with which Ernest rushed from the room, "He will attend the hunt," said she to herself.

Thus, strange to say, Modeste's three lovers all went to Rosembray with hearts full of hope, and enraptured by her adorable charms.

Rosembray, an estate recently purchased by the Duc de

Verneuil with the money that fell to his share of the thousand
million francs voted to legitimize the sale of national property,
is remarkable for a château comparable for magnificence with
those of Mesnière and Balleroy. This noble and imposing
mansion is reached by an immense avenue of ancestral elms
four rows deep, and across a vast courtyard on a slope, like
that of Versailles, with a splendid iron screen and two gate
lodges, and surrounded by large orange trees in tubs. The
façade to this *cour d'honneur* displays two stories of nineteen
windows in each, between two wings at right angles—tall
windows with small panes, set in carved stone arches, and
separated by reeded pilasters. A cornice and balustrade
screen an Italian roof, whence rise stone chimneys marked
by trophies of arms, Rosembray having been built in the reign
of Louis XIV. by a farmer-general named Cottin. The front
towards the park differs from this, having a centre block of
five windows projecting from the main building, with columns
and a noble pediment. The Marigny family, to whom the
possessions of this Cottin came by marriage with his sole
heiress, had a group representing Dawn executed for this
pediment by Coysevox. Below it two genii support a scroll,
on which this motto is inscribed in honor of the King, instead
of the old family device: *Sol nobis benignus.* The great
Louis had made a Duke of the Marquis de Marigny, one of his
most insignificant favorites.

From the top of the semicircular double flight of steps
there is a view over a large lake, as long and wide as the
grand canal of Versailles, starting from the bottom of a slope
of turf worthy of the most English lawn, its banks dotted
with clumps displaying the brightest autumn flowers. Beyond,
on each side, a French formal parterre spreads its squared
beds and paths—pages written in the most majestic style of le
Nôtre. These two gardens are set in a border of wood and
shrubbery, extending the whole length to the extent of thirty
acres, and cleared in places in the English fashion under
Louis XV. The view from the terrace is shut in beyond
by a forest belonging to Rosembray, adjoining two demesnes,

one belonging to the nation, and one to the Crown. It would be hard to find a more beautiful landscape.

Modeste's arrival caused some sensation in the avenue when the carriage was seen with the royal livery of France, escorted by the Master of the Horse, the Colonel, Canalis, and la Brière, all riding, and preceded by an outsider in the Royal livery; behind them came ten servants, among them the Colonel's negro and mulatto, and his elegant britska, in which were the two ladies' maids and the luggage. The first carriage was drawn by four horses mounted by *tigers,* dressed with the spruce perfection insisted on by the Master of the Horse—often better served in such matters than the King himself.

Modeste, as she drove up and saw this minor Versailles, was dazzled by the magnificence of these great folks; she was suddenly conscious of having to meet these famous Duchesses; she dreaded seeming affected, provincial, or parvenu, lost her head completely, and repented of ever having wished for this hunting party.

When the carriage stopped, Modeste happily saw before her an old man in a fair, frizzy wig, with small curls, whose calm smooth, full face wore a paternal smile and an expression of monastic joviality, to which a half downcast look lent something like dignity. The Duchess, a woman of deep devotion, the only daughter of a very wealthy President of the Supreme Court, who had died in 1800, was the mother of four children; very thin and erect, she bore some resemblance to Madame Latournelle, if imagination could be persuaded to embellish the lawyer's wife with the graces of a noble lady-Prioress.

"Ah! how do you do, dear Hortense?" said Mademoiselle d'Hérouville, embracing the Duchess with all the sympathy that was a tie between these two proud spirits; "allow me to introduce to you and to our dear Duke, Mademoiselle de la Bastie, who is a little angel."

"We have heard so much about you, mademoiselle," said the Duchess, "that we have been most eager to have you here."

"We can but regret our lost time," added the Duc de Verneuil, bowing with gallant admiration.

"Monsieur le Comte de la Bastie," added the Master of the Horse, taking the Colonel by the arm, and leading him up to the Duke and Duchess with a tinge of respect in his tone and manner.

The Colonel bowed to the Duchess, the Duke gave him his hand.

"You are very welcome, Monsieur le Comte," said Monsieur de Verneuil. "You are the owner of many treasures," he added, glancing at Modeste.

The Duchess drew Modeste's hand through her arm and led her into a vast drawing-room, where half a score of women were sitting in groups round the fire. The men, led by the Duke, went to walk on the terrace, excepting only Canalis, who went in to pay his respects to the superb Éléonore. She, seated before a tapestry frame, was giving Mademoiselle de Verneuil some hints as to shading.

If Modeste had thrust her finger through with a needle when laying her hand on a cushion, she could not have felt a keener shock than she received from the icy glance, haughty and contemptuous, that the Duchesse de Chaulieu bestowed on her. From the first instant she saw no one but this woman, and guessed who she was. To know to what a pitch the cruelty can go of those sweet creatures who are exalted by our passion, women must be seen together. Modeste might have disarmed any one but Éléonore by her amazed and involuntary admiration; for if she had not known her rival's age, she would have taken her to be a woman of six-and-thirty; but there were greater surprises in store for her!

The poet found himself flung against the wrath of a great lady. Such anger is the most ruthless Sphinx; the face is beaming, all else is savage. Even kings do not know how to reduce the stronghold of exquisitely cold politeness which a mistress can then hide under steel armor. The lovely woman's countenance smiles, and at the same time the steel strikes home: the hand is of steel, the arm, the body, all is steel. Canalis tried to clutch this steel, but his fingers slipped over it as his words slipped from her heart. And the gracious face, the gracious phrases, the gracious manners of the Duchess, concealed from every eye the steel of her cold fury—down to twenty-five degrees below zero. The sight of Modeste's supreme beauty, heightened by her journey, the appearance of the girl, as well dressed as Diane de Maufrigneuse, had fired the powders that reflection had stored up in Éléonore's brain.

All the women had gone to the window to see the wonder of the day step out of the carriage, followed by her three lovers.

"Do not let us show that we are so curious," said Madame de Chaulieu, struck to the heart by Diane's exclamation, "She is divine! Where can such a creature have dropped from?"

And they had fled back to the drawing-room, where each one had composed her countenance, while the Duchesse de Chaulieu felt in her heart a thousand vipers all crying at once to be satisfied.

Mademoiselle d'Hérouville remarked in an undertone, and with marked meaning, to the Duchesse de Verneuil:

"Éléonore is not cordial in her reception of her great Melchior."

"The Duchesse de Maufrigneuse thinks that there is a coolness between them," replied Laure de Verneuil simply. This phrase, so often spoken in the world of fashion, is full of meaning. We feel in it the icy polar blast.

"Why?" asked Modeste of the charming girl who had left the Convent of the Sacred Heart not more than two months since.

"The great man," replied the Duchess, signing to her daughter to be silent, "left her for a fortnight without writing a word to her, after setting out for le Havre, and saying that he had gone for his health."

Modeste gave a little start which struck Laure, Hélène, and Mademoiselle d'Hérouville.

"And meanwhile," the devout Duchess went on, "she was getting him appointed Commander of the Legion of Honor and Minister to Baden."

"Oh, it is very wrong of Canalis, for he owes everything to her," said Mademoiselle d'Hérouville.

"Why did not Madame de Chaulieu come to le Havre?" asked Modeste guilelessly of Hélène.

"My child," said the Duchesse de Verneuil, "she would let herself be killed without speaking a word. Look at her. What a queen! With her head on the block she would still smile, like Mary Stuart—indeed, our handsome Éléonore has the same blood in her veins."

"And she did not write to him?" said Modeste.

"Diane told me," replied the Duchess, prompted to further confidences by an elbow nudge from Mademoiselle d'Hérouville, "that she had sent a very cutting answer to the first letter Canalis wrote to her about ten days ago."

This statement made Modeste color with shame for Canalis; she longed not to crush him under her feet, but to revenge herself by a piece of mischief more cruel than a poniard thrust. She looked proudly at Madame de Chaulieu. That glance was gilded with eight millions of francs.

"Monsieur Melchior!" said she.

All the women looked up, first at the Duchess, who was talking to Canalis over the work-frame, then at this young girl, so ill bred as to disturb two lovers who were settling their quarrel—a thing which is never done in any rank of life.

Diane de Maufrigneuse gave her head a little toss, as much as to say, "The child is in her rights."

Finally, the twelve women smiled at each other, for they were all jealous of a woman of fifty-six who was still handsome enough to dip her hand in the common treasury and steal a young woman's share. Melchior glanced at Modeste with feverish irritability, the hasty look of a master to a servant, while the Duchess bent her head with the air of a lioness interrupted at her meal; her eyes, fixed on the canvas, shot flames of fire, almost red-hot, at the poet while she sifted his very soul with her epigrams, for each sentence was a vengeance for a triple injury.

"Monsieur Melchior!" repeated Modeste, in a voice that asserted its right to be heard.

"What is it, mademoiselle?" asked the poet.

He was obliged to rise, but he stood still half-way between the work-frame, which was near the window, and the fireplace, by which Modeste was sitting on the Duchesse de Verneuil's sofa. What cruel reflections were forced on the ambitious man when he met Éléonore's steady eye. If he should obey Modeste, all was over for ever between the poet and his protectress. If he paid no heed to the girl, it would be an avowal of his serfdom, he would lose the advantages gained by five-and-twenty days of meanness, and fail in the simplest rules of gentlemanly politeness. The greater the folly, the more imperatively the Duchess insisted on it. Modeste's beauty and fortune, set in the opposite scale to Éléonore's influence and established rights, made this hesitancy between the man and his honor as terrible to watch as the peril of a matador in the ring. A man never knows such frightful palpitations as those that seemed to threaten Canalis with an aneurism, anywhere but in front of the gaming-table, where his fortune or his ruin is settled within five minutes.

"Mademoiselle d'Hérouville made me get out of the carriage in such a hurry," said Modeste to Canalis, "that I dropped my handkerchief——"

Canalis gave a highly significant shrug.

"And," she went on, in spite of this impatient gesture, "I had, tied to it, the key of a blotting case, containing an important fragment of a letter; will you be good enough, Melchior, to ask for it——"

Between an angel and a tigress, equally irate, Canalis, who had turned pale, hesitated no longer; the tigress seemed the less dangerous. He was on the point of committing himself when la Brière appeared in the doorway, seeming to Canalis something like the archangel Michael descended from heaven.

"Here, Ernest, Mademoiselle de la Bastie wants you," said the poet, hastily retreating to his chair by the work-frame.

Ernest, on his part, went at once to Modeste without bowing to any one else; he saw her alone, received her instructions with visible joy, and ran off with the unconfessed approbation of every woman present.

"What a position for a poet!" said Modeste to Hélène, pointing to the worsted work at which the Duchess was stitching furiously.

"If you speak to her, if you once look at her, all is ended," said Éléonore to Melchior in a low tone, for his *mezzo termine* had not satisfied her. "And, mind, when I am absent I shall leave other eyes to watch you."

As she spoke, Madame de Chaulieu, a woman of medium height, but rather too fat—as all women are who are still handsome when past fifty—rose, walked towards the group with which Diane de Maufrigneuse was sitting, stepping out with small feet as firm and light as a fawn's. Under her full forms the exquisite refinement was conspicuous with which women of that type are gifted, and which gives them that vigorous nervous system that controls and animates the development of the flesh. It was impossible otherwise to account for her light step, which was amazingly dignified. Only those women whose quarterings of nobility date back to Noah, like Éléonore's, know how to be majestic in spite of being as large as a farmer's wife. A philosopher might, perhaps, have pitied Philoxène, while admiring the happy arrangement of the bodice and the careful details of a morning dress worn with the elegance of a queen and the ease of a girl. Boldly wearing her own abundant and undyed hair, plaited on the top of her head in a coronet like a tower, Éléonore proudly displayed her white neck, her finely shaped bust and shoulders, her dazzling bare arms, ending in hands famous for their beauty. Modeste, like all the Duchess' rivals, saw in her one of those women of whom the others say, "She is past mistress of us all!"

In fact, every one recognized her as one of those few great

ladies who are now become so rare in France. Any attempt to describe how majestic was the carriage of her head, how refined and delicate this or that curve of her neck, what harmony there was in her movements, what dignity in her mien, what nobleness in the perfect agreement of every detail with the whole result in the little arts that are a second nature, and make a woman holy and supreme,—this would be to try to analyze the sublime. We delight in such poetry, as in that of Paganini, without seeking the means, for the cause is a soul making itself visible.

The Duchess bowed, saluting Hélène and her aunt; then she said to Diane in a clear, bright voice without a trace of emotion:

"Is it not time to dress, Duchess?"

And she swept out of the room, accompanied by her daughter-in-law and Mademoiselle d'Hérouville, each giving her an arm. She was speaking in a low voice as she went away with the old maid, who pressed her to her heart, saying, "You are quite charming!" which was as much as to say, "I am wholly yours in return for the service you have just done us."

Mademoiselle d'Hérouville returned to the drawing-room to play her part as spy, and her first glance told Canalis that the Duchess' last words were no vain threat. The apprentice to diplomacy felt he knew too little of the minor science for so severe a struggle, and his wit served him at any rate so far as to enable him to assume a straightforward, if not a dignified attitude. When Ernest returned with Modeste's handkerchief, he took him by the arm and led him out on the lawn.

"My dear fellow," said he, "I am, of all men, not the most unhappy, but the most ridiculous. So I have recourse to you to help me out of the wasps' nest I have got into.—Modeste is a demon; she saw my embarrassment, she mocks at it; she has just spoken to me of two lines of a letter of Madame de Chaulieu's that I was fool enough to trust her with. If she were to show them, I could never make it up again with Éléonore. So, pray, at once ask Modeste for that paper, and tell her from me that I have no views—no pretensions to her hand; I rely on her delicacy, on her honesty as a lady, to behave to me as though we had never met; I entreat her not to speak to me; I beseech her to vouchsafe to be implacable, though I dare not hope that her spite will move her to a sort of jealous wrath that would serve my ends to a miracle. . . Go, I will wait here."

On re-entering the room, Ernest de la Brière saw there a young officer of Havré's company of the Guards, the Vicomte de Sérizy, who had just arrived from Rosny to announce that MADAME was obliged to be present at the opening of the session. This constitutional solemnity was, as is well known, a very important function. Charles X. pronounced a speech in the presence of his whole family, the Dauphiness and MADAME being present in their seats. The choice of the envoy charged with expressing the Princess' regrets was a compliment to Diane. She was supposed to be the immediate object of this fascinating youth's adoration; he was the son of a Minister of State, gentleman-in-waiting, hopeful of high destinies, as being an only son and heir to an immense fortune. The Duchesse de Maufrigneuse, however, only accepted the Viscount's attentions in order to throw light on the age of Madame de Sérizy, who, according to the chronicle repeated behind fans, had won from her the heart of handsome Lucien de Rubempré.

"You, I hope, will do us the pleasure of remaining at Rosembray," said the severe Duchess to the young man.

While keeping her ears open to evil-speaking, the pious lady shut her eyes to the peccadilloes of her guests, who were carefully paired by the Duke; for no one knows what such excellent women will tolerate on the plea of bringing a lost sheep back to the fold by treating it with indulgence.

"We reckoned without the Constitutional Government," said the Duc d'Hérouville, "and Rosembray loses a great honor, Madame la Duchesse——"

"We shall feel all the more at our ease," observed a tall,

lean old man of about seventy-five, dressed in blue cloth, and keeping on his hunting cap by leave of the ladies.

This personage, who was very like the Duc de Bourbon, was no less a man than the Prince de Cadignan, the Master of the Hounds, and one of the last of the French *Grands Seigneurs.*

Just as la Brière was about to slip behind the sofa to beg a minute's speech with Modeste, a man of about eight-and-thirty came in, short, fat, and common-looking.

"My son, the Prince de Loudon," said the Duchesse de Verneuil to Modeste, who could not control an expression of amazement on her youthful features as she saw the man who now bore the name which the General of the Vendée Cavalry had made so famous by his daring and by his execution.

The present Duc de Verneuil was the third son taken by his father into exile, and the only survivor of four children.

"Gaspard," said the Duchess, calling her son to her. The Prince obeyed his mother, who went on as she introduced Modeste:

"Mademoiselle de la Bastie, my dear."

The heir presumptive, whose marriage to Desplein's only daughter was a settled thing, bowed to the girl without seeming struck by her beauty, as his father had been. Modeste thus had an opportunity of comparing the young men of to-day with the old men of the past; for the old Prince de Cadignan had already made her two or three very pretty speeches, proving that he was not less devoted to women than to Royalty. The Duc de Rhétoré, Madame de Chaulieu's eldest son, noted for the style which combines impertinence with easy freedom, had, like the Prince de Loudon, greeted Modeste almost cavalierly.

The reason of this contrast between the sons and the fathers may, perhaps, lie in the fact that the heirs no longer feel themselves to be objects of importance, as their ancestors were, and excuse themselves from the duties of power, since they no longer have anything but its shadow. The fathers still have the fine manners inherent in their vanished grandeur, like mountains gilded by the sunshine, when all round them is in darkness.

At last Ernest succeeded in saying two words to Modeste, who rose.

"My little beauty!" said the Duchess, as she pulled a bell, thinking that Modeste was going to change her dress, "you shall be taken to your rooms."

Ernest went with Modeste to the foot of the great staircase to make the unhappy Melchior's request, and he tried to touch her by describing the poet's miseries.

"He loves her, you see! He is a captive who thought he could break his chain."

"Love! In a man who calculates everything so closely?" retorted Modeste.

"Mademoiselle, you are at the beginning of your life; you do not know its narrow places. Every sort of inconsistency must be forgiven to a man who places himself under the dominion of a woman older than himself, for he is not responsible. Consider how many sacrifices Canalis has offered to that divinity! how he has sown too much seed to scorn the harvest; the Duchess represents to him ten years of devotion and of happiness. You had made the poet forget everything, for, unhappily, he has more vanity than pride; he knew not what he was losing till he saw Madame de Chaulieu again. If you knew Canalis, you would help him. He is a mere child, and is spoiling his life for ever.—You say he calculates everything, but he calculates very badly, like all poets indeed —creatures of impulse, full of childishness, dazzled, like children, by all that shines, and running after it! He has been fond of horses, of pictures; he has yearned for glory; he sells his pictures to get armor and furniture of the style of the Renaissance and of Louis XV.; he now has a grudge against the Government. Admit that his whims are on a grand scale?"

"That will do," said Modeste. "Come," she added, as she saw her father, and beckoned to him to ask him to accompany her, "I will give you that scrap of paper; you can take it to the great man, and assure him of my entire consent to all he wishes, but on one condition. I beg you to give him my best thanks for the pleasure I have enjoyed in seeing him perform for my sole benefit one of the finest pieces of the German theatre. I know now that Goethe's *chef-d'œuvre* is neither *Faust* nor *Egmont"*—and, as Ernest looked at the sprightly girl with a puzzled expression—"it is *Torquato Tasso*," she added. "Desire Monsieur Canalis to read it once more," she went on, smiling. "I particularly desire that you will repeat this to your friend word for word, for it is not an epigram; it is the justification of his conduct—with this difference, that I hope he will become quite sane, thanks to his Éléonore's folly."

The Duchess' head waiting-maid led Modeste and her father to their rooms, where Françoise Cochet had already arranged everything. Their choice elegance surprised the Colonel, and Françoise told him that there were thirty guest-chambers in the same style in the Château.

"That is my idea of a country-house," said Modeste.

"The Comte de la Bastie will have such another built for you," replied the Colonel.

"Here, monsieur," said Modeste, handing the scrap of paper to Ernest, "go and reassure our friend."

The words "our friend" struck the young man. He looked at Modeste to see if there were seriously some community of sentiment such as she seemed to acknowledge; and the girl, understanding the implied question, added:

"Well, go; your friend is waiting."

La Brière colored violently, and went, in a state of doubt, anxiety, and disturbance more terrible than despair. The approach to happiness is to true lovers very like what the poetry of Catholicism has called the Straits of Paradise, to express a dark, difficult, and narrow way, echoing with the last cries of supreme anguish.

An hour later the distinguished party had all met again in the drawing-room, some playing at whist, others chatting, the women busy with fancy-work, while awaiting the dinner-hour. The Master of the Hounds led Monsieur Mignon to talk of China, of his campaigns, of the great Provençal families of Portenduère, l'Estorade, and Maucombe; and he remonstrated with him on not asking for employment, assuring him that nothing would be easier than to obtain a post in the Guards with his full rank as Colonel.

"A man of your birth and fortune can never class himself with the present Opposition," said the Prince with a smile.

This aristocratic society pleased Modeste; and not only that, during her visit she gained a perfection of manner which, but for this revelation, she would never in her life have acquired. If you show a clock to a natural mechanic, it is always enough to reveal to him what mechanism means; the germs within him are at once developed. In the same way, Modeste intuitively assimilated everything that gave distinction to the Duchesses de Maufrigneuse and de Chaulieu. To her each detail was a lesson, where a commonplace woman would have fallen into absurdity by imitating mere manners. A girl of good birth, well informed, with the instincts of Modeste, fell naturally into the right key, and discerned the differences which divide the aristocratic from the middle class, and provincial life from that of the Faubourg Saint-Germain; she caught the almost imperceptible shades; in short, she recognized the grace of a really fine lady, and did not despair of acquiring it.

In the midst of this Olympus she saw that her father and la Brière were infinitely superior to Canalis. The great poet, abdicating his real and indisputable power, that of the intellect, was nothing but a Master of Appeals, eager to become a Minister, anxious for the collar of the Legion of Honor, and obliged to subserve every constellation. Ernest de la Brière, devoid of ambition, was simply himself; while Melchior, eating humble pie, to use a vulgar phrase, paid court to the Prince de Loudon, the Duc de Rhétoré, the Vicomte de Sérizy, the Duc de Maufrigneuse, as though he had no liberty of speech like Colonel Mignon, Comte de la Bastie, proud of his services and of the Emperor Napoleon's esteem. Modeste saw the continued pre-occupation of a wit seeking a point to raise a laugh, a brilliant remark to surprise, or a compliment to flatter the high and mighty personages, on whose level he aimed at keeping himself. In short, here the peacock shed his plumes.

In the course of the evening Modeste went to sit with the Master of the Horse in a recess of the drawing-room; she took him there to put an end to a struggle she could no longer encourage without lowering herself in her own eyes.

"Monsieur le Duc," she began, "if you knew me well, you would know how deeply I am touched by your attentions. It is precisely the high esteem I have for your character, the friendship inspired by such a nature as yours, which makes me anxious not to inflict the smallest wound on your self-respect. Before you came to le Havre I loved sincerely, deeply, and for ever a man who is worthy to be loved, and from whom my affection is still a secret; but I may tell you, and in this I am more sincere than most girls, that if I had not been bound by this voluntary engagement, you would have been my choice, so many and so great are the good qualities I have found in you. A few words dropped by your sister and aunt compel me to say this. If you think it necessary, by to-morrow, before the hunt, my mother shall recall me home under the excuse of serious indisposition. I will not be present without your consent at an entertainment arranged by your kind care, where, if my secret should escape me, I might aggrieve you by an insult to your legitimate pretensions.

"'Why did I come?' you may ask. I might have declined. Be so generous as not to make a crime of an inevitable curiosity. This is not the most delicate part of what I have to communicate. You have firmer friends than you know of in my father and me; and as my fortune was the prime motor in your mind when you came to seek me, without wishing to treat it as a solace to the grief your gallantry requires of you, I may tell you that my father is giving his mind to the matter of the Hérouville lands. His friend

Dumay thinks the scheme feasible, and has been feeling his way to the formation of a company. Gobenheim, Dumay, and my father are each ready with fifteen hundred thousand francs, and undertake to collect the remainder by the confidence they will inspire in the minds of capitalists by taking substantial interest in the business.

"Though I may not have the honor of being the Duchesse d'Hérouville, I am almost certain of putting you in the position to choose her one day with perfect freedom in the exalted sphere to which she belongs.—Oh, let me finish," said she, at a gesture of the Duke's.

"It is easy to see from my brother's agitation," said Mademoiselle d'Hérouville to her niece, "that you have gained a sister."

"Monsieur le Duc, I decided on this on the day of our first ride together, when I heard you lamenting your position. This is what I wanted to tell you; on that day my fate was sealed. If you have not won a wife, you have, at any rate, found friends at Ingouville, if, indeed, you will accept us as friends."

This little speech which Modeste had prepared was uttered with such soul-felt charm that tears rose to the Duke's eyes. He seized Modeste's hand and kissed it.

"Remain here for the hunt," said he. "My small merit has accustomed me to such refusals. But while I accept your friendship and the Colonel's, allow me to assure myself, by inquiring of the most competent experts, that the reclaiming of the marsh lands of Hérouville will involve the Company of which you speak in no risks, but may bring in some profits, before I accept the liberality of your friends.

"You are a noble girl, and though it breaks my heart to be no more than your friend, I shall glory in the title, and prove it to you whenever and wherever I find occasion."

"At any rate, Monsieur le Duc, let us keep the secret to ourselves. My choice will not be announced, unless I am greatly mistaken, till my mother is completely cured; for it is my desire that my plighted husband and I should be blessed with her first glances."

"Ladies," said the Prince de Cadignan at the moment when all were going to bed, "I remember that several of you proposed to follow the hunt with us to-morrow; now I think it my duty to inform you, that if you are bent on being Dianas, you must rise with the dawn. The meet is fixed for half-past eight. I have often in the course of my life seen women display greater courage than men, but only for a few minutes, and you will all need a certain modicum of determination to remain on horseback for a whole day excepting during the halt called for luncheon—a mere snack, as beseems sportsmen and sportswomen.—Are you still all resolved to prove yourselves gallant horsewomen?"

"I, Prince, cannot help myself," said Modeste slily.

"I can answer for myself," said the Duchesse de Chaulieu.

"I know my daughter Diane; she is worthy of her name," replied the Prince. "Well, then, you are all primed for the sport. However, for the sake of Madame and Mademoiselle de Verneuil, who remain at home, I shall do my best to turn the stag to the further end of the pool."

"Do not be uneasy, ladies, the hunters' snack will be served under a splendid marquee," said the Prince de Loudon when the Master of the Hounds had left the room.

Next morning at daybreak everything promised fine weather. The sky, lightly veiled with gray mist, showed through it here and there in patches of pure blue, and it would be entirely cleared before noon by a northwest breeze, which was already sweeping up some little fleecy clouds. As they left the Château, the Master of the Hounds, the Prince de Loudon, and the Duc de Rhétoré, who, having no ladies under their care, started first for the meet, saw the chimneys of the house piercing through the veil-mist in white masses against the russet foliage, which the trees in Normandy never lose till quite the end of a fine autumn.

"The ladies are in luck," said the Prince to the Duc de Rhétoré.

"Oh, in spite of their bravado last night, I fancy they will leave us to hunt without them," replied the Duc de Verneuil.

"Yes, if they had not each a gentleman-in-waiting," retorted the Duke.

At this moment these determined sportsmen—for the Prince de Loudon and the Duc de Rhétoré are of the race of Nimrod, and supposed to be the finest shots of the Faubourg Saint-Germain—heard the noise of an altercation, and rode forward at a gallop to the clearing appointed for the meet, at one of the openings into the Forest of Rosembray, and remarkable for a mossy knoll. This was the subject of the quarrel. The Prince de Loudon, bitten by Anglomania, had placed at the Duke de Verneuil's orders the whole of his stable and kennel, in the English style throughout. On one side of the clearing stood a young Englishman, short, fair, insolent-looking, and cool, speaking French after a fashion, and dressed with the neatness that characterizes Englishmen even of the lowest class. John Barry had a tunic-coat of scarlet cloth belted round the waist, silver buttons with the arms of Verneuil, white doeskin breeches, topboots, a striped waistcoat, and a black velvet collar and cap. In his right hand he held a hunting-crop, and in his left, hanging by a silk cord, was a brass horn. This chief huntsman had with him two large thoroughbred hounds, pure fox-hounds with white coats spotted with tan, high on their legs, with keen noses, small heads, and short ears, high up. This man, one of the most famous huntsmen of the county whence the Prince had sent for him at great expense, ruled over fifteen hunters and sixty English-bred dogs, which cost the Duc de Verneuil enormous sums; though he cared little for sport, he indulged his son in this truly royal taste. The subordinates, men and horses, stood some little way off, and kept perfect silence.

Now on arriving on the ground, John found there three huntsmen with three packs of the King's hounds that had arrived before him in carts; the Prince de Cadignan's three best men, whose figures, both in character and costume, were a perfect contrast with the representative of insolent Albion. These, the Prince's favorites, all wearing three-cornered cocked hats, very low and flat, beneath which grinned tanned, wrinkled, weather-beaten faces, lighted up as it were by their twinkling eyes, were curiously dry, lean, and sinewy men, burnt up with the passion for sport. Each was provided with a large bugle hung about with green worsted cords that left nothing visible but the bell of the trumpet; they kept their dogs in order by the eye and voice. The noble brutes, all splashed with liver-color and black, each with his individual expression, as distinct as Napoleon's soldiers, formed a *posse* of subjects more faithful than those whom the King was at that moment addressing—their eyes lighting up at the slightest sound with a spark that glittered like a diamond—this one from Poitou, short in the loins, broad-shouldered, low on the ground, long-eared, that one an English dog, white, slim in the belly, with short ears, and made for coursing: all the young hounds eager to give tongue, while their elders, seamed with scars, lay quiet, at full length, their heads resting on their fore-paws, and listening on the ground like wild men of the woods.

On seeing the English contingent, the dogs and the King's men looked at each other, asking without saying a word:

"Are we not to hunt by ourselves? Is not this a slur on His Majesty's Royal Hunt?"

After beginning with some banter, the squabble had grown warm between Monsieur Jacquin la Roulie, the old Chief Huntsman of the French force, and John Barry, the young Briton.

While still at some distance the princes guessed what had given rise to the quarrel, and the Master of the Hounds, putting spurs to his horse, ended the matter by asking in a commanding tone:

"Who beat the wood?"

"I, monseigneur," said the Englishman.

"Very good," said the Prince de Cadignan, listening to John Barry's report.

Men and dogs, all alike, were respectful in the presence of the Master of the Hounds, as though all alike recognized his supreme authority. The Prince planned the order of the day; for a hunt is like a battle, and Charles X.'s Master of the Hounds was a Napoleon of the forest. Thanks to the admirable discipline carried out by his orders in stable and kennel, he could give his whole mind to strategy and the science of the chase. He assigned a place in the proceedings of the day to the Prince de Loudon's hounds and men, reserving them, like a cavalry corps, to turn the stag back on the pool, in the event of the King's packs succeeding, as he hoped, in forcing the game into the Royal demesne lying in the distance in front of the Château. He gratified the self-respect of his own old retainers by giving them the hardest work, and that of the Englishman, whom he employed in his own special line, by giving him an opportunity of displaying the strength of limb of his dogs and horses. Thus the two methods would work against each other, and do wonders to excite reciprocal emulation.

"Are we to wait any longer, monseigneur?" asked la Roulie respectfully.

"I understand you, old friend," replied the Prince. "It is late, but——"

"Here come the ladies, for Jupiter scents the fetish odors," said the second huntsman, observing the nose of his favorite hound.

"Fetish?" repeated the Prince de Loudon with a smile.

"He probably means fetid," said the Duc de Rhétoré.

"That is it, no doubt, for everything that does not smell of the kennel is poisonous, according to Monsieur Laravine," replied the Prince.

In point of fact, the three gentlemen could see in the distance a party of sixteen riders, and fluttering at their head the green veils of four ladies. Modeste with her father, the Duc d'Hérouville, and little la Brière, was in front, with the Duchesse de Maufrigneuse attended by the Vicomte de Sérizy. Then came the Duchesse de Chaulieu with Canalis at her side, she smiling at him with no sign of rancor. On reaching the clearing, where the huntsmen, dressed in red, holding their hunting horns, and surrounded by dogs and beaters, formed a group worthy of the brush of Van der Meulen, the Duchesse de Chaulieu, an admirable figure on horseback, though somewhat too stout, drew up close to Modeste, feeling it beneath her dignity to sulk with the young person to whom, the day before, she had not spoken a word.

Just at the moment when the Master of the Hounds had ended his compliments on such fabulous punctuality, Éléonore condescended to remark the splendid whip handle that sparkled in Modeste's little hand, and graciously begged to examine it.

"It is the finest thing in its way that I have ever seen," said she, showing the gem to Diane de Maufrigneuse; "but, indeed, it is in harmony with the owner's whole person," she added, as she returned it to Modeste.

"You will confess, madame" replied Mademoiselle de la Bastie, with a mischievous but tender glance at la Brière, in which he could read an avowal, "that it is a very strange gift as coming from a future husband——"

"Indeed," exclaimed Madame de Maufrigneuse, "I should regard it as a recognition of my rights, remembering Louis XIV."

There were tears in la Brière's eyes; he dropped his bridle, and was ready to fall; but another look from Modeste recalled him to himself, by warning him not to betray his happiness.

The cavalcade set out.

The Duc d'Hérouville said in a low voice to la Brière: "I hope, monsieur, that you will make your wife happy, and if I can in any way serve you, command me; for I should be delighted to contribute to the happiness of two such charming people."

This great day, when such important interests of hearts and fortunes were definitely settled, to the Master of the Hounds offered no other problem but that as to whether the stag would cross the pool, and be killed on the grass slope within sight of the Château; for huntsmen of such experience are like chess players, who can foresee a checkmate many moves ahead. The fortunate old gentleman succeeded to the height of his wishes; the run was splendid, and the ladies relieved him of their presence on the next day but one, which proved to be rainy.

The Duc de Verneuil's guests remained three days at Rosembray. On the last morning the *Gazette de France* contained the announcement that M. le Baron de Canalis was appointed to the rank of Commander of the Legion of Honor and the post of Minister at Carlsruhe.

When, early in the month of December, the Comtesse de la Bastie was operated on by Desplein, and could at last see Ernest de la Brière, she pressed Modeste's hand, and said in her ear:

"I should have chosen him."

Towards the end of February all the documents relating to the acquisition of the estates were signed by the worthy and excellent Latournelle, Monsieur Mignon's attorney in Provence. At this time the family of la Bastie obtained from His Majesty the distinguished honor of his signature to the marriage contract, and the transmission of the title and the arms of la Bastie to Ernest de la Brière, who was authorized to call himself the Vicomte de la Bastie-la Brière. The estate of la Bastie, reconstituted to yield more than a hundred thousand francs a year, was entailed by letters patent registered by the Court in the month of April.

La Brière's witnesses were Canalis and the Minister whose private secretary he had been for five years. Those who signed for the bride were the Duc d'Hérouville and Desplein, for whom the Mignons cherished enduring gratitude, after giving him magnificent proofs of it.

By and by, perhaps, in this long record of our manners, we may meet again with Monsieur and Madame de la Brière-la Bastie, and connoisseurs will then perceive how easy and sweet a tie is marriage when the wife is well informed and clever; for Modeste, who kept her promise of avoiding all the absurdities of pedantry, is still the pride and delight of her husband, of her family, and of her circle of friends.

PARIS, *March-July* 1844.

THE HATED SON

COPYRIGHT, 1898,
BY J. M. DENT & COMPANY

THE HATED SON

To the Baroness James de Rothschild.

I.

HOW THE MOTHER LIVED

ONE winter's night, at about two in the morning, the Comtesse Jeanne d'Hérouville was in such pain that, notwithstanding her inexperience, she understood that these were the pangs of childbirth; and the instinct which leads us to hope for relief from a change of position, prompted her to sit up in bed, either to consider the character of a new form of suffering, or to reflect on her situation.

She was in mortal terror, less of the risk attending the birth of her first child,—a terror to most women,—than of the perils that awaited the babe. To avoid waking her husband, who lay by her side, the poor creature took precautions which her excess of fear made as elaborate as those of an escaping prisoner. Though the pain became more intolerable every minute, she almost ceased to feel it, so intensely did she concentrate her whole strength in the effort to prop herself by resting her clammy hands on the pillow, to relieve her tortured frame from a position which left her powerless.

At the slightest rustle of the immense green silk counterpane under which she had known but little sleep since her marriage, she paused as though she had rung a bell. Compelled to watch the Count, she divided her attention between the creaking folds of the stuff, and a broad weather-browned face whose moustache was close to her shoulder. If a louder breath than usual came through her husband's lips, it filled her with sudden fears that increased the crimson flush brought to her cheeks by her twofold suffering. A criminal who under cover of the night has reached the door of his prison and tries to turn the key he has found in some unyielding lock, without making a sound, is not more timid or more daring.

When the Countess found herself sitting up without having roused her keeper, she gave a little joyful jump that revealed the pathetic guilelessness of her nature; but the smile died half-formed on her burning lips, a reflection clouded the innocent brow, and her long blue eyes resumed their sad expression. She sighed deeply, and with the utmost caution replaced her hands on the conjugal bolster. Then, as though it were the first time in her married life that she was free to act or think, she looked at everything about her, stretching her neck with eager movements, like those of a bird in a cage. To see her, it was easy to discern how full of joy and frolic she once had been, and that fate had cut off her early hopes and transformed her ingenuous liveliness into melancholy.

The room was such as those which, even in our day, some octogenarian housekeepers exhibit to travelers who visit old baronial homes, with the statement, "This is the state bedroom where Louis XIII. once slept." Fine tapestry of a generally brown tone was framed in deep borders of walnut wood, elegantly carved but blackened by time. The beams formed a coffered ceiling ornamented with arabesques of the previous century, and still showing the mottled grain of chestnut. These decorations, gloomy in their coloring, reflected so little light that it was difficult to make out the designs, even when the sun shone straight into the room, which was lofty, broad, and long. And a silver lamp standing on the shelf over the enormous fireplace gave so feeble a light that the quavering gleam might be compared to the misty stars that twinkle for a moment through the gray haze of an autumn night.

The little monsters crouching in the marble carvings of this fireplace, which was opposite the Countess' bed, made such grotesquely hideous faces that she dared not gaze at them. She was afraid of seeing them move, or of hearing a cackle of laughter from their gaping and distorted mouths.

At this moment a terrific storm was growling in the chimney, which echoed every gust, lending it doleful significance; and the vast opening communicated so freely with the sky that the brands on the hearth seemed to breathe, glowing and becoming dark by turns as the wind rose and fell. The escutcheon, with the arms of the Hérouvilles carved in white marble, with all its mantling and the figures of its supporters, gave a monumental effect to the erection which faced the bed, itself a monument to the honor and glory of Hymen.

A modern architect would have been greatly puzzled to decide whether the room had been made for the bed, or the bed for the room. Two Cupids sporting on a walnut-wood tester garlanded with flowers might have passed muster as angels; and the columns of the same wood which supported the canopy were carved with mythological allegories, of which the interpretation might be found either in the Bible or in Ovid's *Metamorphoses*. Remove the bed, and this baldachin would have been equally appropriate in a church over the pulpit or the officials' seats. The couple mounted to this sumptuous couch by three steps. It had a platform all round it, and was hung with two curtains of green watered silk, embroidered in a large and gaudy design of branches, the kind of pattern known as *ramages,* perhaps because the birds introduced were supposed to sing. The folds of these ample curtains were so rigid that at night the silken tissue might have been taken for metal. On the green velvet hanging with gold fringes, at the head of this lordly couch, the superstition of the House of Hérouville had attached a large crucifix, over which the chaplain fixed a branch of box that had been blessed, when, on Palm Sunday, he renewed the holy water in the vessel at the foot of the Cross.

On one side of the fireplace stood a wardrobe of richly carved and costly wood, such as brides still had given them in the country on their wedding day. These old pieces of furniture, now so sought after by collectors, were the treasure-store whence ladies brought out their rich and elegant splendor. They contained lace, bodices, high ruffs, costly gowns, and the satchels, masks, gloves, and veils which were dear to the coquettes of the sixteenth century. On the other side, for symmetry, was a similar piece of furniture, in which the Countess kept her books, papers, and jewels. Antique chairs covered with damask, a large greenish mirror of Venetian manufacture and handsomely framed over a movable toilet table, completed the fittings of the room. The floor was covered by a Persian rug, and its price did honor to the Count's gallantry. On the uppermost broad step of the bed stood a small table, on which the waiting-woman placed every evening a cup of silver or of gold containing a draught prepared with spices.

When we have gone on a few steps in life we know the secret influence exerted over the moods of the mind by place and surroundings. Who is there that has not known bad moments when the things about him have seemed to give some mysterious promise of hope? Happy or miserable, man lends an expression to the most trifling objects that he lives with; he listens to them and consults them, so superstitious is he by nature.

The Countess at this moment let her eyes wander over all the furniture as if each thing had life. She seemed to be appealing to them for help or protection; but their gloomy magnificence struck her as inexorable.

Suddenly the storm increased in violence. The young wife dared hope for no favor as she listened to the threatening heavens, for such changes of weather were, in those credulous times, interpreted in accordance with the mood or the habits of individual minds. She hastily looked round at the two Gothic windows at the end of the room; but the small size of the panes and the close network of lead did not allow her to see the sky and make sure whether the end of the world was at hand, as certain monks declared, greedy of donations. And, indeed, she might well believe in their predictions, for the sound of the angry sea whose waves beat on the castle walls mingled with the war of the tempest, and the rocks seemed to quake.

Though the fits of pain were now more frequent and more severe, the Countess dared not rouse her husband; but she studied his features as if despair had warned her to seek in them some comfort against so many sinister prognostics.

Ominous as everything seemed around the young wife, that face, in spite of the tranquil influence of sleep, looked more ominous still. The glimmer of the lamp, flickering in the gusts, died away at the foot of the bed and only occasionally lighted up the Count's face, so that the dancing gleam gave the sleeping face the agitation of stormy thoughts. The Countess was hardly reassured when she had traced the cause of this effect. Each time that a blast of the gale flung the light across the large face, accentuating the shadows of the many rugosities that characterized it, she fancied that her husband would stare up at her with eyes of unendurable sternness. The Count's brow, as implacable as the war then going on between the Church and the Calvinists, was ominous even in sleep; many wrinkles, graven there by the agitations of a soldier's life, had given it a certain resemblance to the time-eaten heads that we see on monuments of that date; and hair, like the white mossy beards on old oaks, prematurely gray, framed the face ungraciously, while religious intolerance stamped it with brutal passion.

The shape of the aquiline nose, resembling the beak of a bird of prey, the dark puckered ring round a tawny eye, the prominent bones of hollow cheeks, the deep, unbending lines of the face, and the contemptuous pout of the underlip, all revealed ambition and despotism and force, all the more to be dreaded because a narrow skull betrayed a total lack of wit, and courage devoid of generosity. This face was horribly disfigured, too, by a long scar across the right cheek, looking almost like a second mouth. The Count, at the age of two and twenty, eager to distinguish himself in the unhappy religious struggle for which the massacre of Saint Bartholomew's gave the signal, had been terribly wounded at the siege of La Rochelle. The disfigurement of this wound increased his hatred for the heretical party, and by a very natural instinct he included in his antipathy every man with a handsome face. Even before this disaster he had been so ill-favored that no lady would accept his homage. The only passion of his youth had been for a famous beauty known as the Fair Roman. The susceptibility that came of this fresh disfigurement made him diffident to the point of believing it impossible that he could ever inspire a genuine passion, and his temper became so savage that if he ever had a successful love adventure he must have owed it to the terror inspired by his cruelty.

This terrible Catholic's left hand, which lay outside the bed, spread out so as to guard the Countess as a miser guards his treasure, completed the picture of the man; that enormous hand was covered with hair so long, it showed such a network of veins and such strongly marked muscles, that it looked like a branch of beech in the clasp of clinging, yellow ivy shoots. A child studying the Count's face would have recognized in him one of the ogres of which dreadful tales are told by old nurses.

Only to note the length and breadth of the place filled by the Count was enough to show how huge a man he was. His bushy, grizzled eyebrows shaded his eyelids in such a way as to add to the light in his eyes, which sparkled with the ferocious glare of a wolf's at bay in the thicket. Below his leonine nose, a large unkempt moustache—for he scorned the cares of the toilet—hid his upper lip. Happily for the Countess, her husband's large mouth was at this moment speechless; for the softest accents of that hoarse voice made her shudder. Though the Comte d'Herouville was hardly fifty years old, at first sight he might have passed for sixty, so strangely had the fatigues of war marred his face, though they had not injured his strong constitution; but he cared little enough to be taken for a popinjay.

The Countess, who was nearly eighteen, was indeed a contrast to his huge figure, pitiable to behold. She was fair and slender; her chestnut hair, with gleams of gold in it, fell on her neck like a russet cloud, and formed the setting for a delicate face such as Carlo Dolce loved for his ivory-pale Madonnas, who look as if they were sinking under the burden of physical suffering, you might have deemed her an angel sent to mitigate the violent will of the Comte d'Hérouville.

"No, he will not kill us," said she to herself, after gazing for some time at her husband. "Is he not frank, noble, brave, and true to his word? True to his word!" As she thought over this a second time she shuddered violently and seemed stupefied.

To understand the horror of the Countess' immediate position, it is necessary to explain that this nocturnal scene took place in 1591; a period when civil war was raging in France, and the laws were ineffective. The excesses of the Ligue, averse to Henri IV.'s succession to the throne, surpassed all the calamities of the wars of religion. License had indeed reached such a pitch that no one was surprised to see a powerful lord effecting the murder of his enemy, even in broad daylight. When a military manœuvre, undertaken for private ends, was conducted in the name of the King or of the Ligue, it was always cried up by one side or the other. It was thus, indeed, that Balagny, a common soldier, was within an ace of being a sovereign prince at the very gates of France.

As to murders committed in the family circle, if I may

use such a phrase, "no more were they heeded," says a contemporary writer, "than the cutting of a sheaf of straw," unless they were marked by aggravated cruelty. Some time before the King's death, a lady of the Court assassinated a gentleman who had spoken of her in unseemly terms. One of Henri III.'s favorites had said to him:

"And by the Lord, sir, she stabbed him handsomely."

The Comte d'Hérouville, one of the most rabid royalists in Normandy, maintained obedience to the rule of Henri IV. by the severity of his executions in all that part of the province that lay adjacent to Brittany. As head of one of the richest houses in France, he had added considerably to his income from broad lands by marrying, seven months before the night on which this tale opens, Jeanne de Saint-Savin, a young lady who, by a sort of luck that was common enough those days, when men died off like flies, had unexpectedly combined in her own person the wealth of both branches of the Saint-Savin family. Necessity and terror were the only witnesses to this union.

At a banquet given two months later, by the town of Bayeaux to the Comte and Comtesse d'Hérouville in honor of their marriage, a discussion arose, which in those ignorant times was thought preposterous enough; it related to the legitimacy of children born ten months after a woman's widowhood or seven months after the wedding.

"Madame," said the Count, turning brutally on his wife, "as to your giving me a child ten months after my death, I cannot help myself. But I advise you not to begin with a seven-months' babe!"

"Why, what would you do, you old bear?" asked the young Marquis de Verneuil, fancying that the Count was in jest.

"I would wring both their necks at once, mother and child."

So peremptory a reply closed the discussion imprudently opened by a gentleman of Lower Normandy. The guests sat silent, gazing at the pretty young Countess with a sort of terror. They were all fully persuaded that in such an event this ferocious noble would carry out his threat.

The Count's speech had sunk into the soul of the unhappy young wife, and at that instant one of those flashes of foresight that sear the victim like a lightning gleam in the future, warned her that her child would be born at seven months. An inward flame glowed through her from head to foot, concentrating all vitality about her heart so intensely, that she felt as if her body were in a bath of ice. And since then not a day had passed without this chill of secret terror coming to check the most innocent impulses of her soul. The memory of the Count's look and tone of voice as he spoke that sentence of death, could still freeze the Countess' blood and quell her pain while, leaning over that sleeping face, she tried to read in it some signs of the pity she vainly sought when it was waking.

The child, doomed to die before it was born, was struggling now, with increased energy, to come to the light of day, and she moaned, in a voice like a sigh:

"Poor little one——"

But she got no further; there are ideas which no mother can endure. Incapable of reason at such a moment, the Countess felt herself suffocating under an unknown anguish. Two tears overflowed and trickled down her cheeks, leaving two glistening streaks, and hanging from the lower part of her white face like dewdrops from a lily. Who would dare to assert that the infant lives in a neutral sphere which the mother's emotions cannot reach, during those times when the soul enwraps the body and communicates its impressions, when thought stirs the blood, infusing healing balm or liquid poison. Did not the terror that rocked the tree injure the fruit? Were not the words, "Poor little one!" a doom inspired by a vision of the future? The mother shuddered with vehement dread, and her foresight was piercing.

The Count's stinging retort was a link mysteriously binding his wife's past life to this premature childbirth. Those odious suspicions, so publicly proclaimed, had cast on the Countess' memories a light of terror which was reflected on the future. Ever since that disastrous banquet, she had been perpetually striving to chase away a thousand scattered images which she feared as much as any other woman would have delighted in recalling them, and which haunted her in spite of her efforts. She would not allow herself to look back on the happy days when her heart had been free to love. Like some native melody which brings tears to the exile, these reminiscences brought her such delightful feelings that her youthful conscience regarded them as so many crimes, and used them to make the Count's threat seem all the more dreadful; this was the secret horror that tortured the Countess.

Sleeping faces have a certain mildness that is due to the perfect repose of body and brain; but though this truce made little alteration in the hard expression of the Count's features, illusion displays such an attractive mirage to the unhappy, that the girl wife at last took some hope from this apparent peace. The storm, now spending itself in torrents of rain, was audible only as a melancholy moan; fear and pain both gave her a brief respite. As she gazed on the man to whom fate had linked her, the Countess allowed herself to indulge in a day-dream of such intoxicating sweetness that she had not the strength of mind to break the spell.

In a moment, by one of those visions which seem to have some touch of divine power, she saw in a flash the picture of happiness now lost beyond recall.

First, as in a distant dawn of day, Jeanne saw the unpretending home where she had spent her careless childhood,— the green grass-plot, the purling stream, and the little room, the scene of her baby-games. She saw herself plucking flowers, to plant them again, wondering why they always faded without growing, in spite of constant watering. Presently, but at first in dim confusion, the huge town appeared, and the great house blackened by time, whither her mother had taken her at the age of seven. Her mocking memory showed her the elderly faces of the masters who had teased her; and, amid a flood of Italian and Spanish words, repeating songs in her brain to the music of a pretty rebec, she saw her father's figure. She went out to meet the President on his return from the court of justice, she saw him dismount from his mule, by the step, took his hand to mount the stairs, while her prattle chased the anxieties he could not always put off with his black or red gown, trimmed with the black and white fur which in sheer mischief she had clipped with her scissors.

She merely glanced at her aunt's confessor, the Prior of the Convent of Poor Clares, a stern and fanatical priest who was to initiate her into the mysteries of religion. Hardened by the intolerance induced by heresy, this old man was perpetually rattling the chains of Hell; he would talk of nothing but the vengeance of Heaven, and terrified her by impressing on her that she was perpetually in the sight of God. Thus intimidated she dared not lift her eyes, and thenceforth felt nothing but respect for her mother whom she had till then made the partner of all her fun. Religious awe took possession of her youthful soul whenever she saw that well-beloved mother's blue eyes turned on her with an angry look.

Then suddenly she was in her later childhood, while as yet she understood nothing of life. She half laughed at herself as she looked back on the days when her whole joy was to sit at work with her mother in the small tapestried room, to pray in a vast church, to sing a ballad accompanying herself on the rebec, to read a tale of knight-errantry in secret, to pull a flower to pieces out of curiosity, to find out what present her father had in store for the high festival of St. John,—her patron saint,—and to guess at the meaning of speeches left unfinished in her presence. And then with a thought she wiped out these childish joys as we efface a word written in pencil in an album, dismissing the scenes her imagination had seized upon from among those the first sixteen years of her life could offer, to beguile a moment when she was free from pain.

The charm of that limpid ocean was then eclipsed by the glories of a more recent though less tranquil memory. The glad peace of her childhood was far less sweet than any one of the agitations that had come into the last two years of her life,—years rich in delights forever buried in her heart. The Countess suddenly found herself in the middle of an enchanting morning when, quite at the end of the large carved oak room that was used as a dining-room, she saw her handsome cousin for the first time. Her mother's family, alarmed by the riots in Paris, had sent this young courtier to Rouen, hoping that he would learn his duties as a magistrate under the eye of his grand-uncle whose post he might one day hope to fill. The Countess involuntarily smiled as she recalled the swiftness with which she made her escape as she caught sight of this unknown relative. In spite of her quickness in opening and shutting the door, that one glance had left so strong an impression on her mind of the whole scene, that at this moment she seemed to see him exactly as he had looked when he turned round. She had then merely stolen an admiring peep at the taste and magnificence of his Paris-made dress; but now, bolder in her reminiscences, her eye more deliberately studied his cloak of violet velvet embroidered with gold and lined with satin, the spurs that ornamented his boots, the pretty lozenge-shaped slashings of his doublet and trunk hose, and the falling ruff of handsome lace that showed a neck as white as itself. She stroked a face adorned with a small moustache parted and curled up at each end, and with a *royale* of beard like one of the ermine tails in her father's robe.

In the silence and the darkness, her eyes fixed on the silk curtains which she had ceased to see, forgetful of the storm and of her husband, the Countess dared to remember how, after many days which seemed like years so full were they, the garden shut in by old dark walls, and her father's gloomy house seemed to her luminous and golden. She loved and was loved! How, in fear of her mother's stern eye, she had stolen one morning into her father's study to tell her maiden secret, after perching herself on his knees and playing such pretty tricks as had brought a smile to those eloquent lips,—

a smile for which she waited before she said: "And will you be very angry with me if I tell you something?" He had asked her many questions, and she for the first time told her love; and she could hear him now saying: "Well, my child, we will see. If he works hard, if he means to take my place, if you still like him, I will enter into the plot." She had listened no more; she had hugged her father and upset everything, as she flew off to the great lime-tree where every morning, before her formidable mother was up, she kept tryst with the fascinating Georges de Chaverny. The young courtier promised to devour Law and Custom, and he abandoned the splendid adornments of the nobility of the sword to assume the severe dress of a magistrate.

"I like you so much better in black!" she had told him.

It was not true, but the fib had mitigated the lover's vexation at having to throw away his weapons.

The memory of her wiles to cheat her mother, who had seemed sternly severe, revived the joys of her innocent love, authorized and reciprocated: some meeting under the limes where they could move freely and alone; some furtive embraces, stolen kisses,—all the artless first-fruits of a passion never overstepping the limits of modesty. Living through those rapturous days once more, as in a dream she dared to kiss, in empty space, the young face with glowing eyes, the rosy lips that had spoken so perfectly of love.

She had loved Chaverny, poor in riches; but what treasures had she not discovered in a soul as gentle as it was strong?

Then, suddenly, her father had died; Chaverny was not appointed to his place; civil war broke out in flames. By her cousin's help she and her mother had found a secret asylum in a small town of Lower Normandy.

And presently the successive deaths of various relations had left her one of the richest heiresses in France. But with comparative poverty all joy had fled. The ferocious and terrible face of the Comte d'Hérouville, a suitor for her hand, rose up like a thunder-cloud spreading a pall over the gladness of the earth, till now bathed in golden sunshine.

The hapless Countess tried to shake off her memories of the scenes of tears and despair brought about by her persistent refusal. Vaguely she saw the burning of the little town, Chaverny as a Huguenot cast into prison, threatened with death, awaiting a hideous martyrdom. And then came the dreadful night when her mother, pale and dying, fell at her feet. Jeanne could save her cousin—she yielded. It was night; the Count, blood-stained from the fight, was at hand; a priest seemed to spring from the earth, torches, a church; Jeanne was doomed to misery.

Hardly could she say good-bye to the handsome cousin she had rescued.

"Chaverny, if you love me, never see me more!"

She heard her noble lover's retreating steps, and never saw him again. But she cherished his last look in the depths of her heart, the look she so often saw in her dreams bringing light into them.

Like a cat shut up in a lion's cage the young wife was in perpetual dread of her master's claws, ever raised to strike her. The Countess felt it as crime when, on certain days signalized by some unexpected pleasure, she put on the dress that the girl had worn the first time she had seen her lover. If she meant to be happy now it could only be by forgetting the past and thinking only of the future.

"I do not feel that I am guilty," said she to herself; "but if I am guilty in the Count's eyes, is it not the same thing? And perhaps I am. Did not the Holy Virgin conceive without—— ?"

She checked herself.

At this instant, when her ideas were so hazy and her spirit was wandering in the world of fancies, her guilelessness made her ascribe to her lover's last look, projecting his very life, the power exerted over the mother of the Saviour by the angel's visit. But this idea, worthy of the age of innocence to which her dreams had carried her back, vanished at the recollection of a conjugal scene more horrible than death. The poor Countess had no doubts as to the legitimacy of the child that was causing her such anguish. The first night of her married life rose before her in all the horror of martyrdom, followed by many worse, and by more cruel days.

"Ah, poor Chaverny!" cried she with tears, "you who were so gentle, so gracious—you always were good to me!"

She looked round at her husband, as to persuade herself yet that his face promised her the mercy she had paid for so dearly.

The Count was awake. His tawny eyes, as bright as a tiger's, gleamed under his bushy eyebrows, and their gaze had never been more piercing than at this moment. The Countess, terrified by their glare, shrank under the counterpane and lay perfectly still.

"What are these tears for?" asked the Count, sharply, pulling aside the sheet under which his wife was hidden. This voice, which always terrified her, was at this moment tempered to a semblance of kindness which she deemed of good augury.

"I am in great pain," said she.

"Well, sweetheart, and is it a crime to be in pain? Why do you tremble when I look at you? Alas, what must I do to be loved?"

All the wrinkles in his face seemed to gather between his eyebrows.

"I am always a terror to you, I can see it!" he added with a sigh.

Prompted by the instinct of feeble creatures, the Countess interrupted her husband with moans of pain, and then exclaimed: "I fear I may be suffering from a miscarriage. I was walking on the rocks all the afternoon and have perhaps overtired myself——"

As he heard this speech, the Sire d'Hérouville gave his wife a glance so full of suspicion that she turned red and shuddered. He mistook the artless girl's fear of him for the pangs of remorse.

"Perhaps it is the beginning of timely labor?" he asked.

"And if so?" said she.

"If so, and in any case, we must have the help of a skilled leech, and I will go to find one."

The gloomy air with which he spoke froze the Countess: she sank back in the bed with a sigh wrung from her more by a warning of her doom than by the pangs of the imminent crisis. This groan only convinced the Count of the probability of the suspicions aroused in his mind. While affecting a composure to which his tone of voice, his way of moving, and his looks gave the lie, he hastily got up, wrapped himself in his bed-gown that lay in an armchair, and began by locking a door near the fireplace, leading to the state rooms and the grand staircase. On seeing her husband pocket the key a forecast of misfortune oppressed the young wife; she heard him open a door opposite to that he had locked, and go into the room where the d'Hérouvilles slept when they did not honor their wives with their noble company. The Countess knew nothing of this but from hearsay; jealousy kept her husband always at her side. If military service required his absence from the state bed, the Count left more than one Argus at the castle, whose constant watchfulness proved his odious doubts.

In spite of the effort made by the Countess to catch the slightest sound, she heard no more. The Count had made his way into a long corridor adjoining his room, occupying the western wing of the building. His uncle, Cardinal d'Hérouville, an enthusiastic amateur of printed books, had collected there a library of some interest alike from the number and the beauty of the volumes, and prudence had led him to adopt in the walls one of the inventions due to monastic solitude or timidity. A silver chain attached to concealed wires acted on a bell hanging by the bed of a faithful retainer. The Count pulled the chain, a squire of his guard ere long approached, his boots and spurs clanging on the echoing steps of a newel stair in the high turret that flanked the western angle of the castle on the side towards the sea.

As he heard the man come up, the Count went to stir the rust on the iron springs and bolts which closed the secret door from the tower into the gallery, admitting to this sanctuary of learning a man-at-arms whose stalwart build showed him to be worthy of his master. This retainer, only half awake, seemed to have made his way by instinct; the horn lantern he carried threw so dim a light down the long room that his master and he were visible in the gloom like a couple of ghosts.

"Saddle my charger this minute!—and you must come with me."

The order was given with an emphatic ring that startled the man into comprehension; he looked up at the Count, and met so piercing a look that it was like an electric shock.

"Bertrand," the Count added, laying his right hand on his squire's arm, "take off your armor and put on the uniform of a captain of the Spanish guard."

"'Sdeath, monseigneur! What, disguise myself as an adherent of the Ligue? Pardon me, I will obey; but I would as lief be hanged."

The Count, flattered on his weak side, smiled; but to cover this expression, so strongly in contrast with that which characterized his features, he went on roughly:

"Take a horse out of the stable strong enough to enable you to keep up with me. We must fly like bullets shot out of an arquebus. Be ready by the time I am. I will ring."

Bertrand bowed in silence and departed; but when he had gone down a few steps, he said to himself as he heard the howling gale:

"All the devils are loose, by the Mass! I should have been astonished if this one had remained quiet. It was on just such a night that we took Saint-Lô."

The Count returned to his room and found the dress which often did him service in carrying out a stratagem. After putting on a shabby doublet that looked as if it belonged to one of the poor troopers who were so rarely paid by Henri IV., he returned to the room where his wife lay moaning.

"Try to suffer in patience," he said. "I will kill my horse if necessary to come back the quicker and ease your pain."

There was nothing sinister in this speech, and the Countess, taking heart, was on the point of asking a question, when the Count suddenly went on:

"Can you tell me where your masks are kept?"

"My masks?" replied she. "Good God! What do you want with them?"

"Where are they?" he repeated, with his usual violence.

"In the cabinet," said she.

The Countess could not help shuddering when she saw her husband select from among her things a half-mask, which the ladies of that time were as much accustomed to use as ladies of the present day are to wearing gloves. When the Count had put on a shabby gray felt hat with a broken cock's feather, he was quite unrecognizable. He buckled a broad leather belt about his middle, and stuck through it a dagger which he did not usually carry.

These squalid garments gave him so terrible an aspect, and he approached the bed with so strange a look, that the Countess thought her last hour had come.

"Oh, do not kill us!" she cried. "Leave me my child and I will love you well."

"You must feel guilty, indeed, to offer me as a ransom for your sins, the love you lawfully owe me."

The Count's voice sounded lugubrious through the velvet, and these bitter words were emphasized by a look as heavy as lead, crushing the Countess as it fell on her.

"Dear God!" she cried sadly. "Then is innocence fatal?"

"It is not your death that is in question," replied her lord, rousing himself from the brown study into which he had sunk; "but you are required to do exactly, and for love of me, what at this moment I demand of you."

He tossed one of the masks on the bed, and smiled contemptuously as he saw the start of involuntary terror that the light touch of the black velvet caused his wife.

"You will give me but a puny babe!" said he. "When I return, let me find you with this mask over your face. I will not suffer any base-born churl to be able to boast of having seen the Comtesse d'Hérouville."

"Why fetch a man to perform this office?" she asked, in a low voice.

"Heyday, my lady, am not I the master here?" replied the Count.

"What matters a mystery more or less?" said the Countess in despair.

Her lord had disappeared, so the exclamation was not a danger to her; though the oppressor's measures are as far-reaching as the terrors are of his victim. In one of the brief pauses that divided the more violent outbursts of the storm, the Countess heard the tramp of two horses that seemed to be flying across the dangerous sand hills and rocks, above which the old castle was perched. This sound was soon drowned under the thunder of the waves.

She presently found herself a prisoner in this dismal room, alone in the dead of a night by turns ominously calm or threatening, and with no one to help her avert a disaster which was coming on her with rapid strides. The Countess tried to think of some plan for saving this infant conceived in tears, and already her only comfort, the mainspring of her thoughts, the future hope of her affections, her sole and frail hope. Emboldened by a mother's fears, she went to take the little horn which her husband used for summoning his people, opened a window, and made the brass utter its shrill blast which was lost across the waste of waters, like a bubble blown into the air by a child.

She saw how useless was this call unheeded by man, and walked through the rooms hoping that she might not find every escape closed. Having reached the library she sought, but in vain, for some secret exit, she felt all along the wall of books, opened the window nearest to the fore court of the château, and again roused the echoes with the horn, struggling in vain with the uproar of the storm. In her despair she resolved to trust one of her women, though they were all her husband's creatures: but on going into the little oratory she saw that the door leading from this suite of rooms was locked.

This was a terrible discovery. Such elaborate precautions taken to isolate her, implied a purpose of proceeding to some terrible deed.

As the Countess lost all hope, her sufferings became more severe, and more racking. The horror of a possible murder, added to the exhaustion of labor, robbed her of her remaining strength. She was like a shipwrecked wretch who is done for at last by a wave less violent than many he has buffeted through.

The agonizing bewilderment of pain now made her lose all count of time. At the moment when she believed that the child would be born, and she alone and unholpen, when to her other terrors was added the fear of such disaster as her inexperience exposed her to, the Count unexpectedly arrived without her having heard him come. The man appeared like a fiend at the expiration of a compact, claiming the soul that he had bargained for; he growled in a deep voice as he saw his wife's face uncovered, but he adjusted the mask not too clumsily, and, taking her up in his arms, laid her on the bed in her room.

The dread of this apparition and of being thus lifted up made her forget pain for a moment; she could give a furtive glance at the actors in the mysterious scene, and did not recognize Bertrand, who was masked like his master. After hastily lighting some candles, of which the glimmer mingled with the first sunbeams that peered in through the panes, the man went to stand in the corner of a window-bay. There, with his face to the wall, he seemed to be measuring its thickness; and he stood so absolutely still that he might have been taken for a statue.

The Countess then saw standing in the middle of the room a fat little man, quite out of breath, with a bandage over his eyes, and features so distorted by fear that it was impossible to guess what their habitual expression might be.

"By the Rood, master leech," said the Count, restoring the

stranger to the use of his eyes by twitching the bandage roughly down on to his neck, "beware of looking at anything but the miserable creature on whom you are to exercise your skill; or, if you do, I fling you into the river that flows beneath these windows, with a diamond necklace on that will weigh a hundred pounds and more!" And he gave a slight twist to the handkerchief that had served to bandage his bewildered hearer's eyes.

"First see if this is a miscarriage; in that case you answer for her life with your own. If the child is born alive, bring it to me."

Having made this speech, the Count seized the unhappy leech by the middle, lifted him up like a feather, and set him down by the side of the Countess. He then went also to the window, where he stood drumming on the glass with his fingers, looking by turns at his man-at-arms, at the bed, and at the sea, as if promising the expected infant that the waves should be its cradle.

The man whom the Count and Bertrand had with brutal inhumanity snatched from the sweetest slumbers that ever closed mortal eyes, to tie him on to the crupper of a horse which, he might have fancied, had all hell at its heels, was a personage whose physiognomy was characteristic of the period, and whose influence was to be felt on the House of Hérouville.

At no period were the noble classes less informed as to natural science, and never was astrology in greater request than at this time, for never was there a more general desire to read the future. This common ignorance and curiosity had led to the greatest confusion in human acquirements; everything was empirical and personal, for as yet theory had achieved no nomenclature; printing was extremely costly and scientific communication was slow. The Church still persecuted the sciences of investigation based on the analysis of natural phenomena; and persecution engendered secrecy. Hence to the people as to the nobility, physicist, alchemist, mathematician and astronomer, astrologer and necromancer —all were embodied in the leech or medical practitioner. At that time the most scientific leech was suspected of magic; while curing the sick he was expected to cast horoscopes.

Princes patronized the geniuses to whom the future was revealed; they afforded them shelter and paid them pensions. The famous Cornelius Agrippa, who came to France as physician to Henri II., refused to foretell events as Nostradamus did, and Catherine de' Medici dismissed him in favor of Cosimo Ruggieri. Thus those men who were in advance of their age and really worked at science were rarely appreciated; they all inspired the terror that was felt for occult studies and their results.

Without being quite one of those famous mathematicians, the man snatched up by the Count enjoyed in Normandy the equivocal reputation of a leech who undertook mysterious dealings. This man was the sort of wizard who is to this day known to the peasants in various parts of France as a bone-setter (*un rebouteur*). The name is given to men of uncultured genius, who, without any professional study but hereditary tradition, and often by the long practice of which observation is accumulated in a family, can set bones; that is to say, remedy fractured and dislocated limbs, besides curing certain maladies in man and beast, and possessing secrets reputed magical for the treatment of more serious diseases.

Maître Antoine Beauvouloir—this was the bone-setter's name—had not only inherited important lore from his grandfather and father, both famous practitioners, but he was also learned in medicine, and studied natural science. The country folks saw his room full of books and of strange things, which gave his success a tinge of magic. Without regarding him quite as a sorcerer, the people for thirty leagues about treated Antoine Beauvouloir with a respect verging on terror; and, which was far more dangerous for him, he was in possession of secrets of life and death concerning all the noble families of the province.

Like his grandfather and his father, he was famous for his skill in attending childbirths, abortions, and miscarriage.

Now in these troubled times, lapses were common enough and passion violent enough to require the highest nobility sometimes to initiate Maître Beauvouloir into shameful or terrible secrets. His discretion, which was necessary to his safety, was above suspicion, and his patients paid him generously, so that the fortune he had inherited augmented conspicuously.

Always on the road,—sometimes taken by surprise, as we have just seen, sometimes obliged to spend several days in attendance on some great lady,—he was still unmarried; besides, his ill name had hindered some damsels from marrying him. Not so base as to find consolations in the chances of a profession which gave him so much power over feminine weakness, the hapless bone-setter felt himself fitted for such family joys as he might not allow himself. The good man hid a warm heart under the deceptive surface of a cheerful temper that matched his chubby face, his rotund person, the nimbleness of his fat little body, and the bluntness of his speech.

He wished to marry, to have a daughter who might confer his wealth on some man of family; for he did not love his calling as a bone-setter, and longed to raise his family from the discredit it was held in by the prejudices of the time.

However, he derived no small satisfaction from the rejoicing and feasting which commonly succeeded his principal achievements. The habit of finding himself the most important person present on such occasions had weighted his liveliness with a certain grave conceit. His ill-timed jests even were generally well taken in critical moments when he affected a certain masterly deliberateness. Then he was as inquisitive as a pick-lock, as greedy as a greyhound, and as gossiping as a diplomatist who can talk without ever betraying a secret. Barring these faults, developed by the various adventures into which he was brought by his profession, Antoine Beauvouloir passed for being the best soul in Normandy. Although he was one of the few men superior to the spirit of the age, the sound sense of a Normandy countryman had warned him to keep his acquired ideas and discovered truths to himself.

Finding himself by the bed of a woman in labor, the worthy bone-setter recovered his presence of mind. He proceeded to feel the masked lady's pulse, without thinking about her, however; but, under cover of this medical pretence, he could, and did, reflect on his own position. Never, in any of the disgraceful and criminal intrigues where he had been compelled by force to act as a blind instrument, had precautions been taken with so much care as in the present instance. Although his death had often been a matter of deliberation, as a way of securing the success of enterprises in which he had found himself engaged in spite of himself, his life had never seemed more uncertain than at this moment. Before anything he was determined to find out whom he was serving, and thus ascertain the extent of his danger, so as to be able to save his precious skin.

"What is the trouble?" he asked the Countess in an undertone, while arranging her so as to be able to give her the benefit of his experience.

"Do not suffer him to have the child."

"Speak out!" cried the Count in a voice of thunder, which hindered the leech from hearing the victim's last word. "Or else," added the husband, disguising his voice, "say your *In manus*."

"Cry aloud," said Beauvouloir to the lady. "Cry out, by the Mass! This man's jewels will suit your neck no better than mine. Courage, little lady."

"Go gently!" cried the Count.

"My lord is jealous," muttered the operator in a low, sharp tone that was happily drowned in the Countess' cries.

Happily for Maître Beauvouloir, nature was lenient. It was more like abortion than childbirth, so tiny was the infant that presently appeared, and the mother's sufferings were not severe.

THE HATED SON

"By the Blessed Virgin," exclaimed the bone-setter, "this is no miscarriage."

The Count stamped the floor till the boards quaked, and the Countess pinched the leech.

"Aha! Now I understand," thought he. "Then it ought to have been a miscarriage?" he asked in a whisper, and the Countess answered by an affirmative nod, as if she dared not in any other way express herself. "All this is not very clear," thought the good man.

Like all men skilled in this branch of the medical art, Beauvouloir at once perceived that he had to deal with a woman in her first trouble, as he phrased it to himself. Though the modest inexperience of the movements plainly showed the Countess' innocence, the leech, meaning to be smart, exclaimed:

"The lady is as clever at it as if she had never done anything else!"

The Count then said with a coldness that was even more terrible than his fury:

"Give me the child!"

"Do not give it him, for God's sake!" said the mother, whose almost savage cry roused a generous courage in the little man, attaching him much more than he would have thought possible to this child of noble birth whom its father had cast off.

"The child is not born yet; you are clamoring for nothing," he said coldly to the Count, covering up the unhappy infant.

Surprised to hear no cry, the leech examined the child, believing it to be dead; the Count discovered the deception and sprang on him with a single bound.

"By God and all His saints!" the Count yelled, "will you give it to me?" and he snatched up the innocent victim which feebly wailed.

"Take care! It is deformed and scarcely alive," said Maître Beauvouloir, clutching the Count's arm. "A seven-months' child, no doubt."

And with a superior strength given him by his passionate excitement, he held the father's hand, whispering, gasping into his ear:

"Spare yourself the crime; it will not live——"

"Wretch!" said the Count in a fury, as the bone-setter rescued the babe from his hold, "who says I wish the child to die? Do you not see that I am caressing it?"

"Wait till he is eighteen years old before you caress him in that fashion," replied Beauvouloir, reasserting himself. "But," he added, thinking of his own safety, for he had now recognized the Comte d'Hérouville, who in his rage had forgotten to disguise his voice, "have him baptized at once and say nothing of my opinion to the mother, or you will kill her."

The heartfelt joy betrayed by the Count's shrug when he was told that the infant must die, had suggested this speech to the old leech and had saved the child's life. Beauvouloir carried it back forthwith to the mother, who had fainted away, and he pointed to her with an ironical gesture to frighten the Count by the state to which their discussion had reduced her. The Countess, indeed, had heard all, for it is a not uncommon thing for the senses to develop extreme sensitiveness in such critical situations. The cries of her infant lying by her side now brought her back to consciousness as if by magic, and she could have believed that she heard the voice of angels when, under cover of the infant's wailing, the leech said in her ear:

"Take great care of him and he will live to be a hundred. Beauvouloir knows what he is saying."

A heavenly sigh, a covert pressure of the old man's hand were his reward, and before placing the tiny creature in its impatient mother's arms, he carefully examined to see whether the father's "caress," of which the print still remained on its skin, had done no injury to its frail frame.

The almost insane gesture with which the mother hid her babe, and the threatening look she flashed at the Count through the eye-holes of her mask made Beauvouloir shudder.

"She will die if she loses her child too suddenly," he said to the Count.

During the latter part of this scene the Count d'Hérouville seemed to have seen and heard nothing. Motionless, absorbed as it seemed in deep meditation, he was again drumming with his fingers on the window-panes. But at these last words of the leech's he turned upon him with an impulse of frenzied rage, and drew his dagger.

"Contemptible lout!" cried he (*manant*, a nickname used by the Royalists to insult the Leaguers), "impudent rascal! Science, which has earned you the honor of becoming the helpmate of gentlemen when they are fain to prolong or cut short a hereditary race, hardly avails to hinder me from freeing Normandy of a wizard."

Still, to Beauvouloir's great relief, the Count violently thrust the dagger home into its sheath.

"Are you incapable of finding yourself for once in the noble presence of a lord and his lady, without suspecting them of those base calculations which you allow among the common herd, forgetting that they, unlike the gently born, have no plausible motive for them? Am I likely to have state reasons for the action you choose to attribute to me? Kill my son! Take him from his mother! What put such nonsense into your head? Am I a madman?—Why alarm us as to the life of such a strong infant? Villain! I would have you know that I distrusted your braggart vanity. If you could have known the name of the lady you have brought to bed, you would have boasted of having seen her! Pasques Dieu! And you might by excess of precaution have killed perhaps the mother or the child. But remember now, your life shall answer for your discretion and for their doing well!"

The leech was dismayed by this sudden change in the Count's views. This extraordinary fit of affection for the deformed infant frightened him more than the fractious cruelty and gloomy indifference of the Count's previous demeanor. In fact, his tone, as he spoke the last words, betrayed a more elaborate plot to achieve a purpose which was certainly unchanged.

Maître Beauvouloir accounted for this unforeseen revulsion by the promises he had made to the father and the mother.

"I have it!" thought he. "The noble gentleman does not wish to make his wife hate him; he will trust to Providence in the person of an apothecary. I must try to warn the lady that she may watch over her noble babe."

He was approaching the bed, when the Count, who had gone to a closet, stopped him by an imperative word. On seeing the Count hold out a purse to him, Beauvouloir hastened, not without an uneasy satisfaction, to pick up the red net purse, full of gleaming gold, which was scornfully thrown to him.

"Though you ascribed to me the ideas of a villain, I do not think myself exonerated from paying you as a lord should. I say nothing about secrecy. This man," and he pointed to Bertrand, "has no doubt made it plain to you that wherever oak-trees or rivers are to be found, my diamonds and my necklaces are ready for such caitiffs as dare speak of me."

And with these magnanimous words the colossus went slowly up to the speechless leech, noisily drew forward a chair and seemed to bid him be seated, like himself, by the lady's bedside.

"Well, honey," said he, "at last we have a son. It is great joy for us. Are you suffering?"

"No," murmured the Countess.

The mother's astonishment and timidity, and the tardy expressions of the father's spurious satisfaction, all convinced Maître Beauvouloir that some important factor here escaped his usual acumen. His suspicions were not allayed, and he laid his hand on the lady's, less to feel her pulse than to give her a warning.

"The skin is moist," said he. "There is no fear of any

untoward symptoms. There will be a little milk-fever, no doubt; but do not be alarmed; it will be nothing."

The wily leech paused, and pressed the Countess' hand to attract her attention.

"If you wish to have no fears for your child, madame," said he, "keep it always under your own eye. Let it feed for a long time on the milk its little lips are already seeking. Nurse it yourself, and never give it any apothecaries' drugs. The breast is the cure of all infantile complaints. I have seen many a birth at seven months, but never one accompanied by less pain. It is not surprising, the child is so thin. I could put it in a shoe! I do not believe it weighs fifteen ounces. Milk, milk! If he is always lying on your breast you will save him."

These words were emphasized by another pressure of her fingers. In spite of two shafts of flame shot by the Count through the eye-holes of his mask, the good man spoke with the imperturbable gravity of a leech determined to earn his fee.

"How now, bone-setter, you are leaving your old black hat behind you!" said Bertrand, as he escorted the apothecary out of the room.

The motive of the Count's clemency towards his son was based on a legal *et cetera*. At the moment when Beauvouloir rescued him from his clutches, avarice and the usage of Normandy rose before his mind. Each, by a sign as it were, numbed his fingers and silenced his vengeful passions. One suggested to him, "Your wife's property will not come to the family of Hérouville unless through an heir male." The other pictured the Countess as dead and her estates claimed by a collateral branch of the Saint-Savins. Both counseled him to leave the removal of the changeling to the act of nature and await the birth of a second born, strong and healthy, when he might snap his fingers at his wife's chances of living and at his first-born.

He did not see the child, he saw an estate, and suddenly his affection was as large as his ambition. In his anxiety to comply with the requirements of custom, he only wished that this half-dead babe should acquire the appearance of strength.

The mother, who knew the Count's temper, was even more astonished than the leech; she still had some instinctive fears, which she sometimes boldly expressed, for the courage of a mother had in an instant given her strength.

For some days the Count was assiduous in his care of his wife, showing her such attentions as interest dictated, giving them even a show of tenderness. The Countess was quick to perceive that they were for her alone. The father's hatred of his child was visible in the smallest details; he would never look at it or touch it; he would start up suddenly and go away to give orders the instant it was heard to cry; in short, he seemed to forgive it for living only in the hope of its dying.

Even this much of self-restraint was too great an effort for the Count. On the day when he discovered that the mother's keen eye saw, without understanding, the danger that threatened her child, he announced that, on the morrow of the Countess' thanksgiving service, he would leave home, on the pretext of leading his men-at-arms to the assistance of the King.

Such were the circumstances which preceded and surrounded the birth of Étienne d'Hérouville. Even if the Count had not had, as an all-sufficient reason for constantly desiring the death of this disowned son, the fact that he had wished it from the first, even if he would have smothered the odious human instinct of persecuting the victim who has already suffered, and if he had not been under the intolerable necessity of feigning affection for a hapless changeling of whom he believed Chaverny to be the father, poor little Étienne would none the less have been the object of his aversion. The misfortune of his rickety and sickly constitution, aggravated, perhaps, by the paternal caress, was a standing offence to his pride as a father.

Though he execrated handsome men, he no less detested weakly men in whom intelligence supplied the place of strength of body. To please him a man must be ugly, tall, stalwart, and ignorant. Étienne, whose delicate frame compelled him in some sort to devote himself to sedentary studies, was certain to find in his father a relentless foe. His struggle with the giant had begun in his cradle, and his only ally against so formidable an antagonist was his mother's heart; a love which, by a touching law of nature, was increased by the dangers that threatened it.

Left in sudden and utter solitude by her husband's abrupt departure, Jeanne de Saint-Savin owed the only semblance of happiness that could cheer her life to her infant. This child, for whose existence she had suffered on the score of Chaverny, was as dear to her as if he had indeed been the offspring of illicit passion; she nursed him herself and felt no weariness. She would never accept any help from her women; she dressed and undressed the child, taking a fresh pleasure in every little care. This incessant occupation and hourly attention, the punctuality with which she would wake in the night to suckle the child, were unbounded happiness. Joy lighted up her face as she attended to the little creature's needs.

As Étienne's birth had been premature, many little garments were lacking; these she would make herself, and she did it with such perfection as you mistrusted mothers may imagine, who have stitched in gloom and silence for your adored little ones. Each needleful of thread brought with it a memory, a hope, a wish, a thousand thoughts sewn into the stuff with the dainty patterns she embroidered. All these extravagances were repeated to the Comte d'Hérouville and added to the gathering storm. The hours of the day were too few for the myriad interests and elaborate precautions of the devoted mother; they flew, filled with secret happiness.

The leech's warnings were ever present to the Countess. She dreaded everything for the child, the services of the women and the touch of the men-servants; gladly would she never have slept, to be sure that nobody came near Étienne while she was slumbering; he slept by her side. In short, suspicion kept watch over his cradle.

During the Count's absence she even dared to send for the leech, whose name she had not forgotten. Beauvouloir was to her a man to whom she owed an immense debt of gratitude; but above all she wanted to question him as to a thousand matters concerning her son. If Étienne was to be poisoned how should she forefend any such attempt? How should she strengthen his feeble constitution? When should she fitly wean him? If she should die, would Beauvouloir undertake to watch over the poor little one's health?

In reply to the Countess' inquiries Beauvouloir, truly touched, replied that he too feared some scheme to poison Étienne. On this point Madame la Comtesse had nothing to fear so long as she nursed him; and afterwards he advised her always to taste the child's food.

"If, Madame la Comtesse, you should at any time notice any flavor that strikes you as strange, pungent, bitter, strong, briny—anything that startles your taste, reject the food. Let all the child's clothes be washed in your presence, and keep the key of the closet where they lie. And if anything should happen send for me; I will come."

The old bone-setter's advice was stamped on Jeanne's heart, and she begged him to depend on her as one who would do all in her power to serve him. Beauvouloir then confided to her that she had his happiness in her hands.

He briefly told the Countess how that the Comte d'Hérouville, for lack of fair and noble dames to regard him with favor at Court, had in his youth loved a courtesan known as La Belle Romaine, who had previously been mistress to the Cardinal de Lorraine. This woman, whom he had soon deserted, had followed him to Rouen to beseech him in favor of a daughter to whom he would have nothing to say, making her beauty an excuse for refusing to acknowledge her. At the death of this woman in extreme poverty, the poor girl, whose name was Gertrude, and who was even handsomer than her mother, was taken under the protection of a convent of Poor Clares, whose Mother Superior was Mademoiselle de Saint-Savin, the Countess' aunt.

Beauvouloir, having been sent for to attend Gertrude, had fallen madly in love with her.

"If you, Madame la Comtesse," he said in conclusion, "would interfere in this matter, it would not only amply repay anything you may say that you owe me, but make me eternally your debtor."

It would also justify him in coming to the château, which was not without danger in the Count's presence, and sooner or later the Count would no doubt take an interest in such a beautiful girl, and might some day perhaps promote her interests by making him his physician.

The Countess, soft-hearted to all true lovers, promised to help the poor leech. And she did so warmly espouse his cause, that on the occasion of the birth of her second child, when, as was then the custom, she was authorized in asking a favor of her husband, she obtained a marriage portion for Gertrude, and the fair bastard, instead of taking the veil, married Beauvouloir. This little fortune and the bone-setter's savings enabled him to purchase Forcalier, a pretty little place adjoining the lands of Hérouville, which was sold by its owners.

Thus comforted by the worthy leech, the Countess felt her life filled by joys unknown to other women. Every woman indeed is lovely when she presses her babe to her breast to still its cries and soothe its little pains; but even in an Italian picture it would be hard to find a more touching sight than the young Countess as she saw Étienne thriving on her milk, and her own blood, as it were, infusing life into the little creature whose life hung on a thread.

Her face beamed with love as she looked at the adored infant, dreading lest she should indeed discern in him a feature resembling Chaverny, of whom she had too often thought. These reflections, mingling on her brow with the expression of her joy, the brooding eye with which she watched her son, her longing to infuse into him the vitality she felt at her heart, her high hopes, the prettiness of her movements, all composed a picture that won the women about her; the Countess triumphed over spies.

Very soon these two weak creatures were united by common ideas, and understood each other before language could help them to explain themselves. When Étienne began to use his eyes with the wondering eagerness of an infant, they fell on the gloomy panels of the state bedroom. When his youthful ears first appreciated sound, and discerned their indifference, he heard the monotonous dash of the sea as the waves broke against the rocks with a repetition as regular as the pendulum of a clock. Thus place and sound and scenery, all that can strike the senses, prepare the intellect, and form the character, predisposed him to melancholy.

Was not his mother fated to live and die amid clouds of sadness? From the day of his birth he might easily have supposed that she was the only being existing upon earth, have regarded the whole world as a desert, and have been used to the feeling of self-reliance which leads us to live in solitude, and seek for happiness in ourselves by developing the resources of our own mind. Was not the Countess condemned to pass her life alone, and find her all in her boy, who, like her lover, was a victim to persecution?

Like all children who suffer much, Étienne almost always showed the passive temper which was so sweetly like his mother's. The delicacy of his nerves was so great that a sudden sound or the presence of a restless and noisy person gave him a sort of fever. You might have fancied him one of those frail insects for which God seems to temper the wind and the heat of the sun; incapable, as they are, of fighting against the least obstacle, he, like them, simply yielded, unresisting and uncomplaining, to everything that opposed him. This angelic patience filled the Countess with a deep emotion which overruled all the fatigue of the constant attentions his frail health demanded of her.

She could thank God who had placed Étienne in an atmosphere of peace and silence, the only surroundings in which he could grow up happy. His mother's hands, so strong and to him so gentle, would often lift him high up to look out of the pointed windows. From them his eyes, as blue as his mother's, seemed to be taking in the grandeur of the ocean. The pair would sit for hours contemplating the infinite expanse of waters, by turns gloomy or bright, silent or full of sound.

These long meditations were to Étienne an apprenticeship to grief. Almost always his mother's eyes would fill with tears, and during these sad day-dreams Étienne's little face would look like a fine net puckered by too heavy a load. Before long his precocious apprehension of sorrow taught him how much his little play could affect the Countess, and he would try to divert her by such caresses as she bestowed on him to soothe his pain. And his little elfin hands, his babbled words, never failed to dissipate her sadness. If he was weary, his instinctive care for her kept him from complaining.

"Poor, sensitive darling!" cried the Countess, seeing him drop asleep from fatigue after a game which had driven away one of her fits of brooding. "Where are you to live? Who will ever understand you—you, whose tender soul will be wounded by a stern look? You who, like your unhappy mother, will value a kindly smile as something more precious than all else this world can bestow? Angel, your mother loves you! But who will love you in the world? Who will ever suspect the jewel hidden in that frail frame? No one. Like me, you will be alone on earth. God preserve you from ever knowing, as I have done, a love approved by God but thwarted by man."

She sighed and she wept. The easy attitude of her child, as he slept on her knees, brought a melancholy smile to her lips. She gazed at him for long, enjoying one of those raptures which are a secret between a mother and God.

Finding how greatly her voice, with the accompaniment

of a mandolin, could charm her boy, she would sing the pretty ballads of the time, and could fancy she saw on his lips, smeared with milk, the smile with which Georges de Chaverny had been wont to thank her when she laid down her rebec. She blamed herself for thus recalling the past, but she returned to it again and again. And the child, an unconscious accomplice, would smile at the very airs that Chaverny had loved.

When he was eighteen months old the child's delicate health had never yet allowed of his being taken out of the house, but the faint pink that tinged the pallid hue of his cheek, as if the palest petal of a wild rose had been wafted there by the wind, promised life and health. Just as she was beginning to believe in the leech's prognostics, and was rejoicing in having been able, during the Count's absence, to surround her son with the strictest care so as to hedge him in from all danger, letters, written by her husband's secretary, announced his early return.

One morning when the Countess, given up to the wild delight of a mother when she sees her first-born attempt his first steps, was playing with Étienne at games as indescribable as are the joys of memory, she suddenly heard the floor creak under a heavy foot. She had scarcely started to her feet with an involuntary impulse of surprise than she found herself face to face with the Count. She gave a cry; but she tried to remedy this rash error by advancing to meet him, her brow submissively raised for a kiss.

"Why did you not give me warning of your coming?" said she.

"The reception," interrupted the Count, "would have been more cordial, but less genuine."

Then he caught sight of the child. Its frail appearance at first provoked him to a gesture of astonishment and fury; but he controlled his rage and put on a smile.

"I have brought you good news," he went on. "I am made governor of Champagne, and the King promises to create me a duke and a peer of the realm. Besides, we have come into a fortune; that damned Huguenot de Chaverny is dead."

The Countess turned pale, and sank into a chair. She could guess the secret of the sinister glee expressed in her husband's face, and the sight of Étienne seemed to aggravate it.

"Monsieur," said she, in a broken voice, "you are well aware that I had long been attached to my cousin de Chaverny. You will account to God for the pain you are inflicting on me."

At these words the Count's eyes flashed fire; his lips trembled so that he could not speak, so mad was he with rage; he flung his dagger on to the table with such violence that the metal rattled like a thunder-clap.

"Listen to me," said he in his deep voice, "and mark what I say. I will never see nor hear the little monster you have in your arms, for he is your child and none of mine. Has he the least resemblance to me? By God and all his saints! Hide him, I tell you, or else——"

"Merciful Heaven," cried the Countess, "preserve us."

"Silence!" said the big man. "If you do not want me to touch him, never let him come across my path."

"Well, then," said the Countess, finding courage to withstand her tyrant, "swear to me that you will not try to kill him if you never see him anywhere. Can I trust to your honor as a gentleman?"

"What is the meaning of this?" exclaimed the Count.

"Well, kill us both, then," cried she, falling on her knees and clasping the child in her arms.

"Rise, madame; I pledge you my word as a gentleman to do nothing against the life of that misbegotten abortion, so long as he lives on the rocks that fringe the sea below the castle. I will give him the fisherman's house for a residence and the strand for his domain. But woe to him if I ever find him outside those limits."

The Countess burst into bitter weeping.

"But look at him!" said she. "He is your son."

"Madame!"

At this word the terrified mother carried away the child, whose heart was beating like that of a linnet taken from its nest by a country lad.

Whether innocence has a charm which even the most hardened men cannot resist, or whether the Count blamed himself for his violence and feared to crush a woman who was equally necessary for his pleasure and plans, by the time his wife returned his voice was softened as far as lay in his power.

"Jeanne, my sweetheart," said he, "bear me no ill-feeling, give me your hand. It is impossible to know how to take you women. I bring you honors and wealth, pardie! and you receive me like a miscreant falling among caitiffs. My government will necessitate long absences until I can exchange it for that of Normandy; so at least give me cordial looks so long as I sojourn here."

The Countess understood the purport of these words and their affected sweetness could not delude her.

"I know my duty," said she, with a tone of melancholy which her husband took for tenderness.

The timid creature was too pure-minded, too lofty, to attempt, as some cleverer woman would have done, to govern the Count by carefully regulated conduct, a sort of prostitution which to a noble soul seems despicable. She went slowly away to comfort her despair by walking with Étienne.

"By God and His saints! Shall I never be loved?" exclaimed the Count, discerning a tear in his wife's eye as she left him.

Motherly feeling, under these constant threats of danger, acquired in Jeanne a strength of passion such as women throw into a guilty attachment. By a sort of magic, of which every mother's heart has the secret, and which was especially real between the Countess and her boy, she was able to make him understand the peril in which he lived, and taught him to dread his father's presence. The miserable scene he had witnessed remained stamped on his memory and produced a sort of malady. At last he could forecast the Count's appearance with such certainty, that if one of those smiles, of which the dim promise is visible to a mother's eyes, had lighted up his features at the moment when his half-developed senses, sharpened by fear, became aware of his father's tread at some distance, his face would pucker; and the mother's ear was not so quick as her infant's instinct. As he grew older, this faculty, created by dread, increased so much that, like the red savages of America, Étienne could distinguish his father's step and hear his voice at a great distance, and announce his approach. This sympathy, in her terror of her husband, at such an early age, made the child doubly dear to the Countess; and they were so closely united that, like two flowers growing on one stem, they bent to the same gale and revived under the same hopes. They lived but one life.

When the Count departed Jeanne was expecting another child, that was born with much suffering at the period demanded by prejudice; a fine boy, which in a few months' time was so exactly like his father that the Count's aversion for the elder was still further increased.

To save her darling the Countess consented to every plan devised by her husband to promote the happiness and fortunes of their second son. Étienne, promised a cardinal's hat, was driven to the priesthood that Maximilien might inherit the estates and titles of Hérouville. At this cost the poor mother secured peace for the disowned son.

When were two brothers more unlike than Étienne and Maximilien? The younger from his birth loved noise, violent exercise, and warfare; and the Count loved him as passionately as his wife loved Étienne. By a natural though tacit understanding each of them took chief care of the favorite.

The Duke—for by this time Henry IV. had rewarded the great services of the Lord of Hérouville—the Duke not wishing, as he said, to overtax his wife, chose for Maximilien's wet-nurse a sturdy peasant-wife of Beauvais, found by Beauvouloir.

To Jeanne's great joy, he distrusted the mother's influence as much as her nursing, and determined to bring up his boy after his own mind. Maximilien imbibed a holy horror of books and letters; he learned from his father the mechanical arts of military life, to ride on horseback from the earliest age, to fire a gun, and use a dagger. As he grew up the Duke took the boy out hunting that he might acquire the brutal freedom of speech, rough manners, physical strength, and manly look and tone which in his opinion made the accomplished gentleman. At twelve years old the young nobleman was a very ill-licked lion's cub, at least as much to be feared as his father, by whose permission he might and did tyrannize over all who came near him.

Étienne lived in the house on the seashore given to him by his father, and arranged by the Duchess in such a way as to provide him with some of the comforts and pleasures to which he had a right. His mother spent the greater part of the day there. She and her boy wandered together over rocks and beaches; she showed Étienne the delimitation of his little estate of sand, shells, seaweed, and pebbles, and her vehement alarm if he ever crossed the border line of the conceded territory, made him fully understand that death lay outside it. Étienne knew fear for his mother before he trembled for himself; and then while still young he felt a panic at the mere name of the Duc d'Hérouville, which bereft him of all energy, and filled him with the helpless alarm of a girl who falls on her knees to beseech a sign. If he but saw the ominous giant in the distance, or only heard the voice, the dreadful impression that remained to him of the time when his father had cursed him froze his blood. And like a Laplander who pines to death when removed from his native snows, he made a happy home of his hut and the rocks; if he crossed the boundary he was uneasy.

The Duchess, perceiving that the poor child could find happiness nowhere but in a restricted and silent sphere, regretted less the doom imposed upon him; she took advantage of his compulsory vocation to prepare him for a noble life by occupying his loneliness in the pursuit of learning, and she sent for Pierre de Sebonde to dwell at the castle as preceptor to the future Cardinal d'Hérouville. Notwithstanding his being destined to the tonsure, Jeanne de Saint-Savin would not have his education to be exclusively priestly; by her active interference it was largely secular. Beauvouloir was desired to instruct Étienne in the mysteries of natural science; and the Duchess, who superintended his studies to regulate them by the child's strength, amused him by teaching him Italian, and revealing to him the poetic beauties of the language.

While the Duke was leading Maximilien to attack the wild boar at the risk of being badly hurt, Jeanne was guiding Étienne through the Milky Way of Petrarca's sonnets, or the stupendous labyrinth of the *Divina Commedia*.

In compensation for many infirmities, nature had gifted Étienne with so sweet a voice that the pleasure of hearing it was almost irresistible; his mother taught him music. Songs, tender and melancholy, to the accompaniment of the mandolin, were a favorite recreation promised by his mother as the reward of some task set by the Abbé de Sebonde. Étienne would listen to his mother with such passionate admiration as she had never before seen but in the eyes of Chaverny.

The first time the poor soul thus revived her girlhood's memories, she covered her boy's face with frenzied kisses. She blushed when Étienne asked her why she seemed to love him so much more than usual, and then she replied that she loved him more and more every hour. Thus, ere long, she found in the care needed for his soul's discipline and his mental culture, the same joys as she had known in nursing and strengthening her boy's frame.

Though mothers do not always grow up with their sons, the Duchess was one of those who bring into their motherhood the humble devotion of love; she could be both fond and critical. She made it her pride to help Étienne to become in every respect superior to herself, and not to govern him; perhaps she felt herself so strong in her unfathomable affection that she had no fear of seeming small. Only hearts devoid of tenderness crave to domineer; true feeling loves abnegation, which is the virtue of the strong.

If Étienne did not at first understand some demonstration, some abstruse text, or theorem, the poor mother, who would sit by him at his lessons, seemed to long to infuse into him an apprehension of all knowledge, as of old at his faintest cry she had fed him from her breast. And then what a flush of joy crimsoned her cheeks when Étienne saw and took in the meaning of things. She proved, as Pierre de Sebonde said, that a mother lives a double life and that her feelings include two existences.

The Duchess thus enhanced the natural feelings that bind a son to his mother by the added tenderness of a resuscitated passion. Étienne's delicate health led her to continue for some years the care she had devoted to his infancy. She would dress him and put him to bed; none but she ever combed and smoothed, curled and scented her boy's hair. This toilet was one long caress; she kissed the beloved head as often as she touched it lightly with the comb.

Just as a woman delights in being almost a mother to her lover, by rendering some homely service, so this mother in a way treated the child as a lover; she saw some faint likeness in him to the cousin she still loved beyond the tomb. Étienne was like the ghost of Georges seen in the remote heart of a magic mirror, and she would tell herself that there was more of the gentleman than of the priest in the boy.

"If only some woman as loving as I am, would infuse into him the life of love, he might yet be very happy," she often reflected.

But the all-powerful interests which depended on Étienne's becoming a priest would come to her mind, and she would kiss and leave her tears on the hair which the shears of the Church would presently cut away.

In spite of the unjust conditions imposed by the Duke,

in the perspective her eye could picture, piercing the thick darkness of the future, she never saw Étienne as a priest or a cardinal. His father's utter neglectfulness allowed her to preserve her poor boy as yet from taking orders.

"There will always be time enough!" she would say.

And without confessing the thought that lay buried in her heart, she trained Étienne in the fine manners of the Court; she would have him as tender and gentle as Georges de Chaverny. Reduced to a small allowance by the Duke's ambitions, for he himself managed the family estates, spending all his revenues in ostentation, or on his retainers, she had adopted the plainest attire for her own wear, spending nothing on herself, that she might give her son velvet cloaks, high boots trimmed with lace, and doublets of rich materials, handsomely slashed.

These personal privations gave her the delight of the secret sacrifices we hide from those we love. It was a joy to her, as she embroidered a ruff, to think of the day when she should see it on her boy's neck. She alone took charge of Étienne's clothes, linen, perfumes, and dress; and she dressed herself only for him, for she loved to be thought charming by him.

So much care, prompted by an ardor of affection which seemed to penetrate and vitalize her son's frame, had its reward. One day Beauvouloir, the good man who had made himself dear to this outcast heir by his teaching, and whose services were indeed known to the lad, the leech, whose anxious eye made the Duchess quake every time it rested on her fragile idol, pronounced that Étienne might enjoy a long life if no too violent emotions should overtax the delicate constitution.

Étienne was now sixteen.

At this age Étienne was not tall and he never became so; but Georges de Chaverny had been of middle height. His skin, as clear and fine as a little girl's, showed the delicate network of blue veins beneath. His pallor was of the texture of porcelain. His light blue eyes were full of ineffable sweetness and seemed to crave protection of man and woman alike;

the ingratiating softness of a supplicant beamed in his look, and began the charm which the melody of his voice achieved.

Perfect modesty was stamped on every feature. Long chestnut hair, smooth and glossy, was parted over his brow and fell curling at the ends. But his cheeks were pale and worn, and his innocent brow, furrowed with the lines of congenital suffering, was sad to see; while his mouth, though pleasing and furnished with very white teeth, had the sort of fixed smile we see on the lips of the dying. His hands, as white as a woman's, were remarkably well-shaped.

Much thought had given him the habit of holding his head down, like an etiolated plant, and this stoop suited his general appearance; it was like the last touch of grace which a great artist gives to a portrait to enhance its meaning. You might have fancied that a girl's head had been placed on the frail body of a deformed man.

The studious and poetical moods, rich in meditation, in which, like botanists, we scour the fields of the mind, the fruitful comparison of various human ideas, the high thoughts that are born of a perfect apprehension of works of genius, had become the inexhaustible and placid joys of this lonely and dreamy existence.

Flowers, those exquisite creations whose fate so much resembled his own, were the objects of his love. The Duchess, happy in seeing that her son's innocent pastimes were such as would preserve him from the rough contact of social life, which he could no more have endured than some pretty ocean fish could have survived the touch of the sun on the sands, had encouraged Étienne's tastes by giving him Spanish *romanceros,* Italian *motetti,* books, sonnets, and poetry. The Cardinal d'Hérouville's library had been handed over to Étienne; reading was to be the occupation of his life.

Every morning the boy found his wilderness bright with pretty flowers of lovely hues and sweet scent; thus his studies, which his delicate health would not allow him to continue for long at a time, and his play among the rocks, were relieved by endless meditations which would keep him sitting for hours as he looked at his innocent companions, the flowers, or crouching in the shade of a boulder, as he pondered on the mysteries of a seaweed, a moss, or a lichen. He would seek a poem in the cup of a fragrant flower as a bee might rifle it for honey.

Often, indeed, he would simply admire, without arguing over his enjoyment of the delicate tracery of a richly colored petal, the subtle texture of these cups of gold or azure, green or purple, the exquisite and varied beauty of calyx and leaf, their smooth or velvety surface, that were rent— as his soul would be rent—with the slightest touch.

At a later time, a thinker as well as a poet, he discerned the reason of these infinite manifestations of nature that was still the same; for, day by day, he advanced in the interpretation of the sacred Word that is written in every form of creation. These persistent and secret studies carried on in the occult world gave his life the half-torpid appearance of meditative genius.

For long hours Étienne would bask on the sands, a poet unawares. And the sudden advent of a gilded insect, the reflection of the sunbeams from the sea, the twinkling play of the vast and liquid mirror of waters, a shell, a sea-spider— everything was an event and a delight to his guileless soul. To see his mother coming, to hear the soft rustle of her gown, to watch for her, kiss her, speak to her, listen to her, all caused him such acute excitement that some little delay or the least alarm would throw him into a high fever.

All his life was in his soul; and to save the still frail and weakly body from being destroyed by the large emotions of that soul, Étienne needed silence and kindness, peace in the world about him, and a woman's love. For the present his mother could enwrap him in love and kindness; the rocks were silent; flowers and books beguiled his solitude; and finally his little realm of sand and shells, of grass and seaweed, were to him a world perennially bright and new.

Étienne got all the benefit of this absolutely innocuous

physical existence and this poetically noble, moral atmosphere. A boy still in development, a man in mind, he was equally angelic from both points of view. By his mother's guidance, his studies had lifted his emotions to the sphere of intellect. Thus the activity of his mind worked itself out in the abstract world, far from the social life which, if it had not killed him, would have brought him suffering. He lived in the soul and in the mind. After apprehending human thought through reading, he rose to the great first principles that vitalize matter, he felt them in the air and read thoughts written in the sky. In short, he had at an early age climbed to the ethereal heights where he could find fit nourishment for his soul,—a nourishment rare but intoxicating, which inevitably predestined him to woe on the day when this accumulated treasure should clash with the other treasure which a sudden passion brings to the spirit.

Though Jeanne de Saint-Savin sometimes trembled at the thought of that storm, she would comfort herself by a thought suggested by her son's gloomy vocation; for the poor mother knew of no remedy for any evil but the acceptance of a lesser one. Her very joys were full of bitterness.

"He will be a cardinal," she would reflect, "he will live for the arts and be their patron. He will love Art instead of loving a woman, and Art will never betray him."

Thus the happiness of this devoted mother was constantly qualified by the painful thoughts to which Étienne's strange position in his family gave rise. The two brothers had grown up without knowing each other; they had never met; each knew not of his rival's existence. The Duchess had long hoped for some opportunity during her husband's absence when she might bring the two boys together and infuse her soul into them both. She flattered herself that she might engage Maximilien's interest in Étienne by explaining to the younger brother how much care and affection he owed to the elder, in return for the renunciation that had been imposed upon him, and to which, though compulsory, Étienne would be faithful. But this hope, long fondly cherished, had vanished.

THE HATED SON

Far, now, from wishing to make the brothers acquainted, she dreaded a meeting between Étienne and Maximilien even more than between her boy and his father. Maximilien, who could believe in nothing good, would have feared lest Étienne should one day assert his forfeited rights, and would have thrown him into the sea with a stone tied to his neck.

Never had a son so little respect for his mother. As soon as he could reason at all he perceived how small was the Duke's regard for his wife. If the old Governor still preserved some form of politeness in his conduct to the Duchess, Maximilien, hardly ever restrained by his father, caused her a thousand griefs.

Old Bertrand, too, took care that Maximilien should never see Étienne, whose very existence was carefully concealed from him. All the dependents on the château cordially hated the Marquis de Saint-Sever, the name borne by Maximilien; and all who knew of the existence of the elder son regarded him an instrument of vengeance held in reserve by God. Thus Étienne's future prospects were indeed doubtful; he might be persecuted by his brother.

The poor Duchess had no relations to whom she could confide the life and interests of this beloved son; and might not Étienne blame her, if, in the purple robe of Rome, he longed to be such a father as she had been a mother?

These thoughts, and her saddened life, full of unconfessed griefs, were like a long sickness mitigated by gentle treatment. Her spirit craved for skilful kindness, and those about her were cruelly unpractised in gentleness. What mother's heart but must ache continually as she saw her eldest born, a man of heart and intellect, with the promise of true genius, despoiled of all his rights, while the younger, a nature of coarse homespun, devoid even of military talent, was destined to wear the ducal coronet and perpetuate the race? The House of Hérouville was sacrificing its true glory. The gentle Jeanne, incapable of curses, could only bless and weep; but she often raised her eyes to Heaven to wonder at the reason for this strange doom. Her eyes would fill with tears as she reflected that, at her death, her son would in fact be an orphan and the object of a brother's brutality, who knew neither faith nor law.

So much suppressed feeling, her first love never forgotten, her many sorrows unrevealed,—for she concealed her worst griefs from her adored son,—her ever insecure joys and incessant anxieties, had told on her constitution, and sown the seeds of a decline which, far from amending, seemed aggravated day by day. At last a final blow developed consumption. The Duchess tried to point out to her husband the results of Maximilien's training, and was roughly repulsed; she could do nothing to counteract the evil seed that was germinating in her son's heart. She now fell into a state of such evident debility that her illness required the promotion of Beauvouloir to the position of leech in the castle of Hérouville to the Governor of Normandy; so the old bone-setter took up his residence there.

In those days such places were given to the learned who thus found leisure to carry out their studies, and the maintenance needful to enable them to pursue them. Beauvouloir had for some time longed for this position, for his learning and his wealth had made him many and malignant enemies. Notwithstanding the protection of an illustrious family to whom he had done some service in a doubtful case, he had recently been dragged into a criminal trial; and only the intervention of the Governor, at the Duchess' entreaty, had saved him from prosecution. The Duke had no cause to repent of the public protection he afforded to the leech; Beauvouloir saved the Marquis de Saint-Séver from an illness so dangerous that any other doctor must have failed. But the Duchess' malady dated from too far back to be healed, especially when the wound was reopened daily in her own home. When it was evident that the end was approaching for this angel who had been prepared by so much suffering for a happier life eternal, death was hastened by her gloomy forecast of the future.

"What will become of my poor boy without me?" was the thought that constantly recurred like a bitter draught.

At last, when she was obliged to remain in bed, the Duchess faded rapidly to the tomb, for she was then parted from her boy, who was exiled from her pillow by the agreement to which he owed his life. His grief was as great as his mother's. Inspired by the genius born of suppressed feeling, Étienne devised a highly mystical language by which to communicate with his mother. He studied the use of his voice as the most accomplished singer might have done, and came to sing in mournful accents under the Duchess' window whenever Beauvouloir signaled to him that she was alone. Formerly, in his cradle, he had comforted his mother by his intelligent smiles; and now, a poet, he soothed her by the sweetest melody.

"Those strains give me life!" the Duchess would exclaim to Beauvouloir, breathing in the air that wafted the sounds of Étienne's voice.

At last the day came when the disowned son was plunged into enduring regrets. Many a time already had he discerned a mysterious connection between his feelings and the motions of the surges. The spirit of divination of the impulses of matter which he derived from his studies of the occult sciences, made this phenomenon more cogent to him than to many another. During this evening, when he was called to see his mother for the last time, the ocean was stirred by movements which seemed to him passing strange. There was a convulsion of the waters as though the depths of the sea were in travail; it swelled into mounting waves which died on the strand with dismal sounds like the yelping of dogs in torment.

Étienne even said to himself, "What is it that the sea wants of me? It is tossing and complaining like a living thing. My mother has often told me that the ocean was fearfully convulsed on the night when I was born. What is going to befall me?"

This idea kept him standing at his cottage window, his

eyes alternately fixed on the panes of the room where his mother lay and where a low light flickered, and on the waters which were still breaking.

Suddenly Beauvouloir knocked gently at the door, opened it, and showed a face dark with apprehension.

"Monseigneur," said he, "Madame la Duchesse is in such a sad state that she wishes to see you. Every precaution has been taken to forefend any evil that may await you in the castle; but we must be very prudent; and we shall be obliged to go through the Duke's room, the room you were born in."

At these words Étienne's eyes filled with tears, and he exclaimed:

"The ocean was warning me."

He mechanically allowed himself to be conducted to the door of the turret, up which Bertrand had come on the night that saw the birth of the disinherited child. The man was waiting there, lantern in hand. Étienne went up to the Cardinal d'Hérouville's great library, where he was obliged to wait with Beauvouloir, while Bertrand went to open the doors and reconnoitre as to whether the lad could go through without danger.

The Duke did not wake. As they went forward with stealthy steps, Étienne and the leech could not hear a sound in all the castle but the feeble moans of the dying woman. Thus the same circumstances as had attended the boy's birth recurred at his mother's death; the same storm, the same anguish, the same dread of waking the ruthless giant who was now sleeping soundly. To forefend all risk, the henchman took Étienne up in his arms and carried him through the formidable master's room, prepared to make an excuse of the Duchess' dying state, if he should be detected.

Étienne was keenly alive to the fears confessed by these two faithful servants, but the agitation prepared him in some degree for the scene that met his eyes in this lordly room, where he now found himself for the first time since the day when his father's curse had banished him. On the huge bed, which happiness had never visited, he looked for the loved mother, and could hardly find her, so cruelly was she emaciated. As white as the lace she wore, and with scarce a breath left, she collected her strength to take Étienne's hands, trying to give him her whole soul in one long look, as, long since, Chaverny had bequeathed to her his whole life in one farewell. Beauvouloir and Bertrand, the child and his mother, and the sleeping Duke were all once more together. It was the same place, the same scene, the same actors; but here was funereal woe instead of the joys of motherhood, the night of death instead of the morning of life.

At this instant the hurricane, foretold by the loud rollers of the sea ever since sunset, broke loose.

"Dear flower of my life," said Jeanne de Saint-Savin, kissing her son's forehead, "you came into the world in the midst of a tempest, and in a tempest I am going out of it. Between those two hurricanes all has been storm, save in the hours when I have been with you. And now my last joy is one with my last sorrow. Farewell, sweet image of two souls at last to be united! Farewell, my only, my perfect joy, my best-beloved!"

"Ah, let me die with you!" said Étienne, who had lain down by his mother's side.

"It would be the happier fate," said she as the tears stole down her pale cheeks, for, as of old, she read the future. "No one saw him come?" she anxiously asked the two attendants.

At this moment the Duke turned in his bed. They all trembled.

"There is a taint on even my latest joy," cried the Duchess. "Take him away! take him away!"

"Mother, I would rather see you a few minutes longer and die for it," said the poor boy as he fainted away.

At a sign from the Duchess, Bertrand took Étienne in his arms, and showing him once more to his mother, who embraced him with a last look, he stood ready to carry him away at a sign from the dying woman.

"Love him well," she said to the squire and the leech, "for he has no protectors that I can see, save you and God."

Guided by the unerring instinct of a mother, she had discerned the deep pity felt by Bertrand for this eldest son of the powerful race for which he felt the sort of veneration that Jews devote to the Holy City. As to Beauvouloir, the compact between him and the Duchess was of ancient date.

The two true men, touched at seeing their mistress compelled to bequeath the noble youth to their care, promised by a solemn gesture to be the providence of their young lord, and the mother trusted them implicitly.

The Duchess died in the morning, a few hours later; she was mourned by her remaining servants, who pronounced her only funeral panegyric, saying that she was "a gracious dame come down from Paradise."

Étienne sank into the deepest, the most unbroken grief,— a silent grief. He no longer wandered on the shore; he had no heart to read or sing. He would sit the whole day half hidden in a rocky nook, indifferent to the severity of the weather, motionless, as if glued to the granite like one of the lichens that grew on it. He rarely wept, but was absorbed in a single thought, as deep, as infinite as the ocean; and, like the ocean, that thought would assume a thousand aspects, would be dreadful, tempestuous, or calm. This was something more than sorrow; it was a new life, an inevitable fate that had fallen on this noble being who would never smile again. There are griefs which, like blood dropped into running water, tinge the stream but for a time; the flow renews it and restores its purity. But with Étienne the spring was tainted; each wave of time brought the same embittered draught.

Bertrand, in his advancing years, had remained steward of the stables and stud, so as to retain a post of some authority in the household. His residence was not far from the cottage where Étienne lived in retirement, so he was enabled to watch over him with the unfailing constancy and wily simplicity of affection which are characteristic of old soldiers. To talk to this poor boy he set aside all his roughness; he would go gently in wet weather and rouse him from his sorrowful dreaming, to come home with him. He made it his pride to fill the Duchess' place, at any rate so far as that her son should be equally well cared for, if not equally loved. This compassion was indeed akin to tenderness. Étienne accepted his retainer's devotions without complaint or resistance; but the ties between the outcast child and other human beings were too much broken for any ardent affection to find birth in his heart. He allowed himself to be protected, mechanically, as it were, for he had become a sort of hybrid creature between man and a plant, or perhaps between man and God. To what can a being be likened, to whom social law and the false sentiments of the world were unknown, who, while obeying the instincts of his heart, was yet absolutely innocent?

Still, in spite of his deep melancholy, he presently felt the need for loving. He wanted another mother, another soul one with his; but, cut off as he was from all civilization by a wall of brass, it was unlikely that he should meet any other being so flower-like as himself. By dint of seeking for a second self to whom he might confide his thoughts, whose life he might make his own, he fell into sympathy with the ocean. The sea became to him a living and thinking being. Being constantly familiar with that immense creation, whose occult wonders are so strangely unlike those of the land, he discovered the solution of many mysteries. Intimate from his infancy with the measureless waste of waters, sea and sky told him wondrous tales of poesy.

To him variety was ceaseless in that vast expanse, apparently so monotonous. Like all men in whom the soul overmasters the body, he had a keen eye, and could discern at immense distances and with the greatest ease, without fatigue, the most fugitive effects of light, the most transient play of the waves. Even in a perfect calm he found endless variety of hue in the sea, which, like a woman's countenance, had its expression, smiles, fancies, whims: here green and gloomy, there radiantly blue, its gleaming streaks merging in the doubtful brightness of the horizon, or, again, swelling with soft pulses under golden clouds. He witnessed magnificent spectacles of glorious display at sunset, when the day-star shed its crimson glow over the waves like a mantle of splendor.

To him the sea at midday was cheerful, lively, sparkling, when its ripples reflected the sunshine from their myriad dazzling facets; and spoke to him of fathomless melancholy, making him weep, when in a mood of calm and sorrowful resignation, it repeated a cloud-laden sky. He had mastered the wordless speech of this stupendous creation. Its ebb and flow were like musical breathing; each sob expressed a feeling, he understood its deepest meaning. No mariner, no weather prophet, could foretell more exactly than he the least of Ocean's rages, the faintest change of its surface. By the way the surf died on the beach he could foresee a storm or a squall, and read the distant swell and the force of the tide.

When night spread a veil over the sky, he still saw the sea under the twilight and still could hold converse with it; he lived in its teeming life, he felt the tempest in his soul when it was wroth; he drank in its anger in the piping of the storm, and rushed with the huge breakers that dashed in dripping fringes over the boulders; he then felt himself as terrible and as valiant as the waves, gathering himself up as they did with a tremendous backward sweep; he too could be darkly silent, and imitate its sudden fits of forbearance. In short, he had wedded the sea, it was his confidant and his love. In the morning, when he came out on his rocks, as he wandered over the smooth, glistening sand, he could read the mood of the ocean at a glance; he saw its scenery, and seemed to hover over the broad face of the waters like an angel flown down from heaven. If it lay under shifting, elfin white mists as delicate as the veil over a widow's brow, he would watch their swaying motion with lover-like delight, as much fascinated by finding the sea thus coquetting like a woman aroused but still half asleep, as a husband can be to see his bride beautiful with happiness.

THE HATED SON

His mind, thus united to this great divine mind, comforted him in his loneliness, and the thousand fancies of his brain had peopled his strip of wilderness with sublime images. He had at last read in the motions of the sea all its close connection with the mechanism of the sky, and grasped the harmonious unity of nature, from the blade of grass to the shooting stars, which, like seeds driven by the wind, try to find a resting place in the ether.

Thus, as pure as an angel, untainted by the thoughts that debase men, and as guileless as a child, he lived like a sea-weed, like a flower, expanding only with the treasures of a poetical imagination, of a divine knowledge which he alone gauged in its full extent. It was indeed a singular mixture of two orders of creation! Sometimes he was uplifted to God by prayer; and sometimes came down again, humble and resigned to the tranquil enjoyment of an animal. To him the stars were the flowers of the night, the sun was as a father, the birds were his comrades.

He saw his mother's soul in all things; he often saw her in the clouds; he spoke to her and held communion with her in celestial visions; on certain days he could hear her voice, see her smile; in fact there were times when he had not lost her. God seemed to have endowed him with the powers of the ancient recluses, to have given him exquisite internal senses which could pierce to the heart of things. Some amazing mental power enabled him to see further than other men into the secrets of the immortals. His grief and suffering were as bonds that linked him to the world of spirits, and he fared forth into it, aroused by his love, to seek his mother, thus by a sublime similarity of ecstasy repeating the enterprise of Orpheus. He would project himself into the future, or into the heavens, just as he would fly from his rock from one margin of the horizon to the other.

And often when he lay crouching in some deep cave, fantastically wrought in the granite cliff, with an entrance as small as a burrow, where a softened light prevailed as the warm sunbeams peered in through some cranny hung with dainty seaside mosses, a perfect sea-bird's nest,—often he would suddenly fall asleep. The sun, his master, would remind him of his slumbers by marking off the hours during which he had remained oblivious of the scene,—the sea, the golden sands, and the shelly shore. Then, under a light as glorious as that of heaven, he saw the mighty cities of which his books had told him; he wandered about gazing with surprise, but without envy, at courts and kings, battles, men, and buildings. These dreams in broad daylight made him ever fonder of his gentle flowers, his clouds, his sun, his noble granite cliffs. An angel, as it seemed, to attach him more closely to his solitary life, revealed to him the gulfs of the world of sin, and the dreadful jars of civilized life. He felt that his soul would be rent in the wild ocean of mankind and perish, crushed like a pearl which, in the royal progress of a princess, falls from her coronet into the muddy street.

These dreams in broad daylight, made him ever fonder of his gentle
flowers, his clouds, his sun, his noble granite cliffs

II.

HOW THE SON DIED

In 1617, twenty years or more after the terrible night when Étienne was brought into the world, the Duc d'Hérouville, then seventy-six years old, broken and half dead, was sitting at sunset in a vast armchair by the pointed window of his bedroom, in the very spot where the Countess, by the bugle strain wasted in the air, had vainly called for help on man and God.

He might have been a man disinterred from the grave. His powerful face, bereft of its sinister look by age and suffering, was of a pallor almost matching the long locks of white hair that fell round his bald head with its parchment skull. Warlike fanaticism still gleamed in his tawny eyes, though tempered by a more religious feeling. Devotion had, indeed, lent a monastic cast to the countenance that had of yore been so stern, and it now wore a tinge which softened its expression. The glow of sunset shed a tender red light on the still vigorous features; and the broken frame wrapped in a brown gown, by its heavy attitude and the absence of any movement, gave the finishing touch to the picture of monotonous solitude and dreadful repose in a man formerly so full of life and hatred and activity.

"Enough!" said he to his chaplain.

The venerable old man was reading the Gospel, standing in a respectful attitude before his master. The Duke, like the old lions in a beast-garden who are majestic even in their decrepitude, turned to another gray-haired man, holding out a lean arm sprinkled with hairs and sinewy still, though no longer strong.

"Now it is your turn, bone-setter," said he. "See how we stand to-day."

"All is well with you, monseigneur; the fever is past. You will live many a long year yet."

"I would I could see Maximilien here," replied the Duke, with a smile of satisfaction. "My fine boy! He is in command now of a company of arquebusiers under the King. The Maréchal d'Ancre has been good to the lad, and our gracious Queen Marie is trying to find a worthy match for him now that he has been created Duc de Nivron. So my name will be worthily perpetuated. The boy achieved wonders of valor at the assault——"

At this moment Bertrand came in, holding a letter in his hand.

"What is this?" cried the old lord, hastily.

"A missive brought by a courier from the King," replied the squire.

"The King, and not the Queen Mother?" cried the Duke. "What then is happening? Are the Huguenots in arms again? By God and all his saints!" he added, drawing himself up and looking round at the three old men, "I will have out my armed men again, and with Maximilien at my side, Normandy——"

"Sit down again, dear my lord," said the leech, uneasy at seeing the Duke give way to an outburst so dangerous to a sick man.

"Read it, Maître Corbineau," said the Duke, giving the letter to the confessor.

The four figures made a picture full of lessons to the human race. The squire, the priest, and the leech, white with age, all three standing in front of their lord as he sat in his chair, and stealing timid looks at each other, were all possessed by one of those ideas which come upon a man within an inch of the grave. In the strong light of the setting sun, they formed a group of the highest melancholy and strong in contrasts. And the gloomy, solemn room, where for five and twenty years nothing had been altered, was a fit setting for the romantic picture full of burnt-out passions, shadowed by death, full of religion.

"'The Maréchal d'Ancre has been executed on the Pont du Louvre by the King's orders; and then——' O God!"

"Go on," said the Duke.

"'Monseigneur le Duc de Nivron——'

"Well?"

"'Is dead!'"

The Duke's head fell on his breast, he sighed deeply and spoke not. At this word and this sigh the three old men looked at each other. It was as though the noble and wealthy House of Hérouville were disappearing before their eyes like a foundering vessel.

"The Master above us," the Duke added, with a fierce glance heavenwards, "is but ungrateful to me. He forgets the gallant deeds I have done for His holy cause."

"God is avenged," said the priest, solemnly.

"Take this man to the dungeon!" exclaimed the master.

"You can silence me more easily than you can stifle your conscience."

The Duc d'Hérouville was thinking.

"My house is extinct! My name will die!—I must have a son!" he exclaimed after a long pause.

Frightful as was his expression of despair, the leech could not forbear from smiling.

At that moment a song as clear as the evening air, as pure as the sky, as simple as the hue of ocean, rose above the murmur of the waves as if to charm nature. The sadness of the voice, the melody of the strain, fell like perfume on the spirit. The voice came up in gusts, filled the air, and shed balm on every sorrow, or rather soothed them by giving them utterance. The song mingled so perfectly with the sound of the waves that it seemed to rise from the bosom of the waters.

To these old men it was sweeter than the tenderest vows of love could have been to a girl. It conveyed so much religious hope that it echoed in the heart like a voice coming from heaven.

"What is that?" asked the Duke.

"The nightingale singing," replied Bertrand. "All is not lost either for him or for us."

"What is it that you call a nightingale?"

"It is the name we have given to your eldest son, monseigneur," replied Bertrand.

"My son!" cried the old Duke. "Then I have still a son, something to bear my name and perpetuate it?"

He rose to his feet and began to pace the room, now slowly, now in haste; then by a commanding gesture he dismissed his attendants, retaining the priest.

On the following morning the Duke, leaning on his old squire, made his way along the strand and over the rocks to find the son he once had cursed; he saw him from afar, crouching in a cleft in the granite, basking idly in the sun, his head resting on a tuft of fine grass, his feet curled up in a graceful attitude; Étienne suggested a swallow that has alighted to rest.

As soon as the stately old man made his appearance on the shore, and the sound of his steps, deadened by the sand, was audible, mingling with the dash of the waves, Étienne looked round, and with the cry of a startled bird vanished into the rock itself, like a mouse that bolts so swiftly into its hole that we doubt whether it was there.

"Eh! By God and his saints! where has he hidden himself?" exclaimed the Duke, as he reached the projection under which his son had been crouching.

"In there," said Bertrand, pointing to a narrow rift where the stone was worn and polished by the friction of high tides.

"Étienne, my beloved son!" the old man cried.

But the disowned son made no reply.

During a great part of the morning, the old Duke besought and threatened, entreated and scolded by turns, but without obtaining an answer. Now and again he was silent, applying his ear to the opening, but all his old ears could hear was the deep throbbing of Étienne's heart, of which the wild beating was echoed by the cavern.

THE HATED SON

"He at any rate is alive!" said the old father in a heart-rending tone.

By noon, in sheer despair, he was a suppliant.

"Étienne," he said, "my beloved Étienne, God has punished me for misprizing you! He has snatched your brother from me. You are now my one and only child. I love you better than myself. I recognize my errors: I know that it is my blood that flows in your veins with your mother's, and that her misery was of my making. Come to me, I will try to make you forget your wrongs by loving you for all I have lost. Étienne, you are Duc de Nivron, and after me you will be Duc d'Hérouville, Peer of France, Knight of the French orders and of the Golden Fleece, captain of a hundred men of the guard, Grand Bailli of Bessin, Governor and Vice-regent of Normandy, lord of twenty-seven estates including sixty-nine steeples, and Marquis de Saint-Sever. You may marry a prince's daughter. You will be the head of the House of Hérouville. Do you want me to die of grief? Come to me, come or I stay here on my knees, in front of your hiding place, till I see you. Your old father implores you, and humbles himself before his son as if he were praying to God himself!"

The disowned son did not understand this speech bristling with ideas and vanities of which he knew nothing, he only was aware of a revival in his mind of impressions of invincible terror. He remained speechless in agonies of dread.

Towards evening the old man, having exhausted every resource of language, every form of adjuration, every expression of repentance, was seized by a sort of religious contrition. He knelt down on the sand and made a vow.

"I swear to build a chapel to Saint John and Saint Stephen, the patron saints of my wife and son, and to endow a hundred masses to the Virgin, if God and the saints will give me the love of Monsieur le Duc de Nivron, my son here present!"

There he remained on his knees, in deep humiliation, his hands clasped in prayer. But his child not yet coming forth to him, the hope of his race, tears poured from his long-dry eyes and rolled down his withered cheeks.

Just then Étienne, hearing all silent, crept out of the rift from his grotto like a snake longing for the sunshine; he saw the tears of the broken-hearted old man, recognized a genuine sorrow, took his father's hand and kissed it, saying in angelic accents:

"O Mother, forgive!"

In the fever of gladness the Governor of Normandy took his frail heir in his arms, the lad trembling like a girl carried off by force; and feeling him quake he tried to reassure him, kissing him with as much gentleness as he might have used in handling a flower, and finding for him such sweet words as he had never been wont to speak.

"'Fore God, but you are like my poor Jeanne! Dear child," said he, "tell me all you wish. I will give you your heart's desire. Be strong, be well! I will teach you to ride on a jennet as mild and gentle as yourself. No one shall contradict you. By God and all his saints! everything shall bend to you like reeds before the wind. I give you unlimited power here. I myself will obey you as the head of the family."

The father led his son into the state bedroom where his mother had ended her sad life. Étienne went at once to lean against the window where life had begun for him, whence his mother had been in the habit of signaling to him when the persecutor was absent, who now, he knew not wherefore, had become his slave, and seemed as one of those gigantic beings placed at the command of a young prince by a fairy. That fairy was the feudal feeling.

On seeing once more this gloomy room where his eyes had first learned to contemplate the ocean, tears rose to the youth's eyes; the memories of his long sorrows mingling with the dear remembrance of the joys he had known in the only affection that had ever been granted to him—his mother's love—all fell on his heart at once, and seemed to fill it with a poem that was both terrible and beautiful. The

THE HATED SON

emotions of this lad, accustomed to dwell absorbed in ecstasy, as others are accustomed to give themselves up to worldly excitement, had no resemblance to the feelings of ordinary humanity.

"Will he live?" asked the old man, amazed at his son's fragility; he caught himself holding his breath as he bent over him.

"I can live nowhere but here," replied Étienne, simply, having heard him.

"Then this room is yours, my child,"

"What is happening?" asked young d'Hérouville, as he heard all the dwellers in the castle precincts collecting in the guard-room, whither the Duke had summoned them to present his son to them, never doubting of the result.

"Come," was his father's reply, taking him by the hand and leading him into the great hall.

At that period a duke and peer of such estate as the Duc d'Hérouville, having charges and governments, led the life of a sovereign prince; the younger members of the family were fain to serve under him; he had a household with its officers; the first lieutenant of his company of guards was to him what the aides-de-camp now are to a field marshal. Only a few years later the Cardinal de Richelieu maintained a bodyguard. Several of the princes who were allied to the royal family—the Guises, the Condés, the Nevers, the Vendômes—were attended by pages of the best families, a survival of the extinct chivalry. His vast fortune, and the antiquity of the Norman family to which he belonged, as indicated by his name (*herus villa,* the chief's house), had enabled the Duc d'Hérouville to display no less magnificence than others who were his inferiors, such as the Épernons, the Luynes, the Balagnys, the d'Os, the Zamets, who as yet were but parvenus and nevertheless lived like princes.

The Duke seated himself on a chair, under a *solium* or carved wooden canopy, and raised on a few steps, a sort of throne whence in some provinces certain lords of the soil still pronounced sentence in their jurisdiction, a relic of feudal customs which finally ceased under Richelieu's rule. This sort of judge's bench, resembling the wardens' seats in a church, are now rare objects of curiosity.

When Étienne found himself seated here by his father's side, he shuddered at finding him the centre of all eyes.

"Do not tremble," said the Duke, bending his bald head down to his son's ear, "for all these are our own people."

Through the gloom partly lighted by the setting sun, whose beams reddened the windows of the hall, Étienne could see the bailie, the captains and lieutenants at arms, followed by some of their men, the squires, the almoner, the secretaries, the leech, the house-steward, the ushers, the land-steward, the huntsmen and gamekeepers, the retainers, and the footmen. Although this crowd stood in a respectful attitude, caused by the terror the old Duke had inspired even in the most important personages who dwelt under his command and in his province, there was a dull murmur of wondering curiosity. This whisper weighed on Étienne's heart; this was the first time that he had experienced the effect of the heavy atmosphere breathed in a room full of people, and his senses, accustomed to the pure and wholesome sea air, were nauseated with a suddenness that showed the delicacy of his organization. A terrible palpitation, caused by some structural defect of the heart, shook him with its vehement throbs, when his father, determined to appear as a majestic old lion, spoke the following words in solemn tones:

"My good friends, this is my son Étienne, my eldest born, my heir presumptive, the Duc de Nivron, on whom the King will doubtless devolve the offices of his brother now dead. I have brought him before you that you may acknowledge him and obey him as you would me. And I warn you that if any one among you, or any man in the province over which I rule, shall displease the young Duke or cross his will in anything, it were better for that man, if it should come to my ears, that he had never been born. You have heard. Go your ways to your business, and God be with you.

"Maximilien d'Hérouville will be buried here, as soon

as his body has been brought hither. In eight days the whole household will go into mourning. Later we will do honor to the heir, my son Étienne."

"Long live Monseigneur! Long live the Hérouville!" was shouted in voices that made the walls ring.

The footmen brought torches to light up the hall.

These acclamations, the glare of light, the emotions caused by his father's speech, added to what he already felt, made Étienne turn faint. He fell back on the seat, his girlish hand grasped in his father's broad palm.

As the Duke, who had signed to the lieutenant of his company to come closer, was saying: "I am glad, Baron d'Artagnon, to be able to repair my loss;—come and speak to my son," he felt an ice-cold hand in his own, looked round at the Duc de Nivron, and, thinking him dead, gave a cry of terror that startled all present.

Beauvouloir opened the barrier in front of the dais, took the lad up in his arms, and carried him out, saying to his master:

"You might have killed him by not preparing him for this ceremonial."

"Will he not live to have a son, then?" cried the Duke, who had followed Beauvouloir into the state bedroom where the leech laid the young heir on the bed.

"Well, Maître?" asked the father, anxiously.

"It will be nothing," replied the old man, pointing to Étienne, now reviving under the influence of a cordial administered on a lump of sugar, at that time a new and precious substance sold for its weight in gold.

"Here, you old rascal," said the Duke, offering Beauvouloir his purse; "care for him as for a king's son. If he should die in your hands I would cook you myself on a gridiron——"

"If you persist in being so violent the Duc de Nivron will die by your act," said the leech, bluntly. "Leave him and he will sleep."

"Good-night, my best beloved," said the old man, kissing his son's forehead.

"Good-night, father;" replied the youth, and his voice gave the Duke a thrill as he heard him address him for the first time by the name of father.

The Duke took Beauvouloir by the arm and led him into the next room, where he cornered him in a window-bay, saying:

"Now, old rascal, we will have it out."

This speech, the Duke's favorite jest, made the leech smile; he had long since given up bone-setting.

"That I owe you no grudge you know full well. Twice you brought my poor wife through her troubles, you cured my son Maximilien of a sickness; in short, you are one of the family.—Poor boy! I will avenge him; I will answer for the man who killed him!—The whole future of the House of Hérouville is in your hands. Now we must marry this boy without delay. You alone know whether there is in that poor changeling the stuff of which more Hérouvilles may be made. Do you hear me? What do you think?"

"The life he has led on the seashore has been so chaste and pure that nature is sturdier in him than it would have been if he had lived in your world. But so frail a body is always the slave of the soul. Monseigneur Étienne must select his own wife, for in him all will be the work of nature, not the outcome of your will. He will love guilelessly, and by the prompting of his own heart achieve what you want him to do for your name. Marry your son to a lady of rank who is like a mare and he will flee to hide in the rocks. Nay, more; if a sudden alarm would kill him to a certainty, I believe that sudden joy would be equally fatal. To avert disaster I am of opinion that Étienne must be left to find his own way, at his leisure, in the paths of love. Listen to me, monseigneur: though you are a great and puissant prince, you know nothing about these matters. Grant me your entire and unlimited confidence and you shall have a grandson."

"If I have a grandson, by whatever conjuring trick you please, I will get you a patent of nobility. Yes, hard as it may be, from an old rascal you shall be turned into a gentleman, you shall be Beauvouloir Baron de Forcalier. Work it by green or dry, by black magic or white, by masses in church or a meeting at a witches' Sabbath, so long as I have a male descendant all will be well."

"I know of a wizard's meeting that might spoil everything, and that, monseigneur, is you yourself. I know you. To-day you wish for a male grandchild at any cost; to-morrow you will insist on arranging the conditions of the bargain; you will torment your son——"

"God forbid!"

"Well, then, set out for the Court where the Marshal's death and the King's emancipation must have turned everything upside down, and where you must have some business to attend to, were it only to get the Marshal's baton which was promised to you. Leave Monseigneur Étienne to me. But pledge me your honor as a gentleman to approve whatever I do."

The Duke grasped the old man's hand in token of entire confidence and retired to his room.

When the days of a high and puissant noble are in the balance, the leech is an important person in the household, so we need not be surprised at finding an old bone-setter on such familiar terms with the Duc d'Hérouville. Irrespective of the illegitimate relationship which tied him through marriage to this lordly house, and which told in his favor, the learned leech had so often shown his good sense to the Duke's advantage, that he was one of his favorite advisers. Beauvouloir was the Coyctier of this Louis XI.

Still, valuable as was his scientific knowledge, the physician had not so much influence as the old feudal traditions over the Governor of Normandy, still fired with the ferocious passions of religious war. And the faithful servant had understood that the prejudices of a noble would interfere with the father's hopes. Being, in truth, a very learned leech, Beauvouloir felt that for a being so delicately organized as Étienne, marriage ought to be gentle and gradual inspiration which might infuse fresh vigor into him by firing him with the glow of love. As he had said, to insist on any particular woman would be to kill the youth. Above all things to be avoided was frightening the young recluse by the idea of marriage, of which he knew nothing, or by letting him see the end his father had in view. This unconscious poet could know none but such a noble passion as Petrarch's for Laura, as Dante's for Beatrice. Like his mother he was all pure love, all soul; he must have the opportunity of loving placed in his way, and then all must be left to the event. It would not do to command him; an order would seal the springs of life.

Master Antoine Beauvouloir had a child, a daughter, brought up in a way that made her the wife for Étienne. It had been so impossible to foresee the occurrences by which this youth, destined by his father to be a cardinal, had become heir presumptive to the dukedom of Hérouville, that Beauvouloir had never observed the similarity of circumstances in the lives of Étienne and Gabrielle. It was a sudden idea suggested rather by his affection for the two children than by any ambition.

In spite of his skill his wife had died in giving birth to this daughter, who was so delicate that he feared the mother had bequeathed to her child the germs of early death. Beauvouloir adored his Gabrielle as all old men adore an only child. His skill and ceaseless care lent the fragile creature an artificial life; for he cherished her as a gardener nurses an exotic plant. He had kept her from all eyes on his little estate of Forcalier, where she was sheltered from the troubles of the times by the universal good will felt for a man to whom every one about him owed some debt of kindness, while his scientific power commanded a sort of awed respect. By attaching himself to the Hérouville household, he had increased the immunities he enjoyed in the province, and had balked the hostilities of his enemies by his important position as medical attendant to the Governor: but on coming to the castle he had taken care not to bring with him the flower he kept hidden at Forcalier,—an estate of more value from the lands it comprised than from the mansion that stood on it, and on which he founded his hopes of settling his daughter in a manner suited to his views for her.

When promising the Duke a grandson, and exacting his promise to approve of any measure, he suddenly thought of Gabrielle, the gentle girl whose mother had been as completely forgotten by the Duke as his son Étienne had been. He waited till his master had left to put his plan into practice, being aware that, if it should come to the Duke's knowledge, the enormous difficulties which a favorable issue would nullify, would by anticipation prove insuperable.

Beauvouloir's house faced the south, standing on the slope of one of the pleasant hills that enclose the vales of Normandy; a thick wood sheltered it on the north; high walls and clipped hedges and deep ditches enclosed it in impenetrable seclusion. The garden was laid out in terraces down to the river which watered the meadows at the bottom, where a high bank between shrubs made a natural dyke. These hedges screened a covered walk, winding with the windings of the stream, and as deeply buried as a forest path in willows, beeches, and oaks.

From the house to this embankment stretched the rich verdure native to the district, a slope shaded by a grove of foreign trees whose mingled hues made a richly varied background of color: here the silvery tones of a pine stood out against the darker green of elms; there a slim poplar lifted its waving spire in front of a group of old oaks; farther down weeping-willows drooped in pale tresses between burly walnut trees. This copse now afforded shade at all times on the way down from the house to the river path.

In front of the house a terrace walk spread a yellow band of gravel, and it was shadowed by a wooden veranda overgrown with creepers, which, by the month of May, were covered with blossoms up to the first-floor windows.

The garden, though not extensive, was made to seem so by the way it was planned; and points of view, cleverly contrived from the knolls, overlooked the valley where the eye might wander at will. Thus, as instinctive fancy led her, Gabrielle could either retire into the solitude of a sheltered spot where nothing was to be seen but the close grass, and the blue sky between the tree-tops, or gaze far into the distance, her eye following the shading of green hills from the vivid hue of the foreground to the pure depths of the horizon, where they faded into the blue ocean of air, or mingled with the mountain clouds that floated over them.

Tended by her grandmother, and served by her foster-mother, Gabrielle Beauvouloir never left her modest home but to go to the church of which the belfry crowned the hill, and whither she was always escorted by her grandmother, her nurse, and her father's man-servant. Thus she had grown up to the age of seventeen in the sweet ignorance which the scarcity of books made possible, without its seeming extraordinary in a time when a woman of learning was a rare phenomenon. Her home had been like a convent, with added liberty, and without compulsory prayer, where she had dwelt under the eye of a pious woman and the protection of her father, the only man of her acquaintance.

This utter solitude, required in her infancy by her fragile constitution, had been carefully maintained by Beauvouloir. As Gabrielle grew up, indeed, her frail youth was strengthened by the care that was lavished on her and the pure air she breathed. Still, the experienced leech could not fail to mark how the pearly hues about his daughter's eyes would alter, darken, or redden with every emotion; here frailty of body and activity of soul were indicated by signs which long experience enabled him to read; also Gabrielle's heavenly beauty gave him cause for dreading the deeds of violence that were only too common in those times of rebellion and warfare. Thus many reasons had concurred to induce the good man to thicken the shadows and insist on solitude for his daughter, whose sensitive nature was also a cause for alarm; a passion, an abduction, an attack of any kind, would be her death.

Though his child rarely needed reproof, a word of blame crushed her; she brooded over it, it sank into her heart and gave rise to pondering melancholy; she would retire to weep, and weep for long. Thus her moral training had needed as much tender care as her physical training. The old leech dared not tell her the tales which commonly enchant children; they agitated her too deeply. So the father, who by long practice had learned so many things, had been careful to develop his daughter's frame that the body might dull the shocks inflicted by so active a spirit. Gabrielle was his life, his love, his sole desire, and he never hesitated to procure everything that might contribute to the desired end. He kept her from books, pictures, music, every creation of art that could excite her brain. With his mother's help he interested Gabrielle in manual occupations. Tapestry, sewing, and lace-making, the care of flowers, the duties of a housewife, the fruit harvest,—in short, all the most homely tasks of life were the lovely child's daily fare. Beauvouloir bought her pretty spinning-wheels, handsomely inlaid chests, rich carpets, Bernard Palissy's pottery, tables, prie-dieus and chairs finely carved and covered with costly stuffs, embroidered linen, and jewels. With the subtle instinct of a father the old man always chose his gifts from such things as were decorated in the fanciful taste known as Arabesque, which, as it appeals neither to the emotions nor the senses, speaks only to the mind by its purely imaginative inventions.

And so, strangely enough, the life to which a father's hatred had condemned Étienne d'Hérouville, a father's love had provided for Gabrielle. In both the children the soul was like to destroy the body; and, but for the complete solitude that fate had contrived for one, and science had created for the other, both might have succumbed—he to fears, and she to the tide of a too ardent passion of love. But, unfortunately, Gabrielle was not born in a land of heath and moor, amid the sterner aspects of grudging nature, such as the

greatest painters always depict as the background for their
Virgins; she dwelt in a rich and fertile valley. Beauvouloir
could not frustrate the charms of the natural groves, the
happy arrangement of the flower-beds, the cool depth of the
grassy carpet, the love revealed in the twining and climbing
plants.

These living poems have a language of their own, felt
rather than understood by Gabrielle, who would abandon
herself to vague dreams under the leafy shade; and through
the misty ideas which came to her in her admiration of a
cloudless sky, her long study of a landscape, seen under every
aspect lent it by the changing seasons and the variations of
a sea-born atmosphere, where the fogs of England died away
into the bright daylight of France, a distant light dawned on
her mind, the aurora of a day that pierced the darkness in
which her father kept her.

Nor had Beauvouloir been able to exclude Gabrielle from
the influence of divine love; she added to her admiration of
nature adoration of the Creator; she had indeed rushed into
this first outlet afforded to womanly emotions; she truly
loved God, she loved Jesus, the Virgin and the saints; she
loved the Church and its splendor; she was a Catholic after
the pattern of Sainte Theresa, who found in the Saviour
an unfailing spouse, a perpetual marriage. But Gabrielle
accepted this passion of lofty souls with a pathetic simplicity
that might have disarmed the most brutal seducer by the
innocence of its utterance.

Whither would this blameless ignorance lead her? How
was enlightenment to be brought to an intelligence as pure
as the calm waters of a lake that has never mirrored aught
but the blue sky? What image would be stamped on that
fair canvas? Round what tree would the snowy bell-flowers
of that convolvulus open?

The father never asked himself these questions without
an inward shudder.

At this moment the good old man was making his way
homeward on his mule, as slowly as though he would fain

spin out to all eternity the road leading from the Castle of Hérouville to Ourscamp, the village near which lay his estate of Forcalier. His unbounded love for his daughter had led him to conceive of a bold scheme indeed. But one man in the world could make her happy, and that was Étienne. Certainly the angelic son of Jeanne de Saint-Savin and the guileless daughter of Gertrude Marana were twin souls. Any other wife than Gabrielle would terrify and kill the heir presumptive to the dukedom, just as it seemed to Beauvouloir that Gabrielle must die in the arms of any man whose feelings and manners had not the virginal gentleness of Étienne's.

The poor leech had never till now thought of such a thing; fate had plotted and commanded this union. But yet, in the time of Louis XIII. who would dare to marry the son of the Duc d'Hérouville to the daughter of a Normandy bone-setter? Nevertheless from this union alone could the posterity proceed on which the old Duke was so firmly bent. Nature had destined these two lovely creatures for each other, God had brought them half-way by an extraordinary chain of events, and yet human notions and laws set between them an impassable gulf. Although the old man believed that he herein saw the hand of God, in spite, too, of the promise he had extracted from the Duke, he was in the grip of such extreme alarm as he thought of the violence of that ungoverned temper, that he paused as he came to the top of the hill opposite to that of Ourscamp, whence he saw the smoke rising from his own roof between the trees of his orchard. What decided him was his relationship, though illegitimate, a circumstance that might have some influence over his master's mind. And then, having made up his mind, Beauvouloir put his trust in the chances of life; the Duke might die before the marriage; and besides there were precedents: Françoise Mignot, a Dauphiné peasant girl, had lately married the Maréchal de l'Hôpital; the son of the Constable Anne de Montmorency had wedded Diane, the daughter of Henri II. and a Piémontese lady name Philippa Duc.

While he was thus deliberating, his fatherly affection weighing all the probabilities and calculations, the chances for good or evil, and trying to read the future by studying its factors, Gabrielle was in the garden choosing flowers wherewith to fill a vase made by the illustrious potter who did with his glazed clay what Benvenuto Cellini did with metals. Gabrielle had set this jar, decorated with animals in relief, on a table in the middle of the sitting-room, and was arranging the flowers partly to please her grandmother, but partly perhaps as a means of expressing her thoughts.

The tall earthenware vase of Limoges ware, as it was called, was filled and standing finished on the handsome table-cover, and Gabrielle had exclaimed to her grandmother, "There, look——" when Beauvouloir came in.

The girl rushed into her father's arms. After the first effusions Gabrielle wanted the old man to admire the posy and as he looked at it the leech turned a searching gaze on his daughter, making her blush.

"It is high time," said he to himself, understanding the eloquence of these flowers, each of which had certainly been chosen for its form and color, so perfectly was it placed to produce a magical effect in the nosegay.

Gabrielle remained standing, unheeding the spray she had begun in her embroidery. As he looked at his daughter, a tear gathered in Beauvouloir's eye, and gliding down his cheeks, which were a little drawn by a grave expression, fell on to his shirt pulled out in front, in the fashion of the time, between the points of his jerkin above his trunk hose. He tossed off his felt hat with its shabby red feather, to pass his hand over his polished crown.

As he glanced once more at the girl who here—under the dark beams of this room hung with leather and furnished in ebony, with heavy silk curtains, a lofty chimney-place, in a pleasant diffused light—was still all his own, the poor father felt the tears rising and wiped them away. A father who loves his child always longs to keep it young, and the man who can see his daughter pass into the power of a husband without acute grief does not rise superior to higher worlds, but sinks to the meanest depths.

"What ails you, son?" asked his old mother, taking off her spectacles, and seeking in the good man's attitude the reason of a silence that puzzled her in one usually so cheerful.

The physician pointed to his daughter, and the old woman, following the direction of his finger, nodded, as much as to say, "She is a sweet creature."

Who could have failed to enter into Beauvouloir's feelings on seeing the maiden as she appeared in the costume of that time and under the clear sky of Normandy? Gabrielle wore the bodice, open with a point in front and square behind, in which the Italian painters generally dressed their saints and madonnas. This elegant bodice, of sky-blue velvet, as sheeny as that of a dragon-fly, fitted her closely, clasping her figure so as to show off the finely modeled form which it seemed to compress; it showed the mould of her shoulders, back, and waist, as exactly as if designed by the most accomplished artist, and was finished round the throat with an oval slope edged with light embroidery in fawn-colored silk, showing enough to reveal the beauty of her shape, but not enough to suggest desire. A skirt of fawn-colored stuff that continued the flow of the lines presented by the velvet bodice, fell to her feet in narrow, flattened pleats.

Gabrielle was so slender that she looked tall. Her thin arm hung by her side with the inertia that deep meditation imparts to the limbs; and standing thus she was the living model of those artless-looking masterpieces of sculpture which were then appreciated, and which commend themselves to our admiration by the grace of long lines, straight without stiffness, and a firmness of outline that is never lifeless.

No swallow skimming past the window at dusk could show a more delicately marked shape. Her features were small but not mean; her brow and throat were marbled with fine blue veins, tinting the skin like agate and betraying the delicacy of a complexion so transparent that you might have fancied you saw the blood flowing within. This extreme fairness was faintly tinged with pink in the cheeks. Her hair, covered with a little blue velvet bonnet embroidered with pearls, lay on her temples like two streams of beaten gold, and played in curls above her shoulders, but did not cover them. The warm tones of this silken hair showed off the brilliant whiteness of her neck, and by its reflection gave added exquisiteness to the pure form of her face. The eyes, rather long and half-shut between somewhat heavy eyelids, were in harmony with the daintiness of her features and figure; their pearly gray was bright but not vivid; innocence veiled passion.

The thin nose would have seemed as cold as a steel blade but for the rosy, velvety nostrils, so expressive as to be out of harmony with the purity of a dreamy brow, often startled and sometimes mirthful, always serenely lofty. Finally, a pretty little ear attracted the eye, by showing beneath the cap between two locks of hair, a ruby earring in bright contrast with her milky white throat. Hers was not the beauty of the Normandy woman, buxom and stout, nor the beauty of the south, in which passion lends nobility to matter, nor the essentially French beauty that is as fugitive as its expression, nor the cold and melancholy beauty of the north; it was the deep seraphic beauty of the Catholic Church, at once pliant and firm, severe and tender.

"Where could you see a prettier duchess?" said Beauvouloir to himself, as he looked with delight at Gabrielle, who, as she stood leaning forward a little, her neck bent to watch the flight of a bird outside, could only be compared to a gazelle pausing to listen to the murmur of the stream at which it is about to slake its thirst.

"Come and perch here," said Beauvouloir, slapping his leg, and giving the girl a look that promised some confidential speech.

Gabrielle understood and obeyed. She lightly seated herself on her father's knee, and put her arms round his neck, crumpling his ruff a good deal.

"Now, of whom were you thinking when you were plucking those flowers? You never made a finer posy."

"Oh, of many things," said she. "As I admired those

flowers, which seem to be made for us, I wondered for whom we are made,—we human creatures; who the beings are that look at us. You are my father, so I can tell you all I think, and you are so wise that you can explain everything. I feel within me a force, as it would seem, that wants to exert itself; I am struggling with something. When the sky is gray I am almost happy; I am melancholy, but calm. But when the day is fine, and the flowers are sweet, and I am sitting out there on my bench under the honeysuckle and jasmine, I feel as if there were waves inside me surging up against my stillness. Ideas come into my head that seem to hit me and fly away, as the birds fly in the evening; I cannot catch them. Well, and when I have made a posy in which the colors are arranged as they are in tapestry, red against white, and brown mingling with green, when it is full of life and the air blows through it, and the flowers nod, and there is a medley of scents and a tangle of bloom, I fancy I see what is going on in my own mind, and I feel happy. And in church, when the organ sounds and the priest responds, and two distinct strains answer each other, the human voices and the organ, then again I am happy; the harmony rings through my heart; I pray with a warmth that stirs my blood."

As he listened to his daughter, Beauvouloir studied her with a sagacious eye; his gaze looked dull from the sheer force of thought, as the smooth curl of a waterfall seems motionless. He lifted the veil of flesh which hid the secret springs by which the spirit acts on the body; he was watching the various symptoms, which long experience had shown him in all the patients committed to his care, and comparing them with symptoms discernible in that frail form, was half alarmed by the delicate structure of those small bones, and the insubstantiality of the milk-white skin; he tried to bring the teaching of science to bear on the future of this seraphic creature, and he felt giddy at finding himself, as it were, on the edge of a gulf. Gabrielle's too thrilling voice, her too graceful form, made him anxious; and, after questioning her, he questioned himself.

"You are not happy here!" he exclaimed at last, prompted by a crowning idea in conclusion of his meditations.

She faintly bowed her head.

"Then God be with us! I will take you to the Château d'Hérouville," he said with a sigh. "There you can have seabaths, which will strengthen you."

"Do you mean it, father? You are not laughing at your Gabrielle? I have so longed for the castle and the men-at-arms and the captains and monseigneur."

"Yes, my child; your nurse and Jean can accompany you."

"And very soon?"

"To-morrow," said the old man, rushing out into the garden to hide his agitation from his mother and his daughter.

"God is my witness," cried he, "that it is not ambition that prompts this step. My child to save, poor little Étienne to be made happy,—these are my sole motives."

But while he thus questioned himself, he felt in the depths of his conscience an irrepressible satisfaction at the thought that if his plan should succeed, Gabrielle would one day be Duchesse d'Hérouville. There is always the man in the father.

He walked about for a long time, went in to supper, and all the evening rejoiced in contemplating his daughter amid the soft and sober poetry with which he had surrounded her.

When, before going to bed, the grandmother, the nurse, the leech, and Gabrielle knelt down to pray together, he said: "Let us beseech the Lord for His blessing on my plans."

His old mother, who knew what he proposed to do, felt her eyes fill with her few remaining tears. Gabrielle, purely curious, flushed with delight. The father quaked; he feared some disaster.

"After all," said his mother, "do not be so alarmed, Antoine. The Duke will not kill his granddaughter."

"No," replied he, "but he may compel her to marry some ruffianly baron who will destroy her."

THE HATED SON

Next day Gabrielle, mounted on an ass, followed by her nurse on foot and her father riding a mule, and the man leading the two horses loaded with their baggage, set out for the Castle d'Hérouville, which the cavalcade reached only at dusk. To keep the journey a secret Beauvouloir had taken cross roads, starting early in the morning, and he had carried provisions so as to take a meal on the way without being seen at the inns. Thus, without being seen by any of the Duke's people, he went in by night to the house which the disowned son had so long inhabited, and where Bertrand was awaiting him,—the only person he had taken into his confidence.

The old squire helped the leech, the nurse, and the man to unload the horses, carry in the baggage, and settle Beauvouloir's daughter in Étienne's dwelling. When Bertrand saw Gabrielle he stood quite amazed.

"I could fancy it was her mother!" cried he. "She is as slight and fragile as she was; she has the same fair skin and golden hair; the old Duke will love her."

"God grant it!" said Beauvouloir. "But will he confess to his own blood mingled with mine?"

"He cannot disown it," said Bertrand. "Many a time have I waited for him at the door of the Belle Romaine, who lived in the Rue Culture-Sainte Catherine. The Cardinal de Lorraine was obliged to leave her to monseigneur for shame at having been so roughly handled as he came out of her house.

"Monseigneur, who at that time was not much past twenty, must remember that ambush well. He was a bold youth already, and I may say now that he was the leader of the assault."

"He has forgotten all that," said Beauvouloir. "He knows that my wife is dead, but he scarcely remembers that I have a daughter."

"Oh! two old shipmates, as we are, can steer the boat into port," said Bertrand. "And, after all if he is angry and is revenged on our carcasses, they have served their time."

Before his departure the Duc d'Hérouville had forbidden everybody attached to the castle, under heavy penalties, to go down to the shore where Étienne had hitherto passed his life unless the Duc de Nivron himself should desire their company. These orders, suggested by Beauvouloir, who had argued that it was necessary to leave Étienne free to indulge his old habits, secured to Gabrielle and her nurse the absolute privacy of the precincts whence the leech forbade them wander without his permission.

During these two days Étienne had kept his room, the great state room, lingering over the charms of his melancholy reminiscences.

That bed had been his mother's; close to where he stood she had gone through that terrible scene attending his birth when Beauvouloir had saved two lives. She had breathed her woes to this furniture, it was she who had used it, her eyes had often gazed upon those panels; and how often had she come to this window to call or signal to her poor boy, now the absolute master of the castle.

Alone in this room, whither he had last come by stealth, brought by Beauvouloir to kiss his dying mother for the last time, he now brought her to life again, spoke to her, listened to her; he would drink deep of the spring that never runs dry, whence so many songs flow that echo *Super flumina Babylonis*.

On the day after his return Beauvouloir waited on his young master, and gently reproved him for having stayed in the room without going out of it, pointing out to him that it would not do to give up his open-air life and become a prisoner.

"This room is spacious," said the youth; "and here my mother's soul dwells."

However, the leech, by the kindly influence of affection, persuaded Étienne to promise to walk out every day, either on the seashore, or inland through the country, as yet quite unknown to him. Étienne, notwithstanding, still given up to his remembrances, stood at his window all the next day looking out at the sea; it appeared under such various aspects that he fancied he had never seen it so lovely. He varied his contemplation by reading Petrarch, one of his favorite authors, whose poetry went straight to his heart as a monument of constant and single-hearted love. Étienne felt that he had in himself no power for many passions; he could love but once, and in but one way. Though that love would be deep, like all that is unmingled, it would also be calm in its expression, as suave and pure as the Italian poet's sonnets.

As the sun set, this child of solitude began to sing in that marvelous voice which had fallen as a harbinger of hope on ears so insensible to music as those of his father. He gave utterance to his melancholy by variations on an air which he repeated again and again, like the nightingale. This air, ascribed to the late King Henri IV., was not the famous *"Air de Gabrielle"* but one very superior to that in construction; and as a melody as well as an expression of feeling, admirers of Old World compositions will recognize it by the words, also written by the great king. The tune had probably been a reminiscence of those that lulled his childhood in the mountains of Béarn.

> "Viens, Aurore,
> Je t'implore,
> Je suis gai quand je te vois;
> La Bergère
> Qui m'est chère
> Est vermeille comme toi.
> De rosée
> Arrosée,
> La rose a moins de fraîcheur;
> Une hermine
> Est moins fine;
> Le lys a moins de blancheur."

After having thus artlessly expressed his feelings in song, Étienne looked out at the sea and said:

"There is my betrothed—my one and only love."

And again he sang these lines of the ballad:

> "Elle est blonde
> Sans seconde!"

And repeated it as uttering the poetical urgency which rises up in a timid youth, bold only when he is alone. This surging song, with its breaks and its fresh outbursts, interrupted and begun again, till at length it died in a last falling note that grew fainter like the vibrations of a bell, was full of dreams.

At that instant a voice he felt inclined to attribute to some siren risen from the waves, a woman's voice, repeated the air he had just sung, but with the hesitancy natural to a person to whom the power of music is revealed for the first time; he discerned it in the uncertain language of a heart just awakening to the poetry of harmony. Étienne, who by long exercise of his own voice had learned the language of song, in which the soul finds as many means of utterance for its thoughts as it does in speech, could divine all the shy surprise that was revealed in this attempt.

With what religious and mysterious admiration did he listen! The stillness of the evening allowed him to catch every sound, and he thrilled as he heard the rustle of a long trailing dress; he was astonished to perceive in himself—accustomed as he was to surprises of terror that brought him within an inch of death—the sense of balm to his soul which of old had come to him at the approach of his mother.

"Come, Gabrielle, my child," said Beauvouloir's voice. "I have forbidden you to stay out on the shore after sunset. Go in, my girl."

"Gabrielle!" thought Étienne. "What a pretty name!"

Beauvouloir presently appeared on the scene, and roused his master from one of those meditations which are as deep as a dream.

It was quite dark, but the moon was rising.

"Monseigneur," said the old man, "you have not been out to-day. That is not right."

"And I—may I go out on the shore after sunset?" asked Étienne.

The implication conveyed in the question, a first semblance of desire, made the leech smile.

"You have a daughter, Beauvouloir?"

"Yes, my lord, the child of my old age, my beloved little girl. Monseigneur the Duke, your noble father, gave me such strict injunctions to watch over your precious life that, as I could no longer go to Forcalier to see her, I have brought her away, to my great regret; and to conceal her from all eyes I have placed her in the house where your lordship used to live. She is so fragile that I fear every shock, even too strong an emotion; and I have not allowed her to learn anything, she would have killed herself."

"Then she knows nothing?" asked Étienne, surprised.

"She has all the skill of a good housewife; but she has grown up as the plants grow. Ignorance, monseigneur, is a thing as sacred as science. Knowledge and ignorance are two distinct conditions of being; each enwraps the soul as in a winding-sheet. Learning has enabled you to live; ignorance has saved my daughter. The best hidden pearls escape the diver's eye and live happy. I may compare my Gabrielle to a pearl; her complexion has its sheen, her soul is as pure, and till now, my home at Forcalier has been her shell."

"Come with me," said Étienne, wrapping a cloak about him. "I will walk by the sea; the night is soft."

Beauvouloir and his young master walked on in silence to a spot where a beam of light from between the shutters of the fisherman's house shed a path of gold across the sea.

"I cannot express the feelings produced in me by the sight of a ray cast out across the waters," said the bashful youth to the leech. "I have so often watched the window of that room, till the light was extinguished;" and he pointed to the room that had been his mother's.

"Though Gabrielle is so delicate," said Beauvouloir, cheerfully, "it will not hurt her to walk with us; the night is hot and there is no mist in the air. I will go to fetch her. But be careful, monseigneur."

Étienne was too shy to offer to go into the house with Beauvouloir; besides, he was in the stunned condition into which we are thrown by the high tide of ideas and feelings produced by the dawn of passion.

Feeling more free when he found himself alone, as he looked at the moonlit sea he exclaimed:

"The ocean must have passed into my soul!"

The sight of the graceful living statuette that now came out to meet him, silvery in the enveloping moonbeams, increased the beating of Étienne's heart, but yet it was not painful.

"My child," said Beauvouloir, "this is my lord the Duke."

At this instant Étienne longed to be a colossus like his father, he would have rejoiced in seeming strong instead of frail. Every vanity natural to a man and a lover pierced his heart like arrows, and he stood in distressed silence, conscious for the first time of his imperfections.

Embarrassed by her courtesy, he bowed awkwardly in return, and remained close to Beauvouloir, with whom he conversed as they walked along the shore; but Gabrielle's respectful and timid manner gave him courage, and he ventured to address her.

The incident of the song was purely accidental: the leech had prepared nothing; he had believed that in two beings whose hearts had been kept pure by solitude, love would arise with perfect simplicity. Thus Gabrielle's repetition of the strain was a ready-made subject of conversation.

During this walk Étienne was aware of that physical lightness which every man has experienced at the moment when first love transfers the very element of his life into another being. He offered to teach Gabrielle to sing. The poor boy was so happy to be able to show himself superior in any respect, in the eyes of this young girl, that he trembled with joy when she accepted.

At that moment the moonlight fell full on Gabrielle, and allowed Étienne to see certain vague points of resemblance between her and his dead mother. Like Jeanne de Saint-

Savin, Beauvouloir's daughter was slender and delicate; in her, as in the Duchess, suffering and disappointment produced a mysterious grace. She had the dignity particular to those on whom the customs of the world have had no effect, in whom everything is pleasing because everything is natural. But besides this, there was in Gabrielle the blood of the beautiful Italian revived in the third generation, and giving the child the vehement passions of a courtesan in a pure soul; hence an inspired look that fired her eyes, that sanctified her brow, that made her radiate light, as it were, and gave her movements the sparkle of living flame.

Beauvouloir was startled as he noted this, which nowadays might be called the phosphorescence of the mind; the leech regarded it as a forecast of death.

Étienne happened to turn as the girl was craning her neck, like a shy bird peeping out of its nest. Screened by her father, Gabrielle was able to study Étienne at her ease, and her expression was as much of curiosity as of pleasure, of kindliness as of artless boldness. Étienne did not strike her as sickly, only as delicate. She thought him so like herself that there was nothing to frighten her in this lord and master. Étienne's pallid face, his fine hands, his feeble smile, his hair parted into two flat bands ending in curls that fell over his lace ruff, the noble brow lined with youthful sorrow,—all this contrast of luxury and sadness and power and weakness charmed her; for did it not smile on the instinct of motherly protection which lies in the germ in love? Did it not stimulate the need that every woman feels to find something unlike the common herd in the man she means to love?

In both of them new thoughts and new sensations rose up with a vigor and fulness that expanded the soul. They both stood surprised and speechless, for the utterance of a feeling is the less demonstrative in proportion to its depth. Every lasting affection begins in dreamy meditation. It was well, perhaps, that these two should meet for the first time under the mild light of the moon so as not to be too suddenly dazzled by the glories of love; and it was fitting that they should see each other on the margin of the sea, which was the image of the immensity of their feelings. They parted full of each other, each fearing that the other had not been satisfied.

From his high window Étienne looked down on the light in the house that held Gabrielle. During that hour of hope mingled with fear, the young poet found new meaning in Petrarca's sonnets. He had seen a Laura—an exquisite and delightful creature, as pure and golden as a sunbeam, as intelligent as the angels, as dependent as a woman. A clue was supplied to his studies for twenty years, he understood the mystical connection of every kind of beauty; he discerned how much of woman there was in the poetry he delighted in; in fact, he had so long been in love without knowing it, that the past was all merged in the agitations of that lovely night. Gabrielle's likeness to his mother he thought a divine dispensation. His love was no treason to his grief; this love was a continuance of motherhood. He could think of the girl lying under the cottage roof with the same feelings as his mother had known when he was sleeping there.

Nay, the resemblance was a fresh link between the present and the past. The mournful countenance of Jeanne de Saint-Savin rose before him against the cloudy background of memory; he saw her faint smile, he heard her gentle voice, and he bowed his head and wept.

The light in the house below was extinguished. Étienne sang the little ballad of Henri IV. with fresh expression, and from afar Gabrielle's attempts echoed the song. The girl, too, was making her first excursion into the enchanted realm of ecstatic love. This answer filled Étienne's heart with joy; the blood that flowed through his veins lent him such strength as he had never before known; love gave him vigor. Only feeble beings can conceive of the joy of this regeneration in the midst of life. The poor, the suffering, the ill-used, have ineffable moments; so little makes the whole world to them. And Étienne was related by a thousand traits to the Folk of the Dolorous City. His recent aggrandizement caused him nothing but fear, and love was bestowing the invigorating balm of strength; he was in love with love.

Étienne was up betimes in the morning to fly to his old home, where Gabrielle, prompted by curiosity and an eagerness she would not confess to herself, had already dressed her hair and put on her pretty costume. Both were possessed by the wish to meet again; both equally dreaded the outcome of the interview. He, for his part, you may be sure, had chosen his finest lace, his richest wrought cloak, his violet velvet trunks; in fact, he was dressed in the handsome fashion which appeals to our memory when we think of Louis XIII.,—a person as much oppressed in the midst of splendor as Étienne had hitherto been. Nor was their attire the sole point of resemblance between the sovereign and his subject. In Étienne, as in Louis XIII., many sensitive emotions met in contrast: chastity, melancholy, vague but very real suffering, a chivalrous bashfulness, a fear of failing to express sentiments in their purity, a dread of being too suddenly hurried into the joys which noble souls prefer to postpone, the burdensome sense of power, and the instinctive bent towards obedience which is characteristic of those who are indifferent to mere interest, but full of love for all that a great genius has designated as *Astral*.

Though she had indeed no knowledge of the world, it had occurred to Gabrielle that the daughter of a bone-setter, the humble owner of Forcalier, was too far beneath Monseigneur Étienne, Duc de Nivron, heir to the House of Hérouville, for them to be on equal terms; she never thought of the elevating power of love. The girl was too guileless to think of this as an opportunity for aiming at a position in which any other damsel would have been eager to place herself; she had seen nothing but the obstacles.

Loving already, without knowing what love was, she saw her happiness far away and wished to reach it only as a child longs for the golden grapes that it covets but that hang too high. To a girl that could be moved to tears at the sight of a flower and be aware of love in the chants of the liturgy, how deep and strong were the emotions of the past day at the sight of the weakness of her lord, bringing comfort to her own. But Étienne had grown in her mind during the night, she had made him her hope, her strength; she had set him so high that she despaired of reaching up to him.

"Have I your permission to call on you sometimes, to intrude on your domain?" asked the Duke, looking down.

As she saw Étienne so humble, so timid,—for he, on his part, had deified Beauvouloir's daughter,—Gabrielle felt the sceptre he had given her an embarrassment. Still she was immensely flattered and touched by this homage. Women alone know how infinitely bewitching is the respect shown to them by a master. But she feared to deceive herself and, quite as curious as the first woman of them all, she pined to *know*.

"Did you not promise yesterday that you would teach me music?" she replied, hoping that music might afford a pretext for their being together.

If the poor child had but known how Étienne lived, she would have been careful to suggest no doubt. To him speech was the direct expression of the mind, and these words pained him deeply. He had come with a full heart, fearing even a dimness in the light, and he was met with a doubtful reply. His happiness was darkened, he was cast back on his solitude, and the flowers had vanished with which he had beautified it.

Gabrielle, enlightened by the presentiment of sorrow that is peculiar to the angels whose task it is to soothe it, and which is no doubt a heavenly charity, at once perceived the pain she had given. She was so shocked at her own blunder that she longed for God-like power to be able to unveil her heart to Étienne, for she had understood the cruel agitation that can be caused by a reproach or a stern look. She artlessly showed him the clouds that had risen in her soul, forming, as it were, a golden wrapping for the dawn of her affection. One tear from Gabrielle turned Étienne's grief to joy, and then he accused himself of tyranny.

It was a happy thing for them that they thus from the first gauged the measure of each other's heart; they could thus avoid a thousand collisions that would have bruised them. Suddenly, Étienne, feeling that he must entrench himself behind some occupation, led Gabrielle to a table in front of the little window where he had known so much sorrow, and where henceforth he was to gaze on a flower fairer than any he had yet studied. There he opened a book over which they both bent their heads, their curls mingling.

These two, so strong in heart, so feeble in frame, and made beautiful by the grace of suffering, were a touching picture. Gabrielle knew none of woman's arts; she looked at him when he bade her, and the soft beams of their eyes only ceased to regard each other by an impulse of modesty. She had the joy of telling Étienne how much pleasure it gave her to hear his voice; she paid no heed to the meaning of his words when he explained the intervals and value of the notes; she listened, but forgot the melody in the instrument, the idea in the form,—an ingenuous flattery, the first that comes to true love.

Gabrielle thought Étienne handsome; she must feel the velvet of his cloak, touch the lace of his collar. As to Étienne, he was transfigured under the creative light of those bright eyes; they stirred in him a life-giving sap which sparkled in his eyes, shone on his brow, revived, renewed his spirit; and he did not suffer from this fresh play of his faculties, on the contrary, it strengthened him. Happiness was as nourishing milk to this new vitality.

As nothing could divert them from themselves, they remained together not only that day, but every other; for they were all in all to each other from the first, passing the sceptre from hand to hand, playing as a child plays with life. Sitting quite happy on the golden sands, each told the other the story of the past—to him so painful though full of dreams, to her a dream but full of painful joys.

"I never had a mother," said Gabrielle, "but my father was as good as God to me."

"I never had a father," replied the disowned son, "but my mother was all Heaven to me."

Étienne spoke of his youth, his love for his mother, his fondness of flowers. At this Gabrielle exclaimed; on being questioned she blushed and could not explain; then, when a cloud passed over the brow, which death seemed ever to fan with his wing, on which the soul made visible betrayed Étienne's least emotions, she answered:

"I, too, used to love flowers."

Was not this such a confession as maidens make, believing that lovers have been bound even in the past by a common taste? Love always tries to seem old; that is the vanity of children.

Next day Étienne brought her flowers, ordering the rarest, such as of yore his mother would have procured for him. Can any one guess how deeply rooted the fibres may be of a feeling thus reverting to the traditions of maternity, and lavishing on a woman the caressing care by which his mother had beautified his life? To him what dignity there seemed in these trifles which united those two affections!

Flowers and music became the language of their love. Gabrielle replied with posies to those Étienne sent her, such posies as at once showed the old leech that his daughter knew more than he could teach her. The practical ignorance of both the lovers thus formed a dark background against which the slightest incidents of their intimacy, so purely spiritual, stood out in exquisite grace, like the elegant red outline of the figures on a fine Etruscan vase. Each trifling word bore a full tide of meaning, for it was the outcome of their thoughts. Incapable, both, of any boldness, every beginning to them seemed an end. Though absolutely free, they were prisoners to a guilelessness which would have been heartbreaking to either if they had understood the meaning of their vague emotions. They were at once the poets and the poem. Music, the most sensuous of the arts to loving souls, was the interpreter of their ideas, and it was joy to them to repeat the same strain, pouring out their passion in the wide flood of sound in which their spirits spoke unhindered.

Love often thrives in antagonism, in quarreling and peace-making, in the vulgar struggle between mind and matter. But the very first wing-stroke of true love carries it far above these struggles. Two natures cease to be discernible when both are of one essence. Like Genius in its highest expression, Love can dwell in the fiercest light, can endure it and grow in it, and needs no shadow to enhance its beauty.

Gabrielle, in that she was a woman, Étienne, because he had suffered and thought much, soon soared beyond the sphere of vulgar passions and dwelt above it. Like all feeble natures, they were at once soaked in faith, in that heavenly purple which doubles their strength by doubling the soul. To them the sun was always at noon. They soon had that perfect trust in each other which can admit no jealousy, no torturing doubts; their self-sacrifice was always prompt, their admiration unfailing. Under these conditions love brought no pang. Equally feeble, but strong by their union, though the young nobleman had a certain superiority of learning, a certain conventional pre-eminence, the leech's daughter was more than his match in beauty, in loftiness of sentiment, in the refinement she shed on every pleasure.

And so on a sudden the two white doves flew with equal wing under a cloudless sky. Étienne loved and was loved; the present was serene, the future clear; he was master, the castle was his, the sea was there for them both. No anxiety disturbed the harmony of their two-part hymn; the virgin innocence of their senses and their mind made the world seem noble, their thoughts flowed on without an effort. Desire, whose satisfaction blights so many buds, the blot on earthly love, had not yet touched them. Like two Zephyrs seated on one branch of a willow-tree, they still were content with contemplating each other's image in the limpid mirror below. Infinitude satisfied them. They could look at that ocean without craving to sail over it in the white-sailed boat with flower-wreathed ropes, of which Hope is the pilot.

There is a moment in love when it is sufficient to itself, happy in mere living. During that springtime when everything is in bud, the lover will often hide from the woman he loves, to see her better and delight in her more. But Étienne and Gabrielle rushed together into the joys of that childlike time; sometimes as two sisters in their artless confidence, sometimes as two brothers in bold inquiry. Love generally presupposes a slave and a divinity; but these two realized Plato's noble dream; they were but one divinity. They cared for each other in turns.

By and by, slowly, kisses came; but as pure as the lively, happy, harmless sports of young animals making acquaintance with life. The feeling which led them to utter their souls in impassioned song invited them to love through the endless aspects of the same happiness. Their delights gave them no delirium, no wakeful nights. This was the infancy of pleasure, growing up unaware of the fine red flowers that will presently crown its stem. They were familiar, never dreaming of danger, breathing their souls out in a word or in a look, in a kiss or in the long pressure of clasping hands. They innocently boasted of their beauty, and in these idylls invented treasures of language, devising the sweetest exaggerations, the most vehement diminutives imagined by the antique Muse of Tibullus and echoed by Italian poets. On their lips and in their hearts they found the constant play of the foaming wavelets of the sea on the fine sandy shore, all so alike, all so different. Happy, unending fidelity!

Counting by days this time lasted five months; counting by the infinite variety of experience, of thoughts, dreams, and looks, of flowers that blossomed, of hopes fulfilled, of pure delights,—her hair unpinned, elaborately combed out, and then refastened with flowers, conversations interrupted, begun again, and dropped, giddy laughter, feet wetted in the waves, childish hunts for shells hidden among the stones,—by kisses, surprises, embraces,—call it a lifetime and death will justify the word.

Some lives are always dark, worked out under gray skies; but a glorious day when the sun fires a clear atmosphere was the image of the Maytime of their love, during which Étienne hung all the roses of his past life round Gabrielle's neck, and the girl bound up all her future joys with those of her lord.

Étienne had had but one sorrow in his life, his mother's death; he was destined to know but one love, Gabrielle.

The coarse rivality of an ambitious man hurried this honeyed existence to its end.

The Duc d'Hérouville, an old warrior alive to the wiles of others, roughly but skilfully cunning, heard the whispering voice of suspicion after giving the promise demanded of him by Beauvouloir. The Baron d'Artagnon, lieutenant of his company of ordnance, enjoyed his full confidence on all matters of policy. He was a man after the Duke's heart; a sort of butcher, hugely built, tall, of a manly countenance, harsh and stern, a bandit in the service of the King, roughly trained, of an iron will in action but easy to command; a nobleman and ambitious, with the blunt honesty of a soldier and the cunning of a politician. His hand matched his face, the broad, hairy hand of the condottiere. His manners were rude, his speech abrupt and short.

Now the Governor had entrusted his lieutenant to keep an eye on the leech's demeanor with the newly proclaimed heir. In spite of the secrecy maintained with regard to Gabrielle, it was difficult to deceive the commander of a company of ordnance; he heard two voices singing, he saw a light in the evening from the house by the sea. He suspected that Étienne's care of his person, the flowers he sent for, the orders he gave, must concern a woman; and then he met Gabrielle's nurse in the road, fetching some articles of dress from Forcalier, carrying linen or an embroidery frame or some girlish implement.

The soldier determined to see the leech's daughter, and he saw her; he fell in love. Beauvouloir was rich. The Duke would be furious at the good man's audacity. On these facts the Baron d'Artagnon based the edifice of his hopes. The Duke, if he should hear that his son was in love, would certainly want him to marry into some great house, an heiress of landed estate; and to cure Étienne of his passion, all that would be needful was to make Gabrielle faithless by giving her in marriage to a nobleman whose lands were pledged to a money-lender. The Baron himself had no land.

This speculation would have been a grand one with regard to most persons as we find them in the world, but it was destined to fail with Étienne and Gabrielle. Chance, however, had already served the Baron d'Artagnon a good turn.

During his residence in Paris, the Duke had avenged Maximilien's death by killing his son's adversary, and he had heard of an unexpectedly good alliance for Étienne with the heiress to the estates of a branch of the Grandlieu family, a tall and scornful damsel who was, nevertheless, tempted by the hope of one day bearing the name of Duchesse d'Hérouville. The Duke hoped to get his son to marry Mademoiselle de Grandlieu. On hearing that Étienne loved the daughter of a contemptible leech, his hope became a determination. To him this left no question on the matter. The Duke ordered out his coaches and attendants, and made his way from Paris to Rouen, bringing to his château the Comtesse de Grandlieu, her sister, the Marquise de Noirmoutier, and Mademoiselle de Grandlieu, under pretence of showing them the province of Normandy.

For some days before his arrival, though no one knew how the rumor had been spread, everybody, from Hérouville to Rouen, was talking of the young Duc de Nivron's attachment to Gabrielle Beauvouloir, the famous bone-setter's daughter. The good folks of Rouen mentioned it to the old Duke just at the height of a banquet which they were giving him, for the guests were delighted by the notion of annoying the despot of the province. This news excited the Governor's anger to frenzy. He sent orders to the Baron to keep his advent at Hérouville a profound secret, enjoining on him to forefend what he regarded as a disaster.

Meanwhile Étienne and Gabrielle had unwound all the thread of their ball in the vast labyrinth of love, and, equally willing to remain in it, they dreamed of living there. One day they were sitting by the window where so many things had happened. The hours, filled up at first with sweet talk, had led to some thoughtful pauses. They were indeed beginning to feel a vague craving for certain possessions, and had confided to each other their confused notions, reflected from the beautiful imaginings of two pure souls.

During these still, peaceful hours, Étienne had felt his eyes fill with tears more than once as he held Gabrielle's hand pressed to his lips. Like his mother, but happier just now in his love than she had been, the disowned son was gazing at the sea, gold-color on the strand, black in the distance, and swept here and there into long, white breakers foretelling a tempest. Gabrielle, following the instinct of her lover, also looked at the sea and was silent. A mere look, one of those glances in which two souls express their mutual reliance, was enough to communicate their thoughts.

The utmost devotion would have been no sacrifice to Gabrielle nor a demand on Étienne's part. They loved with the sentiment which is so divinely one and unchangeable in every instant of its eternity that sacrifice is unknown to it, and it fears no disappointment nor delay. But Étienne and Gabrielle were absolutely ignorant of what might satisfy the craving which agitated their souls.

When the faint hues of twilight had dropped a veil over the sea, and the silence was unbroken, save by the throbbing of the waves on the strand, Étienne stood up, and Gabrielle did the same in vague alarm, for he had dropped her hand. Étienne put his arms round the girl, clasping her to him with firm and tender pressure, and she, sympathizing with his impulse, leaned on him with weight enough to let him feel that she was indeed his, but not enough to fatigue him. He rested his too-heavy head on her shoulder, his lips touched her throbbing bosom, his long hair fell on her white shoulders and played on her throat. Gabrielle, in her ingenuous passion, bent her head so as to give his more room, and put her arm round his neck to support herself. And thus they stood, without speaking a word, until night had fallen.

The crickets chirped in their holes, and the lovers listened to their song as if to concentrate all their senses in one.

They could only be likened to an angel with feet resting on earth, awaiting the hour in which he might fly back to heaven. They had realized the beautiful dream of Plato's mystical genius—of all who seek a meaning in human life: they were but one soul; they had become the mysterious pearl that should grace the brow of some unknown star, the hope of us all.

"Will you take me home?" said Gabrielle, the first to break this exquisite stillness.

"Why should you go?" replied Étienne.

"We ought always to be together," said she.

"Then stay."

"Yes."

Old Beauvouloir's heavy footfall was heard in the adjoining room. The doctor found the two young people standing apart; through the window he had seen them embracing. Even the purest love craves for mystery.

"This is not right, my child," said he to Gabrielle. "Here still, so late, when it is dark."

"Why not?" said she. "You know that we love each other, and he is master here."

"My children," said the old man, "if you love each other, it is necessary to your happiness that you should be married and spend your lives together. But your union must be subject to the will of my lord the Duke——"

"My father promised to do all I could wish," cried Étienne, eagerly, interrupting Beauvouloir.

"Then write to him, monseigneur," replied the leech. "Tell him your wishes, and give me your letter to send with one which I have just written to him. Bertrand will set out at once and deliver the missives to Monseigneur himself. I have just heard that he is at Rouen, and is bringing with him the heiress of the House of Grandlieu, not for himself, I imagine. If I obeyed my presentiments I should carry off Gabrielle, this very night."

THE HATED SON

"What! divide us?" cried Étienne, half fainting with grief and leaning on the girl.

"Father!" was all she said.

"Gabrielle," said the old man, giving her a phial which he fetched from a table, and which she held under Étienne's nostrils, "my conscience tells me that nature intended you for each other. But I meant to prepare my lord for this union which must contravene all his ideas, and the devil has stolen a march on us! This is Monseigneur le Duc de Nivron," he added to Gabrielle, "and you are the daughter of a humble leech."

"My father swore never to oppose me in anything," said Étienne, calmly.

"Aye, and he swore to me, too, to consent to whatever I might do to provide you with a wife," replied Beauvouloir. "But if he should not keep his word?"

Étienne sat down like one stunned.

"The sea was dark this evening," he said after a short silence.

"If you could ride, monseigneur," said the leech, "I would bid you fly with Gabrielle this very evening. I know you both; any other marriage will be fatal to either. The Duke would of course cast me into his dungeon and leave me to end my days there, on hearing of your flight, but I should die joyful if my death would secure your happiness. But alas! a flight on horseback would risk your life and Gabrielle's too. We must face the Duke's wrath here."

"Here!" echoed poor Étienne.

"We have been betrayed by somebody in the castle who has stirred up your father's choler," said Beauvouloir.

"Come, let us throw ourselves into the sea together," said Étienne, leaning over to speak in Gabrielle's ear, for she was kneeling by her lover's side.

She bowed her head, smiling.

Beauvouloir guessed their purpose.

"Monseigneur," said he, "learning as well as native wit has given you eloquence; love must make you irresistible.

Confess your love to my lord your father, you will confirm my letter, in itself conclusive. All is not lost, I believe. I love my daughter as well as you love her, and I mean to protect her."

Étienne shook his head.

"The sea was very dark this evening," said he.

"It was like a sheet of gold at our feet," replied Gabrielle in a musical voice.

Étienne called for lights, and sat down at his table to write to his father. On one side of his chair Gabrielle knelt in silence, watching him write but not reading the words: she read everything on Étienne's brow. On the other side stood old Beauvouloir, his jovial features unwontedly sad, as sad as this room where Étienne's mother had died. A voice within him cried to the old man:

"He will share his mother's fate!"

The letter finished, Étienne held it out to Beauvouloir, who hurried away to give it to Bertrand.

The old squire's horse stood ready saddled and the man himself was ready: he started and met the Duc d'Hérouville only four leagues away.

"Take me as far as the door of the tower," said Gabrielle to her lover when they were alone.

They went out through the Cardinal's library and down the turret stair, to the door of which Étienne had given Gabrielle the key. Bewildered by his sense of impending evil, the poor boy left in the tower the torch he had brought to light his lady's steps, and went part of the way home with her. But at a short distance from the little garden that bordered this humble dwelling with flowers, the lovers stood still. Emboldened by the vague terror they both felt, in the darkness and stillness they kissed,—the first kiss in which soul and sense combined to communicate a prophetic thrill of pleasure.

Étienne understood the two aspects of love, and Gabrielle fled for fear of being betrayed into something more— what? She knew not.

Just as the Duc de Nivron was going up the tower stair after shutting the door, a shriek of terror from Gabrielle reached his ear, as vivid as a lightning flash that scorches the sight. Étienne flew through the rooms and down the grand staircase, reached the snore and ran towards the house where he saw a light.

On entering the little garden, by the gleam of the candle standing by her nurse's spinning-wheel, Gabrielle saw a man in the chair instead of the good old woman. At the sound of her steps this man had come to meet her and had startled her.

Indeed, the Baron d'Artagnon's appearance was calculated to justify the terror he had caused the girl.

"You are Beauvouloir's daughter—the Duke's leech?" said the soldier, when Gabrielle had a little recovered from the fright.

"Yes, monseigneur."

"I have matters of the highest importance to impart to you. I am the Baron d'Artagnon, lieutenant of the company of ordnance commanded by Monseigneur le Duc d'Hérouville."

Under the circumstances in which the lovers were placed, Gabrielle was struck by this address and the boldness with which is was spoken.

"Your nurse is in there; she may hear us. Come with me," said the Baron.

He went out; Gabrielle followed him. They walked out on to the strand behind the house.

"Fear nothing," said the Baron.

The words would have terrified any one less ignorant; but a simple child who is in love never fears any ill.

"Dear child," said the Baron, trying to infuse some honey into his accents, "you and your father stand on the edge of a gulf into which you will fall to-morrow. I cannot see it without giving you warning. Monseigneur is furious with your father and with you. You he imagines have bewitched his son, and he will see him dead rather than your husband. So much for his son! As to your father, this is the determination my lord has come to: Nine years ago your father was accused of a criminal action, the concealment of a child of noble race at the moment of its birth, at which he assisted. Monseigneur, knowing your father to be innocent, sheltered him from prosecution by law; but he will now have him seized and give him up to justice, applying indeed for a prosecution. Your father will be broken on the wheel; still, in consideration of the services he has done the Duke, he may be let off with hanging. What monseigneur proposes to do with you I know not; but I know this: that you can save Monseigneur de Nivron from his father's rage, save Beauvouloir from the dreadful end that awaits him, and save yourself."

"What must I do?" asked Gabrielle.

"Go and throw yourself at the Duke's feet, declare to him that though his son loves you it is against your will, and tell him that you do not love the young Duke. In proof thereof, offer to marry any man he may select to be your husband. He is generous; he will give you a handsome portion."

"I will do anything but deny my love," said Gabrielle.

"But if it is to save your father, yourself, and Monseigneur de Nivron?"

"Étienne," said she, "will die of it—and so shall I!"

"Monseigneur de Nivron will be sorry to lose you, but he will live—for the honor of his family. You may resign yourself to be only a baron's wife instead of a duchess; and your father will not be killed," said the practical Baron.

At this moment Étienne had reached the house; not seeing Gabrielle, he uttered a piercing cry.

"There he is!" exclaimed the girl. "Let me go to reassure him."

"I will come to-morrow for your answer," said the Baron.

"I will consult my father," she replied.

"You will see him no more. I have just received orders to arrest him and send him to Rouen, chained and under an armed escort," said Artagnon, and he left Gabrielle stricken with terror.

She rushed into the house and found Étienne horrified by the silence which was the old nurse's only reply to his first question:

"Where is she?"

"Here I am," cried the girl; but her voice was toneless, she was deadly pale, and could scarcely stand.

"Where have you been?" said he. "You screamed!"

"Yes, I hit myself against——"

"No, my beloved," replied Étienne, interrupting her, "I heard a man's step."

"Étienne, we have certainly in some way offended God. Kneel down; let us pray. I will tell you all afterwards."

Étienne and Gabrielle knelt on a prie-dieu; the old nurse told her beads.

"O God!" said the girl, with a flight of soul that bore her far above terrestrial space, "if we have not sinned against Thy holy laws, if we have not offended the Church or the King,—we who together are but one, and in whom love shines like the light Thou hast set in a pearl of the sea,— have this mercy on us that we be not divided either in this world or in the next."

"And thou, dear mother, who art in bliss, beseech the Virgin that if Gabrielle and I may not be happy together, we may at least die together, and without suffering. Call us, and we will go to thee."

Then, after their usual evening prayers, Gabrielle told him of her interview with the Baron d'Artagnon.

"Gabrielle!" said the youth, finding courage in the despair of love, "I will stand out against my father."

He kissed her forehead and not her lips, then he returned to the castle, determined to face the terrible man who crushed his whole life. He did not know that Gabrielle's dwelling was surrounded by men-at-arms as soon as he had left it.

When, on the following day Étienne went to see Gabrielle, his grief was great at finding her a prisoner. But the old nurse came out to him with a message to say that Gabrielle would die rather than deny him, and that she knew of a way to evade the vigilance of the guards, and would take refuge in the Cardinal's library where no one would suspect her presence; only she did not know when she might achieve her purpose. So Étienne remained in his room where his heart wore itself out in agonized expectancy.

At three o'clock the Duke and his suite reached the castle, where he expected his guests to supper. And, in fact, at dusk, Madame la Comtesse de Grandlieu, leaning on her daughter's arm, and the Duke with the Marquise de Noirmoutier came up the great staircase in solemn silence, for their master's stern looks had terrified all his retainers.

Though the Baron d'Artagnon had been informed of Gabrielle's escape, he had reported that she was guarded; he feared lest he should have spoiled the success of his own particular scheme, if the Duke should find his plans upset by the girl's flight.

The two terrible men bore on their faces an expression of ferocity but ill-disguised under the affectation of amiability imposed on them by gallantry. The Duke had commanded his son to be in attendance in the hall. When the company came in, the Baron d'Artagnon read in Étienne's dejected looks that he was not yet aware of Gabrielle's escape.

"This is my son," said the old Duke, taking Étienne by the hand and presenting him to the ladies.

Étienne bowed without speaking a word. The Countess and Mademoiselle de Grandlieu exchanged glances which the old man did not fail to note.

"Your daughter will be but ill-matched," said he in an undertone; "was not that your thought?"

"I thought just the contrary, my dear Duke," replied the mother with a smile.

The Marquise de Noirmoutier, who had come with her sister, laughed significantly. The laugh went to Étienne's

THE HATED SON

heart, terrified as he was already by the sight of the tall damsel.

"Well, Monsieur le Duc," said his father in a low voice, with a jovial chuckle, "I have found you a handsome mate, I hope! What do you think of that little girl, my cherub?"

The old Duke had never doubted of his son's submission. To him Étienne was his mother's son, made of the same yielding material.

"If he only has a son he may depart in peace," thought the old man. "Little I care!"

"Father," said the lad in a mild voice, "I do not understand you."

"Come into your room, I have two words to say to you," replied the Duke, going into the great bedroom.

Étienne followed his father. The three ladies, moved by an impulse of curiosity, shared by the Baron d'Artagnon, walked across the vast hall and paused in a group at the door of the state bedchamber, which the Duke had left half open.

"My pretty Benjamin," said the old man, beginning in mild tones, "I have chosen that tall and beautiful damsel to be your wife. She is heiress of the lands belonging to a younger branch of the House of Grandlieu, an old and honest family of the nobility of Brittany. So now, be a gallant youth, and recall the best speeches you have read in your books to make yourself agreeable, and speak gallantly as a preface to acting gallantly."

"Father, is it not a gentleman's first duty to keep his word?"

"Yes."

"Well, then! When I forgave you for my mother's death, dying here, as she did, because she had married you, did not you promise me never to thwart my wishes? 'I myself will obey you as the god of the family!' you said. Now I do not dictate to you, I only claim freedom to act in a matter which concerns only myself: my marriage."

"But as I understood," said the old man, the blood mounting to his face, "you pledged yourself not to hinder the propagation of our noble race."

"You made no conditions," said Étienne. "What love has to do with the propagation of the race I know not. But what I do know is that I love the daughter of your old friend Beauvouloir, the granddaughter of La Belle Romaine."

"But she is dead!" replied the old giant, with an expression of mingled mockery and solemnity that plainly showed his intention of making away with her.

There was a moment of utter silence.

The old Duke then caught sight of the three ladies and the Baron.

At this supreme moment, Étienne, who had so keen a sense of hearing, caught the sound from the library of Gabrielle's voice. She, wishing to let her lover know that she was there, was singing the old ballad:

> "Une hermine
> Est moins fine;
> Le lys a moins de blancheur."

On the wings of this verse the disowned son, who had been cast into a gulf of death by his father's words, soared up to life again.

Though that one spasm of anguish, so suddenly relieved, had struck him to the heart, he collected all his forces, raised his head, and for the first time in his life looked his father in the face, answering scorn with scorn, as he said with deep hatred:

"A gentleman should not lie!"

With one spring he reached the door opposite to that leading into the hall, and called out:

"Gabrielle!"

Then, at once, the gentle creature appeared in the dusk like a lily amid its leaves, trembling in the presence of this trio of mocking women who had overheard Étienne's profession of love.

The old Duke, like a gathering thunder-cloud, had reached a climax of fury that no words can describe; his dark figure stood out against the brilliant dresses of the three court ladies. Most men would have hesitated, at least, between a mésalliance and the extinction of the race; but in this indomitable old man there was the ferocious vein which had hitherto proved a match for every earthly difficulty. He drew the sword on every occasion as the only way he knew of cutting the Gordian knots of life. In the present case, when all his ideas were so utterly upset, his nature was bound to triumph.

Twice detected in a lie by the creature he abhorred, the child he had cursed a thousand times, and now more vehemently than ever at the moment when his despicable weakness—to his father the most despicable kind of weakness—had triumphed over a force he had hitherto deemed omnipotent, the Duke was no longer a father, nor even a man; the tiger rushed out of the den where it lurked. The old man, made young by revengefulness, blasted the sweetest pair of angels that ever vouchsafed to alight on earth, with a look weighted with hatred that dealt death.

"Then die, both of you!—you, vile abortion, the evidence of my dishonor! And you," he said to Gabrielle, "slut with the viper's tongue, who have poisoned my race."

The words carried to the two children's hearts the fell terror of their purpose.

As Étienne saw his father raise his hand and blade over Gabrielle he dropped dead; and Gabrielle, trying to support him, fell dead by his side.

The old man slammed the door on them in a rage, and said to Mademoiselle de Grandlieu:

"I will marry you myself!"

"And are hale enough to have a fine family!" said the Countess in the ear of the old Duke, who had served under seven kings of France.

Paris, 1831-1836.

THE ATHEIST'S MASS

*This is dedicated to Auguste Borget by his friend
De Balzac.*

BIANCHON, a physician to whom science owes a fine system
of theoretical physiology, and who, while still young, made
himself a celebrity in the medical school of Paris, that central
luminary to which European doctors do homage, practised
surgery for a long time before he took up medicine. His
earliest studies were guided by one of the greatest of French
surgeons, the illustrious Desplein, who flashed across science
like a meteor. By the consensus even of his enemies, he took
with him to the tomb an incommunicable method. Like all
men of genius, he had no heirs; he carried everything in him,
and carried it away with him. The glory of a surgeon is like
that of an actor: they live only so long as they are alive, and
their talent leaves no trace when they are gone. Actors and
surgeons, like great singers too, like the executants who by
their performance increase the power of music tenfold, are all
the heroes of a moment.

Desplein is a case in proof of this resemblance in the
destinies of such transient genius. His name, yesterday so
famous, to-day almost forgotten, will survive in his special
department without crossing its limits. For must there not
be some extraordinary circumstances to exalt the name of a
professor from the history of Science to the general history of
the human race? Had Desplein that universal command of
knowledge which makes a man the living word, the great
figure of his age? Desplein had a godlike eye; he saw
into the sufferer and his malady by an intuition, natural or
acquired, which enabled him to grasp the diagnostics peculiar
to the individual, to determine the very time, the hour, the

minute when an operation should be performed, making due allowance for atmospheric conditions and peculiarities of individual temperament. To proceed thus, hand in hand with nature, had he then studied the constant assimilation by living beings, of the elements contained in the atmosphere, or yielded by the earth to man who absorbs them, deriving from them a particular expression of life? Did he work it all out by the power of deduction and analogy, to which we owe the genius' of Cuvier? Be this as it may, this man was in all the secrets of the human frame; he knew it in the past and in the future, emphasizing the present.

But did he epitomize all science in his own person as Hippocrates did and Galen and Aristotle? Did he guide a whole school towards new worlds? No. Though it is impossible to deny that this persistent observer of human chemistry possessed the antique science of the Mages, that is to say, knowledge of the elements in fusion, the causes of life, life antecedent to life, and what it must be in its incubation or ever it *is,* it must be confessed that, unfortunately, everything in him was purely personal. Isolated during his life by his egoism, that egoism is now suicidal of his glory. On his tomb there is no proclaiming statue to repeat to posterity the mysteries which genius seeks out at its own cost.

But perhaps Desplein's genius was answerable for his beliefs, and for that reason mortal. To him the terrestrial atmosphere was a generative envelope; he saw the earth as an egg within its shell; and not being able to determine whether the egg or the hen first was, he would not recognize either the cock or the egg. He believed neither in the antecedent animal nor the surviving spirit of man. Desplein had no doubts; he was positive. His bold and unqualified atheism was like that of many scientific men, the best men in the world, but invincible atheists—atheists such as religious people declare to be impossible. This opinion could scarcely exist otherwise in a man who was accustomed from his youth to dissect the creature above all others—before, during, and after life; to hunt through all his organs without ever finding the individual soul, which is indispensable to religious theory. When he detected a cerebral centre, a nervous centre, and a centre for aërating the blood—the first two so perfectly complementary that in the latter years of his life he came to a conviction that the sense of hearing is not absolutely necessary for hearing, nor the sense of sight for seeing, and that the solar plexus could supply their place without any possibility of doubt—Desplein, thus finding two souls in man, confirmed his atheism by this fact, though it is no evidence against God. This man died, it is said, in final impenitence, as do, unfortunately, many noble geniuses, whom God may forgive.

The life of this man, great as he was, was marred by many meannesses, to use the expression employed by his enemies, who were anxious to diminish his glory, but which it would be more proper to call apparent contradictions. Envious people and fools, having no knowledge of the determinations by which superior spirits are moved, seize at once on superficial inconsistencies, to formulate an accusation and so to pass sentence on them. If, subsequently, the proceedings thus attacked are crowned with success, showing the correlation of the preliminaries and the results, a few of the vanguard of calumnies always survive. In our own day, for instance, Napoleon was condemned by our contemporaries when he spread his eagle's wings to alight in England: only 1822 could explain 1804 and the flatboats at Boulogne.

As, in Desplein, his glory and science were invulnerable, his enemies attacked his odd moods and his temper, whereas, in fact, he was simply characterized by what the English call eccentricity. Sometimes very handsomely dressed, like Crébillon the tragical, he would suddenly affect extreme indifference as to what he wore; he was sometimes seen in a carriage, and sometimes on foot. By turns rough and kind, harsh and covetous on the surface, but capable of offering his whole fortune to his exiled masters—who did him the honor of accepting it for a few days—no man ever gave rise to such contradictory judgments. Although to obtain a black ribbon, which physicians ought not to intrigue for, he was capable of dropping a prayer-book out of his pocket at Court, in his heart he mocked at everything; he had a deep contempt for men, after studying them from above and below, after detecting their genuine expression when performing the most solemn and the meanest acts of their lives.

The qualities of a great man are often federative. If among these colossal spirits one has more talent than wit, his wit is still superior to that of a man of whom it is simply stated that "he is witty." Genius always presupposes moral insight. This insight may be applied to a special subject; but he who can see a flower must be able to see the sun. The man who on hearing a diplomate he had saved ask, "How is the Emperor?" could say, "The courtier is alive; the man will follow!"—that man in not merely a surgeon or a physician, he is prodigiously witty also. Hence a patient and diligent student of human nature will admit Desplein's exorbitant pretensions, and believe—as he himself believed—that he might have been no less great as a minister than he was as a surgeon.

Among the riddles which Desplein's life presents to many of his contemporaries, we have chosen one of the most interesting, because the answer is to be found at the end of the narrative, and will avenge him for some foolish charges.

Of all the students in Desplein's hospital, Horace Bianchon was one of those to whom he most warmly attached himself. Before being a house surgeon at the Hôtel-Dieu, Horace Bianchon had been a medical student lodging in a squalid boarding-house in the *Quartier Latin,* known as the Maison Vauquer. This poor young man had felt there the gnawing of that burning poverty which is a sort of crucible from which great talents are to emerge as pure and incorruptible as diamonds, which may be subjected to any shock without being crushed. In the fierce fire of their unbridled passions they acquire the most impeccable honesty, and get into the habit of fighting the battles which await genius with the constant work by which they coerce their cheated appetites.

Horace was an upright young fellow, incapable of tergiversation on a matter of honor, going to the point without waste of words, and as ready to pledge his cloak for a friend as to give him his time and his night hours. Horace, in short, was one of those friends who are never anxious as to what they may get in return for what they give, feeling sure that they will in their turn get more than they give. Most of his friends felt for him that deeply-seated respect which is inspired by unostentatious virtue, and many of them dreaded his censure. But Horace made no pedantic display of his qualities. He was neither a puritan nor a preacher; he could swear with a grace as he gave his advice, and was always ready for a jollification when occasion offered. A jolly companion, not more prudish than a trooper, as frank and outspoken—not as a sailor, for nowadays sailors are wily diplomates—but as an honest man who has nothing in his life to hide, he walked with his head erect, and a mind content. In short, to put the facts into a word, Horace was the Pylades of more than one Orestes—creditors being regarded as the nearest modern equivalent to the Furies of the ancients.

He carried his poverty with the cheerfulness which is perhaps one of the chief elements of courage, and, like all people who have nothing, he made very few debts. As sober as a camel and active as a stag, he was steadfast in his ideas and his conduct.

The happy phase of Bianchon's life began on the day when the famous surgeon had proof of the qualities and the defects which, these no less than those, make Doctor Horace Bianchon doubly dear to his friends. When a leading clinical practitioner takes a young man to his bosom, that young man has, as they say, his foot in the stirrup. Desplein did not fail to take Bianchon as his assistant to wealthy houses, where some complimentary fee almost always found its way into the student's pocket, and where the mysteries of Paris life were insensibly revealed to the young provincial; he kept him at his side when a consultation was to be held, and gave him occupation; sometimes he would send him to a watering-place with a rich patient; in fact, he was making a practice for him. The consequence was that in the course of time the Tyrant of surgery had a devoted ally. These two men—one at the summit of honor and of his science, enjoying an immense fortune and an immense reputation; the other a humble Omega, having neither fortune nor fame—became intimate friends.

The great Desplein told his house surgeon everything; the disciple knew whether such or such a woman had sat on a chair near the master, or on the famous couch in Desplein's surgery, on which he slept; Bianchon knew the mysteries of that temperament, a compound of the lion and the bull, which at last expanded and enlarged beyond measure the great man's torso, and caused his death by degeneration of the heart. He studied the eccentricities of that busy life, the schemes of that sordid avarice, the hopes of the politician who lurked behind the man of science; he was able to foresee the mortifications that awaited the only sentiment that lay hid in a heart that was steeled, but not of steel.

One day Bianchon spoke to Desplein of a poor water-carrier of the Saint-Jacques district, who had a horrible disease caused by fatigue and want; this wretched Auvergnat had had nothing but potatoes to eat during the dreadful winter of 1821. Desplein left all his visits, and at the risk of killing his horse, he rushed off, followed by Bianchon, to the poor man's dwelling, and saw, himself, to his being removed to a sick house, founded by the famous Dubois in the Faubourg Saint-Denis. Then he went to attend the man, and when he had cured him he gave him the necessary sum to buy a horse and a water-barrel. This Auvergnat distinguished himself by an amusing action. One of his friends fell ill, and he took him at once to Desplein, saying to his benefactor, "I could not have borne to let him go to any one else!"

Rough customer as he was, Desplein grasped the water-carrier's hand, and said, "Bring them all to me."

He got the native of Cantal into the Hôtel-Dieu, where he took the greatest care of him. Bianchon had already observed in his chief a predilection for Auvergnats, and especially for water-carriers; but as Desplein took a sort of pride in his cures at the Hôtel-Dieu, the pupil saw nothing very strange in that.

One day, as he crossed the Place Saint-Sulpice, Bianchon caught sight of his master going into the church at about nine in the morning. Desplein, who at that time never went a step without his cab, was on foot, and slipped in by the door in the Rue du Petit-Lion, as if he were stealing into some house of ill fame. The house surgeon, naturally possessed by curiosity, knowing his master's opinions, and being himself a rabid follower of Cabanis (*Cabaniste en dyable,* with the *y,* which in Rabelais seems to convey an intensity of devilry)— Bianchon stole into the church, and was not a little astonished to see the great Desplein, the atheist, who had no mercy on the angels—who give no work to the lancet, and cannot suffer from fistula or gastritis—in short, this audacious scoffer kneeling humbly, and where? In the Lady Chapel, where he remained through the mass, giving alms for the expenses of the service, alms for the poor, and looking as serious as though he were superintending an operation.

"He has certainly not come here to clear up the question of the Virgin's delivery," said Bianchon to himself, astonished beyond measure. "If I had caught him holding one of the ropes of the canopy on Corpus Christi day, it would be a thing to laugh at; but at this hour, alone, with no one to see— it is surely a thing to marvel at!"

Bianchon did not wish to seem as though he were spying the head surgeon of the Hôtel-Dieu; he went away. As it happened, Desplein asked him to dine with him that day, not at his own house, but at a restaurant. At dessert Bianchon skilfully contrived to talk of the mass, speaking of it as mummery and a farce.

"A farce," said Desplein, "which has cost Christendom more blood than all Napoleon's battles and all Broussais' leeches. The mass is a papal invention, not older than the sixth century, and based on the *Hoc est corpus*. What floods of blood were shed to establish the Fête-Dieu, the Festival of

Corpus Christi—the institution by which Rome established her triumph in the question of the Real Presence, a schism which rent the Church during three centuries! The wars of the Count of Toulouse against the Albigenses were the tail end of that dispute. The Vaudois and the Albigenses refused to recognize this innovation."

In short, Desplein was delighted to disport himself in his most atheistical vein; a flow of Voltairean satire, or, to be accurate, a vile imitation of the *Citateur*.

"Hallo! where is my worshiper of this morning?" said Bianchon to himself.

He said nothing; he began to doubt whether he had really seen his chief at Saint-Sulpice. Desplein would not have troubled himself to tell Bianchon a lie, they knew each other too well; they had already exchanged thoughts on quite equally serious subjects, and discussed systems *de natura rerum*, probing or dissecting them with the knife and scalpel of incredulity.

Three months went by. Bianchon did not attempt to follow the matter up, though it remained stamped on his memory. One day that year, one of the physicians of the Hôtel-Dieu took Desplein by the arm, as if to question him, in Bianchon's presence.

"What were you doing at Saint-Sulpice, my dear master?" said he.

"I went to see a priest who has a diseased knee-bone, and to whom the Duchesse d'Angoulême did me the honor to recommend me," said Desplein.

The questioner took this defeat for an answer; not so Bianchon.

"Oh, he goes to see damaged knees in church!—He went to mass," said the young man to himself.

Bianchon resolved to watch Desplein. He remembered the day and hour when he had detected him going into Saint-Sulpice, and resolved to be there again next year on the same day and at the same hour, to see if he should find him there again. In that case the periodicity of his devotions would justify a scientific investigation; for in such a man there ought to be no direct antagonism of thought and action.

Next year, on the said day and hour, Bianchon, who had already ceased to be Desplein's house surgeon, saw the great man's cab standing at the corner of the Rue de Tournon and the Rue du Petit-Lion, whence his friend jesuitically crept along by the wall of Saint-Sulpice, and once more attended mass in front of the Virgin's altar. It was Desplein, sure enough! The master-surgeon, the atheist at heart, the worshiper by chance. The mystery was greater than ever; the regularity of the phenomenon complicated it. When Desplein had left, Bianchon went to the sacristan, who took charge of the chapel, and asked him whether the gentleman were a constant worshiper.

"For twenty years that I have been here," replied the man, "M. Desplein has come four times a year to attend this mass. He founded it."

"A mass founded by him!" said Bianchon, as he went away. "This is as great a mystery as the Immaculate Conception—an article which alone is enough to make a physician an unbeliever."

Some time elapsed before Doctor Bianchon, though so much his friend, found an opportunity of speaking to Desplein of this incident of his life. Though they met in consultation, or in society, it was difficult to find an hour of confidential solitude when, sitting with their feet on the fire-dogs and their head resting on the back of an armchair, two men tell each other their secrets. At last, seven years later, after the Revolution of 1830, when the mob invaded the Archbishop's residence, when Republican agitators spurred them on to destroy the gilt crosses which flashed like streaks of lightning in the immensity of the ocean of houses; when Incredulity flaunted itself in the streets, side by side with Rebellion, Bianchon once more detected Desplein going into Saint-Sulpice. The doctor followed him, and knelt down by him without the slightest notice or demonstration of surprise from his friend. They both attended this mass of his founding.

"Will you tell me, my dear fellow," said Bianchon, as they left the church, "the reason for your fit of monkishness? I have caught you three times going to mass—— You! You must account to me for this mystery, explain such a flagrant disagreement between your opinions and your conduct. You do not believe in God, and yet you attend mass? My dear master, you are bound to give me an answer."

"I am like a great many devout people, men who on the surface are deeply religious, but quite as much atheists as you or I can be."

And he poured out a torrent of epigrams on certain political personages, of whom the best known gives us, in this century, a new edition of Molière's *Tartufe*.

"All that has nothing to do with my question," retorted Bianchon. "I want to know the reason for what you have just been doing, and why you founded this mass."

"Faith! my dear boy," said Desplein, "I am on the verge of the tomb; I may safely tell you about the beginning of my life."

At this moment Bianchon and the great man were in the Rue des Quatre-Vents, one of the worst streets in Paris. Desplein pointed to the sixth floor of one of the houses looking like obelisks, of which the narrow door opens into a passage with a winding staircase at the end, with windows appropriately termed "borrowed lights"—or, in French, *jours de souffrance*. It was a greenish structure; the ground floor occupied by a furniture-dealer, while each floor seemed to shelter a different and independent form of misery. Throwing up his arm with a vehement gesture, Desplein exclaimed:

"I lived up there for two years."

"I know; Arthez lived there; I went up there almost every day during my first youth; we used to call it then the pickle-jar of great men! What then?"

"The mass I have just attended is connected with some events which took place at the time when I lived in the garret where you say Arthez lived; the one with the window where the clothes line is hanging with linen over a pot of flowers. My early life was so hard, my dear Bianchon, that I may dispute the palm of Paris suffering with any man living. I have endured everything: hunger and thirst, want of money, want of clothes, of shoes, of linen, every cruelty that penury can inflict. I have blown on my frozen fingers in that *pickle-jar of great men,* which I should like to see again, now, with you. I worked through a whole winter, seeing my head steam, and perceiving the atmosphere of my own moisture as we see that of horses on a frosty day. I do not know where a man finds the fulcrum that enables him to hold out against such a life.

"I was alone, with no one to help me, no money to buy books or to pay the expenses of my medical training; I had not a friend; my irascible, touchy, restless temper was against me. No one understood that this irritability was the distress and toil of a man who, at the bottom of the social scale, is struggling to reach the surface. Still, I had, as I may say to you, before whom I need wear no draperies, I had that groundbed of good feeling and keen sensitiveness which must always be the birthright of any man who is strong enough to climb to any height whatever, after having long trampled in the bogs of poverty. I could obtain nothing from my family, nor from my home, beyond my inadequate allowance. In short, at that time, I breakfasted off a roll which the baker in the Rue du Petit-Lion sold me cheap because it was left from yesterday or the day before, and I crumbled it into milk; thus my morning meal cost me but two sous. I dined only every other day in a boarding-house where the meal cost me sixteen sous. You know as well as I what care I must have taken of my clothes and shoes. I hardly know whether in later life we feel grief so deep when a colleague plays us false, as we have known, you and I, on detecting the mocking smile of a gaping seam in a shoe, or hearing the armhole of a coat split. I drank nothing but water; I regarded a café with distant respect. Zoppi's seemed to me a promised land where none but the Lucullus of the *pays Latin* had a right of entry.

'Shall I ever take a cup of coffee there with milk in it?' said I to myself, 'or play a game of dominoes?'

"I threw into my work the fury I felt at my misery. I tried to master positive knowledge so as to acquire the greatest personal value, and merit the position I should hold as soon as I could escape from nothingness. I consumed more oil than bread; the light I burned during these endless nights cost me more than food. It was a long duel, obstinate, with no sort of consolation. I found no sympathy anywhere. To have friends, must we not form connections with young men, have a few sous so as to be able to go tippling with them, and meet them where students congregate? And I had nothing! And no one in Paris can understand that nothing means *nothing*. When I even thought of revealing my beggary, I had that nervous contraction of the throat which makes a sick man believe that a ball rises up from the œsophagus into the larynx.

"In later life I have met people born to wealth who, never having wanted for anything, had never even heard this problem in the rule of three: A young man is to crime as a five-franc piece is to x.—These gilded idiots say to me, 'Why did you get into debt? Why did you involve yourself in such onerous obligations?' They remind me of the princess who, on hearing that the people lacked bread, said, 'Why do not they buy cakes?' I should like to see one of these rich men, who complain that I charge too much for an operation,—yes, I should like to see him alone in Paris without a sou, without a friend, without credit, and forced to work with his five fingers to live at all! What would he do? Where would he go to satisfy his hunger?

"Bianchon, if you have sometimes seen me hard and bitter, it was because I was adding my early sufferings on to the insensibility, the selfishness of which I have seen thousands of instances in the highest circles; or, perhaps, I was thinking of the obstacles which hatred, envy, jealousy, and calumny raised up between me and success. In Paris, when certain people see you ready to set your foot in the stirrup, some pull your coat-tails, others loosen the buckle of the strap that you may fall and crack your skull; one wrenches off your horse's shoes, another steals your whip, and the least treacherous of them all is the man whom you see coming to fire his pistol at you point blank.

"You yourself, my dear boy, are clever enough to make acquaintance before long with the odious and incessant warfare waged by mediocrity against the superior man. If you should drop five-and-twenty louis one day, you will be accused of gambling on the next, and your best friends will report that you have lost twenty-five thousand. If you have a headache, you will be considered mad. If you are a little hasty, no one can live with you. If, to make a stand against this armament of pigmies, you collect your best powers, your best friends will cry out that you want to have everything, that you aim at domineering, at tyranny. In short, your good points will become your faults, your faults will be vices, and your virtues crime.

"If you save a man, you will be said to have killed him; if he reappears on the scene, it will be positive that you have secured the present at the cost of the future. If he is not dead, he will die. Stumble, and you fall! Invent anything of any kind and claim your rights, you will be crotchety, cunning, ill-disposed to rising younger men.

"So, you see, my dear fellow, if I do not believe in God, I believe still less in man. But do not you know in me another Desplein, altogether different from the Desplein whom every one abuses?—However, we will not stir that mud-heap.

"Well, I was living in that house, I was working hard to pass my first examination, and I had no money at all. You know. I had come to one of those moments of extremity when a man says, 'I will enlist.' I had one hope. I expected from my home a box full of linen, a present from one of those old aunts who, knowing nothing of Paris, think of your shirts, while they imagine that their nephew with thirty francs a month is eating ortolans. The box arrived while I was at the schools; it had cost forty francs for carriage. The porter, a German shoemaker living in a loft, had paid the money and kept the box. I walked up and down the Rue des Fossés-Saint-Germain-des-Prés and the Rue de l'École de Médecine without hitting on any scheme which would release my trunk without the payment of the forty francs, which of course I could pay as soon as I should have sold the linen. My stupidity proved to me that surgery was my only vocation. My good fellow, refined souls, whose powers move in a lofty atmosphere, have none of that spirit of intrigue that is fertile in resource and device; their good genius is chance; they do not invent, things come to them.

"At night I went home, at the very moment when my fellow lodger also came in—a water-carrier named Bourgeat, a native of Saint-Flour. We knew each other as two lodgers do who have rooms off the same landing, and who hear each other sleeping, coughing, dressing, and so at last become used to one another. My neighbor informed me that the landlord, to whom I owed three quarters' rent, had turned me out; I must clear out next morning. He himself was also turned out on account of his occupation. I spent the most miserable night of my life. Where was I to get a messenger who could carry my few chattels and my books? How could I pay him and the porter? Where was I to go? I repeated these unanswerable questions again and again, in tears, as madmen repeat their tunes. I fell asleep; poverty has for its friends heavenly slumbers full of beautiful dreams.

"Next morning, just as I was swallowing my little bowl of bread soaked in milk, Bourgeat came in and said to me in his vile Auvergne accent:

"'*Mouchieur l'Étudiant,* I am a poor man, a foundling from the hospital at Saint-Flour, without either father or mother, and not rich enough to marry. You are not fertile in relations either, nor well supplied with the ready? Listen, I have a hand-cart downstairs which I have hired for two sous an hour; it will hold all our goods; if you like, we will try to find lodgings together, since we are both turned out of this. It is not the earthly paradise, when all is said and done.'

THE ATHEIST'S MASS 393

"'I know that, my good Bourgeat,' said I. 'But I am in a great fix. I have a trunk downstairs with a hundred francs' worth of linen in it, out of which I could pay the landlord and all I owe to the porter, and I have not a hundred sous."

"'Pooh! I have a few dibs,' replied Bourgeat joyfully, and he pulled out a greasy old leather purse. 'Keep your linen.'

"Bourgeat paid up my arrears and his own, and settled with the porter. Then he put our furniture and my box of linen in his cart, and pulled it along the street, stopping in front of every house where there was a notice board. I went up to see whether the rooms to let would suit us. At midday we were still wandering about the neighborhood without having found anything. The price was the great difficulty. Bourgeat proposed that we should eat at a wine shop, leaving the cart at the door. Towards evening I discovered, in the Cour de Rohan, Passage du Commerce, at the very top of a house next the roof, two rooms with a staircase between them. Each of us was to pay sixty francs a year. So there we were housed, my humble friend and I. We dined together. Bourgeat, who earned about fifty sous a day, had saved a hundred crowns or so; he would soon be able to gratify his ambition by buying a barrel and a horse. On learning my situation—for he extracted my secrets with a quiet craftiness and good nature, of which the remembrance touches my heart to this day, he gave up for a time the ambition of his whole life; for twenty-two years he had been carrying water in the street, and he now devoted his hundred crowns to my future prospects."

Desplein at these words clutched Bianchon's arm tightly. "He gave me the money for my examination fees! That man, my friend, understood that I had a mission, that the needs of my intellect were greater than his. He looked after me, he called me his boy, he lent me money to buy books, he would come in softly sometimes to watch me at work, and took a mother's care in seeing that I had wholesome and abundant food, instead of the bad and insufficient nourishment I had been condemned to. Bourgeat, a man of about forty, had a

homely, mediæval type of face, a prominent forehead, a head
that a painter might have chosen as a model for that of Lycur-
gus. The poor man's heart was big with affections seeking
an object; he had never been loved but by a poodle that had
died some time since, of which he would talk to me, asking
whether I thought the Church would allow masses to be said
for the repose of its soul. His dog, said he, had been a good
Christian, who for twelve years had accompanied him to
church, never barking, listening to the organ without opening
his mouth, and crouching beside him in a way that made it
seem as though he were praying too.

"This man centered all his affections in me; he looked upon
me as a forlorn and suffering creature, and he became, to me,
the most thoughtful mother, the most considerate benefactor,
the ideal of the virtue which rejoices in its own work. When
I met him in the street, he would throw me a glance of intelligence full of unutterable dignity; he would affect to walk as
though he carried no weight, and seemed happy in seeing me
in good health and well dressed. It was, in fact, the devoted
affection of the lower classes, the love of a girl of the people
transferred to a loftier level. Bourgeat did all my errands,
woke me at night at any fixed hour, trimmed my lamp, cleaned
our landing; as good as a servant as he was as a father, and as
clean as an English girl. He did all the housework. Like
Philopœmen, he sawed our wood, and gave to all he did the
grace of simplicity while preserving his dignity, for he seemed
to understand that the end ennobles every act.

"When I left this good fellow, to be house surgeon at the
Hôtel-Dieu, I felt an indescribable, dull pain, knowing that
he could no longer live with me; but he comforted himself
with the prospect of saving up money enough for me to take
my degree, and he made me promise to go to see him whenever I had a day out: Bourgeat was proud of me. He loved
me for my own sake, and for his own. If you look up my
thesis, you will see that I dedicated it to him.

"During the last year of my residence as house surgeon I
earned enough to repay all I owed to this worthy Auvergnat

by buying him a barrel and a horse. He was furious with rage at learning that I had been depriving myself of spending my money, and yet he was delighted to see his wishes fulfilled; he laughed and scolded, he looked at his barrel, at his horse, and wiped away a tear, as he said, 'It is too bad. What a splendid barrel! You really ought not. Why, that horse is as strong as an Auvergnat!'

"I never saw a more touching scene. Bourgeat insisted on buying for me the case of instruments mounted in silver which you have seen in my room, and which is to me the most precious thing there. Though enchanted with my first success, never did the least sign, the least word, escape him which might imply, 'This man owes all to me!' And yet, but for him, I should have died of want; he had eaten bread rubbed with garlic that I might have coffee to enable me to sit up at night.

"He fell ill. As you may suppose, I passed my nights by his bedside, and the first time I pulled him through; but two years after he had a relapse; in spite of the utmost care, in spite of the greatest exertions of science, he succumbed. No king was ever nursed as he was. Yes, Bianchon, to snatch that man from death I tried unheard-of things. I wanted him to live long enough to show him his work accomplished, to realize all his hopes, to give expression to the only need for gratitude that ever filled my heart, to quench a fire that burns in me to this day.

"Bourgeat, my second father, died in my arms," Desplein went on, after a pause, visibly moved. "He left me everything he possessed by a will he had had made by a public scrivener, dating from the year when we had gone to live in the Cour de Rohan.

"This man's faith was perfect; he loved the Holy Virgin as he might have loved his wife. He was an ardent Catholic. but never said a word to me about my want of religion. When he was dying he entreated me to spare no expense that he might have every possible benefit of clergy. I had a mass said for him every day. Often. in the night, he would tell me of his fears as to his future fate; he feared his life had not been saintly enough. Poor man! he was at work from morning till night. For whom, then, is Paradise—if there be a Paradise? He received the last sacrament like the saint that he was, and his death was worthy of his life.

"I alone followed him to the grave. When I had laid my only benefactor to rest, I looked about to see how I could pay my debt to him; I found he had neither family nor friends, neither wife nor child. But he believed. He had a religious conviction; had I any right to dispute it? He had spoken to me timidly of masses said for the repose of the dead; he would not impress it on me as a duty, thinking that it would be a form of repayment for his services. As soon as I had money enough I paid to Saint-Sulpice the requisite sum for four masses every year. As the only thing I can do for Bourgeat is thus to satisfy his pious wishes, on the days when that mass is said, at the beginning of each season of the year, I go for his sake and say the required prayers; and I say with the good faith of a sceptic—'Great God, if there is a sphere which Thou hast appointed after death for those who have been perfect, remember good Bourgeat; and if he should have anything to suffer, let me suffer it for him, that he may enter all the sooner into what is called Paradise.'

"That, my dear fellow, is as much as a man who holds my opinions can allow himself. But God must be a good fellow; He cannot owe me any grudge. I swear to you, I would give my whole fortune if faith such as Bourgeat's could enter my brain."

Bianchon, who was with Desplein all through his last illness, dares not affirm to this day that the great surgeon died an atheist. Will not those who believe like to fancy that the humble Auvergnat came to open the gate of heaven to his friend, as he did that of the earthly temple on whose pediment we read the words—"A grateful country to its great men."

PARIS, *January* 1836.